MEXICO

JAMES A. MICHENER

MEXICO

RANDOM HOUSE 👁 LARGE PRINT

*This book
is
dedicated to
Conchita Cintrón
La Superba*

Library of Congress Cataloging-in-Publication Data

Michener, James A. (James Albert)
Mexico / by James Michener. — 1st large print ed.
p. cm.
ISBN 0-679-74329-4
1. Mexico—History—Fiction. 2. Large type book. I. Title.
[PS3525.I19M48 1992b] 813'.54—dc20 92-50238

*Manufactured in the United States of America
on acid-free paper using partially recycled fibers*

4689753

Book design by Carole Lowenstein

THIS LARGE PRINT BOOK CARRIES
THE SEAL OF APPROVAL OF N.A.V.H.

CONTENTS

AUTHOR'S NOTE

This is a novel, and the Mexican city of Toledo, its citizens, its Festival of Ixmiq-61 and the three bullfights described in the book are all fictional. The Altomecs, who play a vital part in the narrative, are a fictional composite of several ancient Indian peoples. However, the three toreros who participate in the Saturday fight—matadors Calesero and Pepe Luis Vásquez, and the rejoneadora Conchita Cintrón—are real persons in the history of Mexican bullfighting; I wanted to pay my respects to three friends who helped teach me about their profession. I must add, however, that the situations, incidents and dialogues concerning these toreros are products of my imagination and are not intended to depict any actual events or to change the entirely fictional character of this book.

CHRONOLOGY

INDIANS	PALAFOXES	CLAYS
500 Drunken Builders		
600 Ixmiq begins career		
650 Pyramid built		
900 Nopiltzín discovers pulque	900 Palafoxes in Salamanca	
1000 Altomecs acquire new god		1000 Clays are peasants in England
1130 War God empowered		
1151 Altomecs take Toledo; Xolal slain		
1171 Pyramid enlarged		
1350 Mock battle, Altomecs vs. Aztecs		
1470 Tezozomoc becomes leader		
1477 Gray Eyes born		
1497 Gray Eyes sees hideous goddess		
	1498 Antonio Palafox born	
1503 Xóchitl born		
	1504 Alicia de Guadalquivir born	
1507 Tezozomoc's widow sacrificed		
1519 Ixmiq sacrificed		
1520 Stranger born; goddess destroyed		
	1524 Antonio Palafox to Mexico	1524 Clays become landowners in England
1527 City surrenders	1527 Antonio invades Toledo	
	1529 Professor Palafox burned at stake	
	1531 Building of cathedral at Toledo begun	
	1536 Palafoxes granted 250,000 acres	

INDIANS	PALAFOXES	CLAYS
1538 Gray Eyes lectures		
1540 Stranger baptized and marries Antonio, first bishop	1540 Antonio marries Stranger	
	1544 Hall of Government built	
	1575 House of Tile built	
1600–1700 4 Altomec girls marry Palafox bishops 2,3,4,5 and have 23 children	1600–1700 Palafox bishops 2,3,4,5 marry Altomec girls	1600–1606 Clays contemplate emigrating to America
		1613 Clays arrive in Virginia
	1726 Aqueduct built	1726 Clays acquire Newlands
	1740 A major lode struck at 600 ft. at Mineral	
	1760 Cathedral façade is completed	
		1776 Clays fight in Revolution
	1810 Palafox land cut from over a million to 500,000 acres	
		1823 Jubal Clay born
	1830 Bulls come from Guadalquivir	
		1846 Jubal at war in Mexico
	1847 Alicia in a China Poblano meets Jubal Clay	1847 Jubal at Mineral
1850 Caridad born		
1864 Caridad in mines	1860s Palafax holdings reduced from 500,000 to 250,000 acres	1864 Jubal at Cold Harbor 1864 Clay plantation burned
	1867 Maximilian executed	1866 Clay leaves Virginia 1867 Clay in exile in Toledo
1874 Caridad marries Clay		1874 Clay marries Caridad
	1881 Graziela Palafox born	
		1882 John Clay born in Toledo
	1897 Eduardo Palafox born	
	1906 Graziela marries Clay	1906 John Clay marries Graziela
		1909 Norman Clay born in Toledo
	1910–1914 Revolution takes 150,000 acres of Palafox land	

INDIANS	PALAFOXES	CLAYS
	1911 Gral. Gurza storms Toledo	
		1917 John with AEF in France
	1919 Gral. Gurza assassinated	
		1920 *Pyramid and Cathedral* published; Bull Soldado at Mineral
	1928 Peace in Mexico	1928 John Clay working for oil company
	1933 Palafox girl marries Norman Clay	1933 Norman marries Palafox girl
	1938 Mexico expropriates oil wells	1938 U.S. loses oil wells; John and Norman exiles in Alabama
		1942 Norman on duty in Pacific
1945 Juan Gomez, 17, leaps into ring at Ixmiq-45		
		1950 Norman on duty in Korea
1961 Juan Gomez at Ixmiq-61	1961 Don Eduardo at Ixmiq-61	1961 Norman at Ixmiq-61

MEXICO

THE CACTUS
AND THE
MAGUEY

I HAD BEEN SENT to Mexico to cover a murder, one of a remarkable kind. And since it had not yet happened, I had been ordered to get photographs, too.

I was therefore burdened with unfamiliar gear—a large carrying case of Japanese cameras, some of which could photograph swift action occurring at a distance—and as my rickety bus trundled across central Mexico I wondered what I could do to protect these cameras if I followed my inclination to walk into the city from Kilometer 303.

I knew no one in the crowded bus and the

cameras were far too valuable to entrust to strangers, so I resigned myself to staying on the bus and guarding them the seven remaining kilometers into the city. But as we approached Kilometer 303 the inchoate longing that had always possessed me at this curious spot in the highway surged over me with terrible force, and I was tempted to jump out and leave my cameras to chance.

Fighting back this childish impulse, I slumped in my seat and tried not to look at the road that had always haunted me, but I was powerless to keep my eyes away from it. Like many Mexican boys of good family, at thirteen I had been packed off to Lawrenceville School near Princeton, "to learn some English," my father had grumbled, and sometimes on the green lawn of that excellent school I had stopped and gasped for breath, choked by nostalgia for the road I was now on. Later at Princeton, where there were also many young men from Mexico, I would sometimes seek out boys who had known this area and I would ask haltingly, "Have you ever seen anything lovelier than the view of Toledo from that gash in the hills where the road winds down from Kilometer 303?" And if my friends had ever seen this miraculous spot for themselves we would indulge our homesickness and think of our city of Toledo, the fairest in Mexico, as it displayed its golden iridescence in the late afternoon sun.

As a matter of fact, I think I became a writer because of this scintillating view. It had always been assumed by my parents that I would graduate from Princeton as my ancestors from Virginia had been doing since 1764, and that I would then take one year of graduate work in mining at Colorado and return to the silver mines of Toledo, which my family had been operating for many years. But all this changed in my junior year at college, when I wrote a prize-winning essay that occasioned much favorable comment among the English faculty. It described the view of Toledo from a point just beyond Kilometer 303 as it might have been seen in sequence by an Aztec district governor in 1500, by Cortés in 1524, by a Spanish priest in 1530, by a German traveler in 1660, by an American mining engineer in 1866—that would be my grandfather—and by General Gurza in the revolutionary battles of 1918.

Actually, it is not correct to say that I wrote this essay that was to have such influence in my life. I started it, and the visions came to me so vividly, so directly from the heart of Mexico and from my own memories, that I merely recorded them. In a sense, this prize was a damnable thing, for long after I had become a professional writer I remembered the ease with which I had composed the essay. And I was never again to experience that facility. But the visions I conjured up that day have lived with me forever.

Now they possessed me, and I surrendered myself to them, my glowing memories of Toledo, and I was reacting to them in my sentimental way when I saw through the window of the bus a sight that captured my imagination. Two young Indian women wearing leather sandals, rough-cloth skirts and bright shawls, and with their hair in swaying braids, were walking along the road toward Toledo. Obviously, they were heading for the Festival of Ixmiq, the site of my assignment, and the soft rhythm of their movement, from the undulating braids down to their slim ankles, reminded me of all the Indians I had ever seen walking home from my father's mines, and I wanted to be with them as I had been forty years ago, and I found myself impulsively shouting in Spanish, "Halt the bus! Halt the bus! I'll walk in from here."

As the surprised driver ground down on his ancient brakes and as they squealed back in protest, I looked hurriedly about the bus in search of someone to whom I could entrust my bag of cameras, and it may seem curious to a typical American who might have a prejudiced view of Mexico, but I could hear my Mexican mother saying: "In other parts of Mexico evil men may steal now and then, but in Toledo we have only honest people," Deciding to rely on her judgment, I quickly studied my fellow passengers to identify someone I could trust.

I saw in the rear an unusual-looking fellow who was watching me with aloof but sardonic amusement. He was about twenty-five years old, blond, quite handsome and dressed in what young people called a Pachuca sweater, that is, a huge, woolly, loose-woven affair that looked more like a shaggy tent than an article of clothing. It was much favored by Los Angeles beatniks who were infesting Mexico under one pretense or another and had come to serve as a badge of distinction. Even if the young man had not had his conspicuous blond hair the Pachuca sweater would have assured me that he was an American, for no self-respecting Mexican would have used this sweater for other than its original purpose: to keep sheepherders warm in the mountain pastures.

"You want somebody . . ." the young man asked, leaning slightly forward.

"I wanted to hike into town." For some unaccountable reason I added, "The way I did when I was a boy."

"Memories?" the young man asked with amusement. He reached out with an indolent

gesture to indicate that he was willing to carry
my case and assured me, "I'll sort of . . ." His
voice trailed off.

At this moment an older man seated behind
me intercepted me as I started passing the cameras back to the American youth, and in excellent Spanish asked: "Aren't you John Clay's
son?"

"I am," I replied in Spanish.

"I thought I recognized your father's bearing.
You want me to look after the cameras?"

I considered the question only for a fleeting
moment, during which I compared the undisciplined young American lounging in the back in
his ridiculous Pachuca sweater with the Mexican businessman in his conventional dark suit.
In Spanish I said, "I'd deem it an act of kindness
if you took care of them for me." Thus the motion of my arm, originally directed toward the
young American in the backseat, was easily diverted in flight, as it were, to the Mexican closer
at hand. To the American I apologized: "He'll
know where to deposit them."

The young man laughed—insolently I
thought. With three chopping movements of
his palm as if delivering karate blows, he dismissed me.

"Where are you stopping?" the Mexican businessman asked.

"At the House of Tile," I replied. "Please leave the cameras with Don Anselmo."

"He's dead," the man said simply. "His widow runs the inn."

"She knows me," I replied, starting to dismount, but then I realized that I was about to hike into the city with no camera at all, and it occurred to me that if the event I was concerned about did take place, I might profit from having some good background shots of the festival to provide local color. So I begged the disgusted bus driver to wait for an additional moment while I retrieved one of my rapid-fire Japanese cameras, and with this slung around my neck I stepped down onto the highway at Kilometer 303. The bus accelerated swiftly, leaving a hazy trail of exhaust, and I was alone at four o'clock on an April afternoon at the spot where, above any other in the world, I wanted to be.

But I was not alone for long, for overtaking me with their soft, resolute strides were the two Indian women on their way to the fair, and as I stood somewhat bemused in the road they nodded gravely and passed on. How magnificent they were, those women coming down from the hills to grace the fiesta that their ancestors had initiated more than four hundred years before. They were a timeless part of the red earth of Mexico, and of the restless motion of the earth.

When they nodded to me, their faces were impassive like the basalt statues on Aztec monuments, and yet their eyes glowed with the fire that had consecrated this land. They were the Indians of Mexico, and everything began and ended with them.

I remained motionless as they moved out of sight, held fast I think by a respectful unwillingness to add my ungainly movements to the subdued ballet their soft motions had created, but when the Indian women finally disappeared around the bend ahead, I shifted my camera strap and started slowly along the path they had followed.

For the past two years my magazine had kept me working in the trouble spots of Latin America. I had covered Vice President Nixon's catastrophic tour of the area and Fidel Castro's abominations in Cuba, and I was threatened with burnout. Apparently the home office had become aware of the risk, for Drummond, my editor, who seemed to keep an eye on everything that happened in the world, sent me a telegram that he felt sure would revive me:

> Rumor tells me two Mexican matadors are heading for a showdown in which one of them is likely to force the other to such extremes that it will be the same as murder.

People say Victoriano the filigreed dancer and Juan Gómez the brutal Indian are natural enemies. They're scheduled to compete in a festival at Toledo. Didn't you tell me you were born there? Take a week off. Go there. Catch what you can, but focus on the drama. Pick up camera gear our office Mexico City and get powerful photos.

At first I was inclined to wire back "No thanks" because of professional vanity. This was the casual kind of story I did not like to fool around with; I was a writer and not a photographer. If it had been an important story, the magazine would have sent me a major photographer, and the fact that Drummond hadn't made me suspicious that the whole affair was his device for giving me a vacation I needed without upsetting the home-office accountants. I resented such trickery and had been about to say so in a snippy cable from Havana when I was restrained by a little lecture I gave myself: "Take it easy, Clay. There's every reason you should head for Toledo. As a bullfighting fan you knew this boy Victoriano in Spain, and you've been casually following the career of Gómez for years. With a little brushing up, you could turn out a pretty fair article. And forget the photographer insult. You do know how a Leica works, and the new Japanese cameras can take pictures by themselves."

But even as I reprimanded myself I knew there were other, deeper reasons for accepting the assignment. I was gripped by a memory of Mexico in the spring and the splendor of Toledo and the Festival of Ixmiq. So I took the job, because I wanted to see my homeland again.

If you had asked me: "Isn't this a case of ordinary homesickness?" I'd have had to say: "A man fifty-two years old doesn't indulge in homesickness. This is far more basic." I had been born in Mexico in 1909 of an American father who had also been born there. In 1938, when I was already a mature man and married to a fine Mexican woman, Father and I had been forced to quit the country. The Mexicans had stolen our property and we could not stay. When my wife confronted the thought of moving to Montgomery, Alabama, with me, she couldn't stomach such an exile and divorced me.

It was then that I became a writer, though not a real writer like Scott Fitzgerald, who had also gone to Princeton; I was more like Richard Halliburton, another Princetonian more my age and type. I dabbled in travel books, never successfully, and debased myself by writing as-told-to junk. My magazine found me useful, because without a wife or children I could be dispatched on little notice to cover any hot subject that exploded in Asia, Africa or South America.

It had been in January of this year, 1961, that I caught a glimpse of the gray years that lay ahead of me. I had been in Havana trying to explain Castro's bewildering behavior during his first two years after overthrowing Batista. In 1958 and '59 I'd been a strong Castro supporter, living with him in the mountains, writing articles about him giving him moral support as he marched toward the capital, and rejoicing with his bearded ones as they captured Havana. After that it was all downhill. He lied to me, said he had never been a communist, swore he wanted peace with the United States and laughed at me when I asked: "Fidel, why are you breaking diplomatic relations with us?"

When my onetime hero revealed himself as such a liar and a fraud, I had to evaluate myself, to see if I was any better. What I saw during those three bad days in Cuba did little to reassure me. I had accomplished little. I'd written nothing that would last. I had no wife or children, and I was confused as to whether I was a Mexican or an American.

But as I stood beside the little concrete marker K. 303—indicating the number of kilometers from Mexico City, about one hundred and eighty miles—I felt the good heat of Toledo upon me and suspected that I had done right in accepting the assignment. And when I looked past the marker and at the parched land I knew I had. I had always been fascinated by these cactus plants, with their burden of thick red dust, because for me they were the truest product of the Mexican soil. Unforgiving, bitter and reluctant, they etched themselves against the dark blue sky and stood like gaunt cathedrals. I loved their awkward angularity, the fact that they offered no concession to anyone, and that year after year they were the same. They were very Mexican, these perpetual cactus bushes. Oftentimes an Indian farmer would surround his little plot of land with them, and then the goats had better beware. At first sight they seemed worthless for anything except for functioning as improvised fences, and yet it was they that gave character to the land; without the cactus bushes this would not be Mexico.

One of my earliest fancies had been associated with these unruly and forbidding plants. At about the age of six I developed the idea that my father was controlled by an unseen cactus plant, had indeed sprung from one. He was an angular man, and his sharp beard, when unshaved, resembled the spines I had so often tested. He had both the ruggedness of the cactus and its essential strength. I often thought of him as standing solitary against the sky, the way the cactus did, and in later years when the city of Toledo erected a granite monument to him, that is how his statue stood. Like the cactus, my father had a majestic beauty of his own, and it sprang directly from his unyielding rectitude, for he was one of the best administrators Mexico has ever known. When I was a senior at Princeton with time to restudy my father's famous book I realized that it, even more than he, had a kinship with the cactus. It was sharp, angular, lacking in flowery rhythms, but it achieved a local immortality primarily because it did stand alone, like an isolated cactus bush. It was a completely self-inspired book, like none other that had ever been written about Mexico. And that was the source of its greatness.

I studied the cactus for some time and wished that I had absorbed a little more of its unyielding vigor, just as I occasionally wished that I had inherited more of my father's relentless probity, for I knew myself to be vacillating while he was always sure of where he stood. He lived in a simple world, where categories were rigidly maintained without necessity for explanation: for John Clay, Englishmen were demonstrably superior to Americans, who were obviously better than Spaniards, who were inherently better than Indians, who were infinitely superior to

Negroes. Banks were better than newspapers, Protestants than Catholics, Lee than Grant, and silver much better than gold. Education was good and sex bad. Paved roads were very good and an insecure water supply was an abomination. Hardworking engineers saved the world and soft-living writers corrupted it. Nevertheless, he is now remembered as a writer, for his book, *The Pyramid and the Cathedral,* constructed from the relentless dichotomies of good and evil that he espoused, had somehow caught the inmost spirit of Mexico.

I started hiking down the road, delightfully aware that after a few hundred yards I would see opening before me the prospect of Toledo with its shimmering towers, but as I walked I noticed that in the field to my right the cactus plants had disappeared, for the Indian farmer, whoever he was, had rooted them out and replaced them with orderly rows of that amazing plant, the maguey, and as I walked beside these dark green shrubs, man-high and undulating in the sun, I recalled something my father had told me forty years ago. It could have been in April as we walked that day along a patch of maguey, for I remember that the sun was warm but not oppressive. He stopped and poked at a twisting maguey with his cane and observed, more to himself than to me: "A land is never occupied until the cactus is rooted out and maguey planted."

This was a surprising thing for my father to have said, for to him drinking was an abomination, and it was from these maguey plants, whose mysterious arms twisted about the landscape as if seeking to embrace it, that the Indians had centuries ago learned to brew their intoxicating mezcal drink. I would have expected my father to hate the maguey for that reason. Instead, he reflected: "These are the plants that lend grace and dignity to the land. They're like dancers with beautiful hands. Or like women. They're the better half of life."

I remembered these curious comments when years later I read his book at Princeton and came upon his remarkable evocation of the cactus and the maguey as contrary symbols of the Mexican spirit. Cactus was the inclination to war and destruction. In contrast, "maguey," he had written in a much-quoted passage, "has always been the symbol of peace and construction. From its bruised leaves our ancestors made the paper upon which our records were transcribed; its dried leaves formed the thatch for our homes; its fibers were the threads that made clothing possible; its thorns were the pins and needles our mothers used in bringing us to civilization; its white roots provided the vegetables from which we gained sustenance; and its juice became our honey, our vinegar and after a long while the wine that destroyed us with happiness and immortal visions." Cactus, my father wrote, was the spirit of the lonely hunter; maguey was the inspiration of the artists who had built the pyramids and decorated the cathedrals. One was the male spirit so dominant in Mexican life; the other was the female, the subtle conqueror who invariably triumphed in the end. My father argued that it was not by accident that the Indian worked all his life fighting the cactus and received his only respite from the sweet liquor of the maguey. He had also written that if cactus was the visible spirit of earth's hard core that generated life, the twisting arms of maguey were the green cradle of nature that made life bearable. He ended this comparison with the passage that was later inscribed on his monument: "Where the cactus and the maguey meet, my heart is entwined in the tangle of Mexico."

Here, beside me now in central Mexico, the cactus and the maguey met. For an instant, in these adjoining fields, the unyielding cactus and the wild, aspiring maguey stood side by side, and in them my heart was entangled as my father's had been. I was an American citizen and had helped protect my country in two wars, as a fighter pilot in World War II and as a combat

reporter in Korea, but my spiritual ho
be here, for somehow these two p
helped determine my character.

I now faced some two hundred yards of steeply climbing road, and the work of hiking became demanding, but I was fortified by the assurance that in a few minutes I would once more enjoy the sight that had tempted me to leave the relative comfort of the bus. At last I approached the crest of the hill where the road pursued a ledge between two reddish heights. With my eyes half closed I walked the remaining yards until I felt a fresh breeze greeting me from the other side of the pass. I stopped, opened my eyes wide, and saw before me the vision of my youth. It was the city of Toledo, the old mining city of colonial days, its monuments intact, and it was the fairest sight I had ever known.

To the north, just barely visible beyond the sloping edge of the hill that helped form the pass in which I stood, rose the gaunt and terrible pyramid of the Altomecs. Reddish brown in the sunlight, truncated sharply at the top, its tiers of steps clearly outlined against the mass, it stood mutely as it had for thirteen hundred years. It was enormous, brooding, mysterious. It spoke to me now, as it had nearly half a century before when I was a boy in its shadows, of fearful rites and death and the terror that accompanied an-

‿ient life in Mexico. It was the most westerly of the Mexican pyramids and had been erected in its primitive form sometime in the seventh century by a shadowy civilization known simply as the Drunken Builders, whose domain had been overrun in the year 1151 by one of Mexico's most savage tribes, the Altomecs, whom even the warlike Aztecs had feared. Through the centuries the gaunt old pyramid had witnessed a succession of cultures and had undergone complete resurfacing five separate times. In various rituals during its nine hundred years of religious use, well over a million men had been sacrificed on its altars, their blood running down its steep flanks in rivulets.

There it was. There it was. With relief my eyes left the monstrous pile and looked straight down the road and over the indistinct roofs of the city to where the twin towers of the cathedral rose against the deep blue of the western sky. How subtly beautiful they were, those ancient towers built in 1640 by a Mexican bishop who had studied drawings from Spain and had vainly tried to imagine what his ancestral Salamanca had looked like and the spires of Zaragoza. The spires that he built in Toledo were not soaring pinnacles but honest, sturdy pillars of gray stone. Nestled between them, however, was the most glorious façade in all Mexico. It had been erected by another bishop, in 1760, after the mines had begun to spew out silver, and it was a masterpiece not of silvery gray stone but of marble. Its manifold niches were decorated with the statues of saints, and every aspect of it spoke of poetry and celestial music.

From the hillside overlooking the city I could not see the marvels of this façade, but from the manner in which reflected light shone from the ornaments, I knew that this gem of colonial architecture continued to shed its radiance as it had when I was a boy. Experts from New York and London had termed our cathedral "the acknowledged masterpiece of churrigueresque design." My mother said, "If angels wanted to build a church of their own, they would have to copy ours." My father, who did not much like churrigueresque flamboyance, replied, "They might use it as a model for a wedding cake, but hardly for a church." In this matter I sided with my mother, and although later I was to see such awe-inspiring cathedrals as Chartres and Salisbury, I always thought that our cathedral in Toledo was the most angelic I had ever seen. If I were a Catholic, I would want my church to look like this. Flamboyant it was. Gingerbready it was. But it was also an evocation of the period when Mexico was secure, before the terrible revolutions, and before the corroding doubts of the twentieth century.

And then, off to the right, my eyes sought out what I had really come to see. From my earliest days at the mine I had known the pyramid as a monitory thing whose fierce ghostly priests might torture me if I did not behave, and I had always taken pleasure in the cathedral with its fairy-tale façade, but what had been intimately mine, a definite part of me, were the Arches of Palafox. And there they were! Entering the city from a northeasterly direction, this fantastic line of arches carried an aqueduct from springs that rose beyond the pyramid. Upon the arches depended the city's water supply, and I recall that when I first saw these graceful curves marching over the hills I thought how providential it was that their stony legs were of varied lengths so that they exactly accommodated themselves to all the ups and downs of the rough terrain.

The arches are still the glory of Toledo, and even the most jaded visitor who might be repelled by the pyramid or alienated by a Catholic cathedral has to respond to the subtle rhythms of this aqueduct. Dominating the landscape, its top is a bold line that is absolutely flat, but there is infinite variety in the arches, which grow deep to traverse a valley or fade away to nothing as the water channel rides directly across the crest of a hill. As a boy I used to sit for hours watching the aqueduct, which old Bishop Palafox had built in 1726, and it seemed to me to have been divinely inspired not for the purpose of providing water for our city but for that of linking the pyramid and the cathedral.

I hiked down the road, keeping my eyes fixed on the slope of hill that limited my vision to the right, and with each step another of the bishop's arches came into view until at last I could see the whole magnificent sweep of the Arches of Palafox; but it was not this spectacle that I was seeking. It was something that still lay hidden behind the hill, and I broke into a run, so eager was I to see it again.

As the hill fell away the thing I sought came into view, and I halted, in the middle of the ancient road where stout Cortés had once halted to inspect what he sought. There it was, the old, abandoned silver mine of Toledo. It stood perched against a gray-brown hill, an assembly of roofless buildings, the remnants of a place from which more than $800 million had been dug when a single dollar was worth five today.

This was the Mineral de Toledo, that legendary hole in the earth whose name had been more famous in imperial Spain than that of Lima or any other city in the New World. In those now shattered buildings I had been born and my father before me. Up there my father had resisted General Gurza, the revolutionary wild man who had come to capture the mines. The precious seed bull Soldado had been sequestered in a cave in a successful attempt to salvage the bloodline of the Palafox ranch. Up there General Porfirio Díaz, the benevolent old president, had come in 1909 two years before he fled to exile, driven out by General Gurza and his murderous gang.

The history of our mine had been the history of Mexico, and it was appalling to see it in ruins. Of our Mineral de Toledo it was said that half the wealth of Madrid had been dug by Indians from its deep mouth. Now it was empty, a scar in the earth, but how warm its vacant buildings still seemed. I could almost see, in the distance, my father marching erectly about the property, supervising the excavation of the last ore.

This was Toledo! The pyramid, the cathedral, the arches, and the mine. How deeply entwined my emotions were with this place I did not appreciate till later in life, for when my father took me with him to Alabama I quickly established myself as an ordinary American. I'd already gone to college there, then I served in the American armed forces and dated American girls, though I found none to marry. I worked for an

American publication, ate Southern cooking and forgot things Mexican. But often, in moments of accidental reflection, I caught powerful reminders that I had been born a Mexican, for the sights and sounds and tastes of my childhood days were deeply ingrained. I could not think of myself as only an American, for now, as I stood just west of K. 303 at the point where all of Toledo first became visible, every object of importance that I saw had been built by some ancestor of mine. The pyramid had been raised by one of my Indian forebears. It had been refurbished in 1507 by another ancestor. The earnest Spanish bishop who built the cathedral had had a daughter who played a role in my lineage; the later bishop who had constructed the churrigueresque façade had had a son; and the great bishop who had built the aqueduct had sired fifteen children, one of whom served as an ancestor. The Mineral, of course, had been salvaged by my American grandfather after the Civil War and had been operated in its final days by my father. I could look nowhere without seeing the handiwork of someone in my family, stretching back for more than a thousand years, tied to the harsh red soil of Mexico. For nearly sixty generations my ancestors had stood where I now stood surveying the mountain-rimmed valley of Toledo, and invariably they had

found it gratifying. I recalled the letter my grandfather had written to his young wife in Richmond
in 1847 during the Mexican War while resting at
this spot: "Colonel Robert Lee has dispatched
me on a scouting expedition to inspect the famous silver mines of Toledo, and I am now
halted in sight of this famous city. My guide is a
resident, Captain Palafox of the Mexican army,
leading a troop of his soldiers and mine, and I
must confess that looking down upon his city I
observe a sight as inviting as any I have seen in
my own country, and I trust that it shall be God's
will that as an outcome of this present war these
two lands be joined together. When they are, I
would not be unhappy to live in the area I am
now overseeing, for in my opinion it could produce fine cotton." Years later, after the defeat
of the South, my grandfather would choose exile
in Mexico, where he would be employed as engineer for the mine owned by this young Mexican captain who had brought him to Toledo. In
time the son of that American lieutenant would
marry the niece of that Mexican officer, and they
would be my parents. So, by the fortunes of war
and exile, I became a Palafox of Toledo as well
as a Clay of Richmond.

I think it must have been at that moment when
I renewed my acquaintance with the grandeur of
Toledo that I felt fully the dissatisfaction with my

own accomplishments that had been dogging me for months. "Damn it, Clay, get yourself straightened out. You have twenty more years, maybe thirty. Make them count." As soon as I uttered those last three words I liked them, saw them as the challenge that had been building since my disillusionment in Havana, but how exactly to respond I did not know. However, as I resumed my march toward Toledo I was buoyed by a reassuring thought: Where but in his place of origin can man best find the important answers?

It was five in the evening of a quiet spring day when I entered Toledo along the street I had so much treasured as a boy. It was flanked by rows of brightly colored houses that crowded each inch of space, so that I seemed to be passing down a canyon whose walls were alternately red and green and purple and most of all a brilliant golden yellow. At one corner I could look down another street of similar colors and see the clean new building that replaced the shambles of shacks and warrens that had served as the market when I was young, and I knew that a few more steps would bring me to the central plaza of Toledo, which was the essential heart of the city. One block more . . . half a block . . . and then . . . here I was, in the plaza itself.

For a long time I studied it from where I stood,

and to my pleasure I found little changed. Directly on my right was the historic blue-and-yellow hotel known as the House of Tile, where I would be staying. In the late sun it was more scintillating than ever, each of the tiles that formed the façade flashing like an individual mirror.

Along the north–south axis of the plaza, and fronting on the Avenida Gral. Gurza, so inappropriately named to perpetuate the memory of the rebellious general who had ravaged this part of Mexico, stood the cathedral, its somber silvery-gray towers flanking the delicate luxuriance of its central façade. Not a stone was out of place in this veritable poem of marble, and old women passed through the side portals as they had been doing since 1640.

Facing the cathedral, along the eastern edge of the plaza, was the building that had occupied a curious place in the affections of those city residents who were so vociferously anticlerical during the revolutionary days that they refused to enter the cathedral. Instead they revered this ancient building that had been built in the 1500s by two ancestors of mine, a devout Catholic bishop and his strong-willed Indian wife. Originally a refuge for impoverished old women, later a nunnery of the church, it had become in the 1860s the grandiose Imperial Theater. Its reconstruction had been commissioned by the Austrian Maximilian and his Belgian wife, Carlota, when they ruled Mexico as the emperor and empress and dedicated by them with a performance of Bellini's *Norma.* Rebuilt to Maximilian's specific plans, it represented his understanding of the classical Greek style. In its new incarnation it remained a magnificent building, chaste but royal, and had played a significant role in Mexican history. From its stage the ill-starred emperor had delivered his last address to his reluctant subjects. In one of its dressing rooms he had spent two weeks of his imprisonment, and from its Athenian portals he had climbed into the wagon that had carried him to the fusillade at Querétaro. Later, the famous theater had been the scene of numerous constitutional conventions at which the future of Mexico was hammered out, and it was here that I heard my first opera as a very young child, with Luisa Tetrazzini singing *Aida.*

But the building that gave the plaza a special distinction was the low two-story colonial structure that ran the entire length of the southern side. It had been built in 1544 by my ancestor the first Bishop Palafox, and was in every respect one of the masterpieces of Mexican architecture. Its total aspect epitomized that odd union of Spanish elegance and Indian strength which marked the intellectual history of Mexico. I remember my father's telling me one day as we sat in the plaza facing this dull-red structure, "When our first settlers landed at Jamestown, this building was so old it needed new flooring. In 1607, when America started, our tenth viceroy was paying a state visit to this Hall of Government."

I remember interrupting my father and asking, "When you say 'our settlers,' which country do you mean?"

He replied, "It's possible for a man to belong to two countries."

"At the same time?" I asked incredulously.

"Spiritually, yes," he answered. "I've always considered the old Hall of Government"—he pointed to it—"as the capital of my second nation, just as Richmond has been the tragic capital of my first."

"But you never lived in Richmond. You told me you've never seen it."

"Any spot for which a man's forebears have bled and died will forever be his homeland. Remember that."

Then, as I looked westward from the Hall, I noticed something that held my interest. On the wooden billboards outside the local bullring had been pasted three copies of the flamboyant poster announcing the fights that would take place this weekend. THE FESTIVAL OF IXMIQ-61 shouted the bold black letters, but what mesmerized me were the portraits of the two contenders I had come to photograph and write about. "Mano a Mano!" the words said, meaning a deadly contest involving two matadors. To the left was Victoriano, classically aloof; to the right, Juan Gómez, the stocky Indian, hair hanging down close to his eyes. Victoriano looked down at me as he had when I interviewed him in Spain, and Gómez could have stepped out of the posters and introduced himself: "I'm Juan Gómez. You spoke to me once when I fought in Tijuana." And in that instant I realized that I was on an assignment that was likely to become more complicated than I had supposed when I lightly accepted it. This was Wednesday afternoon, almost evening, and the three fights began on Friday, so I had tonight and Thursday to clarify my thoughts on the matter.

I looked about for some secure point of reference, and at the far opposite end of the plaza, standing near the House of Tile, I saw the guardian spirit of my city, the Indian Ixmiq, who lived in the sixth century after Christ, whom the travelers to Toledo came to honor. Benign, swarthy in burnished bronze, the wiry Indian gazed down upon me, and I felt content. As I approached to tell him "Old man, I've come home," a voice called me from the terrace of tables at the House of Tile. It was the stranger who had carried my cameras to the hotel and he said, "Señor Clay, the bag is safe with the Widow Mier y Palafox."

"Thank you, my good friend," I called back.

"Would you like a beer?" he shouted jovially.

"Later," I replied, for I wanted to be alone.

In English he cried: "I'll give you a rain check." Then he laughed and added: "The statue you're looking for is at the opposite corner."

How well I remembered! It had been a sunny spring day in 1927 and the dedication of the statue had been delayed till I could return from my interview at Princeton, where I would be enrolling in the autumn. Father and I were the only Clays in attendance; the rest of the notables— including all who would be making speeches— were Palafoxes, and since Father and I were members of that extensive clan, the celebration was a family affair. There was music, the firing of a salute, and a boisterous tea afterward on the hotel veranda. The committee that had paid for the statue wanted Father to make a short speech of acknowledgment, but he refused: "If they want to risk a statue while I'm still living, let them go ahead. But I'll have no part of it. Suppose next year I commit a murder. Do they tear it down?"

Now as I approached the statue I gasped, for my father, who had been dead since 1945, was standing before me on that pedestal. His stern gaze was turned away from the cathedral—which was only proper, in view of his attitude toward Catholics—and he looked across the plaza toward the Mineral de Toledo. As I had seen him do so often in life, he held a book in his left hand, with fingers thrust between its pages. His clean-shaven face looked exactly as I remembered it, and it seemed to me that if I were to call him, he would undoubtedly reply.

The carving on the east face said simply JOHN CLAY 1882–1945. Momentarily bewildered by what seemed like the dead come to life, I moved cautiously around the statue. On its northern face it carried in Spanish the title of Father's book: *The Pyramid and the Cathedral.* On the western side, also in Spanish, was the well-known quotation "Where the cactus and the maguey meet, my heart is entwined in the tangle of Mexico." Feeling my own heart equally entwined, I slumped onto one of the exquisite blue-tile benches that lined the plaza and studied this representation of my father as memories haunted me.

In 1943, after I had spent a tour bombing Jap-
anese-held islands in the far Pacific, I was
granted leave for home rest in Alabama, where
I found that my father had rigged a darkroom
where he kept a white sheet hanging on the
wall. Day after day he projected his color slides
onto this sheet and sat and conversed with his
old friends long dead. I must confess that when
I heard about this I suspected that his mind was
faltering, but when I first sat with him and saw
the big, superhuman-sized photograph of the
rancher Don Eduardo Palafox staring down at
me, his full lips almost bursting into speech, it
seemed entirely natural to greet him, so when
Father cried: "Hey there, Don Eduardo! Good
times in the fighting days, eh?" I was not surprised. Indeed, I almost expected Palafox to
reply: "We fooled Gurza and his bandits, didn't
we?" But when I watched my father talking to
his old friends who were no longer here, I felt
deep sorrow for a man who had gone into exile
twice, each time from a land he loved. The first
was when he spiritually cut himself off from Virginia, the Clay homeland, and from Richmond,
the noble city he had never seen. The second
was when he fled Mexico and his legion of
friends there. During that brief respite from war
I vowed that I would never allow myself to be

exiled from any culture that had nourished me, but now in Toledo, as I saluted my father, I felt as deeply isolated as he had ever been. And I could visualize myself in my late sixties as forlorn and bereft as he had been.

My father's exile from Mexico was self-imposed, of course, and he knew he would always have been welcomed among the Mexicans, but after what he called "that dark and evil day of March 18, 1938," he felt that no honest man could possibly live in Mexico, so he left.

I was twenty-nine at the time, visiting him in Toledo on vacation from the magazine. I remember his coming into our home at the Mineral, gasping for breath, and slumping into a chair. "It can result only in war," he mumbled in Spanish. "Only in war."

"What happened?" I asked.

"That madman, President Cárdenas," he gasped.

"What's he done now?"

"He's expropriated the oil wells. We'd better pack."

"You think . . ."

"Think?" he roared at me from his chair. "Of course there'll be war. How else can President Roosevelt react?" Then, seeing my unwillingness to believe that the United States would declare war over some oil wells, he jumped up and cried, "Even a damned fool like Roosevelt will recognize the necessity."

My father had been reared in Southern traditions and was a determined Democrat, but like most of his acquaintances from the South—those gentle and confused people who frequented our Mexican home in the winters—he despised his American president, Roosevelt, almost as much as he did his Mexican president, Cárdenas. "How could two glorious nations like the United States and Mexico get such utter incompetents at the same time?" he would wail.

He waited vainly for Roosevelt to declare war or for some patriot to assassinate Cárdenas, and when neither of these events occurred he fell into a deep depression from which he was never to recover. After giving the two errant presidents eight months to come to their senses, he abruptly shut down the mine, packed all his personal belongings, and gave the Mexico City newspapers a tempestuous interview in which he said that as an honorable man he could not tolerate a nation that expropriated personal property and, moreover, he predicted the decline and fall of Mexico.

He never saw the country again, and when rumors reached him that Mexico, instead of perishing, was yearly better off than it had been the year before, he muttered ominously, "Just wait!"

But his hatred was mainly directed at President Roosevelt, possibly because there were in Alabama other old-timers who enjoyed venting their anger against "that man" in Washington. When in 1940 President Cárdenas was required by the Mexican constitution to retire, my father gave a small banquet at which he said, "My good friends here in Alabama cannot appreciate what a monster of red revolution we have had to suffer in Mexico, but that monster is finished. Now we must bend all our energies to the election of Mr. Willkie."

When Roosevelt won, my father took to his bed for eight days. Thereafter he never spoke the president's name, calling him simply *him* or *that evil man.* Frequently he would write to me, "I cannot understand why God has not punished an evil man who refused to protect the private property of this nation."

When President Roosevelt called me to the White House to decorate me for my work over Japan my father wrote: "It would be highly appreciated in these quarters if you saw fit to leave that medal elsewhere. Your picture naturally appeared in the Alabama papers, from which I got some pleasure, but I saved none of them because you were standing next to him. I noticed with some satisfaction that he appears much older and doubtless God will punish him for his iniquities."

My father's birthday occurred on April 12, and on that day in 1945 I was again home in Alabama recuperating from the banging up I'd suffered when we had to ditch at Iwo Jima, and I was listening to the radio in my room when news came that President Roosevelt had died. I ran down to my father's room and said, "Did you hear? Roosevelt just died!"

He stared at me reproachfully and said, "You're just saying that because it's my birthday."

Recalling his irascible nature, I had to smile, and his presence was so real that I began speaking to his statue: "How strange it is, Father, that you who ignored English in college and read none of the great novels, who concentrated solely on your engineering work, should have written a book of such merit that they put up a statue of you. I, on the other hand, studied all the great novels and always wanted to write but have been able to accomplish nothing of value."

A woman in the plaza, hearing me talking to myself, asked if I was all right, and I said, "No, no es nada, gracias." Then rising and slowly picking my way through the winding, flower-bordered paths of the plaza, I returned to my hotel.

But as I was passing the statue of Ixmiq I saw a long, cream-colored Chrysler speed up and grind its tires to a screeching halt. It was driven by a tall young man wearing an expensive vicuña coat about his shoulders as if it were a cape. Something about his manner made me think that I had seen him before, but his face was masked, and he was soon engulfed by strollers who shouted the magic word "Matador!"

Immediately a crowd swarmed about the Chrysler, but those in front were rudely tossed aside by a man with a firm jaw, blue eyes and a shock of white hair. His arms must have been powerful, for with ease he elbowed his way through the crowd.

"Veneno!" I shouted, for I had known him in Spain. In English his name meant poison, and he had proved himself to be certainly that for any fighting bulls he encountered in the rings of the world.

My use of his name startled him, and he turned in my direction. Recognizing me, he bellowed in the voice he had used to help him dominate the bulls, "Señor Clay! As always, you bring us good fortune."

Just then the slim driver from the front seat and two athletic fellows from the rear seat sprang from the car. All were in their late twenties and all were obviously bullfighters recognized by the crowd, which started shouting their names: "Victoriano! Chucho! Diego!" The four fighting Leals, cold-blooded terrors of the bull-rings, had arrived two days early to rest up for the crucial fights that lay ahead.

I cried: "Victoriano! Over here for a press photo." Turning to see who had spoken, he saw his trusted acquaintance from Madrid and gave me a friendly abrazo.

"Don Norman! You've come to see the fights!"

"And to write about you. To photograph you in your triumph."

Always alert to the value of publicity, he called: "Father! Chucho! Diego! Over here to assist Don Norman," and with a practiced eye he directed his father, white-haired Veneno, to stand to his left, his brother Chucho slightly to the right, and handsome Diego on a somewhat lower level in front between him and his father. It was a more effective tableau than I could have arranged, and the four men kept their poses, even improving on them as I finished a roll of film with my high-speed camera.

At the conclusion I yelled: "Hey, Chucho! Make like you're emptying the car."

Obediently Chucho took the keys from the

driver and whipped open the trunk. The other three came around him and I got a fine shot of the men and the car. Then I shouted, "Chucho, we need a little action. Can you be handing him something?"

Immediately Chucho grabbed a bag and started to hand it to Victoriano, but the matador, obviously the star of the troupe, had had enough. Turning suddenly on his heel, he strode toward me, his lithe body almost snakelike in its grace. Grabbing me by the shoulder, he said, "Take no more pictures, Clay! It's pointless. I'm not going to have a disaster in Toledo!"

"Victoriano!" shouted the white-haired old man, leaping around the car to grab the younger man, and hissed: "Son, never rough up a newspaperman!"

Victoriano repeated: "No more pictures. He's a ghoul, hoping I'll be gored so the pictures will make his story more interesting."

A crowd had gathered, captivated by the excitement of the scene. A husky young workman shouted, "By God, it's Victoriano!" And instantly this fellow had the young man on his shoulders. Immediately others rushed forward to support the figure thus held aloft, and I returned to my camera, but before I could snap the shutter, the crowd had moved across the road and onto the terrace of the hotel.

"Victoriano!" I shouted.

He turned and smiled professionally, knowing that this would be a favorite shot. His two young companions, always mindful that effective photography can make a matador, moved in quickly and took their places by the husky young workman who carried him, and the white-haired old man assumed a pose that showed his craggy profile.

They formed a magnificent pyramid there in the dusk, the godlike young matador, his two rugged assistants and their white-haired father resembling a centaur with a wreath of flowers about his head. I knew I had an extraordinary shot, and so did Victoriano, who twisted his head so that I could catch a more favorable profile.

"Two more!" I pleaded, and the onlookers elbowed in, hoping that I would take their picture as they mingled with the four Leals.

When I finished, the man carrying Victoriano set him carefully down on the steps of the hotel, and the crowd swirled into the hotel. I rewound my film and reloaded my camera. The first of the duelists had arrived, the delicate fencer, but the rowdy swordsman who thrashed about with his saber was still to come. And from his plinth, the little Indian who had started it all, Ixmiq of thirteen hundred years ago, gazed down approvingly.

THE
SPANIARD

VICTORIANO LEAL, slim-hipped and twenty-seven, was considered by many the best matador in Mexico and possibly the world. He was handsome, graceful and a joy to the eye as he led the bull past his chest, and I had come to Mexico to see him duel a stubborn, awkward little Indian, perhaps to the death.

In this contest, which would be taking place in my hometown, I could not be neutral. Victoriano I had known for some years, Gómez I had only spoken to, and that briefly. But each had made himself into a serious matador, worthy of respect and the attention my magazine was willing to focus on them.

I had abandoned Toledo in my voluntary exile long before Victoriano burst onto the taurine scene, but I'd heard rumors of his successes in Mexico so that when I was sent to Spain to write an in-depth article about who might succeed General Franco when the aging dictator died and saw in the papers that Victoriano Leal would be fighting in Madrid on Sunday, I sought permission to interview him. He was told that I was an American writer knowledgeable about bullfighting and that the publicity my magazine might provide could be profitable to him internationally.

When we met, he surprised me by saying: "I am eager to speak with you. Your Ernest Hemingway made many matadors famous by writing about them in English. For me, maybe the same." But our interview would have been quite ordinary except that at one point he asked, "Where did you learn such good Spanish?"

"I was born in a Mexican city you've probably heard of. Toledo of the silver mines."

"Toledo! I've had some of my best afternoons in that plaza!" He paused, then said enthusiastically: "And I've taken part in some great tientas at the Palafox ranch. Don Eduardo, he's like the old-time breeders."

"Don Eduardo is my uncle."

He drew back, studied me and asked carefully: "Don Eduardo? You, a norteamericano? How?"

"My mother was a Palafox and I married Don Eduardo's niece. He's not really my uncle, but it's nearly the same."

"A Palafox!" He shook his head in amazement, and from then on we were friends.

I found myself quite intrigued by this young comer and had a feeling he might one day be a big success. During some of my free hours when I wasn't working on my Franco story, I hung around the bullring and picked up stories about Victoriano and his brilliant bullfighting family. They were so entertaining that I made notes on them in one of the little books I always carry with me. Years later, when Drummond cabled me in Cuba with my Toledo assignment, I was able to dig the old notebook out of my trunk, reconstruct the key moments from Victoriano's past, and cable it all to Drummond before even leaving Havana.

To summarize the history of this brilliant young matador I can do no better than cite the essential passages I had so far sent Drummond.

———

Seville, 1886. It was a hot, song-filled afternoon in the Sierpes, that cramped alleyway that has always served as the heart of Seville. In the small plaza that fronted a restaurant known for the past three hundred years as the Arena, a wedding party was under way celebrating the marriage of a matador, who had gained local fame, and a popular flamenco dancer. All who loved bullfighting were in attendance, but the guest of chief interest was Don Luis Mazzantini, down from Madrid in honor of the occasion, and those who were particularly addicted to the art of running the bulls kept close to the majestic Italian, hoping that he might speak to them.

Don Luis was a phenomenon, one of the most popular fighters in Spain and the most unusual ever to have followed the art. His father was an Italian lyric tenor who had fled the chaos of his homeland to seek refuge in Spain, and his mother was a well-born Spaniard. Don Luis inherited both a love of opera and a passion for bullfighting. He had reached his twenties still torn between the desire to become a principal tenor at La Scala opera house in Milan or to be a master bullfighter in Madrid. After much vacillation he settled upon the latter. He was very tall, finely built and quite bald. He was good in all aspects of the fight, but in the difficult final act of killing he was one of the best who ever lived.

Out of the ring he manifested an interest in liberal politics, the arts, high society and the company of well-bred men and women. It was therefore extremely gratifying that Don Luis had deigned to grace the wedding.

Toward seven in the evening, when the celebration had calmed down somewhat, Don Luis announced with a flourish of his ivory-headed cane: "The main reason I came to Seville was to find an especially skilled peón to accompany me on my grand tour of Mexico. I'm seeking a helper who's superb with the banderillas to show the Mexicans how this art ought to be performed."

He had hardly stopped speaking when a wiry, blue-eyed young man leaped before him and said softly: "I am the man."

Don Luis leaned back, clasped his manicured hands over his cane and studied the intruder. He saw an insolence that he liked, a quick movement that was essential, and an inherent grace that sometimes came with a Sevillian bullfighter. "Your name?" he asked.

"Bernardo Leal," the young man replied.

"Your age?"

"Twenty-six."

"If you're twenty-six and any good, why haven't I heard of you."

"Because you are from Madrid, Don Luis,"

the young man replied with quiet assurance. "In Seville everyone has heard of me. There is no better banderillero."

"You!" the Italian called imperiously to a youth pressing forward to hear the conversation. "You are the bull." And he gave the lad two forks to serve as horns. Then he grabbed two knives and threw them to Leal. "These are your banderillas. Let me see you place a pair power-to-power."

The wedding guests fell back to form a small ring that included Mazzantini, who leaned forward in his chair. The "bull" stood off to one side, pawing with his feet and lowering his head with thumbs pressed against his temples, his forefingers thrust forward like horns.

Bernardo Leal, knowing that his future depended upon this moment, tucked in his shirt and tightened his belt in order to display his trim torso. Mazzantini marked this and approved: "The young man is aware of his lithe figure. That's good." But what the great Italian saw next was much better. Leal raised his arms until they were extended full length above his head and, arching his back, thrust his head and neck forward. Then, with swaying body and mincing steps he started his approach to the bull, and when it charged, snorting like a real animal, Leal broke into a deft run, allowed the bull almost to gore him, leaped into the air like a dancer, and came down with the two knives exactly in the hump of the bull's neck.

"¡Olé!" shouted the wedding guests, rewarding Leal with the traditional cry of praise for a bullfighter who has done well. Mazzantini made no sign of approval, but merely gave a new command: "Now a pair shifting the body."

Leal complied, gaining fresh olés. His examiner, somewhat irritated by the intrusive enthusiasm of the crowd, commanded, "From the barrier."

This was one of the more difficult ways of placing the banderillas, for the fighter had to stand close to the wooden barrier while inciting the bull to charge directly at him. At the last moment the man was supposed to swing clear, place the sticks as the bull thundered past parallel to the barrier, and make his escape from the horns by pressing himself back against the boards.

"You," Mazzantini shouted at some of the guests, "you be the barrier." Quickly the men formed a segment of circle against which Leal took his position. The bull was pawing the pavement and snorting, waiting for the incitement to charge, when young Leal had an inspiration. Grasping the two knives in his right hand, he raised them over his head, caught the free end

with his left, and made believe that he was bringing them down forcefully over the imaginary barrier, thus breaking them in two. Throwing away
the invisible long ends, he displayed the sup-
posedly shortened sticks to the crowd. A great
cheer went up at this gesture, for placing short
sticks against the barrier was extremely perilous.

"Ho, bull, ho!" Leal cried, moving his hips to
attract the animal. The bull pawed again,
snorted furiously, and charged at his tormentor.
With exquisite grace Leal threw his left hip toward the face of the bull, then withdrew the lure
and placed the shortened sticks as the bull
swept past.

The crowd exploded with joy and even Mazzantini applauded politely: "Can you do these
things with a real bull?" Bernardo Leal replied,
in the hearing of all the wedding guests, "Like
you, matador, I do my finest work only with real
bulls."

The tall Italian looked down at the would-be
peón and said, "You shall come with me to Mexico, and I suppose you will never see Seville
again, for if you play with real bulls in that manner, sooner or later they must kill you."

———

Toledo, 1891. Before I explain the significance of this unusual day in the life of Victoriano Leal, who wasn't even born till forty-two years later, I must explain why, in my reports to Drummond in New York, I shied away from using Spanish words in describing the specific acts of the bull-fight. Since Spanish was my first tongue, it would have been natural for me to utilize Spanish words when attempting to describe anything relating to the Spanish world. For example, when I was trailing President Eisenhower through South America I found myself repeatedly falling into using a Spanish vocabulary. Fortunately, at the other end in New York I had a Spanish specialist who knew when to keep my words and when to translate them, but in this bullfight story I could not rely upon such a specialist. Drummond was in charge of features, like this duel of the matadors, and he insisted that stories be kept as simple as possible. I could therefore sympathize with his reactions when he received the following copy from me:

Drummond, you might want to describe briefly old Bernardo Leal's initial appearance in Mexico City in 1886. As *banderillero* in the *cuadrilla* of the *espada* Mazzantini, Leal placed a great pair *uno al sesgo,* but the *toro* *embist*ed quickly from the *medios,* the *banderillas* dangling perfectly from his *morilla,* and viciously lunged at Leal, who was already acknowledging the *olé*s. The crowd gasped and this warned him of the *toro*'s approach, so with four swift strides he struck the *estribo,* vaulted over the *barrera,* and intended landing nimbly in the *callejón.* But the *toro* was too quick, and with his left *cornupeta* caught the *banderillero* in the seat of the pants, lending him an additional impulse that carried him clear over the *tablas,* landing him uninjured in the *tendidas,* where he looked up in surprise to find himself seated among the spectators, who applauded loudly. With perfect composure he bowed, then descended calmly to the *ruedo.*

About two hours after filing this I received spirited reaction from New York, and from the unusual time of its arrival I knew that something had gone wrong. Before I opened the message I thought, "Damn, they're dragging me off this bullfight thing." And I did not want to give up the story because I was hooked on it. My earlier friendship with Victoriano and my immersion in the taurine world now reminded me of the exciting days of my youth when my father would say, "Let's see what's happening at the bullring today," and we would see Luis Freg or Juan Silveti, or even the great Gaona, who was Mexican and the best in the world. Bullfighting had been bred into me. I was therefore relieved to read the telegram:

> Your account of the grandfather's being hoisted into the stands by a mad bull makes fascinating reading. But why so many Spanish words? Are you trying to impress a bunch of beatniks in some San Diego pad? Cut the enchiladas. They are pretentious and useless.

I restudied my dispatch about the grandfather's debut in Mexico City and had to confess that I had used rather more Spanish words than were required, but it was also true that I had used some that could not be avoided if one wanted to narrate accurately what I was trying to describe: the moves of life and death in a bullring. Accordingly I wired back:

> Thanks for your criticism regarding elimination of excessive Spanish, which I confess can be a weakness, but Spanish also produces accuracy, flavor, color, style and the essence of Mexico. Therefore I shall continue to use it discreetly.

This time I received my answer even more quickly than before. The cable read:

> I appreciate the thoughtfulness of your response regarding Spanish and after restudying the problem must acknowledge that philosophically you are entirely right. However if you use one more Spanish word you are fired fired fired repeat fired.

So we worked out a rule that for this story, which had to be read by people who knew neither Spanish nor bullfighting, I would use only those words that had been adopted into English, as proved by any of the unabridged dictionaries of our language. This rule, known as the Drummond Dictate, allowed me a surprising amount of freedom, as I illustrated in my report to New York:

> I am much relieved to find that I am allowed to use almost every essential word required to explain the various stages of the fight, for this will enable me to write intelligibly. The whole afternoon of three matadors facing six bulls, two each in rotation, is not a fight but a *corrida*. The entire class of men who do the fighting are *toreros*. (And although the word *toreador* has been Englished, any Spaniard

or Mexican who used it would be laughed out of the room. It occurs only in *Carmen* and must be left there.) The glamorous entrance of the toreros is the *paseo.* The bottom-rung men who run the bull when he first enters are the *peóns.* In the first major segment of each of the six fights the two men on horseback who try to tire the bull by attacking him with long, steel-tipped oaken lances are *picadors.* In the second part the colorful sticks are *banderillas* to be placed in the bull's hump by *banderilleros.* (Yes, it's in the English dictionary, too.) In the third and most important segment the star of the performance, the *matador,* performs alone in the *faena,* a word that means "the job that has to be done." Working with a dangerously small piece of red cloth, the *muleta,* and the deadly sword, he displays both skill and bravery. If he does well, including killing the bull in an honorable way, he hears cries of "¡Olé!" Those who love bullfighting are *aficionados.* Thus the language of an alien sport, legally banned in the United States and England, has insinuated itself into English.

To return to the story of what happened in the city of Toledo that critical Sunday afternoon in

1891 at the final performance in Mexico of the great Don Luis Mazzantini. He had chosen our plaza for this emotional affair because he wanted to honor his peón de confianza Bernardo Leal, who, some years earlier, had quit working in Mazzantini's troupe to become an apprentice matador on his own. Having done well, he was now eligible to advance to full matador, but this required one of the hallowed rites of bullfighting, the alternativa, or promotion, often translated as "taking the doctorate," as if the aspirant were now a full professor of the taurine art.

Bringing Leal into the ring with him, Mazzantini waited till the first bull of the afternoon came storming out, one that he would normally fight as the lead matador. Gravely he handed Bernardo his sword, his muleta and his bull, embracing him and whispering: "I've taught you what to do. Now do it," and with that act Leal became a full-fledged matador.

From contemporary accounts of that day I learned that Leal had performed so brilliantly that adoring Toledanos carried him on their shoulders to his quarters, where, as always, he expected to find waiting for him in his hotel room the pair of beautiful young women who had accompanied him from Mexico City. Instead he was greeted by a stocky man of sixty who had white muttonchop whiskers and steely blue eyes that marked him as a Spaniard.

"Close the door," he said icily to the matador, who obeyed, thus shutting out a noisy entourage that included two valets.

"Who are you?" Leal asked uneasily, for the man might turn out to be the father of some girl with whom the matador had had an unfortunate relationship.

"Change into some proper clothes, then we'll talk."

When the handsome young matador reappeared in an expensive gray countryman's costume, with shoes of fine leather, a broad-brimmed Spanish rancher's hat and a thin cord tie, his visitor rose, bowed and said, "You look like a true Spaniard. Now, what I have to say I will say briefly. Matador, you waste a noble Spanish life when you fill your rooms with cheap girls like the ones I found here when I arrived."

"Where are they?" Leal asked.

"They are gone, matador," the visitor replied.

"Who are you?" Leal insisted, standing close to the gentleman.

"I am known as Don Alfonso," the man said, fixing his penetrating eyes on Leal's, "but the name is a courtesy. Like you, I am a simple peasant who has prospered in Mexico." He laughed, then drew himself erect so that he was almost as tall as the matador. "But also like you, I am a Spaniard." He hammered his fist into his palm and repeated, "I am a Spaniard."

"What have you to do with me?" Leal pressed.

"I have come to introduce you to your future wife," Don Alfonso replied.

Bernardo Leal did not laugh. Something in his visitor's grave manner inhibited him and he asked, "Where is the girl?"

And Don Alfonso replied with dignity, "In my house, for she is my daughter." He paused, then added with intensity: "You are a Spaniard, matador, and you must not allow your precious blood to be lost among Mexicans."

"Mexico is now my home," Leal began, but whatever he was about to say was cut off when his visitor grabbed him by the back of the neck and thrust him toward the frameless mirror that graced the barren hotel wall.

"Look at your eyes, son!" the determined old man cried. "Look at your skin! Matador, you are a Spaniard. You are too precious to be lost."

He led Leal from the hotel and through the crowds that had come to pay him homage. The girls who had accompanied him from Mexico City fell back and the hangers-on that pursue all matadors stood aside. Through the narrow cobbled streets of Toledo, most gracious of the

Mexican cities and the most Spanish, went the two Spaniards until they came to a white stone wall sixteen feet high on which had been pasted, some days before, a garish red-and-yellow poster proclaiming the arrival in Toledo of the famed Spanish matador Bernardo Leal.

"I tell them they must not place posters on my wall," Don Alfonso complained. "But with Mexicans what can you do?"

He led the way to a huge wooden gate studded with bronze fittings, and after he had jangled the rope for a while, muttering as he did so, "These damned Mexicans!" a barefoot servant swung the heavy portal aside and Bernardo Leal entered for the first time the spacious entrance chambers of his future father-in-law.

He found himself in a corner of Spain. There were the solid wooden trunks carved in Salamanca. Above them were crossed Spanish swords from Seville. And in the patio beyond played a handsomely carved stone fountain copied from one in the ancient city of Ronda. When Don Alfonso's wife appeared the young matador saw she was one of those large-boned, horsey women so common in Spain, and he thought, It was she who sent her husband to fetch me. But the tall Spanish woman had the graciousness of her native land and immediately made Bernardo feel at home.

"This is a most unusual meeting," she said softly, "but I saw you twice in Mexico City and I thought, We Spaniards must stick together.

Quietly, Bernardo repeated what he had told her husband: "I think of myself now as a Mexican."

With equal control, but with much greater force, Don Alfonso's wife replied, "As you grow older, matador, believe me, the heritage of your Spanish blood will come to the fore." She smiled, took Leal by the arm, and said, "Raquel is waiting for us in there. You can appreciate that for her this is a difficult moment."

When the studded doors were swung back, the matador saw standing by a heavy refectory table a girl of twenty-five or so, tall like her mother, big-boned, possibly awkward, but obviously eager to be charming. She was neither beautiful nor ugly, but when she left the massive leather chair upon which she had been leaning, she moved forward with vigor and grace. "I saw you at the bullfight today, matador," she said quietly, "and you were superb."

"If I had seen you there, señorita, I should have dedicated the first bull to you."

"If I wear my best Spanish gown next Sunday, will you do so?"

"I shall be unable to do otherwise," the matador replied.

It was a delightful dinner, candle-lit and opulent. In the course of it Don Alfonso explained that he had come to Mexico thirty-eight years ago and had made his fortune importing goods from Liverpool. At first he had tried living in Mexico City, but had found it oppressive and lacking in culture: "It's so damned Mexican!" Then he had come to Toledo and had stumbled upon this old house that had been built by one of the Palafox men. "Here I have been happy."

"May I visit you during the coming week?" Leal asked.

"We would be desolate if you did not," Don Alfonso replied.

"On Friday I must visit the Palafox bull ranch to supervise the testing of some cows," Leal explained. Then, turning to Raquel, he said, "I would be flattered beyond words if you could accompany our party."

"We will be most happy to accept," the girl's mother quickly replied, having no intention of leaving her daughter alone with any man prior to marriage. And after the pleasant visit to the ranch the young matador dallied in our city and it became apparent that Raquel would marry him and that he would move to Toledo and live in the big Spanish house.

———

Mexico City, 13 December 1903. As a matador's wife, Doña Raquel was unusual in that she was willing to attend the her husband's fights, and she was sitting in the old plaza in Mexico City on the day in 1903 when Bernardo Leal gave a gallant performance. Her eldest son, Justo, eleven at the time, was with her in the seats by the barrier when her husband took the second bull of the afternoon, a wiry, quick Palafox animal, and dominated the beast pretty much as he wished.

Doña Raquel feared all bulls and appreciated their lethal power, but she was also fascinated by her husband's poetic grace, which no other fighter could match. There was something in the manner in which Bernardo worked that projected, a sensation of grave danger linked to exquisite art, and the capacity to accomplish this was rare. She thought proudly, Not even Mazzantini displayed a finer grace than my husband, but when Bernardo finally killed the Palafox beast she closed her eyes and covered her ears as if in surrender to her hitherto repressed fears.

Little Justo, a serious child dedicated to protecting his father's reputation, did not cover his ears at such moments but stayed alert to catch the shouts of "Leal! Leal!" But on this afternoon some of the rowdies seated in the sunny section expressed contempt for the size of the Palafox bull that Bernardo had killed and instead of cheering the matador they jeered him and continued to do so even when the other matador, a famous Mexican, had started to fight the third bull. "Show him how a real Mexican fights real bulls," someone in the crowd shouted.

"Spaniards are always brave with little bulls," another added.

"Liar!" Justo screamed in a high childish treble. Bernardo, leaning against the barrier, looked up at his son and laughed.

Señora Leal did not consider the incident amusing. "Justo!" she whispered.

"I could cut their throats," the boy muttered, not bothering to watch the fight of the second matador.

Doña Raquel slapped her son's hand sharply and said, "No more of that."

"But Father can do it with big bulls, too," her son protested, and breaking from his mother's grasp he dashed to the iron grillwork that separated the good seats from the inexpensive and shouted: "Swine! My father can fight bulls as big as boxcars."

With much embarrassment Doña Raquel recovered her son and the incident might have ended there except that one of Bernardo Leal's partisans in the sunny section bellowed, "The boy's right! Leal is better than any Mexican!"

This challenge was calculated to launch a riot, and it did. Soon the sunny section was a melee with men flying through the air as they dived from the higher tiers to revenge themselves upon enemies seated below. Then, as quickly as it had started, the riot ended, for from the caverns beneath the plaza burst into sunlight the fourth bull of the afternoon, a huge black Palafox animal that weighed more than half a ton. It was intended for the Spaniard Leal.

From the sunny side a voice cried ominously, "Now we'll see what he can do with a real bull."

"You watch!" young Justo shouted back. His mother did not try to silence him, for she was struck with terror at the sight of this monstrous animal.

As if he had vowed to support his son's claims, Bernardo fought the large bull with special grace and skill. He turned and danced with the big cape used at the start of each fight until the crowd sensed that with this big adversary he might even surpass what he had accomplished with his first bull.

And then, at the height of Leal's mastery, the bull suddenly whipped upward with his saberlike left horn, caught Leal in the groin, and threw him into the air. Even before he fell to earth, men were already running into the ring to carry him to the infirmary. But with devilish cunning the maddened bull chopped upward at his victim, and before Leal could drop, the bull's powerful horns threw him back into the air four times, revolving his body upon the horn tips as if he were a rag doll.

"Oh my God!" moaned Doña Raquel.

At last the bull flung the matador far away and onto the sand, whereupon the peóns rushed toward him, but their movement enraged the bull and he charged madly for them. When they fled, his ugly little eyes saw not their swirling capes but the red-stained body on the sand, and with horrifying accuracy he drove his left horn at the inert matador. When the bull's horn first penetrated Bernardo Leal's throat, his wife fainted, and she was spared the ultimate horror of that day, but the boy Justo kept his eyes grimly fixed upon each motion of the bull and its effect on the man.

The Palafox ranch, 1933. Bernardo Leal left two sons, Justo, born in 1892, and Anselmo, born nine years later in 1901. The boys grew up with their mother in the Spanish house in Toledo. They had blue eyes like their parents and fair skin, and throughout their lives the lesson that would live with them longest was not one acquired in school but the one that their old grandfather Don Alfonso had taught them. Often he would grab them by the back of the neck and thrust them before a mirror: "Look at your eyes! Remember that you are Spanish. When it comes time to marry, find some Spanish girl like your mother."

On the streets of Toledo, of course, the boys were Mexican, but once inside the walled garden, whose doors were studded with metal from Spain, they were inheritors of a Spanish tradition. But they were also inheritors of another, more terrible memory, and for this there was no cure, nor has there ever been. In their playroom hung the poster of their father's last fight: ¡PONCIANO DÍAZ AND BERNARDO LEAL WITH BULLS OF PALAFOX! In their mother's room hung a replica of the matador's last suit of lights, slim-waisted and elegant, while in another room known as the chapel because of the silver retable, at which Leal had worshiped before his fights, hung suspended the head of the great Palafox bull that had killed their father.

It was from such memories and mementos that the Leal boys, Justo and Anselmo, derived their obsession with the bulls, but if the Revolution of 1910 had not erupted to break the peaceful passage of days in Toledo, it is hardly likely that either boy would have followed the bulls as a profession. In 1911 General Gurza, the scourge of the north, led his undisciplined rabble into the fair old city, and for three days there was terror. Priests were shot, young girls ravished, and buildings burned. On the evening of the second day four wild-riding pistoleros from Durango rattled the gate at Don Alfonso's big Spanish house, broke their way in, and informed him, "General Gurza will use this house as his headquarters."

"Get out, you rotten Mexican rabble!" the would-be grandee thundered, his muttonchops bristling. These were the last words he spoke, for the invaders instantly shot him, and prepared the way for their general. When Don Alfonso's old horse-faced Spanish wife, screaming, attacked the intruders, they shot her, too. Then they raped the dead couple's daughter and cut the throat of Doña Raquel, the matador's widow. When General Gurza and his men were finally driven from the city, the old Spanish palace was a ruin, its walls knocked down and its tapestries burned by Gurza's drunken lieutenants.

Don Alfonso's business had been failing, and when he died the boys Justo and Anselmo were virtually destitute. But instead of surrendering to despair, Justo, who was a husky nineteen at the time, looked upon his unexpected freedom as a deliverance and at the invitation of the Palafoxes moved himself and his brother to the bull ranch, southwest of Toledo. There he surprised everyone by becoming a master picador. Astride a horse he had natural courage, and with his broad shoulders and powerful arms he had no difficulty driving the long iron-tipped pics deep into the bull's neck muscles. He was a fierce opponent of the bulls and one day a rancher warned, "If you drive the pic so deeply, you may kill the bull."

"I want to," Justo growled.

"You fight that bull as if you hated him like some evil poison," the watcher observed.

"To me all bulls are poison," Justo replied, and from that day his name was Veneno, Poison. As Veneno he appeared in the new plaza in Mexico City, and as Veneno, one of the most famous picadors of his era, he accompanied the Mexican matador Luis Freg to Spain, where he enhanced his reputation.

In Spain Veneno became known as the fearless picador. He would drive his blindfolded horse anywhere to encounter the bull and worked from terrains that a lesser man would not have dared to approach. He exhibited demonic hatred for the bull, and on the days when four or five of his horses were killed under him and he would be prone on the sand, with the infuriated bull trampling him while trying to gore him, it sometimes appeared as if Veneno wanted to fight the bull with his bare hands. That he was not killed before the end of his first season in Spain was a miracle.

All matadors breathed easier when Veneno was in their troupe, for with his cruel, probing lance he punished a bull more severely than any other picador. So during those years, now termed the golden age of bullfighting, Veneno fought repeatedly for most of the giants: Joselito, Belmonte, Gaona. And he came to know as much about bulls as any man who ever fought. The bullfight fans, knowing this, were apt to shout when he rode into the plaza on some pathetic nag whose right eye had been blindfolded so he could not see the bull about to attack and shy away: "¡Olé! Veneno! Kill him with your pic." And this he tried to do. Twice in his career he succeeded in so damaging a bull, his lance driving toward the vulnerable backbone itself, that the animal had to be returned to the corrals, where it died. Normally such an act would have been condemned, but with Veneno it was different, for everyone knew that he wanted to kill bulls to avenge his father.

His brother, Anselmo, never acquired the reputation that Veneno enjoyed. Perhaps because he had been left at home in Toledo on that dreadful afternoon when the bull tore away most of his father's head, he lacked the consuming compulsion of Veneno and failed to attain that mastery of bulls that characterized his brother. He became a minor matador, without class, and moved inconspicuously from one Mexican plaza to the next, brave perhaps but lacking fire. He also tried his luck in Spain but was promptly identified by critics as one who should leave the fighting of bulls to others. But he knew no other occupation, so he continued, one of those semi-tragic men who waste their lives on the periphery of an art that is cruel to horses, bulls and people alike.

Anselmo's only distinction arose from the fact that while on his Spanish tour he contracted marriage with a beautiful girl called Alicia from Seville, in the south. Her father took one look at his son-in-law in the classic ring of Seville and advised: "Son, leave the bulls. They are not for you."

"It is my profession," Anselmo argued.

"I have a meat-packing plant near Cádiz," the girl's father argued. "Work with me."

"My brother and I follow the bulls," Anselmo insisted proudly. "It's in our blood."

"Is your brother married?" the meat-packer asked.

"No."

"Why don't you introduce him to Alicia's cousin?"

When Veneno came south with Belmonte to fight at Seville, the introductions were made, a marriage was arranged, and Veneno promptly had two sons in quick succession. In 1933 Anselmo also had a son, whom he named Victoriano Leal, hoping that the boy would achieve more victories than he had accomplished.

Victoriano was less than a month old when the senior Leals were invited to the Palafox ranch to participate in the testing of some new cows that the ranch had recently purchased in an effort to strengthen the bloodlines and make the offspring bulls more fierce in the fight. Anselmo did not relish these trips to the ranch, for after the sack of their grandfather's Spanish house in Toledo, one of General Gurza's soldiers had turned up with the head of the bull that had killed Bernardo Leal, and Don Eduardo had purchased this grisly souvenir. Now it hung prominently on a wall of the entertainment room at the ranch, marked by a silver plaque that read: "Terremoto of Palafox. This bull of 529 kilos killed the matador Bernardo Leal in Mexico

City 13 December 1903." After more than half
a century the horns were still sharp as daggers
and they terrified Anselmo, but robust Veneno
was in no way dismayed. Unlike his brother, he
appreciated every opportunity to fight Palafox
bulls, and even though on this day he would be
limited to cows, he would nevertheless have
many chances to wound real bulls, to assail
them with an abbreviated pic and to feel them
recoil. If he could not deal with the grown bulls
of Palafox with a heavy pic he would settle for
punishing the young cows with a light one.

So the brothers went by train from Mexico City
to Toledo, where Don Eduardo Palafox met
them for the long drive to the ranch quarters
southwest of town. On the way he confided,
"The reason I wanted you to attend this testing
is that in addition to the new cows, I want you to
see the new seed bull from Spain. He is being
delivered after the testing tomorrow."

"Guadalquivir blood?" Veneno asked.

"Naturally," Don Eduardo replied, and he proposed that they join him in a copa at the long
mahogany bar in the entertainment room, but as
the three men were about to sit down in chairs
built of bull's horns highly polished, interlocked
to form seats and backs, and then made comfortable by cushions of tanned but uncut sheep-
skins, Anselmo found that the chair he had

chosen was one facing the great bull Terremoto, so that whenever he looked up he
found the bull that had killed his father glaring at
him as if the animal was about to charge and kill
the son, too.

"I'll take this seat," Anselmo said, changing
chairs, but Veneno noticed that even when his
brother was safe with his back to the wall, he
kept turning fearfully to look at the bull. When
Don Eduardo left the brothers to greet a movie
actor from Hollywood who had come to see the
testing, Anselmo reached for his brother's hand
and said hesitantly: "Veneno, if anything should
happen to me, promise that—"

"What can happen to either of us?" the valiant picador asked contemptuously.

"He's always in the ring." The frightened man
pointed over his shoulder to Terremoto. "Always waiting."

"I think only of live bulls," Veneno replied with
some savagery. "You should too."

"But if anything does happen, swear you'll
raise my son as if he were a Spaniard."

"What could that mean?" Veneno laughed.
"What in the world do you do to a boy—"

"Make him dress neatly, speak properly . . ."
Anselmo's voice trailed off. "And when the time
comes for him to marry . . ." Again he faltered,
and then with a rush he said: "Brother, we are

strangers in an alien land. To me all Mexicans are General Gurza."

"You talk like a fool, brother."

The testing that day was joyous, with the corral lined with beautiful women, and the hot Toledo sun making the dust golden as the furious cows kicked it aloft as they attacked the horse bearing their tormentor Veneno. When he finished testing the bravery of the cows with his sharp pic—for it was through their mother's line, not the seed bull's, that fighting bulls gained courage—he passed them along to the matadors, who played them with capes, and as each animal left the corral, bleeding a little from the shoulders, where Veneno had stabbed them, the foreman cried, "Number 131. Very brave!" or "Number 132. Cautious, frightened of the horse." The latter would be raised for beef, for she would not be allowed to serve as the mother of a Palafox bull.

When the testing was completed, Don Eduardo stepped into the middle of the little ring and announced, "We are now going to show you our new seed bull from the ranch of Guadalquivir, in Spain."

The crowd applauded and from the cab of a truck a man called, "You ready?"

"Bring him in!" Don Eduardo replied.

The truck backed slowly toward a gate leading to the corral. Dust rose from the wheels to envelop an enormous iron-banded cage whose sides were solid oak. None of the spectators could see into the cage, yet all were fascinated by it and looked at nothing else as it slowly approached the corral entrance.

The dust must have irritated the great seed bull inside, for he was at the end of a journey that had started in distant Andalucía and had included trucks, boats, barges, trains and now trucks again. With demonic force the unseen bull attacked his prison, and the huge oaken box shivered and its iron bands seemed to stretch. Everyone could hear the massive horns stabbing at the sides, and terror was palpable even in the sun. Men who knew bulls looked at each other in apprehension, for no matter how long one worked with these animals, one remained awestruck by their raw power. Again the maddened bull lunged at his cage, and again the huge box shook with his fury. Inside was an animal that could lift a horse on his horns, rush across the diameter of a plaza, and toss the horse over the barrier. An accidental flick of those horns as they passed a matador could throw the man fifteen feet into the air, or gash his leg from knee to thigh.

The unseen bull now started kicking the rear boards of the cage and it became apparent why the cage was banded with iron straps.

"We'll need some men up there," Don Eduardo cried, and the Leal brothers leaped onto the platform that the truck was approaching. The oaken cage would have to be edged over the side of the truck lest there remain a gap between cage and corral in which the costly animal might break a leg. Timbers were called for, and the edging process began, but when it was well under way, and the cage was tipped ever so slightly to permit movement, the bull inside became even more enraged at the unexpected motion, and charged anew at his prison.

Unfortunately, he chose to strike the downhill side and before anyone could warn of the danger, the box tipped and caught the matador Anselmo Leal between its sharp edge and the stone wall of the corral. He gave one cry of terror, and then the great unseen bull himself corrected the accident by lunging at the opposite side of his box, which restored the box's level position.

Anselmo lived for four more years, but his chest had been crushed and he never again faced the bulls. Veneno supported him with the good earnings he made as Mexico's leading picador, and at Anselmo's funeral in 1937 most of the leading bullfight figures of Mexico and some from Spain attended. This ineffectual matador, killed by a bull safely encased in a cage, left only one wish, that he be buried in his wife's city of Seville, in southern Spain, but the dislocations of the Spanish civil war prevented this, and he was sent to a grave in Puebla, a city he had not liked.

Toledo, 1945. One of the most exciting afternoons in the life of Victoriano Leal came when he was twelve years old, for on that sunny afternoon in his home city of Toledo he dressed for the first time in the suit of lights. He was a lean, handsome boy, with a fair complexion, blue eyes and jet-black hair. Including the heavy blue-and-gold bullfighter's suit, he weighed only ninety pounds, but when he stepped into the Toledo plaza with his ceremonial cape drawn about him, it was obvious to everyone that he had at least the physical components required of a stylish matador. More than that, he had presence.

His cousins, Chucho and Diego, had been touring for some time with their father and had gained some fame as the best of the beginners. Chucho was sixteen and already a fine young fighter, while Diego, two years younger, was capable with the sticks. Their father, now in his fifties, naturally served as picador for the exhibitions, riding his horses with erect dignity and punishing the bulls as severely as ever.

The old man, his hair now white, felt that from his three sons, Chucho, Diego and Victoriano—he permitted no separateness regarding his nephew, treating him as a son—he was bound to find at least one worthy matador, and through that boy's achievements he would end his own bullfighting years crowned with glory. He would continue to serve as picador for as long as the years would let him, but he would be serving his own son, and when he himself beat a bull almost to death so that the subsequent part of the fight was easy, he would be accomplishing this not for some stranger but for his own child.

Therefore it was with both apprehension and joy that the white-haired old picador watched his three boys line up for the opening parade in Toledo. To the left, as the crowd faced the youngsters, stood Chucho, the most experienced of the fighters. To the right marched Diego, confident and handsome in his purple suit. And in the middle, as custom required, his bullfighter's hat in his hand, strode the beginner, twelve-year-old Victoriano, wiry as a horseman's whip, and at the boy's first step into the arena his father gasped and a premonition of great force possessed him. "My God!" he cried as his horse moved forward to follow the marching trio. "That middle one is going to be greater than us all!"

It was a sensational day. The calves that customarily appeared for boy matadors were missing that day. Since picadors were being used, older animals had been purchased for the fight, and these beasts would have been too much for most such youthful troupes. Chucho, as if sensing the challenge of his youngest brother, was both valiant and artistic. He had the polished style of a Spanish fighter rather than the awkward ruggedness of the typical Mexican beginner.

Diego, as always, placed the banderillas well, dancing away from the little bulls with both excitement and skill. And as always, old Veneno hammered his pic into the animals just as far as the risk of death would allow, leaving the beasts exhausted and pliant for his sons.

But it was when little Victoriano faced his first formal adversary that the crowd cheered with real excitement. They recognized something different in his manner, a mixture of arrogance and competence that captivated them. Years later in Spain, when I knew Victoriano well, I asked him about his first fight and he said, "You ask me how much I knew, a boy of twelve, about my part

in that first one? Norman, I say with all modesty,
I knew everything. From childhood I'd studied
bulls and matador passes. From hours of study
with Veneno in bare rooms when he traveled to
fights, I had become a master of the big cape,
more than average with the muleta. I made myself do everything, banderillas, sword, how to
bow to the president up in his box, how to dedicate a bull to a pretty girl, then turn and toss my
hat over my shoulder for her to catch. So in my
first fight I was nervous—of course I was—but
I was not afraid, because I knew I was prepared."

At this point in our discussion he hesitated,
thought a long time, and said, "Don't use this,
Norman, in your story, but in that first fight I also
knew something shameful, something quite terrible. I knew that I looked like a matador, and my
brothers didn't. They were too fat, not poetic in
their moves. They couldn't march toward the
bull properly, one foot before the other in a
straight line, and when they stood in front of the
bull they couldn't profile, their spine curved forward, their neck and head pulled way back.
They could not do these things, but I could. The
crowd knew it. I knew it. And I think maybe they
knew it."

"How did that first one end?" I asked, and he
said with no arrogance: "The president awarded

me an ear from my second bull, and with it in my right hand I marched around the arena drinking in the cheers . . . and I've continued marching ever since."

"Is it true that a crowd of boys no bigger than yourself carried you from the ring shouting 'Torero! Torero!' " and he said: "They did."

The effect of Victoriano's first fight on his father was electrifying. The old picador reacted as if he had seen a ghost; a sense of terror seemed to overcome him and for three days he brooded in silence, walking the streets of Toledo and allowing his boys to practice by themselves.

Then he went to see Don Eduardo Palafox, who was lounging at the House of Tile, and asked bluntly, "Did you see the fights on Sunday?"

"They were very good," the elderly rancher replied.

Veneno reached forward, grabbed Don Eduardo's hands and gasped pleadingly: "Tell me, sir. Was he as good as I thought?"

"The little one?"

"Who else?"

The rancher looked at his friend, this ancient enemy of all bulls who had mutilated so many Palafox animals for his matadors, and said slowly, "I think that in young Victoriano you have found what you've been looking for."

As if thrown into the air by some powerful bull, the old picador leaped up, stormed about the tables, and cried, "I'm sure of it, Don Eduardo! I watched that boy as if he were a vision. He is already better than his father ever was. When I see him face a bull I have the feeling I'm seeing his grandfather."

The rancher remained seated, watching the white-haired picador, and when the latter's excitement had subsided he observed, "This boy will be far better than his grandfather."

The words were those that Veneno had wanted to hear, yet he was afraid to believe them. Falling into a chair and clutching Don Eduardo's hand, he pleaded: "Did you see this for yourself or are you merely feeding my hopes?"

"I saw it," Don Eduardo assured him. Then he asked briskly, "Now tell me, where do the boys fight next?"

"Zacatecas, on Sunday."

"I will watch them on that day," Don Eduardo replied, and it was on Sunday, 11 March 1945, in the dusty, mountain town of Zacatecas, where the bullring clings to the side of a hill, that Veneno Leal made his big decision. After the fight he strode, in his heavy picador's costume, to where Don Eduardo Palafox sat and asked the rancher bluntly, "Do you still believe in the boy?"

"Like you," the rancher replied, "I hold to my belief more strongly than before."

"Thank you, Don Eduardo," the powerful old picador replied, wringing his friend's hand. "You have made up my mind."

"Victoriano did it," the rancher said gravely, and the two men separated.

In the barren hotel room in Zacatecas, as the exciting Sunday came to a close, Veneno assembled his three sons and said forcefully, "Tonight we begin our campaign."

"For what?" Chucho asked. He'd had a good afternoon and was pleased.

"For wealth. For fame," the old fighter said simply. "For a place like Belmonte's."

A hush fell over the excited boys, who had been jabbering about the day's adventures. Never before had their father spoken of bullfighting in that way. Staring at Chucho, he said: "Son, today you were adequate. I was proud of you. But you will never have a matador's body. Already you show signs of too much fat." With compassion he watched as these harsh truths paralyzed his older boy, then added: "Starting today you will train yourself to be the best peón bullfighting has ever had. You will master every subtle twist of the art, every trick in running the bull. But, above all, be ready each moment to rush in and save your brother when the bull knocks him down. Save his life with your own if necessary."

Chucho, who could still hear the cheers of the Zacatecas crowd, swallowed his anger, folded his hands resolutely in his lap and looked at his chubby brother Diego, thinking: "I'm twice as good as him. Stand by to protect him? That's crazy."

But then he heard his father saying: "Diego, you're already too stocky. You'll never be a matador. But you have style with the banderillas. That will be your job. Learn to break the sticks across your knee and place the real short ones. The crowds love that."

Now he turned to his youngest son and said: "Victoriano, you shall be the matador, the great figure," and the bleak room fell silent.

It was several years after this crucial night before I came to know Victoriano, but as I queried him in Madrid about this decision in Zacatecas he remembered each moment, each syllable that was said, each look on his brothers' faces: "When my father picked me I thought I might faint. When I was four playing with a pointed stick and a napkin, I dreamed of being a matador. I walked like one, tilted my head like the pictures of Gaona. But I feared that Chucho and maybe even Diego would go ahead of me, so when I heard my father say "You shall be the matador," I was afraid to make a sound. All I could do was look at my brothers. Chucho's shoulders drooped. Diego shrugged as if to say: If I'm to be the banderillero—maybe I knew all along. But I could feel myself standing a little straighter, my chin out just a bit. And in the silence I could hear people cheering—frenzied cheers.

"But it was Father speaking again, in a wild, powerful voice I'd never heard before. 'We will be the Leals!' he shouted as if a spirit possessed him. 'Victoriano will be our matador. Diego will be the stick man like no other. You, Chucho, will be the man who cares for all details. And I will beat the bulls.' A fury came upon him that night. My brothers and me, we'd never before seen him like this, for up to now he'd nursed his dreams in silence, but on this night, he let himself go to reveal his vision."

Fourteen years later Victoriano shivered as he told me what happened next: "Like a madman he raised his powerful right arm, the one he used to hold the pic, and shouted so they could hear him in the hall, 'I will grind the bulls down to the sand. Their knees will buckle and they will fall back. You'll see blood running down their withers and we will destroy them. The four of us, one team! We will destroy them and men shall say of us, 'Those Leals, they know how to fight bulls!' "

Seville, 1959. In 1952 Victoriano Leal had entered the huge plaza in Mexico City to become a full-fledged matador. He was only nineteen at the time, and no boy ever had a less complicated road to the ultimate heights of this difficult art. At twelve he faced his first bull in Toledo. On the following Sunday in Zacatecas three of the most gifted bullfighters in Mexico dedicated their lives to making him preeminent. Two years later, at the age of fourteen, he became a novice with such sensational publicity that he then earned more than many matadors.

He moved from plaza to plaza like a young king, protected in public by Veneno and in the ring by his two skilled brothers. By the time he took his doctorate, in the largest plaza in the world, he was an accomplished fighter, master of all tricks. His particular gift was an excellence with the cape that none of his contemporaries could equal. To watch him unfurl his arabesques before a massive black enemy was to see, in the words of the critic León Ledesma, "a young god sculpturing sunlight."

He was also capable with the banderillas, although with markedly difficult beasts he requested his brother Diego to assume the job; and with the red muleta at the end of the fight he could be exquisite. Again, on bulls that Veneno warned him were apt to be difficult, he forswore exhibitionistic passes and went about the business of killing in a workmanlike manner. He was never good with the sword, veering off to one side at the final moment, but he was competent, and his haunting skill in the earlier portions of the fight encouraged his adherents to overlook his defects at the end.

When I first met Victoriano in Spain he surprised me, as I said, by allowing me to ask more questions than he permitted other newsmen, and when I asked about this he explained, "We're both Toledanos, you and me. But you're also an American, big New York magazine. I want North America to know about the Leals, London too, Argentina."

This emboldened me to ask, "Why do you always refer to the Leals, never to Victoriano?" and he replied: "Without the others I'd not be here today." And from a desk in the spacious room of the house he had purchased for his family he produced a well-thumbed photograph album in which he showed me an almost terrifying series of shots taken by bold cameramen who had sometimes dashed into the ring while some massive bull was trying to gore Victoriano while he lay flat on his back in the sand. In each photograph his life was clearly being saved by one or another of the Leals.

"Tijuana, last year. That's Chucho leading the bull away while he stands almost on me. Very brave, that time."

Of another shot he said: "Nuevo Laredo, this year. Chucho couldn't get to me, but roly-poly Diego came in. Look at him, the horns right in his belly, but he twirled away and took the bull with him."

At the next photograph I started laughing because it showed a tremendous bull standing right over the matador, horns poised to pin him to the ground, and Veneno, the picador, desperately grabbing the bull by the tail and, with bulging muscles, literally hauling the great beast backward and away from his imperiled son. Gravely Victoriano said: "It does look funny, but if our father had not been so brave and so strong, I wouldn't be showing you these shots. We're the Leals. Look at us in the ring," and he continued to flick the pages, permitting me to stop him now and then to study the way his three family members united to help him and, at times, to keep him alive.

"The early newspaper accounts," I said when

he closed the album, "all say that at the beginning, even when you were thirteen and fourteen,
you killed with skill and courage—one of the
things that helped make you famous. Now the
same writers say you're only adequate. What
happened? Some incident like one of those?"
and I pointed to the album.

For the first time since I had met him he
laughed, and through the following years I would
not often see him do this, for he was a young
man of gravity. "You're clever, Norman. Yes, it
was a photograph, but not one of these. When
I look at these, as we just did, I think, 'There I
am, flat on the ground. One puncture from those
horns and I'm dead. But it's the job of the others
to save me, so I lie very still, but with my eyes
wide open so that as soon as they lead the bull
away, I can jump up and run to safety.'" He
laughed again. "But of course, I take my sword
and my muleta with me if I can, because it's still
my responsibility to kill that damned bull."

"What photograph was it that made the difference?" He left the room, taking the album with
him, and returned in a moment with a framed
photograph taken by Cano, the noted taurine
photographer in Madrid. It showed Victoriano in
1953 completing a perfect kill of a huge Miura
bull, the most dangerous breed in the world.
Right over the horn the matador was reaching,

his knuckles touching the hairy skin, a remarkable kill. But the angle at which it was shot
focused not on Victoriano but on the immensity
of the bull. It was a stupendous animal, the
acme of his breed.

For some moments the matador sat staring at
the picture, then said softly: "When I got back in
my room in Madrid and saw this photograph I
said: 'It couldn't be. No man could do that, in
that way, to that bull.' " Laughing nervously, he
said: "Each year the bulls of the mind grow bigger."

When years later I sent Drummond an evaluation of Victoriano that summarized the above
facts, he wired back: "Why use the phrase
'veering off to one side at the final moment'?
Why not use the classic 'at the moment of truth
he chokes'? " I replied in a rather long telegram,
which I hoped would settle this and other Drummond inquiries that had begun to irritate:

> I must make it clear that I will withdraw from
> this bullfight enterprise if your stylists jazz up
> my story with scenes in which the matadors
> quake with fear and pray with parched lips to
> the Virgin of the Macarena just before enter-
> ing the plaza. I have studied this thing at

close quarters for some time and this heroic fear that American authors love to write about is an orgasm of their imagination and not what goes on at all. I've spoken to Victoriano about this a couple of times, and here's a man who knows as much about fear as anyone. After all, his father and grandfather were killed by bulls and he was in the arena once himself when another matador was wiped out. This boy knows. He prays. He carries a silver altar wherever he goes. He wears three gold charms, St. Sebastian, St. Teresa, St. Francis, the last because good old Francis loved animals and is needed to intercede for bullfighters on the day of judgment. He is nervous as hell before a fight, sweats a lot although he's skinny, and has to urinate more often than any matador I've ever seen, but the quaking fear of the novelists simply ain't there. In the course of discussing fear he used a great phrase that you might lift: "If a matador is left alone from one o'clock to four on Sunday afternoon, the bulls of the mind grow larger." I think that about summarizes it. He tells me that before the first serious goring fear can sometimes be remote, but after that no man can fool himself. He knows a bull can kill. He knows that if he goes out often enough, the bulls are bound to hit him, and seriously. But in these days, with penicillin and the sulfas, very few men are killed in the bullring. It is much safer, statistically, to be a matador than to drive racing cars at Indianapolis, markedly safer than to engage in prizefighting, and has about the same risk as playing American football. In one period of ten years, out of 189 full matadors who fought a total of 150,000 bulls only two were killed. But many were seriously wounded and a few were permanently crippled. From talking at length with Victoriano on this I would say that the pre-fight fear of the matador is about the same as the pre–World Series fear of a man like Mickey Mantle facing Sandy Koufax, with this difference, that if Mantle messes things up all he has to face is the jeers of the crowd and a restless night before the game next day, but if the matador slips he may lose a leg or his life. Now, as to this moment-of-truth bit, I positively refuse to let you use the phrase. I've never heard any real torero use it, and I understand it isn't much used by anybody else these days, and for one damned good reason. Bear with me and be sure your writers digest this. In the old days when the phrase originated, the early parts of a fight were pretty sickly affairs, frankly.

I'm sending you old-time photographs of Mazzantini, Lagartijo, Guerrita and Bombita. I want your crowd to study the distance these heroes kept between themselves and the bull. Look at that dilly of Guerrita about to make a pass with five—count 'em—five peóns ringing him with their capes. If the bull wanted to hurt Guerrita he had to fight his way past that whole gang. Look also at the great Mazzantini make a pass with the cloth. He was so far away, the bull couldn't even smell him. So it was through all the fight. But now look at that stupendous photograph of Mazzantini killing. On his toes, all his weight on the sword, right over the horns. One chop of that bull's horns, and Mazzantini goes to the hospital, maybe permanently. That was indeed the moment of truth. And it was called that because all that had gone before was exhibition with the bull in one ballpark and the man in another. But at the moment of the actual kill the matador had to lay his life on the line. Today things are exactly reversed. I'm sending you five photographs that our boy Victoriano selected for me to send you as a summary of what he is like. It's a surprisingly frank assessment and what he said when he explained them was even more so. Number 1: "Look at the size of this beast! Weighs about twelve hundred pounds and he's two inches from my chest." Number 2: "This is cape work when the bull first comes out. This is my version of a pass made famous by our Mexican hero Gaona. Cape flashing way over my head. This time the horns, two inches from my back." Number 3: "I'm in the faena at the end, working with the little muleta low in the left hand. The *pase natural.* Sometimes I fail to do even one, with a stubborn bull. On this day, I remember it clearly, I did five." Number 4: "If you publish your story, please use this one. Fourteen hundred pounds, Concha y Sierra in Seville. See if you could wedge a postage stamp between this horn and my chest." Number 5: "But to be honest I suppose you ought to show this one, too. This is that big bull in Seville again, wonderful animal, deserved better. But I kill the way I can, this time off to one side. When Chucho saw this photo he said, 'You were in Puebla and the bull in Guadalajara.' And I asked him, 'Would you have been any closer?' and he said, 'I tell the girls I would have been.' And then we both laughed."

I really think he wanted me to use Number 5, bad as it makes him look, because he takes bullfighting seriously. If you do use it, print alongside that stupendous photograph of Mazzantini practically throwing himself right onto the horns and you will understand that in today's fighting there is in the final death of the bull no moment of truth. That is a thing of the past, so I don't want your phrasemakers cluttering up my story with words that simply don't apply anymore.

And yet, in the very moment of sending this telegram, I had to admit to myself that there were occasions when decisions of the gravest moral consequence had to be made in the bullring, and such moments did indeed involve the essence of truth. The fact that they so infrequently involved the incident of killing simply meant that their focus had changed. As I filed the message I remembered the critical afternoon in Seville.

Victoriano, now a matador of dazzling accomplishment, had triumphed throughout Mexico and had come to Spain to certify his reputation, for without excellent performances in Seville and Madrid a Mexican bullfighter always remains in the second category, no matter how big he went over in Monterrey or Tijuana. The time had come for Victoriano to submit himself to the first of these acid tests, and he arrived in Seville with his family on Friday afternoon. Veneno, as usual, decided where the troupe should stay, in what rooms, and what food they would eat. He also engaged a Gypsy from Triana to handle the swords and capes during the fight, and a retired matador to help dress Victoriano in the suit of lights. Then Veneno, who loved this hustle and bustle of bullfighting, led his three sons to the historic Café Arena in the Sierpes. They were barely seated when an ancient man in his eighties approached them and said in a high whining voice, "You are Victoriano Leal, the famous Mexican fighter, and you are Veneno, the best of the picadors, but I'll wager you can't guess who I am." He stood back, a thin shadow of a man, and waited for the Leals to speak.

"Somebody I know?" Veneno asked, for he was in a good mood and willing to play games.

"You never saw me before, but your father did."

Veneno leaned forward. "You knew Bernardo?"

"Did he ever tell you about the afternoon he sat at this very table with the great Mazzantini?" the bright-eyed old man cackled.

Veneno dropped his hands into his lap and studied the café. "Was it here that Mazzantini engaged my father for his troupe?"

"Of course!" the old man cried with delight. "Now can you guess . . ."

Veneno turned away from the visitor and said to his sons, "The books all tell about that afternoon. A wedding. A few drinks in the sun. Then Mazzantini proposed this trip to Mexico. It all happened here." In wonder the old picador studied the plaza from which his father had emigrated to Mexico.

The old man, standing on shaky legs, whispered, "So now can you guess who I am?"

Veneno studied the man and suggested: "In 1886 you must have been . . . how old . . . sixteen?"

"I was fourteen," the old man replied, bursting with excitement. "I was a lively boy of fourteen. Doesn't that tell you?"

A grin came over Veneno's creased face and he clapped the old Sevillian on the shoulders: "I know very well who you are." Crying "Ready!" Veneno jumped to his feet, grabbed two knives and handed the old man two forks. Then, despite his bulk, he tried to simulate the agility of his father as he had been in the distant past. The old man cackled with joy and, pawing the ground with his broken sandals, charged with feeble steps, puffed past the picador, who stabbed him gently in the shoulder, and ran clumsily into a chair.

"¡Olé!" shouted the crowd that had gathered with news that the bullfighters had arrived.

With a sweep of his arms, Veneno helped the withered old man to his feet, sat him down at a table, and shouted to the waiters, "Drinks for all!" and a circle of admirers formed around the matador, watching everything he did. Victoriano fell into a kind of trance, blotting out the noise around him, for, as he explained to me later when describing this day that had changed his life and his career, "I was overwhelmed by a kind of vision in which I saw my grandfather fighting his bulls in grand style and my poor father fighting his abominably—that was before he was killed by the bull in the box—and I swore a silent oath, 'I will fight like my grandfather, bravely, alone. I will not depend upon my family to do the dirty work.' And that boast, which I took seriously, accounted for the disaster that overtook me that Sunday in Seville.

"But even as I was making this promise to fight bulls in my own style, not Veneno's, he was shouting to the café crowd that was pressing on me: 'How wonderful it is to be in Sierpes and to know that on Sunday the Leals will bring glory to Seville,' and when the crowd drew even closer so that I was almost smothered, he bellowed:

'Men of Seville, wish us well,' and when they did he embraced the little old man who had awakened these memories and promised, 'On Sunday at half past four, old man, you will meet us at the hotel and you will ride to the plaza with the matador, for in the past you brought our family good luck.' "

When they were in their rooms, free at last of the admirers, Veneno told his sons, "Here it is different. It is in Seville, above all other cities in the world, that a matador has got to prove himself. They tell me the bulls of Guadalquivir are good and big. On Sunday they shall see us triumph." His sons nodded and the family retired, but toward two in the morning Victoriano rose and dressed, and Veneno, who missed little, whispered from his bed, "What is it, son?"

"I'm going to walk in the city," the matador replied.

"I'll dress," Veneno offered.

"No, stay," his son replied, and he slipped from the room to find the freedom he rarely knew in these days of constant adulation. Walking slowly and with no adoring fans at his heels, he roamed the silent streets his grandfather had known before he departed for Mexico. This was the city of Belmonte and Joselito, two of the greatest, the first a suicide in his late years, the second dead in his youth at the horns of a bull.

At the immense cathedral, one of the largest in the world, he found an unlocked side door and entered that vast cavern of aisles and altars waiting in silence for the throngs that would gather on Sunday morning. Kneeling at the gate of one of the many side chapels, he prayed: "Virgin Mary, help me to keep the promise I made myself tonight in the café. Help me to be a man of honor like my grandfather." Remaining on his knees, he could hear nothing, either within the cathedral or without, but then a bird that had taken refuge there but could not find an exit flew down one of the aisles and the matador said, "Bring me good fortune, little bird," and then he went back to the hotel.

It was therefore with heightened emotion that Victoriano rode to the plaza on Sunday, the old man gabbing at his elbow, and when he saw the austerely beautiful bullring, builder and destroyer of reputations, he crossed himself with extra fervor, kissing the fingernail of his right thumb. "Virgin Mary, help me to succeed," he prayed.

Guadalquivir bulls are, by some accident of breeding, among the most deadly in Spain, and through the years they have killed almost as many matadors as the Miuras; yet they have also been the bulls most likely to provide the matador with dramatic opportunities for triumph, as if the bulls were saying to their human adversaries: "Triumph or die."

That afternoon Victoriano triumphed, but it was a triumph mostly of the spirit and not of the right arm. True, he fought exceptionally well and cut one ear from his first Guadalquivir and one from his second, so that the reputation he had carried from Mexico was confirmed. But his more important victory involved his father, Veneno, as the opponent. Up to this time the old picador had masterminded all his son's fights. While Victoriano was occupied with his opening cape work, Veneno obviously had to remain astride his horse in the corrals, unable either to watch the progress of the fight or to direct his son's next moves, but once the cape work ended and the bugles sounded, the old man would spur his horse into the plaza and from then on instruct his son in tactics. There was, of course, a second brief interlude while the picadors were retiring from the ring, but as soon as Veneno dismounted, he would dash back into the alleyway, from where he called out instructions to his son.

And even during the opening passages, when Veneno had to remain in the corrals, he would exercise his will through the person of his older son, Chucho, who inconspicuously advised Victoriano what to do. So in a very real sense,

Victoriano rarely took any action in the ring that was not supervised by other members of his family, and he had become a kind of fighting machine, competent, cool and conditioned. But in Seville this changed.

Before the entrance of the second bull, a typical fierce Guadalquivir, Veneno instructed Chucho, "I size up this bull as dangerous. Keep Victoriano away. He's already cut an ear and the papers will have to say so. Let this bull have its own way."

So while the old picador waited, Chucho advised Victoriano, "Diego and I will handle this one. You stay back."

But the young matador had tasted the thrill of triumph in Seville, and was determined to cap his first performance with an even better display, so after Chucho had run the bull in the preliminary investigations, he, Victoriano, leaped forward with his cape and executed four extremely dangerous passes that launched the fight on a high emotional keel.

Veneno, listening astride his horse in the corrals, knew by the gasping olés that his son was disobeying his instructions, and when after the first series of triumphant shouts he heard another series begin, only to end with a collective agonized gasp, he dropped from his horse and ran to an aperture in time to see Victoriano sprawled on the ground, his pants ripped, with a savage Guadalquivir trying to kill him. By some miracle Chucho got hold of the bull's tail and by brute force restrained the animal from further attacks on his brother. Diego lifted Victoriano from the sand and was about to inspect the wound when the matador shoved him aside, grabbed his fallen cape, and dashed forward to meet the bull again. Veneno, transfixed with fear, stayed at his peephole to watch his son launch a second series of superb passes. Blood was coming from his right leg, but not in gushes.

"Thank God!" the old picador whispered as he remounted.

When he rode into the ring he was as lead picador required by custom to ride counter-clockwise along the barrier, but he did so at unaccustomed speed in order to reach Victoriano, to whom he cried, "Make no further close passes with this bull. He's not reliable. He hooks."

Victoriano, looking up at the austere white-haired figure on the horse, said with unprece-dented independence, "I'm the matador. I'll bring you the bull." And with deft, dancing steps he led the wild animal into range of the pic, whereupon Veneno leaned with furious vigor on his lance, driving the steel shaft so deeply into the bull's back that the Seville men began to shout, "Swine, dog, butcher! Are you trying to kill the bull?" One infuriated spectator began to throw something at Veneno, but police rushed up to intercept him. The crowd continued hurling insults at the white-haired picador, who now swung his horse across the bull's path of escape, thus giving himself opportunity for an even deeper thrust of the lance.

"I will kill this bull," he muttered, bearing down with all the force of his ironlike body. His left foot broke loose from its stirrup, but he pressed on. The bull's left horn, wet with Victoriano's blood, drove against the metal that encased Veneno's right leg, and the picador, seeing his son's blood, drove the lance deeper and deeper. A gush of crimson spurted out along the sides of the pole to which the steel tip was fixed, but still the infuriated old man pressed on.

He was interrupted in his unbridled attack on the bull by his own son. Daringly, Victoriano swept into position between the horse's head and the bull's, and with his cape close to his knees led the bull away until he found a chance to furl the cape spectacularly over his shoulders, teasing the bull away into a series of majestic passes, slow, sweet and marvelous to the eye. Veneno, watching the evil manner in which the bull hooked to the left, prayed.

The dazzling passes ended, a breathless and

perfect creation that brought the audience to its feet with ecstatic cries. A man could attend a dozen fights and not see a series of passes like this. One such performance once a season kept a fighter's reputation alive.

The final portion of the fight threatened to be a typical Victoriano retreat from the excellence of his cape work, and Chucho, mindful of how this bull hooked at the man and not the cloth, issued directions, "Three passes and kill him, or he'll kill you." But Victoriano felt that the moment had come when he must declare his independence from his family's domination, so after giving the mandatory three passes to prove he was a real matador, he proceeded to try a fourth and a fifth, but a Guadalquivir bull is not like others and this one knocked him down and might have killed him had not the Leal brothers swept in with their whirling capes to lead the bull away.

Veneno, rushing in from where the horses were kept, tried to prevent his son from attempting to kill, for it was obvious that the bull had brought blood to the matador's other leg and he could be excused if he allowed himself to be carried from the arena, leaving the bull to the other matadors. But on this day Victoriano refused that honorable escape, for he was after a greater honor, the kind for which his grandfather had been distinguished. Grabbing sword and muleta, he ignored the warnings of the three other Leals, marched directly to the bull, and dispatched him with the kind of perfect thrust he had used years ago when starting in his profession.

It was masterly. The bull dropped almost instantly. The crowd cheered and demanded that he march around the arena as they applauded, but when he started to do so, the pain from his wounds caused him to weave, so the three other Leals caught him, lifted him in the air and took him to the infirmary, where his wounds were cauterized.

He was brought home by his two brothers, followed by a crowd of cheering men who stormed into the hotel room where Veneno sat, solemn and silent. As soon as the matador was placed on the bed, smiling and flushed with triumph, Veneno cried to the mob: "Get out!" One man, who hoped to get a photograph of himself and the matador, tarried, and felt the picador's powerful arms close about him, throwing him into the hall. And then Veneno said to Chucho and Diego: "Get out!" He had not spoken to them in this manner for many years, and they hesitated, whereupon their father with frightening deliberation grabbed each in turn and threw him into the hallway. "What are you going to do?" Chucho cried.

"I am going to explain what it means to be a matador," the old man said. He slammed the door shut and locked it.

In the next ten minutes the awed crowd in the hall heard voices and the sound of smashing furniture. Then there was only Veneno's terrible voice rasping in short sentences: "We created you." . . . "You will not destroy our chances." . . . "You will fight as we direct." After a long time there came a sound of running water. And then silence.

That night Chucho and Diego slept with friends, for it was apparent that the door was not going to be opened. Next morning Victoriano Leal limped down Sierpes to the little plaza of the Café Arena. His left leg was stiff from the bull's sharp horn thrust. One of his eyes was closed and black, and his nose was seriously distended as if it might be broken. But he was a matador. He knew at last what discipline meant, but he also knew that he had faced a major test of manhood and failed.

Mexico City, 1960. The Leals returned from Spain the most famous bullfighting family in the world. They worked together with a cohesion that was almost frightening. Veneno handled contracts and struck extortionate deals, but as he pointed out; "When the Leals fight, the crowds come." Chucho and Diego now performed almost automatically in the ring because of their perfection in their respective arts, while the old picador continued to blast the power out of even the most difficult bulls. Victoriano, of course, was the disciplined matador, a poetic evocation of all that the school of Seville stood for. The critic León Ledesma, who had traveled to Spain to observe the young man's triumphs in that country, reported back to Mexico: "This golden youth, the creation of a notable taurine family, has gained all the laurels Spain has to offer, and if we seek the reason it is because he is a complete matador: at once the essence of lyric poetry and the soul of harsh self-control." Understandably, his countrymen were excited about his return, and when his inaugural fight was announced one Monday, by noon on Tuesday all the fifty-five thousand tickets for Plaza México had been sold.

I did not see the fight, but I did a good deal of reading about it and talked with many who had seen it. Preliminary publicity, of course, had featured the fact that Victoriano Leal, El Triunfador de España, would kill three "noble and exemplary bulls of Palafox," but no mention was made of who the second man would be, and there was no flurry of excitement when it was subsequently announced that the program was to be completed by the routine Mexican hack Juan Gómez.

Since Gómez had been a matador longer than Victoriano, he was entitled to fight first, and with his initial enemy accomplished nothing, as usual. Leal, inspired by the huge crowd that had come to greet him as one who had upheld Mexico's reputation throughout Spain, was brilliant with the cape, fine with the banderilla and poetic with the muleta. If he had killed well, he would surely have won ears and tail and possibly a hoof, too, for his performance was emotionally charged, and no one begrudged him the two ears he carried in triumph three times around the ring while the band played the frenzied Mexican music known as the *diana.*

The trouble started when Victoriano completed his third turn and, accompanied by Chucho and Diego, who picked up the flowers that were thrown at him, moved to the middle of the plaza to acknowledge the continuing cheers. Intoxicated by his magnificent triumph, he succumbed to an urge to glorify himself. Handing the two ears to his brothers, he raised his index fingers: "I am number one."

The crowd roared its confirmation of his claim, but the effect was dampened by the unexpected intrusion of Juan Gómez, who, in his faded blue suit with its tarnished decorations, left the barrier where he should have stayed and shuffled awkwardly to share the middle of the arena. Stopping three feet from Victoriano as the younger matador started to leave the ring, Gómez waited till his opponent had passed, then raised himself on tiptoe, leaned far over imaginary horns, and drove his right palm, as if it were his sword, home. Then, sneering at Victoriano's back, he raised his own forefingers in the air and shouted, "I am the real número uno!" and when cushions began to rain down on him, he maintained his position, his wizened face staring up at the mob, his fingers still aloft, his cracked voice still crying, "I'm número uno!"

A silence fell upon the arena, for this was not an idle gesture. By making it, the bowlegged Indian matador Juan Gómez stripped all the glitter from the afternoon. Victoriano's manipulations of the cape, the dandy's work of placing the banderillas just so, the slow, beautiful movements with the cloth, and the semi-adequate kill at the end—all these were swept away. Juan Gómez, a little Altomec Indian, ignored the triumphant one from Spain and looked across the arena toward the door behind which the four remaining bulls of Palafox hid in darkness. Pointing solemnly to the fateful gate from which his next enemy would soon burst into the arena, he profiled again with his right arm extended forward as if it were a sword, and seemed to be boasting, Thus will I kill my bull! And the crowd waited.

The third Palafox bull of the afternoon weighed thirteen hundred pounds, had a vicious chop to the right, and charged like a fire engine for two thirds of his run, then stopped abruptly to seek his man. With this deadly opponent, Juan Gómez made only four cape passes, but they were close, slow, pure and brimming with emotion. They contained not a single flourish, but they caught at the throats of fifty-five thousand people, and anything Victoriano Leal had accomplished that afternoon was cheapened.

According to his habit, the bowlegged little Indian did not place his own sticks, for he lacked the grace for this part of the fight, but his peóns did acceptably, and when the time came for his work with the muleta, he moved slowly, keeping very close to the dangerous bull. With a minimum of passes, the sturdy fighter chopped his huge enemy down to manageable proportions. "His work," wrote Ledesma the next day, "was filled to the brim with classic agony. We waited in silence for the bull to kill him."

Close, close to death the ugly little man worked, his eyes staring with deadly antagonism at the huge bull.

Then came the time for the kill. So far there had been no embellishments to delight the eye, no arabesques to tease the brain. There had been only a bandy-legged little Indian with dark skin and hair in his eyes playing with life and death against a bull that was obviously intent on ending the game a winner. Now the aching sense of tragedy was to be heightened, for the man seemed hardly tall enough to reach over the horns to kill this huge bull.

But with his left hand he lowered the red cloth, dangling it before his right knee, and with his right hand he clutched the long, point-dipping sword as if it were an extension of his body. He stood perilously close to the bull, and for an agonizing moment of suspense the two adversaries remained motionless. Then deftly, and with exquisite judgment, Gómez flicked the cloth, lured the bull just slightly to one side, took two quick steps, and almost leaped onto the horns. Slowly the tip of the sword found the true entrance. The desperate brown hand pushed on the sword. Slowly it went in . . . in . . . in. Bull and man formed a single paralyzed unit. It seemed as if minutes had passed, but still the man and the horns were one. And then the brown hand flattened itself against the bull's dying neck, the sword blade completely vanished, and the man's palm came away covered with blood.

The moment passed. The bull staggered on a few feet to certain death and the man slipped off the flank in a kind of numb ecstasy. The picture of immortality was broken and from the vast concrete bowl came the sound of breath being released. For two or three seconds there were no olés and no cheers.

His head low toward the sand and not in easy triumph, Juan Gómez mechanically withdrew his sword and slowly marched toward the spot where he must make his traditional report to the president. But before he reached there, the stormy response of the crowd broke over him, cheers such as he had not heard for many years. The music blared and flowers were beginning to cover the sand. Humbly the little Indian bowed to the president, acknowledging his authority. Then, putting his sword in his left hand, he turned to face the crowd and raised his right index finger.

A riot started. The partisans of Victoriano refused to think that one lucky kill entitled this man with a trivial history to dispute the championship with an acknowledged master, who had triumphed in Spain. But this time the tough little Indian was not left alone with only a few supporters in the cheap seats on the sunny side. Many spectators, reviewing in their minds what they had seen that afternoon, must have concluded that there was something more to bullfighting than dancing gestures and poetic passages. There was, in all honesty, a naked moment when man and bull stood equal, with all nonsense gone. This was a fight of life and death, a summary of all we know of man's dark passage, and it deserved a certain dignity. This dignity could not be observed in a hundred afternoons of Victoriano Leal, but this damned little Indian had somehow reminded the plaza of the very essence of bullfighting and life. And now the cheering was more evenly divided.

That night León Ledesma wrote for *The Bullfight:*

> The gauntlet has been thrown down. Rarely has a matador of Victoriano Leal's proven stature been so frontally insulted as after the third bull, when Juan Gómez made fun of him, suggesting to the crowd that Leal knew nothing of the essence of the fight. And rarely has a boastful gesture such as that of Gómez been so immediately backed up by a performance that must have exceeded even his wildest hopes.

The most graceful fighter of our age has been made to look inconsequential by a man who has hitherto shown little but bravery. As we saw this afternoon, the insulting actions of Gómez drove Victoriano to prodigies of effort, and he in turn made Gómez extend himself to ridiculous acts with the fifth bull. I frankly do not like to see a matador take the horn of a maddened bull between his teeth, defying the animal to kill him, but apparently the public loved this rococo gesture of Gómez, for the plaza exploded with cheers and awarded him two ears, in this critic's opinion one more than he deserved.

Yesterday Juan Gómez triumphed. He stole Leal's reception for himself and made the intended hero of the afternoon look pompous. I am sure that Victoriano will not tolerate this indignity, and thus each man will drive the other to more dangerous exploits, and in the end, unless sanity prevails, we shall see one of these matadors goad the other to a display that must end in death.

It was this impending murder that I had been sent to Mexico to cover, and in the nine weeks that had passed since Ledesma's first delineation of the struggle, the two matadors had fought together eight times. The received wisdom in Mexico was that Victoriano would be the victor because he would be supported in a crisis by the cunning of his father, Veneno, and the skill of his brothers, whereas Gómez could rely solely on his own courage.

I did not buy this easy generalization. I feared that Victoriano was not a complete man, was allowed no mind of his own, whereas Gómez was ferociously self-directed and a veteran of both triumph and despair. But as twilight fell I realized that I knew Victoriano but not Gómez and would have to find out more about this stubborn little Indian.

3

THE
RANCHER

BEFORE I could get to my typewriter to start my report on the background of Juan Gómez, I was distracted by the noisy approach of men whose appearance reminded me that I had come not only to observe a series of bull-fights but also to attend a festival honoring Ixmiq, the founder of Toledo. They were a group of nine musicians dressed in brown suede suits with silver ornaments and flowing green ties, oversized tan sombreros and high-heeled cow-boy boots. All were grave of face, especially the three who wore long mustaches, and as they

marched slowly toward me they played a rhythmic Mexican music that from the days of my
childhood had always evoked visions of festival.
They were a band of mariachis from Guadalajara, the home of this uniquely Mexican art, and
they had come to earn money at the Festival of
Ixmiq.

What lively music the mariachis played! The
tempo was always fast, and when they sang, the
words were full of anguish over love or lost
dreams. Besides conventional instruments like
guitars, violins and a deep-voiced mandolin,
which looked like a bass fiddle, there was also
a gourdlike rasp and castanets. They produced
a pleasant sound marked by a heavy unbroken
beat that gave the music an identifiable Mexican
cast. When the leader saw me he stopped his
men abruptly, came over, bowed low, and announced in English, "For our American friend,
'Cielito Lindo,' " and before I could stop them,
the mariachis galloped mechanically into this
song that I was sure they could not like. It was
music for tourists, hammered out in tourist fashion.

At the noisy conclusion the leader tucked his
violin under his arm, bowed again and announced, "Another fine song for the norteamericano, 'San Antonio Rose,' " by this
flattery hoping to win a few dollars from me.

Again the mariachis ground out what they thought I wanted, but before they had reached the first chorus I raised my hand and shouted in rapid Spanish, "Stop that garbage! I want 'Guadalajara'!"

The stolid-faced musicians gaped and the leader asked in Spanish, "You know 'Guadalajara'?"

"Why not?" I snapped. "I'm one of you."

The mariachis grinned and the leader apologized: "We thought you were only a norteamericano." I winced at this pejorative term but said nothing, because I knew that proud Mexicans liked to remind visitors from the north, "Everyone on this continent is an americano, you're a norteamericano. Don't rob us of our name by stealing it for yourselves."

He beat the air twice with his violin bow and the mariachis began to sing, " 'Guadalajara, Guadalajara!' " They pronounced the name Mexican style, which lent the cry an added poignancy: "Wath-a-la-cara." Into this name the singers poured their love of land that was so powerful a force in Mexico, and children who had not yet seen that city of the west paused to hear the sweet song.

The voices gave way to trumpeters who blared out the basic rhythm. Abruptly the trumpets stopped and the troupe sang with unabashed sentimentality, " 'Wath-a-la-cara!' " In close harmony four voices sobbed in conclusion: "How beautiful was that spring in Wath-a-la-cara." A series of minor chords leaped from the strings, while the trumpets danced in furious arabesques above the melodic line, and the song ended in a bath of Mexican emotion. From the terrace of the hotel across the street two travelers from Guadalajara cheered.

The mariachis gathered about me, asking for their fee, but I deferred payment: "You didn't finish 'San Antonio Rose,' so you owe me one more song. I'd like to hear 'The Ballad of General Gurza.' "

The mariachis stopped smiling, and the leader stepped forward deferentially: "Does the señor norteamericano really wish to hear this song?"

"I asked for it."

"Does the señor know—well—perhaps the words—"

"I know the words," I said firmly. "Because I'm also a Mexican. Years ago I used to sing this song up at the mines."

The mariachis relaxed and one asked, "Didn't your American father spank you for singing such a song?"

"He did."

The mariachis made a place for me within

their circle, and the strings ripped out seven quick chords, followed by campfire trumpet calls, whereupon three voices, and mine, began the galloping chant:

"In the year 1916
   President Wilson sent his Yankees
   Into the state of Chihuahua
   To punish our valiant General Gurza.

   "Valiant, valiant General Gurza!
      Let me ride with you.
      I am young,
      But I can fight the americanos.

"Up and down the highways of Durango
   The americanos sought our valiant
      leader.
   Never did they catch him,
   But in the evenings he assaulted them.

   "Valiant, valiant General Gurza!
      Let me fight with you.
      I am young,
      But I can shoot the americanos."

The ballad had many verses detailing the courage of General Gurza as he evaded the troops of President Wilson—pronounced Veel-son in our song—and ended with a typical Mexican conclusion, involving muted trumpet calls and the promise that whenever Mexico was in danger from the Yankees, valiant General Gurza would rise from his grave in the mountains of Chihuahua and lead his ghostly armies to defeat the enemy. Solemnly we chanted the last chorus:

"Valiant, valiant General Gurza!
Let me die with you.
I am young
But my heart aches for Mexico."

The song died away in a crash of trumpet flourishes that would have stopped dead any of President Wilson's Yankees, and I shook hands with the leader of the mariachis. "Those days are gone." I laughed. They bowed and would accept no money, even though I explained that another man had given me some for them.

"No," the leader insisted. "This time we have welcomed you home. Next time we charge you double."

I bowed and said, "Valiant, valiant General Gurza. Always a valiant bandit."

The mariachis laughed at my insult to their national hero and cried, "A valiant bandit," and they resumed their counterclockwise march around the square, leaving me with my memories of the brutal General Gurza. I felt shivery, as I had as a boy when I heard that name mentioned with terror by my mother, who had seen her relatives slain by Gurza. Seeking companionship, I crossed the paved street that separated the statue of Ixmiq from the House of Tile, whose blue-and-yellow façade reflected the last light of day.

In Mexico some buildings are faced with blue tile and they seem cold. Others are fronted with brown-and-yellow tile, and these are garish. But a few, like this hotel, are covered with tile of flowered design in which the leaves are blue and the petals yellow, and that combination yields both warmth and dignity. My hotel had such decoration, and it warmed the heart and extended a welcome to all travelers.

The first Bishop Palafox, who erected the building, did it, he said, as a tribute to his Indian wife, "as fine a helper as any man ever had." It was a lovely building, rather small and intimate in style, and we Palafoxes felt that it was a worthy symbol of both his love and the remarkable qualities of his wife. For almost four hundred years it had served as a kind of rural hotel and in this century it had become the prestigious place for visitors to stay. During the bullfight season, it was obligatory housing for matadors and their troupes.

A classic building of two low stories, it was decorated with bas-reliefs of the saints who protected Toledo. Its façade had originally been of dark stone, but one of the later Bishop Palafoxes had imported blue-and-yellow tile from Spain and redone the face with style. Now the original brownstone saints looked out through frames of colorful tile.

For some happy reason the first Bishop Palafox had made the front of his convent not flat but concave, thus producing at the north end of the square an extended open terrace, which for the last fifty years had been filled with white restaurant tables and wire-backed chairs. During mealtime the tables were covered with red checkered cloths; the rest of the time they stood bare, inviting all who wished to drink.

When I entered the terrace I looked to the left flanking wall and saw, with some satisfaction, that the broken tiles along that side had not been repaired. As a boy I had been stood against those broken tiles week after week to measure my growth, and I remember the day when my head finally reached the line of holes that had caused the tiles to crack. Looking at the tiles now, it seemed impossible that I could ever have been so small. To see these broken tiles was an assurance that things were not going to change in Toledo.

I tapped on one of the white tables and from the heavily carved doorway of the hotel came a large woman of about sixty wearing a black dress and many combs. When she recognized me she cried, "Señor Clay! I was so happy when I received your cable."

"Is the room available?"

"Like always," she said, pointing over her shoulder. "With your cameras in place."

I rubbed my hands and asked, "Is the menu the same?"

The ample woman, known as the Widow Palafox now that her husband, one of the less successful Palafoxes, was dead, disappeared into the hotel and returned with a menu that had become a feature of Mexico. For many years at each Festival of Ixmiq Doña Carmen had been accustomed to serving a traditional Spanish menu so as to help her guests be in the proper mood for the bullfights. Visitors who had once tasted her food during the festival would sometimes come from Mexico City during the fair expressly to enjoy her traditional Spanish feast while lounging on the terrace and listening to the mariachis.

Now the Widow Palafox handed me the menu and I saw that it had not changed. For sixteen pesos, about $1.30, the guest was entitled to five huge courses, each to be selected from many options, but by custom visitors to the festival always included the four special dishes: fish soup of Seville, lima beans and ham hocks of Asturias, and the paella of Valencia, followed by a light caramelized vanilla custard known as flan that provided a fine complement to the heavy Spanish dinner.

Looking at the menu made my mouth water, and I realized with some dismay that it was now only seven o'clock and that the tables would not be set for two more hours, since dinner was not served before nine. I was about to go upstairs to my room, which held extraordinary memories, when I was saved by a loud shout from the plaza and I turned to see one of my father's closest friends darting between taxicabs to overtake me. It was Don Eduardo Palafox, a rich relative of the widow who ran the hotel, the present owner of the Palafox bull ranch and a kind of uncle of mine.

Don Eduardo was now in his mid-sixties, a big, round, bald-headed man with a thin patrician upper lip and a very full lower one, which produced a somewhat puckish appearance. Deep lines radiated from the corners of his eyes while others crisscrossed his ample forehead. He was a happy man and one who was deceptively agile, for although he must have weighed about two hundred and fifty pounds, he now dodged in and out of traffic like an athlete and approached me without being out of breath. "Nephew!" he cried warmly in English. "You made it back to the fair."

"Your bulls fighting?" I asked.

"How would they dare to overlook me?" He laughed, pointing to a bright poster on the opposite side of the hotel: "The Traditional Festival of Ixmiq. Hand to Hand. Victoriano Leal, the Triumphant One from Spain, and Juan Gómez, Both from This State!!!! Bulls of San Mateo, Torrecillas and Palafox." The names of the secondary matadors who would also appear during the festival were listed, along with the names of the peóns and picadors.

"Tell me, Norman," Don Eduardo suggested in Spanish, pulling me down to sit at one of the white tables, "What do you think is going to happen between Leal and Gómez?"

"Simple," I replied. "One of them will goad the other to his death."

"That's what Ledesma wrote," Don Eduardo mused. "Then you count this a real competition, not just something the newspapers have invented?"

"Haven't you seen them fight together?" I asked.

"No, and that's a pity. My bulls have been appearing in the northern plazas, and, as you know, I like to go along with them whenever possible."

"They been any good?" I asked.

Don Eduardo smiled expansively as he ordered beer. "This year the bulls of Palafox have been superb."

"And those for the fair?" I pressed.

"Wonderful," he assured me.

I have been attending bullfights for about forty years and throughout that time a good 95 percent of the bulls have turned out to be cowardly, dangerous and weak in the knees; nevertheless, before every fight those connected with the business assured the world that the next day's bulls would prove truly splendid. Like all ranchers, Don Eduardo enjoyed being described by the press as scrupulous, which implied that when he tested his young bulls and cows, the cowardly ones were turned into beef and not allowed to contaminate the bullrings.

In money matters he was indeed scrupulous. In all human affairs, as my family had cause to know, he was scrupulous, and in politics he had enjoyed preferential treatment by many different governments because of his scrupulousness; but in the raising of bulls for the plazas of Mexico he was, like everyone else in the business, a common crook. So when he assured me that in the plazas to the north his bulls had been outstanding, I translated this to mean: "Out of every six I sent, perhaps one gave a reasonably decent fight. The other five were cowardly, dangerous and weak in the knees."

Now Don Eduardo began reciting the bull breeder's standard complaint: the matadors who work his bulls are never able to get out of them the great performances of which all Palafox bulls are capable. As I drank his beer I began to ignore his complaints and to think of the powerful family of which he was the present head and I a proud though minor part.

As I turned away from him momentarily to study the plaza, where the evening lights were coming on to make the area a postcard portrait of classical Mexico, I remembered that everything I saw in this stately place had been built by an ancestor of mine, one or another of the five bishops Palafox.

I had never before been much interested in the Palafoxes as a clan, being satisfied to know that my mother had been a member, a fact of which she had been inordinately proud. Because she was such a splendid woman I might have become engrossed in family matters had I not married a Palafox, who divorced me. With her departure I lost interest, but now, in this gray period of indecision when I was trying to restructure my life, I found that I was intensely concerned about my varied inheritances and wanted to pursue questions I had previously ignored.

"Uncle Eduardo, didn't I hear you mention last time I was here that there had been two branches of the Palafoxes?"

And he proceeded to remind me of things I must have known as a boy but had ignored at the time. "Still are. In the 1520s two brothers came to Mexico to help Cortés—one a priest, the other a soldier. Each of them had many children. Their descendants' behavior was strange, for the men in the line started by the priest married only Indian women, the soldier's men married only pure-blooded Spanish wives. So, many of the Palafoxes you see today can be quite dark-skinned, but the soldier's line look like typical people from Spain. I'm from that line." He obviously took pride in that pure-blooded ancestry and reminded me that my mother and my wife were also from that branch."

Then he waved the open palm of his right hand back and forth across his face to indicate that he was wiping out such distinctions and said happily, "Anyway, in our family a boy calls any Palafox older than himself uncle. You're one of us, Norman, that's what counts."

"Is all this written down somewhere?"

"Only up here," he said, tapping his head, but then he added brightly, "But in the little museum I've put together in one of the old church buildings up the street, there are paintings and things that tell some of the story."

"You ought to write it down, before it's lost."

He laughed and tapped me on the knee. "You're the writer in the family."

I thought, Would anyone have enough time and daring to unravel the complex story of this family that had played such a vital role in the history of Toledo? And images of compelling power flashed through my mind of the murders and burning I myself had seen as a boy, the crises at the Mineral, and I thought, If one boy in a space of ten or fifteen years saw so much, how much did my ancestors witness in this plaza, at the Mineral, the pyramid? and I felt engulfed by the grand sweep of history.

As from a distance I heard Don Eduardo's cheerful voice: "Well, what do you say?"

"About what?"

"I asked if you would like to join me."

"Where?"

"You haven't heard a word I've been saying."

"I'm sorry, Uncle."

"I invited you to the Tournament of Flowers."

"Is that being held tonight?"

"Yes. Always on the Wednesday. It opens the

fiesta. And I want you to be one of the judges."

I leaned back in my chair with a feeling of distinct pleasure and said, "Father never missed the Tournament. I'd enjoy it and we can dine afterwards."

"Precisely," Don Eduardo agreed, and he and I cut across the plaza to the Imperial Theater, where a distinguished crowd of Toledo citizens, many in evening dress, were gathering for the annual Tournament of Flowers. With the easy grace that comes from years of wielding authority, Don Eduardo introduced me to many who had known my father and then led me backstage past a dozen men dressed in black and so obviously nervous that they had to be the contestants whom I was to help judge. Don Eduardo ignored them and took me to a small room where three judges sat, looking ill at ease. When the head of the Palafox family appeared they rose and bowed stiffly.

"I can never remember your names," Don Eduardo said with the polite contempt wealthy Mexicans have for everyone else. "This is my nephew, the son of John Clay, our author."

The three judges—a dentist, a professor and a self-educated poet—nodded and Don Eduardo announced abruptly, "Señor Clay is going to be one of our judges."

It became apparent that the professor, Dr.

Ruiz Meléndez, did not intend to allow Don Eduardo to ride roughshod over him this year. Pointedly he asked, "Does the norteamericano know Spanish?"

Don Eduardo was impatient and brushed off the inquiry: "Better than I do."

Professor Ruiz seemed ready to combat every position Don Eduardo took: "For judging pretty girls in the United States no Spanish is necessary, but what we shall be doing this evening . . . well, the cultural honor of Toledo is involved."

"Professor," Don Eduardo interrupted bluntly, "my nephew knows more about the cultural honor of Toledo than you will ever know. Now let's get on with the Tournament."

Ruiz Meléndez refused to surrender to Don Eduardo. "I am not convinced that your nephew is the kind of man we require for the task at hand," he said coldly and I thought: He's right, but if he had spoken like that in the old days, some Palafox would have shot him. But these were new days and Don Eduardo laughed good-naturedly.

"You're right, Professor," he chuckled. "We Palafoxes are all idiots when it comes to culture, but we'll have you good men to help us out." Then taking me by the hand he headed for the stage with the command, "Come on, you idiot."

The dentist and the poet smiled discreetly, but the professor remained irritated.

We filed onto the stage of the blue-and-gold theater and I was moved by the sight of the platform on which Emperor Maximilian had behaved with such gallantry at the end of his life. The audience, filling all seats, applauded genteelly as Don Eduardo raised his hand for silence and said, "We are the judges tonight. Four of us you already know." He took a piece of paper from his pocket and read, "Dr. Beltrán, our learned dentist, Luis Solís the poet, and Professor Ruiz Meléndez. I have no right to be here myself, being a rancher, but I came along in case any livestock had to be judged." There was embarrassed laughter at this, and I saw Professor Ruiz wince. "And this stranger," Don Eduardo concluded, "is really no stranger at all. He's John Clay's boy, and we're lucky to have him with us tonight because he's a famous writer himself." I cringed when he said this, for I knew I was at best a journeyman scribbler, at worst a hack. And now he clapped his hands, and shouted gruffly: "Come on. Let's get going."

We judges took our seats on a dais to the side, our feet resting on red carpeting, and when we were settled, from the wings came sixteen charming young ladies, dressed in white eve-

ning gowns and carrying floral bouquets. At first
I thought: Damn! This year it's degenerated into
some local beauty contest; but obviously this
was not the case, for from another entrance
appeared a gorgeous young woman, tall, stately
and with a remarkable grace of movement. An
orchestra struck up a coronation march, and
she was escorted by the sixteen attendants to
a throne that was suddenly revealed at the rear.
There the mayor of Toledo cried: "I crown you
Queen Cristina!" and the stage was set.

Lights were lowered, save for a spot that was
kept focused on the queen, and from the wings
appeared the first contestant, a rather handsome young man in evening dress who seemed
very nervous until he found a place to stand half
facing the audience, half facing the judges.
Then he swallowed, clenched his hands behind
his back, and began to recite three of the sonnets he had composed during the past year.

This was Toledo's Tournament of Flowers,
the annual competition of poets from all parts of
Mexico, and as the first contender recited, the
mellifluous sound of his soft Spanish drifting out
across the audience, I surrendered myself to a
joy I had not known for thirty years. In the United
States no one would think of having a competition of poets, for what our best poets write tends
to be obscure and difficult, and, moreover, our

citizens would be embarrassed to judge or to listen to a group of poets. But in Toledo, where the music of Spanish verse filled the air to the delight of all, poetry was again what it had been throughout history: queen of the verbal arts.

The young man's name was Gonzales, and his sonnets dealt with a day in the country and his reflections on the unhappy fact that tomorrow he would have to go back to work in an office where the lark that he kept hidden inside his coat would find it difficult to sing.

"Do you have larks in Mexico?" I whispered to Don Eduardo.

"Who cares?" He shrugged.

The next poet was a beetle-browed older man named Aquiles Aguilar, and he had composed a Miltonic ode to Princess Cristina, which he delivered with fire and imagination. Turning his back abruptly on the audience, he faced the beautiful girl and poured forth a surprisingly impassioned explanation of what a man who is no longer young thinks when he looks at a girl of twenty. Then, flinging his arms into the air, Señor Aguilar wheeled about to stare at the audience and and cried in a voice trembling with emotion:

> "If tomorrow I must walk where dust
> chokes me,

I shall sing, 'Last night I saw a girl among roses.' "

The audience cheered, and it was obvious that Señor Aguilar was going to stand rather high with the judges, too, for Don Eduardo was clapping heartily and I suspected that he would more or less decide who the winner was to be. As Aguilar took additional bows I thought: He's going to be hard to beat, but so far the sonnets get my vote. But I suspected I might have trouble with my confreres.

The other poets came on, some with hesitant voices, which to me gave a certain poignancy and weight to their poems, and some with a degree of self-assurance that was unjustified by the quality of their compositions, but as I listened to a Señor García Ramos deliver an elegy for a dead child, it suddenly occurred to me that all the poets in this contest were of the Spanish type, or people of very light complexion. Stealing furtive glances at the people in the audience, I saw that all of them were Spanish looking, too. By this I don't mean that they seemed to belong to Spain or to have pure Spanish blood, but that they were the inheritors of the Spanish aristocracy that had ruled Mexico openly from 1523 to 1810 and surreptitiously from 1810 to the present. Among all the contestants and throughout the darkened theater there was not one Indian such as I had seen along the road that afternoon. It was as if Mexico were divided into two nations: the Indians, who worked the fields and the markets, and the Spanish, who ruled from the halls of government.

I turned my attention to the poetry and tried in vain to discover a single allusion to the Indians' side of life, and none appeared. The dead child that Señor—I looked down at my program— García Ramos was lamenting had blue eyes and a fair complexion. The imaginary bird that young Señor Gonzales had kept hidden in his imaginary coat was from Spain. The beauty queen that Señor Aguilar had saluted was a fair Spanish girl.

This discovery led me to study surreptitiously the seventeen girls onstage and I satisfied myself that they were all tall and fair of skin, and were beauties who could have come from Castile and Andalusia.

"Where," I asked myself, "are the beautiful Indian girls I saw on the road today at Kilometer 303? Where are the young women with dark skin that the succession of Palafox bishops had always found so enchanting?"

I looked at my four fellow judges, and each of them was Spanish, too, but when I had satisfied myself that tonight's Tournament of Flowers had been set up to represent only one half of Mexican life, the final contestant appeared, a short, dark, hard-looking Altomec Indian. No one could mistake this poet's genesis, and when, in beginning his recitation, he flashed his left arm, I saw that it lacked a hand, as if he were among the dispossessed. Like his person, his poem was different. It dealt with his ancestors who had built the pyramid and of their ritual dances at the time of harvest. At first I couldn't catch what he was driving at, but after about five minutes of astonishingly powerful imagery, he arrived at the bitter climax:

"Where is our harvest now?
You, with the medals on your chest,
Where have you hidden our harvest?"

The passages that followed were unpleasantly strident and wholly inappropriate for the predominantly Spanish audience, and yet they had a fiery eloquence that held the listeners' attention against their will and kept the audience transfixed with the questions that the Indians of Mexico have been asking for a thousand years.

I was quite unprepared for the ending of the poem, for after a forceful philosophical passage, the one-handed Indian began to dance up and

down on one foot, mimicking the harvest dance
of his ancestors. His motion never became ob-
trusive, nor was it out of place, considering the
words that accompanied it, but it underlined one
fact: that if all the preceding contestants had
been unmistakably Spanish, this one was just as
unmistakably Indian. While chanting the final
stanza he continued his little Altomec dance
and, like me, the audience must have thought
that he had been carried away by his own words.
But this was not the case, for suddenly he
stopped, stood motionless on the stage, his
mutilated left arm close to his side, and concluded his poem:

"I am waiting for the harvest
For which I have danced so long."

He bowed gravely and left the stage. The applause was cautious, to say the least, and he
was not recalled for a second round, but now I
knew who was going to get my vote.

When the judges convened it was clear that
Don Eduardo intended handing down his decision quickly, as his family had been doing for
generations, and it was equally clear that Professor Ruiz Meléndez had no intention of letting
the soi-disant Count Palafox get away with it.
"Well," Don Eduardo said expansively, "it's

quite obvious from the applause that Aguilar was the winner with his fine tribute to our princess. Didn't you think Princess Cristina looked lovely? And certainly the man with the elegy was second, because he showed real feeling. Now, about the third . . ."

"Excuse me," Professor Ruiz interrupted. "I propose that we ballot on these matters."

"We never vote," Don Eduardo explained. "We'll just talk it over for a few minutes. Who did you like for third place, Professor Ruiz?" It was obvious that Don Eduardo was determined to be gracious.

The professor resumed his comment by saying, "So I have prepared some ballots—"

Don Eduardo brushed him aside. "Ballots are ridiculous in a case like this. You, Clay, didn't you agree that Aguilar—"

Trying to maintain control, Professor Ruiz observed, "I hardly think it proper for an American visitor to speak first and to influence judges of a contest that has great importance for Mexican culture."

"Now, that's a damned insulting— Professor Ruiz, as chairman of this committee I demand—"

"Are you chairman?" the professor asked.

"Aren't I?" Don Eduardo asked, showing no resentment. He had usually been chairman of whatever committee there was in Toledo and he had naturally assumed that such was the case tonight.

"No," Professor Ruiz snapped. "I am."

"You are?" Don Eduardo replied with frank astonishment but with no rancor. "Well, in that case, Mr. Chairman, I think that you owe our visitor an apology."

Professor Ruiz bowed. "I agree. Señor Clay, I am sorry. In fact, now that things have been straightened out, I withdraw my objection. Since you are our guest, you have first choice."

I found myself damning Don Eduardo for having projected me into a position where I had either to lie and name my second choice as the winner or insult my Spanish friends by stating frankly that I preferred the Indian. To save myself I said, "You are indeed most gracious, Professor Ruiz, but I agree with you that I ought not speak first in an affair so close to the heart of Mexicans."

"You are a charming guest," the chairman acknowledged, "but I insist upon knowing your choice."

I swallowed hard, looked away from Don Eduardo, and said firmly, "I preferred . . ." And then I couldn't think of the Indian's name and ended lamely, ". . . the Indian with one hand."

Don Eduardo exploded. "But good God, Norman! It was never intended that the prize should go to one of them. We had him on the program only because he's a local boy."

"I liked his poem," I repeated stubbornly.

"I should have left you at the hotel," the rancher snapped with disgust. "Well, anyway, the rest of us know that Aguilar—"

Professor Ruiz Meléndez astonished me by saying abruptly, "I agree with Señor Clay. The man with one hand was clearly the winner."

"Now, wait a minute!" Don Eduardo protested. "If we are stupid enough to name him for first prize it will be an insult to our city. For as long as I can remember, the Festival of Ixmiq has been divided up so that the cultured people win all the prizes indoors while the Indians win everything outdoors. I insist—"

"Who was your choice, Dr. Beltrán?" the chairman interrupted.

"I much preferred Señor Aguilar and his ode to Princess Cristina." It was interesting to me that these men spoke of the young girl as if she really were a princess, as if the make-believe of the festival had entered their minds as well as their imaginations.

"Then it's up to you, Señor Solís," the chairman said.

"Now look, Solís," Don Eduardo interrupted. "You're a poet and you know that the poetry prize has always been reserved for—"

"Don Eduardo!" Professor Ruiz snapped. "Please allow the gentleman to speak his own mind."

In a soft, conciliatory voice the little poet said, "I liked Aguilar and the ode."

"Good!" Don Eduardo shouted. "Aguilar first, the elegy second, and if you want to put the one-handed Indian third, it's all right with me." He reached for the door that led back to the stage where he was prepared to announce his decision, but Professor Ruiz, now very red in the face, halted him.

"I will announce the winners," the doctor said icily, "and we have not yet decided on second and third place."

"How many are in favor of the elegy for second place?" Don Eduardo blustered. "Good. That's three, and that means he's in second place. The Indian can be third."

"Don Eduardo," Professor Ruiz said, trying not to shout, "that is no way to decide second place. It ignores completely the fact that the Indian won two nominations for first—"

"But the elegy just got three votes for second. You heard it. Me, Beltrán and Solís."

"Do you mean . . ." the professor spluttered

and Señor Solís spoke up softly: "I believe that Don Eduardo is right. This is not the year to give the young intruder second place. If we accord him third position, it will be an adequate gesture."

"My view entirely," Don Eduardo agreed affably. Then, clapping Beltrán on the back, he suggested: "And yours, too, I should think."

"Mine too," Beltrán said. He liked Don Eduardo. In fact, he liked all the Palafoxes and hoped to get to know them better.

"What do you think?" Professor Ruiz asked me.

I was disgusted by my uncle's steamroller tactics and saw no reason for hiding that fact, so I said: "To deny this man first place is an error, but to rob him of second is a disgrace."

"Now, wait a minute!" Don Eduardo cried. "You're an American and you don't understand the peculiarities of our situation. You have no right to butt into Mexican problems. It simply isn't right—"

"Do you think it's right to pervert a judgment for the reasons you're giving?" I snapped.

"Maybe not right." Don Eduardo laughed. "But expedient." He opened the door to the stage, and before I could even reach my seat he was announcing to the expectant audience: "The judges have agreed unanimously that the winner of the Tournament of Flowers is Señor Aquiles Aguilar for his inspired . . ." The cheering audience drowned out his last words.

A few minutes later Don Eduardo had his arm about me, leading me back to the House of Tile and saying, "You saw for yourself! The one-handed fellow was pleased as punch to get recognition in third position. Just as it should have been, because what you don't know is that if we had forced him into first place he would have been embarrassed." Without a bit of resentment for my having fought him in the committee, Don Eduardo sat himself beside me and shouted to the Widow Palafox: "Carmen! Carmen! Two of your best dinners."

As we sat down at the table I reached for one of Doña Carmen's crisp peasant rolls and said, as she handed us the menus: "Same as always, and I'm glad nothing's changed."

She corrected me: "One thing's changed." And with a pudgy finger she pointed at a warning printed in English: "Because of the unusual consumption of bread during the Festival of Ixmiq, there will be a charge of fifty centavos for each roll."

I looked up with surprise. The whole idea of dining at the House of Tile was that since 1910 the menu during the fair had not changed—you sat on the terrace and ate what you had always eaten. But now there was a charge for the bread. "What's happened?" I asked with some dismay.

"The norteamericanos happened, that's what happened," Doña Carmen snorted.

"What do you mean?" I countered.

"In the old days, when no one had heard of our festival, decent Mexicans, homesick for Spain, came here and ate in a decent manner," she explained. "Then fools wrote about us in your magazine, with photographs of the food, and now each year we get many norteamericanos."

"Why should that increase the price of bread?" I asked.

"We're glad to get the norteamericanos," she assured me. "They behave well and spend money, and I have many friends among the tourists, people who come back year after year. But they do create a problem with the bread."

"What problem?" I asked with irritation.

"When a Mexican comes," she explained, "he eats one roll, and we take this into account in our price, which you must admit is reasonable."

"No complaint," I said. "In the States a meal like this would cost twice as much."

"So I'm told," she nodded. "But here is the trouble. Apparently in the States there is no bread. Because whenever an American sits at this table he does just what you have done. He sees the basket of rolls, grabs one, and says, "I haven't tasted bread like this since I was a boy." And he eats not one roll but four and kills my whole budget."

I felt self-conscious, sitting there with a half-eaten roll in my hand, but I knew that what she said was true. In civilized America we no longer had bread; we had something sanitized and puffy that no self-respecting man would want to eat. I remember working on an article that our magazine ran some years back in which four scientists claimed that our bread was not only a sad travesty of what the staff of life should be, but that it was actually poisonous as well. I seem to recall that when boys in my class at Lawrenceville forced rats to eat it, either the rats died or their hair fell out.

But here in the peasant culture of Mexico there was still bread made from the simple ground wheat of the countryside, filled with impurities and flavor, and when we Americans tasted it after many years of chewing paste, we devoured it like starving pigs. "Look!" Doña Carmen said as two tourists who had come to the fair sat down at a nearby table. The woman looked about her and said: "Isn't this a charming plaza? Listen to the music!" But her husband cried: "Oh boy! Look at that bread!" He was well on his way to consuming his third roll before the meal even started.

"So now we have to charge," Doña Carmen said, shrugging her shoulders.

"Put me down for three. I love your soup and your rice, but what I really came for was your bread."

"And look at that one in the corner," Doña Carmen muttered in disgust. She pointed to one of the tables where an American sat wolfing down the rolls, and I saw that it was the blond young man from the bus, still dressed in his outsized, rumpled Pachuca sweater.

"I don't think he's hungry for bread," I told Doña Carmen. "I think he's just hungry."

"Do you suppose he has money?" the proprietress asked.

"If he doesn't, Don Eduardo will pay," I assured her.

"I like to see young people eat," my uncle said. Then he added: "Looks like we're going to have music," and he was correct, for the tourist couple at the next table had summoned a mariachi band to play for them during the meal, but they had called a band quite different from the flashily dressed and somewhat mechanical musicians we'd heard earlier. This was a group of Altomec peasants who had come down from

Durango to see the fair and to pick up what pennies they could by offering themselves as mariachis. They had no uniforms, no big hats, not even shoes. Nor did they have the customary instruments of the real mariachis. There were only six—a bass drummer, a snare drummer, two clarinet players, a huge guitarist and a tall, thin man with an extremely sad face and a dented trumpet. They looked an epitome of the real Mexico, and on their faded blue pants and worn sandals there was dust.

"What shall we play for you, señor?" I heard the bass drummer ask in Spanish.

"We don't know," the husband replied in English.

The leader shrugged his shoulders, consulted with his companions, and told them in Spanish: " 'Cielito Lindo' and 'San Antonio Rose' for the norteamericanos," and I thought: This is going to be pretty bad, so I said to Don Eduardo, "I'd better speak to them."

I went to the other table and asked in English, "Excuse me, but could I be of help with the mariachis?"

"You might tell them to play some real Mexican music."

"If you would permit me."

"Oh, please do!" the wife pleaded. "We don't

want to hear American music on our first visit in Toledo."

"I thought you wouldn't," I said. I then turned to the mariachis and said in Spanish: "These visitors love the music of Mexico. Please play only the real songs of your country."

"Like what?" the leader asked suspiciously.

I gave some examples of wonderful songs rarely heard, ending with: "And you might give them a battle cry like 'The Ballad of General Gurza.'"

The men's eyes lighted up with pleasure—all, that is, except those of the tall, sad trumpeter, who merely fingered the valves on his instrument, as if warming up. I bowed to the tourists and returned to Don Eduardo.

With two quick waves of his drumstick, the leader started the music, but I was not prepared for what followed, for in the first blaring passages of a robust folk dance the lean trumpeter unloosed a cascade of purity such as I have rarely heard matched in any orchestra. He played passionately, his hollow cheeks distended with air, his thin lips wedged against the mouthpiece, and his tongue ripping out triple and sextuple passages. He was truly a heavenly trumpeter, lost in some Durango village, and whenever he rested it was to gain fresh strength

for some new display of virtuosity. He never
smiled, and always seemed removed from the
simple realities. Throughout the time of the Festival of Ixmiq I saw him only as a disembodied
talent who mysteriously produced music of the
angels. In the nights to come I would often hear
his tongue-splitting rhythms echoing in various
parts of the plaza, and no one could confuse
him with the other mariachis. His companions
seemed to recognize this, for when during a
song the time came for him to rest, they merely
limped through their part of the music, waiting till
his liquid trumpet sound exploded once more
behind them, and then they would play with
added spirit. Now, as they wound through the
final passages of the vigorous dance, I sat back
contented.

"I've never heard a better trumpeter," I told
Don Eduardo.

"I've often thought," the old rancher mused
as we waited for our soup, "that a lot of people
from other parts of the world are going to be
surprised when they enter heaven and find that
God entertains himself with mariachi music."
But then he suddenly scowled, as the new selection began. He asked abruptly: "Did you tell
them to play that?"

"I did," I confessed.

"You have a curious taste. To sing of General

Gurza in this place." And he pointed to the bro- ken tiles on the wall in back of where the maria- chis stood, the tiles against which I had been measured as a boy. Having rebuked me, Don Eduardo fell silent and I could tell that he was recalling his encounters with the murderous general who had been the scourge of Toledo. And I recalled my own experiences.

General Gurza had come roaring into Toledo on one of his periodic raids to rob the city's citizens. I was at the Mineral when Gurza led a detachment to the mines in a search for silver, and I was sure they were going to shoot us. Father whispered: "Stay very still. Say nothing," and we watched as Gurza and his men over- looked several tons of black ore from which sil- ver could be extracted. They ransacked our quarters, and had the calf been sequestered there according to the original plan, both he and we would have been shot.

At the end of the search, General Gurza as- sembled our family and I remember standing in front of my mother, hoping to protect her, and I could feel her legs trembling. The general was not my idea of a general at all, for he certainly did not look like any of my tin soldiers, with brightly colored uniforms and colored bands across their chests. General Gurza was a big man, both taller and heavier than my father. He had a round face with a black mustache, and wore a huge sombrero and silver-studded chaps. He carried a shotgun. And on his hips were two pistols, while crossing his chest was a bandolier, with here and there a cartridge missing.

He nudged me in the stomach with his rifle and asked: "When you grow up will you fight for the Revolution?" I said, "I don't know what a revolution is. But I'm going to fight against you and help my mother."

General Gurza laughed, poked the gun deeper into my stomach, and said, "When you grow up you'll know better." He then made a short speech in which he said that he had found what he had come for. He whistled sharply without moving his lips, and from our stables four of his men approached leading one of our miners with his hands tied and a rope around his neck. "This is what we are going to do with all our enemies," he said. And without further ado the four soldiers threw the rope over a beam projecting from the cloisters and hanged the man. Because our cloisters were not high, the man's feet were never far from the ground, and he seemed to dance in our faces. I could feel my mother's knees start to give way behind me and I cried: "Mother's going to fall down." My father leaped to catch her, but General Gurza got there first and, dropping his gun, he carried her to a table. When she opened her eyes she expected to see my father but instead looked directly into the eyes of the general. His black mustache must have been only a few inches from her face, and she began to scream.

This angered the general particularly because he thought that she must be an American, since she was married to one. He slapped her, then laughed and said: "We don't hurt norteamericanos—if they remain neutral." He then directed my father to come to him, and with the dead miner's body swinging between them, the two men discussed how the silver from the Mineral was to be delivered to the general's forces and what records were to be kept. I remember how the interview ended. General Gurza said: "You understand, Mr. Clay, that if any of this silver falls into the hands of Carranza we shall have to shoot you?"

My father replied: "But I thought you were fighting for Carranza."

General Gurza scowled and said, "That was last month. Now he's our enemy. No silver to him."

"I understand," my father said, and the two men shook hands as if they were bankers. But when the time came to leave, some of Gurza's men saw the dangling body and were apparently infuriated by the sight, for they began shooting at it from horseback, and many of the shots went wild, ricocheting down our cloisters. All the way back to the gate the men kept up their wild shooting, and when they had ridden safely down the hill, my father systematically inspected all the workers to be sure none were hurt, then gave orders to cut down the dead man and bury him. When the others were busy with this task, he and I went cautiously to the cave below the slag heap and satisfied ourselves that Soldado was safe. Father directed me to give the calf some hay, and we left the animal content and eating.

Well, I thought now, sitting on the terrace of the House of Tile, that was a rare peaceful moment in a turbulent past.

"Where were you in those years?" I asked Don Eduardo, who was attacking his soup.

"What do you mean, 'those years'?" he asked without looking up. He loved food.

"I was thinking of the years when we hid Soldado from the Gurza troops," I explained.

He put his spoon down, thought a moment, and said, "That would have been 1916 to about 1919, I guess. I was hiding out in Mexico City, working like the devil with Carranza to keep control of my lands. I didn't succeed."

Laughing at his own incompetence, he said,

"In 1536 we Palafoxes were granted a quarter of a million choice acres and by 1580 this had grown, by thefts from Church and state, to a third of a million. By 1740, due to shrewd management and further thefts from everyone in sight, our holdings had increased to over a million acres and the labor of nearly a hundred and twenty thousand Indians, who were for all practical purposes our slaves." At this point in the narration he sighed.

"In the 1810 War of Independence, of course, the Conde de Palafox sided with the Spaniards, so that when relative peace came he was penalized by the victorious Mexicans, who took back half his vast holdings."

In the 1860s the Palafoxes guessed wrong again and supported the Austrian usurper, Emperor Maximilian, as did all decent people, and when the rabble shot him to restore Mexican independence, they also shot the then conde, whereupon the Palafox holdings fell to about two hundred and fifty thousand acres. In the Revolution of 1916, as we have seen, Don Eduardo came out strongly against General Gurza and lost another hundred and fifty thousand. Finally, in 1936, the family guessed wrong again and fought President Cárdenas, who had the land courts legally divest the Palafoxes of most of their remaining acreage.

"As a result of always being on the wrong side," Don Eduardo concluded, "our once-vast Palafox dominion now consists of nine thousand arid acres of bull ranch in a corner of our state, the skeletons of a few haciendas that General Gurza gutted, and the abandoned Mineral."

But if the Palafoxes invariably guessed wrong about the advantageous political affiliation, thereby losing their land, they displayed canny judgment where investments were concerned, thereby maintaining their family security. With the business acumen that had always marked the Spanish branch of the family the Palafoxes had invested in railroads, in French mercantile companies, and more recently in Swiss and American pharmaceutical corporations, so that while their land holdings were steadily diminishing, their equity in the business wealth of the world rose comfortably. In 1961 the family was at least as wealthy as it had ever been, and with this wealth the members had been able to buy favor with whatever administration was in power, regardless of its politics.

But the principal fame of the family derived from the fact that old Don Eduardo Palafox, who under a better system of government would have inherited the title conde, raised the best bulls in Mexico and probably the best anywhere in the world except Spain. It was not unusual for

Cardinal Palafox, while on church duty in other parts of Latin America or the United States, to be greeted with the enthusiastic comment "I saw your bulls in Mexico City and they were tremendous."

The young bull Soldado, who had survived for three months in our cave as my responsibility, turned out to be one of the memorable seed bulls of history, and his offspring accounted for much of the glory accruing to the name Palafox. On the last day of the fair we would see his latest descendants, and I looked across to the white wall where the poster blared the news: "The Traditional Festival of Ixmiq. Bulls of Palafox."

I said, "Don Eduardo, when your first bull comes out on Sunday, I am going to salute him like a grandson. After all, he sprang from my cave."

The big rancher laughed and leaned back, wiping the Valencian rice from his heavy under-lip. "Do you know why I like bullfighting so much?" he asked.

"Because you make a fortune on the bad bulls you sell," I suggested.

He chuckled and said: "You know I lose money raising those damned animals. We all do. But I like the essential battle of life. In this city my people have been fighting through four centuries. Not one of the buildings you can see from here was erected except after some shattering fight. No one wanted the cathedral there, or the new façade, or the expensive theater. No one except some Palafox. What happened to the Miers? Doña Carmen's family? They owned more land than we did, but when General Gurza approached, they quit like chickens of no strain." He paused and picked at a tooth with his little finger. When he had dislodged a bit of clam he said, "We have fought the Altomecs in the hills, and the king in Madrid, and the pope in Rome, and General Gurza in Mexico City. I fought President Cárdenas through every court in Mexico, but we still parted good friends. Do you know what Cárdenas said when he confirmed the decision of the land courts that confiscated our acres? He said, 'Don Eduardo, I think you are the father of your best bulls.' In a sense, I am."

"I'll bet that on Sunday five of your six animals will be disgraceful."

"Accepted, but remember that if only one is good, he's the one that'll be remembered." He laughed, then grew sober. "Here comes the matador now," he said.

I turned to see what had captured his attention, and watched a beat-up black Cadillac, about six years old, come speeding into the plaza and stop abruptly with protesting brakes before the terrace where we sat. At the wheel was a gnome-like man of about fifty, a black fedora jammed over his eyes and a cigar stuck between his teeth. Sharing the front seat with him were two middle-aged bullfighters who looked like gangsters. Quickly the three jumped out and started untying ropes that had kept bundles secure on top of the Cadillac on its trip from Mexico City. One of the men paused to open the rear door nearest me, and from it stepped a flashily dressed, attractive young woman, followed by a smallish, tense, very dark man in his early thirties. As soon as he appeared, a crowd gathered while keeping at a respectful distance, and little boys began calling to others, "It's Juan Gómez!"

The crowd increased and some youth who had seen many movies gave a low wolf whistle, at which the girl smiled. Gómez, the matador, with no emotion on his face, forced a passageway through the crowd and went into the hotel. As he passed my table he looked at Don Eduardo and stopped to embrace him.

"May the bulls be good," the matador said.

"May you have much luck," the rancher replied.

Then Gómez disappeared, while the gnome-like man supervised the unloading of the costumes, the swords, the lances and the odd leather baskets in which the matador's hats were carried. Gómez was now among us, and Don Eduardo observed, as the mariachis paraded about the square, their trumpeters filling the night with the music of Mexico, "Tonight they sleep under one roof, Victoriano and Gómez. Do you think they'll be valiant on Friday?"

"People who saw them fight in Puebla say they almost made you forget Manolete," I replied.

"May their luck be good," the old rancher said. He crossed himself, kissed his thumb, and threw the benediction over his shoulder and into the House of Tile, where the two matadors were resting.

4

THE INDIAN

I SPENT Wednesday night after the poetry competition and all day Thursday in a forced explosion of energy I had not displayed since my all-night cramming for exams at Princeton. Consulting experts, borrowing their newspaper clippings regarding memorable fights, and even conducting hurried interviews with Juan Gómez and his manager, I was able to construct a mental image of the bowlegged Indian. Then, when I had my room organized as a workstation, my typewriter on a table away from the sun, my pile of white paper neatly within

reach and fresh carbons at hand, I plunged into
the task of grinding out the type of story that
New York treasured: good guy versus bad, all-
white versus all-black, premonitions of tragedy
to come, plus a general breathlessness to keep
the story line galloping ahead. As the pages
piled up, I was not unhappy with what I was
accomplishing, for I took professional pride in
my ability to write quickly and accurately while
fitting my data into the patterns that Drummond
liked.

What we have in the three-day festival that
starts tomorrow, Friday, is a Spanish celebration dating back about two hundred years
but based upon Indian rituals almost two
thousand years old. It's appropriate, therefore, that our protagonists should represent
almost ideally the two historic strains of Mexican history: the ancient Indian, the recent
Spanish.

The Spaniard I've already given you in detail:
slim, tall, blue-eyed and with exceptional poetry of movement. You have my photos of
him that I've caught in other plazas and earlier in Spain and they show the charismatic
Victoriano, but use those that emphasize his
elegant style. I haven't sent you too much on

Gómez yet, but he's different, a grubby little Indian peasant with no elegance whatever, only a brutal determination to get the job done and a willingness to risk his life in doing it. Fortunately for us, he looks like what he is: awkward, a stumpy little guy with a head of dark hair encroaching on his eyebrows, and legs that are decidedly bowed. Taciturn, moody, afraid of the press, he is not a likable matador.

So I see Ixmiq-61 as a duel between the two faces of Mexico, the Spaniard versus the Indian. Also: sunlight versus shadow, hero versus villain, beauty versus ugliness—and, above all, a young man protected by three extremely canny bullfight operators versus an older fellow assisted by a beat-up codger who poses as a manager but who really uses Gómez as a last-chance meal ticket, and a brassy dame who believes Gómez will help her become a flamenco entertainer in Spain but who will drop him instantly if something better comes along.

As I pushed my chair back to stare out the window at the plaza, I was not entirely happy with my facile comparison of the two matadors, for I suspected that in stressing their obvious differences I was missing essentials. A few days earlier I had telegraphed New York a brief report on Gómez and their response proved that the home office had adopted my simplification, because the art editor had cabled me: "Be sure get moody shot Gómez working bull deep in shadows." Drummond himself cabled: "Essential you provide us with numerous incidents that show good guy in peril and bad guy momentarily triumphant." In our shop Victoriano had become certified as the good guy.

Thus, through words and photographs we were prejudging an event that had not yet happened, and I could detect in the communications reaching me from New York evidence that the editors had become emotionally involved in this duel between the matadors. Late Thursday afternoon, a few hours after dropping off my latest dispatch at the cable office, I was startled by a messenger who brought to my room an urgent cable from Drummond that asked: "Highbrow philosophizing aside, which matador do you think is likely to die?"

Sitting at my desk, I stared at my typewriter and grumbled: They're forcing me to make a prediction I'm not capable of making. Then as I blinked and restudied the cable I realized that it did not represent a business query. It was a personal question from Drummond as a man, not an editor, one who had become caught up in the struggle between Victoriano and Gómez and after a long day at work and a cocktail at some bar or bistro had shot me an honest inquiry. I was not required to answer, and yet as I sat there, my head resting on my hands as dusk fell and my room grew dark, I found that I wanted to give him an answer.

"It's the Spaniard who will die," I said aloud, and I could see the culmination of this insane contest. Juan Gómez, the relentless little Indian, would continue to fight the bulls with increasing valor, "tickling their tonsils with his elbows," as the bullfighters described it, and he would goad Victoriano into executing more and more arabesques until the final afternoon of the festival when in the lengthening shadows a bull would suddenly hook to the left, and Victoriano would hang suspended for a long forty seconds, after which he would be dead.

And then I must have lost all sense of morality because I found myself praying, "Dear God, if he has to die, let it be now, at the height of the festival, with the bands playing and not at the end of the fight but at the beginning, while the light is still good, so that the camera can catch the full detail as he dangles from the horn."

I regained my senses. "Jesus Christ!" I gasped. "What am I saying?" But before my self-disgust could drive the grisly prayer from my mind I had to admit that what I had prayed for was what I actually wanted. If Victoriano was doomed, let the swift horn thrust come at the Festival of Ixmiq, early in the afternoon on a sunny day when the light was good—not for *the* photographers, but for *this* photographer, me. "If there's to be a story, let it be a good one, a classic of the bullring. Let me write a story that cuts right to the heart of the bullring, at the heart of Mexico itself. Purged of all nonsense. Just the bare truth."

But as I shifted my gaze from my desk I could see Drummond working at his own desk in New York and thinking exactly the way I had been thinking in Mexico. I could picture him unwilling to leave the office and breaking out a bottle of porter while he arranged imaginary headlines and calculated: If one of them has to die, as Clay claims, let it be the one who makes the best story for us. And he would be juggling the copy and the photographs I'd not yet sent him, because the events had not yet happened, and I could hear him assuring himself: We can't go wrong playing Victoriano as the doomed hero, young and handsome, hounded to his death by the evil little man . . . that's not bad. Pictures here and here. Left page we'll use that great shot of him being carried in glory out of the ring in Mexico City with girls throwing flowers at him. Facing page the same golden face but this time held aloft by a bull's horn. The black horn coming right out of his chest. Then on the inside pages the eight flashbacks of the family history, with that stupendous thing of his grandfather pinned to the sand by the bull's horn through his head. Those old-time photographs always carry a wallop. It isn't till pages five and six that we get our first shot of the bowlegged little Mexican who caused it all.

As soon as he thinks of the bowlegged little Mexican, he would be faced with a crucial editorial problem, and I could see him brushing his dummy aside and asking: But how do we play it if it isn't Victoriano who dies but the little Mexican? It was at this point that he would wire me for my opinion. He was now facing up to his problem and I had no doubt he would come up with one of the noble-sounding phrases for which he was famous: "And thus we see why it is that men fight bulls and sometimes die on their horns."

I could feel myself becoming irritated at all this speculation, but as an obedient field worker I would continue to send him all the instructive information I could find on Gómez, trusting that something I said would illuminate the story— however it came out. But as I brooded about my work so far, I realized that nothing I had said about Gómez had represented the real man. I had been using him simply as if he were the Indian half of Mexico counterpoised against the Spanish component. I had been describing him as darkness opposed to light, as fate imperiling the exquisite. I had set up in my mind a phony preconception of what was going to happen— the death of Victoriano Leal—and this act had determined my observations of Gómez. I had been describing a man only as he functioned in the life and death of another, and this was wrong.

All the books I had ever read about Mexico, and the thesis I had written at Princeton about my homeland, had been flawed by a fatal weakness. Spaniards had spoken of the country as it affected Spain's quest for Catholics and bars of silver. Americans like my father had explained how it looked from the American point of view. In his *The Pyramid and the Cathedral* he had tried to reassure the American reader that, after all, Mexico was a reasonably decent place because in many respects it was almost up to American standards. But of Mexico as a unique land, with its own promise and its own problems, no one had written. And least of all the Mexicans themselves. For anyone in this land who took up his pen did so either as a Spanish apologist, or as an Indian, or as an anti-American, or as a pro-Russian. But as a Mexican? Never.

Since truth to a Mexican and to an American almost always differed, I now realized that everything I had so far written about the matador Juan Gómez had been constructed strictly from the point of view of an American writing about an Indian who was about to cause the death of a Spaniard. Now I was wide awake, and as sleep was impossible, on that quiet Thursday evening after I had filed my report, I left the House of Tile to walk in the plaza. There, gazing at the contrasting Spanish and Indian structures in the silvery moonlight, I said to myself: Forget your personal hang-ups, forget your desire for the perfect headline that sells magazines—if you were forced to describe Juan Gómez as he actually is, in relation to no one else, to no symbols, how would you do it?

Finding no easy answer, I sat on one of the benches that lined the plaza and stared alternately at the cathedral of Bishop Palafox and at the pyramid of the ancient Drunken Builders while struggling to reach some understanding of this stolid Indian matador. Out of the grubby incidents I had heard about his career I recalled one incident in particular that seemed to epitomize the hardships he constantly had to confront. It involved a frantic midnight auto trip from Acapulco to Mexico City.

About three years ago, before his competition with Victoriano Leal had provided him with real money, Juan Gómez was a full-fledged matador, but with a chaotic past, a dismal present and a rather limited future. He had accomplished little, was beset by leeches who kept him poor, and had no logical reason to expect his luck to change. He fought about six times a year and at fees that barely kept him from starvation. He could not afford to maintain a regular troupe of his own, as affluent matadors did, but was forced to rely upon any picadors or peóns he could get cheap and sought to ingratiate himself with the unions by accepting whomever they sent.

He had picked up a striking-looking girl named Lucha González, a strident singer who also tried to dance and was reasonably good with the castanets. When he managed to find a bullfight, he contributed to their upkeep, but much of the time he was forced to rely upon the modest amounts of money she earned from her engagements. Lucha, whose name was the accepted abbreviation for one of the most popular girl's names in Mexico, María de la Luz (Virgin Mary of the Light), was about two inches taller than her matador, a fact that he was never able to forget. One day she saw in an American magazine an advertisement for elevator shoes and the promise "Now you can be taller than she is." She could not read English, of course, but she caught the idea conveyed by the picture and had a friend write a letter to New York, sending the twenty dollars that she had saved. It had not been easy to measure her matador's feet, but one night when he was asleep she had pulled away the covers and made on paper a rough outline of his feet.

When the shoes arrived and she handed them to Gómez he noticed the exaggerated heels, trickily camouflaged, and began to laugh. But, actually, his vanity was wounded and thereafter he never loved Lucha as much as he had before.

At the time I'm speaking of, Gómez had been awarded a third-rate contract for a fight in Acapulco, with bulls that were not acceptable for the big ring in Mexico City. He had been offered $750 for the afternoon, but of this amount he had to pay $110 for his troupe, $88 for travel and hotel bills, and a kickback of $150 to the impresario. Laundry, care for his suit, and $44 for bribing the newspaper critics meant that he earned, for an afternoon of fighting dangerous bulls, about $300, most of which he had to spend at the cafés to create the illusion that he was an important matador. It is true that for some of his fights he earned considerably more, but for the past four years he had kept for himself less than two thousand dollars a year, out of which he had had to pay for five months in the hospital.

In fact, his Acapulco engagement would have been financially disastrous had it not been for Lucha, who by persistent phone calls had forced one of the big American hotels to sign her on as an entertainer for a two-week period. As so often before, her earnings enabled the matador to live, and when the fight was over Lucha kept on singing while her matador in his high-heeled shoes strutted aimlessly about the cafés.

His work in the Acapulco bullring had not been impressive, for the animals were atrocious, but he had been at least as good as the other matadors and patently braver, so that during the long week after the fight he won a good deal of favorable comment in the cafés, especially since he was spending what remained of his earnings on drinks for the parasites that clung to him. At midnight on a Saturday, six days after his appearance in the ring, considerable excitement was caused by a man who ran from café to café crying, "Phone call for the matador! Impresario in Mexico City calling urgently."

Lucha herself had told me about that night in Acapulco. I'd been working on a story about illegal Mexican immigrants in San Antonio, Texas, and chanced to see a newspaper item about a Sunday bullfight across the border in Nuevo Laredo. Since it was only a two-hour drive south, I decided to go because I'd heard that this Mexican matador Juan Gómez was a real bulldog and I was eager to see what he could do.

After the fight, in which he performed well, I sought him out, showed him my credentials and asked if we could talk. His manager, a tough character with a long cigar, grabbed my card, studied it and nodded, whereupon Gómez led me to a café overlooking the Rio Grande. The featured entertainer was an ersatz flamenco singer-dancer who joined us at our table. "This is my friend, Lucha González," the matador said, but she corrected him: "I'm his manager. Cigarro here thinks he is, but I'm boss." And when we got around to talking about that night in Acapulco she proved that she was boss, for she dominated the conversation.

"I'm singing one of my best songs when this man rushes up shouting 'Telephone for Juan

Gómez! Impresario in Mexico City! Needs him
for the fight tomorrow!' So I jump off the stage
and run to help the man find Juan. I'm thinking:
My God! Mexico City! The big plaza!"

As we talked she looked lovingly at her matador and said: "I find him in that big café by the
ocean, wearing that checkered suit I got him in
Mexico City, a string tie, his Andalusian hat and
the polished shoes from New York. A proper-
looking matador. When the messenger shouts
'Gómez! The impresario in Mexico City wants
you for a fight! Tomorrow! On our phone!' a
change comes over Juan."

She paused, smiled at Juan again and said as
if recalling a fairy tale: "He was so handsome
when he rose, straightened his jacket and
walked through the streets to the telephone with
men behind us shouting to others: 'Gómez,
called to Mexico City for a big fight tomorrow!' I
was proud to be walking with him, and when we
reached the phone the news was exciting:
'We're in trouble, Gómez. All tickets have been
sold for tomorrow's fight. We were supposed to
have the hero from Venezuela. But his plane
was grounded in Bogotá, no way he can get
here. Can you rush right up here and be ready
to fight at four?' "

Now Gómez interrupted: "I told him: 'I'll be

there,' and he said: 'Matador, you've saved the honor of Mexico.' "

"But tell him what the pig said when I asked him about the fee," Lucha cried, and Gómez fell silent, so she spoke: "He told Juan, 'We'll arrange that later,' but he was helpful about the trip: 'If you drive out of Acapulco right away, say by one o'clock, you have less than two hundred miles to go. That should put you here by seven, easy. Then you can catch some sleep, Cigarro can select your bulls at noon, you get a little more sleep and you'll be bright-eyed for the fight at four.' "

Lucha, who had been listening in, could not accept this evasion. Grabbing the phone, she said: "Señor Irizaba, how much for Gómez?" and when the suave voice of the impresario assured her: "We'll settle that later," she exploded, and as she talked I had a chance to study this forceful, crudely handsome woman. In her thirties, she had obviously trailed from one nightclub to another through most of Mexico and even in the American border towns. Now, stuck in Nuevo Laredo in a fifth-rate joint, she recalled that night in Acapulco, and despite the mournful tale she was about to relate her sense of comedy made her chuckle.

"Now it seems funny. Then it was a fight, real

bad," and she explained how, when the call from Mexico City ended she had warned Gómez: "That man is a liar. He's using you, For you there will be no fight in the capital tomorrow."

"You heard him, Lucha," Gómez had argued. "The Venezolano is stranded in Bogotá. Irizaba has to find someone—with a strong reputation."

The proud woman lowered her voice as she told me: "In those days my man here had no reputation, strong or weak. So I knew it was a lie on Irizaba's part. He was calling Juan simply to have him on hand if the matador he really wanted, someone much better known, couldn't come." But again she laughed as she touched my arm: "When Juan left the phone and the men in the café asked how much he would be getting for the fight, he told them 'Three thousand dollars,' but they must have known it would have been more like six hundred, and there he was, likely to get nothing."

At this parading of his shame, Gómez winced, and as Lucha continued in her energetic way I caught a glimpse of the bullfighter's life. As a woman who had engineered her own café appearances, she knew how unreliable Mexican managers of such places could be, and she'd had a few bad experiences in the States, too, so she had told Juan firmly: "You cannot drive to Mexico City this time of night. For nothing."

He had said: "But there's a chance. If I could have a big day in the capital—"

"You'll have no day—none—not with that worm Irisaba."

She told me: "We continued the argument for nearly half an hour, didn't we, Juan?" He nodded: "It was bitter. She knew I had no chance, and maybe I knew it, too. But that's what a matador is, a man who takes chances."

"How did it end?" I asked, and they both spoke at once, each giving the other credit for decent behavior in what had become a brawl, but in the end Gómez had issued an ultimatum: "In fifteen minutes Cigarro and I leave for the capital. Come with us or stay here, you choose."

Realizing that her man meant what he said, she had temporized: "Let me sing my next set. You know we live on my singing and I can't just walk out—"

"I'll wait," he had replied, and that night, at a quarter to two, with Cigarro at the wheel and Lucha and Gómez trying to sleep in the backseat, the Cadillac roared out of the seaside resort, entered the mountains and drove due north toward the capital. From time to time the rear-seat passengers awakened to watch Cigarro speed through some sleeping village at seventy miles an hour or scatter a flock of chickens sleeping on the warm pavement—through Iguala, famous in Mexican history for its role in revolutions; through Taxco, with its old buildings of great beauty; and into Cuernavaca, with its exquisite residences occupied by rich American tourists.

As they finished the treacherous trip through the mountains and reached the plateau on which Mexico City rested, Cigarro had slowed to a halt: "Juan, I'm tired. You like to drive?" but Lucha objected: "He needs sleep." She climbed into the front seat to take the wheel and guided the old car into the outskirts of Mexico City and then along its crowded streets. Passing cafés in which she had sung, she started humming one of her favorite songs and made her way to a cheap hotel. There she argued with the custodian that since it was now seven in the morning, she would expect to pay only for the coming day. At seven-thirty Cigarro and his matador were asleep, so she drove on to an all-night café where the patrons remembered her and there she joined in a few songs.

At half after eleven she was back in the hotel, bringing Gómez hot water for shaving and at ten to twelve she had both him and Cigarro ready for noontime events at the arena.

Unlike most matadors, who were superstitious to an incapacitating degree and who refused ever to look at their bulls until the animals burst into the arena for the final fight, Juan Gómez insisted upon being present at the midday selection of the beasts. He had felt, even as a boy, that he could never learn enough about the animals and felt there was always the possibility that at the noon choosing he might detect some characteristic in his beast that would enable him to produce a great fight. The only weakness in this theory was that he rarely produced a superb afternoon, while men who never saw their bulls sometimes did.

But when the matador and his entourage entered the corrals where the bulls would be assigned to each matador, Lucha was shocked, for she saw immediately that not only were the representatives of the other two fighters for that day present, but also the men who were to have served the Venezuelan visitor, plus the agents of four other well-known matadors, each with a more glittering reputation than Juan Gómez.

She felt sick. "The bastards!" she muttered. "Oh, those filthy bastards!"

Gómez, trying to protect the slim hope that he would be chosen for the fight, tried to silence her lest she destroy the chances he never had, but she brushed him aside, elbowed her way

through the crowd of men inspecting the six
placid bulls in the corrals, located the impresario
Irizaba, a tall, corpulent man in his sixties whose
left eye twitched, and began screaming at him:
"You stinking son-of-a-bitch! Bringing all these
men here for no purpose. You swine!"

Her fury was so great and her attempts to
claw at Irizaba became so ferocious that he ordered two of his helpers to restrain her while he
fled to the security of his upstairs office overlooking the corrals, but he did not escape un-
scathed, for as he retreated, Lucha, though held
firmly in the grip of two strong men, succeeded
in giving him a painful kick.

Agents for the other disappointed matadors,
thinking to protect whatever chances Gómez
might have for fighting in the capital, dragged
Lucha away, and when she was safely outside
the plaza, they returned to Gómez and said: "If
you ever want to fight here, apologize to Irizaba.
He'll understand. Just say the woman got out of
control." He said: "No one can step on her toes.
I learned and so did he," and he pointed to
Cigarro standing by the corrals.

Throwing Lucha out of the plaza solved nothing. Still steaming mad over what had been
done to Gómez, she found another entrance
and rushed up the stairs to Irizaba's office,
where she broke open his door and shouted at

him: "We drove all night. So did those three others. Are you going to pay us for our trouble?"

Irizaba was terrified of her. He kept moving about behind his big desk to protect himself. She would have torn him apart.

"How did it end?" I asked, and Gómez deferred to Lucha, who said: "The fat one told me: 'What I'm willing to do, since the matadors are already here, I'll give each of you two seats— free, you understand—for the fight,' and he pushed two of them at me."

"What did you do?" I asked, and she said bitterly: "Didn't even touch them. Saw the location and flicked them away with my fingernail, told him: 'You would! Cheap seats way up there. For a full matador. How shameful. You give us good seats down there, or—' "

"Did he?" I asked.

"He knew he had to."

"And did you take them? I'd have thought—"

Gómez responded: "Of course we took them. A matador can never see enough bulls. Always something different. That's how he learns." Then he told me something I did not know: "And quite a few times in bullfight history some matador just watching in the stands has stepped in, with no cape, to handle a bull who has leaped in among the crowd. We save lives, because with bulls you can never be sure."

———

Bullfighting is an ugly business. For a few lucky men it offers a life of brilliance if they are either brave enough or canny enough to dominate it. But for most it is a sad, bitter, dirty existence that lasts only a few years and that leaves men either maimed or emotionally scarred for the rest of their lives. Here is the story, as I heard it from Juan Gómez and his friends, of how he became committed to this dismal world.

Even now I could hear his soft voice with its heavy Indian accent as he spoke reluctantly of his early years: "I was born in a small mud hut near a village beyond the pyramid. Altomec Indians, no land of our own. Father, always white cotton pants, you know the kind, rope for a belt, very thin shirt, front ends tucked over the rope, back ends flapped across skinny bottom." He said that for some years his stolid father had fought in the armies of General Gurza, hoping to win for his family a better life, but all he had gained from this excursion into the revolution was an additional cotton shirt. He had been present at the second sacking of Toledo, but while the more prudent of Gurza's men were stripping the cathedral he had been trying unsuccessfully to rape a nineteen-year-old girl. He had thus missed his one chance to profit from the Revolution, for the other soldiers got the cathedral's rich silver ornaments.

In the month of Juan's birth the Gómez family was overtaken by retribution, for a large group of conservatives, banded together by priests and calling themselves Cristeros—Men of Christ—swept over much of Toledo state sacking villages and murdering everyone suspected of having served with General Gurza. One evening at sunset the Cristeros came roaring in from the plains of central Mexico and in an act of supreme irony shot Juan's father.

I say this was ironic because in those last wild and evil years that plagued Mexico, when good men were driven to murder, the peasant Gómez had taken into his home a Catholic priest who would otherwise have been assassinated by the old remnants of Gurza's rebellious army, and for three years the Gómez family had hidden this priest, dressing him as an ordinary workman and allowing him, at great peril to themselves, to conduct Mass in their mud hut. It was surprising that Gómez had done this, for he had been a vigorous if ineffectual revolutionary who had at one time hated priests, but he explained his action simply: "I am tired of killing. Priests should not be killed."

The matador said of his father: "When he was raping and tearing down churches, God watched over him. But when he repented and protected a priest in our home, God killed him. He sent men who shouted, 'Long live Christ the King!' as they murdered and burned, and they shot him."

The Widow Gómez was left with two sons, Raúl, aged five, and Juan, aged one month. The priest stayed with them for several months to help till the fields that the dead man had worked for others, and for some time the boys grew up thinking he was their father. But when the Cristeros departed, some old Gurza partisans reported the priest's existence in the village, and government forces, strongly anti-Catholic, came to find him and perhaps shoot him, but by the time they arrived Father López had been warned and had escaped. I can speak with some authority about these particular matters, because when Father López fled from the village in northwest Toledo state, he was taken in by my family at the mine, and I remember that he occupied a room next to mine. Father López said that it was a miracle that he, a hunted priest, should have been saved first by a soldier from General Gurza's armies and next by a Protestant who feared Catholics. My father, who had rescued Padre López after a midnight ride in an old Ford car, growled that there the similarity ended, "because you are not welcome to conduct any Masses in this house." Nevertheless, the redoubtable priest did hold secret Masses in what was called the bull-cave, and to them came the workmen at the mines, even though some were known to be spies for the revolutionists.

How the Widow Gómez, now left with two sons and no man to help her, survived, the matador never told me, but in those dreadful years it was not uncommon for half the women of a village to be widowed. Husbands who had supported the revolution were killed by the Cristeros, and those good men who were suspected of being Catholics were shot by the revolutionists. Take my own typical case. Before I was fourteen I had seen the city of Toledo occupied four different times and burned twice. I had seen not less than twenty men hanged and numerous others shot, and later I had watched some of the most gentle men and women I had ever known rise up in the Cristero movement and strike back with murderous fury. That was the Mexico of my youth, and it was the Mexico in which Juan Gómez grew up with his widowed mother.

The boy had one year of education. Then the village school was burned by the Cristeros, and he roamed the countryside earning what pennies he could. Of these years he told me: "I could sign my name but I couldn't read. Still have trouble with big words. But a kind neighbor told me: 'Go down to Toledo and find the Pala- fox ranch. They hire boys.' So I walked south, with one pair of pants and one shirt. Cold day in January when I walked through the big gate. Didn't even know it was a place where they raised fighting bulls. Never seen one.''

At the small stone bullring inside the ranch many automobiles were parked and a crowd of ragged boys like himself milled about. ''What's happening?'' he asked. A boy said: ''La tienta,'' and when he asked ''What's that?'' the boy said in astonishment: ''If you don't know, why are you here?'' He said: ''To get a job,'' and the boy said impatiently: ''Armillita is testing the cows.''

''Who's Armillita?'' he asked.

Staring at him in amazement, they pushed him from the gate, deeming him unworthy of being allowed to enter if he did not even know who Armillita was. A few moments later the gate was opened from inside and a big round man whom he later knew as Don Eduardo Palafox appeared. ''Let the boys in,'' he commanded, and the men who had been keeping the raga- muffins out now graciously admitted them.

''Sit over there,'' a gruff man ordered, ''and if one of you dares to jump into the ring, his throat will be cut.''

At this moment a red gate on the far side of

the little ring swung open and for the first time
Juan Gómez watched an animal charge into an
arena. A flush of excitement swept over him as
he saw a tall Indian walk up to the fighting animal and begin to dominate it with his red-and-
yellow cape. In his motions there was not only
grace but discipline in how he controlled his
body as he suspensefully evaded the animal's
horns.

"Is that Armillita?" he whispered to the other
boys. Their looks of contempt satisfied him that
it was, but he still did not know who Armillita
was. So he selected an intense-looking boy at
his right, older than the rest, and asked: "Who
is Armillita?" And the boy replied without taking
his eyes off the matador, "The best."

This did not satisfy Juan, who asked further:
"Does he always fight bulls?"

The boys almost interrupted the testing of the
animals with their wild shouts. "That's not a bull,
you idiot!" one cried. "He can't tell a bull from
a cow!"

The interruption had attracted Armillita's attention, and when the time came for a rest he
pointed to the boy at Juan's right and asked:
"Want to try?" In a flash the boy leaped the low
barrier, ran to the matador and grabbed a cape.
Then, with the tall professional at his back, he
approached the two-year-old cow. The other

boys sat silent as their companion walked slowly and with the exaggerated posture adopted by matadors—head back, torso arched—marched toward the waiting animal. Suddenly there was a charge of black fury as the tormented cow sought something she could hook into, but the boy anticipated her motion and with some skill led her into his cape.

"¡Olé!" shouted the crowd that had come to see the testing. This inspired the boy and four more times he led the cow past his belt, leaning into her flanks as she sped by. On the sixth pass he dropped the end of the cape, which he had been holding in his left hand, gave a pirouette and sent the animal chasing the end of the sculptured cloth as it etched an arc across the sand.

"¡Olé!" the crowd called again, and the boy was sent back to his perch with a nod of approval from Armillita himself. Obviously, the young man had been practicing for many months and obviously he was intending to be a bullfighter. The other boys treated him with respect. He did not return to sit alongside Juan Gómez, but sat apart, flushed with excitement.

Toward the end of the afternoon Don Eduardo Palafox, whom the boys near Juan identified as the owner of the ranch, announced that he intended testing a three-year-old bull that he was planning to assign to the cows as a seed bull, and he was requesting the two matadors to try this animal to see if he had the courage required of any bull chosen for this important purpose. The crowd murmured its pleasure, for many testings would go by without the rancher's throwing out a real bull for the matadors. Such an event was equally significant to the owner of the bull, for it represented a substantial gamble. A three-year-old fighting bull worth more than a thousand dollars in an arena was being thrown into the trial ring, and if the animal proved himself inadequate for seed purposes there was no alternative for an honorable rancher but to destroy him, for the bull could never be sold to fight in another ring. At three a bull had such capacity to learn, and could remember so long, that if he were tested today and allowed at some future date to go into a real fight, he would remember what to do and he would almost surely kill the matador.

There was, of course, one alternative that a disappointed rancher could adopt if he was wholly unscrupulous: he could lie about the bull, deny that it had ever been tested, and sell it to one of the inconsequential plazas, where third- and fourth-rate matadors would have to battle it, at enormous risk. No ranchers were completely honest—Don Eduardo, for example, repeatedly lied about the ages of his bulls and was often guilty, just before the weighing in, of feeding them salted grain so they would drink an abnormal amount of water, which would illegally inflate their weight—but those ranchers with scruples refused to send out once-fought bulls, and Don Eduardo had never done so. Furthermore, even if he had been so inclined he could hardly risk it now, for to throw out a real bull in the presence of Armillita and the other matador meant that the testing had to be honest; too many informed people were present to watch the progress of the bull and what happened to him in the event he proved cowardly. Therefore, when Don Eduardo announced the testing of a potential seed bull there was honest excitement, for he was gambling a thousand dollars.

The pleasant informality that had marked the testing of the young cows was now gone. Serious men on larger horses tested their pics against the stonework. Those with capes moved into carefully studied positions and Armillita stood well behind a barrier, biting the edge of his cape with his teeth. The cows were dismissed. A bull was about to appear.

"It was at this point," Gómez told me, "I realized the bull had been led into a cage directly beneath where I was sitting. I could feel the force of the bull as it charged against its prison.

The wood I was sitting on trembled, and the other boys pressed their eyes to cracks to see the animal that had such power. I didn't. I allowed the messages sent by the horns as they smashed into the timbers to pass into my body. I felt a new, strange power. The world was shaking. Then from a spot just below me the bull thundered into the plaza."

He was a handsome young animal of about six hundred pounds. His black horns were wide and sharp. His tail was sleek, with a tangle of brambles at the tip, and his flanks were marked with blood from minor scratches he had inflicted on himself while fighting the sides of his cage. He was a real bull, and with a mighty rush he charged at the various bits of cloth that the fighters flashed at him in planned sequence from one safe spot after another, so that all could inspect his qualities.

After he had made six such charges, throwing his left foot in the air as he tried to trample and hook at the same time, Armillita moved into the arena and with his cape began a series of exquisite passes that showed the bull off to great advantage. It looked as if the animal would be as good as everyone had hoped.

At this point Armillita withdrew and allowed the junior matador to try his luck, and with him, too, the bull was excellent. Then came a surprise, for Armillita motioned to the boy in the stands and said, "Now try a real bull." Nimbly the tense young man leaped down to a part of the ring well away from where the bull was charging the barrier. Taking a cape that hung from an inside wall, he started the traditional march of the matador toward the enemy, his feet moving cautiously, his hands jerking the cape in rhythms to attract the bull, and his husky, fear-filled voice calling, "Eh, bull! Eh, come here!"

The young bull charged and Juan saw that the boy froze into position, held his hands low, and somehow took the bull past. The crowd shouted its pleasure and the boy tried again, but this time the wary bull turned too soon and caught the young fighter with the flat of his left horn, tossing him far to one side. Instantly two things happened. The bull, having found his target, wheeled abruptly, reversed his direction and came thundering back at the fallen boy. But the trained matadors, anticipating this, nimbly interposed themselves and with their flashing capes lured the bull away.

This was the first time Juan had seen anybody knocked down by a bull and he was impressed with three things: the power of the bull, whose sudden flick of a horn could send a human being sprawling; the deftness with which the real matadors slipped in to lead the animal where they wanted it; and the courage with which the fallen boy leaped to his feet, recovered his cape and continued fighting the bull as if nothing had happened. This awe-inspiring sequence of events affected Juan Gómez so profoundly that, without realizing he had done so, he at that very moment committed himself to bullfighting, inwardly vowing: "I will know bulls. I will be quick. And I will be brave."

But what happened next gave his first experience with the bulls that touch of tragedy which is never far from the bullring. The successful beginner climbed back to his perch in the improvised stands, flushed and joyous. The real matador finished with a few ornamental passes, and the men below with the big books in which the ranch records were kept looked pleased. They had found a new seed bull, and that was always a happy moment, for a fine bull might sire as many as three hundred fighting bulls and bring glory to his ranch. For example, Soldado, the Palafox bull who hid in our cave at the Mineral, had, in the years from 1920 through 1930, fathered 366 splendid bulls, at least eleven of which were remembered in Mexican annals as immortal—that is, they had either killed matadors in the ring or had fought so stupendously that they had been accorded, in death, the adulation of the crowd and two or more turns about the sand they had defended so well. Now it looked as if Palafox had found another in the historic sequence of great sires that reached back through Soldado and Marinero to the ancient bull ranches of Spain.

But when the picadors came out, on big horses and with real barbs, the young bull became frightened. From a distance he looked as if he intended to charge, but each time he drew near the horse and the man he grew cautious. Then, when he did charge halfheartedly, and felt the barb cutting into his shoulder, he leaped, recoiled and retreated.

A silence fell over the plaza, for the spectators were seeing something they wished they were not. They pleaded with the bull to show his courage. "Now, now!" they coaxed as he edged reluctantly toward the next horse. Armillita led the bull repeatedly right into the flanks of the horse, but cautiously the bull drew back, refusing to give battle. In the ring no bullfighter looked anywhere but at the bull. By no trick or gesture did any spectator betray the fact that he recognized a bull as a coward. That was for the rancher to decide. The fighters acted as if they had a bull with spirit, and no one shrugged his shoulders in disgust, although each was inclined to do so.

After the eighth unsuccessful attempt to get the bull to face the horses, Don Eduardo shouted, "Shoot him." The crowd gasped, because sometimes such a bull was returned to the corrals and sold later for beef, or if the rancher really needed the money, secretly sold to some remote plaza. But Don Eduardo turned his back on the bull and repeated, "Shoot him."

Three trained oxen were turned into the plaza and with uncanny cunning surrounded the bull and lured him back to the corrals. A cadaverous man in charro costume carrying a gun left the box near Don Eduardo's. There were a few moments of apprehensive silence, a shot, and a wave of sorrow swept through the little plaza. But before anyone could speak Don Eduardo hurried into the ring shouting merrily, "Let's have one more cow. You, son! Do you want to be a bullfighter?" He pointed directly at Juan Gómez, whom he had not noticed before, and the little Indian boy saw that the big rancher had tears in his eyes. Mesmerized, Juan nodded his head and felt the other boys pushing him into the ring.

He was dizzy with emotion and hardly heard the low, strong voice of Armillita as the big matador whispered, "Hold the cape like this." With uncertain hands the little Indian grabbed at the cape. He dropped one end and the boys laughed. Reaching for that end, he lost the other, then succeeded in getting the entire cape tangled in his feet.

Then something happened. He felt a tremendous hand on his left shoulder, pressing in toward the bone. He looked up and saw that it belonged to Armillita, who was saying: "Keep your feet still. If the cow knocks you over, it won't hurt."

The gate swung open and a feisty black cow, hardly a year old, burst into the arena. She charged at whatever she saw, and the matadors prudently drew Juan back to a safe area, spreading their capes to lure the animal. But she needed no lures. Anything that moved was her enemy, and as she flashed past, Juan thought, Isn't it strange that the bull should have been so cowardly and the cow so brave?

"Watch me," Armillita called as he ran into the ring to give the determined little cow her first passes. The crowd cheered as the animal charged again and again at the tall matador, trying vainly to knock him down, and one could hear in the repeated olés both relief from the tragedy of the bull and the wish that it was not the cow but the bull that had been brave.

Now a firm hand was placed in the middle of Juan's back, and he felt himself pushed awkwardly into the ring. The crowd shouted encouragement, but before the first applause had died, the cow spotted the boy and charged at him with even greater fury than before. Ineptly Juan tried to protect himself with the cape, but his feet became tangled with the cloth, and the cow hit him with full force, her blunt and still unformed horns making a kind of cradle in which she lifted him, throwing him some six feet into the air.

This was the moment of decision, when a human being flying through the air thinks, I am going to be killed. In this instant, if that thought overpowers the boy or the man he can never become a bullfighter; but if, as in the case of little Juan Gómez, the imperiled one dismisses that first fear and follows it with the vow "I will conquer this bull," then there is a chance that courage will prevail.

At the moment of crashing down onto the sand Juan laughed: "It's not a bull. It's a cow."

He struggled to regain his footing, but his rear was covered by the red cape, and this attracted the cow, who gave him a second tremendous thrust. The crowd cheered, while the matadors, knowing that the cow could not hurt the boy too badly, stayed off to one side, ready to rescue him if he fell into real danger.

Again he tried to get up and again the little cow knocked him around like a football, but at one point the animal charged well past him, giving him time to straighten himself up. From a distance he heard someone crying, "Stand firm," and he planted his feet in what he considered an advantageous spot and recovered control of the cape. He did not have to cry "Eh, bull!" at this one, for as soon as she saw the cape, she whirled about, charged, and caught Gómez on the side, catapulting him once more into the air.

He got up and stood near the middle of the ring. Flicking the cape as he had seen Armillita do, he shouted at the cow and she came toward him like a locomotive. This time he managed the cape correctly, and for the first time in his life led a wild animal directly past his waist. He could hear Armillita shout, "¡Olé!" and from that moment his soul belonged to the bullring.

"I hiked home that evening in a daze," he told me. "The stars came out and as I entered my village and saw its meanness, and the ugly mud house in which I lived, I discovered the power that would keep me moving back and forth across Mexico." It was some weeks before he found the courage to tell his mother of his plans, and when he did she started crying, saying that the government had taken his older brother away to school and now Juan wanted to become a bullfighter, and someday he would be brought home dead. He ended the argument by heading down the road toward the city of Toledo and whatever bullrings he could find en route.

With no proper attire, no money, no friends and not even the ability to read and write, he drifted from Toledo to León to Torreón to Guadalajara. In the second city he met a friendly, soft-spoken man who told him that in return for certain favors he would guarantee to make Juan Gómez a first-class matador, as he had done for others, and he did actually give Juan an old suit and two swords and an opportunity to fight in a small ring out in the country. But after three months with the man Juan decided: "This is no way to live," and ran away, taking with him the suit and the swords.

He was now a bullfighter, with one pair of pants, one shirt, worn shoes and a torn cape in which he folded all his belongings as would-be matadors had done for generations. At fifteen he fought seven times in villages few had ever heard of. At sixteen, in the remote town of Rio Grande de Zacatecas, he tried to fight a bull seven years old weighing half a ton. One of the townsmen said, "This bull has fought so many times that when you come into the ring, he salutes and tells you where to stand. That's so he can kill you better." With this bull Juan had no luck whatever. Four times the huge, wily animal knocked him down, and four times, with that fearlessness which was to mark his career, Juan got up and tried again. But on the fifth try the bull caught him in the right leg and ripped a deep gash thirteen inches long. For a while it looked as if he might lose his leg, but a doctor in Aguascalientes heard of his plight and had him brought to that city, where he was able to save the limb.

At sixteen Juan Gómez, limping rather badly, had earned as a bullfighter exactly one hundred and twenty dollars. Most of his fights had paid nothing, for boys were expected to risk their lives for the practice they got from fighting fourth-rate bulls in fifth-rate plazas. And this Juan was willing to do. While the drain tubes were still in the upper part of his leg to keep the wound clean of pus, he had fought two incredible animals that had been hauled from one plaza to another. This was near Aguascalientes, and when he reported with his tubes back in place to the doctor who had saved his leg he had expected a severe lecture, but that man said simply, "If you don't have courage when you're young, you'll never have it."

But when the leg refused to grow strong, and he was generally debilitated, he had to hike penniless back to his mother, who had managed to keep alive in the mysterious ways women do in small villages. She put him to bed and nursed him back to strength, telling him sharply: "You will soon be seventeen, and you must find yourself a decent job." She sent him to a friend in the city of Toledo, and this friend got him work distributing beer. Hefting the heavy cases gave Juan Gómez those extraordinary shoulders that were later to enable him to kill bulls with such overpowering skill.

It was arranged between Juan and his boss that whenever an informal bullfight was planned for some village near Toledo, he was free to try his luck, for the man was a bullfight fan and took pride in having one of his force appear before real bulls. But what Juan liked best about his job was that once each year, during the Festival of Ixmiq, he was allowed to manage the brewer's stand at the bullfights. There, as he sold cold beer to the patrons, he could watch the leading matadors for three afternoons in a row, and in order to ensure himself more time to study the fighters he employed at his own expense young boys to sell the beer. It was under such arrangements that he attended the festival in 1945, at the age of seventeen.

There would be great fights that year, with the final gala presenting Armillita, the ace of the Mexicans, Solórzano, the stately gentleman, and Silverio Pérez, the darling of the mob and a man who could do wonders if he happened to draw a good bull. Above-average fights on Friday and Saturday had generated excitement, so that on Sunday Juan felt impelled to undertake a move he had been planning for some time. He appeared early at the plaza, arranging his beer as carefully as a housewife arranging her teacups for a party. He coached his boys on the parts of the ring each was to cover, then allocated the bottles. When the crowds began to enter, he was everywhere, encouraging them to buy, and although, true to his Indian heritage, he was never exuberant, there was about him this day an unusual alertness and quickness of action that his helpers noticed.

"What's going on, Juan?" they asked as he rushed beer to all parts of the plaza.

"Sell the beer," he ordered, and by the time the fifth bull out of the six of the afternoon was ready to be killed, most of the bottles were gone. Scooping up his money, he ran to one of the spectators connected with the brewery, a man named Jiménez, and said abruptly: "Hold this." Then he was gone.

What happened next has found its way into the modern annals of bullfighting in Mexico, and if you listen long enough you can hear some pretty wild accounts of that sixth bull of Ixmiq-45, but I prefer to blow away the myths and report what I believe actually happened.

When the final bull of the feria rushed out, the
crowd knew that this animal, though on the
small side, was bound to give a good fight, and
a roar of hopeful encouragement filled the
plaza. Although the Festival of Ixmiq usually
commanded the best bulls available, this year's
lot had not been exceptional, but this last one
was excellent with the cape and very powerful
against the horses. He took five punishing
thrusts of the pic and would have accepted
more if the horses had not been ordered from
the ring. Silverio, the matador who on his first
bull had performed badly, now presented himself to the judge, asked permission to kill the
bull, and turned to dedicate the animal to the
crowd, always a popular gesture and one likely
to win an extra ear or a tail if the bull was superb.

But as Silverio turned to face the center of the
ring from which he would dedicate the bull, he
groaned and cried: "Oh, hell! Look at that!"

From the barrier in front of the beer stands a
young man with a limp in his right leg had
dropped into the arena, carrying a stick that
could be used as an imitation sword and a
length of red cloth draped over a second stick.
Juan Gómez had decided to present himself to
the people of Toledo, and if he could escape the
policemen, peóns, matadors and general attendants who were already trying to catch him,

he might win two minutes—he would need no more—in which to prove what he could do with a full-grown bull.

"Damn that boy!" Silverio mumbled as he ran across the arena to try to keep the espontáneo (spontaneous volunteer from the audience) from spoiling his fine bull. The matador's third-string péon, a tall wiry man with the pinched face of a gargoyle, hurried from an opposite direction crying: "I get him, matador." As the peón neared Gómez he made a wild lunge at the boy's legs, but Gómez anticipated this and escaped.

This motion carried him toward the bull, so while still running he adjusted his cloth, whipping it vigorously with his right hand in order to make it fall free and at the same time attract the bull. The animal, still panting from his encounter with the horses and the pain from the banderillas, caught sight of the fleeing boy and made a quick, unexpected charge. The crowd gasped as bull and boy approached the point of contact, then cheered wildly as the boy planted his feet like a real matador, dropped his right hand close to the sand, and led the bull past in a thundering charge.

"¡Olé!" came the great approval.

Now the boy had to escape the clutches of the dozen or more men bearing down on him while trying to position himself properly for the next charge of the agitated bull, whose confusion and anger were heightened by the large number of people in the ring. Deftly he sidestepped both the wizened peón and Armillita, the senior matador, who half an hour ago had considered his work for the afternoon ended with the killing of the fourth bull, but now was back in the ring to help remove the boy.

A man who tended the horses tackled the boy and succeeded in getting a grip on Juan's left leg, but only for a moment, and for the second time Juan faced the bull. Placing the cloth in his left hand, for the most dangerous of the regular passes, he called to the bull and brought him past in a beautifully executed gesture.

The crowd leaped to its feet with one gigantic "¡Olé!" and began throwing things at the men who were trying to eject the young fighter.

"Let him finish the job!" the men in the sun began shouting.

"To-re-ro!" others cried in mockery of the men who were trying to clear the arena.

But this time the skinny old peón was not to be denied, for he pinned Gómez against the barrier and seemed about to knock him to the ground when the boy gave a violent thrust with his right elbow, knocking the peón backward onto the sand and almost rendering him unconscious. But in falling, the peón kept hold of the boy's improvised muleta and carried it with him, so that when Juan broke free he faced the bull with only a wooden sword and no cloth for protection. Seeing the bull about to charge, he hesitated in awful fear. From the stands he heard the unanimous shout of "No, no!"

As the bull hurtled toward him he instinctively dropped his left hand as if it held the protecting cloth, trusting that this motion would deceive the animal. And for a second it did, enough for the tip of the deadly horn to move past the body, but then the lure failed, and the bull turned. The horn caught Juan in the chest and sent him flying through the air, away from the men who were trying to catch him. Quickly the bull wheeled and bore down upon the fallen boy. With one deft drive the left horn passed under the boy and tossed him backward, still away from the men who might have rescued him.

Again the bull wheeled, satisfied that it had at last found a solid enemy and not a fluttering piece of cloth. This time the animal exercised greater care but succeeded only in piercing the boy's right pant leg, making a ripping sound that all could hear and throwing him into the air. He would have fallen directly on the horns had not Armillita at that moment caught the bull by the tail and given it a savage twist. Bellowing with pain, the bull turned to attack his new enemy, and Gómez fell limp on the sand.

The first man to reach him was the third matador's peón, the tall man with the gargoyle face, and instead of helping Gómez to his feet, this peón began beating him in the face. "You son-of-a-bitch!" he kept shouting. "You ruined a good bull."

Now a dozen hands clutched at him and started rushing him toward a gate that had been thrown open. When the gate slammed shut a policeman started jabbing his rifle butt into Juan's stomach, whereupon the crowd, awed by Juan's bravery, began hurling beer bottles at the policeman.

At this juncture Silverio, always the calculating showman, realized that although his enviable bull had been ruined by the intrusion, there might be a way to retain his popularity with the crowd. Rushing to the barrier as if on a mission of life and death, he demanded that the burly policeman release the boy. With a grandiose gesture, which the crowd approved with ecstatic shouting, the matador summoned Juan back into the ring, wiped away the blood on his forehead caused by one of the beer bottles, and embraced him. "You can fight," the matador shouted into the boy's ear. "But don't ever fight my bull again." With the hand that embraced the boy he twisted the skin on Juan's neck until the boy winced. But, uncowed, Juan said to the matador, as if thanking him for a kindness: "See if you can do as well." Then, turning abruptly, he walked at a stately pace not to the nearest gate but to a distant one, arching his back like a true matador and throwing insolent glances at the crowd, who rewarded him with an ovation.

That night Juan Gómez washed the gash in his forehead, pressed his only shirt, tied the rope around his pants and went out to watch the bullfighters as they lounged in their usual manner before the House of Tile. At the first of the two big tables sat Armillita. At the other was Solórzano, surrounded by admirers, and Silverio, the idol of this part of Mexico. There was exciting talk as the three afternoons of the festival were reviewed, and waiters hurried about with trays of beer and toasted corn. For some time Juan loitered in the plaza across from the hotel in shadows near the statue of Ixmiq, but finally the allure of bullfighting proved too great and he ventured onto the terrace of the hotel itself.

Unfortunately, the first to spot him was the old peón with whom he had brawled in the arena, and this man called out, in the near-illiterate jargon that bullfighters use: "You not come here. Ruined our best bull entire fair."

Men at various tables turned to inspect the boy and Solórzano asked, "Your face hurt?"

"No," Juan said.

"Have a beer," a big man at another table suggested, and Juan realized with delight that it was Don Eduardo, at whose ranch he had first tasted the thrill of bullfighting. Hoping that Palafox would remember him, he said: "I was the boy you aided at your testing, the day you shot your seed bull."

This unfortunate statement brought Don Eduardo such unpleasant memories that he turned away, indicating the end of the conversation.

Although ill at ease, Juan continued to hover about the matadors' tables, saying to Armillita: "You were very good today, matador," and hoping that the great one would remember what had happened at the testing, but the matador merely grunted: "Regular."

Juan moved on to where six aficionados were explaining to Silverio exactly how it was he had killed the third bull. Not realizing how improper it was for him to speak to Silverio, since he had ruined the matador's final bull, he elbowed his way up to the table and said: "You were very good in your first bull, matador." Looking up in surprise to see the boy standing over him, Silverio, always the gracious showman, smiled and said: "You too were excellent. You intend to follow the bulls?" Before Juan could reply, the hostile peón hauled him away from Silverio.

"I asking you," the skinny peón repeated, "who invite you ruin our bull?"

Juan pushed him away so that he could return to answer Silverio's question, which the matador had by now forgotten.

He tried to escape the peón, who continued to hound him. In frustration, Juan turned and, lashing out with his fists, knocked the peón down. Immediately some picadors and other peóns who had resented the boy's intrusion both now and in the ring closed in on him and began punching him until he collapsed.

"Throw him out!" one of the picadors cried, and police came to haul the inert body off to jail. In the morning the owner of the brewery came to the jail and demanded, "Where's the money from the festival?"

"I gave it to Jiménez," Juan explained.

"He's disappeared," the man snapped. "Fistfighting, jumping into the ring, causing me nothing but embarrassment. You're fired."

But the 1945 Festival of Ixmiq was not an entire loss for Juan Gómez. Three different photographers had caught impressive shots of his action with the last bull, and one had taken a fine photo of Juan passing the bull with his bare hand. It was widely published throughout Mexico with the caption "Thus fights Juan Gómez." With the last pennies he had saved from his brewery salary, Juan purchased glossy copies of each of the photographs, and bundling his property once more in his cape, he set out to conquer Mexico in earnest.

He never saw his mother again, for she died while he was in jail in Torreón. Famished, he had robbed a store to get food and had been caught, and if his mother never heard of his disgrace, he did not hear of her death.

He was now an acknowledged apprentice with the right to demand a formal contract for his fights, but he got so few that he was always ready to fight for nothing. If he heard that a village was planning a fiesta, he would hike and steal rides and jump trains for three days to get there in hopes that he might face the bulls. He fought animals that had already killed men, animals that were blind in one eye, animals that had horns whose tips were so badly battered that if they caught a man in the stomach he was sure to be killed by the dirt-stained ends. He lived on beans and tortillas, and sometimes on water. He weighed less than a hundred and twenty pounds, and when he had the fever after a wound he sometimes dropped to a hundred and ten.

It was a pitiful life, from 1945 through 1950, lightened only by a few superb afternoons with the bulls and an occasional meeting with some country girl enchanted by bullfighters from the city. Three times in hunger and desperation he returned to the soft-spoken man in León who was always ready to take him back and who forgave him for the things he had stolen on his earlier renunciations of what the easy-living man had to offer. Once the León man actually did arrange a major fight for him in Irapuato, and Juan had been extremely good.

"See how easy it would be?" the persuasive man argued. "I can get you fights like that every month." But at the height of his pleasure over the Irapuato success, Juan announced for the last time, "I will never be back. I'll conquer the bulls some other way."

When he was twenty, the mother of a girl he dated in a small town near Monterrey taught him how to read, and he could now follow what was said about him in the sporting sheets. For the most part his life was spent going from one plaza to the next. Although he earned little, he did learn about bulls. At every chance, he would spend weeks at the ranches watching the bulls.

He was content to sit all day, studying the animals, and he came to know when they would lift their heads, when they would move. He could tell which neck muscles tensed before the animals lunged. Few men his age knew as much about bulls.

One day in 1950, while lounging in a Guadalajara café hoping vaguely that something would turn up regarding a testing that was supposed to take place for a group of American tourists, he heard a stranger shout in English: "Cigarro, you ugly bastard! Remember that night in Tijuana!" and when he turned to see who this Cigarro might be he saw it was Silverio's peón, the gargoyle-faced one who had chased him around the ring at Ixmiq-45 and had beat him up later at the House of Tile. The ugly one was now seated with a local girl who tried to sing flamenco songs in bars, and as soon as he saw Gómez he recognized the espontáneo who had given him so much trouble in Toledo. "Stay away!" he growled. "You not welcome here." Juan ignored the peón and bowed stiffly to the girl. "I heard you sing the other night. You were fantastic." This was a word much used by bullfighters and meant that the event so described was ordinary.

The singer smiled graciously and asked, "Will you be at the testing tomorrow?"

"Oh, it's tomorrow?" Juan replied, betraying the fact that he had not been invited.

"I say you not welcome," Cigarro grumbled, showing obvious displeasure with the singer for having betrayed the secret of the testing.

"Could I ride up to the ranch with you?" Juan asked bluntly.

"No," Cigarro snapped.

Next day at the testing, to which Juan had hiked during the night, Cigarro went so far as to suggest to the owner that Gómez be prevented from participating. "I didn't invite him," he explained.

The rancher shrugged and said, "Well, he's here. Let him make one or two passes."

Cigarro was leaning against the improvised stands, talking with the singer, when Juan's first cow came out and the peón warned the girl, "This one not a matador. He know nothing. Rancher being polite to him."

Here I must interrupt my narrative to mention Drummond's reaction to my rendition of Cigarro's speech, which was a rough translation of the peón's Spanish. Drummond wanted to know: "What is this guy speaking, Chinese?" and I had to explain my problem:

Toreros of the second category often use a verbal shorthand consisting of grunts, abbreviated words, sentences with no verbs and an arcane lingo. Some years ago a matador enjoying a season of unbroken triumphs wanted a bumper sticker for his Cadillac that proclaimed "The whole world is wonderful," and this could be expressed in good Spanish as "Todo el mundo es maravilloso," but in his argot the sentence came out "To er mundo e ueno," with the last two words being pronounced "a waaaay-no." That's the problem I have with translating Cigarro's speech into English.

Drummond wired back: "Appreciate your difficulties but make him sound less Mongolian."

Cigarro's near-illiteracy was explained by his birth to a landless peasant family in southern Mexico. His militant father, prepared to die in his fight to gain a little field of his own, had named his son Emiliano Gutiérrez, proclaiming at his baptism: "He will be a revolutionary leader of the peasants like Emiliano Zapata," but when the boy turned bullfighter instead he threw him out of the Gutiérrez shack: "No son of mine will fight bulls instead of landlords," and the boy started his frustrating chase after the bulls.

Emiliano's life followed the torero's time-honored course of action: as an impoverished boy walking from one village feria to another, as an impoverished man serving as peón to a full-fledged matador. One night in a small village he saw a motion picture in which the hero smoked long Cuban cigars that made him look important, and he was so impressed that he instantly adopted the habit, buying cigars whenever he had a few pesos to spare. With Cigarro as his professional name he became a competent peón, never of the top category but so brave and trustworthy that he found constant employment and his gargoyle face became familiar in Mexican plazas.

Now, in 1950, at the testing for the American tourists, since Cigarro had not seen Gómez for some years he was unprepared for what the young apprentice had learned in the interim and was impressed by what he saw. Juan kept the cape low, his feet solidly rooted in the sand but spread apart. He had an emotional style, in the pure tradition of fighting, and he cut a reasonably good if small figure.

Cigarro leaned forward, and when the testing passed on to the work with the cloth and the make-believe sword, he began chomping nervously on his long cigar. What he saw moved him profoundly, and when the cow was about to be returned to the corrals he called, "Gómez, suppose you got to kill that one? How?"

Juan did not comprehend the importance of

the question, and thought that the peón was trying to humiliate him because of the long-forgotten fight at Ixmiq-45, but the young Indian so loved the bulls that any chance to work with them struck fire in his heart. "Eh!" he shouted to the men working the gates. "Bring that one back."

He was too late. The cow kicked savagely at the swinging gate, lunged at something inside the corral and vanished. She was a stalwart beast and had attacked the horses eight times, as if with her still-unformed horns she would destroy them. "I could have shown you how to kill with that one," Juan cried with some disappointment.

The rancher interrupted. "Later we plan to throw out a four-year-old bull with one horn broken off. We'll fight that one to the death—for the Americans."

"How does a bull lose a horn?" one of the tourists asked.

"Fighting with other bulls," the rancher explained. "This one charged a tree on the range."

"Is the animal useless then?" the tourist asked.

"He's a glorious bull," the rancher said sadly. "But he cannot be sold."

The testing continued, and at the appearance of Juan's second cow, Cigarro left his singer and

went down into the ring with the young apprentice. "Let me see you work with cape in back,"
he suggested, and Gómez unfurled four handsome passes with the cape behind his shoulders and his exposed body facing the horns.

"You make passes on knees?" Cigarro queried.

Instantly, Juan dropped onto the sand and
showed the small crowd six daring passes, with
the little cow almost on top of him each time.
"With real bull not so brave?" the peón asked,
chomping his cigar.

"When the real bull comes, you'll see,"
Gómez snapped. Cigarro returned to where the
rancher was sitting and asked, "What you plan
for fighting one-horned one?"

"I thought I'd let the matadors figure it out for
themselves," the rancher replied.

"Maybe better he do killing," Cigarro suggested, pointing to Juan Gómez, who was playing the cow with great skill. Then Cigarro, who
appreciated the politics of bullfighting, added,
"Your bulls so fine, Don Wiliulfo, any matador
looks good such bull. I like see this boy fight fine
bull."

"All right," the rancher agreed. "If the others
don't object."

Quietly, in his best political manner, Cigarro
moved among the matadors and convinced

them that the apprentice Juan Gómez should be allowed to kill the one-horned bull. Although at first each of the professionals protested, as if to defend his honor, each accorded the privilege to the young Indian, for with a one-horned bull you could never entirely predict the reactions.

So when the four-year-old exploded from the corrals, a lithe, excellent beast that would have graced Plaza México itself were it not for the missing horn, the senior matadors took a few passes with the cape and demonstrated their mastery. One, retiring to the barrier after a fine series, thought, Let the boy have this one. They won't pic it enough and the killing will be very difficult.

In the cape work Gómez was able to show little of his skill, for the professionals monopolized the fine animal, but when it came time to lead the powerful bull to the horses, the apprentice seemed to establish a personal harmony with the animal, and by deft twists of the cape led the angry beast directly onto the horses, where a picador from Guadalajara—certainly not one of the best—did a rather bad job of lancing. As the senior matadors had foreseen, this fine animal was going to enter the last part of the fight improperly prepared, and whoever had to kill him would have much work to do.

"Take out the horse!" the rancher shouted,

and the picador ingloriously retreated. The regular matadors now each took two or three passes
with the muleta and the real sword, and the
small crowd cheered dutifully. The bull, more
agitated than hurt by the picador, was proving
difficult.

Then Cigarro shouted, "You, Gómez," and by
common consent the professional matadors
withdrew, holding positions by the barrier from
which they could dash out to save the boy if it
became necessary to do so.

Slowly, with the matador's time-honored posturing of placing one foot directly before the
other and the back arched in a handsome line,
Juan Gómez approached the one-horned bull. It
was the right horn that was missing, but the left
was a deadly instrument, straight and extremely
sharp. All the bull's defenses had been built
around this solitary weapon, and with it he attacked vigorously.

In one respect, Gómez was lucky that the bull
had only one horn and that one his left, because
this made it obligatory that the fighter use the
greatest pass in bullfighting, the one in which
the man stands with the bull to his right, with the
sword in his right hand but placed behind his
back, and with the red muleta in his left, a dramatically small target when not spread out by
the sword. What gives this pass, called simply

the natural, its extraordinary weight of emotion, is that the man offers first to the enraged bull not the sword, nor the cloth, but his own un-protected body, which the bull must pass before it can hit the muleta. When the bull charges, if the man has miscalculated by even one inch, the animal's left horn will pierce unopposed the man's right stomach. But if the man has judged wisely, and if he knows his animal, the bull, while seeking the cloth, will thunder past the immobi-lized sword, past the exposed body of the man, and into the cloth held only by the left hand. In such a pass, perfectly performed, the bull's left horn will graze the man and the bull's forward hump, wounded by the banderillas, will leave flecks of blood upon the suit of lights.

So now Juan Gómez slowly approached the one-horned bull, crying softly, "Eh, bull! Eh, my brave friend! Come here and taste the cloth!"

The bull, confused by the poor quality of his fight against the horse, pawed the earth and tested the air with his powerful left horn. He saw something moving toward him, a thin vertical line and an inviting square of red movement. Then his small black eyes focused perfectly, and he charged.

With a stupendous rush of power the bull drove for the cloth, his left horn ripping past Gómez's body, and even as he lunged into the unresisting cloth he sensed that he had been diverted to the wrong target. Where his error lay he obviously did not know, but if he was allowed to charge as often as he wished, sooner or later he would piece together the mystery, and on some final charge he would follow not the lure but the man, and he would drive that lethal left horn completely through whatever he hit.

Leaning against the stands, Cigarro gasped. To the singer he whispered, "This boy, he learned."

Four more times the Indian gave the bull the natural pass, and each time the searching horn seemed to come closer. The rancher put his hands over his face and moaned, "Why does a bull like this have to be killed in secret? Look at him charge!"

But what the crowd looked at was not the bull's superb charge but at the brown-skinned apprentice who had now dropped to his knees in the middle of the ring. One of the senior matadors advised, "Not there, son. Over by the barrier." But Gómez stayed where he was and from this position passed the bull three times, leaning far backward on the third pass to escape the probing horn.

The crowd was overcome by his bravery and everyone, even the matadors, shouted, "¡Olé! ¡Olé!" The singer shouted: "To-re-ro!" the cry that needs a thousand voices in unison to make it truly effective. Nervously the others laughed at her, grateful for this release from tension.

The time had now come for Juan to kill the one-horned bull, and Cigarro leaned forward anxiously to see what would happen, for he felt that if the Indian boy could really go in over the horns. . . . Then he relaxed. This bull had no right horn, and at the moment of death it is only the right horn that can kill the matador, for it is over this dreadful weapon that the man must reach, his full chest exposed.

"This not anything," Cigarro explained to the singer. "Anybody kill a bull with no right horn."

But as he spoke, Gómez profiled before the animal, threw his left knee forward to provoke the charge, then lunged with perfect timing so that his body and the bull's great hulk formed for a moment a perfect union of man and beast. The slim sword flashed in the air and plunged toward the bull's exposed shoulder, through which it would have to find its way in order to cause a lethal wound.

The kill was so perfectly executed that the crowd burst into cheers, but, just as suddenly, fell silent when the sword, which had struck bone, flexed nearly double, snapped back into a straight line, and arched serenely through the air, falling point down into the sand, where it quivered for a singing moment before slowly dropping.

Gómez, cursing his bad luck at hitting bone on an otherwise superb kill, recovered the sword and made ready to try again. The rancher called reassuringly, "That last was a perfect kill. Good luck."

Again Gómez postured before the animal in solitude. Again his body leaped forward to meet the bull's deadly charge. And again the sword struck bone. This time it zinged musically as it flashed through its high arc, which carried it toward the spot where Cigarro and the singer sat. As Gómez, cursing, stopped to recover his weapon, he saw two faces. Cigarro's pinched and ugly countenance was nodding gravely and he was throwing the apprentice an imaginary kiss. It was apparent that after many years of searching Cigarro had found himself a real bullfighter, and as his scarred face continued nodding he was negotiating a contract. The second face belonged to Lucha González, and from the manner in which her dark eyes flashed it was apparent that she too had found her matador. Of course, he wasn't yet a matador, but she was convinced that he soon would be.

Striding back to the bull, who stood ready to defend himself again, Juan Gómez whispered,

"All right, little bull! You have brought me glory, and now I shall—"

There were voices behind him. The rancher was shouting, "Gómez! Come back! We want that bull."

The Indian did not fully understand and thought that he was being warned not to attempt his third effort on such terrain, for the bull was indeed dangerous. But he felt that he knew bulls better than the senior matadors, better than the rancher and certainly better than the peóns. He would kill this valiant beast where he stood, and he prepared to do so.

Then strange things happened. One of the senior matadors dashed out from the barrier and with a red cape started swinging the bull away, and two peóns grabbed Gómez from behind. Dazed, he looked up at the improvised stands and shouted, "It's my bull!"

The gate to the corral was swinging open and two oxen were crowding into the plaza. Juan interpreted this to mean that the bull was being taken away from him alive because of his bad luck in killing, and he fought to break loose from the men who held him. He was determined to kill the animal before it could return to the corrals, and then he saw Cigarro's ecstatic face. The wiry peón had lit a big cigar and was smiling like a gargoyle.

"They are sparing the life of your great bull!" he shouted. "What a superb afternoon!"

And then Juan Gómez saw the thing happen, the thing that tears at the heart of a bullfighter. The oxen nudged at the perplexed but defiant bull, and at first the brave beast was willing to fight against them, for he was still determined to defend his life against all adversaries. But then he smelled their indifference, tentatively poked at one with his left horn, pawed the earth and looked for the men he had been fighting. Finding no one, he ran in a small circle as if proclaiming his sovereignty over that plaza, and dashed with terrible force at some unknown enemy in the darkness.

The crowd cheered as the valiant beast disappeared, for they knew that he would be used in later years as stud for the ranch. Gómez, at last realizing what was happening, whispered, "Go off, little bull! You find me a manager." He then walked slowly and with dignity across the ring to where Cigarro waited by the barrier.

"Six months, bowlegs," the péon was assuring him expansively, "you be matador, contracts Plaza de México. But that one you keep away from," he warned, indicating with a toss of his ugly head the singer, who was watching everything.

Cigarro kept his promise. In late December of 1950 Juan Gómez took his doctorate with bulls of Palafox in the great ring at Mexico City. When he marched out of the darkness he gasped, for towering above him in the concrete bowl were more than fifty thousand people. In the front row, with a bright shawl over the barrier, as if she were a real Spaniard, sat Lucha González wearing flowers. Cigarro was in the alleyway, reprieved from wearing the suit of lights any longer, now that he was a full-fledged manager, and when the time came for Gómez to dedicate the first bull of the afternoon, the one handed him by the senior matador as a traditional gesture of sponsorship, it was inevitable that he offer this animal to Lucha. His gesture was popular with the crowd, and his kill was good. He gained no ears but he was accorded a turn around the huge plaza while some in the stands bellowed, "¡Olé!" feeling that they were assisting at the birth of a real matador.

After that nothing happened. Juan Gómez became merely one of thirty-one Mexican matadors. He had no wealthy patron to underwrite stories about him for the major papers or to force him upon the provincial impresarios. His

reputation was not sufficient to warrant repeated invitations back to Plaza México, where
a matador had to have a name in order to fill the
huge arena. He was merely another matador of
no great distinction, and the remorseless grind
resumed.

A fight in Torreón in April was followed by
another in Orizaba in early June. A hurried
phone call from a village of two thousand in
remote Jalisco would suffice for July, and in August there might be nothing. He was not important enough to be invited to the Festival of Ixmiq,
and the years went by with one more Mexican
matador at the near-starvation level. In spite of
this he was required by bullfighting convention
always to look sharply dressed, to pay bribes to
the newspaper critics, and to convey at all hours
a sense of success and grandeur. More than
some, Juan Gómez was able to accomplish
these requisites, for he had three factors operating on his behalf.

In Cigarro, his manager, he had a solid friend.
This peón had experienced a life much like
Juan's, working for matadors who underpaid
him and before bulls that had often sent him to
the infirmary. He had been far too ugly to marry
a wealthy girl and financially unable to marry any
other kind, but through all his years of loneliness
he had kept alive one vision. In Mexico City, not

far from the great plaza of the cathedral, there was a café frequented only by bullfighters, actors and newspapermen. It was called the Tupinamba, and around its white marble tables swirled the gossip of the bullring. During his long apprenticeship Cigarro had been unable to afford the Tupinamba, and had had to content himself with watching its exciting life from the sidewalk, but he had sworn that someday he would be a famous matador with the best table at the Tupi. When that vision faded because of his ineptitude with the bulls, he decided to become a peón in the regular troupe of some successful matador, which would entitle him to sit in the Tupi, but since he was not a first-rate peón he failed to achieve this dream also. He then built his life on the hope that in his fifties he would stumble upon a young fighter of promise who would require a manager, and then he would sit day after day in the Tupinambo, organizing his matador's professional career. This last dream he had achieved, and he now lounged each day in the Tupi, issuing statements of great gravity. With the little money he had acquired during the preceding thirty years, he played the role of manager, giving his matador an emotional security few fighters enjoyed. He never doubted that someday Mexico would discover what a classic matador it had in Juan

Gómez, and until that fateful day he, Cigarro, would continue to wait in the Tupinambo for the best contracts available in the smaller plazas.

The two other factors that bolstered the ego of Juan Gómez were self-generated. First, it was becoming widely acknowledged that although he was not particularly accomplished with either the cape or the cloth, as a killer of bulls he was the best Mexico could provide. In his fights this small Altomec Indian demonstrated what the culminating moment of the afternoon should be as he stood before the bull, profiled, kicked out his left knee, and threw himself like a man bent on suicide right over the horns.

The second factor was a towering sense of honor. When he walked into the Tupinamba to speak to Cigarro, he moved with visible dignity, imparting a clear sense of his status as a matador. He was a wiry bundle of aggressions and defenses, and for the slightest slur he would fight anyone. In the bullring he allowed no one, not even Armillita himself, to tell him what to do. For even if a matador of the top category tried to tell him how to behave in the ring, Gómez would say coldly, "When you kill the way I do, I listen." León Ledesma, the critic, wrote of him: "He is the only man in Mexico, since the death of General Gurza, who can challenge the entire nation to a fistfight merely by the way he enters a room. He is a man of honor."

But there was one area in which Juan's carefully cultivated sense of honor did not operate, and this lapse caused genuine anguish. He had been picked up by Cigarro in January of 1950, and two weeks later he had stolen the ugly man's girl. At first, adhering to some kind of code of ethics, Lucha González had tried to suppress her preference for the young bullfighter, for Cigarro had been good to her and had been largely instrumental in getting her started as a singer-dancer. But in the end her passion for the self-possessed young Indian had been too great, and one night in Torreón she had brazenly moved herself and her one bag out of Cigarro's room and down the hall to Juan's.

The hurt to Cigarro's ego would never heal. On that first miserable night he had tried to kill his matador, but Gómez, bewildered by Lucha's action, had first held him off, then beaten him about the face. Cigarro, bleeding badly, had then tried to kill Lucha, but she started screaming and the police were called. The affair got into the newspapers, for bullfighters' brawls always made good reading, and later on it was largely this highly publicized love affair between Lucha and Gómez that enabled Cigarro to arrange the contracts that Gómez did get.

And so this curious trio, held together by poverty, ambition and the love of bullfighting, moved back and forth along the lesser highways of Mexico. Cigarro, having at last found himself a matador, stayed with Gómez even though he daily suffered from the indignity of having had his woman stolen. The Indian, having attained for himself a life that was not totally wretched, stayed with his surly manager, for he suspected that he would never find another half as capable. And Lucha González supported both of them with her ersatz flamenco. Pathetically loyal to her two bullfighters in Mexico City, if she ever made it to Seville she could have said good-bye to them without shedding a tear.

For nine years the trio fought bulls and managers and hotel owners and moving picture directors who refused to give Lucha the singing roles to which she felt entitled. They grew older, and Cigarro definitively passed the age at which he could again don the suit of lights. Lucha grew no prettier and her whiskey-soaked voice became harsh, which made her imitation flamenco sound better. And Juan Gómez scurried back and forth, always seeking the bulls. He was now thirty-two years old, an age when successful matadors in Spain have already retired, and he

had never known real success. He still awaited
an invitation to fight in Spain or Peru, where
there was good money, or at the Festival of
Ixmiq. Yet he never grew disconsolate. Cigarro
told him: "No man in world kill the way you do."
And that was enough.

Then, in early 1960, Cigarro was sitting at his
usual table in the Tupinamba, flicking cigar
ashes and trying to look important, when a
flunky from the impresario of Plaza de México
drifted by, pretending not to see him because it
was important that Cigarro open this particular
conversation.

"Hello, Moreno!" the ugly one called.

"Oh, it's you!" the tricky negotiator replied,
and the discussion was launched. Moreno intimated that the forthcoming fights were to be
the best ever held in Mexico City. "Like the days
of Manolete," Moreno suggested. "This young
fellow Victoriano Leal! Ahhhh!"

"You've got him booked?" Cigarro asked
warily. In this business nothing could be certified
until the day after it had happened and the critics had been paid off.

"Fight after fight," Moreno assured him.
"When Leal's through with us he'll be the richest
bullfighter in the world."

"High fees, eh?" Cigarro asked evenly.

"Fantastic. Five thousand, six thousand dollars for one afternoon," Moreno said, picking his teeth.

Cigarro looked at him coldly: "And how much you pay my torero?"

Without changing his blasé expression Moreno said: "Nine hundred dollars and not a penny more."

Cigarro stalled for time. "That's what you pay picadors."

"Of course," Moreno replied.

"What I thinking"—Cigarro stalled, for much was at stake—"was the people all want to see Victoriano. I admit you frankly my torero not so popular—"

Moreno suspected that this might be a trap, but he did want to clinch one point, so he quickly said: "Quite honestly, Cigarro, we couldn't afford two other first-class matadors on the same bill with Victoriano. There isn't that much money in Mexico."

"So you plan get my torero almost nothing," Cigarro joked.

Moreno laughed expansively: "In Morelia, where I come from, nine hundred dollars is not called nothing."

Cigarro laughed with equal heartiness, then pointed at the negotiator with his cigar. "It also good we show our torero Plaza México again."

"My friend," Moreno agreed warmly, "those

were my thoughts exactly. What an afternoon for Gómez! Fifty-five thousand people. How long's it been since he's fought before a crowd like that?"

"What I thinking," Cigarro suggested slowly, "was everyone want to welcome Victoriano back home his successful tour, why don't you give public a real thrill? Victoriano, Gómez, mano a mano?"

At the sound of this phrase, which meant hand to hand as in mortal combat, with only two matadors, instead of three, each fighting three bulls in a deadly duel, Moreno snapped to attention, for he saw the possibility of a series of such duels across Mexico. Abandoning his easy comradely air, he asked cautiously, "How much would Gómez expect? For killing three bulls instead of two?"

"Only thirteen hundred dollars," Cigarro replied evenly. He knew that this would prove an alluring offer and was not surprised when Moreno asked abruptly, "Can you wait here?"

"I'm here all day," Cigarro replied.

"Don't leave," Moreno snapped.

When he was gone, Cigarro began to sweat.

"Virgin the Hills," he prayed, evoking the patron of his childhood, "let him fall my trap. Let him give us hand to hand, and my torero make great scandal—for fifty-five thousand people to

see. Let there be riot, challenge, or maybe
something. Dear Virgin . . . dear Virgin . . . let
there be something furious."

That night when Cigarro finally reached Juan
Gómez, he found that the impresario had already informed the Indian of the mano-a-mano
fight with Victoriano. He said to Gómez: "This
got to be day of decision, matador. Something
got to happen in that ring that—explode. You
got to insult Victoriano, or take away one of his
bulls, or knock Veneno from horse. Matador!
The Virgin herself gonna smile on this day, but
the scandal we got to fix ourselves."

They plotted long into the night, trying to devise something that would justify outrageous
behavior and electrify the vast crowd into demanding a rematch between the two matadors.
"What we got to lose?" Cigarro asked, his
palms up. "Suppose we go to jail? Long time
ago Lorenzo Garza go to jail every year and
each time more popular. Juan, on Sunday some
fantastic thing got to happen."

The plan they agreed upon was this: on his
first bull Juan Gómez would make the supreme
effort of his career and if successful would win
the adulation of the crowd; since Victoriano
would be pressing to do well, he would undoubtedly be nervous with his first animal; Gómez

would work even harder with his second bull and capitalize on the crowd's sympathy for a fighter who was Mexican to the core; then on Leal's second animal Gómez would intrude on the passes as the bull came away from the horses, would insist upon more than his share of turns, and would do everything he could to humiliate his opponent.

"Old Veneno not gonna like it," Cigarro said confidently. "That one never gonna let you insult his torero. But Veneno not too popular with public. They think he boss his boy. So you got to make your fight with Veneno, and maybe . . ." The skinny one chomped on his cigar and whispered with diabolic satisfaction, "Juanito, little matador, on Sunday there will be riot in Plaza México. Every man will want you fight Victoriano again next Sunday and next after that." Then he grew sober: "But it all depend on your first bull. You got to be fantastic."

I've explained what happened. The first Palafox bull was unmanageable, and Juan accomplished little with it, whereas Victoriano's first bull was what they called "a boxcar on rails," charging back and forth with power and insistence. With this bull Leal performed brilliantly, and Cigarro had a sickening suspicion that the day was lost. While Victoriano was running around the arena, holding the two ears aloft in the traditional gesture of triumph, Cigarro was sweating and trying to reassure his matador.

Then salvation came. Cigarro told me how it had happened: "When Victoriano running with the two ears, everybody cheering and music, my stomach knocking with my knees, I see no chance for Gómez to make much and we probably leave Plaza de México no fame, no contracts. But then Victoriano raise two fingers to say he number one. My fighter his honor been offended, he raised his finger to tell public *he* number one. So the big riot come, and after that, contracts come all the time."

It was now late Thursday evening. As I sat with my uncle at a big table on the House of Tile terrace, I thought of the two matadors asleep in their rooms above and said to Don Eduardo: "I'll wager they're nervous up there. Could be their biggest fight of the year." But before my uncle could respond we were surprised by the sight of Veneno and his three sons at the entrance to the hotel. They had probably come down for a midnight drink of seltzer and a look at the festival crowds that still followed mariachi bands around the plaza. Waiters cleared the big round table that dominated the center of the dining

area, and there the four Leals ensconced themselves like royalty, the way leading toreros had
been doing for the past half century. Immediately a crowd gathered to gape at the bullfighters while Veneno, savoring the adulation,
bowed condescendingly to the aficionados.

Whispering to my uncle, I said: "He's intolerable, the way he poses as a great torero. But
you have to admit, he's built Victoriano into a
masterpiece," and when Don Eduardo turned to
study the young man, so relaxed, so gracious in
accepting adoration from his fans, he had to
agree: "He is a credit to the profession. And we
can be proud that he's a Mexican." I thought,
but had not the courage to say: "A Mexican
trying to behave like a Spaniard."

At this moment Victoriano, realizing that the
breeder of the bulls he would be fighting was at
our table, rose, lifted his glass of seltzer and said
loud enough for all on the Terrace to hear: "I
drink to your Festival of Ixmiq."

We were prevented from joining the toast by
the nervous intrusion of a waiter who hurried to
our table whispering breathlessly: "Gentlemen,
I'm mortified, but the matador Juan Gómez and
his party are coming down, and by right they
ought to occupy this table."

"Naturally." Don Eduardo nodded, although
by any kind of seniority he was entitled to it. But

he appreciated the restaurant's difficulty should one matador enjoy a better table than his adversary. Consequently we rose and moved to a smaller table, and we were sitting there when Gómez, Cigarro and the singer Lucha González appeared. To my surprise, she did not stop at the table but with a brief nod toward the Leals passed them and went alone to the café-bar, where she was greeted by the manager. In a moment she was singing. Now that her matador was winning contracts that paid three or four thousand dollars a fight, she was no longer responsible for the support of her entourage, but peasant wisdom was strong in Lucha González and she knew that in the life of a matador disaster was always close at hand. Tonight Juan Gómez had money; next week he might be dead; so she would capitalize on his transitory fame and earn as much money for herself as possible. Gazing across the public square between numbers, she was probably thinking, If I earn enough, perhaps I'll get to Spain whether my matador gets there or not.

And so we sat in the late hours before the first bullfight of the Festival of Ixmiq-61. Don Eduardo Palafox, inheritor of so much that characterized the best in Toledo—the cathedral, the arches, the governor's palace and the bull ranch—sat like any breeder assuring himself

that his bulls were bound to be good. Doña Carmen Mier y Palafox occupied a rear table, supervising her waiters. At their table the Leals
basked in the adulation of the crowd and pretended not to know that sitting close at hand
were Cigarro and Juan Gómez, whose attention
was focused on the singer in the nearby café.

From the opposite side of the public square
came the golden notes of the five barefoot
mariachis and their sad-eyed soloist with his
trumpet borrowed from the angels, and as they
approached the soaring trumpet obliterated all
other impressions of the night—and all thoughts
of the possibility of death for the next day.

> Guadalajara, Guadalajara!
> You taste like rain-soaked earth
> And distant little springs. . . .
> O, unforgettable little springs,
> Unforgettable like that afternoon
> When rain from the hill
> Kept us from going to Tlaquepaque. . . .

The trumpeter played a coda that would have
melted any Mexican heart that heard it, and I
wondered what had happened on that day long
ago when sudden rain prevented someone from
having a picnic at Tlaquepaque.

The mariachis passed, and from the café we

could hear the rough voice of Lucha González improvising flamenco songs and clicking her heels. As the various sounds blended with the hum of conversation at the tables I found myself staring at the benign statue of the long-forgotten Altomec Indian Ixmiq, whose stony smile was eternal and granted us benediction.

5

INDIAN
ANCESTORS:
THE BUILDERS

OWARD MIDNIGHT, while there was still noisy activity in the plaza, the Widow Palafox came to my table, tapped me on the arm and whispered, "Your package of manuscript reached the airport and will be in New York at just about this time. You owe the messenger but we paid and will put it on your bill."

She led me through the ancient doorway and onto a small patio that I had loved as a child. There was the stone fountain on which I had played and the mass of brightly colored flowers that had always bloomed in such profusion. We

climbed a series of stone steps to the second
floor of the hotel, where a broad cloister ran
completely around the upper section of the
patio, into which it dropped tendrils of flowering
plants. The heart of the hotel had always been
this quiet patio of weathered stone, echoing
cloister and abundant flowers.

The widow took me along the cloister until
she reached a door on the plaza side, and pushing this open she led me into a room famous in
the history of Mexico. It was no ordinary room:
its sides were extremely irregular, since they
had to follow the wandering walls of the hotel
front, and its haphazardly placed windows had
always looked down upon the cathedral and for
the last century upon the statue of Ixmiq as well.

When the widow moved the door, a faint
creaking that dated back to 1575, when the
structure was built, told me that I was home, for
it was in this room that my mother and I had
hidden in 1918 during the second sacking of
Toledo, when to continue living at the Mineral
was impossible. It was from the largest of the
windows that at the age of nine I had looked
down on the rapists and the firing squads. I remember standing there and announcing matter-
of-factly to my mother: "They're going to shoot
some more." She had hurried over and when
she saw who the victims were to be—the seven

good people from the very building in which we had found refuge—she had screamed, "Oh God! No!" One of General Gurza's men who commanded the firing squad turned momentarily from his duties and pumped a couple of revolver bullets at us, which had missed the window but splattered the surrounding stones, where the chips they tore away left shallow pockmarks that were still visible in the light from the terrace below.

"I was standing here when the executions took place," I remarked to the widow.

"They were crazy days," she mumbled.

"After the captain shot at us, my mother hid on the floor but I crept back and peeked out to watch the squad do its work."

"That hole in the wall," the widow explained, pointing to a prepared space over the bed, "is for a plaque that one of the historical societies is going to put here."

"Let's make it a little larger and add, 'Norman Clay slept here, too.'"

"May your sleep be good," the widow said, closing the squeaking door.

The room held such vivid memories that it even evoked the history of my powerful Indian ancestors.

When I was about ten years old and living once more at the Mineral, my father who, as an engineer and a scientist, was interested in speculating on historical might-have-beens, said: "At breakfast when we were talking about the choices that men sometimes have to make, you told me: 'It doesn't matter.' Well, making the proper choice can matter, Norman, and I want you to remember an excellent example of how a decision that must at the time have seemed of no consequence turned out to be vitally significant." To demonstrate this, he reached for a stick with which he drew in the sand a Y, saying:

"This will stand for a decision that had to be made about four thousand years ago by some people from eastern Asia, probably from Siberia, who crossed over the Bering Strait and hiked southward through Alaska and the western United States." (In later years I often wondered how my father could have known about this migration of our Indian ancestors, because during his time the relics of this Siberian trek had not yet been uncovered in Alaska; perhaps he was merely guessing. Of course, on one point he was quite wrong; we now know that the migrations from Asia took place not four thousand years ago but more like twenty thousand or possibly forty.)

"These Indians wandering south from Alaska came at last to San Diego," my father explained, "and they held a council to discuss what to do next. Some said, 'Let's continue down the coastline, because we've been doing that for three hundred years and it's familiar territory,' but others argued, 'Let's leave the coastline and strike out inland.' The upshot was that each group went its own way. No one could have foretold that one group had made a brilliant choice and that the other had chosen disaster."

I remember looking at the two arms of the Y and asked, "Which one did right?"

"Visualize the map of California," he said, "and think."

I tried to do this, but all I could remember was the map in my Mexican schoolbook, and it showed California merely as one of the lands stolen from Mexico by the United States, so I could not deduce the point my father was trying to make.

"Was the arm pointing to the sea the good one?" I asked.

"It led to California Baja," my father said grimly, and I instantly recalled what I had learned about that brutal, barren peninsula of heat and waterless sand. "Centuries later, when the Spaniards explored that desolate land, they found that the Indians who had gone there had degenerated close to the animal level. They lived almost without what we call a culture—no houses, not even clothing. They had no decent food and almost no water, and although the ocean about them was full of fish, they had never learned how to catch them. They were as pathetic as human beings can be and still live."

My father continued: "The other Indians chose the arm leading inland, and ultimately they reached the rich and fertile lands and, later, gold. They built three of the greatest civilizations of ancient times—the Aztecs of Mexico, the Maya of Yucatán and Guatemala and the Incas of Peru."

We stood for some minutes in silence. Then my father concluded his lecture with a statement that haunts me still, forty years after it was uttered: "You say choice means nothing? Norman, if your Indian ancestors had gone west you might now be an idiot. Thank your stars they came down through Toledo, for with the courage and the intelligence you inherited from that crowd you can become anything you wish."

Since my father's death scholars have concluded that the Indians who made the right choice reached the high valley of Toledo about twenty thousand years ago, but, as I said before, some argue it might have been as much as forty thousand years ago. At any rate, from a level thirty feet below the bottom of our pyramid, archaeologists have excavated charcoal remains that radium analysis puts at not less than five thousand years old, while along the edges of the prehistoric lake that once filled the entire valley others have dug up the skeletons of elephants killed by spears at least fifteen thousand years ago.

I have spent many idle hours, on plane trips or when my eyes were too tired to read, trying to visualize these ancient Indians of the primitive period, and at times they have seemed very real to me. Fifteen thousand years before the birth of Christ they had developed some kind of civilization in the high valley. They chipped out rude spear points for hunting and carved dishes for serving food. We know little about them, but they must have feared the gods, worshiped the sun, and wondered about the accidents of birth and death. From the day of my first talks on this subject with my father I never forgot that where I lived at the Mineral, men had been living for thousands of years, and you could not say that of Richmond, Virginia or Princeton.

Therefore, when in the early years of the seventh century a certain tribe of Indians gained control of the high valley, its members, some of whom we now know by name, seemed to me almost like close relatives, and when the story is told that sometime around the year 600 one of these men became leader of the tribe and began building the great pyramid, he becomes so real that he fairly shouts at me from the distant past, and the fact that the oral traditions of Toledo indicate that he was one of my ancestors gives me great pleasure.

In the year 600 the high valley looked pretty much as it does today. The last volcano had erupted some four thousand years earlier; the fantastically old lake had finally dried up; and the mountains stood exactly as they do today. In the intervening years the great piles of rock have lost possibly an inch and a half in height, due to wind erosion, but probably no more.

Far to the north, still living in caves along jungle rivers, hid the uncivilized tribes who were eventually to develop into the Altomecs and the Aztecs, but in these years they were of no consequence. To the south, living in splendid palaces decorated with silver, gold and jade, were the Mayas, whose gaudily dressed messengers sometimes reached the high valley to arrange treaties of commerce. In the valley itself my ancestors were well established, a tribe of slim, fairly tall, dark-skinned Indians who had no real name but who were known throughout central Mexico simply as the Builders, for they had the capacity to construct finer edifices than any other peoples in the area. They knew how to quarry huge blocks of rock and transport them for miles, and they could make bricks with which to build their lesser structures.

Shortly after the year 600 a leader with a new kind of vision gained control of the tribe. He was Ixmiq, and today in Toledo a statue and a yearly festival honor his name. He had a tightly controlled personality that was ideal for exerting leadership, so for nearly fifty years he ruled unchallenged, and this gave him time to accomplish many important projects.

Waiting for an auspicious day on the calendar, he announced to his council, "I have in mind to erect a holy place for our gods ten or twenty times larger than any we have attempted before." Before his advisers could protest he added, "And we shall build it not here in the city but in a special area that shall hereafter be reserved for holy rites."

He forthwith led his elders from the rude palace, which then occupied the site of today's cathedral, and took them in a northerly direction some distance from the city to where the pyramid now stands. Using piles of stones, he directed his men to lay out what seemed to them a gigantic square, but which was only about half the size of the pyramid as we now know it. His councilors protested that such a building was impossible to build, but Ixmiq insisted on its construction.

His workmen spent two years scraping away the loose earth until they reached firm earth or solid rock. He then divided the tribe into several units, which were assigned particular duties, and appointed a captain for each. Some went to live at the quarries and remained there for thirty years, passing their entire lives chipping rock. Others were the transport teams, who, with constantly increasing skill, mastered the trick of moving twenty- and thirty-ton rocks into position. Most of the men worked at the pyramid itself, inching the great blocks into position and then filling in the central portion of the structure with basketfuls of rubble, so that year by year the structure rose more impressively, and always with a flat top that grew smaller as the pyramid grew in height. These were years of peace in the high valley, nearly six centuries going by without an arrow being shot against an enemy, so that it was not imprudent for Ixmiq to assign his people to widely scattered areas and to a task that utilized the efforts of the entire community.

When the huge pile had reached the intended height, it was leveled off and its spacious flat top was laid in huge blocks that took six years to work into place. Then a beautiful wooden altar was constructed so that when a priest stood at it he faced east. Four gods shared the altar and their statues lined it, with their faces turned to the west. The most important was the god of rain, for he was responsible for the flowers and the grain. Next came the sun god, the goddess of earth and a mysterious god who represented flowers, poetry, music, statesmanship and the family, and was carved in the form of a serpent with a bird's head and scales of flowers.

The pyramid of Ixmiq was a monument to peace and in the fortieth year, when it neared completion, the ceremonies that consecrated it were testimonials to peace and to one of the gentlest societies that ever existed in Mexico, or indeed, anywhere else on the American continents. The dedication ceremonies, insofar as we can reconstruct them from old carvings, consisted of prayers, dancing, the offering of hundreds of thousands of flowers, and a gigantic feast that lasted for three days. It is notable that for the first four hundred and fifty years of this pyramid's existence not a single human life was sacrificed on its altar, or lost in any other way, except for the occasional case later on when some drunken priest or reveler accidentally tumbled from its height and broke his neck.

It was a pyramid of joy and beauty, a worthy monument to the benign gods and to the farsighted man who had built it. In City-of-the-Pyra-mid, as the area came to be called, irrigation projects brought water from the hills down to the flat land, where flowers and vegetables were grown in abundance. Honey was collected from bees kept among the flowers, and turkeys were raised both in enclosures and in large guarded fields. Fish were available in the rivers and were kept in ponds.

The Builders dressed well in cloth made of cotton, hemp and feathers, while leaders like Ixmiq ornamented themselves with gold and silver carved with religious symbolism, which workmen also applied to some of the finest pottery ever made in the Americas. Many little statues have come down to us, representing one or another of the four major deities, and each seems to be a god whom a family could have cherished. When I was a boy we had in our home a clay figure of the earth goddess, and she was a delightful fat little woman smiling and making the land fruitful with her blessing. Whenever we looked at her we felt good, and I can think of no primitive gods that were gentler than those of Toledo. I know of few civilizations that came so close to providing an ideal life for their people.

Carved hieroglyphics have been recovered

outlining Ixmiq's code of laws, and although it is likely that we are misreading some of them, it is not conceivable that we have misunderstood them all. In Toledo, in the year 650, a woman whose husband had died leaving her with children not yet old enough to work was given a share of the produce of land owned by families with grown sons. On the other hand, a woman who committed adultery once was publicly shamed; on the second offense she was killed. It was conspicuous in the law of Ixmiq that priests had nothing to do with the execution of criminals; this was carried out by civil officials. In fact, in the entire history of these six centuries there is no record of priests being other than the spiritual heads of the community. They lived intimately with the gods and advised the populace of decisions made in heaven.

We have one old stone, dug out of the pyramid in the 1950s, which shows a dignified leader who might have been Ixmiq. He is depicted as a stocky man with a long, straight nose, high cheekbones, Oriental eyes and powerful arms. He wore a towering headdress, probably ornamented in gold and silver, that must have stood about two feet high and that had feathers and flowers streaming from it in profusion. He carried a scepter topped by an animal's head, a ceremonial robe of cotton and feathers, and a bunch of flowers. He was naked to the waist, but wore a kind of sarong and sandals.

Ixmiq certainly was in touch with the Mayas to the far south and with the nondescript tribes that flourished to the southeast around what is now Mexico City, for he had a zoo in which he kept animals from distant areas and in it were birds from the seacoast areas controlled by the Mayas. But he seems to have been ignorant of the dreadful Altomec and Aztec tribes that were gathering strength in their caves to the north.

It is impossible to guess how large City-of-the-Pyramid was in those early days, but my father once estimated that it would have required no fewer than fifteen hundred men to work constantly for forty years to build the first pyramid, and he guessed that each man would have to be served by three others who quarried and transported the building blocks. This would mean about six thousand men, or a total population of somewhere around twenty thousand people. We know from excavations undertaken at the time of the building of the cathedral and the aqueduct that these people, whatever their number, lived in a sprawling Indian city built of mud and wood and located around the plaza that now serves as the center of modern Toledo.

I stress these matters because throughout my adult life I have been irritated by people who glibly suppose that Spaniards brought civilization to Mexican people who had previously been barbarians, when this was clearly not the case.

In the year 600 the civilizations of Spain and Mexico were roughly comparable, except for the fact that the former had profited from the invention of the wheel, the development of the alphabet and the knowledge of how to smelt hard metals. In any event I choose to measure advances in civilization by noting such things as soundness in the organization of the state, the humaneness of the religion, the care given to the indigent, the protection of trade, the advances in sciences such as astronomy, and the cultivation of music, dancing, poetry and other arts. In these vital respects my ancestors in City-of-the-Pyramid were just about even with my ancestors in Spain and infinitely far ahead of all who shivered in caves in what would become Virginia.

In the matter of astronomy, Ixmiq was incredible. He calculated the orbits of the planets and based his century on the movements of Venus, whose behavior he had calculated within an error of only a few days. Unaided, so far as we know, by a single hint from Europe or Asia, Ixmiq solved most of the major problems of keeping

time and had even discovered that in the year of
365 days that he had devised, even if he added
four days every thirteen years, at the end of his
fifty-two-year cycle he would still be one day
short of the world's exact movement, so for that
time he added an extra day. It is possible that he
may have borrowed his major concepts from the
Mayas, but everything he took he perfected.

I have mentioned the portrait believed to be
that of Ixmiq; there is another—but some argue
that it is not Ixmiq—which shows a man as I like
to think he must have been. He is seated in the
center of a huge stone carving and about him
are flutes, trumpets, drums made of snakeskin,
and shell horns; pitch pine from the forest
serves as a torch. The ground seems to be covered with woven mats and ambassadors are
waiting to talk with him.

Ixmiq had fifteen or twenty wives and from
one of these sprang the line that ruled City-of-
the-Pyramid for nearly half a millennium. Around
the year 900 one of these descendants known
as Nopiltzín inherited the kingdom, which was
now somewhat changed from the days of Ixmiq.
For one thing, the pyramid had been rebuilt
twice in the interim and was now approaching its
present size. The enlargements had been accomplished by the simple process of resurfacing the entire structure with two or three layers

of new rocks quarried from the original site. Just when these resurfacings took place we do not know, but each probably occupied the community for fifteen or twenty years, for with any enlargement the number of blocks required to cover the structure increased considerably. Thus in 900, when Nopiltzín took command, each side of the huge edifice was five hundred feet long with a height of about two hundred feet, producing an enormous flat top for the various wooden temples that now crowded the platform.

The effectiveness of the pyramid as a religious edifice had also been enhanced by a simple improvement. Ixmiq's original structure had resembled an Egyptian pyramid, with straight, unbroken edges running from the ground to the platform above, but in subsequent rebuildings four huge setbacks had been constructed, yielding four spacious terraces on which religious celebrations could be held. Furthermore, to provide a series of terraces, the angle of incline between the various terraces varied sharply, with the result that a worshiper standing at the base of the pyramid and looking upward could see only so far as the edge of the first terrace; the great temples at the top were no longer visible and the pyramid seemed to soar into the clouds.

Up the southern face led a steep flight of steps, which paused four times at the terraces, and it must have been one of the most exciting experiences in Mexico to climb these steps, not knowing what one was to find at the topmost level; at the apex one came upon a broad platform, now larger than in the days of Ixmiq, containing four temples to the rain god, the gods of earth and sun, and the mysterious serpent god that protected all things of beauty. There had still, in the days of Nopiltzín, been no man sacrificed to these gods, although turkeys, flowers, musical instruments and cakes were regularly offered at the four altars.

It is difficult for me to write of what happened next, because it shows my Indians in a poor light, and this provides fuel for Christian apologists who preach that when Hernán Cortés invaded Mexico in 1519 he found it occupied by barbarians to whom he brought both civilization and Christianity. Even in 900 Nopiltzín's people were not barbarians, but they became so lax in guarding their marvelous civilization that they allowed real barbarians to overrun them.

The events I am about to discuss are genuinely historic, for they derive from records uncovered by archaeologists. Such records, of course, were written in hieroglyphics and not in words, for our Indians had no alphabet, but they are at least as substantial as many related to Europe's Middle Ages. But in the reign of Nopiltzín, when the building of pyramids had long since stopped, the civilization of the high valley fell into a curious state of apathy. When wars ceased there was nothing to excite the passions of the citizens; when building halted, there was nothing to engage their energies.

Some years ago I helped excavate an ancient quarry site that proved, by carbon dating, that no significant activity had occurred there for a period of three hundred years. How did the team of which I was the reporter know this? Because at the site we unearthed much pottery from the early Ixmiq age and each subsequent period down to 900. Then for three hundred years, through the 1100s, we found no local pottery of any kind, and when I asked the leader of our dig what this signified he explained: "We often see this phenomenon in Near East digs. It means the locals had acquired enough wealth that they could stop making things for themselves and import them from other regions in which workmen remained at their kilns." But at the upper edge of this dead period comes a flood of Altomec pottery that can be positively dated to about 1200. The record was as clear to us as if work sheets had been kept at the site.

Worship of the old gods seems also to have

diminished and a tradition arose that the flowered serpent had left the area to return at some
future date. Because the high valley was not
plagued by droughts, the god of rain was taken
more or less for granted. The sun god lost his
fury, and the goddess of earth grew prettier and
less motherly in her pottery representations.
Peaceful trade relations to the east, south and
west had reached their maximum advantage,
and practically every good thing known to Mexico at large was now available in City-of-the-
Pyramid.

In the year 900, during the reign of Nopiltzín,
life was probably as good in the high valley as
it was anywhere on earth, but some of the older
priests, led by their superior, Ixbalanque, eighty
years old and clothed with wisdom and power,
questioned the status quo. Their view was ably
voiced by a fiery younger prelate: "Our citizens
are growing soft. They pay no attention to the
old virtues. The king ought to launch some significant project to enlist his people's energies."
When his companions agreed, it fell to High
Priest Ixbalanque to present their concern to the
king.

It's not easy, at this distance from the year
900, to define the relationship between the old
priest Ixbalanque and the young king Nopilitzín,
but it is possible to gain some idea of the story

from what the old murals show and what the archaeologists have been able to uncover. Power and responsibility among the Builders was cunningly divided: the king controlled short-term decisions, the high priest those on which the long-term welfare of the people depended. The king could declare war and prosecute it; the high priest determined the terms of peace, but since no wars occurred for long periods, these powers remained in limbo. The king could collect taxes, but the priest decided how the money should be spent for the welfare of the people. And underlying all was the tacit understanding that the king could never depose the high priest, while the latter could and sometimes did depose a king who had become ineffective or corrupt.

Nevertheless, it was traditional for the high priest always to defer in private speech and in public display to the king, using Builder words which were equivalents of our "Sire" and "Majesty." Thus the illusion was maintained that the king ruled and the high priest merely counseled, and for centuries the system worked. It was on the basis of this understanding that High Priest Ixbalanque asked for a private session with King Nopiltzín.

Ixbalanque: My Ruler, I feel it is imperative that we resurface the pyramid.

Nopiltzín: Ridiculous. It's as big as it ever need be.

Ixbalanque: For a pyramid dedicated to the gods it can never be said that it is high enough.

Nopiltzín: There is, however, a limit to how we can waste men's work.

Ixbalanque: Would you consider building a new pyramid altogether?

Nopiltzín: Equally foolish.

Ixbalanque: Powerful One, I've studied the crest of a small hill off to the northeast, and it occurs to me that with no more effort than it would take to resurface our present pyramid we could build one there that could be seen for miles. Whoever entered the valley would know that we served the gods.

Nopiltzín: I cannot sentence my people to the folly of building useless pyramids. Why do you argue this way?

Ixbalanque: Because I have the concern of our people at heart.

Nopiltzín: And do pyramids in any way increase the welfare of our city?

Ixbalanque: No, but engagement upon projects of enormous size does. It binds our society together and keeps all parts strong.

Nopiltzín: Now, exactly what is it you want to do?

Ixbalanque: I want to engage our city in some

project so stupendous that those who come in later years will say, "They were crazy to try so much." Because then I know we will all grow stronger. We'll have something to work for.

Nopiltzín: Why do you keep saying the people need something to work for? Our people have enough food. They have many celebrations with music and flowers. What more do they need?

Ixbalanque: I want the spirit of the gods to motivate this place as it used to. I want our people to dedicate themselves to something.

Nopiltzín: I don't understand a word you're saying.

Ixbalanque: Great One, let me tell you what I mean. Last month, when our scouts captured that stranger who said he came from the north I was present when we interrogated him. I watched the blaze of wonder that came into his eyes when he saw our canals and our abundance and our pyramid, and I could sense that he wanted similar things for his people. I can imagine him now, telling his savage tribe about the majesty of our city.

Nopiltzín: I don't follow you at all.

Ixbalanque: It was the look in his eyes that I'm talking about. That look of inspiration and wonder. Go out into your city, Powerful One, and see if you can any longer find that look in the eyes of your people.

Nopiltzín: There will be no new pyramid. This discussion is over.

What the king did, in lieu of building a pyramid, is remembered as one of the turning points in the history of Mexico, and certainly in the history of the Builder Indians. He had for some time been experimenting with the maguey bushes that grew luxuriantly along the edges of his palace grounds. He loved the dark green plants that threw twisting arms into the air and he suspected that the poetic joyousness of the maguey sprang from some secret hidden in its heart, and this secret he proposed to uncover.

After he had dissected several dozen plants, he found that each held a certain amount of honey water, a fact that had been known to the Indians for several thousand years. It occurred to King Nopiltzín that this honey water must contain the secret of the maguey, and he tried putting it to many different uses, such as medication for a cut finger or fertilizer for other plants, but his experiments led nowhere. In disgust he abandoned the project, forgetting a small store of the honey water that he had put into a clay jar wrapped in cotton cloth.

Some three weeks later he wanted to reuse the clay jar and found that the honey water had turned into an opaque whitish substance thicker than water. He threw this out, but in so doing some of it got on his fingers and out of curiosity he tasted it. He found to his surprise that the whitish fluid made his gums tingle slightly and had a wholly pleasing taste. Tilting the jar to his lips, he drained the the few remaining drops, which he found more than palatable.

Nopiltzín, realizing that he had found something that might prove to be of interest, recalled the various steps he had followed and extracted a new supply of honey water from the maguey, stored it in the same clay jar, wrapped it in the same cloth and set it aside, planning to open the jar at the end of three weeks. When the time came, however, he found himself preoccupied with further proposals being made by the priest Ixbalanque, who was insisting upon further discussion of the pyramid project. It was Ixbalanque's contention, after protracted consideration of the king's objections, that the people of the high valley would continue to find themselves in growing confusion unless their energies were directed toward some significant community undertaking, but now the elderly priest had an entirely new plan.

Ixbalanque: Powerful One, if the rebuilding of the pyramid is impractical, why not introduce some new god, or elevate one of the old ones to a position of preeminence?

Nopiltzín: What good would this serve? Our

present gods have proved more than adequate.

Ixbalanque: I sometimes think that you do not appreciate the great loss our community has suffered with the flight of the flowered serpent.

Nopiltzín: We have other gods. The loss of one is of no significance.

Ixbalanque: I believe you might be overlooking two important points. The god who has fled protected those elements of our life that gave mystery and meaning to the people, and for such a deity to depart is a sad loss. But I suspect that even more significant, in the long run, is the fact that a god has been lost without another of equal importance arising to take his place.

Nopiltzín: Now how can that be of any worry to the people?

Ixbalanque: They're not worried about it. Apparently they don't even realize that the flowered serpent has really fled. And you're not worried about it. But the spirit of this great valley is worried.

Nopiltzín: How can you claim that?

Ixbalanque: Because when a god departs an emptiness is left, whether at the moment we appreciate the fact or not. In time a restlessness sets in. The people become apprehensive. Life has lost a little of its meaning and the city is in danger.

Nopiltzín: What are you driving at, Ixbalanque?

Ixbalanque: Revered Ruler, I've spent much time thinking about your objections to the pyramid, and although I am as sure as ever that I am right in this matter, I do see why you don't want to disturb the city and launch a project that might take thirty or forty years to complete. The people don't want it. You don't want it. And some of the other priests don't want it. All right. The pyramid idea is dead.

Nopiltzín: I'm glad you've come to your senses.

Ixbalanque: I surrender that idea on the ground of expense. What I now propose will cost nothing. I propose that the empty place in our circle of gods be filled by the veneration of your ancestor Ixmiq, whose spirit broods over this valley.

Nopiltzín: Ixmiq? In some quarters he's remembered only as the mad builder who drove his people to construct useless buildings throughout the valley.

Ixbalanque: He is remembered elsewhere as the man who gave this city character.

Nopiltzín: Ixmiq? I find no affinity in my heart for Ixmiq. I would feel no pleasure in elevating

Ixmiq to the top of the pyramid. None at all. Ixmiq stands for nothing that I stand for.

Ixbalanque: If Ixmiq is unacceptable, we could establish a new god.

Nopiltzín: What would this accomplish?

Ixbalanque: There would be a sense of vitality in the air. Women would grow more flowers with which to decorate the temple of the new god. There would be a fresh spirit at the top of the pyramid.

Nopiltzín: I was thinking just the other night that at last you priests have the temples atop the pyramid nicely arranged. To add another would cause confusion.

Ixbalanque: I see we're getting nowhere. You fail to understand a thing I'm talking about.

Nopiltzín: I'm afraid that's right. But I will listen to this extent. Suppose we were to create a new god—but no buildings, mind you. What kind of god would it be?

Ixbalanque: I have given great thought to this, and I wish to speak without being interrupted, for it is important to this valley that what I have to say be fully understood by the king.

Nopiltzín: I will be most attentive, for up to now I haven't understood anything.

Ixbalanque: The god who left us, the serpent with flowery scales, represented the joyous things of life but also those that are most difficult to comprehend. Who has seen the spirit of beauty? Who has ever touched music, or the genesis of a clay bowl? Who knows what makes one man an artist and another completely unskilled? With the flight of the serpent we have lost our god of beauty. Now I see no reason to try to create another in his place, but it does occur to me that there is a real and dangerous emptiness in our life, and this must be remedied, or I honestly fear that our great city will begin to fall apart. I have therefore come to the conclusion that we should have a god who goes far beyond what the flowery serpent represented. I would propose a god who represented nothing of substance, perhaps a god of the nether sky, or of the darkness that comes when lightning has vanished, or of this valley, or of what you and I might think about the day after tomorrow. I believe that such a god might capture the imagination of our people, and at times I suspect that it might accomplish more even than the rebuilding of the pyramid.

Nopiltzín: I find all this talk extremely vague.

Ixbalanque: May I give you this illustration to ponder? Do you remember when we had the last visit from the ambassadors of Tenayuca-by-the-Lake? They spoke of their great god Tezcatlipoca, and when we tried to identify who he was they said simply, "The god of the smoking mirror." I remember that you smiled, for who has ever heard of a mirror that smoked? When I asked further, they said, "The god of the hall where gods live." I did not understand this, so I pressed them, and they replied, "The god of good things done by the sun." I pointed out that they already had a god of the sun, but they replied, "Tezcatlipoca is the god of redness but also the god of blueness. He is the god of sun, but also the god of night. He is the god of the warm south but also of the cold north. And it is improper to speak of Tezcatlipoca as *he* at all, for Tezcatlipoca is simply Tezcatlipoca."

Nopiltzín: I was bewildered by what they said.

Ixbalanque: Is it not possible that the greatness of Tenayuca-by-the-Lake derives from such a god?

Nopiltzín: Have you ever seen Tenayuca? Who says it's great?

Ixbalanque: Its ambassadors.

Nopiltzín: Who believes ambassadors? I've seen our city and I've seen our simple, honest gods: rain, earth, sun. Do you know what I think, Ixbalanque? I think it was a good thing when the flowered serpent left us. He was far too difficult for our people to understand.

Ixbalanque: I warn you, Nopiltzín, if you do not restore something like him our people will perish.

It was following a week of such argument, for the high priest was so deeply disturbed about the future of his city that he was determined to challenge the king, that Nopiltzín happened to remember the long-forgotten clay jar and its contents of honey water. With some excitement he hurried to the dark corner where he had placed it, unwound the damp cotton cloth and smelled the contents. There was the same tempting pungency. Then he tasted, and there was the same tingling in the mouth. It never occurred to the king that any by-product of the maguey could be harmful to men of the high valley, so without fear he took a substantial amount of the liquid into his mouth, and to his delight the large drink was even more satisfying than the small. He allowed the new liquid to remain in his mouth for a moment, then swallowed it. Down into his stomach the tickling stuff passed, and its course was totally pleasing, but exactly how joyous it was going to be the king did not then appreciate.

Gratified by the tastiness of his converted honey water, Nopiltzín took four or five additional gulps, and now the magic of the maguey began to work. The small room in which Nopiltzín had hidden his clay jar became larger, and the mean floors acquired a certain sheen. The walls became appreciably more ornate than those of the royal room, which were covered with cotton-and-silver cloth. The wind, which had been blowing from the north a few moments before, now swung around to the south and changed to a soft breeze that induced a feeling of languor.

The king looked out a window to see what had caused this sudden shift in the wind and he saw walking along the palace grounds the older sister of one of his queens. For the first time he realized how beautiful this girl was.

"Greetings, Coxlal!" the king called.

The woman turned in surprise and bowed to Nopiltzín.

"Where are you going?" he shouted rather more loudly than the distance required.

"I'm to pick some flowers for the queen," she explained.

"Well, pick some for me too," Nopiltzín shouted as the surprised woman moved off toward the gardens.

He felt very good, took another long drink of the liquid and, when he found that this had exhausted the supply, threw the clay jar hard against the splendid wall. The sound of shattering fragments as they fell to the beautiful floor pleased him and he cried to no one in particular: "I'd like to talk with Ixbalanque again. That man

had some powerful ideas that I didn't fully understand."

He left the small room and hurried through the
palace, and whereas the distances between
rooms had sometimes seemed excessive to
him, on this day they seemed entirely functional
and he was impressed at how charmingly his
grandfather had laid out the sprawling palace.
He banged his way unannounced into the
priests' quarters and shouted in what he intended to be a commanding voice: "Ixbalanque!
I want to talk to you!"

The high priest hurried from an inner sanctum
and bowed with precisely the degree of deference due the royal leader, but before he was
able to rise he felt the king's right hand slam
down on his shoulder and heard him cry in a
voice louder than usual: "Ixbalanque, my friend,
let's go somewhere quiet, because now I see
everything clearly and appreciate what you've
been talking about."

The priest was pleased and led his king to a
quiet arbor overlooking the pyramid, and here
Nopiltzín shouted expansively, pointing to the
pyramid: "We're going to put a new face on that
pile of rocks that will reach from here to here."
He indicated dimensions far greater than those
the the high priest had suggested.

"You mean," Ixbalanque asked, "that we can proceed?"

"In days to come," the king said, embracing his priest once more, "the people of this valley will look back upon us as two of the greatest builders the Builders have ever produced. That pyramid is going to be so large—" He stopped abruptly and turned away from the great structure. "Explain again about this curious god the Tenayucans have. What is a smoking mirror?"

Not to be sidetracked by the sudden digression, Ixbalanque replied, "If we're going to resurface the pyramid, there will probably be no need for—"

"Tell me about Tezcatli . . ." As his tongue twisted over the unfamiliar name he started to giggle. Quickly recovering his dignity, he moved back a few paces and bellowed: "Tell me about him."

Ixbalanque was frightened. He could see that the king was afflicted with some strange malady, and it would be dreadful if Nopiltzín were to fall seriously sick before the rebuilding of the pyramid was actually launched. Every precaution must be taken to ensure the king's health, so the priest suggested, "Shall I take you back to your quarters?"

"You shall not!" Nopiltzín bellowed. "You'll sit

here and tell me about Tezcatli . . ." Again he could get no further.

Seeking to humor the sick man, Ixbalanque began, "The god Tezcatlipoca stands for the reconciliation of things that cannot be reconciled." The old man stopped, for he was afraid that the king was in no condition to comprehend such matters, but he soon resumed, for he had become convinced that any community must pay allegiance to two kinds of gods.

"We must placate the gods who control our immediate destinies—the rain god, the earth god and the god of fertility—but we should also worship some deity who represents a higher order of thought and who is not concerned with arbitrating day-to-day problems. Perhaps he is the god from whom the lesser ones derive their power. Perhaps he is a god infinitely removed from temporary questions of power, but if we do not direct ourselves to such a god . . ."

When the old priest paused to look directly at his king, he saw that the monarch had fallen asleep. He didn't hear a word I said, Ixbalanque reflected, which is probably a good thing, because it might have confused him and prevented us from going ahead with the pyramid. Then he noticed that the king's jaw was slack and that his forehead was sweating profusely while his right arm and shoulder twitched spasmodically. It was apparent that Nopiltzín was much sicker than Ixbalanque had originally suspected, so the latter called for help, but when the servants were carrying the inert king off to bed he suddenly regained consciousness and, seeing some tame rabbits on the lawn, broke away to follow the animals, shouting: "I'll be a rabbit and I'll be the new god!" Then he saw the old priest and ran over to embrace him. "Don't worry, old friend," he mumbled. "Now everything is very clear. It's as if a hundred suns have risen." With this jubilant remark he collapsed completely, with a beatific smile.

That night, after the king had been put to bed, Ixbalanque went to a temple at the crest of the pyramid where he convened a meeting of his priests. "We face a difficult situation," he told them. "King Nopiltzín has been struck by a fatal malady and might leave us at any moment."

"The fever?"

"Worse. Loss of his mind." Allowing his subordinates time to grasp the ominous news, he resumed: "The king has authorized us to resurface the pyramid, as we had proposed, but if he dies before we start, the new king—"

"What we must do," one of the priests advised, "is start immediately to resurface, because if the task is fairly begun, the new king won't feel free to halt it."

That night the priests remained in the temples atop the pyramid praying that King Nopiltzín would recover from his illness and survive long enough to let them begin the resurfacing. At dawn the high priest hurried down the long avenue to the royal palace to inspect Nopiltzín's health and to gain final permission for initiating the vast project.

He found the king in a vile humor, but more distressing was the fact that Nopiltzín had no recollection of having authorized the rebuilding of the pyramid. In some confusion Ixbalanque pleaded, "Don't you remember looking at the pyramid and saying that we would make the new version even longer and higher than I had proposed?"

"Are you insane?" Nopiltzín growled.

"But we agreed on it," Ixbalanque argued, "and I want to start digging the trenches today."

"Then you get yourself a little stick and start digging," Nopiltzín snapped.

Ixbalanque decided to be direct: "Are you ill?"

Nopiltzín's features relaxed slightly and he said: "I do not feel well, but I'm sure the giddiness will pass. The important thing is that last evening for a moment I saw everything very clearly. I know just what we are going to do about the gods."

"What?" Ixbalanque asked with undisguised eagerness.

"I'll tell you later," Nopiltzín parried. "But there are two things I'll tell you right now. We're not going to build any pyramid. And we're not going to import from Tenayuca-by-the-Lake any god who represents nothing but vague contradictions."

"What are we going to do?" Ixbalanque pleaded.

"You'll be most surprised."

When the high priest left, Nopiltzín went out among his maguey plants and with an obsidian knife—although my ancestors of that period had not discovered durable metal, they did know how to give hard rock a cutting edge—cut down into the heart of several plants and drew out by sucking through a hollow gourd enough honey water to fill eight clay jars. These he wrapped in damp cloth for storing in the dark, and at the end of three anxious weeks he sampled the results.

He was elated because the honey water had once more transformed itself into the exciting beverage that he had tasted earlier. Closing the curtains that protected his apartment, he began to drink the liquor seriously, and before long the animated visions that had so pleased him at the first testing returned. Knowing that many problems beset the high priest, he summoned Ixbalanque, threw his arms about the old man, and cried in a half-tearful voice, "Ixbalanque, you are going to get your god!"

The priest struggled to free himself from the embrace and asked: "Will you remember tomorrow what you say today?"

Nopiltzín ignored this and said, "I have discovered a new god."

"Where?"

"In the heart of the maguey plant."

The king led Ixbalanque into the darkened room where the eight clay jars stood and pointed to his treasure. "A god lies hidden there, Ixbalanque, and I shall introduce you to him." Going to one of the jars, the king poured his guest a substantial helping of the liquid and invited the priest to drink. With some apprehension Ixbalanque lifted the cup to his lips and for the first time tasted the beverage that was to become known as pulque.

As the afternoon wore on, Ixbalanque noticed that under the influence of pulque the king became more and more expansive while he, Ixbalanque, became increasingly suspicious. He could feel the strange liquid altering his normal behavior and tried to fight against it; he had the distinct suspicion that the pulque was usurping a function that any man should keep for himself or allocate to the gods. He was on the point of formulating what that function was when Nopilt-zín grabbed a flute and began playing delicious music, whereupon Ixbalanque found himself a drum, and after only a few moments of frenzied playing, the entire situation began to clear up for the high priest.

"We play better than the temple musicians," Ixbalanque announced gravely.

"We're going to have a temple on top of the new pyramid—"

"Are we going ahead with the rebuilding after all?"

"Old friend, if you want a new pyramid, you get a new pyramid. See that tree over there? We're going to put so many blocks of stone on that old pyramid that it will be higher than the tree."

"Marvelous," Ixbalanque shouted, banging his drum with renewed vigor.

For five or six hours the king and the high priest drank pulque and rearranged the business of the high valley. There would be a new pyramid and new laws, grouchy elderly officials would be demoted, and the high priest would arrange a marriage between the king and his wife's oldest sister, even though such a union was forbidden by custom. In the sixth hour the king began to run around on all fours like a rabbit and he invited the high priest to do the same.

"No," Ixbalanque said, "if you are the rabbit, I am the coyote, and I'm going to catch you!"

Together the two leaders of the state crawled around the king's chambers, Nopiltzín leaping like a rabbit and Ixbalanque yelping like a coyote, until the chase became so noisy that the queen sent her older sister to see what was happening. When that austere and ugly woman pushed aside the curtains, she was aghast to find the two men rolling around the floor, but this reaction soon turned to utter confusion when the king saw her, leaped across the room on all fours, and grabbed her by the knees, pulling her down onto the floor beside him.

"I've found my darling little rabbit!" he shouted.

"Oh no!" the high priest barked in protest. "Only coyotes can have little rabbits." He leaped past the king and started biting the queen's sister on the forearm, whereupon she screamed, and he suddenly came to his senses. In amazement and confusion he rose, brushed himself off and looked down at his king, who was still groveling on the floor, holding the woman by the knees.

"Nopiltzín!" the priest cried. "Get up!"

With some difficulty, for he had been drinking

for some hours before the arrival of the high priest, Nopiltzín released his sister-in-law and staggered to his feet. The astonished woman adjusted her clothing and fled, while the king banged himself on the temples to clear his head. Mouthing ill-formed words, he asked: "What were we doing, down on the floor? I've always thought of her as the ugliest woman in the high valley."

That night Ixbalanque, once more in command of his reasoning powers, walked disconsolately among the temples atop the pyramid, and in trying to understand what had happened that confusing afternoon he reached several frightening conclusions. Under questioning, after the queen's sister had left, Nopiltzín had assured his priest that the strange liquid had consistently reliable power: the same results had been achieved with each batch. Furthermore, it could be easily made. Finally, when one was drinking it, a god did indeed seem to inhabit one. There was a sense of excitement and colors seemed brighter. What was most shocking was that during the time when the god of pulque had been in command, the queen's sister had actually been a rather attractive woman, so that when he, Ixbalanque, had attacked her and started nibbling her arm, what he had really wanted to do was to drive the king away, tear off the woman's clothes and enjoy her.

"There will be no new pyramid," the high priest admitted in the darkness that enveloped the top of the pyramid. "The god of the smoking mirror, which might have saved us, will not be welcome. The flowered serpent is gone with his sponsorship of beauty, and I'm afraid that all we have accomplished in the high valley is in danger." He looked down at the sleeping city, then one of the loveliest and best governed in Mexico, and sensed accurately that the great decline had begun, that subtle dry rot that overtakes societies when vision and grand design have been surrendered. In anguish he went to the dormitory where his priests slept and cried: "Brothers! I need your counsel!" and long after midnight the guardians of the high valley's conscience debated the most danger-filled question the clergy ever had to confront: "The king seems to have lost control of his powers to govern. Shall we depose him?" The younger men listened in bewilderment as Ixbalanque reported the king's curious behavior while saying nothing of his own when he was galloping about as a coyote.

Relying only on what the high priest had told them, the group could reach no conclusion

about deposing the king, and Ixbalanque was
left with the dismal realization that he must act
but had no idea of what that action should be.
In his confusion he asked two of his senior advisers to walk with him among the temples he
and they were supposed to serve and protect,
and in the darkness he revealed the cause of his
consternation.

"It has a potent magic. It's made from the
liquid at the heart of the maguey, so it must be
sacred. When you drink it, you weigh less. Your
eyes see colors more clearly. Your tongue is
loosened and you become a golden-voiced ora-
tor." At this point he stopped, looked out over
the valley below and confided: "When I drank
some of the new liquid and looked at Coxlal, the
queen's ugly sister, she became sixteen years
old, a ravishing princess."

"It must be magic," one of the priests said.
"We must protect our city from the king's mad-
ness."

In the dark hour before dawn, Ixbalanque
faced the critical problem: "I think we must consider carefully the king's future," and now his
colleagues knew he was speaking of deposition.
Beating his fists against his chest, Ixbalanque
cried: "I should have forced a change years ago.
Well, I'll perform my duties now," and he returned to the dormitory, where he roused his two

advisers and whispered: "The king must go. This city must be saved." And he hastened down the long flight of stone steps to the level below, where he went immediately to his quarters and prepared for the painful meeting at which he would inform the king that his reign was over.

But one of the priests who had learned of the decision scurried down the stone steps in the breaking dawn and alerted the king to what was afoot, so that when Ixbalanque appeared at the palace, the king was waiting with two henchmen secreted behind a wall. Since Nopiltzín had spent the previous night drinking huge drafts of pulque, his capacity for understanding what the high priest wanted to tell him was severely blunted, but at the first sign that Ixbalanque had come to recommend abdication, he flew into a towering rage and, summoning his two thugs, shouted: "Kill him!" and the obsidian daggers, gleaming black in the morning sunlight, plunged into the chest of the high priest.

As he fell at the king's feet he looked up to see his drunken monarch and mumbled: "We shall have a new god, but it won't be the one we need," and he perished, the one man who might have saved the civilization of the Builders.

For the next two hundred years, roughly 900 to 1100, which is not an insignificant length of time as the lives of nations go, City-of-the-Pyramid enjoyed one of the greatest levels of human happiness ever attained by an early organized community. There was no war. no hunger, no forced labor on state projects, no human sacrifice, no grinding social injustice. Some were rich and some were poor, but the gap between the two was not immense. There was an army of sorts, but it played no significant role in the affairs of state. Adultery was punished severely so as to protect the family, and there was even a rude educational system that enabled even the poorest of boys to rise to the priesthood.

What gave City-of-the-Pyramid its greatest distinction, however, was its worship of the god of pulque. The beverage was fermented in great amounts at maguey plantations, which now occupied fields that had once produced only cactus. For mile after mile the spidery arms of the blue-green maguey twisted into the air like the flames of earth, and one of the most common sights in the high valley was the maguey harvester passing among his plants, armed with a hollow gourd, one end of which he pressed into the heart of the plant while the other end was kept in his mouth. Then, by sucking vigorously, he drew up the honey water, depositing it in large gourd buckets which carried it to the fermenting areas, where it was transformed into pulque, the beer, the wine of Mexico.

One of the curiosities of history is that the god of pulque was named Four Hundred Rabbits, since the king who had discovered the drink felt that any man, given enough pulque, could be as carefree as four hundred rabbits. There was a temple to Four Hundred Rabbits—not a large one because the high valley's energy for building had long since been dissipated. The god was represented by a green stone statue of a rabbit with ears like a maguey leaf, and he was perpetually surrounded by flowers of four colors. A troupe of dancers was usually in attendance at his temple and the outer walls of the little structure were festooned with gourds and garlands of fruit. Celebrations in honor of Four Hundred Rabbits consisted of music and singing, the burning of nopal-and-rubber incense, and all who worshiped the god were supposed to be gentle, happy and, above all, kind. It is no exaggeration to say that Four Hundred Rabbits was the loveliest god who ever reigned in Mexico.

Although I'm an American and not a trained historian, I believe I'm entitled to make a judgment about the reign of King Nopiltzín because, through a quirk of Mexican history, I was born a lineal descendant of the king: my grandfather married an Indian woman who sprang directly from his line. So when I try to evaluate his performance I am speaking not of some Indian stranger long dead but of my own ancestor. My summary of his reign is this. The god of pulque acquired a significance greater than that of any other deity. No priest like Ixbalanque tried to call the city back to its high destiny, and the king, unlike tough old Ixmiq, did not dream of building a city so powerful and vast that it would be a monumental tribute to the gods. Instead, king and priest alike worshiped fairly constantly at the shrine of Four Hundred Rabbits, and a hazy indifference settled over the city and the entire valley.

I am convinced by various murals that life in the latter years of Nopiltzín's reign was very good indeed. There is evidence from some of the memorials dug up around Mexico City that other states looked upon City-of-the-Pyramid as the apex of accomplishment, and the decorated pottery and featherwork produced in the high valley was treasured even as far south as present-day Guatemala. Some of the songs composed in those years are still sung in Mexico, including the one that accompanies the hilarious pulque dance that tourists love to photograph: the singers jig up and down on one foot like rabbits while bystanders bark like coyotes.

Tradition claims that Nopiltzín himself composed both the music and the dance.

But after his death the city began to decline.
As the years passed, artists in the rest of Mexico
began to depict City-of-the-Pyramid not as a triangle accompanied by a flute but as an Indian
dignitary whose many headdresses were
cocked to one side, as if he were drunk. The
envy of others had given way to contempt, even
by local artists.

And there was an ominous development
whose menace the rulers of the city were too
befuddled by pulque to appreciate. From time to
time, starting in the year 992, when Nopiltzín
was long dead, a strange group of Indians who
occupied caves far to the north began wandering down to the high valley; we know this from
the decorated pottery of the period. Invariably
they are depicted as barbarians, ugly and ferocious people lacking the graciousness that had
marked the citizens of City-of-thePyramid. We
find not a shred of evidence that any of the
pulque people appreciated the significance of
these stragglers. Just as the rest of civilized
Mexico now treated the Builders with contempt,
so the latter dismissed the northern barbarians
as insignificant.

One aspect of this darkening period around
the year 1000 saddens me, for it reflects on

what I had come to think of as "my people." The descendents of Ixmiq, those fine people who had built some of the grandest structures in all the Americas, would be known in history only as the Drunken Builders, a name taken from the days of their decline. This misnomer has deluded many into thinking that men who were habitually drunk could have built those enduring memorials. I think those ancestors of mine should more generously be termed the Beautiful Builders Who Took to Drink. But I know that's too cumbersome, for historians, like us journalists, seem always to prefer the simplification, whether it represents the truth or not.

INDIAN ANCESTORS: THE ALTOMECS

AT THE BEGINNING of the tenth century, when Nopiltzín was preoccupied with the discovery of pulque, there existed in a series of dark caves along a network of rivers that ran through the steaming jungles several hundred miles north of Mexico City a tribe of Indians who for three or four thousand years, at least, and possibly much longer, had kept alive in their tribal traditions memory of an age when they had lived in a high place. This recollection was so persistent that after the Conquest the tribe was given the name Altomec, a mixture of Spanish and Indian meaning "Those who seek a high place," but during the time of which I speak they were called by others either the Cave People or the Followers of Glittering-Fish Color-Bird.

They were a short-statured, very dark people. Their standard of living was abysmal. In three or four thousand years, huddling in their caves, they had failed to invent cloth, or to develop any simple decoration for their pottery, or to tame the turkey. But they had made two discoveries that were to remake the history of Mexico. Along with their relatives, the Aztecs, who were a little more advanced, the Cave People had learned the effectiveness of organized tribal action, and they had found a god ideally suited to lead them.

Their capacity for unified movement was remarkable, and all during the first half of the eleventh century their rulers sent out disciplined bodies of men to scout the rest of Mexico in the search for a new homesite, for it had become apparent that continued life in the caves was not desirable. Some of these scouting parties penetrated as far south as the areas beyond Guatemala. Others had spied upon the lands of the Drunken Builders, and these had reported favorably on that domain.

Sometime about 1050 the Cave People decided to abandon the caves. Loading their men and women with heavy burdens, they set forth with rude implements, statues of their god weighing thousands of pounds, seeds, gourd baskets, totems of one kind or another and hundreds of small children. Each year, from September to April, they moved a few miles from their old camping ground to a new site, where in the spring they planted the seeds they had been carrying through the winter. For five months they tended their crops and during another month they harvested, and then they pushed south. Scouting parties were constantly probing the areas ahead and for a period of ten years it was intended that they would settle somewhere in the Yucatán peninsula. It was a strange fact that most of the people in the areas spied upon by these nomads were not aware of their presence, so stealthy were their operations. But they did leave a trail, for wherever they probed, a few local men would mysteriously disappear; Glittering-Fish Color-Bird required the constant sacrifice of young warriors.

The powerful god of the Cave People acquired its name Glittering-Fish Color-Bird in this curious way.

Sometime around the birth of Christ the Cave People had seen in a river a fish whose scales seemed to be made of some glittering substance that caught the sun and held it prisoner. After three days of marveling at the phenomenon, the priests proclaimed the fish a god, for it was apparent that it had some control over the sun, and for six or seven hundred years it was worshiped as one of the Cave People's principal deities.

In the year 753, three hundred years before the Cave People set forth on their tribal journey through Mexico, one of their scouting parties brought back from Guatemala a dead specimen of that extraordinary bird the quetzal, whose bright bronze-green and red plumage and immensely long tail would excite all Indian tribes who saw it. The priests were convinced that no such bird could have been placed on earth without the direct intervention of the gods, so on the spot they added the divinity of this colorful bird to that of the glittering fish to create one god.

When trying to explain Glittering-Fish Color-Bird to people who do not know Mexico, I have found it helpful to remind them that the god was a composite whose two halves had originated seven centuries apart. Glittering-Fish was a primal god who could be represented by any kind of shimmering material, and since the Cave People had no metal of any kind, they used waxy leaves, fish scales, polished bones and human teeth to indicate the glittering quality of their deity. The glitter also represented the movement of water that brought fish, the move-

ment of the heavens that brought the growing
seasons, and the radiance of the sun. Thus Glittering-Fish was one of the most practical gods
in Mexican history, and one of the most service-
able, for he served as intermediary with the rivers, the fields, the flowers and the life-giving
sun.

The attributes of glorious Color-Bird, represented by feathers, flowers and iridescent
stones, were the intangible virtues such as love
of beauty—even though the Cave People were
deficient in this—honesty and loyalty. Color-Bird
was worshiped by displaying before him featherwork, bouquets of flowers and costumed dancers. The figure chosen to represent this benign
deity was, appropriately, an androgynous figure
with a benevolent countenance and an all-em-
bracing smile.

About the year 1000, a small group of priests
serving the Cave People decided that their tribe
might be better guided if their rather languid god
Glittering-Fish Color-Bird was replaced by one
with more clearly defined manly virtues. One of
the younger priests, a man of vision and vigor,
argued: "If we are ever to move south into the
good lands we've been scouting, we'll meet
enemies who will want to prevent us from coming into their territory. Since we'll have to fight
them to gain what we need, we must have a god

who will lead us in battle." So slowly the priests began to transform Glittering-Fish Color-Bird into a more commanding figure with more rigorous demands. His smile became a scowl, his hands held not flowers but obsidian-studded maces. He now gave the impression of being eager to lead men into battle rather than to protect them in their homes and fields.

This new god, taller and bigger than his predecessor, demanded for tribute not flowers and colored feathers but war clubs, obsidian daggers and shields made of closely woven matting. At his stone feet a hollow was kept filled with short lengths of wood to feed the fire that smoldered perpetually, producing soot that darkened the figure and gave it a menacing look.

The transformed god transformed his worshipers. Under his triumphant guidance the Cave People moved slowly but steadily south, thrusting aside small communities of Indians less well organized than they and occupying always more attractive land. In these first years of their migration they met no armed resistance, but they felt confident that if battle was forced upon them they would win.

Even with their new, belligerent god the Cave People might have proved a commendable force in Mexican history if they had not remained totally ignorant. If their priests had been aware of the extraordinary discoveries in astronomy made a thousand years before by Indians in other parts of Mexico they would not have found it necessary to initiate the horrible rites that have severely damaged their image in later years.

For more than three thousand years, learned men in various parts of Mexico, priests and astronomers alike, had been aware that in what we now call the month of December the sun wandered each day farther and farther south until, as the twenty-first of December approached, it looked as if it might continue its flight south until it disappeared altogether. Primitive men must have feared that it would never return, so curious rites, mainly involving sacrifices, were invented to lure it back, and since they invariably worked, they became fixed in religious practices. But thoughtful men deduced the rules governing the seasons and realized that the sun was bound to return to perform its functions whether or not it was appeased by rites of any kind. Had the Cave People known this simple fact the abominations I am about to describe would not have happened.

The Cave priests repeatedly told their people: "We sacrificed to our gods, and the sun came back. If we had not, our crops would never have grown and we would have starved," and the listeners agreed, for they saw that the sun did return. But as the first millennium ended, the priests argued: "Since you are determined to move south in search of better living, sooner or later we will encounter strong tribes who will forbid us to touch their land. So we need his continued help in new and more persuasive ways to ask our god to help us. To a god leading us in battle, the offering of fruit and flowers is no longer proper. Our god deserves the ultimate sacrifice, a human being, one a day in the critical period, so that he not only will dissuade the sun from leaving us in the chill darkness but also will guarantee our victory in battle."

When one listener asked, "How will the sacrificial man be chosen?" the high priest replied quickly: "No member of the Cave People will ever be selected. We will offer only enemy soldiers we have captured in battle. The best and the bravest, men of valor. Our god will recognize them as major gifts and will be eager to help us, so let us accept this new form of worship gladly."

On a day in mid-December when the sun was perilously low, citizens assembled in the area facing the image of the new god and watched as a prisoner from a recently vanquished tribe was brought forth, a handsome young warrior who had fought with valor and who now stared defiantly at his captors. He was half led, half dragged toward a huge rounded log, and four priests, grabbing his ankles and wrists, lifted him high in the air and then brought him down forcefully on his back across the log. In this position the young warrior looked into the eyes of a ferocious priest who approached with a long, sharp dagger, which he drove into the prisoner's chest under the last rib and across the belly. Reaching with his left hand into the cavity to tear out the living heart, he offered it as food for the god of battle.

The people were awed by the terrible power of their new god, that he could command such a sacrifice, and in the days that followed they watched five successive ritual murders. After the final sacrifice everyone gathered in a public square to spend the night in prayer and religious ritual, imploring the sun to return. As dawn approached, a priest who was monitoring the sun's movement turned to the waiting crowd and shouted triumphantly: "The sun has halted his flight south. He's coming back to save us."

Later, in a year when no prisoners were taken for the good reason that this barren part of Mexico had no inhabitants, December approached with no captives to sacrifice. But the ritual had become so sacred, so vital, in the life of the Cave People, that it was an easy transition from

sacrificing enemy warriors to plunging the obsidian knife into the chest of the tribe's own
warriors. Within the space of a mere fifty years
the priests had convinced the Cave People that
this was the noblest way to leave this earth, a
death that was more to be desired than life itself.

In their first encounters with other tribes, the
wandering Cave People gained significant victories, and so grateful were they to Glittering-Fish
Color-Bird that they dropped the complex double name and referred to him thereafter simply
as War God. His original attributes were ignored,
and few in the tribe remembered that he had
once been their god of fertility and beauty.

After they had been wandering for thirty years
in the general direction of Yucatán, they encamped somewhere in north-central Mexico—
the place has never been identified—which was
entirely different from their riverbank home: it
was a broad, arid plain whose fields were surrounded by cactus. Here they stayed for about
half a century to recoup strength, during which
they introduced certain innovations. First, they
were so impressed by the cactus plant that
when there was no one surviving who could remember the caves they renamed themselves
the Cactus People. Second, from the tanned
skins of large snakes that infested the area they
built themselves a huge drum that they beat

whenever they were to offer a human sacrifice. Third, they were so fascinated by the soaring eagles that guarded the cactus plains that they adopted the habit of dressing their chief warriors in costumes that made them look like eagles, and it was these fighters who would soon be dreaded by much of Mexico.

A fourth change was one that occurred in the hearts of the people, for when the leaders decided that the time was ripe for a major thrust at some area in which they could settle permanently and cease their aimless wandering, the priests advised: "For an adventure of this magnitude, in which we may have to wage prolonged war against well-prepared adversaries, we should carry with us a powerful image of our god, one that reminds us of his strength and our enemies of his power." (Up to this time other peoples had been known as strangers; now anyone not of their clan carried automatically the label of enemy.)

Accordingly a hideous image was carved that represented a tyrant who sat in judgment not only of captives hauled before him but also of his own people. Held between his knees was a stone bowl, into which were thrown the still-pulsing human hearts ripped from the chests of living men. Smoke, emblem of the power of fire, curled about the figure, which in the years of its horrible existence became blackened with soot, and always there was that bottomless bowl into which heart after heart was thrown.

After the harvest period in the year 1130 the Cactus People held a convocation where in a two-day period they sacrificed four hundred and eighty men, of whom nineteen were Drunken Builders who had been surprised on a hunting trip. They were the first Indians from the high valley to die at the hands of War God. The military leaders and the priests presented the people with options: "One scouting party proposes yearly marches until the rich lands of Yucatán are reached, and rich they are, but the distance is endless, requiring so many years to traverse, that some of you would not live to see it." The people shouted down this proposal, so the leaders continued: "Other scouts have found a lake region only two years distant. But it has no high land in the vicinity except smoking volcanoes." To this the people cried: "We want no burning mountain," and it was rejected. At this impasse, the high priest spoke: "There is one land that I myself have seen. It lies not far away, set among hills. It is a high valley, the kind of land our people have always sought, and it contains a man-made mountain upon which the present inhabitants have erected their temple. It almost looks as if it were waiting for our War God."

"Are the people living there warlike?" the king asked.

"We've engaged them in minor skirmishes," the high priest assured him, "and they are easy prey. War God has assured us that we can capture their city."

At the time of this meeting, City-of-the-Pyramid and its supporting countryside counted a population of about sixty thousand, whereas the nomadic Cactus People could not have numbered more than five thousand; furthermore, each year upward of a hundred of the best Cactus warriors were sacrificed to War God, which constantly weakened the tribe, but on the other hand the weak, the worn-out and the blind were also killed off, which constantly strengthened it.

The elite warriors that remained were among the most effective fighting men in Mexico and the idea of engaging an enemy twelve times their number in no way disturbed them. From having defeated many different tribes they had accumulated some of the most advanced weapons of the age: obsidian war clubs, shields of hardened wood, mechanical spear-throwers, and sharp-tipped arrows. Their War God was decorated with turquoise and silver, which made him flash when fires were lighted at his feet and magnified his aura of evil menace.

The Cactus People were convinced that sixty

thousand lackadaisical Drunken Builders could not withstand them. Therefore, in the year 1130 the Cactus People decided to move slowly but with constant pressure against City-of-the-Pyramid and occupy it. For the first fifteen years of this slow encroachment the Drunken Builders were not even aware that hostile forces were approaching, but in the spring of 1145 they awakened to the fact that the nomads were encamped only sixty miles away. Although there was consternation, no one knew what to do about the distressing situation.

During these critical years, the king of the Drunken Builders was Tlotsin, a descendant of Nopiltzín, the discoverer of pulque, and of all that his ancestors had accomplished in the high valley Tlotsín appreciated most the brewing of this beverage. He could not be called a hopeless drunkard, but he did find solace in drink.

In 1145, when the Cactus People were a definite threat, Tlotsín was thirty-three and married to a keen-eyed girl of twenty named Xolal, who was particularly sensitive to the danger posed by the invaders because her father had been sent as an ambassador to the Cactus People some years earlier when they were still some hundred miles to the north and they had promptly sacrificed him to their War God. At the time Xolal had wanted the king to dispatch a force to punish the murderers, but Tlotsín, who was then wooing her, argued: "They're barbarians! You've got to take into account that they don't know the customs of civilized states."

"They killed an ambassador," Xolal protested.

"They probably don't know what an ambassador is," Tlotsín rationalized.

"They're a hideous people and they worship a hideous god," Xolal said.

"Our scouts tell me there are only four or five thousand of them," the king said lightly. "Two generations ago they were living in caves."

But when, in 1146, the Cactus People sent an armed group within a few miles of the city and captured a band of Tlotsín's people, hauling all the men back to their camp to serve as living sacrifices, City-of-the-Pyramid was finally forced to acknowledge the existence of a powerful enemy.

"They worship a monstrous god," reported a man who had escaped from his captors. "He feeds only on human hearts. Any man captured by them is stretched across an altar and his heart is ripped out while he is still breathing."

The escaped prisoner's description of the god did not so much terrify the Drunken Builders as fascinate them, and men began to speculate on what life would be like if the invaders triumphed.

There was discussion of how it would feel to be flung across an altar with a knife at one's chest, and it was generally concluded that any god that could command such devotion must be more important than the pallid ones worshiped in City-of-the-Pyramid.

"There's only a handful of them," Tlotsín temporized, "and it isn't logical to suppose that they could cause trouble to a large city like ours."

Xolal, who made every effort to discover as much as she could about the enemy, became convinced that they did intend to occupy the high valley permanently, and she argued: "They are few now, and they have not yet crossed the mountains into our valley. Let us drive them back now, lest they invade our fields and, strengthened by our food supply, become too strong for us to oppose."

In fairness to King Tlotsín, it must be said that there was not much he could do, for during the golden age of the Drunken Builders there had been no knowledge of war and therefore no need for an army. Complacently Tlotsín took refuge in the thought, Something will happen and they will go away.

But when Xolal persisted in arguing for defensive action King Tlotsín produced a map that showed the high valley secure within its rim of hills and explained indulgently, "The Cactus

People are here beyond the hills, and we are safe inside. Before they reach us they must pass Valley-of-Plenty, which has always been our outpost, and when they see how strong we are"—he pointed triumphantly at the distant valley—"their scouts will report how many we are and how few they are, and they will depart along this river."

To this reasoning Xolal replied, "Three years ago they were far away and we did nothing. Next year they will occupy Valley-of-Plenty and it will be theirs."

"If that occurs," the king replied resolutely, "we shall have to do something."

In 1147, as Xolal had predicted, the Cactus People and their puissant god moved to the crest of the protecting hills, but to her surprise they did not attack Valley-of-Plenty. Instead they waited for their own meager crops to ripen, after which their priests decreed that anyone with even a slight physical defect must be killed off. Eighty of the best warriors were also sacrificed, and at the height of the religious frenzy thus induced, the Cactus People rushed through the passes and down into Valley-of-Plenty, capturing or killing all those at the Drunken Builder outpost. They sacrificed every one of their captives and rededicated the area as Valley-of-the-Dead, a name that has continued to this day.

"Now we have got to do something," King Tlotsín said, and he summoned his advisers, who argued back and forth futilely all through the winter of 1148. When the autumn came, more Drunken Builders were captured and there was another ghastly series of sacrifices, after which the Cactus People moved closer to the city.

Some of the younger men, encouraged by Xolal, proposed conscripting an army that would drive the invaders away, but King Tlotsín opposed this with determination. "We would only anger them," he cautioned, and the year progressed with still no decision, except that a delegation of ambassadors was dispatched. This time the Cactus People did not cut out the emissaries' hearts. "See!" Tlotsín said to his advisers. "They are becoming civilized."

"Did our ambassadors win any concessions?" Queen Xolal demanded.

"No," the king replied, "but at least they weren't sacrificed, and that's progress." The Cactus People made progress in another direction, too. When the crops were in, they moved even closer to the city.

The year 1149 was a critical one, for it became evident that if the Cactus People were to usurp any more fields the Drunken Builders would begin to experience shortages in food.

Now something had to be done, so against his better judgment King Tlotsín authorized the formation of a battle corps that would march against the intruders and convince them that they must come no nearer the city. It was an exciting day when the corps assembled and its inexperienced generals fortified themselves with liberal drafts of pulque, which gave them all the courage they needed. There were banners and drums and flutes and ferocious-looking headdresses designed to frighten the enemy.

Some four thousand men marched out from City-of-the-Pyramid and against them the Cactus People dispatched seven hundred rock-hard warriors. Sustained by an absolute belief in their War God, these skilled warriors hacked their way right into the middle of the enemy army and with no great struggle carried off more than twelve hundred prisoners.

That afternoon, while the remnants of King Tlotsín's demoralized army were creeping back to the city, the Cactus People hauled their god to the scene of battle, and while the appalled citizens of the city looked down from the terraces of their pyramid, the captives were lined up and led one by one to the altar, across which they were stretched by powerful priests while their hearts were ripped out and fed to the hungry War God. The citizens of City-of-the-Pyramid could identify their husbands and sons as they came before the awful deity, and they could hear their final shrieks of agony as the swift daggers plunged into their breasts. They could also see the smoking fires as they enveloped the god and the bowl of pulsating hearts that was constantly replenished.

The aftermath of this terrifying day could not have been predicted. The Cactus People made no effort to assault the city. They merely kept their god on the spot where he had gained a significant victory and from time to time his priests sacrificed whatever captives were taken on raids throughout the countryside. The harvest of 1149 was garnered and a thanksgiving celebration was held, at which over three hundred victims were sacrificed in plain view of any who wanted to watch from City-of-the-Pyramid. In 1150 new crops were planted and in the autumn of that year they were harvested to the accompaniment of a celebration fully as bloody as those that had preceded. The next year a new crop was planted, this time less than a hundred yards from the northern base of the pyramid.

Within the city a great debate was being waged. In his public speeches King Tlotsín maintained that within a year or so the Cactus People would go away, but sometimes when he drank in private with his closest advisers he would say in the fourth or fifth hour, "Now I see it all very clearly. We should have opposed them when they were camped beyond the hills. Before they captured our grain fields." But when his council asked him directly, "What shall we now do?" he never had any clear idea. He kept repeating: "I feel sure that sooner or later they will go away."

Queen Xolal in these days moved among the people trying to make them rise to some supreme effort. She often argued, "Granted that we were defeated that first time, and granted that we lost some of our best men. Look at the Cactus People! Each year they willingly sacrifice many of their bravest warriors and each year they return stronger than before. We too could muster our strength." To her despair, her pleas went unheeded because the great snakeskin drum beyond the pyramid would begin to throb and the people would throng to the walls and rooftops to watch yet another gruesome scene of bloody sacrifice; becoming transfixed by the barbarity, they would wonder among themselves: "How many of us will they sacrifice when they capture the city?" And it was an appalling fact that as the sacrifices continued, the people of the city became increasingly engrossed in conjecturing when it was going to happen to them, and how it would feel, and how great the War God must be if he could command such devotion; so before Xolal could devise a plan to ward off disaster, and before the drunken king could make up his mind on what to do, the city had virtually surrendered from within.

In midsummer of the year 1151 the Cactus People simply walked into City-of-the-Pyramid and occupied all buildings. There was no fighting, no massacre, not even any negotiation. They came in not from the north, which would have disturbed their ripening crops, but from the east, where the roads were good.

July, August and September passed without a single Drunken Builder being killed by the Cactus People. They were, of course, pressed into service for harvesting the crops, and some six thousand were assigned the task of tearing down everything on top of the pyramid to make way for an imposing temple in which was to be seated the hideous statue of War God. Since the Cactus People admitted that, unlike the Drunken Builders, they were not skilled craftsmen, they appointed a team of the best local stone carvers to construct a new statue of War God, and it is interesting to note that we have on clay tablets fine portraits of the old version in wood and the new in stone—you can study them at the Palafox Museum in Toledo—and what is most notable is that in the new stone version every trace of the original god who had nourished these people in the caves is gone. There is a slight indication of a glittering fish, but the iridescence comes from jewels in the handle of a war club, and there is a hint of a quetzal feather, but it is really the hair of a victim. The new god who was to occupy the apex of the ancient pyramid was remorseless, warlike and terrifying; and he clasped between his knees a bowl of stone much deeper and wider than the original one.

As the end of harvest approached, and as the newly carved image of War God was installed in the temple atop the pyramid, a pall of nervous apprehension hung over the city and men whispered to one another: "I wonder if I'll be taken?"

When the harvest was in and all work on the pyramid had been completed, the great snakeskin drum began to throb and its echoes penetrated to the limits of the city. Gaunt priests, their ears pierced with cactus spines, their hair matted with human blood, appeared at the base of the pyramid, and scores of men were lined up at various points throughout the city. Then it became obvious to the horror of all that the entire corps of six thousand men who had worked on the pyramid was to be sacrificed. The number was almost too vast to comprehend, but the

Cactus People had decided that in this greatest of all celebrations they must outdo themselves in expressing gratitude to their god. For such an occasion six thousand human hearts were not excessive.

The victims were paraded through the streets along which they had once reeled in drunken revelry, and their compatriots, watching them go, could only think, This must be a most powerful god who now sits atop our pyramid. There were gasps of surprise when the final procession formed and it was seen that at its head marched King Tlotsín, a tall, imposing Indian of thirty-nine—an ancestor of mine in direct line. That day, the chronicles tell us, he wore a kind of numbed look, but he also smiled. In a simpler time, when a king could drink as he liked and postpone decisions to another day, Tlotsín would have been an adequate ruler; even now as he marched to the base of the pyramid he failed to realize how wretchedly he had met the challenge of his reign. The Cactus People, willing to accommodate a captive king who would shortly initiate the installation of the new god, had allowed him as much pulque as he wished, and he had drunk generously. When, in the solemn procession, he passed some old friend he would nod in a kind of daze and pass on with his fatuous smile unchanged. He knew where he was marching, but he was able to erase that knowledge from his mind.

But when he came at last to the pyramid itself, leading his six thousand, he saw his beautiful queen, Xolal; he realized that she had been set aside as a prize for one of the Cactus People's leaders, and the foolish smile left his face. "Xolal," he mumbled, but his brain would not form the words he wished to say, and he could only look at her dumbly.

Breaking loose from the Cactus People who surrounded her, Xolal leaped to her husband's side and, standing before him as a shield, started to cry, "Men of the city! Defend yourselves at last!" Before she could continue her exhortations, an eagle warrior, his terrible mask in place, slammed his hand across her mouth. Biting the hand, she broke loose again and shouted: "Men! Men! You must resist," With a sweep of his obsidian dagger the eagle warrior cut Xolal's throat and silenced her forever. She fell backward against her husband, then slumped to the ground, but as she fell she trailed a line of blood down his body.

Tlotsín marched up the steep steps of the pyramid, flanked on either side by a Cactus warrior. At last he reached the topmost terrace of the pyramid and there he saw for the first time the god who had captured his city. War God sat with his massive hands on his knees, between which rested a beautiful unstained bowl adorned with human skulls. The head of the god was wreathed in carved snakes. His eyes were made of turquoise and his teeth of opal. About his neck he wore a chain of carved skulls and his ankles were festooned with little stone hearts. His visage was terrifying beyond Tlotsín's imagination, and his gaze was focused on a convex slab of stone. The captive king was hurled down on the stone with such force that his breath was knocked out, and as he lay supine he saw for the first and last time the flashing of a long, beautiful knife. It was his royal heart that first stained the massive bowl. His broken body was the first to pitch headlong down the steep eastern flank of the pyramid.

From that day on the Drunken Builders ceased to exist as a nation. The shock was so great that they never recovered. In subsequent bloody orgies their men were systematically eliminated and their women routinely violated by the conquerors. Native blood became so diluted that within a hundred years it is doubtful that one pure-blooded Drunken Builder survived. I am descended from the daughter of King Tlotsín and Queen Xolal who was taken by one of the eagle warriors and who was, my family's chronicles claim, a good and faithful wife, whose descendants were a line of warriors who for more than three hundred years spread terror throughout central Mexico.

About twenty years after the Cactus People had occupied the city their priests advised the king: "For more than a hundred years our people have grown strong through wandering and fighting. But now that we have our own city and the comforts that go with it we are becoming weak, and soon no one will fear our eagle warriors. There are no more important battles to be fought, so let us engage on some massive project that will stimulate the people and keep them strong." When the king asked what such a project might be they said, "Let us put a new face on the old pyramid built by our enemies. Let us make it a Cactus pyramid decorated with our gods and our figures."

In 1171, therefore, the final resurfacing of the great pyramid was authorized. Half the surviving Drunken Builders were moved to the quarries and the other half put to work on the pyramid itself. The present vast outlines of the structure were laid out—691 feet on each side, 219 feet high—and the ambitious operation began. But the Cactus People quickly saw that they lacked both the artists and the knowledge required for such an undertaking, so they turned over the supervisory job to the last of the Drunken

Builder experts, and the pyramid as we know it today is the final poetic flowering of those gifted master builders.

A good many critics have said that the southern stairway is one of the marvels of world architecture and I recall the joy with which my father and I used to study its exquisite details. The functional part, of course, is the stairs themselves; each has a carved riser showing the flowers and animals of the region. One shows birds flying and it has been widely reproduced, for the scene is the essence of flight, so handsomely executed that one can almost feel the stone wings whizzing by in the eddies of air.

But the risers, exquisite as they are, have never been as universally admired as the accompanying frieze of eagle warriors, one of the treasures of Mexican art. At the top of the stairway stands a low, roofless wall along which march a row of warriors in bas-relief, each different from the others but all wearing eagle masks in which the upper beak of the bird juts out from the forehead and the lower from beneath the chin. What has always impressed me about the frieze is that such minute details as the feathers on each eagle helmet are superbly carved.

Sometime in the thirteenth century, when the final work on the pyramid was completed, most of the surviving Drunken Builders had their hearts ripped out in a ghastly celebration that lasted six days. In a photo essay I did for an art magazine in Germany I calculated that this noble pyramid had witnessed during the nearly four centuries from 1151 through 1519 no less than one million human sacrifices. During the preceding five hundred years of Drunken Builder occupation, none had died, but in Cactus times an average of about three thousand human beings were sacrificed each year. What is appalling is that for the most part only the young and strong were sacrificed. Year by year their hearts were burned so that the smoke could make the temple look more forbidding and their bodies were thrown down the steep steps to be hauled away by slaves to rot in pits. Thus the pyramid and all connected with it was a stinking place of abominable death; yet, paradoxically, from the spirit it generated rose the greatness of the Cactus People.

And they did become a great people; of that there can be no question. They voluntarily adopted every desirable trait of the Drunken Builders, even taking over their advanced language. Once the Builders' gods had been removed from the top of the pyramid, they were reinstated in lesser temples and honored for their own special virtues. The Cactus People improved every aspect of Builder agriculture, built better roads and found new sources of water. For their pottery they adopted Builder design, but they also made the clay objects stronger and more functional. Once they had learned how to domesticate animals they maintained huge turkey farms, and they even made improvements in the manufacture of pulque. Numerous archaeologists have pointed out that just as the Romans borrowed from the Greeks, always improving what they took, and just as the Japanese borrowed in the same improving way from the Chinese, so the Cactus People absorbed Builder culture and made each item better, until in the period from 1350 to 1527—when the Spaniards finally reached the high valley— the Cactus civilization was one of the most advanced in the Americas, surpassing in some respects both the nearby Aztec and the distant Inca in Peru.

Because the Cactus People learned to keep picture records, we have a substantial history of their nation, one with names and dates in a fairly reliable chronology. German and English experts have written books on the subject and we know far more about these warlike people of Toledo than we do about any of the Indians who inhabited the United States. To take only one example, we know exactly how they planted corn, in what month and with what fertilizer. We know how and where it was gathered and stored, and we have specific lists of how much was apportioned to each kind of family, and what amount had to be paid back in taxes.

But mostly we know about the wars, for under the pressure of War God the Cactus People terrorized the entire central Mexican plateau. They regularly ranged from Guadalajara on the west to Puebla on the east, never seeking territorial conquest but only captives who could be sacrificed to their insatiable god. Their most consistent enemies were the Aztecs, from the lake on whose borders present-day Mexico City stands, and the wars between these two strong nations were prolonged and bloody. What the two tribes fought about is never specified, and there is substantial suspicion that the leaders of the two groups initiated wars solely for the purpose of keeping their warriors occupied.

In fact, in one year around 1350 all ostensible reasons for fighting seem to have been exhausted, so in a formal agreement worked out by ambassadors from the two nations the ninety leading warriors from each side met on a field of flowers halfway between the cities and a mock battle was held, which in subsequent reenactments became known as the Tournament of Flowers. I use the phrase "mock battle" with some hesitancy because according to the ground rules observed at the tournament, prisoners captured by either side were hauled back to the home capitals, there to be sacrificed with due pomp to War God in the case of the Cactus People and to an equally evil god, Huitzilopochtli, in the case of the Aztecs. Later, if the records are read in a certain way, historians believe that the murderous tournament was held not on an impartial middle field but one year in Mexico City and the next in City-of-the-Pyramid on what one archaeologist has called "a home-and-home schedule."

One aspect of this ceremonial war was particularly reprehensible. When either side required prisoners for some unusually important ceremonial, for which ordinary captives from ordinary tribes would not suffice, a full-fledged war would be launched with the best generals from each side leading their troops, unaware that some months earlier ambassadors had secretly arranged that this year one side would win and be allowed to capture the two or three hundred prisoners they needed, with the firm agreement that in some subsequent year, when the priests on the other side were calling for prime prisoners, the leaders on the opposing side would manipulate a reciprocal betrayal of their army. When the faked battle was over—"faked" is hardly the right word, for men did die—the betrayed prisoners were led off to ritual slaughter, and, so far as we know, none protested the treachery.

There has been much speculation as to why, year after year, the finest men of the Cactus People allowed such things to happen and why they went so willingly to their death, for there is substantial proof that it was with exaltation that they climbed the steep steps of the pyramids. I once asked my father about this abomination and he said, "Young men like you often think that the worst thing in the world is death. And you shudder at the behavior of your Indian ancestors. But I can think of a hundred civilizations that developed propaganda that convinced their youth that to die for one cause or another was the noblest act of all or that to perish in the arms of a certain religion ensured perpetual life. Every man who climbed these steps was sure he was going straight to heaven, and someday you'll probably find a flight of stairs that you'll be willing to climb." In later years I often thought of my father's words as I got into a B-29 and then felt it climb high into the sky for our bombing runs against Japan.

An incident in which one of my ancestors was involved will illustrate my father's argument. Sometime around 1470, when Aztec and Cactus culture had reached a high level of sophistication, City-of-the-Pyramid developed a general of unusual prowess called Tezozomoc, and under his leadership the Cactus People extended their fringe of feudatory states almost to Guadalajara. In nineteen major battles he was not defeated, and his victories were gained principally because he outguessed the enemy and deployed his troops in sudden and unexpected patterns. Long before his time the Indians had stumbled upon the universal trick of sending forth what appeared to be the main but small body of troops, so that the enemy would be lured into attacking in force; when the battle was joined the real power of the first army would strike from some unexpected quarter, catching the main body of the enemy off balance; and wily generals defended themselves against this maneuver. It was Tezozomoc who developed the tactic of sending forth one weak force, then supporting it with another almost as weak, so that when the enemy fell upon the second force, thinking it to be Tezozomoc's trap, the principal body of the Cactus warriors rushed forth to easy victory.

From his nineteen triumphs Tezozomoc had led back to the pyramid no less than twenty-five thousand captives, who were duly sacrificed, and each one who died enhanced the general's reputation a little more, so that his fame reached as far as Yucatán, and at places as distant as modern Veracruz there have been found clay tablets celebrating his accomplishments.

It was natural that the Aztecs, who were twice defeated by this great warrior, should lust for his heart to be fed to their war god, so they launched a major effort to capture him, but Tezozomoc defeated them handily. In 1483 ambassadors from the Aztecs secretly approached the Cactus leaders and arranged for Tezozomoc to be betrayed, in return for which the Aztecs would allow Cactus ambassadors free entry to trading posts in the Pachuca area. When the Aztecs returned home, three Cactus ambassadors, according to plan, were slain in the Pachuca hills, and this gave the Cactus leaders an adequate cause for war, with unsuspecting Tezozomoc at the head of the Cactus army. In the height of battle, during which the wily eagle warrior was preparing a new kind of trap for the Aztecs, he was left without protection as planned and was taken captive.

There was much rejoicing in the Aztec capital when his capture became known, and he was hauled into the city imprisoned in a cage decorated with silver and gold, and for eleven days the residents were free to inspect the greatest warrior of his time. On the twelfth day, when he was to be sacrificed, a multitude crowded the plaza, including King Tizoc, the uncle of the boy who was later to become Moctezuma II. In ceremonial robes, Tezozo-moc was led to the sacrificial stone, a huge flat disk big enough for six or seven men to stand upon, and a rope attached to the center was tied around Tezozomoc's waist. The captive warrior could move only in a restricted circle, and under these conditions he was handed a war club with which to defend himself, but in-stead of a club edged with sharp obsidian he got one decorated with delicate feathers that fluttered in the air when he swung it.

Against one seminaked man were arrayed twenty fully armed warriors. The massive crowd had gathered hoping for an unusual spectacle, and they were not disappointed. The chronicles of the time are specific in stating that Tezozo-moc defended himself so adroitly and overcame the handicap of his tether with such skill, that he stood off the twenty Aztecs, disarmed many and killed three. After about a half hour he was bleeding from numerous gashes and his breath was coming in painful gasps. He was about to collapse, when with a violent effort he flung him-self outward to the fullest extent allowed by the tether, and with a powerful swing of the club crushed the heads of two opponents. With that mighty effort he fell senseless on the disk, his last thought being that before he wakened he would be with the gods. But when the priests started to lay hands on him, the populace voiced their protest violently and Moctezuma's uncle, the king, announced: "This man shall be general of my armies!"

For three years the great Cactus warrior led the Aztecs to victories on the extended fronts of their empire. He fought the Tlaxcaltecas, the Pueblas, the Oaxacans and the Pachucans and from each foray he returned with many captives and much booty. But in 1486 the time came when it was unavoidable that he lead the Aztecs against his own Cactus People, and this he refused to do. Presenting himself before King Tizoc he said: "I have led your armies to victory at many parts of your empire, and I would willingly continue to do so, for I have never known men braver than the Aztecs. But I cannot lead your army against my own people. If you press me to do so, I would be a traitor and this would be a shameful conclusion to my life. So the time is at hand when I must offer myself as a sacrifice to your war god, and this I do willingly, for I have served him long and would join my companions in heaven."

Of his own accord, the great Indian warrior Tezozomoc, who if he had lived might have successfully countered the wiles of Cortés, dressed himself in ceremonial robes, both Aztec and Cactus, and, while drums throbbed and flutes shrilled warlike music, marched alone up the steep steps to the altar of Huitzilopochtli the war god, where priests laid reverent hands on him and conveyed him to the convex slab, where his heart was ripped out and fed to the god. When news of his death reached City-of-the-Pyramid no one lamented. His daughter, known to history as Lady Gray Eyes, was nine years old at the time, and when she was told of her father's death in the remote Aztec capital and of the manner in which he died, she said gravely: "He should have died in battle."

Because the Indians of this later age focused their attention and their art so strongly on death and in such hideous forms, history has dealt rather harshly with them, as if they were barbarians whose sole concern was human sacrifice. This was not so, and in order to strike a balance in evaluating my ancestors I have always liked to think of Lady Gray Eyes, one of the great people of Mexican history.

She was given her peculiar name not by fellow Indians but by Europeans who came to Mexico from abroad and who, in their moment of victory over the Cactus People, came into contact with this resolute woman. They noticed that her eyes were not the usual jet-black but a kind

of gray—this could have been an illusion because she was certainly not of mixed blood, but
her eyes were, as one of the conquerors wrote,
"of a soft gray color that could turn to steel as
she gritted her teeth and fought to protect the
rights of her people."

As the daughter of Tezozomoc, she was naturally brought up in a warlike world; she never
saw her father after she was six and maintained
only a dim memory of what he was like, but in
later life Spanish chroniclers recorded what she
told them:

> I think of him not at war but in our home at
> the edge of the city that later became
> Toledo. We had about an acre of land on
> which slaves he had taken in battle grew
> vegetables and raised turkeys. In fields
> somewhat removed from the house he also
> raised a lot of cotton, and I remember him
> primarily tending his garden.
>
> My mother was encouraged to weave, and
> she had slave women who worked under her
> direction making a cloth that other cities
> cherished. As a little girl I wore dresses
> made of cotton, feathers and silver strands,
> all miraculously woven together so that I
> looked like a silvery bird in flight.

I was very fond of a candy made from cactus, but my father made me recite songs to him before I could have any. At six I couldn't have known anything but children's songs, but he enjoyed them and I remember that he often joined me.

He assured me even then that I was destined to be the wife of the king, so that later when he sacrificed himself, my mother continued to impress upon me the importance of my future duties, and I learned not only about sewing and weaving and the making of tortillas but also about the management of a house that contained many rooms and many servants. I was especially good at music and played the flute in the quietness of our home, and at one time I must have known most of the songs of my people.

Most Spaniards I have met have asked me what I thought about human sacrifice, and I have grown tired of explaining that up until the age of twenty-one I had never seen the rite and did not really comprehend it. My mother, I noticed, kept us at home whenever the great drum sounded at the pyramid, and even on the days that celebrated my father's greatest triumphs, when thousands of captives were executed, my mother refused to attend. I remember when I was six and Father returned triumphantly from Guadalajara. After the drum stopped beating, he came home, washed, played with me and then tended his garden. I can't recall ever having heard sacrifices mentioned in my home, and that is why my reaction to the Mother Goddess was so unexpected and so spectacular.

In two short articles my magazine once asked me to write about the Cactus People, I tried to speak well of them, for there was much about these ancestors of mine that was admirable, but I admit that my task would have been easier if the Mother Goddess had not become part of their history.

In the late 1400s, when the triumph of War God was as complete as it could be, and when there were no further refinements in the grisly rites honoring him, a convocation of priests of City-of-the-Pyramid convened and heard the high priest reason in this manner: "If our War God is wholly omnipotent, and if there is nothing further we can do to honor him directly, we ought to consider other oblique ways in which to pay him respect. And it seems to me that what we have overlooked is the fact that he could never have become so powerful if he had not had a mother even more terrible than he."

Consequently, to fulfill a religious need, the Cactus priests created a Mother Goddess who as a sheer abomination has never been equaled. Her head was two horned serpents on the verge of devouring each other. Her hands were talons, each tearing apart a human heart. Her breasts were coiled vipers, and her navel was an eagle's beak plucking out the eyes of an infant. Her skirt was a writhing mass of snakes and her feet were the teeth of animals rending flesh. She wore a necklace of human hearts, rings of human eyes and beads of teeth. Hers was the most repulsive statue ever carved in Mexico, a squat, sullen, hideous travesty of both god and woman. When she was unveiled, in her own temple atop a small pyramid that occupied the space where the cathedral now stands, there was revelry and feasting, for it was recognized that a worthy goddess had at last been found to accompany War God in his lonely rule of the high valley.

What made the Mother Goddess such a dreaded deity was the refinement in torture that the priests had devised for her: since she was the mother of War God, she was satisfied only with perfect things, so each year only the youths who were flawless in every way were set aside for her. Since she also represented mother-hood, she was also entitled to numerous sacri-fices to empower her to ensure continued fertility, and therefore hundreds of victims were thrown alive into huge fires that roared at her feet.

When, in her twenty-second year, Lady Gray Eyes first saw the rites she was so overcome that she would have fainted had not her strong-minded mother gripped her arm and whispered: "If you disgrace yourself before the Mother Goddess you too will be chosen as a sacrifice." Lady Gray Eyes thus learned the need for ex-treme discretion. Because her reputation was unsullied by any suspicion that she was less than devout, there were no obstacles to her marrying the young king, who was much in love with her.

The position of the young queen at this crucial moment in history was a curious one. There was no way in which she could have known that powerful strangers from Europe were about to land in Cuba and would soon be heading for Mexico, but she sensed that great change was in the wind. This nebulous suspicion made her feel that Cactus society could not remain as it was, especially the hideousness of Mother God-dess and the abomination whereby the priests

were able to convince the Cactus women that
their noblest function in life was to produce
handsome, intelligent sons to be sacrificed at
the feet of the Mother Goddess. "It's evil," she
muttered to herself as she contemplated the
perverting of motherhood and the waste of
human lives. "No woman can want to see her
son, her brother or her husband slain in such a
horrible way. Killing scores so the sun will come
back north! Of course it will return! It always has
and always will."

When she asked her mother: "Surely you
know that the sun will always come back,
whether the goddess has victims or not?" her
mother drew back and counseled: "Daughter,
don't think along those lines or you'll endanger
the king." But when Lady Gray Eyes asked:
"Surely you must deplore the ritual sacrificing of
our best young men?" her mother nodded.
"Yes." She would say nothing more.

From that moment Lady Gray Eyes became a
kind of subversive citizen. By patient listening
and oblique questioning she began to probe the
minds of others, which led her to suspect that
many women had sickened of the bloody rites
and that a general revulsion against them was
developing among the population. However,
she was not yet daring enough to speak openly,

as noted in a report by the wife of a Cactus general:

> She overtook me one morning as I was drawing water at the well and asked me casually, "How is your son?" and I replied, "He was taken, you know." That was how we phrased it when the priests selected your son. Very quietly she asked: "And do you miss him?" We were forbidden to discuss such matters, but she was the queen and this made me feel free to speak, so I said: "Yes, I do," and tears, which were rigidly forbidden, came to my eyes. And for a moment I wept, but when I looked at her, she was as hard as rock, all of her, hands clenched, teeth gritting together and her remarkable eyes tearless but almost flashing fire, and I knew that she and I thought alike. That accidental meeting was why, when the great test came, I stood with her and handled one of the wooden levers.

The secret opposition launched by Lady Gray Eyes came to a head in 1507. Since that autumn marked the end of a fifty-two-year cycle that coincided with some important date regarding the movement of the sun and the planet Venus, the high priest ordained ceremonies that were especially gruesome. "To ensure the regeneration of the world," he explained, "we must all make unusually difficult sacrifices."

It had long been a belief of the Cactus People that with the culmination of any fifty-two-year cycle the world might end and the sun not rise. Only by extraordinary human sacrifice could the sun be coaxed from darkness and a tradition had developed that when the cycle ended, all human possessions had to be destroyed so that life could begin anew with the rebirth of the world. Accordingly, as the year 1507 drew to a close, there was wholesale destruction of personal belongings; and here Lady Gray Eyes first came into open conflict with her gods. Her father had left her a shield that he had worn in battle against the Guadalajarans, but before he had given it to her he had decorated it with designs drawn by his own hands, and from the age of six she had treasured it. This shield she was determined not to sacrifice, even though she was warned that for a queen to hold back anything of value would especially incense the gods and cause them to terminate the world instantly. When she went to hide the shield in a closet whose door was masked, she found that her mother had already secreted there many objects of sentimental value.

What had led to this initial break with the gods was a series of events so profoundly malignant that Lady Gray Eyes later told the chroniclers: "If I had suffered those cruelties without revulsion and anger I would have been less than human." What happened was that the high priest of the Mother Goddess required for the ceremony of relighting the world a man of exemplary character, a man of vital importance to the kingdom whose sacrifice would mean a grievous loss to the city; only by kindling a sacred fire on his living heart as he lay with his chest cut open would the sun be lured back to embark on its next cycle of fifty-two years.

The man they had chosen was her own kin, the king's learned brother, and when she heard of the decision Lady Gray Eyes cried to her mother: "This is senseless. He's the wisest man in the kingdom. We need him."

"Ssssssh!" the mother warned. "You may think these things, but you must never speak them."

The king's brother was killed, the ritual of fire was completed; and obediently the sun rose again. The priests then launched an orgy of sacrifice to celebrate the rebirth of the world: hundreds were killed, then more hundreds, then thousands until the mind was numb from counting and the air was thick with smoke. In her quarters as Lady Gray Eyes listened with mounting anger to the throbbing drum she was oppressed by the thought that for the past three hundred years there must have been countless women like herself who had hated this abomination of endless sacrifice but had never spoken out because of fear.

The horror did not end with her brother-in-law's murder. A disaffected servant reported to the priests of the Mother Goddess that the queen's mother, the widow of General Tezozomoc, had sequestered personal treasures and not destroyed them to ensure the rebirth of the world. An inspecting party had been immediately dispatched to the royal palace, where the servant led them to the secret closet where they found the hidden items. Among them, of course, was General Tezozomoc's shield, which would have incriminated the queen herself had not her mother stepped forth and calmly said: "The shield was given me by my husband."

She was hauled off to the temple of the Mother Goddess. Even the king was powerless to intervene; and the brave old woman prevented Lady Gray Eyes from confessing that she too was a culprit. I will not describe what the priests did to the old woman, nor how her cries of denunciation, before she was burned, ignited

the first public doubts about the horrible Goddess who ruled City-of-the-Pyramid.

When Lady Gray Eyes looked at the twin-ser-
pent head of the Mother Goddess, obscured by
steam and smoke and smeared with the blood
of her mother, she vowed: "This terror must
stop." The destruction of this appalling goddess
now became an obsession, and during the years
from 1507 to 1518 she made discreet investigations that convinced her that the city was full of
people who were as disgusted and disaffected
as she but could only stand by helplessly. In
later years she said of these days: "So we lived
in a terrible darkness, desperately hoping for the
rediscovery of peace and the rebirth of human
love. But after many years of fearful silence it
became the general opinion that the salvation of
our city would come not from within but from
without—that some act from the outside world
would rescue us—but the likelihood of this
seemed so remote, and a thing so futile to hope
for, that I concluded that salvation must come
from within, and I dedicated myself to the destruction of the terrible goddess."

As the year 1519 dawned with its customary
savage ceremonies, the full power of the Mother
Goddess was brought to bear against Lady Gray
Eyes. One afternoon as she was sitting in her

garden she was approached by a trio of senior priests who were so supercilious in manner that she had an instant premonition of disaster. "Revered Highness," said their leader, "we bring joyous news. Your son—"

"Which one?" she asked, trembling.

"Your second, Ixmiq, named after the builder of our sacred pyramid."

"Yes?"

"He has the honor of having been chosen this year's Perfect Youth."

She did not cry out, for she had been taught from childhood that that was not allowed. Her father and her nurses had preached: "It is the duty of women to bear sons for the glory of the Mother Goddess. Some become warriors in her defense. Some are sacrificed to prove our respect. And each year some mother is honored above all others by having her son chosen as the Perfect Youth."

Biting her lip to prevent herself from shrieking at these miserable men, she sat immobile, her mind in a frenzy, as the priests went to the house, called forth her nineteen-year-old son, Ixmiq, and led him away. He was allowed no farewell words, no last embrace, for priests had learned from past experience that such acts were apt to create exhibitions of weakness unworthy of the Mother Goddess, so the queen was forced to remain sitting there as her radiant son left his home for the last time.

Young Ixmiq was moved into a small sacred palace, where he was daily anointed with oil, bedecked with flowers and cloth of gold, and taught to play the flute. He ate only the most exquisite of foods and was constantly massaged by priests so that no ungainly fat should accumulate on his athletic body. He was encouraged to play games and sing, and at night he was watched by four priests lest he catch cold and diminish his health. His long hair was plaited with flowers, and he was sprinkled with perfume.

For eleven months, Ixmiq led a cloistered existence. He was allowed to see his royal father now and again, but he was not permitted to talk with his mother, for the priests had found in earlier years that such a meeting sometimes unmanned the Perfect Youth and induced melancholy, which had no place in their plans for him; furthermore, Lady Gray Eyes was suspect because her mother had sinned against the Mother Goddess.

On the first day of the twelfth month four of the most beautiful young girls of the city were brought into the sacred palace, where in the presence of Ixmiq they were undressed by a priest, who said simply: "Enjoy them." And from then on the girls were constantly with the Perfect Youth, enticing him to lose himself in sensual pleasures.

This was a cynical move on the part of the priests: they had found that if a young man came to the last days completely debilitated through sexual excess he was more apt to be submissive and not mar the culminating sacred moment of the year by resisting and creating a scene. But for further insurance they introduced into his diet during this last month substantial amounts of mescaline, a narcotic derived from cactus buds, and this ensured both an initial sexual excitement and a subsequent lassitude.

But this year the plans of the priests went awry. There was among the four young girls sent to serve Ixmiq an exquisite child of sixteen named Xóchitl, who was the last to sleep with Ixmiq because she was the youngest. But once he discovered her he loved her so intensely that he wished to have nothing more to do with the others. The priests noticed this with dismay, for experience had taught them that if a Perfect Youth formed any strong attachment for one particular girl among the customary four, he was apt to dread the moment of separation and behave badly at the ceremony that would end his life. After consultation, therefore, the priests decided to whisk Xóchitl away from the palace and to substitute for her a somewhat older girl, but when they did this, Ixmiq refused to leave his quarters, where he remained secluded, pensively playing the flute. When the priests asked why he was being so solitary, he replied: "I am waiting for Xóchitl."

It was apparent that unless the young girl was returned to Ixmiq there was going to be trouble, so the priests brought her back but threatened: "Unless you keep Ixmiq from loving you, when he dies you will be burned alive." But when they thrust the girl back into the room, she ran to Ixmiq and they embraced passionately, and for the last eleven days of the month they stayed together. The other three girls could do nothing, for Ixmiq refused to associate with anyone but Xóchitl, and when the priests tried to drag him away he was sufficiently in control to feign hysteria: "If you take her away I'll scream, and lunge at you and create a great noise at your ceremony." Seething with rage, they were forced to retreat.

When they were gone, Ixmiq laughed at the success of his ruse, and drew Xóchitl to him, saying bravely: "It won't be too painful, little bird. For one month you'll be my wife. Lots of young men marry and either go off to war and death, or are chosen for some important sacrifice. It happens."

"But what of the children we should have? I want to have your children."

"Maybe I'll leave you with a son," he said consolingly. When she drew back and said almost in tears, "I can't pray to a creature like Mother Goddess for aid in becoming pregnant," he could think of no god in the Cactus pantheon to whom a young woman could pray for help.

In the quiet of their luxurious prison they could take consolation only in the fact that he had succeeded in convincing the priests that he loved her, and that she was able to share his last days even if she did so at mortal danger to herself.

On the last day of the year 1519, when Ixmiq was given food that was drugged almost to the point of causing nausea so that his eyes were dull and heavy, he was anointed for the last time and dressed in robes of unusual splendor. Flowers and jewels were woven into his hair and sandals with golden buckles were put on his feet. He clasped Xóchitl to his bosom and whispered: "You are my wife."

He then left the palace and, one of the most handsome young men ever to have performed this rite, he walked in a kind of golden haze through the streets of the city, and as he walked he played occasionally on one or another of his flutes. It was a day of complete beauty, with the sun that lit his face making his jewels shimmer. The king, his father, was proud of his son's regal bearing, but Lady Gray Eyes clenched her fists, barely restraining her grief and anger.

The priests, who were aware through their spies that the queen had been asking dangerous questions but were not yet strong enough to offend the king by attacking her openly, had arranged that she not be present at the final rites lest she call out and distress her son. She was therefore excused from witnessing the final act, and for this she was grateful.

Toward three in the afternoon, when the sun had noticeably declined and birds were beginning to sing before roosting, Ixmiq walked gallantly toward the temple of the Mother Goddess, and now a hush fell over the multitude that followed him. The priests fell away and prayed that their selection would behave himself well. Stepping upon the first stone of the stairway leading to the altar, he turned to face the crowd, raised his hands above his head, and broke one of the flutes. Throwing the pieces gaily over his shoulder, he ascended to the next step, where he broke another flute. At the small terrace that separated the two flights of stairs, he paused to play a brief song, after which he broke the flute he had been using, and in this manner he came to the top of the stairs and to the altar, where he broke his last flute and threw the two parts out to the silent and admiring crowd. He should then have presented himself impassively to the five waiting priests—four to bind him and one to kill—but instead he threw his arms into the air and screamed in agony so that all could hear: "Xóchitl, Xóchitl!" The outraged priests grabbed him and smashed him so hard on the sacrificial disk that his back was broken and his senses were gone even before the knife plunged into his chest.

Thus the year 1520 got off to an ominous start, and rumors of events that could not be understood were blamed on Ixmiq and his misbehavior at the sacrifice. One of Lady Gray Eyes' uncles, the wise man Xaca who served as an ambassador to the Aztecs in the great city to the southeast, returned with staggering news: "A frightening group of men, gods perhaps from another world, white of skin and speaking a strange language, have come to the jungles at the feet of the great volcanoes. They are served by lesser gods that run on four feet and carry the strangers on their backs. And both the men and the lesser gods protect themselves with a heavy cloth that glistens in the sun and cannot be pierced by arrows."

All the priests and wise men in the city were assembled to analyze Ambassador Xaca's report, and after each frightening item had been analyzed and rejected as absurd, the priests' only proposal was that Xaca should be sacrificed to Mother Goddess as a liar and one who did not have her welfare at heart. But others, who struggled to understand the new mysteries, argued: "Let us accept what Xaca has said and try to determine what it means," so the ambassador was spared to repeat what he had been told, but when the priests hammered at him: "Did you see the white-faced men? Did you see the lesser gods with four feet? Did you touch the garment that cannot be pierced?" he had to answer no, and was again discredited and sentenced to death as a deranged menace. Only the courage of the king wrested him from the priests and allowed him to escape back to the safer climate of the Aztec capital, where men now had painful proof that a new force had entered Mexican life.

With the ambassador gone, there was a strong movement to blame Lady Gray Eyes for the dangers that were threatening Mexico, for she had certainly abetted her son in his abysmal behavior. For the moment, the king remained strong enough to protect her as he had his ambassador, but events were unfolding with such speed and mystery that even he had begun to suspect her loyalty to the gods who had made his Cactus People strong.

Most of all, the priests were determined to execute Xóchitl because they believed that the sixteen-year-old girl had bewitched the Perfect Youth and had kept him from performing his duties in proper style. But they could not find her, for on the day Ixmiq was sacrificed Lady Gray Eyes had anticipated the priests' intentions and had secreted her in a cave under the royal palace, where the queen attended her as her pregnancy advanced.

"All this senseless sacrifice must soon end," the queen said. "Xóchitl, the priests may kill you and me, as they seem determined to do, but this evil can't go on much longer." Once she took the girl's hands in hers and asked, "Tell me the truth, before you were sent to my son, did you realize how evil all this was?"

"I knew," Xóchitl said. "My mother told me."

"Oh my child, thank you!" Lady Gray Eyes started to weep and now it was the girl who comforted her.

"When my son is born," Xóchitl promised, "I shall tell him the truth. So far it's been only women telling other women."

At these words Lady Gray Eyes felt new tears well in her eyes and she clasped the young girl

in her arms. "I had forgotten how to weep," the
queen said.

In July, the seventh month of Xóchitl's pregnancy, Lady Gray Eyes came into the cave in
some excitement and carrying a package. "I
must tell you what has happened," she began.
Then abruptly she stopped speaking and began
to kiss Xóchitl. "My beloved daughter," she
whispered, "you are the only one to whom I can
speak. Have a strong child. Have a son as beautiful as his father."

"I know I will," Xóchitl replied.

"This must remain a secret between us,"
Lady Gray Eyes insisted as she unrolled a
length of parchment. "My Uncle Xaca, ambassador to the Aztecs, sent to me secretly a picture of the gods whom the strangers worship,
and here they are!" In the dim light of the cave
the queen and her pregnant daughter-in-law unrolled the parchment and saw a drawing of a
serene mother fondly holding on her knee a boy
of one or two years, and in silence the two
women contemplated the picture for a long time.

Finally Xóchitl asked: "What kind of gods are
they?"

"You can see," Lady Gray Eyes replied. "A
mother whose head is not a serpent. A son
whose hands are not caked with blood."

Again the two women reflected upon the

enormous moral chasm that separated the new gods from the ones they knew. Neither spoke, but years later Lady Gray Eyes reported what happened: "So we sat there in the cave, my pregnant daughter and I, and I thought, For all these years we've been hiding in caves and worshiping hideous gods, while in other parts of the world people could look at the sky and worship human beings like themselves who could weep. But what impressed us most that day was that the mother had a benign smile as if she loved everyone and hated none, and the difference between this kind of god and the ones we had known was so great that later, when we comprehended it more fully, Xóchitl said, 'My son shall be born to these gods,' and it was so."

But after the child's birth—it was a girl whom they named Stranger, as if she had come from nowhere so that she could not be traced back to her condemned mother—Xóchitl sought sunlight and was detected by the priests and captured. For the part she had played in ruining the ultimate celebration of the Perfect Youth, she was sentenced to death, and both the king and his queen were forced to witness her execution. Xóchitl, one of the most memorable of my ancestors, was the first Christian to die for her faith in Mexico and was later sanctified as Santa María of the Cave.

When Xóchitl stood before the Mother Goddess, she thought of the new gods, and when she looked down at Lady Gray Eyes, she knew that she was also thinking of Mary and the infant Christ. But when she turned to face death she saw five priests, their hair matted with blood, their fingernails black with caked blood, their bodies foul with tattoos and more blood. She saw a goddess whose head was a pair of serpents and whose entire being was an abomination. She looked up at the walls of the temple and they were black with smoke and blood, and fear, and death. The only clean thing she saw that day was the obsidian knife, and soon even that would be stained with blood.

With miraculous strength she broke free from the priests and shouted, "The evil god must die! A new god is coming!" She was quickly seized and thrown on the convex slab, and hers was the last human heart on which the most obscene of all Mexican gods ever feasted.

That night, while the priests were in convocation to consider what steps must be taken to protect the city from the heresy that Xóchitl had pronounced, Lady Gray Eyes, wrapped in a gray serape such as peasant women wore, left the palace, and hurried through back streets to the home of the general's wife who had been brave enough to weep openly because her son had been needlessly sacrificed. Slipping in by the back entrance, she signaled the woman to join her in the garden, where they could speak.

"Do you remember that day when we talked of your son, and you wept?"

"Yes, and I wondered why you didn't weep, too."

"I did, but I did it secretly. On many nights I have gone to sleep with tears."

"Why have you come to see me?"

"Because the time has come." For some moments the two women allowed these fateful words to hang in the air, then the general's wife said: "I've waited for you to call me."

"Do you know others we can trust?"

"Many, many."

"Can you bring me two others like yourself?"

"Fifty."

"No. We must rely on only a few trusted women. Find me two more like yourself." When the woman nodded, Gray Eyes added: "And each of us must bring a log—a piece of strong wood. Not so long that it will attract attention, but long enough to do the job."

"What job?"

For a moment Gray Eyes was afraid to utter the fateful words and was silent, but finally she said in cold, measured tones: "The destruction of that despicable goddess."

The general's wife said only: "Four of us, armed with logs. It shall be. But when?"

"If we delay, someone or something will betray us. The deed must be done tomorrow midnight after the last priest makes his rounds."

The general's wife grasped the queen with both hands: "We are committed—to the death," and they parted.

Next night the four conspirators waited nervously at separate hiding places till midnight approached, then one at a time they crept to the top of the pyramid, three of the women carrying heavy logs, Gray Eyes a length of rope. They did not assemble at the top until midnight rituals had been completed, then, when the last priest had departed, they crept to the goddess, and there Gray Eyes took upon herself the terrifying task of climbing that repulsive statue and fastening the rope around her neck. Working her way down, she ran quickly to the free end of the rope and began tugging while her three helpers, using the logs, tried to dislodge the horrible creature from her pedestal.

For a terrifying moment it seemed as if they were not strong enough to topple the Mother Goddess, but when Gray Eyes gave a mighty pull, the monster quivered, and as the three women threw their full weight on the logs, the leverage broke the statue loose and with a resounding crash it fell and broke into fragments. According to plan, the four women sped from the scene the moment the statue appeared certain to crash, and they were far down the steps of the pyramid by the time a dozen priests were surveying the wreckage of their terrible goddess.

Three hundred years after that memorable night a German archaeologist recovered most of the fragments of the Mother Goddess, and the reassembled deity can now be seen in the Palafox museum, as repulsive as she was then.

I now move forward to a happier time, to 1601, when a document particularly precious to those who were born in the old City-of-the-Pyramid was written in the corner room of the House of Tile, the one I now occupied, by the girl who was born in the cave, Stranger, the first Christian child of the high valley:

> After my mother, Xóchitl, was sacrificed to the Mother Goddess the priests suspected that she had left behind a baby and they searched for me in order to kill me, too, but I was well hidden by my grandmother, Lady Gray Eyes, who brought me up. I never con-

sidered her as my grandmother but as my real mother, for she instructed me in all ways.

She was the first of our people to become a baptized Christian, even though she performed the rite herself and assured the Spanish priest who tried to rebaptize her later, "I've already been a Christian for seven years." When he said: "But that's impossible. There were no priests here at that time," she replied, "We won't argue about it." And after the king's death, it was she who kept our people together until they had adjusted to the Spanish ways.

But what I wish to relate today is what my grandmother told me when I was fourteen years old.

To catch the flavor of what my grandmother said that long afternoon when we sat in the garden, you must remember that she spoke in the year 1535, when the Spaniards were in complete command. She was fifty-eight years old and I think she wanted to reassure me that living by the rules of our Cactus People could be just as rewarding as living by those of Spain. She had accepted Christianity joyously, but that did not mean that she approved of all she saw in Spanish behavior. But I will let her speak for herself.

Gray Eyes: You are now fourteen and from the changes in your body it is clear that when you wish you may bear a child. This poses a great problem for girls, for there are many men who are willing to help her have a child, but there are few who are willing to understand the full responsibility of this act. Certainly I would lie to you if I denied that conceiving children is pleasant, and it is a constant temptation to do so, for in this world there are many attractive men.

Stranger: Why is it that in a marriage there is always only one woman and one man?

Gray Eyes: Through many centuries we have found that that's the best way. Choose your man and be faithful to him in all things. Why men do not behave the same way with one woman I will not go into now; possibly it was because in the old days we killed so many of our best men in the temples that there were always surplus women to be taken care of and one man had to share himself with many wives. At any rate, for you there is to be one man, and he is to be your life. I have lived that way and have found it satisfactory.

Stranger: How does a girl learn to choose the right man?

Gray Eyes: I've heard from women who have known many men that they're generally much alike. Certainly I have never seen in men anything that would justify a woman's abandoning her good name and her family for one rather than another. Besides, if you are caught in adultery you will be stoned to death.

Stranger: If they're all alike, then it doesn't matter which one I choose, does it?

Gray Eyes: Now wait! Burn this into your mind. If you're fortunate and make the right choice the relationship between a man and woman can be like the rising of the sun or the love of a mother for her child. My mother told me that when General Tezozomoc returned from battle she could feel the earth tremble while he was still a mile away, so secure and steady was his step. I never once saw my father angry at my mother and she worshiped him so much that she went to her death because she treasured even the things he had touched. Keep that as your definition of love between a woman and a man.

Stranger: You speak as if most people don't find that kind.

Gray Eyes: Your father did. Cherish this memory of how you came to be born. Your father was offered the four most beautiful girls in the kingdom and he preferred your mother above the others, and as I have told you many times, when your mother was taken from him he grew sick and sat by himself and would not speak until she was returned. He chose your mother alone, and in the last moment of his life he called her name because he wanted to affirm his love for her in opposition to what the priests called "an honorable death." Never forget that you were born of such a love.

Stranger: You seem to know men rather well. In your opinion, would that Spanish lieutenant who's been coming to our home—

Gray Eyes: Keep away from that young man. Far away. You're destined for some significant marriage, as great perhaps as my mother's to General Tezozomoc or mine to the king. You're an important young woman, Stranger, destined for an important marriage.

Stranger: I can't imagine myself brave like

you or beautiful like my mother. How will I ever find the kind of man you're describing? What chance have I?

Gray Eyes: You face the problem that all women face. In the days before you're married you must seek and find the kind of man who is capable of the love that has marked your family, and if you find him, cling to him forever, more even than you cling to your family, or your god, or your country. But if you are unfortunate and do not find him, then hold on to whatever you are given, for it is an honorable thing simply to be a good wife. And if you are wise you will never let your husband know whether you are disappointed or not. I myself lived loyally with the king for many years yet I hated his policies, his gods, and even his manner of eating.

Stranger: First you say "Marry an important man," then you say "Marry a man who will love you." How can I do both?

Gray Eyes: That's the problem all young women face. You'll find a way. Good women usually do. But let's stop worrying about who you're going to marry. In due course that will be solved. Your real problem is how you are going to behave when you are married. When you're head of a household there are two things you must attend to. Spend your husband's money wisely and be neat, for I do not know which is worse, a sloppy woman or a spendthrift. Reprimand your husband when necessary, but never nag. And although it may at first seem unfair, you will in the end gain much pleasure by accommodating your wishes to his.

Stranger: But people say you were very strong-minded. I'm told that all the time, as if people expected me to be the same.

Gray Eyes: They speak the truth. I did fight against the cruel god, but in public I always supported my husband, no matter what I said to him at home. And if this task seems odious or impossible, remember that during the last years of my married life, while I fought against the gods in private, I tried to do so in a manner that would not bring shame to the king.

Stranger: I can't imagine myself fighting any battles, or being strong enough to overthrow a war god. Times are different.

Gray Eyes: Child, I'm appalled to hear you say that. It's true that I led the fight against the evil gods, but I was supported by hundreds of ordinary women who didn't need any instruction from me. They'd decided for themselves that the old gods had to go. I could never have done what I did without their support. You fight the battle that confronts you at the time, and invariably there is one that has to be fought. Remember that long before the Spaniards came many of us, leaders and common people, had reached the conclusion that there could be only one God. There can now be no doubt of this, and it is a good thing that our evil gods have been replaced; but never forget that it was not the Spaniards but your own people who destroyed the old gods. Therefore worship the true God with pride, knowing that your people came to Him of their own accord.

Stranger: But the Spaniards refuse to believe that. They say awful things about us.

Gray Eyes: Never allow anyone to ridicule the Cactus People. Fight back. Remind them that we were the one city that the Spaniards did not conquer. We were brave to the end, and if General Tezozomoc had lived I think we could have withstood the Spaniards. As it is, we should be glad they came, for it made our work of destroying the old gods easier. But do not let anyone claim that we were savages, or that we lived like animals, or that we were nothing before the Spaniards came. The cloth you were wrapped in when you were born was woven of rich cotton and silver and quetzal feathers, and it was much finer than any the Spaniards have shown us since.

Stranger: When I listen to them I become so angry that sometimes I hate Spain.

Gray Eyes: You mustn't do that, Stranger. The probability is that it'll be a Spaniard you'll marry.

Stranger: How can you say that? When you just told me to stay away from the lieutenant?

Gray Eyes: Because I think it will be your task to bring the Cactus People and the Spaniards together. And to accomplish that you shall have to marry a Spaniard of some importance, one who is powerful enough to make a difference. But when you do, remember me and make me proud. Carry yourself like a princess. Keep your eyes fixed straight ahead and move regally. Walk like a princess, for you are descended from a great general, a good king, and the fairest young man our city could produce. You were born in wisdom, for it was with her own mind that your grandmother discovered the new God. You are the daughter of a people that was never humiliated.

THE
CRITIC

O N FRIDAY MORNING I was awakened by something that formed the most distasteful part of any assignment overseas. It was a telegram that read:

> Big boss has assured O. J. Haggard of Tulsa that you will get his party tickets to the festival and explain bullfighting. Haggard very big in oil. Good guy. Helped finance our purchase paper mills. Commiserations but this a must. Drummond.

I had barely digested this unwelcome message when the Widow Palafox was banging on
my door with the news that Haggard and his
party had arrived and where could she put
them? I didn't know Haggard but I could be sure
he was a jerk. However, I also knew that if he
were a minor jerk Drummond would have got
him off my neck, so I told the widow, "If these
people don't get rooms, I get fired."

"They're very important?" she asked.

"Sí, muy importantes. How many in the
party?"

"Five. One couple. Man and daughter. One
widow."

"Oh my God," I groaned. "We'll never be able
to find five tickets."

I shaved, climbed into my festival clothes—
baggy white Mexican pants with a rope for a
belt, white shirt, red bandanna—and started apprehensively down to the lobby. When I got
there the Widow Palafox pointed to the big table
out on the terrace at which sat my Tulsa visitors,
five expensively dressed, solid-looking Americans who were now my responsibility. Gritting
my teeth. I went out to meet them and was
pleasantly surprised by the urbane manner in
which O. J. Haggard, a sixty-year-old suntanned
oilman, did his best to put me at ease.

"You're Clay, I'm sure," he said with abundant charm. His white teeth gleamed and he pressed my elbow. "Let's get one thing straight. We're imposing on you and I know it. But we did want to see the fights and your—" He was going to say "your boss," but he was delicate: "and your office said they'd ask you to help."

"My—" I also paused. "My office doesn't know how tough it is to get tickets."

Mr. Haggard led me to one side and whispered, "Look, Clay, these characters are loaded. Do them good to spend some of it. You get the tickets, no matter the cost, and add a healthy commission for yourself. I mean it when I say I'm embarrassed about barging in this way. Now let me introduce my friends," he said more loudly. "This is my wife, Helen Haggard. This is my disreputable redneck partner, Ed Grim, and his pretty daughter, Penny. With no wife, Ed has to serve as both parents. And this is the queen of our gang, Mrs. Elsie Evans. When her husband was alive he was the rainmaker for our team. We miss him."

I was beginning to like the oilman, so I said frankly, "With enough money we can get tickets, but rooms—"

"Son!" he cried expansively, although I was a man over fifty, "you're talking to a gang of dirty-neck Oklahoma oil people. You think characters like us worry about beds? We're used to sleeping on rigging platforms. And our wives are just as tough. Half of them never wore shoes till they were sixteen. They'll sleep where I tell 'em to sleep. But, seriously, could you square us away on this bullfight business?"

"I can explain some of it," I said gingerly.

"The big boss told me you used to live in Mexico," Haggard probed.

"Until I went to Lawrenceville."

"Hey, gang!" Haggard said. "Clay here says he can explain bullfighting."

"Hooray for the bull!" redneck Grim shouted, whereupon his daughter said rather bluntly: "Daddy, don't make a fool of yourself."

The authority with which she said this and the way in which her father accepted her rebuke made me pay closer attention to this young heiress from Tulsa. First of all, she had a wealth of red hair, not the fire-engine red of which my roommate at college once said: "I wouldn't allow hair like that to be near an open can of gasoline." Hers was more like what my wife used to call burnt orange, real red but with a touch of amber. She wore it with a line of bangs straight across her forehead, the rest pulled back, with a darker red ribbon disciplining a ponytail in back. She was about five feet six, slim, attractively formed and dressed, and with a puckish smile that seemed to proclaim: "I don't take myself too seriously."

In my reporting I had always had difficulty describing females. If they were under sixteen they were girls, if older than eighteen, young women. In my four days with Penny Grim I found that she followed the same categories. When talking of frivolous subjects that might interest high school kids she referred to herself and her friends as girls, but if the topic contained even a shred of mature substance, she became in her own words a young woman. She had come to participate in a gaudy Mexican festival, hoping no doubt to encounter experiences that would justify the long trip south. I wished the redhead well, but I did not want to teach either her or her elders the mysteries of bullfighting.

From dismal experience I had learned what every other American stationed in Mexico learns: that yokels from the home office don't really want to know anything serious about bullfighting and that a man can waste a lot of time and money proving it. But at that moment I saw coming at us from across the plaza a man who once seen could never be forgotten, the one in all Mexico who could best explain the aesthetic, historical and moral significance of the bullfight.

"Here comes our expert!" I cried with enthusiasm, for the newcomer could relieve me of the onerous task of trying to explain and defend what we would be seeing the next three afternoons. He was a huge man, taller than most Mexicans and much more rotund. Indeed, his enormous girth caused him to waddle from side to side like a duck, but it was his costume that riveted attention. Even on this relatively warm day he wore a large, flowing black cape that came down to his ankles. On his head was an expensive caballero's broad-rimmed hat, also black. When he was a few feet from the steps leading to the terrace he spotted me and cried: "Señor Clay! You've come down from New York to lie about us again. Greetings, and watch your step."

With that he bounded up the three steps with surprising agility, took me in his bearlike arms and embraced me. Then he saw the Widow Palafox, and with another leap grabbed her in his arms, crying in his penetrating voice: "Still poisoning the public, you Borgia?" Then, facing us all, he said with no hint of jollity: "It would not be Ixmiq if one could not sit on this terrace and catch a breath of old Mexico. Widow Palafox, allow them to change nothing."

Breaking in to make introductions, I said to my table: "We're unbelievably lucky. This is León Ledesma, born in Spain, thrown out by the Fascists, now a citizen of Mexico and our foremost bullfight critic. He has arrived just in time to answer your questions." Reaching for a chair, I invited him to sit at our table, and he took his place between Mrs. Evans and Penny Grim, saying as he did so, "I may be a big hulk, but I'm not stupid," and to the delight of the two women, he kissed their wrists.

'I've known Señor Ledesma, during my various writing stints in Mexico, for many years. He's younger than me, but he's taught me much of what I know about bullfighting. Maestro, let us have your classic spiel about the eighteen bulls in a typical three-day festival."

"That's as good an introduction as anyone could make to our national art form. Yes, bullfighting is not a sport. It's an art, ancient, unique and difficult to comprehend. During the next three days you'll have the rare opportunity, for such festivals don't happen too often, of seeing eighteen bulls in action."

He smiled at the Oklahomans and ticked off on his fat fingers: "You'll have Friday, Saturday, Sunday, three fights, six bulls each day, eighteen in all. Forget the matadors and the picadors and the peóns."

"But I came to see the matadors," Penny said, twisting her head to look at him. "Now you tell me to forget them."

"I guess that's the real reason we came," her father said. "She badgered me. Said she'd seen all the American football players she needed. She was a cheerleader in high school, you know, one of the best baton twirlers in the state. Finished second in the big competition. Told me that now she wanted to see the real thing, a matador."

"Properly so," Ledesma said. "But for now the important thing is the bull. Focus on him and you'll penetrate the secret of the fight."

"Where did you learn such excellent English?" Mr. Haggard asked, and Ledesma said offhandedly: "Also French, German and Italian. When you're a fugitive from your homeland, you know you must learn the languages of your future countries."

"Are these special bulls?" Mrs. Haggard asked.

"Yes," Ledesma snapped, growing somewhat impatient at these interruptions of a set speech he had been using for years. "Now the way to attend a bullfight is this. Admit before you go that you're not going to enjoy a single thing you see. Of your eighteen bulls, three are bound to be complete catastrophes. They will be mean, uncontrollable and cowardly. You have no idea how horrible their deaths will be. The matador will be scared green and he will stand way over here like this. . . ." Nimbly, Ledesma leaped to his feet and grabbed a butter knife. Burlesquing a matador with a bad bull, he stabbed futilely at the imaginary animal. "Once, twice, nine times, ten times. You count. The poor matador will try to kill that damned animal until the beast looks like a pincushion. You, madam, will get very sick and you will want to vomit. You, madam, will vomit. It will be horrible, disgraceful, without a single bit of art or beauty."

"Does this always happen?" Haggard asked.

"Always. Inevitably, some bulls are bad," Ledesma replied with finality. "The only way to avoid such catastrophes is to stay home."

He returned to his seat. "So three of the eighteen will be total catastrophes, and anything bad you want to say about bullfighting will be justified. It will be worse than disgraceful. It will be revolting. The next six bulls won't be much better. They'll refuse to fight. They'll hook to one side or the other. They won't run true and they won't show much action of any kind. The matadors will sweat and curse and try all manner of tricks. But to no avail. These six fights will be so dull that you, sir, will say, "Let's get the hell out of here!" And if I happen to overhear, I may join you, because you've never seen anything more dull than these six bad fights will be. If you were allowed to carry a gun I would not blame you if you tried to shoot the matador. He will deserve it."

He laughed and ordered a bottle of beer. "We've now seen half the bulls and not one has been worth watching. The next six will be what they call regular, more or less acceptable. (In Spanish, regu*lahr*.) That is, they'll be cowardly and inept, but from time to time they will charge with terrifying force, so each bull will cause one or two incidents that may please you. But since each will also cause a hundred incidents that are downright boring, I can't promise you much excitement. The horses won't be in the right places, the banderillas won't go in properly. And on each of these so-called regular bulls the matadors will mess up the first two or three attempts to kill. Frankly, you're going to find these fights rather tedious and I wouldn't blame you if you all leave after the second. I'm warning you that bullfighting can be very miserable indeed.

"That leaves three bulls—on the average one for each afternoon, but they could all appear on one program, say this afternoon. Now they won't be great bulls, but they might be good. And here's the tragedy. By the time these reasonably good bulls appear, the matadors will have been so unnerved by the bad ones that in all probability they'll accomplish nothing. Properly handled, these good bulls would charge, but the matadors will not be able to make them do it. The bulls will also be capable of dying bravely, but the men will no longer be brave. We have an old saying in this business that is lamentably true: 'When there are bulls there are no men, and when there are men there are no bulls.' And that's the way it will be." He threw his hands on the table palms down.

"You don't paint a very exciting prospect," Haggard said with some interest.

"In the eighteen bulls," Ledesma warned, "there will occur perhaps three details that could honestly be called thrilling. But they'll happen so fast, and so unexpectedly, that you won't really understand what it was you saw. There will be a blur, a moment of exquisite suspense, and then the blur again. You'll probably miss it."

O. J. Haggard was apparently not satisfied with this answer. "If that's true, Señor Ledesma, why do people bother to go?"

Ledesma thought for a moment, put his fat hands together, and stared directly at the Oklahoman, "Because, Señor Visitor, out of two hundred bulls there will ultimately come one that shows extraordinary bravery. And on that day the old parable will not apply, for there will be a bull and there will also be a man. And for twelve minutes out there on the sand you will see something that occurs nowhere else on this earth, the perfect duel between life and death. You will see sunlight sculptured by a flaming cape. You will see stark power ripping at a defended horse. You will see men on their toes daintily throwing their lives upon the horns, and at the end you will watch a man with a frail piece of cloth play a bull to death. People will scream with insanity from the tension. Horses far from the scene will neigh, and when it is all over you will sit limp as death yourself."

The fat critic relaxed his hands and sat silent. No one spoke, so he added quietly, "Of course, this happens only once in every two hundred bulls, or three hundred, or perhaps a thousand. When it does, all Mexico remembers the name of that bull and it's inscribed on plaques and written down in books. We won't see such a bull in Toledo. Chances are all against it. But if you ever do see such a bull, my dear visitors, you will realize that this is the most profound experience a man can have, except for his first success with love." He said laughingly, "That's what keeps us coming back to the bullrings. We know that the six bulls for today will be bad, but we hope against hope that tomorrow one will be good. Now I must wash."

"Señor Ledesma!" Mrs. Evans interrupted. "We're about to visit the pyramid. Won't you please join us."

"I really can't," the critic apologized. "Long trip."

"We'll wait till you wash up," Mrs. Evans insisted, placing her hand on the fat man's arm. "You speak so eloquently."

I was glad that she said this, for I was never with Ledesma when I didn't learn something. He was a clown but he was also an Aristotle. The woman's obvious goodwill charmed him and he said: "All right! Let me wash my face, and you, madam, shall ride to the pyramids with me in that red Mercedes over there. These peasants can ride in their Cadillacs." In a few minutes he was back with us, and we started for the ancient center of the Altomecs.

When we reassembled before the pyramid, Ledesma said, "I have never had any desire to be a guide, for you spend your life showing people things they don't want to see, but whether a man wants to or not, he ought to see this pyramid."

"Did they hold human sacrifices here?" Grim asked, and Ledesma explained how every fifty-two years, when the Cactus People feared the world might be coming to end, they conducted a cruel number of human sacrifices to lure the sun back.

"What do you mean by 'cruel number'?" Grim asked, and Ledesma snapped; "In the thousands. But even in normal years they killed regularly, to keep their people frightened of their power."

"Could we climb up and see where it happened?" Mrs. Evans asked, and he replied, "Years ago I grew too fat to climb this pile of rocks, but if any of you want to imagine that you're human sacrifices trying to lure the sun back on the fifty-second year, go ahead. I'll wait here and be the priest that catches your bodies as the boys topside roll them down."

Mrs. Evans said, "I'm going. Anyone else?" Four of us finally climbed to the top and the first thing I did was point eastward to the gaunt smokestacks and say, "That's the Mineral, where I grew up."

We surveyed the countryside and Mr. Haggard asked, "Is that shimmering white thing over there the cathedral?" I looked toward Toledo and saw the resplendent church.

"That's it."

"Where's the bullring?"

"Behind the cathedral," I explained. "Can't seem to see it from here."

"But it's in that area?" Haggard asked. "I always orient myself to the topography," he explained. "These old Indians certainly picked themselves a site, didn't they?" He turned around several times, admiring the valley that the pyramid commanded, but constantly his eyes were drawn back to that distant white façade. "Come to think of it," he added, "those Catholics didn't do so bad, either, did they?"

But my eyes were on the Mineral, set empty and forlorn against the hills that it had robbed of such stupendous treasure. I could see the Indians toiling up the deep hole in the earth, each lugging his burden of ore, and I could imagine the secret cave where we had hidden the prize bull and my room in which we had saved the life of Father López. My mother and father had been an important part of that old mine and I was proud of their contribution.

While I was describing the Mineral to the men, Mrs. Evans had discovered the frieze of eagle warriors and, calling me over, said: "There's something about these figures, half-man, half-eagle, that seems the perfect exemplification of force, predatory and fearful."

I told her: "I remember the first time I saw them. I said to Father, 'But they don't have beards!' and he asked, 'Why should they wear beards?' and I explained, 'In my books the bad men always have beards,' and he told me that these eagle warriors were neither bad nor good, just soldiers with the characteristics of eagles."

When Mr. Grim joined us he took one look at the eagles and said: "I want to get down. This

place specializes in cruelty. Too scary." He
jumped from the top platform to the first step
and his weight dislodged a heavy stone, which
went careening down the face of the pyramid.
"My God!" Mrs. Evans screamed. "Do be careful!" and from below came the calm, even voice
of Ledesma: "I don't care if you kill yourself up
there, but don't kill us down here."

When we joined him at the foot of the steps
he astounded me by taking both my hands and
saying apologetically, "You must excuse me,
Norman, but now I have to speak poorly of your
sainted father, for almost every glib conclusion
he reached in his famous book *The Pyramid and
the Cathedral* was wrong."

Mrs. Evans spoke for me. "The librarian in
Tulsa told us, when she heard we were coming
here for the festival, that we had to read that
book. We did, all of us, I think." She looked at
Penny, who said eagerly, "Yes, I read it. A super
book. It was so neat in explaining things."

"What did it say that impressed me so
much?" Mrs. Evans asked. "That this pyramid,
big and brutal, symbolized the Indian heritage of
Mexico? That the cathedral down there, so
heavenly beautiful in its façade, represented the
lyrical grace of the Spanish inheritance?" We all
agreed, especially me, for that had been Father's thesis, but I have to insist that he did not

take sides—he claimed not that one was better than the other, but just that they were fundamentally different. Ledesma took me by the arm and led me along a path that led westward from the bottom of the steps we had just descended, and as we walked he said: "Forgive me for what I just said about your father. No fault of his. When he wrote he couldn't have known that what we're about to see existed, deep down under this pile of rubble." And he led us to another triumph of pre-Columbian Mexican art.

"About ten years ago, long after Norman's father had written his book and left Mexico, archaeologists excavated at this site along the base of the pyramid a mound that had for some years tantalized their imaginations, and look what they uncovered!"

He showed us a miracle, a terrace some hundred and fifty yards long and twenty wide, its surface composed of delicately tinted red paving blocks laid down in gently swaying patterns that led the eye toward the distant hills that rim the plateau. Along three of its sides run benches, built of a darker red stone and providing a resting area for several hundred people. But the wonder of the terrace, and the feature from which it takes its name, is the procession of bas-relief jaguars that march above the backs of the benches. In all there are a hundred and nineteen animals, each about three feet long and each completely different from its companions. Some of the jaguars are laughing, some are snarling, some scratch themselves, one feeds her young, and others chase deer. But there they are, a hundred and nineteen beasts, the joy of the jungle, the soft counterpoint to the eagle-studded pyramid.

"We call this the Terrace of the Jaguars," Ledesma said reverently. "How exquisite it is, how lyrical, how soft and gentle. How did these beasts get here? In Mexico they live only inland of the ocean shore. What are they doing on this terrace in Toledo? They were brought here, I think, not as living animals but as ideas in the imagination of artists whom the Altomecs, the Cactus People as they are called, captured during raids in the vicinity of Veracruz or maybe even distant Yucatán. And here, in stone, they were brought to life, a procession of the most beautiful animals ever carved in Mexico."

After we had had a chance to study the animals, each almost springing to life, he continued: "These supple jaguars, hiding at the very foot of the pyramid, deny every generalization made by John Clay. He said this was a cruel place, but the jaguars are depicted as gentle. He said this was a haunt of eagles, but the jaguars bring us down to earth. He pointed out that the hill of the pyramid was lonely and treeless and forsaken, but our jaguars live on in their lush jungle. He said he could find in the pyramid only harshness. Yet all the while, under his very feet as he wrote, existed this superb Terrace of the Jaguars, which represents all the virtues whose absence he mourned.

"I have no way of knowing, but I like to think that this terrace was erected so that after the grisly ceremonies of the pyramid were completed, the kings and the townspeople and even the weary, bloodstained priests could congregate here in the late afternoon to watch the sun, whose rising had been so cruel and punctuated with the screams of those sacrificed, sink among the western mountains. I'm sure that here musicians played, and women danced, and men recited epics of the race. Much of what John Clay told us about the pyramid is wrong, for he spoke only of its brutal force. The poetry that existed beside it, and which must always exist if men are to survive, was momentarily hidden from his view."

Since he had spoken harshly of my father's book, I wanted him to know that I bore no grudge, for he was right. If Father had known of the jaguars, he'd have said everything Ledesma had just pointed out. So I was about to speak when Mrs. Evans said: "Señor Ledesma, leaning back in that corner among your jaguars, you do indeed look like an Altomec priest."

"Nothing sweeter will be said to me this day," he replied graciously, "but frankly I have always judged myself better fitted for managing the tribe's finances than conducting the religious sacrifices. You will find me here daily, counting the bags of silver."

He relaxed as priests must have done long ago and Haggard resumed a conversation that had been under way while we were atop the pyramid: "So what can we expect of today's matadors?"

"Nothing. Today will be very bad," Ledesma replied.

"Why?" Haggard pressed.

Ledesma reached over and rapped the oilman on the knuckles. "You haven't learned your lesson. Don't start with the matadors. Always start with the bulls."

"But I like the matadors," Penny broke in. "That's why we came. Or at least I did."

"And so you should, at your age, Señorita Penny, but your father's a grown man. He should know better."

"What do we know about the bulls?" Haggard asked.

"This is a very expensive festival," Ledesma explained. "And with all the money going to the matadors, the bulls for the first two fights are the cheapest you can get. Those for tomorrow are horrible, and those for today pretty bad. They save the expensive Palafox bulls for last so that we can go home with a good taste in our mouths."

"Now can we get to the matadors?"

"All right. Now then—Victoriano, goaded by the pressures from Gómez, will try to show off, but he will be nervous and incapable of doing much. Gómez will as usual be very brave, but with these bulls he will accomplish little."

"How about the third man?"

"Paquito de Monterrey? Nothing. Nothing."

"Then why is he fighting at such an important fair?"

"Because, like the bulls, he comes cheap, and that's the honest fact."

As I relaxed below the jaguars and looked out across the sleeping valley whose riches had attracted the ancient Altomecs, I listened to Ledesma's cynical comments about bullfighting and modern Mexico and reflected on the things he had told me on my previous visits to Mexico, when we had knocked around in bullfight circles. He had been born forty-four years ago in Valencia, the seaport east of Madrid, and as a boy had wanted to be a bullfighter. Lacking physical grace, he had become a critic, and was now Mexico's best, primarily because he had failed so completely as a torero; now, whenever he judged a matador, it was with a coldness of heart, for he muttered to himself: "All right, matador, prove you're as brave as I was."

As a boy torero León had been both skillful and unusually brave. Unfortunately, he had also been fat, and this the Spanish public would not tolerate. In the old days there had been half a dozen toreros named Gordito—the little fat guy—and one had been the premier fighter of his age, but just as older musical audiences had tolerated obese sopranos like Tetrazzini whereas modern audiences would not, so the more sophisticated aficionados of Ledesma's day refused to accept any fat boy as a serious matador, and Ledesma's lasting memory of his adventures in the ring were the echoes of a laughter that still haunted him. The debacle had occurred in a rural village near Valencia called Burriana, whose name for no known reason was thought to be comical in itself. There he had gone at the age of eighteen to help kill a set of vicious old animals that had often been fought before.

Now as we stood with the Americans on the beautiful terrace I asked: "Could you tell us about that day in Burriana?" and he shrugged, saying somewhat bitterly, "If you have a taste for tragedy, I have one for comedy." When he started his account it was obvious that he took a perverse delight in the recitation of his woes.

"Those bulls of Burriana had developed into wily adversaries, and the two would-be matadors who were fighting with me—they later became moderately well known—showed themselves to be scared to death of the treacherous beasts. Not me. Biting my lip I swore, 'I will not run from my bull.' So I was foolishly brave, committing myself to acts of heroism quite beyond what my two wiser companions would dare, and for a few delicious moments there in Burriana I knew what it felt like to be a true torero, for I was discovering that although I was afraid of death, I was even more afraid of behaving dishonorably. Also, I hoped that after the disgraceful performances of my companions, I would be applauded so loudly that reports of my triumph would get into the Valencia papers and no doubt into those of Madrid, as well, and my career would be launched.

"But when I attempted a heroic pass that should have been used only with an honest bull, my tricky animal turned swiftly, bumped me with his forehead, and rolled me in the sand unhurt. The crowd began to laugh. At first I did not hear the laughter, for I was experiencing the instinctive fear that overwhelms a matador when he has been tossed. I rose, faced the dangerous animal again, and attempted another pass. Again the bull tossed me, rolling me over and over in the sand like a ball of butter. The audience howled. This time I heard the laughter the minute it began, and swore: 'I'll show them how a Valenciano fights.' And with real bravery I attacked the bull, but the hilarity had reached a point at which even the other aspirants along the barrier had to join in.

"Goaded and gored, I finally addressed myself to the death of the bull and managed a beautiful kill, one that ought to have earned me a standing ovation. Instead it brought a hearty wave of laughter. It wasn't derisive laughter, it was encouraging, cheerful and sympathetic laughter, but for the last twenty-six years it would echo back and forth in my brain. I'd been braver than others that day, but for my courage I'd been awarded not praise but laughter."

However, an even greater indignity awaited him in Valencia, and I wondered if he had the courage to reveal it to the Americans, but he was in a talkative mood and when I asked: "Would you care to tell them about what happened in Valencia?" he laughed: "He's only doing this because I spoke unkindly of his father. However"—here he swept his right hand as if about to salaam—"two nights after the di-

saster in Burriana I was visited at home by the
manager of a troupe of bullfighters who had
become popular in central Spain, the Charlots of
Valencia. The clowns and this man said frankly:
'León, we've been looking everywhere for a fat
boy who is brave and funny. I didn't see you at
Burriana, but my friends did and they say you
were hilarious.' He paused dramatically, and it
was obvious he was offering me a job.

" 'I've seen your comic bullfighters,' I said.
'Some of your men are very brave—' "

"The manager grew expansive and said:
'Frankly, León, as a comedian you'll make a lot
more money than most of the serious fighters.
For one thing, there isn't so much competition,
and for another, when the bull does hit you he's
a lot smaller and doesn't do so much damage.' "

" 'But I hadn't intended becoming a comic
bullfighter,' " I said.

"The manager drew back in some surprise.
'You mean that with your build you expected—'
His dark face broke into a smile. 'León!' he
remonstrated in a friendly way. 'Surely you
never thought that the public . . .'

"I did not allow the tears to come into my
eyes, but with difficulty I kept myself from betraying my anger. 'I think you had better go,' I
said. And as the manager disappeared down the
dark Valencia street his laughter was added to

that of the men from Burriana, and with it died any dreams I had of being the new phenomenon."

It was odd that Ledesma had even attempted to become a bullfighter, because, as he had told me, he was good at books, and toreros customarily do not have that ability. When his aspirations in bullfighting were drowned in laughter, he diverted his energies to education, with the well-formulated idea of becoming a bullfight critic. He learned French and English, philosophy and history. He had a keen inclination toward art criticism, which permitted him to fit the aesthetic of bullfighting into the larger aesthetic that encompassed Velázquez and Goya. He was especially well informed on the ballet and its accompanying music and sometimes felt that with a little luck and a very different body he might have become an excellent dancer.

As a potential bullfight critic he had one prohibitive weakness, insofar as the art was practiced in Spain: he was Republican, whereas almost everyone else connected with the art was Fascist, and in the Civil War that convulsed Spain and that murdered not only his Republican father but also León's idol, García Lorca, he fought on the side of the Loyalists as bravely as he had in the bullring of Burriana. When the war became obviously hopeless, he had escaped to

France, where his language skill enabled him to pass for some months as a Frenchman, and then on to Mexico, where he found a congenial home. There, in 1938, he published a book of poems in which he bade farewell to Spain and announced himself a permanent Mexican citizen. His poems were graciously received, but what caught the attention of the public was a short work he had added at the last moment. He called it "Lament for García Lorca," and this rang a bell with the public, for that famous poet had made bullfight history by writing early in his career "Lament for Ignacio Sánchez Mejías," a charismatic torero killed in the ring. Lorca's poem began "A las cinco de la tarde" (at five in the afternoon), and if you recited those six words in the hearing of an aficionado, he might well quote the next eight or ten lines of the famous poem. Anyway, Ledesma's happy invention projected him into the world of bullfight journalism and shortly thereafter he became second-string critic for a leading paper and subsequently the country's major critic, his reputation evolving from his style and courage. Literate Mexicans grew to love his long, sometimes apparently diffuse essays on the art, for no matter how much he seemed to digress, he always made some shrewd point. In reading him one came to know Seneca, Unamuno, García Lorca,

Ortega y Gasset and the music of de Falla,
Granados, Turina and Albéniz, and his refer-
ences to these giants carried Mexicans close to
the heart of Spain. But Ledesma did not stop
there. His citations were just as apt to be drawn
from Goethe, Shakespeare, Hugo, Tolstoy and
Montaigne. At first he rarely cited American writers, for during the years of his education in Valencia none were known in Spain, but in recent
years he often referred to the fact that when
Ernest Hemingway received the Nobel Prize he
had had the decency to tell Pío Baroja that the
prize was really Baroja's. "In this old man, Spain
had an immortal genius," Ledesma often
pointed out, "and we ignored him as if he were
a filthy dog. It's to our shame that we left it to an
American to publish the old man's greatness."
Later, when Ledesma bullied a Mexican pub-
lisher into bringing out a selection of Baroja's
novels, the people of Mexico saw that Baroja
was truly worth the fuss that Ledesma had been
making.

The critic's courage was proverbial. He was
willing to say anything, no matter how outrageous, in print and then to defend it with his fists
if necessary. In his forties he took to carrying a
cane, with which he lashed out at anyone who
tried to assault him for his views. His code was
simple: matadors get paid well for fighting bulls,

so let them show some courage as well as skill. In identifying rascals he was remorseless, and some of his better essays concerned the chicanery of the bullring; but in his willingness to praise young men who had not yet established firm reputations he was also courageous. And so the fat boy had become, by force of wisdom and courage, a major voice in Mexican bullfighting, and a man whom I admired and whose friendship I treasured.

Just as he had been attracted as a boy to the impossible, bullfighting, so as a man he was drawn to an equal impossibility—he was always falling in love with the most petite and fragile-looking actress in Mexico and saw nothing incongruous in the disparity in size between him and his lady love. Any Hollywood actress who weighed less than one hundred and ten pounds was sure, upon her arrival in Mexico City, to be visited by an amorous León Ledesma. Usually he terrified the girls until he began to talk, and then his scintillating jokes, often directed at himself, had a good chance of winning them over. A bachelor, he kept a modern apartment on the Reforma decorated with a Goya etching of a bullfight and a Picasso drawing of mountebanks. Each afternoon he took a cab down into the heart of the city, where he ensconced himself in the famous café Tupinamba, at a table not far from that occupied by the manager Cigarro.

It was the Tupinamba part of Ledesma's life that cast an ugly shadow upon his character, for in his actions in the café he was not a likable man. But he was honest about his behavior. In the afternoons when he planted himself at his favorite table it was customary for people connected with bullfighting to stop by and pay homage to the emperor. A tradition had grown up, now observed with the iron force of custom, that Ledesma was never to pay for anything. He made a decent salary, if you counted his radio and television contracts, but even the poorest aspirant knew that it was he, and not Ledesma, who had to pay for the hot chocolate and the sandwiches.

This, of course, was petty graft, which the bullfight industry willingly paid in hopes of winning favorable comment from Ledesma. But the additional tribute this powerful man exacted was not petty, and after the minor actors of the day had paid for his drinks and had disappeared, the major ones came on. I once saw old Veneno himself, when his son Victoriano was already at the height of his fame, sidle up to the imperial table, sit down and ask bluntly, "How much do you want this week, León, for a strong article in favor of my son?"

"How much will he be getting at Plaza México?" Ledesma countered.

"Four thousand, five hundred dollars," Veneno replied honestly, for he could be sure that Ledesma would have the accurate figures.

"Under those circumstances, four hundred and fifty dollars would be about right," Ledesma replied. The money was paid, and next Monday morning Ledesma's column carried a poetic review in which Victoriano was compared to Michelangelo.

Almost no one could hope to make his way in the bullfight world without paying tribute to this influential critic. From leading matadors he took as much as 10 percent of their earnings for especially fine essays. From a beginner, who could scarcely pay for his rented suit, he would content himself with a few dollars, but they had to be paid. If any aspirant dared ignore Ledesma, the latter poured scorn upon him and sometimes hounded him out of Mexico City. Even established matadors felt the fury of his pen if they thoughtlessly failed to pay him the tribute he felt himself entitled to.

His salary from the newspaper was two thousand dollars a year. In outright graft paid down for favorable notices, he earned upward of twenty-five thousand. He took from the bullfight racket not only his chocolate at the Tupinamba and hard cash, but also most of his meals, his Mercedes-Benz, many of his hand-tailored suits, his shirts, his shoes, and even flowers for his hundred-pound actresses. Almost every month he praised the stoic Seneca, yet in the same week he lived like the Roman sybarite Seneca. In fact, in Mexico City the Spanish critic Ledesma accepted just about the same amount of graft that in imperial Rome the Spanish politician Seneca had taken, which was probably why Ledesma considered Seneca the greatest Spaniard who had ever lived.

Still, I would never claim that Ledesma was corrupt. Some years ago he told me, as we sat in the Tupinamba, with me paying for his chocolate, "In bullfighting there is no score. The uninitiated cannot possibly tell who won. Of the fifty-five thousand people who will see the fight tomorrow, not fifty will know what they actually saw until they read the paper and satisfy themselves as to what I say they saw. I am the mind of bullfighting, the eyes, and the conscience."

"The conscience?" I asked sarcastically.

"Yes, the conscience," he repeated. "Don't allow the fact that you have just seen Veneno pay me nearly five hundred dollars for a good report on his son to obscure your judgment. If his son proves to be very bad tomorrow I won't say that he was perfect. I'll just refrain from saying he was stinking." He sipped his Spanish chocolate, a bitter, dark drink, and continued. "Everyone who reads the paper knows that I get paid large sums for my opinions, but they also know that fundamentally I tell the truth. I allow no man to buy my vision of the truth. What they buy is my exuberance, and if they pay, I deliver."

I thought of those remarkable statements as I studied Ledesma now, lounging there among the poetic jaguars, and I was about to pass unfavorable judgment on him when a surprising thing happened. To the Terrace of the Jaguars came two waiters from the House of Tile riding a three-wheeled motorcycle, towing behind them a small cart, from which they produced a folding table, a cloth, napkins, knives, forks and spoons, and a delicious picnic that he had ordered from the Widow Palafox and paid for with his own funds.

"For my friends from Tulsa. When I visit you there I shall expect much more expensive treatment," and he ordered "Dos Equis for everyone."

"What's that?" Ed Grim asked and the critic explained: "Best beer in the world. In English Two Exes from the trademark XX." As we enjoyed our pre-fight luncheon I felt that Ledesma should clarify the curious relationship that existed among the three principals in today's fight:

Victoriano the Spaniard, Gómez the Indian and León Ledesma, who had practically engineered the series of mano a manos that had been conducted throughout Mexico.

"León," I asked, "why did you spend so much effort initiating this series? You get no salary from the impresarios, not directly, that is."

"I love bullfighting. I cherish seeing two good matadors with different styles duel with each other."

"But the real reason," I goaded.

"He knows damned well the real reason," he said to the Oklahomans. "Because I love the way Victoriano conducts himself. And I despise Juan Gómez."

"Do you want to tell us why you hate Gómez?"

"I don't want to, but the seven of us may never be together again, and if I do tell, it'll be a story you'll take home with you as almost the soul of Mexico—certainly the soul of Mexican bullfighting."

"Please share it with us," Mrs. Evans begged. He took a lingering drink of his Dos Equis, wiped his lips and told us: "I think everyone connected with bullfighting hopes that one day he will see a lad of thirteen or fourteen who has all the movements of a natural-born matador. All of us. I'm told that in the United States there are men like me who dream of finding in the ghetto a black boy who has the skills to become a great basketball player. Don't your men adopt that boy, give him every opportunity, and don't you even arrange for the boy to get free education at a university?"

Mr. Haggard laughed and pointed at Ed Grim: "He's paying the costs of two boys like that at Oklahoma State right now."

"Then you'll understand what I thought when I say that one day in a fish market I saw this perfect boy, Ignacio Molina, fourteen years old, with a small cloth in his hands giving passes to another boy playing the bull. He was a dream— arched back, marvelous profile, head of black hair, hands that wove magic and, most important of all, no fat bottom."

"Any parents?" Mrs. Haggard asked, and Ledesma said, "I suppose so, but they never mattered."

"And you took him under your control?" she asked.

"Understand, there aren't many would-be matadors a critic in my position would care to risk his reputation on. Nacho, that's what they called him, was the one."

"Tell them what happened in Torreón," I said, mentioning the city in northern Mexico.

For almost a minute Ledesma sat staring at

his thumbs, there against the perfect jaguars. Finally he began to talk about that disastrous Sunday afternoon *a las cinco de la tarde:* "My boy Nacho was head of the cartel. Boy from Saltillo fighting second, no talent whatever. And a nothing Altomec Indian boy, Juan Gómez, as the junior. All the boys seventeen or eighteen. All in the years when they had to prove themselves or quit."

"Let me get it straight," Ed Grim said. "These are not the matadors we'll be seeing today and the next two afternoons?"

"You'll see Juan Gómez. Neither of the others."

"So what happened?"

"Painful to relate. When we're all in the waiting area before the opening parade, I try to organize the fight to protect Nacho. I give instructions, who's to do what, how the expert peóns I've hired are to see he doesn't get into trouble. Then the devil must have warned me that I had a potential enemy in Gómez, because I warned him, 'You stay away from our bull when Nacho takes him away from the picadors.' And what do you suppose that insolent Indian does? He comes slowly up to Nacho, studies him carefully like he's buying a horse, and spits on his shoes. Then he whips around like a hawk, glares at me and says, 'Fat boy, tell your torero to do his own protecting.' Then he takes his position in the middle for the opening parade."

"You mean," Haggard asked, "that he challenged you before others, and you a major critic? He must have been insane."

"At times he is."

"What did you do?"

"They tell me I grew black in the face. I wanted to strangle that damned Indian, but the music started and the three young would-be matadors marched out into the sunlight. And as I watched the Indian strut into the arena I swore, I'll handle that Altomec later."

"Did you?"

"He handled me. Most grievously he handled me."

"Would you care to tell us?" Mrs. Evans asked, and he nodded, drew himself back against the jaguars and said: "It happened on the last bull of the day. Gómez had the gall to come to where I was and dedicate his bull to me: "Protector of the public, lover of bulls and master of the matadors." Men around me started laughing, so I told Nacho, "Make him look foolish," and Nacho did. Moving in on Gómez, he did a series of splendid passes, cape behind his back, but on the last one the bull turned back too quickly, caught him in the middle of the chest and heaved him in the air, catching him again on the way down."

"Dead?" Grim asked and Ledesma nodded, and we fell silent.

Finally Mrs. Haggard asked, "Did you ever find another boy?" and he said, "Mine died at Torreón."

I had never before seen León so willing to talk about his disasters, so I probed: "But if you hate Gómez so much—despise him, really—why have you gone out of your way to promote and even sponsor these hand-to-hand fights?"

"Because, miraculously, we have two fighters who represent the best of their competing styles. And if the world is to be kept in balance, it requires one like Gómez to underline the brilliance of one like Victoriano. So even though Gómez pays me nothing, I'm forced by the respect I have for bullfighting to speak the truth, and the truth is he's a courageous fighter. One of the bravest."

"Did I hear you say that the matadors pay you for good notices?" Haggard asked.

"That's how I earn my living."

"Does your paper know that?"

"They encourage it. Allows them to pay me less."

Haggard was shocked by this inside view of

Mexican criticism, but Young Penny Grim was proving rather sharper than I had supposed, and would not be sidetracked, for she asked, "Hating him as you do, are you able to be unprejudiced?"

He reached out to pat her hand. "I go to each hand-to-hand praying that the next bull will throw that damned Indian in the air eleven times and puncture his heart on each descent."

"Do you think that's the way it will end?" I asked, and he said, "I'm sure of it. Victoriano has style, but Gómez has only raw courage. And in real life, style beats courage every time. So the better Victoriano becomes, the more Gómez will have to take risks. Until one day he brings on his own death." He ground his fat knuckles into the table as if he were crushing the bow-legged little Altomec.

After our delicious luncheon we thanked Ledesma for his thoughtfulness in arranging for it. Mrs. Evans spoke for all of us when she said: "Señor Ledesma, you've been so kind to us here at the pyramid that we wonder if you'd spare a few more minutes and accompany us to the cathedral." He started to reply that he wanted to be at the ring at noon to watch the sorting of the bulls, but he stopped and reconsidered. "A visit there would help all of you understand the fights better, but I'm afraid Brother Clay won't appreciate it because I shall have to point out again that his sainted father had it all wrong."

"I can take it," I said. "I associate with you, León, to learn things I was not clever enough to see for myself. And I'm not teasing." Indeed I was not. In my efforts to sort out my priorities, specifically what I wanted to do with the rest of my life, I kept thinking about Mexico, and to attempt to understand this tangled, magnificent land with its constant revolutions would require all the brainpower I had. And it occurred to me that León and I were curiously similar, each of us an alien—he a Spaniard, I an American—so that we saw the nation from the perspective of an outsider. I needed to know what he knew, and was eager to hear what he had to say about the cathedral, which had been so important to my father.

"I'll take you!" he decided abruptly. "Thus I will complete my own preparation, and you, Mrs. Evans, shall again ride with me, if you are not a coward."

The sprightly widow jumped into the Mercedes, and with a roar she and the critic started back to town, but after a few hundred yards he spun the car perilously in a circle, roared back and shouted while negotiating a second circle, "We'll convene in the plaza facing the front of the cathedral." Then dust flew from beneath his tires, and he disappeared toward town.

We reached the plaza before he did, for apparently he and Mrs. Evans had stopped somewhere in town to make a purchase. When he did arrive he carried a rather bulky package under his arm, and when he joined us he made up for lost time, for he exploded into almost frenzied praise of the ornate façade that graced the cathedral. "Unique in the world, I mean the beautiful item and the ugly word that names it. Churrigueresque. That's the name of the architectural style you see, but what it means I do not know, except that it denotes a twisting, dancing, flaming creation, as you can see."

Allowing us some minutes to appreciate the glorious façade, he resumed with an observation I will never forget: "But we must not allow ourselves to be seduced by this lovely façade, for it hides an ugly secret, precisely the way our ugly pyramid hid a beautiful secret, the Terrace of the Jaguars. John Clay, not having been permitted to see either of the secrets, fell into understandable error, the brutal Indian pyramid competing with the delicate, lovely cathedral, each a false description."

"What do you mean?" Mrs. Evans asked. He

said: "Come with me, children," and led us to the south side of the cathedral where he stopped us before a very old fountain, which sent its water leaping into the sunlight. "For decades scholars have wondered why this statue of the first Bishop Palafox, our city's builder, had been stuck in this out-of-the-way place rather than in the spacious plaza we just left, for to tell you the truth our Palafoxes are not a reticent breed. At the bullfights, watch their present leader, Don Eduardo, breeder of bulls. If one of his bulls does especially well, and the crowd demands that he take a bow, he's allowed to enter the ring and garner the applause, but he'll jump in whether there's any real applause or not. I've heard two handclaps bring him in for bows. So if our first Palafox chose this inconspicuous corner for his fountain, there must have been a reason."

After giving us time to think about this, he explained, "In 1953, again well after the death of John Clay—so what I'm about to say does not reflect on his leadership—archaeologists pulled down the stucco facing of the old fortress-church opposite and laid bare one of the rude, rough statements of the earliest Spanish architecture. Over there you see the outdoor pulpit built in 1527 from which Fray Antonio converted the Altomecs."

Leaving the fountain, we crossed over to the old chapel, where Ledesma marched about indicating its features. "Look at the brutal form of this sanctuary. Its grand low arches are as profound as the pyramid and not a bit different, for the Spaniards used Indian architects. It has no ornament, no single extraneous line of beauty. The consecrated rock from which the friar first preached stands just as it was stolen from the ruined temple of the Mother Goddess. This crude holy place is the heart of the Catholic Church in the plateau region. Our church did not conquer and convert the Indians because we had the delicate churrigueresque architecture that John Clay held to be the essence of Catholicism in Mexico. We triumphed because we spoke from the solid rock of the land we had invaded. Our first chapels were low and powerful, like the temples from whose flanks the stones were stolen. We did not introduce completely new gods to our Altomec Indians; we adopted those we found and gave them the names of Spanish saints. Nor did we indulge in any sentimental piety." He paused. "If we had been Indian peasants in those early days, we'd have gathered here to listen to some Spanish priest shout theology at us in words we could barely understand. Spanish soldiers with their guns at the ready would have lined those battlements up there, and if a strong-minded Indian like Mr. Haggard even so much as opened his mouth in protest—bang, bang! You, Mr. Haggard, were dead."

He laughed, then said gravely, "I've grown to love this rude chapel that lay so long hidden beneath the stucco of respectability. It reminds me that the conquest of Mexico, my adopted home, was a harsh and often cynical affair. Here I see the nonsense of history ripped away, the soft words and the guileful lies and the distortions of the truth. We Spaniards were a hard people, and if when we had the land properly subdued we did find time to build a marble façade that dances for joy, we were cautious enough first to kill and subjugate."

When we finished inspecting the remnants of Toledo's earliest Spanish structure, Ledesma surprised me by leading us into the interior of the cathedral, because ever since that day in 1911 when General Gurza's troops had sacked Toledo and ravaged the cathedral few guides bothered to take their American tourists inside. Prior to that vandalism, the church had been famous for its three high altars of pure silver, its Virgins with faces of gold and rubies, and its ornate swaying lanterns sixty feet above the aisles. These too were of pure silver. It was a cathedral known throughout the Catholic world as the ideal example of a rich man's devotion to God, and it had been brought into being by the fifth Bishop Palafox, who had badgered his wealthy cousin to pay the bill.

The sacking had been started by an Altomec Indian from Chihuahua State who had learned to read and who had shouted from the main entrance: "Soldiers! Look at the silver in here! Our grandfathers mined that silver and it belongs to us." Three hours later there was no silver, and the looters, as they left with the marvelous lanterns, paused to fire several hundred volleys into the stone statues that helped support the walls.

In subsequent years no effort was made to rebuild the interior, and the once-great cathedral of Toledo had remained a glittering shell containing nothing of importance. In 1935 my father, a Protestant, had proposed that the citizens of the city contribute toward the reconstruction, but his proposal was made during the presidency of General Cárdenas, a powerful anti-cleric who would later expropriate the oil wells, and his government would not permit even voluntary contributions to be used for such purposes.

So now, as we entered the church of the Palafoxes, we saw barren walls pockmarked with bullets. The three main altars each had cheap wooden constructions showing ghastly Christs and even more ghastly saints; the wings of the angels were painted with cheap gilt and the garments were gray with dust. The church was kept viable only because of the inherent sanctity of the altars.

I could not at first understand why Ledesma had brought us into this gloomy memorial, repellent with its dirt and tawdriness, but obviously he had some plan in mind, for he led us directly to a spot between two ribs of the vaulting, and there he pointed to the Eleventh Station of the Cross. It was a carving I had not bothered to look at before, but at first glance it fitted in well with the rest of the interior; it was gray and dusty.

It was in the form of a tall rectangle, carved from several stout pieces of wood that had been nailed together. At the top was Jesus Christ, crowned with thorns and nailed to the cross, his torso covered by a dirty purple cloth that hung about his loins. Lower down and to his right and left were the two thieves on their crosses, and they were notable in that they wore the gold-and-silver satin pantaloons of the conquistadors. On a lower semicircle, repeating the lines of the crosses, knelt the Virgin Mary clothed in a dusty purple velvet cut in the style of 1500,

Mary Magdalene in scarlet velvet, and Elizabeth in brilliant huntsman's green.

Neither the carving nor the design merited comment, but the figure of Christ did, for simple human agony has rarely been more revoltingly depicted. From his contorted brow hung the crown of thorns, each spike cutting visibly into his already purplish flesh and sending drops of blood dripping across his wan countenance. His arms, legs and shins had been gashed, as they probably had been at Gethsemane, with deep saber slashes that had broken the bones and sent reddish-purple blood coursing down his extremities. Most horrible, however, was the centurion's lance thrust into his side, for in this particular statue the wound was actually big enough to permit any doubting Thomas to thrust his fingers in up to the wrist and thus to be convinced that Jesus Christ actually did die upon a cross.

I recoiled from the horrible scene, as did the women in the party. Mrs. Evans caught her breath: "It's sickening. I think I'll go."

Ledesma said quietly: "But it was this that I wanted you to see."

"What has a monstrosity like this to do with religion?" O. J. Haggard asked.

"With ordinary religion, nothing," Ledesma

replied slowly. "But with Christianity, every-thing." He then began speaking as if he were addressing a class, and he would not permit any of us to leave. "You asked to be brought here, Mrs. Evans, and now you must in fairness stay."

"I did not want to see this," Mrs. Evans pro-tested in a stricken voice.

"This afternoon you will not want to see the bulls die," he reminded her, "but that is why you have come to Mexico. To see death."

He stood below the Eleventh Station and said: "The cardinal principle of Christianity is that Jesus Christ died for us. He died on a cross, suffering the most extreme agony, with his arms and legs broken, as you see here. He did not die quickly, but he slowly bled to death.

"We have, I am afraid, tried to hide this fact from ourselves. We depict Jesus in flowing white robes, or with insignificant little needle pricks on his brow, or lying serenely in a sepul-cher. The inescapable fact is that he came from a violent God, into a violent world, to save vio-lent men from a terribly violent hell. We fool ourselves in the most bitter mockery if we try for the sake of prettiness to gloss over the terrifying fact that Jesus Christ died in the agony you see depicted there, and by and large, only the Span-ish peoples have been brave enough to ac-knowledge that fact. Have you never wondered why it was that Spain perpetually defended the faith, even though it cost us our empire and our position in the European sun? Why was it that Spain alone poured forth her blood to save the Church of Christ? Because we Spaniards, led by men like Seneca, García Lorca and Cervantes, have never been afraid of death. Always re-member Cervantes's arrogant last words, 'Yes-terday they gave me Extreme Unction, so today I take my pen in hand.' That's the way a man should face death, the way Jesus did, the way Seneca did. He said: 'Give me the cup.' We don't know what García Lorca said, nor even how he died, but I can imagine him saying, not anything profound or poetic, but something to-tally banal like 'Let me stand over there.' To be in a Spanish mind, or in a Spanish cathedral, is to be near death.

"Mrs. Evans, why do you suppose God chose this instrumentality, this horrible crucifixion, to save us? Don't you suppose that someone as generous and as loving as God could have de-vised an alternative way? Why do you suppose he elected to impress this bloody scene on our conscience as the only true way to salvation?

"Let's imagine that God had decided to turn his duties over to a women's club in Tulsa, Okla-homa. Don't you suppose that the good women could figure out a more tasteful way to denote the salvation of the world? You could use doves or Easter lilies or any of a hundred other delicate and wonderful symbols of peace and serenity of the soul. I am quite satisfied that you women would come up with something much better than what God used. For He chose blood. He chose the most cruel form of death that men of that time knew. It wasn't death. It was outright torture. And He did it, I think, in order to show us how insignificantly mortal we are."

He stood in the shadows of this ruined church and made us study the awful crucifixion. No one of us who saw that bloody statue could ever doubt that Jesus Christ had been tormented beyond human endurance. Ed Grim was the first to speak: "Don't those goddamned satin pants on the two thieves look ridiculous?"

"It's all ridiculous," Ledesma agreed brightly, moving from the shadows. "This magnificent interior gutted because a few greedy soldiers wanted silver. What could be more ridiculous than that?" He waved his arms expansively, then said softly: "All that you will see this afternoon will be ridiculous. Truthfully, you would be wiser not to attend the bullfights."

"Will they be as bad as . . ." Mrs. Evans paused. "As bad as this?" She pointed to the crucifixion.

"They will be exactly the same," Ledesma replied. "They will be very sickening, and Americans ought not to look at them."

Grim said: "If we've driven all this distance and paid all this money for tickets, I'm sure goin' to see the fights." Mrs. Evans agreed and the Haggards said: "The only sensible thing to do," and Penny Grim said: "I came to see matadors and I intend to see them." Upon the unanimous agreement, Ledesma said: "So if you're determined to go, you should do so prepared to understand what you're going to see—the spiritual significance I mean. The technical details of this and that you can get from any of the little handbooks." From the packet he had purchased on the way down from the pyramid he handed each of us that day's special English-language edition of a newspaper that contained a long article by Ledesma in polished translation.

"It will explain what I've been driving at. Take a look and I'll see you later." With that he left us in the church, but as he went he called back: "And study the carving from time to time as you read, since they're both about death." And so we six Americans sat in the bleak cathedral and read what would be for the Oklahomans their first taste of Mexican sports writing. Ledesma's essay bore a cryptic title.

Earth and Flame

Today many readers of this newspaper will make the pilgrimage to Toledo for the Festival of Ixmiq-61 and those who have been guided by friends will have studied John Clay's masterpiece, *The Pyramid and the Cathedral,* and will thus discover some of the values inherent in Toledo.

But in another sense this book will be poor preparation for the bullfights at Toledo, for Clay suggests that the soul of Mexico can be comprehended only if one counterbalances the Indian pyramid against the Spanish cathedral, as if the two were mutually exclusive yet somehow symbiotic. Of course, when we drive to the festival and see at Kilometer 303 the finest view in Mexico, we will for a moment contrast the pyramid and the cathedral, and if we stop with that surface contrast, we shall be able to adopt John Clay's thesis with ease. But if we plan our excursion to Toledo so that we have time to inspect the city, and if we attend the bullfights in a spirit of exploration, we may in some oblique way stumble upon the essential mystery of Mexico. To accomplish this we must visit the pyramid of the Altomecs before we see our first fight, and as we approach this grisly scene of sacrifice we will see it exactly as John Clay knew it when he wrote. There is the brutal pile and aloft the hideous altar. Down that steep flank the bodies were thrown and the implacable blue sky is exactly the way it was a thousand years ago. It is the essential monument of Indian Mexico.

As we reach the top we shall see again the eagle warriors, those powerful figures that so enchanted Clay. Their finely sculptured heads wearing the eagle masks show men indescribably cruel in purpose, and the blend of human and animal is a masterly accomplishment of both the sculptor and the psychologist.

(At this point in his reading O. J. Haggard put down his paper and asked: "When do we get to the bullfighting?" I replied: "But the whole piece is about bullfighting.")

In fact, if I were required to select the one work of art that best typified central Mexico, I would choose these fierce men, half brutal warrior, half soaring eagle. They summarize our ancient heritage, and in selecting them for his eulogies John Clay spoke for us all.

Had he in 1920 known the Altomec bull-fighter Juan Gómez he would probably have agreed that in Gómez the eagle warriors lived again.

From the pyramid one should move directly to the cathedral. It is best seen in the early morning from across the plaza near the Imperial Theater, for only from this spot can one appreciate the glorious churrigueresque façade of Bishop Palafox. It is extraordinary, this twisting, convoluted, magic assembly of white marble and fluted columns and saints standing in niches. For two hundred years people have been studying this amazing pile of architecture—indeed, this is a perfect year in which to study it again, for we are in the two hundredth anniversary of its completion—and I suppose that in the centuries to come its fame will grow and even more will visit it. But I suspect that no one has ever really seen it nor ever will, because even as you look, its components constantly shift in their relationship to one another. When I last studied it, during an early dawn at the last Festival of Ixmiq, I swear I caught Saint Anthony dancing. Of course, whenever I looked directly at him, he stood dutifully in his niche like a boy in school, but when my eyes wandered, I could catch him dancing up and down and teasing Saint Margaret, who shied away from his impertinent attentions. This is the glory of the churrigueresque as it is epitomized in Toledo: that it cries to unyielding marble and traditional Gothic: "I am weary of buildings standing stiffly in the cold. Let's dance." And dance this great façade does. Even its stoutest columns are in motion.

Of course, the reader will understand that I am writing not about the façade of Toledo but about the matador Victoriano Leal, for the arabesques that he is able to carve with his magical cape are also cries of longing. And like the façade, this poetic torero, this glory of Mexico, does dance, and he sets our hearts on fire.

So there we have the easy symbolism of Mexico, all neatly wrapped up in one set of bullfights. Juan Gómez is the cold, stolid Indian of the pyramid and Victoriano Leal is the poetic dancer of the cathedral, all explained in the clever words of our visitor from the North, John Clay. But I am sorry to have to tell you now that every conclusion John Clay drew was wrong and that he is the worst possible guide to the Festival of Ixmiq.

I say this not in rudeness and not in criticism of Clay, but simply because he could not have known what we now know; he could not have avoided his tremendous and misleading errors, but we can. To do so we must double back to the pyramid. This time we don't climb the steps to the fierce eagle warriors. We stay below, walk a few steps to the west and feast our eyes on the elegant jaguars who march sedately about the terrace that bears their name. They are the other aspect of the brutal pyramid, and we must keep them in mind when we are too hasty in denouncing the pyramid. It isn't all brutality as Clay would have us believe.

(I had a strange reaction to this mild castigation of my father, whom I revered. During our morning visit to the pyramid Ledesma had been careful to apologize for having to disagree with Father, but I had thought this unnecessary, because the criticism was just. Father had been wrong in dichotomizing the bad Indian pyramid and the good Spanish cathedral. Mexico was like the huge snake that appears as one of the symbols on its colorful flag. It is a twisting, writhing entity that no one can really grasp, hold still and study. Ledesma was not criticizing my father; he was helping educate me: "Quit accepting snap judgments. Look carefully and honestly at the conflicting data and reach your own conclusions." And just at that point my eyes fell upon almost the same words in Ledesma's essay.)

The same kind of correction must be made at the cathedral, so let's march back there and look not at the scintillating façade but off to one side at the almost ugly outdoor chapel in which the Indians had to worship while Spanish soldiers guarded them with guns. Just as the harsh pyramid had its gentle side, so did the graceful cathedral have its brutality.

To understand how these two apparent contradictions apply to bullfighting, and especially to the duel between Victoriano and Gómez, I want you to leave Mexico and accompany me to a very large room in Madrid that many consider the most beautiful in the world. It is on the second floor of the Prado, the city's huge treasure-filled art museum, and it contains more than a dozen superb canvases by Velázquez.

Half the people represented are Spanish kings, queens and royal children. They are foppish or elegant or aloof. The other half are peasants drinking wine as they rest after toiling in the field or women weaving the fabrics that made Spain famous for that art; these strong men and women live on Spanish soil, drink Spanish wine, and eat Spanish bread soaked in Spanish olive oil. Even the noblemen exhibit the stolidity of Spanish life, and if in a certain light they appear almost stupid, this is an illusion; what appears to be stupidity is in reality merely the enormous force of character that allowed Spain to stand firm against innovation, against doctrinal change, and even against the lessons of the New World. The rugged power of the Spaniard has never been better exhibited than in the paintings of Velázquez, and if a stranger were to ask me: "What is a Spaniard?" I would take him to this room and point to these earthy men and women.

But if he persisted: "I do not want to see how you look. I want to see how you are," then I would have to lead him to that smaller, darker room where the canvases of El Greco hang, luminous as if lit with a green flame. And there, as we studied the attenuated tortured figures with faces expressing pure anguish, I would say, "Here you see the Spanish soul."

In attempting to understand Spain, one confronts both the solidity of Velázquez and the spirituality of El Greco, and we have now identified the true dichotomy that inspires the duel between Juan Gómez and Victoriano Leal. It does not spring from a surface difference between Indians and Spaniards, nor between the paganism of the pyramid and the idealism of the cathedral, nor even between the harshness of the cactus and the soaring beauty of the maguey. It is not an either-or disjunction. It springs from the conflict that exists in Spanish life itself. It is the battle between earth and flame. It is a dichotomy in which all men are imprisoned, but which the Spaniard alone is willing to exhibit as an open fact.

(At this point in his reading Ed Grim threw down the mimeographed sheets and said, "I came here to see a bullfight, not get an art lecture. Where's the bullring?" I pointed down the Avenue Gral. Gurza and said: "Walk one block beyond the cathedral, it'll be on the right." He jammed on his panama hat and asked: "Will I be able to recognize it when I see it?" I said: "Possibly not. It's crowded in among other buildings." Turning to his daughter, he asked, "You coming with me?" She tapped the essay:

"Nope. This is beginning to make sense, and I want to see how it comes out." Ignoring her and speaking to me, he said: "I'll find it. I'll be able to smell the horses." And he left. The rest of us continued reading.)

It would be an error to assume airily that Velázquez and Juan Gómez represent the brutal earthly body of man, while El Greco and Victoriano Leal represent the ethereal flame of man's spirit. I think the difference is much subtler than that. Velázquez's people are humanity, with all their limitations and powers. His kings are vain, foolish people who reign for a little while, then pass their authority on to others who are no less stupid than themselves. His peasants sweat a while in the sun, grow old and die, their places being taken by others exactly the same. This is how the world revolves. This is how men actually live, and there is in his paintings a sense of down-to-earth dignity that men like El Greco can never achieve, just as in the pyramid of which we have been speaking there is an inescapable, foursquare rightness that the ornate cathedral can simply never challenge. It is not that Velázquez restricts himself to the corporeal world and El Greco to the spiritual. That is too easy a disjunction. What has happened is that Velázquez has depicted the ultimate meaning of life by approaching it through the earthly body, whereas El Greco has reached for the same goal by denying the body, by contorting it and abusing it, and by concentrating on the deepest psychological forces that animate man. But the goal of each is exactly the same.

I said earlier that the men who built the pyramids were driven also to build the Terrace of the Jaguars, whereas the priests who built the cathedral were also motivated to build the squat, brutish open-air chapel. Similarly, Velázquez often gives us glimpses of the most exquisite poetry, while El Greco is not loath occasionally to portray people who are distinctly earthbound. The dichotomy of which we are speaking thus lies within each man, and forms two parts of his being. As a Spaniard, I am at once part Velázquez and part El Greco. As a Mexican going to the bullfights at Toledo I am at the same time part Juan Gómez, brutal and stupid, and part Victoriano Leal, the lyric poet; and the greatness of this series of fights we have been witnessing since the first of the year is that these two men disclose to us aspects of our own secret life, and each contains an essential part of the other.

These conflicting aspects of man are also exhibited in the great writers of Spain, for a man who writes cannot escape spreading out on paper a major proportion of what he thinks, whereas artists in other categories can sometimes avoid this, or obscure it. In order to investigate the ideas I have in mind, I am going to discuss the two most representative writers Spain has so far produced.

(O. J. Haggard asked cautiously: "In Mexico do they call stuff like this sports writing?" I replied: "In Mexico they don't regard bullfighting as a sport. It's an art." Mrs. Evans put a finger on a line to mark where she stopped and asked: "But do other writers about bullfighting go on like this?" I answered: "I bought a book the other day that was supposed to be about bullfighting, but the outsider would have thought it was an essay on religion." Mrs. Evans shook her head ruefully and observed: "To me it seems very pretentious. In Tulsa I'm afraid this young man wouldn't get very far reporting on football.")

I should first like to discuss Federico García Lorca, for he epitomizes physically, intellectually, spiritually and artistically one part of the Spanish nature. His life was his principal work of art.

No people that I know hold poetry in such high esteem as the speakers of Spanish, and it is not unusual to see in either Madrid or Mexico City a man and his wife strolling down a street, he reciting from García Lorca while she holds the prompt book. Exactly why García Lorca should have captured the Hispanic mind is difficult to say. His awkwardness in playwriting often leaves me embarrassed. For example, the plotting of *Blood Wedding* is quite pedestrian, while his *House of Bernarda Alba* comes straight from eighteenth-century Gothic. To appreciate how deficient the Spaniard was, you must compare his plot devices and characterizations with those of Goethe and Eugene O'Neill.

But when I get to the words of Lorca and forget his silly plots, I conclude that in his poetry he stands second to none, and it is for this that we prize and praise him. I wonder if there has ever been another Spanish writer who could compress into so few words the agony of life, as when in *Blood Wedding* the bridegroom's mother confesses: "Always in my breast there's a shriek standing tiptoe that I have to fight back and keep hidden under my shawls." How brilliantly he compresses the action of *Yerma* into a single song sung by the ghostly offstage voice:

> "When you were fancy-free,
>   You and I could never see.
>   But now that you're a wife
>   You have become my life."

Little wonder that Lorca, who wrote so emotionally about bullfighting, has become the acknowledged poet laureate of the plaza, for in its intense and compressed drama he found the summation of the tragedy he sought. The literary counterpart of El Greco, he exhibits the same leaping flame of passion, and also like El Greco, his artistic ambitions override his technical skills—he thus becomes the patron of matadors like Victoriano Leal, whose artistic aspirations are greater than their basic skills. Yet with García Lorca there is always something more. He speaks to us Spaniards with a fury that no other poet commands, and we instantly recognize the authority of his speech.

But let us now turn to a writer from a much earlier age, one whom I consider the greatest Spaniard who has ever lived, and that includes the painters, the musicians, the philosophers and the kings. Lucius Annaeus Seneca, born in 4 B.C., that year in which historians believe Jesus too was born, began his life in Spain. But, like the sensible lad he was, he quickly moved to Rome, where his wit, his stalwart character and his skill at playwriting attracted such favorable attention that in time he became chief counselor to Emperor Nero, and as long as Seneca remained in control, Nero was an exemplary ruler. Seneca was also a notable administrator, Rome's leading dramatist, the conscience of the empire, and one of the capital's most brilliant intellects. In Spain we cherish his memory because he was the first man of any intellectual substance to become a Christian and is thus the spiritual father of Catholicism in Spain. At his death he was the most distinguished man in the world who had so far embraced the new religion, and his advice to the Roman world was as profound as Saint Paul's to the world at large. Seneca's dealt with more immediate problems: "God is not to be worshiped with sacrifices and blood; for what pleasure can He have in the slaughter of the innocent? He is to be worshiped only with a pure mind, a good and honest purpose. Temples need not be built for Him with stones piled high upon high; He is to be consecrated in the breast of each."

The impact of Seneca upon the Spanish mind is felt daily, and the contradictions that plagued him continue to plague Spain. He was subject to keen passions, yet he preached a calm and even cautious adjustment to conflicting forces. He was the supreme stoic, taking nothing too seriously, yet he feared death. In literary style he was ornate, but in the essentials of life austere. I have always considered myself a disciple of Seneca's, and I would rather talk with him for half an hour than with any other Spaniard who has ever lived; yet often his down-to-earth realism irritates me because it can be so prosaic. He is par excellence the Velázquez of the written word: the glowing man of earth.

And so we have the intellectual battle lines drawn for our visit to Toledo: there is the earth of Velázquez and Seneca directly opposed to the flame of El Greco and Lorca. There is the earthy style of the bowlegged Altomec Indian Juan Gómez directly opposed to the fiery arabesques of Sevillian

Victoriano Leal. And the Festival of Ixmiq will show us a classic confrontation of these two concepts.

(Here O. J. Haggard interrupted with "I never heard of Seneca. How come—if he's as good as this fellow says?" His wife added, "And I never heard of Lorca. Is he any good?" Mrs. Evans observed: "After John's death I went to New York, as you know, and I saw a group of actors do *Blood Wedding* in a little theater off-Broadway." Haggard asked: "Was it any good?" And Mrs. Evans replied: "It was terribly intense," at which Haggard pressed: "But was it any good?" and she said bluntly: "Yes. At the time I didn't think so, but it occurred to me later that after seeing it I thought about *Blood Wedding* five times for every once that I recalled the usual Broadway play." Haggard grunted and said, "Then it was good." They resumed reading and came to the first major point of Ledesma's essay.)

But it is not the differences between Seneca and García Lorca that bind them together in our minds as the supreme examples of Spanish thought. It is their similarity, and when I say what this is each reader will understand why these two writers now serve as the apostles of bullfighting. Seneca and Lorca are concerned primarily with death, and every Spaniard, whether he lives in Pamplona or Peru, is similarly preoccupied with this ultimate mystery. It was not by accident that in the long history of Spain no two Spaniards ever died more appropriately than Seneca and García Lorca. At the height of his fame, when his plays commanded the Roman theater and his shafts of wit monopolized Roman conversation, Seneca was ordered by an insane Nero to commit suicide. And now what at times had seemed to be weakness in Seneca's character, especially his tendency to shift with each new wind that blew from the Roman Forum, was seen to be the Stoic's honest adjustment to the necessities of life. When it came time for Seneca to die, he lifted the poisoned cup fearlessly to his lips, and Rome saw a Spaniard die a noble death. Not even Socrates, in similar circumstances, met his end with greater dignity.

It would have been unforgivable had his final act been flawed, for in life Seneca was preoccupied with death, and his philosophy could be summed up in his statement that "the whole of life is nothing but a preparation for death."

In my studies I have had to read a great deal of English literature, and I never found an author who seemed honestly convinced that man is inescapably mortal, that one day he is going to die. There is something infuriating about the English writers' assumptions about immortality, and the Spanish reader soon tires of such writing because he is accustomed to a literature that lives each day with death. If Spaniards are preoccupied with death, it is because our greatest men have taught us to be so. If we love bullfights it is because we subconsciously know that this is the world's only art form that depicts our preoccupation. That is why the reflections of Seneca are so important to all who follow the bulls. He is our philosopher and guide, and the death that he contemplated so sublimely is the death we watch being acted out each afternoon.

And a fascinating aspect of this inescapable denouement is that we cannot predict how death will strike, or at whom. Nero proved that, for sometimes when a fight between the lions and the Christians in his arena

proved dull, or when the lions killed everyone too soon, he instructed his guards to
grab at random a score of spectators and
toss them into the ring to feed the beasts.
Thus a man who had paid that morning to
watch Christians being eaten suddenly
found himself being part of the feast. Decade after decade, in the various bullrings of
the world an enraged animal occasionally
will not only leap the barrier that defines the
ring in which he is supposed to fight but will
vault into the rows of spectators in the
stands and kill one or two. Like Nero's Romans, those who paid to watch a fight
become the fight.

(O. J. Haggard asked quietly, "Have you
found the Mexicans preoccupied with death?"
and I replied, "When I was a little boy living at
the Mineral, General Gurza came by and
hanged one of our men from a pole that stuck
out from the kitchen, and the man's legs dan-
gled above the place where we prepared food.
I asked my father why we did not cut him down,
and my father pointed out that General Gurza
had left a soldier in the patio with instructions to
keep the man's body hanging there, so that, in
the general's words, 'We would all remember

what death was.' " Haggard concluded: "I prefer the English preoccupation with life. I say, 'Let's kid ourselves as long as possible that the old bastard is going to pass us by.' ")

At long last, this was the conclusion of Ledesma's piece:

If it is true as I claim that we are all Spaniards inexorably marching toward death, it is no less true that we are all stubborn Mexicans holding on like peasants to life on earth. Unquestionably we are, like Seneca, obligated to consider how we shall die, but we must not forget that for most of his life Seneca lived surrounded by the luxuries of imperial Rome and ignored death; nor should we forget that García Lorca, who lived with death like a brother, spent the best years of his life in New York, where he lived vigorously.

We are tragic men, but we are also comic. We march to death, but we get drunk on the way. I cannot identify Juan Gómez with the pyramid or Velázquez or Seneca, nor can I see Victoriano Leal as his opposite in those categories. It is true, however, that I see these two matadors approaching the problem of death from two different philosophies, but just as the pyramid contains the Terrace of the Jaguars, so each of these men contains the best elements of the other.

Which matador do I prefer? As a child of Spain I should elect him who stands closest to death, and that is Juan Gómez, who knows how to kill, but I must make an un-Spanish choice and say I prefer him who best depicts the flaming heart of life, and that is Victoriano Leal, who knows what grace is.

So to those traveling to Toledo I give the benediction that the great Spanish philosopher Miguel de Unamuno bestowed upon us all: "May God deny you peace, but grant you glory." Gentlemen, to the bulls!

O. J. Haggard was first to finish the essay. As he stepped out of the cathedral and into the bright noonday sunlight he said: "Too much like a tomb in here. Too much death." One by one, as each of us finished reading, we too went outside, glad for the life-filled plaza and the sun.

We saw Ed Grim leaving a café by the bullring, and as he approached us he called out in his hearty voice: "I was waiting in the bar till you finished your philosophy lesson."

"We're done," Haggard said.

"You know any more about bullfighting than when you started?"

"No."

"Well, I do," the red-necked man growled. "This bullfighting is a racket. When I went to the box office to buy us five seats for each of the three days, the poster said in Spanish, but with English beside it, that the cost was seven dollars each—that's one hundred five dollars in all—but when I tried to give the man in the booth the money, he called an interpreter who explained, 'Sorry. All seats sold.' So I looked around for a scalper and a mangy-looking character stepped forward. 'I just happen to have five good seats for today.' When I asked how much, he said, 'Twenty-five dollars each.' I almost gagged but paid him. Then he said: 'How about five each for the next two fights?' and I agreed. What else could I do? I cashed a traveler's check and paid him three hundred eighty-five."

"You overpaid," his daughter said. "Fifteen times twenty-five is only three hundred seventy-five."

"He demanded a tip. For just standing there he made a cool two hundred dollars or more."

"I make it two hundred seventy dollars," Penny said quietly, and he growled: "But what really gagged me—when I gave him the money he went around to the back door of the ticket office and gave the same clerk I had talked to fifteen times seven dollars, that's one hundred five dollars. And without even blushing he came back to me and handed over the tickets. At those prices I guess the fat boy has a right to throw around some fancy words." Pointing to one of the newspapers, he asked: "He continue to lay it on pretty thick?"

"He didn't hold anything back," Haggard said.

Penny Grim cried: "He's come for us," and ran to tell him, "That essay was fantastic. You did beat around the bush, but in the end I think I caught what you were trying to say."

"Which was?" I liked the way he took the young girl seriously, and I listened when she asked hesitantly, "Maybe that life is more complex than we think? Two faces to everything? Pyramid, cathedral, the two matadors? One time we see it one way, next time another?"

"See what, for instance?"

She looked at him and then at Mrs. Evans as if seeking permission. "But there's always death—to make things equal. Is that it?"

"Yes," he said soberly. "You read with marked intelligence, señorita. But you're too young to worry about death."

"Not so. Last year my mother died."

He studied her carefully, took her hand and kissed it. Her father, seeing this, came and put his arm around her, then told Ledesma: "I read only part of your essay. Much too deep for me. But I'm glad one of our family knew what you were shooting at. I wondered if you were just throwing words around for effect."

Again León bowed. "Sir, you're as clever as your beautiful daughter. You saw through me. Shameless exhibitionism. I do it for two good reasons. To impress my Mexican readers with the fact that I've read books. And because I get paid by the word." And he led us from the church back to the House of Tile for drinks before the afternoon fight. As with the picnic lunch, he paid for them.

FRIDAY
FIGHT

THROUGH THE YEARS visitors to the Festival of Ixmiq have established certain revered traditions. From one o'clock to three, lunch on the Terrace to partake of the Widow Palafox's enormous meal. Three to four, a brief siesta. Four-fifteen sharp, back on the Terrace to applaud as the three matadors elbow their way through the cheering guests and climb into their conspicuous limousines for their journey to the fights. Four-fifteen, march down Avenida Gral. Gurza to the historic bullring of Toledo. Five

sharp, cheer the entrance parade of the matadors as the corrida begins.

On this Friday, of course, we broke the ritual,
for we'd had our picnic lunch at the pyramid and
a protracted stay at the cathedral reading Ledesma's essay, so it was a quarter to three when
we returned to the House of Tile, just in time for
the Oklahomans to take a siesta and for me to
participate in one of the hallowed rites of bullfighting: dressing the matador. From time im-
memorial, meaning from about 1820, it had
been the custom for grown men who loved bullfighting and adored their favorite matadors to
visit the hotel suites in which the toreros
climbed, sometimes awkwardly, into their suit of
lights, that ancient costume so bright in its vivid
colors and so heavy with brocade and even bits
of metal adornment. Since it was believed that
attending a matador in this ritual proved your
allegiance to him, his rented rooms were apt to
be crowded.

Because I was a confirmed bullfight junkie, as
soon as I reached my room I dressed myself
hastily for the fight, then hurried down the hall to
the Leal rooms, where I explained to the guardian of the door: "Norman Clay, New York photographer here to get some shots of the
matador." I did not, on such occasions, use the

word "writer," because that might bar me. Everyone who was trying to force his way into the sanctuary claimed to be a writer, but a man with an expensive Japanese camera with a motor drive who might really take a picture that would appear in a paper was welcomed.

Inside the crowded room I found activities that were pleasantly familiar. In that corner a group of important Toledo aficionados was talking with Veneno regarding details of the afternoon fight. "How were the bulls at the sorting?" "Precious." This was the code word for "Stupendous." Always the bulls at three o'clock in the matador's room are precious. At seven later that evening they would be more accurately described as disappointing *ratones,* little mice. "How did you do in the lottery?" "Magnificent. We drew the two best animals." At seven it will be acknowledged that the two beasts our man drew in the choosing were the poorest of the lot. With the bulls that other matador was lucky enough to receive we'd have cut ears and tails.

I loved this artificial ritual and even threw in my contribution. When asked what television company I worked for, I said: "Magazine in New York. They'll print maybe four full pages of this fight. The home office sees it as sensational." And I was treated with respect. But I was not concerned about my reception: I wanted to know what Veneno would be telling his three sons. Now a reverential hush fell over the room as the toreros entered into serious discussion. And when I edged my way into where they had gathered I heard the familiar litany.

"At the selection we got the two best. They're precious. But the bulls Gómez got are pretty good, too. His man Cigarro drove hard bargains in arranging the pairs. Between us we took the best ones, and I'm afraid the boy" (he was referring to Paquito de Monterrey, who was fighting for almost nothing) "may have drawn two bad ones. We'll see."

A Toledo valet, hired for the occasion, moved back and forth between the rooms of the suite, laying out the glittering gold and silver costumes to be worn that day. Victoriano and his two brothers, each in a white shirt without tie or jacket, smoked cigarettes as conversation lagged and fell into a long silence in which the four toreros thought of nothing but the coming test. And the ghost that haunted the room was Juan Gómez.

"What we must do"—Veneno finally broke the silence—"is to play cautious with our first animal. Frankly, it's a very bad bull and today Gómez has the better of us in the draw." At this unprecedented honesty Victoriano stared sullen-eyed out the window. He preferred never to hear of his bulls, and certainly never to see them until that vital moment when they burst into the arena seeking an opponent. Even then, during the early moments, he remained safe behind the barrier that protected toreros not in the ring, keeping the gathered edge of his cape over his eyes, choosing when to lower it and look at his enemy for the first time.

But no matter where he looked, here in this quiet room, he could see Juan Gómez and hear his father's droning rasping voice, filled with experience. "With the first bull we will comply—get it over with. Gómez may be strong with his, and it may look as if he's better. So with our second bull we've got to cut at least one ear and maybe two."

Diego, the younger son, who would have to place the banderillas if the first bull was bad, observed: "At the sorting I thought our first bull hooked to the right. Be careful."

Veneno continued, driven to talk by the importance of this fight. "If we can get rid of that first mouse without a disaster, everything will be all right, Victoriano." I noticed that at these empty words Victoriano winced, as if weary of the passive role his father had forced him to play. He was about to break another of his rules against discussions of the bulls prior to a fight, when a noisy group of well-wishers from Mexico City pushed their way into the room crying: "Good luck, matador!" One said, "We were at the sorting, and you got the best ones." Another assured Victoriano: "Your bulls, so precious!" After they left, the buzzing echo of their lies continued. Three-thirty came as a relief, and the four Leals, who had of course eaten nothing (they did not want a bull's horn to rip into their gut and find it crammed with half-digested food because that way led to septicemia and death) started the ritual dressing.

Veneno and his sons dressed without the valet's help, but there was one operation in which the toreros had to enlist aid—forcing the very tight crotch of their pants up into position. To help their father climb into his extra-heavy leather pants, Chucho and Diego waited until he had eased his legs partway into the suit, aware that he could not possibly finish the job of pulling the boardlike trousers up into proper position. The traditional way to solve this problem was for the boys to pass a rolled-up towel between the legs of the suit, each to grab one end, and pull strenuously upward until the suit seated itself protectively around the picador's belly, groin and buttocks. It was not an elegant operation but it worked.

When Veneno was satisfied he was properly clad, he grabbed one end of the towel and passed it between his son's legs so that Chucho could ease himself into his expensive suit. Victoriano, as the matador, was dressed by the hired valet until time for the towel act, when half a dozen eager watchers stepped forward, hopeful of being allowed the supreme honor of being allowed to hold one end. If Victoriano was killed that day, the two lucky men who had given assistance could forever afterward boast, "I dressed the matador for his last fight." The valet pointed to the most prosperous-looking and said, "You two! The towel!" The lucky chosen bowed as if being presented at court.

As Mexico's first family of bullfighting, the Leals were expected to look good, and by four o'clock they did. Victoriano was dressed in a new suit imported from Seville, silver and white ornamented with disks of shimmering gold. It fitted so snugly and its seams were so well hidden that the slim young matador did indeed seem to be made of lights. Veneno, to ensure success on this opening day, was wearing his lucky suit, a dark blue studded with silver. Chucho was in maroon and Diego gleamed in green. As they waited for the mariachis to signal the hour for departure, Victoriano lounged awkwardly in a chair, silent as always, as if brooding on the fact that the entire burden of the afternoon fell on him, and not on his father and brothers. Chucho stood smoking by the window while his younger brother Diego, seated backwards in a chair, pressed his teeth against the back. Veneno, now encased in many pounds of protective gear, which the bulls would attack many times that afternoon, found it more comfortable to remain standing by the door. They were stiffly immobile, nervously thinking of Juan Gómez and the bulls, when León Ledesma entered.

"Good luck, matador!" the critic called across the room. "I saw the bulls," he lied. "They were precious."

"Good crowd?" Veneno asked, not because he wanted an answer but because he wanted no more comment about bulls.

"Complete," Ledesma assured them. "Everyone wants to see Victoriano."

"Any wind?" the matador asked anxiously. If he had not been so completely laced into his suit he would have liked to go to the urinal. Someday, he thought, a bull's horn was going to hit him in the bladder and the damned thing wouldn't be empty and all the penicillin in the world wouldn't save him. "Any wind?" he asked again.

"None," Ledesma assured him. The matador left his chair and went to the window. The trees in the park were blowing as if in a gale. He asked for a cigarette.

"I came to tell you," Ledesma said quietly, "the crowd will demand that Victoriano place at least two pairs of sticks. If he doesn't do it voluntarily you can expect the Indian to force the issue. If I were you, I'd place sticks in the first bull, bad as they say he is." The big man left the room without waiting for a reply, and in a moment the mariachis began their frenetic rendition of "Hail to the Matadors." The Leals leaped toward the door with an eagerness that betrayed their anxiety over this first of the fights.

At three that afternoon, in a smaller room and with no hired valet to tend the costumes, and only a handful of sycophantic visitors, Juan Gómez began an idle conversation with his manager, Cigarro, and Lucha González. That he allowed a woman in his room at such a time was evidence that this matador, too, was nervous. He needed the assurance she gave him. Casual visitors, like myself, drifted in and out; most of them had first stopped by to see the Leals, with whom their sympathies lay, and few had anything substantial to tell Gómez.

Unlike his opponent, the bowlegged little Indian liked to watch the sorting of his bulls even though, by tradition, a matador's manager made the final selection, and matadors rarely stooped to handle such details. Gómez and Cigarro, however, went to the sorting with prearranged signals, and Cigarro rarely assented to any division of the bulls that his matador had not first approved. I once asked Gómez why he attended when other matadors didn't, and he replied, "A matador never knows enough about bulls. I always think, Today I may see the one important thing that will give the bull away." He also differed from Victoriano in that when the bugle sounded for his bull to enter the ring, he did not cover his eyes with his cape but fixed himself behind the barrier, cape folded low, staring with painful intensity at the dark chute from which the bull would catapult into the arena. In this long instant of waiting he held his breath and not until the bull tore into the daylight, his horns attacking the sun, would Gómez release his captive breath with a guttural "Ahhhh! He is here!" Until the bull was dragged out dead the little Indian rarely took his eyes away from that dark menace. Even when dedicating the animal to some influential person or to Lucha, a gesture always applauded by the fans who liked the idea of a matador's being in love with a singer, he seemed to be watching not the honoree but the all-important bull.

He was obsessed with bulls but confused as to what he thought about them. Before any fight he saw them as evil incarnations of some primitive force against which men had always had to fight. They were the timeless enemy replete with evil tricks for destroying men, and he found pleasure in killing them before they killed him. In pursuit of this goal, within the ring, he was remorseless. But in the final moments of a fight, when he and the bull remained alone in the ring, all picadors and stick men and peóns gone, he experienced a surge of remorse at being obligated to kill this honorable creature who had defended himself so courageously. It was in those moments that spectators overheard him talking in gentle accents to his bull, "Eh, torito. Now, my friend, over this way." And he would not have been able to explain why he said these things, except that at this point in the bullfight he loved bulls and did really think of them as his friends.

On this afternoon he complained bitterly about the bulls he had been given. "They are miserable. How can a rancher send out such *ratones*?"

"Yours are as good as Victoriano's," Cigarro claimed defensively.

"Fit for a village fair, no more," Gómez said contemptuously. The three were silent for a few moments until Lucha suggested, "They do it for money, that's why."

"What the hell are you talking about?" Gómez snapped.

"The damned ranchers. They sell these *ratones* and call them bulls just to get money."

Gómez turned and looked at his girl. "What in hell did you suppose they do it for? Why do you suppose I fight? Why do you sing?"

"All right!" Lucha rasped. "So you're growing afraid of Leal. Don't take it out on me."

Gómez stalked over to Lucha. "What was that you said about me and Victoriano?" He drew back as if to strike the tall girl, then muttered, "Don't ever use the word *afraid* around me." He slumped into a chair and took a little water from the carafe on the side table, not as much as he would have liked but enough to drive away the dry taste. He did not swallow, merely gargled and spit into a spittoon.

"How do you see the fight?" he asked Cigarro. He wanted to talk about the bulls.

Lucha interrupted, taking a chair by the door. "If I was you, Juan, I'd do everything I knew with the first bull and scare the pants off that pretty boy."

"How do you see it?" he repeated, ignoring the girl.

"Leal got Ledesma, other critics paid off," Cigarro rationalized in his mumbled shorthand. "You not let me work out deal with Ledesma.

Don't matter much whether you good or bad. Nobody gonna read about it one way or other."

"It matters," Gómez said.

"And where it matter," Cigarro argued, changing his ground, "right here in Toledo. You do real good here, you gonna get contracts next year's festival. Lousy impresario won't want give them, he do what Ledesma say. But public will demand it. Juan, you got to be twice as good as Victoriano. You got to throw everything you got at first bull."

"Isn't that what I just said?" Lucha asked.

The men continued to ignore her and Cigarro continued: "It ain't only Ixmiq. Lot of small-town impresarios here. They ain't seen way you been fightin' against Leal. They just read the papers and in the papers you don't look as good as you really are. Remember, they all prayin' you be lousy, 'cause then they can believe Ledesma and go back to sleep." He stopped abruptly, walked up and down the room several times, then came to stand directly over his matador, staring down at him.

"Juan, this festival you gonna be great. I feel it. How about lettin' me slip Ledesma a couple hundred so he'll tell the world?"

The little Indian, ignoring the suggestion, reiterated his primary concern: "Cigarro, tell me the truth. Can that first bull be fought?"

"Hard to do but possible," the manager grunted. "Second looks better. But I'm puttin' him last so audience go out happy."

The two men fell silent. It wasn't yet time to dress and there were no visitors in the room interesting enough to talk with. Lucha, looking out the window, said, "There comes that fat son-of-a-bitch with a bunch of Americans. I'd like to spit in his eye."

Aimlessly Juan Gómez went to the window to see not his enemy Ledesma but an even greater enemy, a substantial breeze rustling the leaves in the park. "Jesus," he said, "I'll bet Leal's scared to death with that wind blowing."

"Not much wind," Cigarro grunted.

"You're not fighting." The Indian dropped into a chair and asked his manager, "You ever feel like you want to get back into uniform?" Gómez indicated the faded purple cape that Lucha had laid out for him.

Cigarro studied the matador's uniform and shook his head. "I got somethin' better than suit of lights. I got the best bullfighter in the world. Juan, do one thing today. Kill that first bull real good."

"What time is it?" Gómez asked.

"Three-fifteen," Lucha replied. It was still fifteen minutes before her matador could begin to dress, and the bulls in his mind were growing bigger.

"I'd hate to be Leal with that wind blowing," Gómez observed to no one.

"Wind dropped," Cigarro said, and one of the visitors went to the window and repeated: "Yes, the wind's dropping."

"Who's doing the fighting?" Gómez asked again, then leaned forward intently. "You know, Cigarro, I wish you were in lights today. This young fellow, Paquito, he may need help with the *ratones* you and Veneno gave him in the lottery."

"Let him look for himself," the old peón growled.

"You used to look out for a lot of them," Gómez countered. "The reason I wanted you for my manager, you were so good in the ring."

"In ten more years Paquito be good, too," Cigarro insisted. "Only way he'll be good, the way you made it. Fight anything comes into the ring."

At last Lucha cried brightly, "Well, it's three-thirty," and the restless matador immediately began to undress. Strangers pressing at the doorway to see the torero were told: "You've got to get out now," and grudgingly departed.

With Lucha handing Cigarro the worn bits of apparel, and the manager pulling and molding

the clothes against his matador's legs, the intricate ritual of dressing the bullfighter proceeded.
When part of the tinsel tore off the old purple
suit, Lucha mended it with a needle she carried.
"You can afford a new suit," she chided.

"A good suit costs money," snapped Gómez,
irritated to have a woman present while he was
dressing, but as always Lucha insisted on staying, and her matador surrendered, for she was
the one force in his life on which he believed he
could rely.

The ritual was momentarily interrupted when
the door was pushed open and Ledesma thrust
his large face into the room. "Good luck, matador,' he said with just a hint of snideness. When
he saw Lucha he smiled condescendingly, and
to me it looked as if he pitied a matador who
allowed a woman to help him dress.

"I hope the bull jumps the barrier," Gómez
growled, turning away rudely from the critic. "I'd
like to see you running." Wiggling his right hand
deftly, he imitated the fat man running from the
bull.

"I never run," Ledesma replied blandly.
"Don't you. Courage is the only virtue you
have." He left and Lucha continued handing
Cigarro the various parts of the matador's costume. When it came time to use the towel to
force the skintight pants into position, she

handed me one end and worked the other herself.

At last Juan Gómez stood fully attired in the center of the room. His thick black hair crept from under his cornered hat and the muscles of his bowlegs strained against the faded purple cloth. His capable shoulders moved easily as he tested the suit, and his dark face assumed the Indian mask it would retain until the fight was ended. He did not have the commanding figure of a great fighter, the lithe body that could curl around the path of a mad bull, but he did have a rugged physique that made one think he could wrestle a bull bare-handed.

It would not be accurate for me to say, "I also participated in the dressing of Paquito de Monterrey," because it didn't happen in that conventional way. I was more or less dragooned into watching. The blond young American in the Pachuca sweater I'd met on the bus came to the door of the Gómez suite and, when the guard would not allow him to enter, signaled that I join him in the hall. When I did he surprised me. "This kid Paquito is in that cheap hotel over there, and no one's paying attention to him. Go there with your camera and at least take his picture."

It required only a few minutes to reach the young matador's room and in that time my guide reminded me of his own name and background. "Name in the States, Richard Martin. Down here where I'm doing a bit of bullfighting, Ricardo Martín, heavy accent on that last syllable."

"From where?"

"Idaho and San Diego."

At Paquito's mean quarters I found him with his suit of lights carefully laid out on the bed, his two peóns and picador standing by with their suits, and three or four local aficionados. It was the lower rung of the ladder that matadors had to climb and I understood why Ricardo had wanted me to lend it some semblance of dignity. "This is Señor Clay, famous photographer from New York. He wants some photos."

I had no desire whatever for shots of one more beginning fighter, but looking at the brilliant red suit of lights on the bed, I said with feigned enthusiasm, "I could use some of shots of you being dressed—very colorful," and in that way I watched the third of that day's matadors put on his suit. When it came time to do the towel routine with the tight pants, I handed my camera to Ricardo and asked him to shoot me as I handled one end of the towel while we crammed the picador into his heavy pants and Paquito into his lighter ones.

When the four toreros were properly dressed, we rushed down back paths to enter the House of Tile from the rear so we could join the other two matadors when they came down to get into the limousines that would take them to the bull-ring. In this way it would look to the public as if the kid from Monterrey had also stayed in the expensive hotel, and this was important, for in the pecking order of matadors, maintaining a first-rate appearance is obligatory.

Ricardo Martín served as scout for us, and soon he whispered: "They're coming down," and with the skill of master spies on a secret mission, Paquito and his men insinuated themselves into the general milieu of the hotel stairways and halls so that they appeared to have stayed there for some time.

On the Terrace I watched as Juan Gómez and Cigarro overtook the four Leals. Briefly the two matadors stared impersonally at each other, then bowed ceremonially as Paquito de Monterrey and his shabby troupe, picked up for pennies, joined them. A little overeagerly, the young matador greeted the other two as each group climbed into its own limousine for the drive of a few blocks to the plaza.

As soon as the limousines left, the guests of the hotel began to congregate for their own less formal parade to the bullring. With two cameras slung from my neck, two notepads and three pens stuffed into the various pockets of my safari jacket, I led the Oklahomans down the sunny canyon of Avenida Gral. Gurza, flanked with brightly colored houses of blue and cerise and green. "This couldn't be anywhere but Mexico," Mrs. Evans cried. "And there's nowhere else in the world I would rather be today than right here."

My own thoughts were more complex. Watching the three matadors dress in the colorful uniforms they used when challenging death, I took macabre satisfaction as a workman in knowing that if anything did go wrong in this first fight justifying a magazine article, I would have those fascinating photos of how men dressed for this strange occupation. But even if nothing happened till the last day I'd still have the good shots of the two principals. Those of Paquito would be of no account, except for their brilliant color.

My reverie was broken by a sound totally inappropriate for a bullfight.

From well beyond the cathedral on land that was usually vacant came the tinkling music of a merry-go-round, the soaring tunes from a Ferris wheel. Yes, for as long as I could remember, street fairs had been held there to coincide with the bullfights of Ixmiq, so the childish music was a vital part of my childhood.

Before long we pedestrians had caught up with the matadors, whose limousines were constantly halted by crowds of Indians far too poor to afford tickets to the fight but who crowded the Avenida for a glimpse of the toreros. Impassive, they did not cheer as Spaniards would have, but the manner in which their dark eyes followed the four handsome men showed they appreciated the Leals' fame. When Gómez rode past, an Altomec like themselves, they gazed at him in silence and he stared back with stony Indian dignity. I was walking beside the matador's car when it was halted by a mass of sandal-shod Altomecs, from whom not a flicker of an eye betrayed the fact that they wished him well.

Finally the policemen had to open a path for the limousines, and I caught a great shot of Paquito de Monterrey nodding to the crowd, which re-formed like a wave behind his passage. When the Indians engulfed me again, silent and earnest, I was assailed by another assault on my senses. It was the inviting smell of chiles and tripe frying in deep fat, reinforced by the aroma of lemonade and sweet oranges. I was no longer an American journalist but a little Mexican boy holding his father's hand as we hurried to the bullring of Toledo to revel in the Festival of Ixmiq. But even my revered father was eclipsed in my memory by the Indian woman in a shawl who bent over a shallow pan, frying tortillas to accompany the tripe. As I looked at her I thought: She must have operated that stand when I was a boy, selling her wares at the same corner for half a century. I forgot the bullfighters and the rich Oklahomans and asked in colloquial Spanish, "Old mother, may I take your picture, for I used to live here, long ago."

Without halting the trained motions of her hands, she looked up at me but not a flicker of reaction crossed her dark face. She simply stared, her blank, Indian face rimmed by the bright fringes of her shawl. I took the picture, and she returned her attention to her tortillas and tripe.

At last we reached the ring, whose big wooden gates stood slightly ajar to admit us to the shady section where the Oklahomans, using the tickets Mr. Grim had bought from the scalper, had seats as good as the extortionist had promised—second row. As an accredited journalist I was allowed to roam the passageway between the spectators and the red board fence behind which the matadors stood for protection when not fighting in the ring.

At five minutes of five, six workmen in white

pants and blue cotton shirts hauled from the center of the ring an enormous plastic bottle that directed the spectators to "Demand Coca-Cola." Perched on chairs atop the roof, a police band played bullfight music while the rusty hands of the old German clock imported in 1883 creaked their way toward the starting hour. The legal authority who would supervise the fight and ensure compliance with custom was always a local luminary who perched in a gala box at the highest point in the stands. Called the president, he started the festivities by waving a small white handkerchief, whereupon drums rolled, a trumpet sounded, and the rooftop musicians broke into the traditional accompaniment for the fight to begin.

The big red doors through which the matadors would soon enter in their resplendent parade were opened and out rode an elderly man astride a fine white horse. The *alguacil,* as he was called, the constable enforcing the decisions of the president, was handsomely dressed in the frilled costume of the eighteenth century, and made a fine figure as he rode in a stately manner across the ring to ask permission to open the small red door through which the bulls would explode into the ring. Petitioning the president, he received a big brass key, which he held high in the air as he galloped back to disappear through the big doors to hand the ceremonial key to the attendant who guarded the small door from which the six bulls would emerge, one by one.

No matter how many times you have seen the entrance of bullfighters it is always a thrilling experience. They come out not in single file, for that would denigrate the fellow in last position, but side by side, as if all were equal, which is the case as the fight begins. From my safe spot in the passageway I slipped out into the middle of the ring itself, snapping a fast series of color pictures. Through my viewfinder I could see the three matadors as they marched in the order prescribed centuries ago: to my left as I photographed them the senior matador, in this case Juan Gómez in his faded purple suit; on the extreme right, second in point of experience, Victoriano in silver and white; and always in the middle the youngest, in this case Paquito the kid from Monterrey, in scarlet.

When they reached our side of the arena, the one in the shade for the first-class patrons, they spent some minutes in a pleasant ritual. Searching the stands for some beautiful woman sitting in the first row, they draped over the railing before her their ceremonial capes, the richly brocaded garments used only in the opening parade. Then they tested their real capes, the judge nodded to a trumpeter, who rose and sent forth the exciting Moorish bugle cry that traditionally heralds the appearance of the bull. The brassy notes rose impressively, then fell away in mournful cascades, ending in an Oriental wail. The crowd roared and across the ring from where the matadors waited a red gate swung open. From a dark passageway beneath the stands there came a bellowing, a black flash of power and a swirl of dust as the bull torpedoed into the sunlight. Braking with his front feet, he gazed momentarily left and right until, catching sight of a flickering cape, with the mad instinct of his breed he launched a furious charge at his enemy.

Sensing the bull's great power, the crowd roared encouragement and men yelled to their seatmates, "This one looks good!" When the bull saw the red barrier looming, the cheers died, for he cowardly veered away from contact with it, forefeet splayed in the air and horns slashing wildly. Those who knew bulls muttered, "Another disaster," and they were right.

With this bull, who got worse as the fight progressed, Gómez could do nothing. The bull would not follow the cape, nor charge at the picadors, nor allow the banderilleros to place their sticks. By the time Gómez marched out with his sword to attempt a kill, Cigarro was shouting: "This one, nothing. Finish him how you can," but the Gómez sense of honor would not allow that. Six times he tried to do a decent job and six times he struck bone, the sword flying back in a lovely arc and landing point down in the sand. On the seventh try Gómez wounded the beast, but the bull refused to fall. Slowly he paraded around the rim of the arena, refusing to die. The trumpet sounded, warning Gómez to finish this travesty, but he was powerless to do so.

At last the bull staggered sideways and fell. A dagger man leaped out on foot to stab the fallen animal at the base of the skull, and the dismal fight was over.

In the plaza, reactions to this opening fight were varied. The red-necked Oklahoman shouted to his party, with some relief, "I'm glad Ledesma warned us most of the fights are like this. It was even worse than he said."

Mrs. Evans told her companion weakly, "Señor Ledesma intimated this morning that he thought Americans were somehow degenerate because we couldn't tolerate bullfights. How can anyone tolerate this?"

Ledesma, parading through the passageway to chat with friends, saw the Oklahomans and cried in English, "Well, what do you think?"

O. J. Haggard asked, "Was this one of the three that you described as disasters?"

"Oh, no! I'd rate this as one of the better fights. The matador was at least trying."

"My God!" Haggard gasped. "Even with that awful business at the end?"

"Of course!" Ledesma replied with no irony. "A real disaster comes when everything goes wrong and those devils over there"—he pointed to the sunny side—"begin to act up. This time they could see that Gómez was doing his best with a bad bull. You wait. When a real disaster comes, you'll recognize it." He passed on to greet an impresario from the north.

"This is one of the better fights?" Haggard repeated to his group. "I don't think I want to see a disaster."

"You will!" Ed Grim assured him. "From what Ledesma said, by the time this is through, it'll be sickening."

Under the stands, in private quarters reserved for the ranchers, Don Fernando Murillo, the breeder who had supplied the bulls for that day, looked at his friends as his first bull was hauled out. Shrugging his shoulders, he said, "Well, it wasn't one of our best bulls, but it wasn't too bad." Nobody dared ask him what a really bad one would look like. Knowing that if even one bull fought well, the bad ones would be forgiven, they listened respectfully when the breeder predicted, "This next one should yield ears and tail. On the range it looked precious." It was a lie, but uttering it gave him hope.

In the passageway Cigarro, his trademark cigar arrogantly jutted upward toward the crowd, was dismayed but could express his concern to no one. In his matador's first performance there was honor, but none of the grace and excitement that would make a visiting impresario want to contract the Indian for future fights. "Not likely Ixmiq next year," Cigarro mused. "But there's another bull today, three more on Sunday. Maybe something happen." And if nothing happened today, it would be Cigarro's job to make something happen. "Maybe a riot, maybe Juan insult Veneno—oh, anything."

In the patio, where the picadors waited for the second bull, old Veneno astride his horse reflected: "This damned Gómez has guts. Whew! Those horns. Thank the Virgin my son didn't have to fight that one. Now if he can only do something with his own bull." Even as he worried about his son, his thoughts remained on the performance he had just witnessed. "That damned Gómez! Suppose a man with that much guts gets a good bull on his second?" He licked his lips and tasted salt.

Juan Gómez, using a towel to clean his sag-

ging face, thought, God, they build these bulls of
concrete. Seven tries! It's a wonder they didn't
throw the bottles at me today. Maybe the next
bull, maybe the next." He refused to think of the
two tosses he had received, or of his miraculous
escape from the horns as Victoriano swept out
from the barrier like a protecting angel, flapping
wings of magenta and yellow. Those things he
would think of later, but his mind flashed back to
the images he had seen. Since Gómez was of
the school of matadors who preached, "Never
take your eye from the bull's head," even when
he was flying downward in his swift flight toward
the horns, he was looking to see where he
would land and could picture the swift and terrible upward rush of those black-tipped, silver-
based horns as they sought him in the air. He
had landed between them and, with his sharp
eyes still watching everything, had slipped back
off the bull's forehead and down along his wet
flanks. With almost childlike relief he had
watched the approach of the bull's tail as it her-
alded his escape from the horns. Thoughts he
could postpone, but sights he could not, and
again the abrupt appearance of Victoriano and
his rescuing cape flashed before him. "Glad he
was quick," the little Indian grunted to himself.
His face now clean, he moved along the pas-

sageway to where Lucha sat. "You mind if I dedicate the next bull to you?"

"Go ahead," the singer said. "You hurt?"

"No," the little matador grunted, and moved on to where Ledesma was talking with the impresario from the north.

"Lot of courage, matador," Ledesma said in greeting.

"Will you say so tomorrow?" Gómez snapped.

"If you want good notices, you know what to do."

"You miserable son-of-a-bitch," Gómez growled, but the critic replied with "Good luck on your next bull," as he moved off.

Here it might be helpful if I added an explanatory word. Whenever I'm talking to people who know nothing of bullfighting, or writing for them, I remind myself, They probably think the big, heavy capes that are so important in three quarters of the fight are red. That's completely wrong. The capes are magenta or a dull yellow, and they dominate the opening running, the matador's first passes, the work with the picadors and positioning the bull for the sticks. Only at the dead end of the fight is a red cloth used, and it's about half the size of the cape, but it's in at the death and that's what counts. They've

conducted tests and the bull is in no way enraged by the red color. The simple fact is, he
sees it better, but he'll charge anything that
moves, no matter the color. He is a killer, not an
art fancier.

In the passageway Victoriano Leal stood
mumbling with his furled cape already over his
eyes. "That damned Indian. On a bull like that
he should have suffered a disaster." In the folds
of his cape he shook his head. "If mine's the
same kind, what can I do? But it won't be that
kind. It won't be. There goes the trumpet. Now
the gates. Now the bull. He takes the first cape.
The second. Now he's running my way. Now!
Now!" He dropped the cape from his eyes and
saw a handsome thousand-pound bull on the
other side of the barrier. Already the crowd was
crying its approval of this animal's charges, and
on the spur of the moment Victoriano rushed
into the ring, his cape ready, calling, "No, Chucho. He's mine."

With delicate movements the tall young man
goaded the bull, then dropped his hands very
low toward the ground so that the top of the
cape came no higher than his knees. The bull
charged true, sought the cape, buried his sharp
horns in its pliant folds, and thundered past with
tremendous force. Victoriano kept his feet firmly
planted in the sand and arched his back grace-

fully to incite the bull to attempt another charge. Again the huge beast hammered at the cape, and again the crowd sensed the subjugation of great animal force by cool human intellect.

"¡Olé!" shouted the audience, the first of the stormy cries that this Festival was to hear.

"¡Olé!" everyone shouted again as the great bull was brought back. In the breeder's box under the stands, Don Fernando breathed easier. "Like I said, two ears and a tail." On the roof, the band began to play.

When the Leal family got a good bull, it knew what to do. Now Chucho, who directed the fight until his father entered the ring, cried, "Two more passes, Victoriano. Then the half." In compliance, the young matador executed two wonderfully suave passes and finished with an exhibition that earned shouts of approval. He started the next as if he were about to make a normal pass but, as the bull approached, cut the pass in half, pulled the cape close to his body, and gave the bull no target at all so that the animal brushed very close to his left leg. It was a moment of exquisite art.

"¡Olé!" shouted the crowd.

In the passageway Juan Gómez muttered, "I get a complete bitch but he gets a freight train that runs back and forth on rails." He spit.

When the trumpet summoned the picadors

and the gates opened, old Veneno galloped in like a white-haired centaur lusting for combat. He quickly guided his horse into position, studied the bull and waited for Chucho and Diego to lure the animal into the first pic. Testing his right stirrup, against which the bull would strike, he brandished his wooden pole and watched each motion of the beast, aware that in the next few minutes he would be required to make judgments that might determine the outcome of this fight.

Now the bull spied the horse. With a powerful lunge that strengthened the crowd's belief that here was a fine animal, he ripped at the horse with his right horn as Veneno reared in his stirrups, bore down with all his weight, and drove his lance sharply into the hump just back of the neck muscles. This was a dangerous moment, for one never knew how a bull would react to his first sharp stab of pain, and the picador had to be prepared for anything.

This bull was brave. Spreading his hind feet, he braced himself against his unknown adversary and drove ahead like a ten-ton truck plodding uphill. The lance quivered. The horse began to buckle at the knees from the force of the drive, but still Veneno pushed deeper. "We'll see how he takes this one," he grunted furiously as he leaned far out over the bull's horns to push home another lance.

The crowd, aware it was seeing a picador at his best, began to cheer, until it realized Veneno's intent was not merely to punish but to completely destroy the bull. "Let him go!" the men in the sunny seats shouted as the crowd began to boo and curse the old man. Someone threw a cushion, which bounced off his stout hat, but still he drove the iron-tipped lance deeper into the bull's neck. Dark red blood appeared on the animal's flank.

At this point, with the neck muscles damaged so that the bull could no longer carry his head high, Victoriano interposed himself between the horse and the bull and deftly drew the animal away from the picador, utilizing a pass which I had earlier described to Drummond as "poetry flowing over sand." Inciting the bull from a distance with cape low and extended, the matador seemed prepared to execute a normal pass until, when the bull was halfway into his charge, he suddenly pirouetted and twisted the cape about his body, leaving the enraged animal only a flicker of cloth at which to lunge. By the time the bull had turned to charge again, the man was again waiting with the tantalizing cloth, which he once more wound about his body.

"Now you see what Madrid saw!" a partisan shouted.

At the end of the seventh pass, as if Victoriano had planned the maneuver from the start of the series, the bull was left in position before old Veneno's horse, which it charged with such power that horse and picador were thrown to the ground. There was a moment of frenzy, during which the bull tried to gore the fallen man, but Victoriano protected his father with his cape while Paquito de Monterrey, with a series of skilled passes, led the bull away and kept him occupied until Veneno was able to re-mount. From his subterranean position the breeder, who had remained in hiding during the disaster with his first bull, began waving in regal gestures to friends he knew. This bull was not exceptionally good, but it was acceptable, and everyone knew it.

Now old Veneno, shaken and dusty, faced one of the most tantalizing decisions in bullfighting: should he give the powerful bull a third pic, which would weaken the animal and make him easier for Victoriano to handle at the kill, or should he allow his son to make the grand gesture, sure to be popular with the crowd, of petitioning the president to "dismiss the picadors, this brave bull has been punished enough"? It would seem that all evidence would be in favor of the first choice, but there was a catch that might endanger Victoriano's chances for a stupendous triumph.

The rule of the ring was: "After the first pic, the matador whose bull it is has the right to lead the bull away and try to make a series of brilliant passes." After the second pic the matador next below him, in this case Paquito de Monterrey, had taken the bull from the fallen Veneno and made a few passes. Now, if there was a third pic, Juan Gómez, as next in line, could step in, take the fine bull and perhaps launch a series of passes that would eclipse Victoriano, and make a muddle of the afternoon. It was a difficult decision, and I, along with all the other aficionados in the plaza, appreciated Veneno's dilemma.

Victoriano thought: Veneno won't risk a third pic. That's all right with me. He gave the beast hell on the first one. But if he does go for a third pic, it's all right too, because even if Gómez does pull something good, I can still recover with the sticks. I'll show them banderillas they never saw before.

Juan Gómez stood impassively in the escapeway and thought: The old bastard doesn't want to give me a crack at his precious bull. But he knows his son's a coward, so he'll want to destroy the beast. If he tries it, I know what I'm going to do. He waited.

Cigarro, chomping his cigar, was exultant: "This may be it. Veneno's going to go for a third pic and Juan'll tear that bull apart. Now the festival really starts." Outside the arena the merry-go-round played children's songs.

The decision was made by the bull, who sought further battle with the horses, and headed at a trot toward the reserve picador. This unexpected turn dismayed the Leals. The bull would get a third pic, but it wouldn't be as effective as Veneno's and, what was worse, Gómez would get his chance to show.

The Leals swung into action. Chucho rushed across the sand to intercept the galloping bull as Diego leaped the barrier and threw himself in front of the reserve picador. Veneno spurred his horse into a favorable position while Victoriano, with four swift, immaculate passes, drew the bull directly onto the lance of the old man. "Jesus," Cigarro whistled in admiration.

"Those clever bastards!" Gómez snarled. "But wait."

It was nearly two minutes before the little Indian had an opportunity to show what he could accomplish with a good bull, for Veneneo was demonstrating how a wily picador could do a matador's work for him. His third pic, delivered in defensive surprise, as if he were astonished that the bull had switched from the second picador to him of its own volition, was perfect, placed far enough back to damage the bull yet forward enough to permit and encourage the animal to keep lunging ahead. With quick, terrible applications of his right arm, the old man drove the pic deeply home until he could feel bone.

The bull tried to disengage, not through fear but because his backbone seemed about to explode. Veneno allowed no escape, deftly swinging his horse into a tight circle, so that when the bull tried to break away the horse's body was across his path. Man and bull and horse entered into a stately waltz, with the bull always turning to the right to escape but the horse turning a little faster, the man leaning far out of his saddle so that his entire weight drove the pic closer to the backbone. Aficionados called this maneuver "the carioca," and when a bull danced it for two or three minutes, especially with rugged Veneno leading the steps, he was apt to be finished.

During the dance Juan Gómez waited patiently with his cape gathered about his chest, inconspicuously shifting his feet so as to be in position for what he had in mind. Astride the horse Veneno caught a glimpse of him. "That damned little Indian, there he waits like a pauper hoping for scraps at a banquet."

Finally the carioca ended and the bull, gush-ing blood, staggered free. A matador who rushed in would have accomplished nothing, but Juan Gómez, understanding bulls better, waited until the animal recovered his senses. Then the Indian electrified the crowd by swinging his bright cape over his shoulders as if wearing it against a storm, his unprotected body facing the bull. When he extended his right arm a small triangle of yellow cloth presented itself to the bull, but to get to it the animal had to pass under the man's arm and very close to his right leg.

"Eh, torito!" Gómez cried, and the beast charged directly at the small triangle of cape. With thundering speed he passed under the man's arm, brushing his leg with his horn.

"¡Olé!" cried the crowd as the bull turned quickly to a new attack. There again was the fragment of cape, this time raised by the matador's left arm. With a new burst of fury the bull drove at it and again passed under the man's arm. Back and forth, under alternate arms, the bull roared.

The crowd shouted its approval of one of the finest series of passes that would be exhibited during the festival, and back in the corrals old Veneno swore. "I should never have taken that last pic. What's that damned Indian doing out there?"

Veneno, goaded by the Indian's brilliance,

was thinking intelligently; his son was not. Victoriano, aware that Gómez was exciting the public, could only think bitterly and disjointedly: I didn't want that third pic. Why is that Indian so damned lucky with my bull after his failure with his? What can I do to regain control of my bull? And most important, I wish they'd stop ordering me what to do, as if I knew nothing. This is their fault.

The Indian's final pass sent the bull off to the barrier and left Gómez where he had intended to be, alone in the center of the ring. Keeping an eye on the distant bull, he acknowledged the applause that bombarded him. Scarcely moving his body, he bowed his head three times, then, with an eye on the bull, strode with insulting arrogance back to the barrier.

"You see that?" O. J. Haggard asked his group. "I feel weak."

One of the impresarios from the north said to the woman he was with: "These damned Indians know something about emotion the rest of us don't. You see how he kept the bull tied to him in the middle of each pass? Fantastic."

Despite his cry for freedom to direct his own actions, Victoriano now looked for signals from his father, who had returned on foot to the passageway, and the old man indicated the boys were to put on an act that had proved popular elsewhere. As Chucho and Diego made ready to place the sticks, the audience protested in unison with loud cries of "No! No!" Chucho, pretending not to understand what the commotion was about, actually incited the bull as if intending to go through with his job, but as he did so Victoriano moved into the ring and looked up at the crowd as if uncertain of their desires. Using a schoolboy's self-effacing gesture, he pantomimed, "You mean you want little old *me* to place the sticks?"

Gómez, who had seen the act before, thought: This is sickening, but the audience shrieked with approval when the matador signaled that he would place his own banderillas.

But Chucho pretended not to see Victoriano and began a slow run toward the bull, whereupon Victoriano feigned anger and ran to intercept him. For a few carefully timed moments they wrestled not far from the startled bull, who, as they had anticipated, was too surprised to charge. After a sharp scuffle Victoriano grabbed the sticks and dismissed his brother, who sulked back toward the barrier with broad gestures indicating he couldn't understand what the fuss was all about.

The nonsense over, Victoriano now dedicated himself and the banderillas to the crowd— always a popular gesture—and began the most colorful single feature of any bullfight. Across the ring, moving in a heel-and-toe rhythm peculiar to bullfighters, he proceeded in a straight line toward the bull, his back arched in a graceful half-circle, arms high above his head with fingertips pointing downward as they held the banderillas. Standing alternately on flat feet and on tiptoe, Victoriano broke into a run just as the bull did likewise, and the two met for a fraction of a second precisely calculated by the matador. The horns missed but the barbs sped home.

"That's impossible!" O. J. Haggard shouted to his crowd.

"But he did it," the red-necked oilman rebutted.

One of the differences between bullfighting in Mexico and in Spain was that the mother country's matadors were like Juan Gómez—they knew that placing the sticks, albeit dramatic, was the easiest part of the fight and considered it beneath their dignity; but in Mexico it was traditional for even the greatest matadors not only to place their own sticks but also to use spectacular styles that squeezed the last ounce of emotion from the ritual.

Victoriano now profited from the Mexican tradition. His placement of two more excellent pairs halted the fight while he took a turn of the ring as the crowd exploded in approval. Cigars, flowers and goatskin wine bottles cluttered the sand, and occasionally the matador picked up a flask and squirted a thin stream of red wine into his mouth.

"I guess that takes care of the Indian," Veneno said comfortably.

"A dancing boy who wins his laurels with the sticks," Juan Gómez muttered to Cigarro in complete contempt.

As Victoriano finished his tour of the plaza garnering still more cheers, he thought: I've won them back. You do what you have to do, and those were good banderillas. But even three pairs don't add up to one good kill. I'd like to get back to the way I did it years ago, before they took over. He then bowed before the president, asked for permission to kill his bull, and, always the shrewd calculator, reasoned: I'll make the dedication to Ledesma. They'll like that. And it did bring cheers. Then, turning abruptly to the bull he cried "Eh, toro!"

From where I stood it looked as if the bull charged before Victoriano was fully prepared, which would have excused what happened next; as the bull came at him he instinctively moved backward a few inches. The bull turned and charged again; and this time, with no excuse, he shuffled backward as before, revealing his fear. Fans who knew bullfighting began to whistle, and this stiffened his resolve, for he launched three fine, low passes and turned the whistles into cheers.

Heartened by the applause, he spontaneously decided to try a series of naturals, with the cloth kept low in the left hand and the sword behind his back in the right. "You're too far away!" Veneno cautioned his son, who began to move in slightly, edging his feet toward the bull in a shuffling dance.

Suddenly, like a charge of dynamite, the bull boomed forward at the cloth. Suavely and with much skill Victoriano led him past. Three times in quick succession the beast doubled back to strike the target, and on each passage Victoriano gave him only a drooping area of red cloth in front of his left knee. The passes were long and slow and liquid, as good as the crowd would ever see.

Clicking my rapid-fire camera, I shouted to Ledesma in Spanish: "New York will grab that series. Show the readers what the *pase natural* can be." And he called back in English, "Now you know why I love this boy. He'll save bullfighting in Mexico."

On the last natural Victoriano was given an opportunity to display one of his surefire tricks. When the bull charged, as soon as the tip of his left horn was safely past Leal's stomach, the matador pushed his body hard against the bull to leave a smear of blood on the silver-and-white suit. The Oklahomans shouted to one another, "Did you see that?" One of the women gushed that it was the most thrilling thing she had ever seen, but Juan Gómez, leaning against the barrier, sneered: "They've been leaning into bulls like that for thirty years—always after the horn is past."

From the barrier Veneno called, "Kill him quick. No fooling around." Victoriano nodded assent, but approached the bull as if he intended another dramatic pass. "No!" Veneno commanded, and regretfully his son surrendered whatever plans he might have had, gave the bull four hurried passes, then prepared for the kill.

"Not yet!" roared the crowd, sensing that the animal had several more minutes of excellent play. Victoriano appealed to them with his hands spread in a pleading gesture as if asking, "Do you demand still more of me?"

"Yes! Yes!" shouted the crowd.

This presented Veneno with another difficult decision: if his son gave a bad, hasty kill before the bull was properly prepared, all trophies would be lost; but if Victoriano began a new series of passes this bull, learning rapidly, might gore him. The last natural had been far too risky.

"Kill now," Veneno growled to his son, and to himself he muttered, "And may the Virgin make it a good one."

When I saw what Victoriano was about to do I thought: I wish Drummond and his moment-of-truth gang could catch a load of this. The bull had been a strong, courageous animal, deserving of a real fight to the end, and what was about to happen to him was a disgrace. Victoriano ran in a wide circle, made no attempt to go in over the horn, and assassinated his enemy. The brave bull would have needed horns six feet long to have had a chance of catching the distant man. Yet I had to admit that Leal had managed his kill with an illusion of bravery that appealed to the crowd.

While the handsome young matador ran around the arena showing the two black ears he had been awarded, Cigarro came up to me and growled: "You get a picture of that kill?"

"Yep."

"Every photographer got dozen shots showing kills like that, but they never print."

"Why not?"

"Because old Veneno, fight ends, he pays off photographers," Cigarro explained.

"If my story's ever published there'll be one page with Leal killing the way he just did and directly across will be Gómez killing the way he does. Even the little old lady in Dubuque will be able to see the difference."

Cigarro spat into the sand: "If you publish in America only, how they gonna hurt Leal?"

When I heard O. J. Haggard say, "That was really something. Made the Indian look like a beginner," I had to agree that Cigarro had a point.

On the third bull, Paquito de Monterrey in his bright red suit was pathetically out of his class. On the cape work following the pics both Leal and Gómez made him look foolish, a disadvantage from which he was unable to recover. Of such drab performances the critics customarily report: "He complied."

The fourth bull was Gómez's test case, for if the Indian wished to reestablish his reputation in the festival after what Victoriano had accomplished, he had to do well. When his bull came out with feet high and head tossing wildly, chopping viciously at everything in sight, he groaned and muttered, "God, he's worse than the first. But he does charge."

He allowed his peóns to give the bull more preliminary runs than usual, and when the crowd protested he insolently directed his men to take the bull around once more. With some relief he noticed the animal was powerful and willing, but wild as a summer storm. At last he entered the ring himself and tried two classic passes. He launched them well, but the bull was so agitated—so loose, as the matadors say—that Juan was forced to shift his feet or the beast would have run over him. The crowd made no comment, but down in the caverns the breeder predicted, "A great matador could make something of this bull. You watch."

Gómez, beginning to sweat, tried two more classic passes, but again the bull gained terrain and forced him backward. This time the crowd booed. To end the opening section Gómez tried to give his bull one of the half passes Victoriano had used with such effect, and he planted himself properly and with much dignity, but the skittish bull roared past so wildly that Gómez did not just move, he ran, clumsily and without even attempting his pass. The crowd did not boo; its laughter was much worse.

Gómez recovered his composure and tried again. This time the wild, horn-swinging animal lunged past like a runaway truck, but nevertheless Gómez completed his pass. When the picadors appeared Cigarro advised them, "Lay in a ton."

In the routine passes that followed the pics none of the matadors was able to accomplish much. Gómez tried. The other two went through spurious motions, thinking, This isn't my bull. I don't have to prove anything.

When it came time for the banderillas, the peóns placed three perfunctory pairs, keeping well back from the rambunctious horns. At the dedication of the bull, Lucha González found herself wishing it could be given to someone else, for she suspected there was going to be very little honor out of this beast, but when Gómez came before her, she had to accept graciously and the crowd applauded.

Cigarro, watching his former mistress accepting the dedication like a queen acknowledging a suitor's bow, thought, She always know how to behave good, suppose she want to. Then he turned to Gómez: "Don't have to prove nothin', Juan. Kill and be done."

But Gómez had never been able to be content with finishing a bad job badly. His sense of honor would not permit that, so now as he slowly approached the difficult animal I could hear him chanting, "Come to me, torito. I'll teach you how to dance." And I thought, That bull weighs half a ton but to him it's his little toro. The bull did not move, so Gómez, maintaining his shuffling gait, crept closer. "Come to me, torito," he whispered, "and I will make you immortal." Ever closer to the dark horns he moved.

It was only then that I awakened to what this tremendously brave little Indian was going to do. With no flamboyance, no dazzling passes that caused the crowd to shout "¡Olé!" he was going to move right up to the bull's nose and with a long series of low, chopping passes, pulling the neck this way, then that, he was going to tire the bull's great muscles so that he became docile and manageable. This was the art of toreo at its finest, the unspectacular but heroic act of a man dominating a wild bull, dispelling his rambunctiousness, taming him with one masterly low pass after another.

Then suddenly, to the surprise of both the bull and the crowd, Gómez stood upright, feet resolutely planted, and with a high pass that brought the bull's horns close to his head, he wrenched the animal's head high, as high as it could go, stretching the tired neck muscles in the opposite direction. As the bull turned and came back, head still high, Gómez dropped the red cloth and down crashed the head, and the horns, and the exhausted neck muscles. The fight was over. The fractious bull had surrendered. The man had won.

León Ledesma observed grudgingly to an impresario from the north, "We won't see better fighting this year."

"How does he have the guts?" the impresario asked.

"He's an Indian."

"I'd give him a contract if he had a little style."

When Gómez came to the barrier for a drink of water, he told me, "Not sixteen people in this plaza realize what I've done. No cheers. Nothing for me. Well, I've subdued the bull, now I'll subdue the crowd."

In order to understand what he did next, you must know that his series of masterly passes had left the bull perplexed and uncertain as to how or when to charge. The matador was about to risk his life on the assumption that he knew more than the bull himself about the animal's intentions. Carefully testing the bull's eyes, and watching his confusion, Gómez walked slowly up to the black snout. With great control, so that no sudden action might alarm the animal, Gómez dropped to one knee, his face only a few inches from the bull's. When the confused beast gave no sign of moving, Juan dropped his other knee to a position from which flight was impossible. If he had guessed wrong and the bull charged, he was dead.

"Look what he's doing now!" Ledesma groaned.

"This craziness is his only hold on the public," the impresario replied. "It sickens me."

The crowd, remembering how difficult this bull had been, fell silent. Cigarro looked away and prayed. Veneno thought: 'This damned Indian! Why is he allowed to do such ridiculous things? This isn't bullfighting.' Victoriano thought: He's better than that. León Ledesma, disgusted that a classic matador should resort to such cheap exhibitionism, muttered to the impresario from the north, "Get me a gun. If the son-of-a-bitch does the telephone act I'll shoot him."

On the ground Gómez leaned forward until his forehead touched the bull's. For five long seconds he stared at the animal's dark and hairy face, then slowly he drew back. The crowd roared approval of the vulgar display, and from the cheap seats a man who had lugged a set of batteries into the arena for just such a moment began ringing a bell, which echoed through the stadium, while the sunny side chanted: "Teléfono, teléfono!" In the passageway León Ledesma groaned: "I refuse to look. Tell me when it's over."

In the center of the ring, still on his knees before the bull, Juan Gómez cocked his ear as if listening to the bell ringing in the stands. Then, with his left hand he grasped the bewildered bull's right horn and slowly pulled it down until its tip was level with his own left ear. In agonizing silence he brought the tip of the horn directly into his ear, and for almost ten seconds he kept it there, carrying on an imaginary conversation. One chop of the great black head and Gómez would be dead.

No one moved. No one applauded. In the un-bearable suspense the little Indian matador slowly drew back from the horn and began a slow pirouette on his knees until he had turned completely around, exposing his back to the horns, his brown face gazing up at the crowd. Dropping his sword and cloth, he raised his hands in a gesture of supplication.

There was a suppressed gasp from the crowd and Ledesma asked the impresario, "What's he doing now?"

"Knees, back to the bull."

"That cheap, cheap bastard," Ledesma mut-tered.

The mighty roars that engulfed the arena sig-nified that Gómez had gotten to his feet, and Ledesma turned to look at the bowlegged little matador just as the bull, unlocked from the spell into which he had fallen, charged with tremen-dous power. Deftly, Gómez kept him under con-trol with three fine, low passes. As the great beast wheeled his half ton of muscle and bone in the sand, the crowd recognized the risks the matador had taken.

When he came to the barrier to get his sword for the kill, Gómez asked me unemotionally, "You get good pictures of that?"

"The best," I assured him.

"Get pictures of this kill, too," he said bluntly.

He went in hard and true, right over the horns. As the bull took a dozen faltering steps and dropped dead, the crowd shouted wildly. Instead of acknowledging the cheers, Juan Gómez did the sort of thing that made other matadors hate him. He ignored the crowd and marched over to the cave-like room from which the rancher had been watching his bulls.

"Come out, Don Fernando," Gómez insisted, and the hangers-on pushed the rancher into the passage and out into the ring. Together the two men, the bandy-legged little Indian and the tall rancher, circled the arena, and as he passed us I heard Gómez say: "If you give us brave bulls they don't have to be suave. It's my job to make them suave."

The crowd knew that the rancher should properly have taken a turn in the arena after Victoriano's bull, a truly fine animal, and not after the Indian's, which was unruly. But Gómez, by his courage and skill, had made the wild bull good and now he insulted the Leals, disdained the crowd that had applauded them, and scorned León Ledesma, who had been paid to publicize them. Veneno, watching the goings-on in the ring, thought: I'd like to get my pic into that Indian, just once.

His family didn't accomplish much with their second bull, which was not as difficult as the one Gómez had just fought but far too ugly for Victoriano to play around with. The matador allowed his brothers to place the sticks and engineered a halfway decent kill, which produced neither boos nor applause. As the bull was being dragged out Victoriano thought: "One good one, one bad one. Just like Gómez. The day's a draw. But on Sunday, with Palafox bulls, we'll show him how to fight." The trumpet sounded for the last bull of the afternoon.

It belonged, naturally, to Paquito. The young man's manager warned him of the important people here. "If you want contracts, do something."

Unfortunately for Paquito, his last bull was another bad one. The young fellow, although lacking the skill of Juan Gómez, nevertheless tried to emulate him in subduing the dangerous animal by courage alone. Ledesma, watching carefully since he had received a small purse to say something good about the boy, was worried: "This is going to be pretty bad."

But Paquito's placement of the sticks was an impressive show of bravery, and the audience warmed to him. Encouraged, by the time he took the cloth and sword for the final act of the fight, he was prepared to try some special feat that would save the day for him, as Gómez by bravery alone had rescued his. But it was apparent to those of us in the passage that the young torero was not sure what his gesture ought to be, and in this uncertain frame of mind he went out to face the bull.

His first pass was a lucky one. By accident Paquito had planted himself where the bull intended going, and the resulting fusion of man and beast was both artistic and exciting. "¡Olé!" cried the crowd, hopeful they were going to see something after all. Spurred on, the young man achieved three more thrilling passes, and the loud cries of encouragement from the cheap seats tempted him to try a pass that most matadors reserved for what they called the stop-and-go bulls, the perfect animals that charge along straight and true lines. This pass, called the manoletina after the greatest matador of recent years, required Paquito to keep the sword and cloth in his right hand, as if for a regular pass, with the tip of the cloth in his left hand behind his back. Thus the target area provided by the cloth was markedly diminished, and the matador had to pass the bull under his right arm and very close to his body.

Juan Gómez, watching the attempt, mused: "I wouldn't try it with this bull." Victoriano said nothing but by instinct edged a few steps closer so that if the bull caught the boy there would be a better chance of rescue. Old Veneno, also reacting to instinct, motioned Chucho and Diego nearer the barrier so they might leap into the ring if trouble developed, then relaxed upon seeing that his sons had anticipated him.

I saw Léon Ledesma glance at Paquito's manager as if to ask, "You think this is all right?" The manager nodded and pointed to a group of impresarios. Ledesma came over to stand by me and said, "Well, if he manages it, I'll have something to write about."

"Me, too," I said. "If the kid does something really fine, maybe we'll use it in the story. Show them how tough this racket really is," but the journalist in me was thinking: So far we lack a good-focus shot of a man actually being tossed—if he tries the manoletina with this bull, he's going right up in the air. Eyes on my view finder, I heard the young matador calling, "Eh, toro!"

By luck he persuaded the animal to charge directly under his right arm, the banderillas in the beast's back clattering noisily across the matador's chest. It was a tremendous pass and the crowd bellowed, "¡Olé!" Veneno, although it was no business of his, ran to the barrier and shouted, "That's enough," but the boy's manager, hoping to impress the impresarios from the north, shouted, "Keep it going."

Paquito, deluded by the roar of the crowd, launched the pass again, and again he brought the powerful bull close to his ribs. Confident that he had learned how to dominate this bull, he shut his ears to the advice being shouted at him by older men and elected to give one more display of his courage, a pass that had become his specialty in the small plazas where smaller bulls are fought. This time his luck failed him, and as the huge bull bore down, people started screaming: "¡Cuidado! Take care!" But the warning came too late.

With a ripping sound the bull's right horn tore into the boy's left side. There was a confusion of legs and arms spinning in the air and then a collective gasp in the arena as the boy fell awkwardly back upon the horns. With lightning speed the animal tossed the boy three times, catching him on each descent in some new attitude, so that the two deadly horns chopped deep into the rectum and the chest and the face and the neck. With a violent toss of his powerful head, the bull threw the young matador hard against the boards, then wheeled for a last assault and plunged his red-stained horns into the limp body, crushing it against the barrier.

Everyone knew the boy was dead. In one flashing moment the celebrated competition between Leal and Gómez had exploded into a tragedy of which they were not a part. I saw it all through the viewfinder of my rapid-fire camera and, as I automatically clicked the pictures that were later to become famous in bullfight circles, I thought: I'm shooting the wrong man. This one's wearing the scarlet suit. I got a tremendous shot of the four Leals wrestling with the bull, old Veneno holding the tail while Victoriano tried to save the boy. Finally, as I photographed the arena workmen in blue pants and white shirts bearing the broken body toward the infirmary, I had another ugly thought: That blood smearing those white shirts will tell the whole story.

But what I remember most about the death of Paquito is that in the hush of hauling him away I could see the top of the Ferris wheel as it moved slowly through the sky.

When the ring was emptied, Juan Gómez stalked out to kill Paquito's bull, for it was the senior matador's obligation to see that the fight ended as planned even though a man had died. In mordant silence, Gómez led the animal to the proper location for a kill, quieted it with four carefully executed passes, then profiled as always. I wanted to shout, Don't try that, Juan. He's not your bull and he's proved he's deadly. You'll be forgiven if you kill this one with a Victoriano side swipe.

He refused the temptation; he would kill as he always had. When the bull started an unexpected charge, Gómez calmly surrendered his stance, and encouraged the animal to gallop away and release its wild fury. But again, with those low, knowledgeable passes he tamed the bull and again he profiled. This time he drove in deep, right over the still-red horns that had caught Paquito. The bull staggered sideways and fell.

Like a bowlegged gnome in a fairy tale, Juan Gómez came silently back to the barrier, his dignity restored, his teléfono forgiven.

9

THE
MEANING
OF DEATH

A S SOON AS I could elbow my way through
the crowd that lingered in the bullring, still
shocked by the tragic death of Paquito, I
reached the Avenida Gral. Gurza and rushed
along pathways that led through the central
plaza. My task was to get my story and my sixteen rolls of film to New York as rapidly as possible.

As I took the steps leading to the Terrace I
called for the Widow Palafox and gave her two
commissions: "Call that man with the light

plane. He must fly my films to Mexico City airport to catch one of the big planes heading north. And see if the man at the telegraph office will stand by till I get my copy done."

I ran up the stairs to my room and started typing as fast as I could, but soon realized that I knew practically nothing about the dead matador. But as I tried to flesh out the few facts known to me, I had the good luck to hear coming into the House of Tile the troupe of Juan Gómez. Dashing out the door and down the stairs I was able to grab Cigarro and bring him back to my room, where he sat on a chair beside me and, in his near-illiterate manner, told me all he knew about Paquito de Monterrey.

"Poor family. Mother ran boardinghouse maybe. Two daughters work there doing what? Father gone, long ago. Maybe work in Texas don't send no money. Paquito, real name Francisco, in English Frankie, learn passes in the street. . . ."

So the story went of a Mexican boy who wanted to be a bullfighter to escape the ugly poverty of his childhood. With me typing as fast as I could we put down each scrap of information, including the fact that Paquito had once been a choirboy in a storefront church operated by an uncle. I would leave it to New York to sort out the basic story and clean up my sentence structures, but as I was about to end my story I had an afterthought:

> I believe you will find film cassette Color #9 a shot of me helping to dress Paquito prior to the fight. Me holding towel between his legs, he with red jacket draped on chair.

I was satisfied that with such an unusual photograph the story would be sure to run. Thanking Cigarro for his valuable help, I ran downstairs and back through the plaza to the telegraph office. On the way I came upon a group of male singers accompanied by two guitars, and when I heard their words I was satisfied that Paquito de Monterrey had already found a secure place in taurine history.

When a matador is killed in the bullring it is customary for local poets to launch his immortality with a series of folk poems, which occasionally approach high standards. For example, many Americans are familiar with García Lorca's lament for the death of his torero friend Ignacio Sánchez Mejías. I was not surprised, therefore, as I hurried through the crowds to hear this group of musicians offering a mournful ballad, which they had written, words and music, in the relatively brief time in which I composed

my story. It was called, the brass-voiced lead
singer announced with his handheld bullhorn,
"Lament for Paquito de Monterrey."

"He had an eighth-grade education,
    Could write and read the finest books.
He will be mourned by the entire
        population,
For he was a young man of the most
    commanding looks.

"Weep for Paquito!
His cup of tragedy is full,
Killed by Bonito,
That unfair and disgraceful bull.

"His sainted mother lives in Monterrey,
Where Mexican workmen make the
    world's finest glass.
Now her son must be laid away
Because he failed to make the proper
    pass.

"Weep for Paquito!
Through all of Mexico's fair lands.
Killed by Bonito
On Toledo's bloodstained sands."

Within two days we would be hearing this lament over the radio from Mexico City, and by the

end of the week it would be popular throughout the nation, for Mexico reveled in its sorrow whenever a matador was killed. Paquito's lament contained two phrases that were obligatory for such songs. Any bull that succeeded in killing his matador was thenceforth known as "that unfair and disgraceful bull," as if no one realized that when men fight wild animals the beast must sometimes win. Yet at the moment of vilifying the lethal animal, the public also enshrined his memory, so that throughout Mexico men who loved the art would thenceforth never say: "There was this promising kid from Monterrey who was killed by a bull." They would invariably say: "Remember when Paquito was killed by Bonito?" Thus the matador Balderas was killed not by a bull but by Cobijero, Joselito by Bailador, and Manolete by Islero.

The second requirement for a good lament was that it contain the phrase "his sainted mother." This was a convention of which I did not entirely approve, for most of the bullfighters I knew had mothers who had thrown them out of the house at the age of nine. The last time a leading matador died in the ring, his mother was accorded the compulsory sainthood in spite of the fact that up to that particular moment she had run a house of prostitution whose three principal attractions were her own daughters, the sisters of the dead matador. In fact, he had become a bullfighter principally because he grew tired of whispering to any man who looked like an American tourist a touching appeal his mother had taught him: "You like to sleep with my seestair, very clean."

I had no idea what Paquito's mother was like. Chances were she was an old harpy, but nevertheless the mariachis continued wailing about "his sainted mother," and accompanied by this phrase the young matador achieved immortality. His fame was guaranteed by the series of pictures I had taken showing the bull goring him to death. When our magazine ran this sequence Drummond labeled it, with his customary reserve, "the greatest series of bullfight pictures ever taken." I had seen better taken by German refugees in Spain using old-style Leicas, but who was I to contradict my editor?

It was half past ten before I completed the dispatch of story and film to New York, and as I walked back toward my hotel I was assailed by humiliating regrets: I ought to have written something new and perceptive about this sudden, dramatic death, but all I came up with was the same old guff. "Today the Festival of Izmiq in the beautiful colonial city of Toledo saw the career of a promising young matador snuffed out by an enraged bull. His loving family in Monterrey, who depended upon his earnings in the ring, was left destitute. Etc., etc." I had even stooped so low as to quote from the newly composed "Lament."

> Weep for Paquito!
> His cup of tragedy is full.
> Killed by Bonito,
> That unfair and disgraceful bull.

What was even more deplorable than the junk I'd written was my personal reaction to the death: "Damn it all, the wrong man died. The background pictures, the story line—all wasted. Now, if it had been Victoriano or Gómez, the piece would've had significance."

Once before I'd been tempted into such shameful speculation regarding my work. It had occurred during a battle in Korea. Early one Sunday morning I had gone out to photograph the operations of a patrol-in-strength and we had penetrated fairly deeply into Chinese lines when we were hit by considerable enemy fire. We fought our way free and lost only six dead. Some of our men had behaved rather well and I felt sure that I had caught some unusual battle-action pictures.

But as we climbed the rugged Korean mountains that led back to our trenches I realized that this damned patrol had gone out on Sunday, which would be Saturday back in New York, and no matter how fast I filed, my story would miss the next week's edition, and by the week after that no one would give a damn about a casual night action in Korea that was already two weeks old. I had wasted a good story, and I must have been under strain because I remember snapping at the lieutenant who had led the patrol: "You stupid jerk! Why couldn't we have gone out on Friday?"

"What the hell are you talking about?" the young officer asked.

"Well, if we'd gone on Friday I could have gotten this film back in time and you would've had your picture in the magazine."

Very seriously he replied, "But Friday was impossible because we were shifting units at the front." We considered this for a moment, after which he added brightly, "But we might have gone on Saturday? Could you have made the deadline then?"

"Yes," I snapped. And neither of us saw anything ridiculous about our trying to move up by one day a patrol in which six young men from Texas and Minnesota and Oklahoma had been killed.

It was that way when you were a writer. You wanted life to adjust to patterns you had devised. Now the Festival of Ixmiq was shot to hell because the wrong man had died. I told Drummond:

> Looks to me as if the story we had planned is dead. I feel certain that the Leal-Gómez bit is washed up and whereas the Ixmiq idea had a lot of merit originally, whatever happens from here on out has now got to be anticlimactic. I might as well come home but I'll stay to see the finish as a kind of vacation.

I felt sure Drummond would agree with my analysis, for with the shots of Paquito taking the horn so dramatically already in the magazine, there would be no need for a second story and I ought to fly back to New York. But did I want to follow that suggestion, even though I had made it? Clearly no! I wanted to remain in Mexico, to see the conclusion of this feria, to ascertain what steps I should take next to clarify my own life.

I was now in front of the cathedral, to which small groups of men and women clothed in black were coming, summoned by the bronze bells that tolled mournfully, for when a matador died it was customary to hold memorial services. In a curious way I thought I might have played a role in goading him to take the extra chances that resulted in his death. I recalled how, in the lonely room where he dressed, he had been so appreciative that I had come to photograph him. Perhaps he tried those dramatic passes in hopes I'd catch some good shots of him for the newspapers. Of all the visitors to Toledo, I was the one most obligated to attend his wake.

Behind me the mariachis sang their own benediction:

"At the manoletina he was by far the best,
Knowing no fear with any bull.
But now he has got to be laid to rest,
Because Bonito made him look like a
    fool."

It was about eleven that night when I joined the crowd that would be attending the service for Paquito, and as I moved along I became aware of a small man in his mid-sixties who was hurrying toward me. For a moment I did not recognize him, for he was dressed in an ordinary blue business suit, but he obviously knew who I was, so I asked in Spanish, "Don't I know you?"

"Sure, you do," he replied in the American vernacular he loved. "Father Gregorio. I taught you your catechism in the cathedral class you attended in the good days."

"I remember! Mother was determined to make me a good Catholic. She failed. You failed."

"Only because your father never allowed me a clean shot at you." He chuckled.

"Is it true? Did you remain right here in the heart of Toledo? General Gurza's troops searching for secret priests like you all the time?"

"God allowed me to achieve that act of faith."

"How did you have the courage?"

"The help of good people like your mother. Prayer. I was no great hero, Norman. A job to be done. Who could refuse?"

I was confused to see my old friend in street clothes, for although I had witnessed the intense religious hatred that accompanied the revolution, I had forgotten that Mexican law still maintained a strict ban against clerical garb, except within the limits of church property. A rather satisfactory concordat had been worked out between church and state, but even so the state insisted, "We would rather not see priests on the street," so they were forced to wear ordinary clothes.

"I haven't seen you for years," I said with real pleasure. "Are you still stationed in Toledo?"

"In the cathedral," he said proudly. "I'm not

the principal priest, but tonight I'm conducting a Mass for the dead bullfighter."

"I'm attending," I said.

"I'll be proud to have a son of John Clay and Graziela Palafox join me," he assured me. "You like to talk with me while I change?"

We did not enter the main door of the cathedral but went down the side street that contained the open-air chapel, but before we reached the old fortress-church of which it was a part, we ducked into a small side door that led to the cathedral. "The old fortress," he said, "no longer pertains to the cathedral."

"What happened?"

"The state appropriated it for an orphanage." He spoke with no bitterness, but it was apparent that he resented the dismemberment of his church, for throughout history the huge cathedral and the even larger fortress-church had formed one unit, and to think of one divorced from the other was for me, and apparently for Father Gregorio, too, impossible.

"The state has treated you badly, Father," I said as we entered the room where the priests dressed, but to my surprise he corrected me, saying brightly, "It's not too bad, Norman. We now worship openly, and not in secret as we did when you were a boy." Then, as he slipped into his cassock, he added, "There are many things we object to in the present arrangement, but the Church does have freedom to exist. Do you remember when you had to come see me in secret?"

I said, "That was a bad time, Father. We never knew who would be hanged next."

He adjusted his chasuble and remarked, "Those were the cherished days, Norman, when God tested us. Today, when I say Mass it is with a deep conviction." I studied him as he made final preparations to welcome into eternity the soul of a dead bullfighter, and he seemed hardly changed from the days when I first knew him in hiding in the House of Tile. He was sixty-six, a small man, about five feet three, weighing a hundred and twenty. He retained the nervous excitement he had always found in pastoral work, and although I had reason to think that like many Mexican priests he was deficient in education, since seminaries were not allowed in Mexico, he had acquired a satisfactory vocabulary and a constantly deepening understanding of God's ways with rural communities. His street clothes were shabby, but now that they were covered by his clerical vestments he seemed taller and better groomed. He carried his Bible as if it were his personal book and he had developed the habit of looking directly at people; he had done this consciously after long years of hiding, during which he had been afraid to look at anyone lest he betray the fact that he was a clandestine priest. He had escaped death more miraculously than most of his generation, for the revolutionary troops heard of his subterranean Masses and were determined to trap him, but where a wiser man might have been betrayed by his own cleverness, this simple, earthy priest had muddled along and survived with his love of God.

One day, in the quiet years that followed the Revolution, one of General Gurza's colonels had visited the House of Tile as a private citizen and had said to the Widow Palafox, "If we had known you was hidin' that priest Gregorio we would of strung you up."

"He was a good priest," the proprietess assured the colonel. "If you had shot him you'd have destroyed a man who was to accomplish a lot for Mexico."

"One thing honest, señora," the illiterate colonel probed. "Did Gregorio conduct secret Masses here at the House?"

"Yes," she replied. "I warned him not to. The servants warned him not to. And the soldier you left as guard warned him not to."

"My soldier?" the colonel asked.

"Yes, we bought him off. He knew about the bull at the Mineral—and the priest."

"You can always buy a Mexican soldier." The colonel laughed. "So the little priest went right ahead?"

"Regularly."

"He had courage," the colonel agreed. "One night we almost caught him. A little village south of here. Damned little rat ran down a hole in the earth."

"That's why he was so strong," the widow explained. "Close to the earth yet close to God."

"About a year ago, when the trouble had ended, I slipped into a church to hear what kind of nonsense he was preachin'. I sat in the back and he looked at me across the heads of the people, and we nodded."

Now Father Gregorio, who no longer had to run, showed me the passageway into the nave of the cathedral. As I slipped from the hidden door I saw the five Oklahomans, dressed in formal clothes, and from the manner in which they hesitated about taking seats I knew they had never worshiped in a Catholic church before, so I joined them.

When O. J. Haggard saw me approaching he came forward and whispered with the exag-

gerated solemnity that Protestants use in Catholic churches, "Say, I'm glad to see you. Where
do we sit?"

"Anywhere," I explained and led them to a
spot from which we could see Father Gregorio
as he stood at the altar. As we sat down, I noticed that Mrs. Evans had tears in her eyes, so
I said, "In bullfighting death happens."

"I had a son about his age," she replied. "He
was lost over Germany."

I started to say, "I'm sorry," but Mrs. Evans
seemed like a woman who did not want routine
condolences, so I said, "I flew over Japan. In
some ways that was easier. Less flak."

"From what I hear, it was never easy. You had
to fly over great distances of water, didn't you?"
She found a seat next to me and said, "I wasn't
prepared for what I saw today."

"Nobody ever is," I replied. "The bull is so
terribly swift when he finally hits the target."

"It's something primitive and overpowering,"
she answered. "I suppose the explosion of an
airplane in midflight is the same."

"Is that how your son died?" I asked.

"Yes. Other planes in the formation saw his
explode. His wingmen came to visit us in Oklahoma and they assured us his death must have
been instantaneous."

We stopped talking and watched the Mass. In

the bleak, scarred cathedral a few inadequate lights cast ghostly shadows that took my eyes back to the Station of the Cross which we had studied that morning. There again I saw Christ dying in agony on his cross and I noticed that the wounds of Christ were not greatly dissimilar to those that the bull had inflicted on the young matador. I asked Mrs. Evans, "Have you noticed how much of what Señor Ledesma said this morning about death became relevant when real death intruded this afternoon?"

"It seems almost irreligious to say it, but this bloodstained Station of the Cross was a perfect introduction to the fight we saw. I'm not sure I can stand two more fights at this level of intensity."

From the great altar of the cathedral, which must have been a stunning structure when it was covered with silver and precious stones, Father Gregorio droned on and I tried to ascertain what element of the people of Toledo had come to attend the melancholy Mass, but I could reach no conclusion, for the audience seemed to represent a cross section of the entire population. There were Indian women who had probably not been able to afford the bullfight. There were men who luxuriated in the emotionalism of the night. There were young boys who wanted to be bullfighters and there were whole families who would be indignant if a bullfighter were to ask for their daughter in marriage. No common trait characterized this motley crowd, yet they had all come in obedience to a common passion. They sought to understand the significance of death.

The night reminded me of experiences I'd had at our air base during the Korean War. Whenever there was a major disaster we would work like demons to clear up the mess, but later we'd want to congregate and talk about it, as if we'd suddenly started living on a higher plane of consciousness. Invariably someone said, for example, "Wasn't it awful about Larry and his crew?" But Larry and his crew, in dying, produced in the living an added appreciation of life. In later years I often thought of fighter pilots and bullfighters as identical—that is, I thought of them with equal respect and, if they died, with equal reverence.

Mrs. Evans touched my arm and said, "Look! Your friends have all come to mourn," and in various parts of the cathedral, clustered together in different groups, sat Veneno and his sons in shadow, Juan Gómez and his crew near a pillar still pockmarked with revolutionary bullets, and León Ledesma and Ricardo Martín, both silent and somber. And beyond them, sitting alone, was the tall, thin, beetle-browed poet, Aquiles Aguilar, who had won the poetry prize the night before at the Tournament of Flowers. He was writing, and I was sure that he was using the cathedral and the Mass as inspiration for his own elegy on the death of the young matador.

From where I sat I could see the four handsome Leals, a battered arch and the Station of the Cross that showed the crucifixion. The shadows were deep behind the men and the vaulting of the desecrated cathedral seemed like an archway to death. Kneeling in the aisle, I framed the old picador and his sons and clicked the shutter before they were aware of me, but the slight noise alerted them and, like the actors they were, they understood at once what I was after; so each set his face a little more overtly in an expression of grief. I could not then foresee that one of these photographs would ultimately be used in half a dozen different books as a classic representation of toreros contemplating death. But what I did appreciate even then was that of my half-dozen shots, the one that came out best was the one I took before the four Leals had begun to pose. In this one their grief was not so obvious, so the picture was more compelling.

When the Mass ended near midnight I approached the poet Aguilar, who had been writing in the shadows, and said in Spanish, "Excuse me, sir, but I heard that you work in Don Eduardo's museum. I'm taking some visitors from the States around Toledo. Could we one day . . . ?"

"Of course!" the tall, angular man said with the enthusiasm that amateurs have for a field in which they have done some work. When we were all outside the cathedral he said, in English, "It's a museum Don Eduardo has supported for years. Not very good, but it'll show you what bullfighting's all about."

"Where did you learn such good English?" O. J. Haggard asked.

"Worked as a druggist in Texas," the poet replied.

"You Mexicans put us to shame," Haggard said.

"We like to talk," the poet laughed. "To think of being locked up in Texas without being able to talk the language would drive a Mexican crazy." Impulsively he stopped us under a streetlight and asked, "Would you like to hear the poem I have just completed about the death of Paquito?"

"Oh, yes!" Mrs. Evans cried.

"We'll go into the bar," Haggard suggested, pointing to the cantina where Lucha González sang.

"Poems are not for bars," Aguilar said stiffly.

"At least not this poem." He spoke quickly, switching back and forth between English and Spanish, which I didn't bother to translate.

"Make a circle for the poet," Ed Grim cried, and something in his voice betrayed the contempt he felt for both Mexicans and poets. We all sensed this, so Mrs. Evans quickly said, "Stand here by me, where the light's better," and I said, "Señor Aguilar won first prize last night in the big poetry contest."

"He did!" Mrs. Evans repeated. "Señor, may I congratulate you?" She said this so simply, with such exquisite rightness, that the poet had to forget the earlier insult. "It was an ode," he explained, "to our local beauty queen. She was the prettiest girl I saw yesterday. You are the prettiest tonight." The other women clapped.

"And now the poem," Mrs. Evans said.

"It's in Spanish, of course," Aguilar explained. "I'll read it in that language first, because Spanish is the language of poetry, and then I'll give a rough translation in English, which is the language for making money." Forthwith he launched into an impassioned recitation of his reactions to the death of a young bullfighter, and as his voice rose in the quiet night air, a crowd began to gather under the streetlight. When the poem reached its climax, I saw that from the terrace of the House of Tile had come the blond young American in the Pachuca sweater, and he listened intently as the agitated poet declaimed his threnody. When the last words had died away the young man pushed his way through the crowd, came up to the poet and said in hesitant Spanish, "Maestro, you have spoken for all of us." Without waiting for comment, he abruptly left us.

"In English," Aguilar explained, "the ideas in the poem are more restrained, and of course they won't rhyme." As he started to improvise, it was natural that those in the crowd who could not understand English should start to drift away, but I was surprised at the number who remained to hear the awkward words:

"Death, who lives near the aqueduct,
  Called for him a little sooner than for us.
  There was dancing and sweet candies
    and festival
  And death did a little jig with a red
    cape."

I could see Grim trying to figure this one out, and even Mr. Haggard was looking a little speculative, apparently of the opinion that whereas it might be pretty good in Spanish, in English it was pretty bad.

"This next part gets rather difficult," Aguilar

apologized. He tried twice to put his words into an alien tongue, then crumpled up the paper and cried, "Damn English." He sighed, unfolded the poem and tried again:

"Water from the aqueduct where death
     lives
   Cools my sorrow. And the pyramid
   Is able to accommodate itself to one
     more loss.
   In the cathedral I try to weep, but there is
     dancing.
   Paquito is no more, but the bull's head
     will be mounted."

He ended with a flourish and once more assured us, "In Spanish it's better."

"I don't get it," Grim exploded. "I just don't get it. What's this about the aqueduct?"

Señor Aguilar was not the least embarrassed by the question. "What I'm trying to do," he explained patiently, "is to indicate that this young man from Monterrey was killed in Toledo."

"Then why didn't you say so?" the oilman asked.

"It's got to be done with symbols," the poet expounded. "You don't just say, 'Paquito was killed in Toledo.' "

"I would," the oilman snapped.

"That's because you're not a poet," Aguilar said in Spanish. The crowd laughed.

Aguilar translated his comment and, to show that he had enjoyed the oilman's reactions, threw his arm about Grim's shoulder and said, "Off we go the Terrace for a goodnight copa," and the poetry reading ended in harmony.

To my surprise, Mrs. Evans, agitated by the afternoon tragedy, wanted to escape any frivolity at the hotel. "Could we," she asked tentatively, "go back to that chapel?"

"It's midnight, but if you wish . . ."

"I do." She told the others, "I've asked Mr. Clay to show me the outdoor chapel again," and the manner in which she spoke indicated that she intended going alone with me. At this Ed Grim cried, "Laura! He's young enough to be your son!" She replied, "I wish I had a son like him." And off we went.

When we were seated on a tile bench in the small plaza that faced the outdoor chapel Mrs. Evans said, "That was an amusing remark Ed made about your being young enough to be my son. We've just come from Cuernavaca, as you probably know, and what impressed me there —throughout all Mexico for that matter—is the astonishing number of American widows who live in Mexico and who are invariably attended

by handsome young American men from Yale
and Princeton. Nobody ever told me this was
going on."

"Were you envious?" I asked.

The sixty-four-year-old widow laughed and
said, "I might have been. Even a sensible
woman might have been. It's most flattering to
be attended by an attractive young man. But
one evening in the hotel I saw a particularly
good-looking widow in her sixties, silver-gray
hair and all that, who was accompanied by a
broad-shouldered young god, probably in his
late twenties, and I was thinking, How handsome they both are, when I realized that this
young blond god was the son of a poor Oklahoma druggist. I had represented my husband
on the committee that had selected him for a
scholarship to Yale, where he had played football and done very well in his studies. It was the
same boy, a boy of really outstanding talent, and
here he was in Mexico, working as a paid escort."

"Good work, if you can get it," I observed.

"But not for a young boy with promise. I was
so distressed that one morning I introduced myself to the young man, telling him of my past
interest in his career, and he wasn't the least
embarrassed. 'Who'd want to go back to Oklahoma?' he asked. I pointed out that people of

accomplishment lived there and he replied, 'It's all right if you like oil and heifers.' He said that one week of Yale had convinced him that Oklahoma wasn't for him. When I asked him why he hadn't taken a job in New York or somewhere he said, 'I may marry Ethel and then I'll have a job in New York, just as you suggest.' When I asked what, he said, 'Managing her money—on Wall Street.' I felt like telling him that Oklahoma was glad to be rid of him, but instead I started to cry, and do you know why? Not for him and his lack of principle, but because the first substantial check I wrote after my husband's death was my contribution to the scholarship fund for Yale. And this pathetic creature had won that scholarship. I had intended helping some deserving boy start in the world, and my good money . . ."

She blew her nose and, regaining her composure, she said, "My visit to Mexico has had some rather emotional overtones, as you can guess, but none equal to this day's. I'd like to talk with that Ledesma man for hours. So many people you meet say nothing." She pointed to the low arches of the outdoor chapel and said, "I lived with my husband for forty-two years, and until I heard Señor Ledesma chattering this morning I never even dimly understood what marriage was all about."

"I don't recall his saying anything about marriage," I replied, "although if you're around him long enough you're bound to hear him say something about everything."

"It was while he was talking about the cathedral. He said there were two entrances to any edifice. And of course there are, but in sixty-four years of life I didn't discover this for myself."

"In what particular?" I asked.

The widow sat staring at the strong low entrance to the fortress-church. She tapped her fingers against the tile bench and watched the night shadows play back and forth across the carved stones. At another bench a young couple were kissing and from the corner bar up the street we could hear the faint echo of Lucha González's singing. It was a beautiful night and for a long time we said nothing. Then she observed, "There are two entrances to any marriage, the low, brutal, honest one down the side street and the highly ornamented, delicate one up front. And I never realized that his entrance was just as valid as the one I preferred."

I decided to let this comment stand by itself, for with my record I was certainly no one to comment on marriage, but Mrs. Evans followed up by observing, "In ten years—think of it, only five hundred weeks—I will probably be dead and this cathedral will still be here and this plaza and the ghosts of the Spanish soldiers who stood on those ramparts to fire at the Indians. I was fascinated by the bullfight today and by that gaunt poet, and the matadors. I think I shall die a sounder woman for having experienced today."

This was getting too deep for me, so I said, "We'd better get back to the hotel and have some supper."

When we reached the Terrace we found that the other Oklahomans had collared Ledesma, who sprawled in his chair explaining the day's fight and any other topic that came up.

Ed Grim cried, "Ah, the lovers back from the cemetery. Remember what the old man said to his wife, 'When I think of our beautiful daughter laying out there in the cemetery, I almost wish she was dead.' "

"Not funny," Haggard said, making a place for us at the table that the Widow Palafox was about to cover with food.

"I enjoyed your observations so much this morning," Mrs. Evans told the critic, "that I'm sorry I wasn't here when you started tonight."

"I've said nothing so far," Ledesma assured her. "But later on I'll be brilliant."

"He's lying," Haggard interrupted. "He's been giving us a fascinating comparison of payola in Mexico and in the United States."

Delighted to be able to repeat himself, Ledesma said, "All I said was that I never write a word about bullfighting until I have been amply paid by the fighters I'm discussing. I feel that the men involved are better paymasters than some impersonal cash register in a newspaper office. When a bullfighter pays me, I've got to write interestingly."

"Don't you ever wish," Haggard asked, "that you could avoid all this . . . this . . ."

"Sycophancy?" Ledesma asked.

"I was thinking of back-scratching." Haggard laughed. "Your word's better."

"And yours more colorful."

"Thank you. But wouldn't you prefer being paid a decent wage by your paper, instead of being bribed, so that you could write only the truth?"

"There's the problem," Ledesma cried, spreading his hands. "In Mexico we feel that the simplest way to ensure relative truth is to pass around ample payola. The government does it, the Church, the businessmen, the movie actresses. For example, this morning Mrs. Evans here forced me into admitting that I preferred Juan Gómez's style of fighting, but believe me I would never say so in public unless he paid me to do so. To me, payment sanctifies my judgment."

"We Americans find all this very disagree-
able," Haggard said.

"But do you?" Ledesma countered. "I've
watched businessmen of sixteen different countries come down here to Mexico in search of
markets. And which ones, do you suppose,
adapted themselves most quickly and easily to
our system of handing out graft for everything?
You norteamericanos. Invariably your people
make the best crooks. For clever fraud I'd have
to put the British first, because fraud requires
finesse, but for downright thievery and corrup-
tion of public officials, I'd take a typical norteamericano every time. Ask Clay. He's a
Mexican."

The Oklahomans turned to me and I said, "I'd
like to object to the bad character Ledesma
gives us North Americans, but I can't. I've recently come back from a long trip through Latin
America and practically every aspect of daily
living is controlled by blatant graft. For example,
tonight when I tried to get my films off to New
York I had to bribe the owner of the shipping
office who claimed to have lost the key, the
maid who said the electricity couldn't be turned
on, and the official who took it to Mexico City. So
there is constant bribery. But the people who
accommodate themselves most easily to it, and

who become experts in the art, are, as Ledesma says, the Americans."

"Let me cite a case," Ledesma began to expatiate. "This afternoon in the bullring a young man was killed." He crossed himself. "Now every single act of that tragedy was manured in graft. The suit the young man wore had cost him double because of a crooked valet. The sword he used had been stolen from a richer matador. His salary had been manipulated by his thieving manager, and what I shall say about him in the paper tomorrow was paid for in advance. Could you find a more completely dishonest event?" He paused dramatically and looked at the Oklahomans. "Yes," he said. "Not long ago in the United States a college with a good reputation went to a high school with an equally good reputation and said, 'You have this fine basketball player. We need him to attract large crowds to pay for our posh arena. But his high school marks are low. Will you make them high enough so that we can admit him?' The school raised the marks. The college lowered its standards. The coach paid the boy as if he were a professional. The boy took almost no classes but was nevertheless declared eligible. Everybody— how you say it—winked at everybody else, so what did the boy do? He entered into a compact with gamblers to throw important games. The gamblers paid off the police so they could bet freely and make a lot of money. And writers like me in your papers said nothing about the whole dirty business, although they knew what was happening. Do you know why such behavior is so much worse than bullfighting?" He stared at Mr. Haggard.

"How do you know so much about basketball?" Haggard asked evasively.

"Because I'm a philosopher, and it's my business to know," Ledesma replied. "And I also know this. Bullfighting corrupts only the fringes of society, the unimportant make-believe element. But your basketball scandals corrupt the very heart of your nation—the universities, the young men of promise, the police. And there is also this significant difference. In basketball nothing is honest. Everything has been corrupted from the university president down to the home of the high school player. In bullfighting every human element has been corrupted. Difference is, the bull remains honest, and since the lottery that determines which matador draws which pair of bulls might mean the difference between life and death, it too has remained incorruptible."

There was a long silence, and then Haggard, who was looking past my shoulder, cried, "There's the young man!" and I looked around

to see the blond American in the shaggy Pachuca sweater. Haggard rose and drew the
young fellow into the circle, finding a chair for
him and saying, "We owe you a real debt, young
man. The Widow Palafox told us you gave up
your room for us."

"She paid me double what I was paying to
give it up," the young man replied. Noticing the
critic, he jumped to his feet and bowed. "You're
León Ledesma," he said in Spanish.

"I am," the critic replied.

"I'm Ricardo Martín," the boy said, giving his
last name the Spanish pronunciation by accent-
ing the last syllable.

"Is that an American name?" Haggard asked.

"I was . . ." Once more the young man became inarticulate, and then, finally, he said,
"Name's Richard Martin Caldwell."

"Where you from?" Ed Grim asked.

"Boise, Idaho."

"Marvelous country," the Oklahoman said.
"Good hunting, fishing, all that."

"What you doing in Mexico?" the red-necked
man persisted.

The young fellow thought for a moment and
started to speak. No words came and he
hunched sideways in his chair, as if he had decided not to reply. Then he saw Ledesma and

said in a rush, "Came down here to be a bullfighter."

"You what?" Grim exclaimed.

"I . . . well . . ." he fumbled, longer than usual,
as if the explanation he had at the end of his
tongue were too preposterous to throw out into
a public discussion. "There was this G.I. Bill."

"What war were you in?" Grim asked with
open contempt.

"Korean," the boy replied. Then staring forcefully at his questioner he added, "Marine."

"You were a Marine?" the Oklahoman
shouted. "I was a Marine. Shake, buddy." The
two shook hands awkwardly.

"I shouldn't think you could use G.I. funds to
study bullfighting?" Mrs. Evans observed.

"You can't," the boy said. "But . . . well . . ."

"Are you at Mexico City College?" Ledesma
intruded.

"Yes, sir."

"Quite a few of your G.I.s used their scholarship funds to come to Mexico," Ledesma explained. "They couldn't get into our university,
of course, but they do attend Mexico City College, an American school, and half a dozen or
more are studying to be bullfighters—on the
side, that is."

"An American boy wants to be a bullfighter?" Grim asked. "What does your father say?"

The young man hunched up his ridiculous oversized sweater and started to speak but said nothing. His silence was broken by the arrival of food, and Mr. Haggard said, "Son, dinner is on me."

"I . . ." the young man began, but seeing the food, he apparently felt that no further comment was required. I was interested in his verbal hesitancy, because if I could judge he was twenty-five or twenty-six and seemed to have at least an average intelligence. He ate with passable manners and used his napkin to wipe his mouth after the fish soup.

"How'd you get interested in bullfighting?" Grim asked. "In Idaho?"

"After Korea I was stationed—"

"Wait a minute," the Oklahoman interrupted. "How old are you?"

"I don't think—"

"I mean, you must of been in diapers when you enlisted in the Marines." The red-necked man spoke with pride in the boy's early enlistment.

"My father missed World War Two. Exempted because of me. But he's a very military man."

"Army, Navy?" the Oklahoman asked.

"Nothing. Just make-believe military," the boy

said. By the manner in which he attacked the Valencian rice he indicated that he was not interested in further conversation, but Mrs. Evans asked quietly, "How old were you when you went into the Marines?"

"Sixteen. My old man lied about my age. Said every red-blooded American . . ."

"I don't like the way you speak of your father," Grim protested. "What's the matter? Weren't you proud to be a Marine?"

Without looking up the boy said, "You talk just like my old man."

"Now, wait a minute!" the Oklahoman snapped.

"O.K., so you were a big hero," the boy said, still not looking up.

"What the hell are you, a beatnik or something?"

"Like I said, you were a big hero. It's O.K."

"Marine or no Marine," Grim shouted. "You don't talk to me—" He belligerently rose from his chair but the young man remained seated, eating his rice.

It was Mrs. Evans who broke the tension, and she did it by using Mr. Grim's real name. "Sit down, Chester," she commanded.

At this the boy threw down his napkin and said, "I might of known his name was Chester."

"That does it!" the red-necked ex-Marine bel-

lowed. He grabbed for the boy's throat but
caught only the Pachuca sweater, which pulled
out to a ridiculous length, so that one of the
antagonists stood on one side of the table and
the other clear across it.

Mrs. Evans began to laugh. "You look so ridiculous," she cried, and the other Oklahomans
also began laughing. Chester's daughter said,
"Sit down, Daddy. You're making a fool of yourself."

When the red-necked ex-Marine let go of the
sweater collar, it flopped back around the boy's
neck, and this caused more laughter. "Where in
the world did you get such a sweater?" Mrs.
Evans asked.

"Sort of a . . ." the boy began.

"It's a uniform affected by students," Ledesma explained. "Where did you see your first
bullfight?"

It was obvious that Ricardo Martín was just as
impressed by the bullfight critic as he was an-
noyed by the Oklahomans, so he turned directly
to Ledesma and addressed him exclusively, "I
get home from Korea—"

"Does that mean you were wounded and sent
home as a hero?" Ledesma asked perceptively.

The boy squirmed in his chair and rolled up
the sleeves of his sweater until it looked even
more ludicrous than before. "Well . . ." he fum-

bled. "Couple of medals. So they station me at San Diego . . . recruiting . . . high schools."

"And there you saw a bullfight?" I suggested, recalling the time I'd driven down from an interview I was doing in Hollywood to see the border fights.

"Not so simple. There was this coffee joint. A guy singing ballads . . . a guitar. Real gone. Real far out. On off time we used to go there, and some of them were mad about bullfighting . . . flamenco . . . you know . . ."

"So one Sunday they took you to Tijuana," I guessed.

"Yep."

"You liked it from the start?"

"First day, Juan Gómez. Boom!" He used his right arm like a sword and plunged it into an imaginary bull.

"So when did you decide to become a bullfighter?" I continued, eager to understand the phenomenon of American boys who underwent great sacrifices to become toreros.

Again he became fidgety and I thought he might not reply, but apparently he wanted so much to talk with Ledesma that he was willing to share his thoughts with me, too. Turning to Ed Grim, he said, "You won't like this, but I mean no offense." He spoke so softly and with such obvious goodwill that Mrs. Evans laughed and said, "Chester wouldn't dare raise trouble with a Marine who has medals. What did you get them for?"

Ricardo ignored the question and said to Ledesma, "So one day I was sitting in this coffee shop in San Diego . . . in civvies . . . and I was sort of joining the gang in some music and my father had driven down from Idaho to visit me at the base. . . . He was always mad about Marine bases and parades and me in uniform. . . . So he's disappointed I'm not there and they send him to the coffee joint and when he sticks his nose inside there's this smoke and the smell of java and this guy playing a guitar and me sitting in the corner playing a recorder, and he takes one look at me sitting there in civvies and he yells, 'My God, what are you doing with a flute?' And right there I know I wanted to be a bullfighter. Because I want to be as much unlike that pathetic crock of . . .'"

"Has he ever visited you here in Mexico?" Mrs. Evans asked.

"Once. He says, 'What you doin' in a spick college?' When he sees my new name is Ricardo Martín . . ." He gave the name its Spanish pronunciation, then explained, "My mother's name was Martin. From Denver."

"Does he send you any money?" Mrs. Evans asked.

"You know why he came down here?" Ricardo addressed this question to Ledesma. "He's been named chairman of the Idaho Civil War Centenary Commission and he's all mad for staging replicas of the major battles. He's going to be General Lee and he came down for me to be his aide, General Beauregard." He stopped and ate some more rice. "Imagine! When the Civil War was fought Idaho was a prairie. You ever stop to think that everyone like my old man who is mad for the Civil War wants to be General Lee. Nobody ever wants to be General Grant. My old man is no more related to the South—"

"I ought to smash you right in the mouth," Ed Grim muttered. "Who the hell are you to . . ."

Ricardo ignored the threat and said to Ledesma, "But, anyway, my old man's going to be hightailing it all over Idaho as General Lee and I'm going to be in Mexico fighting bulls."

"Have you had any fights?" I asked.

"Village fairs."

"Ever fight with picadors?" Ledesma probed and his question was significant. For if Ricardo said yes, it indicated that he had fought bulls of some size, for picadors are not employed against scrubs.

"I had a novillada at San Bernardo."

Ledesma nodded approvingly.

"Have you fought real bulls?" Mrs. Evans asked.

"Of course," Ricardo said.

"Have you actually killed a bull?" Mrs. Evans pursued.

"Eight . . . ten . . ."

"Are you any good?" O. J. Haggard asked.

"Yes," the young man replied.

"Do you mean to say—" Grim began.

"Yes," the young man said quietly, "I mean to say that I'm going to be a bullfighter."

"Why would a decent American kid . . ." the red-necked man began, but Mrs. Evans didn't hear the finish of the question nor Ricardo's reply, for she was recalling with amusement the fact that in Cuernavaca she had used exactly the same phrase when chiding the druggist's son who had graduated from Yale to become a paid escort. She thought: Older generations have trouble dealing with the ambitions of the young. She therefore broke the thread of interrogation by interrupting whatever Chester and the boy were fighting about to say, "Ricardo, when I was in Cuernavaca I met more than a dozen young American boys like you who were . . . well . . . they . . ."

"Escorts?" Ricardo asked with no surprise.

"Yes. They seemed to have reasonably satisfactory lives worked out for themselves. Why would you choose bullfighting instead of the easier way?''

"That's the first intelligent question I've been asked here tonight," the quiet young man said. Quickly he corrected himself, saying to Ledesma, "Except yours about the picadors, but that was specialized." Ledesma, gratified by the young man's payment of moral graft, as it were, nodded condescendingly and the young bullfighter continued: "As a matter of fact, I tried being an escort once. When you want to be a bullfighter you'll try anything—absolutely anything." He whipped about to me and asked, "You got anybody you want killed?"

Mrs. Evans resumed her questioning: "Didn't it work?"

"For some proud men it's impossible to romance an older woman."

At this remark the red-necked man gasped, leaned across the table, and slapped the young bullfighter across the face. "No man can talk like that in front of my daughter," he said, but the effect of his words was diminished by the fact that when he said them, Penny started giggling at the ridiculousness of it all. To my surprise Ricardo took no notice of the blow and continued talking solely with Mrs. Evans: "So after three months in Cuernavaca and Acapulco I quit.''

"How do the others explain the fact that they don't?" Mrs. Evans asked.

"Good heavens, Elsie!" Grim protested. "You'd think you were trying to line up an escort for yourself."

"I'm interested in what women my age do to solve their problems," Mrs. Evans replied firmly.

"What problems?" Ed asked.

"The problem of meaning in life," Mrs. Evans said. "When a husband dies and the children are gone and your eyes are too weak for constant reading, what in hell does a woman do? Apparently a good many take the hard-earned money their husbands left them and spend it on young men in Mexico."

"It's repulsive," Haggard said, reaching for the lima beans and ham hocks.

"It's not repulsive," Mrs. Evans argued.

"He just said it was," Grim replied, pointing with his fork at Ricardo.

"He said it was repulsive to him," Mrs. Evans responded, "and properly so, for young men should be interested in young girls, but I don't think he gave any opinion about how the women who were paying the bills—"

"Ethel!" Grim shouted. "What the hell's happened to you? If Paul heard you—"

"He wouldn't understand a word I was saying, and that's a pity."

"Was Paul a lot like my old man?" the young bullfighter asked.

"No," Mrs. Evans corrected. "He was a fine, thoughtful, hardworking man with whom I lived for forty-two years without even remotely comprehending what he was all about. Maybe when you're older you'll say the same about your father."

"Stupid jerks remain stupid jerks," the boy insisted. Then quickly he turned to warn Ed Grim, "And if you ever touch me again, Pop, I'll tear you limb from limb, you miserable son-of-a-bitch."

Grim rose automatically to the insult, as Ricardo knew he would have to, and lunged for the young man, who stood him off with two light-ning-quick jabs that did no harm.

"Sit down, Chester!" Mr. Haggard com-manded with some irritation. "We came to see the fights in the bullring." Not rising from his chair, he said to Ricardo, "I'd appreciate it if you'd apologize to Chester, for that last remark was out of line. He had a right to knock your block off."

"I apologize," Ricardo said honestly. "I with-draw those words, Mr. Grim. And I apologize to you too, Miss Grim. But your father has strong opinions, as I'm sure you know." When Grim said, "I knew no Marine could be all bad," the table relaxed.

Mrs. Evans turned to Ledesma. "I've been so impressed by your opinions—I wonder if you'd drive me out to the pyramid again? It's been haunting me all day and I'd like to see it by moonlight."

Ledesma groaned: "I will not go back to that pile of bloodied rocks." When Mrs. Evans said, "But you must," he replied: "On this day of death I will show you something appropriate to the occasion, something unique in the New World," and Mrs. Evans cried: "Let's go!" Ledesma banged on the table and cried: "Widow Palafox! Watch our plates while we descend into the past."

The widow appeared on the Terrace to warn that if anyone got up from the table, when he or she returned the food would be gone, for it was now one in the morning. So we ate in big gulps, then hurried toward Mrs. Evans's Cadillac, but on the way she nudged me and revealed her growing interest in Ricardo: "Fetch him. He ought to see it if it's significant." Soon we were piled into the big car and with me at the wheel and Ledesma guiding me, we drove a short distance west on the León highway to a place where a grove of cypresses gave it a funereal aspect. Ledesma routed out the caretaker, gave him some pesos and asked him to turn on the lights, and when this was done we saw among the trees the kind of stone monument common in Mexican cemeteries. This one provided a portal that led us down a flight of steep steps to a geological miracle, a cavern in the same rock layer that held the silver ore at the Mineral, except that here it provided an atmosphere with zero humidity.

"For ten thousand years," Ledesma told us, "no moisture entered this place, and with modern machinery none is allowed in now. The result? Voilà!" and with that he carefully opened first a huge wooden gate, allowing us to enter a small antechamber guarded by a small, tightly fitted steel doorway leading to whatever was hidden inside. Switching on another light, he opened this last door and led us into a subterranean miracle that had not yet been opened to the public when I lived in Toledo.

It was a gallery about eighty feet long and twenty feet wide that had been cut into solid rock millennia ago by some underground force, perhaps a long-vanished stream or a readjustment of volcanic lava, and then sealed off by some mysterious agency. It formed a perfect catacomb, its sides lined by dozens of amazing figures, men and women of all ages and sizes who had died hundreds of years ago and been chosen, because of wealth or local fame, for the honor of this burial spot. Now they stood erect, still dressed in the fine clothes they had worn at their funerals. Time had not touched them. Their bodies had not turned to dust or been attacked by worms. Their clothes had not raveled or been wasted by moisture. They were an awesome assemblage, these mummies of Toledo created by nature.

"Could they be of wax?" Mrs. Evans asked. "Like Madame Tussaud's?"

"No artifice here," Ledesma said. "These are the people of Toledo, preserved forever."

As the others moved down the corridor as in a reception line where they were greeting the dead citizens in formal dress, I heard behind me a startled cry, but not one of fright, and when I turned I saw Penny Grim standing with mouth agape before the exquisite figure of a Chinese woman, perhaps thirty years old when she died. But what differentiated her from the other mummies was her radiant costume, as pristine as it had been when it served as her burial gown. Of Oriental design, it had been made of precious fabrics that she might have brought with her when she crossed the Pacific from the Philippines to Acapulco. It contained also bejeweled silks and satins that must have come from Japan, and it was so gorgeous that Penny cried,

"Oh, Mr. Clay! Isn't she magnificent? Even I would look beautiful in a dress like hers." Prematurely the Chinese woman had died of some unknown cause, but here she was, as if living, and the mystery surrounding her seemed to give life to all the other figures in the catacomb. This was a grand ball celebrating the Festival of Ixmiq in 1710, so vivid and real that I expected to hear music from the Negro dance band that would have played.

"Aha!" Ledesma cried as he came upon us. "I see you've found our lovely China Poblana. Doesn't she look as if you could ask her for the next dance?"

Mrs. Evans asked, "What's a China Poblana?" and León was about to explain when he was called to the other end of the corridor by Ricardo: "What's this mean?" and we went down to see the contorted head of a man who had obviously been hanged and entombed with a portion of the rope about his neck.

As we four stood in silence in the presence of what seemed a double death—the hanging and the entombment—Martín began speaking quietly, without the reticence he had shown before. As though we had never left the Terrace, where we had been talking about bullfighting, he said vehemently, "I am going to be a bullfighter. I've known death in Korea, and it's frightening, this afternoon I saw a man killed by bulls, and that's frightening too. But nothing can scare me away from what I've determined to do. I—am—going —to—be—a—bullfighter."

"Do you have the skill?" Mrs. Evans asked in the darkness.

"I'm not the best," Ricardo answered. "But I'm a professional. Better than sixty percent— no, eighty percent of the Mexicans fighting today. I have all the passes, all the knowledge. Mrs. Evans, I know more about bullfighting than your husband did about oil."

"You sound like him, son. Same determination."

"Can you keep your feet still?" I asked.

"I can."

"Everybody can—till he's hit once," Ledesma replied. "You ever been hit?"

Quickly he rolled up his pant legs and showed us three separate horn wounds above his knees. "This I got fighting a bull seven years old that had been fought a dozen times before. I made four great passes, even though I knew he was going to hit me. So I got it, and I was in a grubby little hospital in Michoacán for three weeks. Next time I fought I was just as brave and got it here. Back to a different hospital. And on the next fight after that—" Realizing his voice was rising, he stopped speaking.

"Back to the good old hospital sheets?" Ledesma asked.

"Yes," he said in a very low, controlled voice. "And one month later I fought my first fight with picadors and look—" Like every would-be matador, Ricardo carried in his wallet a set of glossy photographs, which he now produced. It was too dark to see them well, for the electric light was not strong, but we could discern a vast hulk of animal rushing past a slim young man. "Look at those feet," he cried exultantly. "You ever see feet firmer on the ground than those, Mr. Clay?"

I replied that in the catacomb I couldn't see, and he said: "You can take my word for it."

Mrs. Evans asked, "Do you get good marks in college?"

Ricardo relapsed into his former style: "Well . . . you know how it is . . . like mostly A's . . . blah . . . blah . . ."

"Stop that!" Mrs. Evans cried impatiently. "How can a boy your age talk like that?"

"Because it is mostly blah," he replied coldly. "My old man's a jerk. You saw him tonight at dinner. Like Chester, he thinks he can solve things by getting into a Civil War uniform and belting somebody. He loved Mexico because the peóns are like serfs. He says the strong have got to rule. He was absolutely mad about war, but he wangled a deferment. My mother is one of the most beautifully stupid women on earth. They invented television because she was around. She takes westerns seriously and honest-to-God wonders if the hero will win this week. When horses stumble on the TV she cries, and she dreads Thursday nights because she's afraid Eliot Ness might get shot.

"That was my world, Mrs. Evans. So I leave it and go to Korea, and half my buddies are killed in a war that makes no sense at all. You ever hike down from a reservoir in North Korea in mid-winter, just because some colossal jerk wearing stars made a mistake? So I'm back home safe in San Diego trying to con other kids into joining up for future wars and my old man writes me, 'I hate to think of you. . . .' I could quote you the whole letter by heart, Mrs. Evans, but he was humiliated at the golf club because the war in Korea was still going on while his son was recruiting in San Diego. You want to hear the end of that letter? And may God knock off the rock above this cave if I miss a word. 'Richard, it is the duty of every man in uniform constantly to seek out the enemy and destroy him. Your place is back in Korea and I'm going to see the general and get you a transfer back to real duty.' "

He paused to stare at the hanged man, then

asked, "Can either of you even imagine what Korea was like in winter?"

"I was there," I said.

"During the retreat from what we called Stream X?"

"Yes."

We looked at each other in the gloom and Mrs. Evans asked, "Was it that bad?"

Ricardo ignored the question and said with some humor, "You saw me tonight when Chester tried to start a fight. To me it makes no difference what one more jerk in the world does—including my father. That time when he yelled at me, 'What in hell are you doing with a flute?' I started laughing, and I laughed so hard that everyone in the coffee house joined in and I jumped around the floor shouting, 'I am the great god Pan, down in the reeds by the river.' And my old man just stood there. And here I am, among the dead."

"And in the future?" Mrs. Evans asked.

"Oh, no! You don't trap me on that one. The future is now. This festival. These fights. And nothing more. I'm not going to think about what it all meant when I'm stowed away standing here with these dummies. Nor what I'll be doing when I'm forty, because the way the world is going I probably won't be around when I'm forty. I'm here now. That's enough, and I'm going to fight bulls. No one's going to stop me. And do you know why I'm willing to risk everything to do it?"

"Why?" I asked.

Stepping away from the hanged man, he walked a few steps toward the distant exit, then said: "I'm doing it, I think, because I want to bring the world back into focus: In the United States we talk about peace, but actually we love war. Look at the way men like my father idealize the Civil War. They're hungry to go riding off with the cavalry and always will be. My mother says, 'Wouldn't it be horrible if the Russians atom-bombed Detroit someday?' If it doesn't happen before she dies she's going to be disappointed. She's even drawn a map calculating how many poor Detroiters are going to be killed. Six hundred thousand was her latest guess, but of course Moscow's bound to lose a lot more. We aren't at all the way we say we are, or the way newspaper editorials write about us. We're violent. We love war."

"I can't believe it," Mrs. Evans snapped.

"I went back home once and while I was in Boise my mom sat before the television and watched murder, rape, acid throwing, suicide, kidnapping, gunplay and strangling. I don't know how many people were killed—more than twenty just while I watched with her. And every time a gun went off, she hunched up her shoulders and punched at the screen. Whenever a girl was hauled out of a car to be raped or cut up she moved forward to see better. And after a week, a month, six years of this, she says to me, 'How can you be mixed up with something so violent as bullfighting?'

"So I've decided," he said, "to slash through my father's irrationalism and my mother's sentimentality and get face-to-face with the essence of the matter. I don't want to waste my life watching mayhem on television. I don't want to make my father feel good by fighting on his behalf in Korea. I don't want to bomb Moscow and I don't want six hundred thousand people to die in Detroit. I want to be a man standing alone, and I will stake my life in an honorable game of death against an honorable enemy who will kill me if he gets a chance. Like you, Mrs. Evans, like my mother, like my father, like my country, I'm preoccupied with death, and I've wrestled with the old bastard several times. I know that in the end he's got to win, but with me he'll have a damned good tussle."

We had been speaking at the far end of the corridor, so now I turned and walked slowly back toward the entrance, and as I passed along the lifelike figures it was as if they were introducing themselves. "I'm Pablo, the apothecary, in 1726." This stout fellow was "Miguel, butcher,

1747." Then came the carpenter, the learned lawyer who argued cases in Mexico City. Then came a crisp voice: "I'm Enrique, the engineer who repaired the aqueduct after the flood in 1759." The nurse who saved lives during the plague, the seamstress, the nun María de la Luz, who was sainted because of the care with which she brought abandoned infants to Jesus. Then came the deep magisterial voice from a dominant figure in a red cape, "I am the first Bishop Palafox, builder of the plaza."

The names, the stories intoxicated me and for a moment I had the feeling that they were calling me to come back to their city, to tell their story. "Your father did a grand job on the historical significance and the battles, but we were the people to whom those things happened. Come back. You knew us. You can see us. You hear our voices. We are still alive, in your mind and heart."

Deeply moved, I walked on. Ahead waited the Chinese woman in her resplendent costume. I leaned forward, hungry to hear her words, but the spell was broken by a living woman who took my arm and whispered, "You seem as enchanted by her as I am." It was Penny Grim, and she asked as she moved closer, "Who was this one?"

I had no intention of sharing a family secret, but the emotional moment made me recall wounds that I would have preferred to forget: "In our family plantation near Richmond, Virginia, we had a large doll, a copy of this figure. Same stance, same rich fabrics. I never saw it, of course—it was long before my time. But I heard my father describe her. The doll played an important role in getting the Clays down here, from Virginia to Mexico."

"Is that all you're going to tell me?" she asked, and I said, "I've already said too much." I heard others approaching between the ranks of the dead, so, bowing to the China Poblana, I joined them.

When we reached the steel gate that protected the cave, Ledesma stopped, wrapped his black cape around him and spoke: "Farewell, good citizens of Toledo. You, Judge Espinosa in the robes of which you were so proud. You, road-robber García with your neck awry. And you, adorable lass from China. Give us your blessing as we return to our petty festival, aware that far sooner than we think we shall be standing here with you, erect and proud through the centuries."

Ledesma switched off the light. The steel gate clanged shut, and then the wooden one. We climbed up the stairs to rejoin the cypress trees, and in the Cadillac as we returned to our hotel there was little talk.

When we reached the Terrace at two in the morning we found the two main tables occupied, by the Leals and by Gómez and his troupe. Beside them in the front rank were two of the three matadors who were fighting tomorrow, accompanied by their assistants. All rose to greet Ledesma, who gravely acknowledged the gesture of respect. There was not the customary exuberance that one associated with the Festival of Ixmiq, for when a matador has just died in the ring a deep solemnity settles over the bullfighting fraternity, and men sit humbly in silence, reflecting on the fact that tomorrow they too may die. In the distance mariachis sang and, closer at hand, Lucha González shouted her flamenco songs.

After we had seated ourselves at some of the rear tables and ordered some good Mexican beer, I indicated to the waiter that he must serve Señor Ledesma first, and with my right hand passing low over the floor as if it held a red cloth I said, "Señor Critic, I send you your beer with a pase natural."

Ledesma laughed condescendingly and said,

"I'm afraid you have it backwards, Clay. You can't give the pase natural with the right hand."

"What's that?" Veneno called from his front table. He was a classicist who honored the traditions of bullfighting. "Did I hear someone say the pase natural cannot be given with the right hand?"

"Of course it can't," Cigarro broke in from his table. He knew only what he had been taught in Mexico. "Everybody knows it can be given only with the left hand," and the two main tables were now engaged in battle.

Victoriano, who felt obligated to support his father, leaped to his feet, grabbed a tablecloth and a knife, which he used as a sword, and showed clearly that the pase natural could also be given with the right hand. Whereupon Juan Gómez jumped up from his table to support Cigarro: "See! It must be with the left hand, always the left."

Now Ledesma entered into the debate. "Any fool who claims the natural can be given with the right hand is an idiot."

I shouted in Spanish, "Cossío himself says clearly that the natural can be given with the right hand," and, with a table cover jerked from a nearby table I illustrated what the outstanding authority on bullfighting had said.

Now there was a flurry of cloths and knives

and extended hands, and Ricardo Martín was
arguing in excited Spanish with one of the Leals,
and old Veneno's booming voice echoed back
and forth, as he bellowed, "The natural can be
given either way—left is better but right is also
allowed." At the height of the argument Mrs.
Evans tugged my arm. "What's it all about?"
she asked.

"People take bullfighting seriously." I
laughed.

All the matadors were now engaged, and
many of the bystanders. Table covers and handkerchiefs and bare hands wove patterns
through the night air like figures in a ballet, and
she said, "It's refreshing to see men taking a
question of aesthetics seriously."

"What are you doing?" Cigarro yelled at me in
Spanish. "Telling this woman that the pase natural can be given with the right hand?" He
shoved me aside and with grandiose gestures,
posturing as I had never seen him do before, he
showed Mrs. Evans the true natural, according
to his training. To my surprise, he was quickly
supported by Ledesma, the man he hated, who
explained, "Mrs. Evans, only foreigners and
damned fools contend that this pass can be
given with the right hand."

"Then Cossío, the smartest man who ever
wrote about bullfighting—"

"Don't quote Cossío to me!" Ledesma shouted.

"Look, Cigarro—" I began to reason with him, but with disdain the gnome-like man pushed me away and growled with deep contempt, "I would rather not speak with a man who claims that pase natural can be given with the right hand."

Turning his back on me, he chose to form a partnership with his enemy Ledesma, and shoulder to shoulder this unlikely pair moved off to defend their left-hand-only orthodoxy against misguided men in another part of the Terrace. And so the tension of this night of death was broken by good-natured threats, wild flapping of table linen, loud shouting and impassioned debate.

SPANISH ANCESTORS:
IN SPAIN

DURING my college years I frequently found myself in trouble with certain professors, ardent Presbyterians mostly, who promulgated with vigor the notorious Black Legend, which held that Spanish culture, especially as manifested in Spain's colonies in the New World, was somehow degenerate and certainly less moral than what either England or France exhibited in their territories. The college's handful of students with Spanish names or backgrounds chafed under this constant denigration because they knew it to be grossly unjust.

"This is a Presbyterian college," a boy from Ecuador explained. "There's a strong influence of John Knox, and he hated Catholics. To be a good Presbyterian you almost have to despise Catholic Spaniards."

When I pointed out that although I had a Spanish background I was a Protestant, the group wanted to know how that had happened and I said, "As long as I was under my mother's domination I was a Catholic, but after they separated my father made me a Protestant, like him."

A very wealthy boy from Bolivia whose father owned tin mines voiced an opinion that he believed settled the matter: "The hatred comes from Spain's introduction of the Inquisition at about the time Columbus discovered the Americas. Protestant textbook writers do love to include in their history books those horrible woodcuts of Catholics burning Jews and Protestants alive." I remember that when he said this he sighed: "It's a cross we have to bear, because it did happen," but the boy from Ecuador was more contentious: "What infuriates me, in England and New England they burned and hanged just as many witches as we did Protestants and Jews, but the professors don't harp on it. They don't fill the textbooks with pictures of those infamies. We get the Black Legend thrown at us, but they get praise heaped on them because of Shakespeare and Queen Elizabeth."

The young men from South America elected not to fight back against their professors in an attempt to defend Spain against the infamous charges of the Black Legend, but I was not reluctant to engage in the battle. "I'm proud of what Spain gave to the world. Cervantes, Velázquez, bringing civilization to the New World." I doubt that I changed any professorial attitudes, for the Black Legend was a convenient cudgel with which to lambaste Catholic Spain, and the Inquisition was an institution easy to hate, but my public defense of Spain did gain me friends among the Hispanic students.

One evening, after a particularly vigorous attack by one professor and my valiant attempt at refutation, the young fellow from Bolivia asked me: "Sometimes you say you're an American, sometimes a Mexican. Who are you? And why do you defend Spain so vigorously?"

"I'm both, American and Mexican Indian, but spiritually I'm heavily Spanish. And I know what I'm talking about, better than any of the professors, because the Inquisition touched my family with a cruel and heavy hand. They talk abstract principles. I talk reality."

It was late in the winter of 1524 in Salamanca

in western Spain that Mexico became linked to my Spanish heritage. This is how it happened:

The University of Salamanca, which then stood in premier position, was playing host to a convocation of learned men from Europe's three other principal universities: Bologna, in Italy; the Sorbonne, in France; and upstart Oxford, from England.

This particular convocation had been summoned to deal with interpretations of religious matters that were of interest to the Catholic world, particularly the schismatic effect of occurrences in Germany, where the monk Martin Luther had been causing trouble. When the more weighty concerns of Church doctrine had been settled, the professors turned their attention to a curious letter that had been sent from Antwerp, then as preeminent in trade as Salamanca was in learning. It had been submitted by a group of merchants who were perplexed by a matter of business morals and who sought guidance from the professors. The letter read, in part:

> What confuses us in Antwerp is this. If the broker Gregorio fears God and wishes to live within His law, but if he also makes his living as a broker and wishes to prosper, how must

he deal with the merchant Klaus who comes to him one day and says, "Broker Gregorio, next week begins the Fair of Mid-Lent here in Antwerp and to conduct my business I require one thousand ducats which I don't have. Do you give them to me in cash and I will repay them three months later at the May Fair at Medina del Campo in Spain." To this request of the merchant, the broker Gregorio replies, "I will give you the thousand ducats here in Antwerp but when you repay them three months hence in Medina del Campo you must pay me not only the thousand ducats which you owe me but one hundred more to cover my expense in transferring the money, my risk of loss, and my salaries to my assistants."

We desire to know, learned doctors, whether the action of the broker Gregorio in supplying the money and charging for the risks he is taking falls under the category of usury, which is forbidden by Holy Writ, or whether it is not, as we merchants hold, a necessary and permissible exercise of business and thus excused from the condemnation which is properly placed on lending money at interest, which we admit is forbidden by the Bible.

The issue posed by the merchants of Antwerp was clear-cut, and one that would worry the Church for centuries, but the professors at Salamanca could find no logical reason for abandoning traditional interpretations of the laws against usury. They therefore easily decided that the broker Gregorio was transgressing God's law if he gave the merchant Klaus one thousand ducats in March and took back eleven hundred—or any other amount above one thousand—in May. Accordingly, the convocation composed a reply which read in part that "the transaction is usury and is forbidden on pain of death," and that in the transaction described, "the broker Gregorio does nothing to make his money increase, therefore such increase must be held to be illegal and against the will of God." But before the document was signed one of the professors from Salamanca who for some years had been weighing this perplexing problem of interest charged for the use of money rose to offer a further consideration that he felt his colleagues had overlooked. He said, "Have we spent enough time inspecting all aspects of this matter? We are answering it, I fear, in terms of Antwerp and Medina del Campo when what we ought to weigh is its effect upon Mexico."

A whisper of consternation passed among the

doctors, and the chairman of the meeting, one
Maestro Mateo, a fierce Dominican who had
begun to suspect the orthodoxy of the protesting savant, replied brusquely, "Professor Palafox, the law of God is immutable and applies
now and forever both to Medina del Campo here
at home and to Mexico far overseas. Usury is
usury and must be forever forbidden."

"I grant that, Maestro Mateo," the professor
replied humbly, for as a mere professor he was
of the laity, whereas the man to whom he spoke
was an ordained clergyman. "I am sure that
usury as such will always be outlawed in respectable nations, but I suspect that with the
opening up of vast and rich lands overseas we
are going to have to develop new concepts of
trade, for if the trader Klaus, whom we have
been discussing, wants to operate in Mexico, he
will have to borrow funds from some broker, and
if Gregorio risks sending his wealth so far
abroad, he will be entitled to some kind of substantial reward, and it will not be usurious."

"Professor Palafox," the maestro thundered,
"usury is usury and we must allow the merchants of Antwerp no Mexican loophole through
which they can defile the law of the church."

Professor Palafox believed that he had a new
concept of the unfolding world, one that merited—nay, even demanded—attention: "You

ask, revered sir, what new fact has emerged that might force us to alter our previous dictates? Distance. In the hypothetical transaction we've been pondering, the broker Gregorio resides in Antwerp. The merchant Klaus offers to repay him later in Medina del Campo in Spain. A great distance apart, but not insurmountable, so the risk in making the loan is not preposterous." Since it was obvious that young Palafox was about to make an important point, his listeners leaned forward to catch his words: "But for a merchant to charter a ship that will sail to Darien, then hire a mule caravan to cross that isthmus and charter another ship to take him down the coast to Peru to fetch his precious metal, and then double back along the same perilous route—that constitutes a risk that justifies a special reward."

Some of his listeners were impressed by this modern reasoning, but not Maestro Mateo: "Do you argue that mere distance and added risk excuse a lender from the sin of usury?"

"No, reverend Professor. What I argue is that there is a universe of difference between a commercial journey from Antwerp to Medina requiring a few weeks, and one from Seville to Peru and back, which will require more than a year and unimagined risks. Such a risk requires a new definition."

"But never a new morality."

"What I'm trying to point out," Palafox said, forging ahead, "is that with the discovery of Mexico and Peru new patterns of business life must be worked out, and I believe that we would be well advised to send some other kind of answer to the merchants of Antwerp. Let us think this matter—"

"Palafox!" Maestro Mateo thundered.

"Yes, reverend Maestro."

"Be silent!" And the reply was sent as planned, which meant merely that the merchant Klaus still had to have his thousand ducats, that he still had to borrow them from the broker Gregorio, that interest was charged as always, that borrower and lender incurred mortal sin, and that honest business had to be conducted outside the purview of the Church. One unforeseen result did occur, however, for one of the professors from Oxford was so impressed by the statements of Palafox that when he returned to England he launched his own investigation of these matters, and although he never brought himself to break with Church rule on this question, one of his students did, and in time England devised a new interpretation of lending money, and upon this new understanding of sharing risk the industrial greatness of England was built, while Spain, refusing to reconsider the matter, crushed those incipient industrial developments that might have strengthened the nation.

When the convocation ended, Professor Palafox lingered for some time in the beautiful plaza that faced the university, and as he stood there waiting he could catch a promise of spring in the breeze that blew up from the river. On one of the walls his name was carved, in honor of the high degree he had won many years before at the university, and through that small arch leading to the cloisters he had marched on the day he had been chosen professor of civil law. This was his spiritual home, and he was distressed when Maestro Mateo bristled by without speaking. Professors from Bologna and the Sorbonne, who would soon be leaving on their dangerous journeys homeward, stopped to argue with Palafox and it was apparent that none had appreciated his stance.

"Do you honestly believe," a Frenchman asked in crisp Latin, "that one of these days lending money at interest will be held to be different from usury and that the Church will permit it?"

"Let's not argue about it," Palafox said quietly. "It's obvious that I failed to make myself clear."

"You were very clear," the French professor corrected. "But you were also very wrong. Let's go to my rooms to argue this matter further."

"I can't, much as I would like to, because I'm waiting for my sons."

"Are they at the university?" the Frenchman inquired.

"The older is. A month ago he was ordained a priest. Right here."

"How fortunate you are, Palafox. Will he become a professor, too?"

Palafox smiled and said, "In secrecy, I'm waiting to tell him that the university has invited him to become instructor in Church law."

"How excellent!" the Frenchman cried with real enthusiasm. "May I wait with you to meet the lucky young man?"

The two professors stood near the center of the plaza and the Frenchman said, "At the Sorbonne we look to Salamanca as the rugged, permanent defense of the faith. I think the preeminence of your university stems from its dedication to permanent truths. That was why this afternoon we were somewhat shocked to hear a professor from Salamanca raise the questions you did."

"On one point you're wrong," Palafox replied. "The preeminence of this university comes from

its powerful dedication to the truth, and I'm trying to discover the changes our nations must
make if they are to accommodate themselves to
the discovery of the New World. Believe me,
Europe will never again be as it was."

Even the hint of change was distasteful to the
Frenchman and he dropped the subject, asking
idly, "How many students do you teach at Salamanca now?"

"This year we shall have seven thousand,"
Palafox replied. "Hernán Cortés, as you probably know, attended our university and his fame
has made us popular."

"Are these your sons?" the Frenchman
asked as two young Spaniards, the older tall,
austere and slim, the younger a robust fellow
with an infectious smile, approached with the
eagerness of young men who had so far experienced no major disappointments.

"Antonio! Timoteo!" Palafox called, and from
their father's enthusiasm the Frenchman could
see that the professor took unusual pride in his
sons.

"The older boy's the priest?"

"Of course."

"And the younger one's to be a soldier?"

"In Spanish families that's the rule."

"Your father must be proud of you," the

Frenchman said to the young men, and Palafox replied, "That I am. Are they not two fine fellows?"

The French scholar did not reply, for he was comparing the older son, Antonio, with the many young Frenchmen he had helped enter the ministry of Jesus Christ, and he quickly saw that Antonio Palafox was not cast in the predictable mold. But the young man would undoubtedly make an exceptional priest; he would never be a devout mystic dealing with the ultimate problems of his religion, nor a patient rural agent of the Church bringing his religion to peasants. More likely he would be a churchly administrator or a general-extraordinary of the Church's political wing. The Frenchman reflected: He's beginning as a professor. He'll end as either the emperor's adviser or the pope. After all, Borgia was pope, and he was from Spain.

When the introductions were completed, the French professor took Timoteo, the soldier-son, by the arm and said conspiratorily, "Your father has news of interest for your brother. Guide me to your home and we'll wait for them there."

As they departed, Professor Palafox suggested to Antonio, "Let us go to the plaza for some wine," and his son replied: "How unusual for you to suggest that. You've spent years advising us to steer clear of wine. Your news must be spectacular."

"It is," his father said as he led the way through Salamanca's ancient and narrow streets, down which had marched Roman soldiers and Carthaginians and Vandals and Moors. Finally Professor Palafox could keep his secret no longer and blurted out, "Today it happened!"

"What did?"

"At a formal meeting, before convocation, you were chosen our next professor of Church law." To the older man's surprise, his son showed no excitement at the news, and there followed an embarrassing pause, which the professor tried to fill by repeating lamely, ". . . of Church law."

The two men were now in one of the narrowest alleys leading to the vast central plaza of the city, and the young priest stopped abruptly so that he blocked his father's progress, saying, "I can't take the professorship. I'm joining Cortés in Mexico."

Professor Palafox was stunned by the announcement. He tried to speak but felt himself choked not only by the oppressive alley walls and his son's blocking of the way but also by the upheavals of the age. He looked at his tall son and imagined the brilliant future the boy could win here at home: a professorship; association with scholars throughout Europe; a cardinal's cap; perhaps a preferment offered by the king. "Antonio," he cried, "your world is here. Let your brother go to Mexico."

"I am called there," the young priest replied.

"Who called? You know nothing about Mexico!"

"I haven't spoken to you about this," the young man replied, still blocking the alley, "but I've been concerned about it for many months. If you ask me who called, I can only reply that God did."

Professor Palafox shrugged his shoulders and looked dumbly past his son toward the huge plaza, where he could see the familiar sights of Salamanca: muleteers down from the hills with casks of wine; silversmiths from Antwerp tending their shops; scholars from Oxford in gaudy crimson caps; and alluring young girls wasting time before the night. This was the meeting place of the world, and his brilliant son was prepared to cast it away for an adventure in Mexico. "Can't you reconsider?" he asked.

"No," his son replied. At this moment the setting sun threw such shafts of golden light across the plaza that Palafox senior caught an impression of oceans and mountains and people with faces of burnished gold, and he muttered, "It's Mexico," acknowledging to himself that if he were young and full of promise he too would want to join Cortés in that distant land. He broke the tension with a laugh, grasped his son's arm and cried, "Let's get that wine and drink to Mexico."

When they were seated so that the pageant of the plaza was before them, the stocky professor laughed at himself: Ridiculous. This afternoon at the convocation I argued that we must adjust to the reality of Mexico. I was rather persuasive, too, but I convinced no one. Now my son says, "I'm going to adjust to the reality of Mexico," and I grow afraid. We're very stupid, we human beings.

The eager young priest took several large gulps of wine, then set his glass down and explained energetically, "I'll work in Mexico for six or eight years, Father. The basic reason I'm doing this is to help establish the rule of God in the New World, but a more personal reason is that I believe preferment in Church and government here in Spain will henceforth come to those who know Mexico."

The wisdom of this rationalization pleased Professor Palafox, and he observed, "When you return, you'll be twice as valuable to your Church—and also to Spain."

"You must reserve the professorship for me," his son replied.

"That can be arranged," Palafox senior assured him. He snapped his fingers to order more wine, then observed: "It'll be exciting to think of you working with Captain Cortés in the building of Mexico while I stay here at the university trying to explain what's happening in the world of business and morals."

At this remark the young priest frowned. "As I was leaving the hall just now, Maestro Mateo stormed in, all furious over some argument you had pursued in the convocation. He said to several of his companions, 'This damned Palafox is going to strangle himself on Mexico.' What did he mean?"

"An argument," the professor replied.

"What argument can there be about Mexico?" the priest asked.

Palafox took the wine from the waiter and poured himself and his son substantial drinks. "I reason, Antonio, that the advent of Mexico changes many things we used to consider fixed for all time."

"For example?" Antonio asked.

"Take your case. You go there as priest to the army. What is your responsibility to the king, to the Church, to the army and to the Indians?"

"Very simple," the priest replied easily. "First,

I'm to save the Indians for God, and this takes precedence over all. Second, I'm to protect the souls of our soldiers. Third, I'm to help win a new land for our king."

"Good," the professor agreed, his eyes flashing with the joy of anticipated debate. "But what do you do when your first responsibility, converting Indians, conflicts with your third, winning a new land?"

"There'll be no conflict," the priest affirmed.

Professor Palafox leaned back and smiled at his son. "You're very young, Antonio. You can't even imagine the snake pit of conflict and confusion you're entering. It was something like this I was talking about today."

Antonio, befuddled somewhat by the wine, did not comprehend what his father was talking about but he did remember one thing clearly. "Father," he warned, "when Maestro Mateo railed against you, he was not speaking idly. In fact, he was about to say something important when he saw me and caught himself. I still don't understand what it was you said about Mexico, but do be careful."

"Let me put it simply," the professor said. "When great wealth intrudes upon any established situation, new concepts are required to manage it. Our glorious nation has stumbled upon that wealth—"

"Stumbled?" Antonio gasped. "I would say that God in His wisdom has led his favored people to the discovery—"

"Is that how you'd say it?" Palafox asked.

"Of course," Antonio replied.

"Let's go home and tell Timoteo the news," Palafox suggested. "With you in Mexico he must become the next professor in our family."

The two men left the plaza and wandered unsteadily through narrow streets until they reached a little square that overlooked the river Tormes and the antique Roman bridge that carried the main Spanish road south to Seville. Here they entered a house of modest appearance, whose front wall crowded the street but whose dark interior gave way to a small patio containing a Roman statue found one day in Salamanca, a fragment of Greek marble and a bronze horse that had been cast in the Spanish capital, Toledo. But what gave the patio its essential character were the flowers, some planted in formal rows in the soil, others strewn in profusion in clay pots. It was the private garden of a man who loved nature and during all the years that Fray Antonio could remember it had provided the Palafoxes with a sense of serenity.

Now as the two men entered this tranquil area Antonio confessed, "This was the one thing that might have kept me from Mexico. I would have enjoyed being a professor here and inheriting your garden." Then he shook his head as if to clear it and said, "But there is also Mexico, and I think it may be a bigger garden than this."

"You'll still come back and inherit mine," the professor said. "When you're a bishop."

"Of course!" the priest agreed. He was about to speak further when he saw that his younger brother, accompanied by the French professor, was waiting on one of the garden benches.

Young Timoteo, then twenty-two years old and honed to a fine edge by his anticipation of life, rose and said, "Professor Desmoulins and I have been talking about your meeting today, Father."

"Could I speak with you alone?" the Frenchman asked in Latin.

"My sons are privy to all I know," Palafox replied, and something in the manner in which the Spanish professor indicated that his boys were to sit with him made the Frenchman suspect that in this house there was no woman and that a widowed man had raised his sons as both father and mother.

"Very well," Desmoulins nodded. "Perhaps it's better that the young men hear what I have to say. Their influence could be decisive." He coughed, and as a man considerably older than Palafox, assumed a paternal attitude. "Young

men, this afternoon while your father was waiting to inform the priest here of his appointment
to a post at the university, I had occasion to
reprimand him—gently, of course—for heretical
ideas that he had propounded at the convocation."

At the word "heretical," Antonio raised his
eyebrows and leaned forward. "Did you say heretical?"

"I used the word now, although I did not do so
this afternoon," the Frenchman replied, "because after I left you in the university square I
was joined by three other professors whose
names I may not divulge, and it was their opinion, first expressed by Maestro Mateo, that Dominican with the probing mind, that in today's
arguments your father came terribly close to
heresy."

With the mention of the dread word, Timoteo
moved closer to his father, as if to protect him,
but Antonio drew back. The Frenchman
resumed, "So I have come to advise your father
that tomorrow there will be spies in his lecture
hall, directed to report to Maestro Mateo, and if
your father is a prudent man he will recant his
approach to heresy."

There was an uneasy pause while the visiting
professor and the Palafox sons waited for their

father to speak. Finally he said, "Is speculation heresy?"

"Some things are settled by divine law," Professor Desmoulins reminded him.

"But the movement of business and the operation of forces—"

"Don't finish the sentence," the Frenchman begged. To the boys he said as he rose to go, "It's your duty to prevail upon your father, for he has entered upon a course of reasoning that could end in heresy."

At the gate, Desmoulins told the two young men: "I wish you'd accompany me to your father's lecture tomorrow. I want you to sense for yourselves the danger in which he might find himself." Antonio explained that he could not join them, since he himself would be teaching at that hour, but Timoteo eagerly accepted: "I'll see if I can identify the spies that've been reporting on Father," and the four men laughed as if that possibility really were a joke.

The lecture room was typical of that period, very large, with an earthen floor on which the scholars sat before low wooden benches that served as desks. Each length of wood was deeply carved with the names of girls, some of whom had lived and died in Salamanca more than a hundred years before, inflaming the minds of youthful scholars, then passing on to become fishwives and loom tenders, and finally old crones begging in the plaza.

The lecture room had only one small window, which shed a cold north light on a stool and a desk at which sat a clerk who kept the roll of the class and who from time to time droned out passages from ancient Latin texts on which Professor Palafox, standing in a kind of elevated pulpit, was required to comment. This morning the clerk chanted a text from the distinguished Córdoban philosopher, Averroës, who in 1190 had made his own interpretation of Saint Augustine's famous observation: "For who would not rather have his pantry full of meat than mice? This is not strange, for a man will often pay more for a horse than for a servant, for a ring than for a maid."

The dark room was hushed when Professor Palafox began speaking. Without committing himself, he referred to Aristotle and Saint Thomas Aquinas. He squared Averroës with Saint Augustine and cited the responses of learned men from Bologna and Oxford. His erudition was enormous, for speaking without notes he gave in twenty minutes a fairly complete gloss on the text, quoting many authorities verbatim.

Now came the time when he was required to express his own reaction to the text, and no one moved as he put his hands firmly on the wooden lectern and said, "I hold with Saint Augustine that prudent men will sometimes pay more for an ingenious ring than for a serving maid, for the value that men place upon an object is determined not by any external standard of worth but by their own desire for that object and their estimate of the good its possession will do them."

The more critical members of the audience sighed with relief as Palafox firmly supported the traditional Salamanca view regarding these matters, and some even took pleasure from the brilliant manner in which he marshaled his facts in support of the dictates laid down by the pope in Rome.

"Our Church is on solid ground when it condemns usury as an immoral act in which gold and silver beget profits for which they have done no constructive work. Only a living creature, acting in conformance with the laws of God, can beget another living creature. Gold and silver, being inanimate, must not be allowed to procreate."

When the savants applauded this unequivocal proof of his orthodoxy, Palafox sought to quench any flicker of doubt about his doctrinal purity by reconfirming the Salamancan dogma:

"As we terminate this thoughtful convocation, let us restate the permanent truth that these difficult matters will be settled as they have always been settled, by our wise attention to the will of God, by our careful study of His word, and by the learned dictates of His church. It is inconceivable that the truth could reside outside these sources, and it is our duty to reconcile our business behavior to the truth as it shall be revealed. Thus there can be no quarrel between the merchant and the Church, the peasant and his king, nor Bologna and Oxford. We are all obligated to work within the conscience of the Church."

These sentiments rescued Professor Palafox from the charge of heresy. They relieved the anxiety felt by Professor Desmoulins, and they enabled young Antonio Palafox to leave Salamanca with his mind at rest.

On the first day of May in 1524 Antonio Palafox, a priest of the Franciscan order, said goodbye for the last time to the flower-filled patio of the professor's house and marched down to the riverbank to join a military party that had assembled for the long and dangerous march to Seville. He was accompanied, in this part of the journey, by his father, a man who was not afraid to express emotion at the milestones of life and therefore wept, and by hard-muscled Timoteo, who was already vacillating between the priesthood and the army. The three proceeded to the Roman bridge, where a confused and apprehensive group of travelers was receiving harsh marching orders from the captain who would be responsible for their safety.

"Will you pray for us?" Professor Palafox asked his son, and the three stood aside from the others while the tall young priest asked for blessing upon their various ventures.

"You!" the captain shouted. "This horse is for you."

With agility Fray Antonio leaped astride the animal and moved to the head of the column, from which he turned for one last glance at his father, the spires of the great University of Salamanca, and the benevolent little alleys down which he would run no more. The captain shouted "Halloooo!" and the ungainly troop started across the bridge.

On the other side of the river the captain abandoned the principal highway, which led down the west side of Spain, and turned sharply toward the southeast, whose forbidding mountains he would have to penetrate on his journey to the capital city of Toledo, where an additional complement of travelers to Seville would be acquired. Riding back and forth along the column, he warned his charges, "We're entering dangerous territory. Obey commands." And those on foot, as well as the creaking wagons bearing the luggage and the troops at the rear, drew closer together.

As Fray Antonio rode toward the mountains he had a chance to see how glorious the peak of springtime could be in Spain, for he was attended by a swooping covey of red-and-gold birds whose wingtips seemed to have been dipped in bronze. The bee-eaters of the central plateau, they were exquisite in the sunlight, and the young priest wondered sadly whether he would ever see such brilliant creatures in Mexico.

The hillsides glowed with yellow gorse, protected by old pine trees whose lower branches had been torn off by peasants seeking firewood. The gnarled cork trees, their valuable skin peeled back year after year, were home to hawks, those swift, fiery, dedicated birds who policed the highways as Spain policed the oceans.

Wherever Antonio looked there were red pop-

pies and buttercups and daisies and blue corn-
flowers—the entire countryside appeared to be
almost an extension of his father's patio garden.
But what impressed him most was something he
had not seen before, and in his memoirs, from
which I am drawing for this account, he referred
to this as a kind of benediction for his departure
from Salamanca: "There were before us constantly as we rode a breed of swallows who
dipped and swerved across our path as if with
their wings they were bidding us Godspeed."

It was no mean thing, in the year 1524, to be
a young Spaniard on his way from the world's
principal university to the compelling wonders of
Spain's new colony of Mexico. Spain was then
the major nation of the world, with no near com-
petitor in sight. It controlled the landmass of
Europe and ruled the oceans. The New World
was Spain's, and the mines of Mexico and Peru
were beginning to pour into Seville that constant
supply of gold and silver which was to further
enrich the wealthy. The most learned scholars
were Spanish, as were the foremost admirals,
the shrewdest money changers and the best
weavers. In 1524 England was a puny power
and France was torn with dissension. Germany
was nothing and the Italian states were mere
appendages to Spanish dominion.

What was even more important, however,

was that Spain formed the powerful right arm of the Catholic Church and was the source from which the popes derived their temporal power and their security. The Spanish people, freed from the yoke of Islam as recently as 1492, knew how to appreciate the sweet blessings of their Church and were more willing than the citizens of any other European nation to dedicate their lives and their wealth to its support.

Therefore, to be a vigorous young Spaniard in 1524 was to be a man at the very center of world power, a man secure in the conviction that he represented the leading nation on earth and the religion that would soon confound schismatics. It was in this spirit that Spaniards set forth to colonize Mexico, and Fray Antonio was pleased when the captain of the troop reprimanded three Flemish merchants who were on their way to Seville and warned them how they must comport themselves.

"You have to watch these foreigners," the captain later whispered to the priest, and the latter agreed.

In this arrogant frame of mind Fray Antonio entered upon the transit of the Guadarrama Mountains, which cut Salamanca off from Toledo, and as the wagons creaked their way up the northern approaches to the summit he could visualize his future clearly: he would spend six or eight years in the Christianization of Mexico, after which he would return to his professorship and to the problem of winning promotion in the Church. But as the troop began its descent along the southern trails it was attacked by the bandits who preyed upon this area. In the battle that ensued several of the marauders were shot and Fray Antonio was called upon to administer extreme unction to a hairy-faced rogue who wished to die with the blessing of his Church. For some nights a vision of the dying man haunted the priest and he reflected: Men's lives don't always turn out as they intended—that one may have wanted to be an honorable merchant. The nights were cold, and perhaps they induced in the young priest a fever; in later years he concluded that he had experienced a vision in those mountains.

One night, trying to find warmth in the thin mattress that covered the cold rocks on which he slept, he looked up at the dark sky and saw the Gothic peaks of the mountains twisting and writhing among the stars, and from this experience came his first vision of himself as the builder of great cities stretching in grandeur across the plains of Mexico. Each city resembled those woodcuts of the previous century that depicted the holy city of God, but whenever Fray Antonio rubbed his eyes to study the cities

more closely, their soaring towers became the
peaks of the mountains in which the troop was
encamped. He watched the dawn come over
the Guadarramas, proving again that his imaginary towers were merely mountain crests, and
he rose shivering to shake the dream from him.
He laughed as he thought, I'm to be in Mexico
only eight years, but the city I've been dreaming
about would take sixty to build. But that night the
vision returned stronger than ever, and he
awoke that morning in a kind of fear. Am I leaving Spain forever? he asked himself, his heart
pounding with anxiety.

In this kind of semihysteria over the possibility
of never seeing Spain again, the young priest
allowed his horse to carry him down the last
rocky passes and out onto the warm, flowering
plain that reached out from the river Tagus, and
as the troop marched along its gentle meander-
ing a general excitement overtook them, so that
those who had made the trip before began to
spur their horses, and the captain hurried up to
the laggard priest to warn, "We'd better move
to the head of the column or we'll miss it."

"What?" Fray Antonio asked, still distracted
by his vision of a tall city.

"You'll see," the captain called back as he led
his horse at a gallop to the crest of a hill, where
Antonio joined him to look down upon one of the

memorable sights of Europe, an allurement that had bewitched the minds of Romans and Vandals and Muslims for nearly two thousand years: the view of Toledo seen from the east, with the city rising high upon a rock, encircled almost completely by a river and its tumbling gorges. In physical grandeur no other city could compare with Toledo, and in the rugged architecture that rose from behind its walls—bastions that had withstood eighty different sieges, some lasting as long as three years—there was a Spanish grandeur that shone in the afternoon sun.

At his first glimpse of this unparalleled view Fray Antonio cried exultantly, "I shall name my city Toledo!"

"What city?" the captain asked.

"The one I'm required to build in Mexico," Antonio explained, as if he were definitely committed to staying in Mexico for many years.

"You better get there first," the captain grunted. "There are pirates."

Fray Antonio laughed at the warning and began spurring his horse. "Why the hurry?" the captain asked.

"We must enter Toledo before they close the gates," the eager priest replied.

The captain laughed and said, "We won't reach the walls before dusk," and the necessity of camping outside the city was so disappointing to the young priest that he asked if a forced march might not accomplish the entry, but the captain merely asked, "With these wagons?"

That night as he camped beside the river Tagus outside the walls of Toledo, Antonio was profoundly affected by an epiphany that would have a lasting influence on his life. Of this experience he wrote:

> All through the long night I heard mysterious birds singing in the darkness, birds I did not know and whose plumage I could not guess about, but they talked with me. And across the silent river on whose banks we had pitched our tents I could hear the voices of those within the walled city and I could see flickering lights move back and forth along the battlements and once I heard a watchman call out, "Ho, Esteban!" and I spent more than an hour trying to picture Esteban and what he was doing in Toledo that night.
>
> I watched the city as it passed through the various phases of the night and it occurred to me, unable as I was to sleep from the excitement of the journey, that most men live outside a walled city and are aware of the life within solely because they hear muffled voices or see flickering lights whose mean-

ing they do not comprehend. Or they hear a man cry "Ho, Esteban!" although who cried or why or who Esteban was or what he was doing they will never know.

And it seemed to me that we live in this darkness outside the walled city only because of our ignorance. We know neither present life nor the fullness of God's life hereafter, and it would be wise if we dedicated ourselves to the task of moving from the darkness and into the city of light, where voices speak openly to one another, man to man, and God to man.

But when these thoughts possessed me a donkey brayed, for it was nearing dawn, and I lay on my pack staring at the walled city, and I thought: But those fortunate ones who are in the city tonight do not appreciate where they are or who they are, and perhaps it is only those of us who camp outside, waiting for admission, who appreciate what the city is.

And as dawn broke, with our porters making a great noise assembling our party for the fording of the river and our entry into the city, I thought: A city can be truly occupied only by those who appreciate its significance, and it is of no real consequence whether a man be within the walls or out, so long as he has aspiration. And I concluded that faith is of this character, and it alone saves men; for when toward nine we entered the gateway through the powerful walls the city inside was nothing of what I had imagined, and I was happier outside at night attended by the mysterious birds and hope than I was inside, for Toledo is much more compelling seen from across the river than it is inside the walls.

In 1524 Toledo was a city of spiritual grandeur rather than one of worldly display, for only recently it had suffered from communal riots that had destroyed the city's treasures and destroyed many buildings. But in rebuilding from the somber ruins the Catholic Church had made the city the spiritual head of Spain, and from within its walls the kings of Spain ruled. There were libraries in Toledo and art schools, but there were also smithies where flexible steel swords were forged.

The sturdy cathedral, more fortress than church, left a deep impression on young Fray Antonio, for it reminded him of something that his father had said about Spain but which he had forgotten. He was kneeling before the high altar to report his safe conduct across the mountains when a beggar, who waited impatiently for the long prayer to finish, finally interrupted with a hoarse whisper, "Father, if, as they say, you're sailing to Mexico, you must pray at the column on your right."

"Why?" the young man asked.

"It will protect you from pirates," the beggar whispered.

"How could that be?" Antonio queried.

"Because it is the pillar of Abu Walid, the Muslim saint whom we worship in Toledo, and he will save you from his countrymen, who are pirates." The old beggar asked for alms and shuffled away to tell others of the Muslim who had his place in a Christian cathedral.

That night, dining at a Franciscan monastery, Antonio asked how it could be that a Muslim was revered as a saint in Toledo, and an older priest explained that centuries ago, when Muslim, Jew and Christian occupied the city in an uneasy truce, King Alfonso gave the Muslims his word that they could live unmolested in Toledo, but during his absence at war, his wife roused the Christians and there was a massacre of the Moors, so that upon his return King Alfonso felt obligated to execute his headstrong queen, but before he could do so, Abu Walid, saintly leader of the Muslims, came to him and reasoned,

"King Alfonso, the uprising was a thing of the heat of the moment. The queen and her courtiers must be forgiven by you. They have been by us."

The old Franciscan ended, "As we carry the might of Spain to far lands and our religion to strange people, it would be a good thing to remember Abu Walid of Toledo. He died a Muslim, devout in the will of the Prophet, but he also died a Christian saint, because he had taught us charity."

"Did Abu Walid become a Christian?" Antonio asked.

"We made him one," the old priest equivocated.

"My father used to speak in exactly the same way." Antonio laughed.

"Did he know Abu Walid?" the old priest asked.

"No. He was speaking of merchants. He maintained that they did God's work and must be brought within the family of God. He often argued about this with his fellow professors."

"What was your father's name?"

"Palafox, of Salamanca," Fray Antonio replied.

A shadow fell across the face of the older priest and after a moment he said, "When you reach Seville you should write your father and advise him to use more caution in his reasoning. At the cardinal's palace there have been inquiries about him.''

''Is that true?'' Antonio asked. ''But if you were able to absorb a Muslim into your faith, surely you can absorb—''

''Ah, yes, but that was five centuries ago. Today, with schismatics everywhere, well . . .'' The old man shrugged his shoulders. ''We must be more cautious. Jews, Arabs, followers of Luther, usurers . . . I doubt if the Church was ever so beset by enemies.''

On the following day Fray Antonio was summoned by the captain of the troop to a private residence behind whose iron-studded doors and grilled windows waited a gentleman who was to be of considerable importance to the Palafoxes and whose descendants were also to play a significant role in my life. He was the sixty-six-year-old marquis of Guadalquivir, one of the heroes in the expulsion of the Muslims from Spain. King Ferdinand and Queen Isabella of Aragon had given him the responsibility of trapping the last Moorish army in Granada and destroying it, and in 1492 he had done so with some brilliance. He gained as a reward his title plus vast lands along the river after which he was named. He was tall, black-haired and with a mustache that fell past the corners of his mouth. When he rose from his leather chair to greet Fray Antonio, he bounded forward and grasped the younger man's hand with a powerful grip.

He came to the point: "You are determined to go to Mexico?"

"Yes."

"Good. I have letters for Captain Cortés dealing with the salvation of Indian souls. Carry them with you to ensure safe transit."

"I would be honored," the priest said quietly, and the marquis noted his look of authority and thought: I like priests who act like soldiers. Because of this favorable opinion he launched into a much fuller discussion of state affairs than he had intended.

"The king has asked me to work out a plan to bring the Indians into the Church. It's rather difficult to talk with the king. He speaks no Spanish and I no German. But we've decided on a system. Indians will be kept on the land and the man who owns the land will own the Indians, but their spiritual lives—that's for you priests to handle, of course. You see any reason why this plan won't work?"

"None at all," Fray Antonio replied enthusiastically. "The men who supervise the Indians will be devout Catholics and will naturally have uppermost in their minds the welfare of their charges, and the priests will be able to halt any chance excesses that arise. In this way we shall win the natives from barbarism on the one hand and from idolatry on the other."

"It won't be that simple," the marquis warned, and thus began a stimulating series of conversations between Guadalquivir and the young priest, during whose stay in Toledo the marquis discussed all particulars of the Mexican mission. The more Antonio saw of the powerful soldier the more he understood why Spain led the world.

It was in the marquis's fortified home that Antonio saw his first dispatch from Captain Cortés, a soldierly report of expeditions to the west and south plus a hopeful report of the riches to be found throughout the new nation. At one point the marquis threw the soiled sheets on his leather-covered table and cried, "From what he says, they don't sound like savages. Father, what if we are dealing with civilized people to be embraced as equals and not the barbarians you speak of as children in darkness?"

"You've read the accounts of their gods," Antonio replied, and this truth snuffed out the glimmering possibility that the marquis had seen flickering through the Cortés report.

Nevertheless, the wily old campaigner came back to the subject many times. "Father, only

two things matter. Winning souls to Jesus Christ
and establishing a rich commonwealth. When
you speak with Captain Cortés, remind him of
this. When I conquered the Muslims, the first
thing I did was assure them that Spain needed
them. When we reach Córdoba I'll show you
how we won the Arabs over."

"Does that mean you're riding with us to Seville?" Antonio asked with an excitement that
pleased the soldier.

"My home is in Seville. My daughters are
there. And the ranch the king gave me bestrides
the Guadalquivir, hence my title. The ride
south'll give me a chance to know you better,
and I could profit from that." Antonio accepted
this compliment with dignity, whereupon the soldier clapped him on the shoulder and said,
"When you come back from Mexico, you must
work close to the king. He needs men like you."

"When I come back," Antonio replied, "I
should like to work close to you," at which the
general grunted.

The caravan that struggled out of the pinna-
cled city of Toledo some days later was entirely
different from the one that had left the university
city of Salamanca, for the road ahead was not
an insecure trail over mountains but a major
highway between the capital of Spain and its
principal commercial port. The soldiers now

numbered an even ninety, of whom more than half were mounted; all had an air of gallantry and the powerful dignity of the Spanish court. A convoy of sixteen carts creaked along, bearing large quantities of goods for Mexico, while in the middle of the convoy, well protected by soldiers, a private carriage bounced up and down on its leather hinges. It carried on each door a blue-and-gold armorial crest and was sufficiently commodious for the marquis, his secretary and young Fray Antonio Palafox, who sat day after day absorbing the old soldier's theory of governing new dominions.

"When the Muslims ruled Spain from North Africa," the crusty old warrior complained, "they sent their dregs to rule us. We're doing the same in Mexico. The finest soldiers stay at home. Look at the captain of this troop. You ever see a better man? He won't go to Mexico. And so far the nobility we've sent to help Cortés. What are they? Not a decent man among them." Antonio sensed that the marquis, whose title dated only from 1492, felt irritated by the true grandees of Spain, some of whose titles went back to pre-Muslim times.

"The only group sending out first-class men"—the words sounded so impressive in Spanish: *hombres de la primera categoría*—"is the Church. When you get to Mexico, Antonio, you'll find you're smarter and more dedicated than the men you have to deal with. Therefore be shrewd. See to it that the land gets a good government."

"In such matters what can a priest do?" Antonio asked.

The old general poked the young priest in the ribs and winked at his secretary. "What can a priest do!" the marquis teased. "When I was in charge of high-spirited troops . . . I hated to see priests come along because I knew they would try to discipline my men. Well, that's wine that's been drunk. But have you noticed, Fray Tomás, how every time on this trip we mention building new cities this young priest's eyes light up like candles? What are you dreaming, Antonio? Are you going to build one long city across Mexico?"

"I am dreaming mostly of souls, now in darkness," Antonio replied.

"Yesterday, when our carriage was bogged down, I was most impressed by the practical way you found stones as a fulcrum for our levers." Almost unconsciously, the old soldier slipped into using the familiar form of the Spanish *tú* and from this time on Guadalquivir spoke to the young priest as if he were his son.

"I have no sons," the marquis observed at one point, "and that's a pity, for I possess a name worthy of perpetuation. I do have daughters, and they're providing grandsons, so all's well."

As they approached Córdoba, that burnished jewel of Muhammadan power in Spain, the old marquis observed, "Always remember this city as an example of how Spain governs. We fought the Moors in Córdoba for six hundred years. When we conquered them we preserved their city, their mosques, their language, their cooking. And the more of their life we absorbed, the stronger we became. In Mexico we must do the same."

The old man spoke so forcefully on this somewhat unusual theme that Fray Antonio asked, "In the conquest of the Moors did you experience something—"

The general put his right hand on the priest's knee and said, "At the conquest of Granada . . . , at the moment of victory . . ." He hesitated. "There was an insolent young Moor who had fought against us . . . very brave . . ." Again he paused. Twice he tried to continue his narration and twice he choked. Finally he managed to finish his account.

"A man does many things he regrets, priest. Those that involve women he's able in time to forget, because men were made to war with women and that's part of the fun of life. But the abuses he commits on other men haunt him.

The older he grows, the more they haunt him."

"What did you do to the young Moor?" Antonio asked.

"When we captured him, I had him garroted," the general replied. "And ever since, I have wondered what this young leader might have accomplished in Spain. When we wanted to appoint a Muslim to govern the regions outside Granada, where was he? Where was this fiery, brave young man?"

The old general rubbed his hands, as if washing them and thereby erasing his memories.

Together the marquis and the priest hiked about the former imperial city of the Arabs, now a somnolent minor capital of the Spaniards, and as they progressed through the narrow streets the marquis pointed out hundreds of Moorish relics of a type not known in northern cities like Salamanca.

"One of the reasons why we rule the world," the marquis reflected, "is that we absorb the best from everybody we conquer, yet we remain Spanish."

"I should think that our grandeur came rather from our love of God and His Holy Church," Antonio said simply.

Guadalquivir stared at the priest, then growled, "Maybe you're right."

At last the caravan re-formed for the five-day march into Seville, and on the evening of the final encampment Antonio said, "I shall deplore seeing the end of our pilgrimage."

"Good trip," the old man grunted, as if to dismiss the subject.

But Antonio, finding in the general the kind of solid human being that his father was, was reluctant to have their association end so abruptly, and added, "Riding with you, sir, has been like talking with my father again."

The marquis replied, "None of my daughters has the least understanding of what we've been talking about." Once more he spoke with such finality that the conversation seemed ended.

But again Antonio tried to reopen it: "I hope that when I reach Mexico I'll be able to accomplish some of the things you spoke of."

"You'll be lucky if you accomplish anything," the marquis growled, and since he rebuffed all efforts to maintain the conversation, Antonio watched the towers of Seville as they rose mysteriously across the flatlands that bordered the river Guadalquivir. The sight of one soaring tower that dominated the city tempted the old general to revert to his major theme: "It's a Moorish tower, the best in Spain. When our priests decided to build a cathedral, they stuck

it at the foot of the Moorish tower, sprinkled holy
water over it, and claimed it for their own. Sensible people."

When at last the caravan drew up at the edge
of the pleasing plaza that stretched out from the
foot of the Moorish tower, the captain of the
troop rode up to the marquis's carriage, bowed
and announced, "Sir, we are home," whereupon the passengers alighted for Antonio's first
glimpse of the richest city in the world.

He was fascinated by the enormous new cathedral, finished only five years before, and
spent some time inspecting how it had been put
together. At his elbow the marquis mumbled,
"When the priests wished to commemorate Seville's redemption from the Moors they announced, 'We shall build a church so big that all
who come after us will cry, "They were insane."'" From a door the two men looked
down a nave of such astonishing length that it
seemed to end not in some distant wall but in
the shadows of faith, and Antonio whispered, "If
a man is going to honor God, his monument
should be of insane size." At this the marquis
clapped him on the shoulder and muttered,
"Poor Captain Cortés. Where will he find the
money to pay for the follies you intend to commit?"

When the travelers had paid homage to the

twin glories of Seville—the Moorish tower and
its Christian cathedral—the attention of the marquis was directed to the huge wooden platform
that filled one end of the plaza, and he growled,
"What's that for?" Since he was one of the senior magistrates of the city, several attendants
hurried up to whisper their replies, whereupon
his face grew grave and he took Antonio by the
arm.

"Back into the carriage," he said simply.

"I must recover my horse," the priest explained, "and find the Franciscan monastery."

"You're living with me," the marquis growled.
"I have many horses." And he dragged the surprised young man into the carriage, pulling away
the curtains so that Antonio could see the imposing plaza and the formidable stone wall
through which they passed into a quiet courtyard filled with orange trees. Footmen hurried to
take charge of the horses and to welcome the
hero of Granada.

The quiet residence they had entered was an
astonishment to the young priest from the north,
for he had not yet seen the subtle grandeur of
Moorish architecture as applied to private
homes. If I describe in some detail what he saw
on that May evening in 1524 I do so only because on a March evening in 1932 I stood in the
same courtyard, under similar orange trees, and

gazed at those arabesque walls, those Moorish arches, and those paneled ceilings whose traceries were as intricate and alien to my background as they were to Antonio's four centuries earlier.

The reception room was entered through arches of green-and-purple marble, across floors of rich orange tile, and past walls of shimmering black and white. The room itself was decorated with hundreds of thousands of minute tiles in many different colors, and the massive stone fountain that filled the central area was carved from African marble in the shape of lions and desert serpents. Three windows, high in the wall, admitted light through the most delicate marble tracery that Antonio had ever seen, and there were a dozen other ornate refinements.

"This isn't a house," the young priest whispered. "It's a mirage." Even more so was the young woman who now rushed in to greet her father.

"Leticia," the marquis mumbled gravely by way of introduction. "And this one is Fray Antonio Palafox, of Salamanca. He's heading for Mexico, and I wish I were going with him."

As a young man early dedicated to the priesthood, Antonio had never known much about girls, and Leticia's spirited entrance flustered him. As he watched her elfin pirouettes and the manner in which she tilted her head delightfully this way and that as she smiled at him, he felt dizzy. He was entranced by the way her silken dress accentuated the exquisite form of her body. But it was her smile, hesitant at times, then bubbling with warmth and enthusiasm that truly captivated him. He was in the presence of a girl destined to fill the dreams of young men, and although he had no realization of what was happening to him, she was instantly aware of her effect upon him. Despite her careful upbringing, she found pleasure in charming this young man, and the fact that he was a priest, and therefore a forbidden target for her wiles, she found to be an extra challenge. After greeting her father, she held out her hands toward Antonio and asked sweetly: "Do you wish to see the work so far completed in our little garden?" Antonio stammered: "I've already seen the garden," and he indicated the spacious courtyard with the orange trees. Mocking him gently, she said, "I've heard that in the north houses have one garden. In Seville that wouldn't do," and she led both Antonio and her father into an inner garden luxuriant with flowers and pillars rescued from Roman cities that had existed in the southern seacoast cities of Spain long before the days of Christ. The architecture of the garden, however, was Moorish and of an intricacy that excelled anything Antonio had so far seen. Looking at the ancient pillars, he said to the marquis, "This has a pagan quality."

"It *is* pagan," the marquis growled. He was about to expand on this when a knight arrived who bore a message from the governor.

"You and the priest intended for Mexico are invited to participate in the ceremonies tomorrow," the messenger informed the marquis.

Apparently the ceremonies were involved with the structure in the plaza, for the general frowned and asked, "Is this a command?"

"Yes," the messenger replied.

"At what time?" Guadalquivir asked.

"The governor's party convenes at half after five in the morning," the knight replied and the general snapped, "Agreed," whereupon the messenger left.

"What are the ceremonies for?" Antonio asked.

Before the marquis could reply his daughter blurted: "They're going to burn the heretics tomorrow."

"Leticia!" the old man growled.

"Well, they are. Five were caught relapsing after previous conversions, and two Jews reject all overtures of the Church and say they will die in their own religion."

"Where do you hear such things?" the marquis asked.

"Father Tomás told me," she explained.

"You go in and see about dinner," the general suggested, and the somewhat hesitant manner in which he spoke indicated clearly that he was not at all sure that Leticia would obey, but this time she did, passing close to the young priest and whispering, "You'll see I was right."

The two men walked up and down the lush garden, breathing in the powerful fragrance, and Antonio was fascinated by the Moorish tower that could be glimpsed through one of the archways in the wall. For some time they said nothing, but finally the marquis observed tentatively, "Very distressing . . . what happens tomorrow."

He obviously felt constrained from speaking freely, so the young priest said cautiously, "You know, sir, I'm a Franciscan."

"I forgot," the general said, exhaling audibly. "May I speak freely?"

"About the heretics?"

"Are you apprehensive, too?" the soldier asked.

"It hasn't reached Salamanca yet . . . the burning, that is," Antonio replied with extreme caution.

"It's necessary, you understand," Guadalquivir said, supporting the official line. "We've got to weed out the Jews."

"And the professing Muslims."

"And the followers of Luther."

"And all obvious enemies of the Church."

"This we admit," Guadalquivir said. "But when the burning started, it was not intended—"

"Whom are you speaking of now?" Antonio asked guardedly.

The general picked up a switch and struck his leg with it. "I'm just as willing as the next man to burn Jews," he announced firmly. "But . . ."

It was obvious that he had not the courage to finish the remark. While Father Antonio was considering how to divert the discussion to a new track, he noticed through the archway that a flock of swallows, perhaps three hundred or more, had started to descend on the Moorish tower, and he was captivated by the marvelous way in which they dipped and turned and seemed to ignore the tower until unpredictably they darted into their nests. He watched the birds for some minutes, and then observed abruptly, "You know, sir, that the job of rooting out heretics was given to the Dominicans, and it was intended that they restrict themselves to Jews and Moors. But in the last dozen years they've become much bolder." There was a painful silence, during which the last of the swallows flew home and night fell over Seville. In the darkness the priest added, "And when our church itself was about to ask the Holy Father to restrain the Dominicans, this new difficulty broke out with Martin Luther, and now the Dominicans have become more arrogant than ever."

Without looking at the priest, but with caution lest someone had entered the garden while they were talking, the marquis observed, "Tomorrow, for the first time, they will burn Spaniards . . . like you and me."

"How do you know?" Antonio asked.

"Messengers came to Córdoba. Two men that I know will burn. One fought with me in Granada."

"Can you do nothing?"

"Nothing," Guadalquivir said simply. "The judgment was to have been executed last week. I tried to escape by delaying my return. But the Dominicans demanded my presence—to give the thing public sanction—so they delayed."

"This time there are no Jews and Moors?" Antonio asked.

"Only Spaniards," the marquis replied. What later happened was to prove him wrong.

"Hallooo!" Leticia called from the interior of the house. Bearing a candle whose flickering light heightened her natural beauty, she came into the garden and announced, "The evening meal is ready, Father." But it was apparent that she was speaking not to her father but to the priest, for it was to him that she went with her candle, arousing in him a most unpriestly thought: She moves among those Roman pillars as if she were one of the vestal virgins I've read about. She's like those silvery swallows seeking her nightfall nest. This unfortunate imagery of Roman villas, virgins and her sleeping quarters became so powerful that night when he went to bed he could not sleep; he continued to see her, with her soft dress flowing behind her, and the night passed in a torment that was as strange as it was intense.

At four in the morning, his eyes heavy with sleeplessness, he rose as was his custom to offer his Sunday prayers, and from the third floor of the Moorish palace he looked down on the wooden platform in the plaza, where workmen were busy arranging tall-backed chairs, each emblazoned with the seal of the Holy Inquisition, the colors somber in the light of flickering torches. Because of the gravity of this day, Antonio stayed at his prayers for nearly an hour and was found in that position by the servant who came at five to waken him.

In the next hurried hour the young priest dressed in his finest robes, was forced into eating a large breakfast because, as the marquis warned, "Today there will be no food till nightfall," greeted Doña Leticia, who was apparently going to attend the ceremonies, and watched in the courtyard as the marquis mounted an Arabian horse and rode out in the predawn shadows to join the other nobles of the countryside, whose presence was required to lend authority to the day's events.

At half past five the new bronze bells in the Moorish tower began tolling slowly, their reverberations summoning the thousands of spectators who would attend, each assured of forty days' plenary indulgence if he or she watched with care as the Church cleansed itself of heresy. At sunrise the huge plaza was jammed with families, most of whom had brought their children, who were encouraged to run back and forth to tire themselves out, so that during the blazing heat of midday they would sleep.

At six a small cannon was fired; the clanging bells increased their tempo; and from the huge wooden gates of the Alcazar, the Moorish fortress that stood not far from the cathedral, appeared the doleful procession of the forty-one who had been caught in one dereliction or another and had been found guilty by the judges of the Inquisition, against whose decision there was no appeal, neither to the king in Toledo nor to the pope in Rome. The first to appear in the march to the plaza of judgment were not the condemned but a group of city and church officials, accompanied by a troop of soldiers and four clerks of the Inquisition, who bore silver caskets covered with velvet and containing the list of offenses committed by the condemned. These were followed by eight Dominican friars, whose effect upon the public was electric, for each carried a long oak stave topped by a cluster of silver rings that jangled furiously when the friars hammered the staves against the cobbles, and it was this terrifying sound that prepared the way for the condemned.

The forty-one miserable prisoners had already been in solitary cells for periods of up to three years, awaiting trial, so that their complexions were pale and ghostly. Some, who had clung desperately to forbidden religions, were very old and walked with such infirmity that whatever worldly punishment they were to receive could be of little consequence to them, but of great agony and significance to their children. Each prisoner carried four badges of dishonor: an unlit wax taper, which signified that the light of the Church had gone out in the sinner's soul; a rope around the neck, each of whose gnarled knots indicated that the wearer would receive one hundred lashes as part of his or her punishment; a tall, conical dunce's cap whose tip danced back and forth as the wearer stumbled in fear; and, worst of all, a bright yellow sackcloth robe with a high collar and a train that trailed in the dust. The last was decorated in front with a flaming red cross, and for more than fifty years after the final judgment of this day, it would hang in churches throughout Spain, clearly labeled with the name of the heretic who had worn it, thus proclaiming forever the holy sin of that family, so that the descendants of the condemned could never hold office in Spain, or become priests, or serve as officers in the army, or collect taxes, or travel overseas, or do anything but expiate in poverty and despair the sins of their ancestor.

At the rear of the procession came seven who were accorded special attention, for their dunce's caps were taller than the rest and decorated with twisting red flames fed by embroidered devils, and although the crowds had been pressing forward to stare at the guilty, when these seven passed, even the most curious fell back. Each was attended by two Dominican friars who consoled those who had at the last minute abjured their error so that they might die in the bosom of the Church, and expostulated with those who had refused.

Behind the condemned rode the marquis of

Guadalquivir, his handsome old face a mask, and following him on spirited horses came six other nobles of the region, after whom the lesser priests of the various congregations of Seville appeared. Marching with the Franciscans was Antonio Palafox, whose lips were already dry; as he entered the area of the plaza he saw that one of the best seats on the platform was taken by Leticia.

The Holy Inquisition made these Sunday judgments as impressive as possible, for by this means heresy could be controlled, and now, with the multitude assembled, a minor priest conducted Mass and asked blessing upon what was to follow, whereupon the Grand Inquisitor rose and, addressing the condemned as they stood in their bright robes of shame, preached to them for two and a half hours on the disgrace they had brought upon themselves and the grief they had caused the Church.

When he finished, the two senior secretaries of the tribunal marched solemnly to two facing pulpits decorated in black velvet, from which they intoned alternately the dread accusations against the condemned. Since it required many minutes to recite the evil these forty-one had accomplished, the day dragged on.

The guilty were divided into three major categories. There were some who had committed serious but not crucial offenses against the church—such as stealing religious funds or committing open adultery—and these were sentenced to two or three hundred lashes and a year or two in jail. With intense joy most of these learned that their yellow robes would not be hung in the churches, which meant that they could at some future date rejoin the community without fatal prejudice to their children. Of the forty-one, nineteen received this indulgence. When this decision was announced their tapers were relit, signifying that they had again been received into the Church.

Fifteen of the condemned, and their families, heard a more dreadful judgment. These had committed major offenses against the Church; some had once been Jews and had publicly converted to Christianity, only to backslide in secret, and their neighbors had reported them to the Inquisition; others had been Muhammadans and had done the same; still others, and they received the most crushing sentences, had listened to the allurements of the crazy monk Martin Luther; and two had written mystical poetry that could not clearly be identified as subversive but that the judges felt certain had to be. These fifteen were stripped of all possessions, were given from sixty to a hundred lashings each, were condemned to perpetual solitary imprisonment, and were advised that their robes would hang forever in their local churches: "And when the robe you are wearing shall disintegrate with time," the clerk read, "another shall be made on your behalf and hung in its place so that as long as the church lasts your infamy will be known." But their tapers were relighted.

The clerks now came to the cases of the seven who were still being prayed over by the untiring priests, and with real sorrow the officials of the Inquisition turned to inform the civil government that these seven had been so persistent in their error that the Church could no longer hope for their regeneration. In the curious phrase of the time, the clerks read, "And so we relax the prisoner Domingo Tablada to the civil authorities." This circumlocution meant simply that the irreconcilable one had no further relation to the Church and would be burned to death by civil authority. During the entire course of the Inquisition in Spain, that institution never executed a single criminal.

It was late in the afternoon when the mayor of Seville notified the marquis of Guadalquivir that his attendance would also be required at the burning, which was to take place this time on a broad field outside the city and near the banks of the river Guadalquivir. Hiding his repugnance, the old general summoned his horse and asked that one be found for his confessor, Father Antonio, and the two men rode to the execution ground, but as they did so they passed a string of carriages in which fashionable families were hurrying to the fires, and from the window of one Leticia waved to her father and the priest from Salamanca. The old marquis affected not to see her, but the priest waved back, feeling in his stomach that it was odd for such a girl to be engaged in such a mission.

At the edge of the river Guadalquivir, near a grove of olive trees, seven stakes had been driven into the ground and surrounded with piles of wood, over which rough steps had been built leading to small platforms on which the condemned and the priests could stand. To these seven stakes the heretics were led.

At five of the stakes a ceremony occurred that had a profound effect upon the multitude gathered in the dusty field, for prior to the lighting of the fires, priests won last-minute recantations. When the clergy indicated that this man or that woman had been saved, a joyous cry arose, whereupon an official of the Inquisition hurried up the wooden steps bearing a lighted torch from which he relit the prisoner's cold wax taper, signifying that the condemned was about to die in the arms of the Church. More important to the crowd, and perhaps to the condemned, was the fact that at this moment two burly executioners reached around from behind the stake and with powerful hands garroted the prisoner, thus saving him from the agonies of being burned while still alive. When the strangling was accomplished, the executioners leaped nimbly down, ignited the pyres and immolated the already dead bodies of the reconciled heretics.

But at the last two pyres, one containing a Jewish woman, the other a Christian friend of the marquis, no reconciliation was possible. The four priests involved with these two obdurate souls prayed and wept and implored to no avail. The Jewish woman cried loudly, "I am going to die. Let me die in my own faith."

"Look at those terrible fires," a young priest pleaded, tears streaming down his face.

"Let me die," the resolute woman repeated.

"No! No!" the priest begged.

When it was obvious that his pleas would be fruitless, the executioners moved up the steps to remove the two clergymen, and one went peacefully, but the other, determined to save the woman from the terrible ordeal that faced her, refused to be dragged away. Clinging to the woman's yellow robe, he cried in anguish, "Abjure! Abjure!" but she refused, and he was dragged down the improvised steps as the executioners prepared to set fire to the wood.

Even then the young priest would not surrender, but flung himself onto the pyre and, staring up at the Jewish woman, begged her to recant, and as the flames crept closer to his fingers he was at last dragged away.

For more than ten minutes the Jewish woman was immobile and silent, but when the faggots burst into full flame and burned away her dunce's cap and her hair and the smoke began to strangle her, in her last extremity she uttered an appalling shriek, which seemed to knock the young priest to the ground, where he groveled in agony, praying.

An official of the Inquisition, watching his disgraceful performance, muttered to an assistant, "That one will bear watching."

"We won't have him attend any more of the condemned," the assistant assured his superior.

"Who is he?" the official asked.

"A Franciscan," the assistant replied, with some disgust. The senior official shook his head and directed his attention to the seventh stake, where the marquis of Guadalquivir had ascended the platform to speak with the condemned.

"Esteban, recant," the marquis pleaded. "Martin Luther is a fraud. He offers no salvation."

"I am like the Jewess," the doomed man replied. "I have my own religion."

"Save yourself this agony," the soldier begged.

"I have lived the worst of my agony, and now you must live yours," the prisoner replied.

"As your former general, I command you to recant."

"I defy you, and I defy him," the condemned man replied, indicating the priest.

The executioner, hearing this new blasphemy, clapped his hand over the man's mouth while the marquis and the two priests were led away. The fire was lit, and the man to be burned watched the flames falter and flicker along the edge of the pyre. It seemed they would not fully catch the first time and he laughed. The old general looked at his friend and wondered what potent evil had taken possession of the man. Then a burst of flame intervened between them and the last the marquis saw of the man at the stake was a pair of eyes calmly watching the flames as they approached his face. From this pyre there was no last-minute outcry.

The official of the Inquisition, watching the behavior of the marquis at the seventh stake, observed to his assistant, "There's another we might well watch."

"He's the hero of Granada," the assistant warned.

The official turned coldly as the hot flames writhed nearby and observed, "No one is too powerful or too mighty."

It is a matter of record in my family that on the spring day in 1524 when my ancestor Fray Antonio Palafox was watching the seven heretics burned in Seville, another ancestor, the Altomec Indian Lady Gray Eyes, was secretly explaining to her granddaughter in City-of-the-Pyramid the mystery of the new gods who would shortly rescue Mexico from barbarism. "This is a Mother who loves," Lady Gray Eyes repeated, pointing to her treasured image, "and this is her Son, who has come in gentleness to save us."

The child Stranger could not comprehend, for she had never known a god of mercy, so Lady Gray Eyes explained once more. "Here we suffer under evil gods, and men are constantly killed. But soon these gentle gods of the newcomers will occupy our temples, and injustice will end." She could say no more, but as she clutched the emblazoned parchment to her cheek she felt her tears drifting across it. How long must we wait for the gods of mercy? she prayed silently.

That evening in Seville, while Lady Gray Eyes waited in the noontime heat of Mexico, Fray Antonio, the agency of salvation for whom she waited, rode away disconsolately from the burning plain. Ahead, in equal confusion of spirit, rode the marquis of Guadalquivir, but the crowds through which the horses moved appeared to experience no distress. They had enjoyed the burnings, which brought drama to an otherwise drab week, and their merriment as they trudged back to the city supported the contention of many authorities that a good public execution now and then did wonders for the morale of a city. Furthermore, it demonstrated the cohesiveness of Spain as it gathered strength for the salvation of the New World; Mexico might lie in remote parts of the world, but its presence was constantly felt in Seville, where the galleons stood in the river for all to see.

Something of this excitement overtook Fray Antonio as he rode through the crowds, so that whereas he was repelled by the populace's reaction to the burnings, he was nevertheless impressed by their sense of loyalty to the Church and to the nation that buttressed it. Dire enemies like Martin Luther were abroad, and they required strict measures to keep them from polluting both the Church and the country, and he did not doubt that he would encounter the same enemies in Mexico. He hoped that he would have the courage to combat them, but even as he expressed the wish he called to mind the young priest who had tried vainly to save the soul of the Jewish woman as the fires consumed her, and he knew instinctively that it had been this young priest, and not the executioners, who had spoken for humanity and God on that burning afternoon.

It was in this confused frame of mind that Fray Antonio returned to the center of the city and followed the marquis as the latter rode past the cathedral, past the Moorish tower and across the plaza to his palace. When the two men reached the high wall that protected the residence, they saw that the brass-studded gates were open and that Leticia's carriage was depositing her in the orange-tree courtyard. Seeing her father approach, she waited in the doorway while the carriage wheeled about the graveled circle and departed. She now ran up to him crying, "You looked handsome in the procession, Father."

"I was surprised to see you—especially at the stakes," he said reprovingly, but his words had little effect on Leticia, who led the way into the arabesque interior, saying, "I'm starved. We'll eat now."

But the marquis was still distraught from the death of his former companion and could not erase from his memory the eyes of the be-witched man as he stared back through the flames, so he told his daughter, "Arrange for us to eat a little later. Father Antonio and I will be in the garden." He led the priest into the private garden, where the Roman columns reminded him of the stakes at which the heretics had burned. When he was alone with the young priest he abandoned the caution that had marked the discussion on Saturday night and said with visible agitation, "No man can predict where this will end. Even as I was pleading with my friend to recant, the Dominicans were mark-ing me. I could be next . . . or the emperor." He strode back and forth along the garden paths for some minutes and then said with great force, "Antonio, when you get to Mexico you must pre-vent this evil thing from taking root."

The priest drew back. "Evil thing?"

The old marquis showed no inclination to re-treat. "Yes, evil. The last twenty years have seen the evil of burning Jews and Moors."

The priest gasped and recalled, "Last eve-ning we agreed that the Church must extirpate

Jews and Moors who practice their abominations secretly."

"Isolate? Imprison? Perhaps," the marquis
snapped. "Burn alive? No!"

Again the priest drew back in alarm. "I will
keep your thoughts secret," he mumbled.

"Don't bother. I'm an old man and I've always
been willing to fight the enemies that might destroy Spain."

"You consider the Holy Inquisition an
enemy?" Antonio asked with dry lips.

"Yes," the marquis said bluntly.

"But last evening . . ."

"Last evening I had not seen my friend burn
to death," the old man said forcefully.

Dressed in a shimmering gown of lace and
silk, drawn tightly about the waist, Leticia appeared to announce dinner. But once more her
father asked her to wait, and while she stood
framed in the doorway with the light behind her,
Fray Antonio was trapped in the dilemma she
had devised. As a young man he wanted to
enjoy the ravishing sight of the exquisite form
the shadows revealed, but as a priest who had
already taken holy orders he knew that he must
not. His confusion was solved by the marquis,
who took his arm and led him to the opposite
end of the garden, where he said quietly: "The
important matter, Father Antonio, is that when

you reach Mexico you must use your influence to prevent this from happening there. Promise me."

But Antonio was looking past the marquis and toward the doorway, and his thoughts were becoming so jumbled—the attack on the Inquisition was as disturbing as the presence of the girl silhouetted by the light—that he suddenly became dizzy and felt that he had to leave the garden. He went past Leticia, who did not move, so that he had to brush against her, and into the courtyard. Asking the servants to open the huge gates, he ran out into the city, calling over his shoulder, "I shall come back later."

We know from the records in our family that in profound spiritual and sexual agitation he walked along the banks of the Guadalquivir and back to the site of the burning, where townspeople had whittled away the charred stumps of the seven stakes, selling fragments as souvenirs, those from the stake where the Jewess had died bringing the highest prices. He studied this grisly business for more than an hour, then came back to the heart of the city and to that street which for more than a thousand years has enraptured the minds of all who visit Seville, the winding, narrow alley called Sierpes, its name meaning Serpent. From the town hall it creeps between shops whose upper floors are almost connected; it passes cafés where Gypsies dance; it winds through markets heavy with fruit and fish; it is the center for silversmiths and booksellers and the carvers of rosaries. It is the most extraordinary passageway in Spain.

Had Antonio Palafox been a muleteer down from Salamanca, or a student on vacation, it could have been predicted that he would seek out this renowned alleyway, but for a young priest to be there walking alone in the night occasioned some surprise. A Gypsy girl from one of the smaller cafés shrugged her shoulders and said to her companions, "Why not?"

She followed Antonio until he reached a darkened part of the Sierpes, then accosted him: "Would you like to see my room?"

He looked at her in the shadows and realized with hunger how much he would like to join her. "Yes," he said, and she quickly ducked out of the Sierpes and motioned him to follow.

With both apprehension and desire he trailed some distance behind her, and she must have feared that he would lose his courage, for she fell back and took him by the hand, the first time any girl of mature age had done so, and he became less fearful. But when they reached her room near the riverbank and he saw how miser-

able it was, and how wretched she was in spite
of her youthful beauty, he felt a deep revulsion
and fled.

He wandered through the city for three hours,
tormented by the events of the day: the impassioned sermon of the Inquisition leader, the
burnings, the wild attempt of the young priest to
save the Jewess, the memory of Leticia in the
doorway and the repugnant encounter with the
Gypsy. It was after midnight when he realized
how tired and hungry he was, and headed back
for the marquis's palace. When he banged on
the gates he was surprised at how promptly they
were opened, but then he saw that Leticia had
remained waiting for him just inside the courtyard. She had at her side a silver tray of wine
and cheese, which she offered to him, and as he
ate he saw that she was still dressed in the silk
and lace drawn tightly about the waist. When he
was finished she took a candle and led him not
to his room but to hers.

By the time the galleon was loaded for the long
trip to Mexico, it was apparent to the marquis
that his headstrong daughter and the priest had
fallen in love, and he suspected that not all the
night sounds he had been hearing along the
corridors were due to the wind. He was aware

that Spanish custom required him to do something about his daughter's honor, but he had
already successfully married off his older
daughters and recognized what a lot of nonsense went into the procedure; with Leticia he
was inclined to let nature follow a somewhat
simpler course. Furthermore, he was in no way
repelled by the idea of a priest's taking a wife,
for the custom had been commonplace
throughout Spain until the late 1490s, when Ferdinand and Isabella had tried to stamp out the
practice, with no success. So there were still
many priests throughout Spain who had wives
and children. The marquis imagined that in Mexico conditions must be much the same.

On the day of the galleon's departure, the old
marquis led Antonio once more into the garden
with the pillars and asked bluntly, "Have you
talked with my daughter about taking her to
Mexico?"

Antonio blushed and replied, "I could not appear before Cortés with a wife."

"Not at first, perhaps," the old soldier
growled. "But in Mexico these things are no
different than in Spain. Later—"

"Later I would be proud to be your son," Antonio replied.

"You are already my son," the marquis responded. "Leticia is headstrong. My future here

is uncertain. It might be better if she were safe in Mexico."

A month later they rode together, the marquis, Leticia and Antonio, to the dock where the galleon was preparing to stand out into the river for the long journey down the Guadalquivir to the sea, and at the ship's side they said farewell. The young priest wanted desperately to kiss Leticia good-bye, but they had done this through most of the night and now they merely gazed at each other.

Antonio had had no previous experience that would have enabled him to gauge how seriously Leticia had taken their nights together, but as for himself, he was shattered by the thought of leaving her, and as the noisy preparations were being made aboard ship for sailing down the river, he was tormented by the agony of leaving her. Then he clenched his fists and mumbled: "God forgive me for this transgression. Let me put it behind me," and he turned away from Leticia.

"Man the ropes!" came the captain's cry.

"Aye, aye!"

"Up the anchor!"

"On deck and lashed down."

"We sail!" and the creaking galleon was warped out into the river, laden with nails and horses and handsome leatherwork and the flexi-

ble steel swords of Toledo and empowering letters from the emperor.

At the last moment, as the ship broke away
from shore, Antonio looked frantically for Leticia, but she had turned to enter her father's
carriage. "Leticia!" he bellowed like a lovesick
boy of seventeen, and she heard him. From the
step of her carriage she swung around and, seeing his anguished face, with the tips of her fingers imitating the flight of swallows she threw
him a kiss.

11

SPANISH ANCESTORS:
IN MEXICO

B ECAUSE these were the good years when voyages from Seville to Veracruz were not threatened by pirates, English, Dutch or French, all lusting for the precious metals of the New World coming eastward from Mexico and the riches of Spain, traveling westward—the leisurely month-long sail across the Atlantic—was a delightful experience. Antonio conducted morning and evening prayers. He conversed with the captain, who had made two such voyages before. And he watched as the navigator marked off on his parchment chart each day's slow progress. It was a gentle introduction to a new world and a new life.

Antonio was awed by his first sight of Mexico—a snowcapped volcano rising majestically out of the clouds that hung over the ocean. He later recorded his sensations at that moment: "I felt as if the finger of God were indicating my new home to me, and I entertained the disturbing premonition that once I had set foot on the mighty land hidden beneath that finger I might never be allowed to depart."

He landed at the swampy port of Veracruz, and before the rowboat in which he was ferried ashore had gone ten feet he was covered with buzzing insects that punctured his skin in hundreds of places that began to itch. This was his introduction to mosquitoes. Ashore he found mud, filth, vegetation so dense it could be penetrated only with axes, and a few Spanish settlers covered with unfamiliar kinds of sores. A priest from Salamanca stumbled up, a shivering wreck of a man, weeping with joy at seeing a fellow clergyman.

"I'm going home . . . on that ship," the sick priest mumbled, but before he could explain why, he fell to coughing and spitting blood, whereupon a soldier, thin as death, led him away.

What impressed Antonio more than the fellow

priest, however, was his first sight of the Indians of Mexico, who now crowded in to inspect the new arrivals. They were for the most part naked, squat and blank-faced, displaying none of the superiority either of intellect or physical endowment that was supposed to mark the adversaries of Cortés, for they were jungle primitives, as he found out, whom the Spaniards had enlisted into forced-labor gangs. And it became obvious that false reports had been circulated throughout Spain in order to lure young men to a strange country with an unhealthy climate.

This suspicion was fortified wherever Antonio looked, for in late 1524 the port of Veracruz had already become what it was to be throughout the centuries of Spanish occupation: one of the ugliest and least hospitable anchorages along the Atlantic, the deplorable gateway to a noble land. For three miserable days Antonio languished there in the intense heat amid the sickening swarm of mosquitoes, catching not even one glimpse of the greater civilization he had come to Christianize. Without exception the Indians he saw were low brutes, while the Spaniards he talked with were disillusioned adventurers. From a rude room crawling with bugs he sent his first letter home to his brother, Timoteo, reporting his disgust with the new land. In spite of its harsh tone, it has become an epis-

tle much honored in Mexican literary history because of its honest appraisal of daily life in that
early period.

We eat strange foods prepared in filth, fight
strange insects whose wiles are superior to
ours, and are attended constantly by as low
and mean a body of natives as it has pleased
God to put on this earth. Many mumble that
they have been deceived, and if I were you,
Timoteo, and not a man of the Church, and
if someone invited me to join Cortés in Mexico, I would most quickly say no, for this is a
mean land unless one has a taste for bugs
that bite with a most furious intensity. What
has impressed me most, I think, is that the air
seems so unusually heavy, as if it were compressed by weights and laid oppressively
over all things. One breathes, and the air he
inhales is hot and wet and heavy. One
sweats all day, but the heavy air keeps
pressing upon him, making him ever more
damp. From the ocean, on our first sight of
Mexico, we beheld a majestic volcano rising
above the clouds, but on land we see nothing, absolutely nothing, to inspire the mind or
gladden the heart. We live at the foot of that
volcano, whose slopes are forever hidden
from us, swamped in a green maze of jungle

whose trees produce no fruit. I take solace in only one thing. The stolid brutes I see, the brown-skinned Indians, require the saving grace of Jesus Christ like no other human beings I have ever witnessed, and that I shall be the agent for bringing the light of God into those empty eyes is the only boon among the manifold disappointments of Mexico.

Antonio's disillusionment continued during the long march from Veracruz to the capital, for the route was ugly, forbidding and dangerous, and the Indians encountered were even less civilized than those at the port. Yet once, during a night that was refreshingly cold, the young priest awoke to adjust his blankets that had slipped off, and he happened to look through a clearing in the trees toward the moonlit sky, where a gigantic peak, snow-white and perfect in its conical beauty, rose serenely in the heavens. He gasped and looked again, but before he could verify that he had actually seen the lovely mountain a veil of clouds enveloped it, and in the succeeding days he saw nothing of it, so that he was again convinced that he had come to a land of chimeras.

But on the eleventh day the troop of newcomers broke out of the jungle, leaving the tangled vines and the insects, to discover themselves on a vast plateau bigger than any in Spain, rimmed by volcanoes even more majestic than the one Antonio thought he had seen at night and marked by carefully tilled fields that bespoke an organized society. As the Spaniards marched through the cool morning they felt the oppressive humidity of the coastal areas replaced by the most bracing air in Mexico: the cool, crisp air of the upland plateaus.

To Antonio's disappointment, the troop skirted the cities that Cortés had conquered on his way to the capital. Tlaxcala lay to the north, an intriguing city enclosed by a brick wall. Mighty Puebla and holy Cholula lay hidden in the south, but evidences of their power were visible everywhere in the good roads, the canals and the rich fields. From time to time groups of tall Indians in good raiment passed on official business, and Antonio studied their faces to find them not unlike his own and marked with an equal intelligence.

Fed by such evidence, his judgments of Mexico began to soften, a fact that he reported in his second letter to Timoteo:

I fear I was too hasty in Vera Cruz when I condemned this land as barbaric, for the upland areas provide quite a different impression, and along the well-paved road one meets tall, straight men of obvious breeding and capacity. To win these men to God would prove a substantial victory, and now I am eager where before I was depressed. But I think that much of this change has been due to the salubrious air that has attended us once we broke free of the jungle. Here among the volcanoes it seems to rush joyously into one's lungs, urging one on to explore the next bend in the road. For three days I have been amazed at the beauty of this new land.

More important, however, to our family history was a more secret letter, which he wrote to Leticia in Seville and which was taken to her by a sailor returning to that port city:

I dare not address you as my dearest or my beloved, for the rules of my life and my chosen occupation forbid that. But in the night watches aboard ship, in the steamy fastness of the jungle, and when the great volcanoes gleam down at me like guideposts, I am tormented by our nights together. In a saner moment this morning, as I saw the new land opening ahead of me, now that the jungle is gone, I had the wild thought that Mexico needs women like you, women with grace and courage, women capable of building a new nation in a new land, and my heart called out "She should be here." If you were, even though we could not be wed, I would feel extraordinary strength. In my imagination you are in Mexico.

———

It was on the fourteenth day of his travel that Fray Antonio received impressions that would never fade from his memory during the fifty-six years that he was to labor in Mexico, for toward noon his troop approached the enormous lake across which lay the shimmering City of Mexico. Even though its highest pagan towers had already been pulled down by the conquerors, it still presented an imposing face to the newcomers, who were enthralled by its grandeur.

Its general aspect, seen from across the lake, was a light gold broken by the greenery of many trees. Its houses and public buildings were of uneven height, which lent the city a kind of rippling quality well fitted to a metropolis surrounded by water. About its shores there was a constant movement of boats whose passengers, wearing bright garments and the plumage of brilliant birds, could occasionally be seen. But what principally characterized the city was its sense of extreme solidity and efficient operation, an impression that grew stronger with each step the Spaniards took along the causeway that led across the lake.

The soldiers who were seeing the great city for the first time thought: It has already been looted. How fortunate the first ones must have been. But Antonio, renewing the sense of dedication that had possessed him in Salamanca, thought, What an admirable city to win for God, and as specific houses began to take shape and as he saw the physical beauty of what the Aztecs had accomplished, the conviction grew that here was a prize worth any effort required for its salvation.

He was now in the area where small boats abounded, and he could see their cargo—the fish, the myriad strange fruits, the corn, the woven cloth, the threads of gold and the brilliance of the feathers—and it occurred to him that not even in Salamanca had he seen such riches. He entertained for the first time the suspicion that this rude, violent land of Mexico with its towering volcanoes would one day be more powerful than Spain. Spiritual battles of greater significance would be fought here, and in generations to come, Mexico would loom larger in the world than its mother country. "I must send for Timoteo quickly," he decided. "He's the kind of man this country needs."

He had now reached the portals to the city itself, and from the watchtowers friendly Spaniards called down greetings to the new troops; Captain Cortés, hearing the news of their arrival, hurried to greet them at the gateway. With marked deference the conqueror first welcomed the priest and found to his pleasure that Antonio was from Salamanca. Then he quickly passed on to soldiers to ascertain how many and how worthy they were, for he was already engaged in vast new conquests that had carried the flag of Spain to Guatemala and was planning others that would in later years consolidate all the territory between the City of Mexico and what would later be called California.

When he had satisfied himself that the troops were able, he returned to Antonio and led him by the arm into the heart of the city, where for three years the able young priest served the conqueror in an administrative capacity.

Two significant events occurred during Antonio's service in the capital, the second deriving its importance from the first. In 1525, after he had worked in Mexico for less than a year, he received an anguished letter from his brother, Timoteo, advising him that their father, the Salamanca professor, had been arrested by the Holy Inquisition on charges of heresy:

After you left, Antonio, Father kept repeating
in his lectures that with the discovery of great
riches in Peru and Mexico and with the costs
of developing them so exorbitant, new ways
of financing the industries must be found,
and although he was always careful to add
that the new ideas he was proposing would
have to be developed within the teaching of
the Church, many interpreted his words as
justifying usury, so that Maestro Mateo, his
relentless Dominican adversary, was able to
bring the charge of heresy against him in a
public accusation. The Inquisition hauled
him away to their dungeons, where I was
allowed to see him and I found him in good
spirits, even though his right arm had been
broken during the torture. He thinks he will
escape with lashes and a reprimand, but
there are others who fear he may be imprisoned for life or even executed. If you can
think of anyone to whom we can apply for
help, please do so at once, for you and I are
in danger, too.

Fray Antonio was shaken by his brother's letter,
for he knew how unlikely it was that a man
charged with intellectual heresy could ever clear
himself, and he could visualize the extreme tortures to which his father was being subjected in

the attempt to force his admission of sin. Walking through the streets of the New World, Antonio thought constantly of the Old and caught himself wishing that his father had been less outspoken on matters that were of no real concern but which nevertheless put him at odds with the teachings of the Church. Why did he have to speculate on such matters? he asked himself again and again.

In response to his brother's plea for help, Antonio drafted a long letter of supplication to the marquis of Guadalquivir—the letter still exists in our family files—but he did not send it, realizing that on the one hand the marquis would be powerless and on the other that this particular nobleman was not an appropriate one to appeal to, since he was himself probably suspected by the Inquisition, so that any intervention from him might work to Professor Palafox's detriment. There was nothing Antonio could do to help his father but wait for the infrequent ships that reached Veracruz with dispatches from Spain.

He did, however, have to consider what might happen to him and his brother if their father was convicted of major heresy and his yellow robe of shame hung in the cathedral at Salamanca as an evidence of proscription. Since he, Antonio, was already a priest he could not be disbarred from the clergy, but his advancement would be forever halted and he would be looked upon with suspicion. But the case of Timoteo was more serious: he had not yet taken orders, nor had he joined the army, and if his father was convicted by the Inquisition, he would be permanently shut off from either career. It therefore seemed essential to get Timoteo established quickly, and this matter preoccupied Antonio as he worked.

It was in this frame of mind, beset by uncertainties and apprehensive over his father's fate, that Antonio was walking one day near the palace in which Cortés lived and happened to come upon an Altomec Indian who had hiked in from the west carrying some raw silver, the metal that had helped place Professor Palafox in a dungeon and his younger son in jeopardy. Asking the Indian if he could examine the silver, Antonio weighed it in his hand. "Father was right," he muttered to himself. "This is the real power, and he's in jail because he spoke in defense of it. Well, I will get this power for myself."

In that moment, standing by a canal in the City of Mexico, Fray Antonio Palafox was seized by the conviction that to possess silver was to possess authority and power. He knew instinctively that somewhere in the west, probably in the unconquered area around City-of-the-Pyramid, there must be silver mines of magnitude, and he believed that if his family could gain control of those mines, it would be in a position to fight back against whatever judgment the Inquisition might dictate against his father.

That night he dispatched a letter, which is still retained by the Palafox family, addressed to his brother, who had remained at his classes at the University of Salamanca:

> My dearest brother Timoteo,
>
> This day I have satisfied myself that certain rumors that have been whispered are true. Keep this letter private on pain of condemnation, but somewhere in the west the Altomec Indians possess a secret that could be of great importance to our family. Enlist at once in the service of Captain Cortés and meet me in Mexico, where I shall share with you what I already know.
>
>   Your brother, Antonio.

He hoped that Timoteo would appreciate the importance of getting into the army before the Inquisition handed down its judgment, but on this matter he was apprehensive, for he knew that his brother's great love for his father might prevent him from leaving Salamanca while the professor's fate was still uncertain.

Decisions of the Holy Inquisition were never reached in a hurry, and it was not unusual for trials to drag on through three or four years, for although the Dominicans were remorseless once heresy was proved to their satisfaction, they were not arbitrary in finding guilt where none had been proved, so with dogged dedication they might devote years to following leads that would either condemn or acquit. Of course, during those years whoever they were investigating languished in prison to be brought out for periodic torture at the hands of the Dominicans, who sought to clarify some obscure point in the testimony. Complete acquittal was unheard of, but there were hundreds of instances each year in which the accused were let off with four or five sessions of torture, stiff fines and public humiliation, after which they were welcomed back into normal citizenship. Such an outcome was prayed for in the case of Professor Palafox during the four years from 1525 to 1529 that he lay in the dungeon.

Throughout the first two years of this anxious period Fray Antonio worked diligently to convince Captain Cortés of his dedication to Church and emperor, so that the ruler of Mexico assured him, "No matter what happens to your father, your future in Mexico is secure," and he gave his young assistant additional responsibilities. As soon as Antonio felt safe under Cortés, he started quietly suggesting that he, Palafox, be sent to subdue the Altomecs. At first Cortés replied that those Indians were the most dangerous remaining enemy in Mexico, and he refused to hear of Antonio's marching against them, saying, "I have no captain whom I can spare to accompany you."

"I could serve as captain," Antonio replied and Cortés laughed.

"You'd do better than the fools we send, but you remain my priest."

In 1527, Cortés finally acceded to Antonio's request and the expedition was authorized. It was as a kind of soldier-priest that the first Palafox approached the high valley, for although a captain of minor category had been sent along to command the troops, Cortés knew that in the field young Fray Antonio would quickly establish and exercise superior authority. Of his first view of the Altomec capital, the soldier-priest wrote:

> The idea of building a great new city in Mexico had possessed me ever since my vision of Toledo in Spain, and when I first saw the City of Mexico I was pleased to discover that my new land could provide the bricks, the masons and the artists required for building a city. But I had always imagined myself

starting from nothing, on an empty plain filled with cactus and maguey, and when I asked men who had explored for Cortés "Where is the wild land that no one wants?" they all said "The land of the Altomecs. It's as wild as its owners." It was with this destination in mind that I led my donkey along rough Indian trails, assuring the soldiers who accompanied me, "Soon we'll be there." And then one morning as we climbed a hilly pass that carried us into a high valley we saw with astonishment that we were looking down upon a fine Altomec city with a towering pyramid, temples beyond counting, gardens and substantial homes, a metropolis requiring only a cathedral and a name. I asked the captain to halt the troops, and from our summit I proclaimed, "This shall be the city of Toledo," whereupon we fell upon our knees to give thanks to God, and we were in this position when the Altomecs attacked.

The conquest of City-of-the-Pyramid required fifteen weeks of uninterrupted fighting, during which the incompetent captain of the troops several times lost heart and would have abandoned the siege had not Fray Antonio forbidden him to do so. The Altomecs were terrifying enemies, who charged with feather headdresses and the faces of eagles. Neither horses nor bullets nor Spanish bravery discouraged them, and they seemed not to care how many warriors they lost in their counterattacks. Their defense of City-of-the-Pyramid became one of the highlights of Mexican history, for in the end neither side won. An honorable truce was arranged on the Altomec principle that "this could go on forever, and that would be foolish, for we are both strong peoples." The peace treaty was later represented in murals by Indian artists, such as Rivera and Orozco, who took pride in this siege as proof of their ancestors' courage. Several times in my father's book, *The Pyramid and the Cathedral,* he referred proudly to the fact that, alone of the Mexican tribes, the Altomecs had never been defeated by the Spaniards, and as a child he taught me to be proud of my Altomec blood, for it was the blood of heroes.

At the same time my Palafox uncles took care to teach me, "Never forget, Norman, that it was a Palafox who took control of this city. When the others were afraid and would have run back to Mexico City, Fray Antonio stood fast. Read what he wrote about the battle."

During the siege a strange event took place, from which each army seemed to derive strength to continue the fight. Each morning during the fifteen bitter weeks, about half an hour before dawn, atop the pyramid that commanded the city, a slack-headed drum began throbbing, sending its echoes throughout the city and across our encampment, which crowded the walls. And this drum exercised a spell on all who heard it, for to the Altomecs it was a summons by their horrible gods to offer fresh human sacrifices, which took place at sunrise atop the pyramid so that all of us could see, and we observed with horror that the condemned were apparently not slaves but the bravest warriors we had been fighting against in previous days, for at times we could recognize them, or thought we could. Nor did the condemned struggle or appear in any way to protest their fate, but marched gladly to the stone slab where their hearts were torn out by foul and bloodstained priests. To us Spaniards the drum was a command to new battles, and each time we heard it I summoned the leaders of our force and conducted prayers for the poor victims about to be sacrificed, and if our prayers had any power, some of those unfortunates gained heaven.

Through the first eight weeks the hatred of the Spaniards for the rites of human sacrifice that they were forced to observe was based simply on moral outrage, but early in the ninth week events occurred that stunned the Spaniards and left them grimly determined to humble this arrogant city and lay waste its evil pyramid. At dawn the drum had sent its echoes pulsating over the encampment and Fray Antonio had summoned his captain to prayer, when to his horror he discovered that the day's living sacrifice was to be one of their own companions who had been captured along with several others some weeks before by the Indians. This time there was a violent struggle at the altar, and in the Spanish camp prayers ceased while in horrified fascination the soldiers watched the death throes of their friend.

From that moment on, the battle for City-of-the-Pyramid degenerated into barbaric ruthlessness, for each morning the Spaniards assembled in mute rage to watch the priests atop the pyramid cut out the heart of another comrade, and during the course of the day the invaders killed—not always quickly—any Indians they caught. But what provided the ultimate horror was an incident that occurred in the eleventh week: on the walls of the city in full sight of the Spaniards there was a small parade of feathered Altomecs accompanied by three Spanish soldiers, or so it seemed until it became apparent that the three were not alive—they had been skinned alive, with their heads left on, and Altomec priests had crawled into the white skins, pulling the heads down upon their own, so that the dead bodies walked and looked much as they had in life.

Groups of outraged Spaniards leaped toward the walls to avenge their comrades, but they were driven back, and that night Fray Antonio erased from the minds of his companions any thought of retreat from this dreadful city. "We are engaged with demons from hell," he preached in the darkness, "and we have been chosen by God to humiliate this enemy, to destroy his temples, and to convert all we find to the love of Jesus Christ." In the days that followed, it was Fray Antonio who led the troops, and his tall, stoop-shouldered body, dressed always in black, became a symbol of his men's determination, but as the fifteenth week dawned the two armies remained in stalemate: the Altomecs showed no signs of irresolution and continued to sacrifice Spaniards at dawn or to flay them alive at midday, while the Fray's Spaniards pressed the siege and engaged in their own tortures.

Then what is known in history as the Miracle of Toledo occurred, for at nine o'clock on Thursday morning, after what appeared to the Spaniards to have been a scuffle inside the city, a dignified woman of about fifty appeared at the principal gate leading a beautiful little girl, and the Spaniards saw, to their surprise, that the woman was carrying aloft a parchment banner showing the Holy Virgin and the Christ Child. A cry went up and fighting ceased; Fray Antonio and the captain were sent for. In great solemnity, as in numerous later reenactments of the event, the woman and the child approached the priest and the soldiers.

From the troops came the shout "It is a miracle!" And when the woman reached Fray Antonio, who had been wondering how long he could sustain the courage of his army, he knelt before the banner, bringing it down to his lips and kissing it, as each new governor of Toledo has been required to do for the past four hundred years.

The occupation of the city was arranged by interpreters, and the woman summoned from within the walls the military leaders, who ratified the arrangements not as a surrender, for they remained willing to fight, but as a decision between equals. Before noon that day Fray Antonio led his soldiers to the pyramid, which he and the woman climbed, accompanied by sixteen Spanish veterans and about fifty Altomec women. At the top of the pyramid the Spaniards and the Indians ransacked the temples, smashed the drum, and with the aid of long poles tumbled the hideous idols down the face of the pyramid.

In the next five days the Spaniards destroyed more than two thousand Altomec statues, burned nearly half a mile of tanned animal hides on which the history of the city had been recorded, and eradicated almost all visible signs of culture. During the first of these days Fray Antonio, caught up in a religious frenzy, led the rampaging troops, but on the morning of the fourth day, when much had already been lost, Lady Gray Eyes and her little granddaughter came before the priest and by means of an interpreter indicated that he was to come with them. They led him to a crypt in the palace containing the most valuable codices—those now in the Vatican—and urged that these records of the Altomecs be saved. All that I have related about my Indian ancestors, their triumphs and their defeats, has been taken from those few precious records that Lady Gray Eyes managed to rescue.

This was the year 1527, the year in which Lady Gray Eyes arranged her truce with Fray Antonio Palafox and deposited with him the parchment bearing the portrait of the Virgin and Child. Thanks to the intervention of the queen, the pacification of the Altomecs was speedy, and before the end of the year Fray Antonio had completed his fortress-church and started the mass conversion of the people, but he was disturbed by the refusal of Lady Gray Eyes to be baptized in the blood of the Lord or to permit her granddaughter to undergo the rite. Obstinately she insisted, "I have been a Christian for six years," and she explained how the parchment had effected her conversion.

Fray Antonio, a purist, reasoned, "But that's impossible. There were no priests here at the time."

"We won't argue about it," she replied, and although she was instrumental in making her people undergo formal baptism, she forswore the rite for herself.

One day Fray Antonio asked her, "If you were powerful enough to make your generals surrender the city—"

"We did not surrender," she argued.

"I mean, if you were strong enough to end the war, why didn't you do so sooner?"

"For a very good reason," she explained. "Our men are warriors. My father was the bravest of all the Altomec generals, and if we had surrendered cravenly, we would now be living in shame. But we fought you to a truce, and now we are free to live with honor."

One day she added a strange observation: "Men are men and they are happiest when they live as men. Our men wanted to test themselves against the Spaniards, and they did."

Fray Antonio asked, "What did you do during the long weeks of the siege?"

The queen replied, "Each morning, when the drum sounded, I spread the parchment on the floor and knelt before it with my granddaughter, and we prayed."

"At the same moment I was praying, too," the young priest confided. "What did you pray for?"

"For your victory," the queen said simply.

"Then why did you not end the siege sooner?" the priest repeated in some irritation.

"Because there is a proper time for all things, and unless you had spent an appropriate amount of blood and courage winning this city, you would not have appreciated it when you took it."

"I see. . . ." he said simply, and then shifted to a familiar argument: "Lady Gray Eyes, at the next services you must be baptized."

"That occurred a long time ago," she replied. "In blood."

"True baptism is in the love of the Lord," he argued.

"I have known that love for seven years," she replied. "It was in such love that I gave you the city when your soldiers proved powerless to take it."

"Let me at least baptize the child," the priest pleaded. "She will have a long life in this city and therefore ought to be a Christian."

"She is already a Christian," the queen insisted.

"Who made her so?" the priest demanded.

"I did."

Her negative attitude on the matter was fortified one afternoon as she walked through her city and came upon a group of young girls laughing with Spanish soldiers and apparently waiting for a minor priest. "What are you doing?" she demanded.

"We are waiting to be baptized," the girls said.

"Why?" she inquired.

"Because we desire to have babies with the Spaniards," the girls explained, "but they refuse to sleep with us unless we are baptized."

The queen was not pleased to hear this, and the more she saw young girls undergoing baptism so that Spaniards would accept them as sexual partners, the more determined she became that her granddaughter, still far from marriageable age, would not be baptized.

"You are not to look at Spanish men," she warned the girl constantly. When Fray Antonio

came to her house, the old palace of the Altomec kings, to argue over the child's soul, Lady
Gray Eyes ably rebuffed him. "We were Christians years ago," she insisted during one visit,
"and the only remaining reason for baptism
does not apply to my granddaughter."

"What reason are you referring to?" the priest
asked.

"So that she might sleep with a Spaniard,"
Lady Gray Eyes elaborated.

The priest slapped his forehead and exclaimed, "Is that the only reason you can see for
baptism?"

"If one is already a Christian—yes," the
queen replied.

Fray Antonio now switched to the question
that had for some time been plaguing him. "I see
that your granddaughter wears many ceremonial bracelets," he observed.

"Girls always do," the queen replied.

"But these are of silver," the priest continued
smoothly.

"The royal family always wore silver," Lady
Gray Eyes explained.

"Where did they get it?" Fray Antonio asked,
trying to mask his excitement.

"I never knew," the queen replied.

"But surely . . . you must have heard . . ."

"Doubtless the king knew, but—"

"Did the Altomecs have a mine?"

"This was the sort of thing that would never concern me," the queen replied, and no amount of subsequent questioning could dislodge her from her placid indifference to the matter. She quickly perceived, we know from what her granddaughter later wrote, that the young priest was inflamed with a lust for silver and she was determined to use this as a leverage against him, but no one ever learned whether or not she ever knew where the mines were. Her granddaughter, when she later wrote of these matters, was of the opinion that the queen did know, but if so she kept the secret.

The reason why most chroniclers suspect that Lady Gray Eyes did indeed know was that when Fray Antonio made an impassioned plea to the Altomecs for enough silver to cast a statue of the Virgin in that metal, the queen thought this an excellent idea and quickly the necessary ore appeared, from what sources Antonio never discovered.

When he applied pressure for further supplies to send to Spain, he encountered opposition. "Why should we Altomecs send silver to a king in Spain?" the queen asked suspiciously.

"Because he is the greatest king in Christendom," Antonio explained.

"He is not our king," Lady Gray Eyes retorted.

"But he is. You are all his children."

"Our king is God, who is in heaven," the queen replied, and no more silver was forthcoming, a fact that was intensely upsetting to the priest.

For two years Fray Antonio concentrated on building his first edifice in Toledo, and it represented his dual responsibilities: winning land and slaves for the king, winning souls for God. He did force Altomecs to become the king's slaves, but he allowed them to work only on building the cathedral, which, under his constant supervision, became a rugged fortress-church with walls as thick as a man is tall and doors studded with bolts to ward off murderous Altomecs. For the Spanish soldiers a little wooden church was hidden safely inside the fort, within the square, and this accounted for the name of the construction, the fortress-church. Today, of course, the church has vanished but the fortress remains, and along the south wall you can still see one of the famous memorials of the pacification of Mexico. It is the austere outdoor altar, constructed in the simplest lines by Altomec Indians whom Fray Antonio had taught to use the chisels he had imported from Spain. In the early years of the occupation it was considered too dangerous to admit Indians into the heart of a fortress-church lest they rise in sudden revolt and massacre the Spaniards, but at the same time the priests never lost sight of the fact that they were in Mexico to convert the Indians, so the compromise of the outdoor altar was conceived. To this altar, through the solid wall, was cut a narrow tunnel just wide enough for one priest to pass to the outdoor chapel, where in the open air there might be assembled four or five thousand Indians who had come to hear the message of Jesus. Under these precautions, if the Indians did rebel they could murder the priest who officiated before them, but they could not force their way into the fortress through the narrow tunnel, which could be easily blocked from within.

Furthermore, whenever the priest conducted worship from his outside altar, a company of soldiers manned the battlements above him, so that if trouble erupted the armed men could fire point-blank into the crowd. For the first eleven years of his service in Toledo, this soldier-priest never led his Indians in prayer without the assurance of some twenty armed men ready to spray musket fire among the worshipers.

But it was neither the fort nor the altar that occupied Fray Antonio's principal energies. He constantly took detachments of his soldiers into the hills, searching for the silver that he knew to be there, and constantly the prize eluded him. When Bishop Zumárraga came from Mexico City to inspect the fortress-church, he was so impressed with the way in which Fray Antonio had subdued the old pagan city that he wished to take the young man back to the capital with him. "We need your energies," Zumárraga explained.

Fray Antonio demurred modestly, saying, "My work is with the Altomecs."

With the bishop safely back in the capital, Fray Antonio was free to resume his obsessive search for the mines, but he met with no success. What made his failure the more galling was that from time to time his Altomec converts would appear with pieces of pure metal such as the one he had first seen or with silver bangles, and it infuriated him that they knew the secret of the mines while he did not.

Then in 1529 matters in Spain's Toledo took a dramatic turn. In midsummer Fray Antonio received word that his father had finally been judged guilty by the Holy Inquisition and, because of the gravity of his heresy against the financial stability of the empire—a sin that furthermore smacked of Lutheranism—had been burned at the stake in the public square of Salamanca. He had, a friend related, been strangled before the fires reached him.

For some weeks Fray Antonio moved in a kind of daze. His first thoughts were not of his father but of the little garden of flowers that the Palafoxes had nourished over many generations. He saw the bright blooms crowded out by weeds and in the cathedral a yellow robe of shame bearing his father's name and the proscription against all Palafoxes for as long as time should last. He then thought of his brother, Timoteo, and what would happen to him, and for several nights he prayed that the fiery young fellow might control his temper. He hoped that Timoteo had already slipped into the army, for if he had not, entrance now would be impossible and the boy would be reduced to beggary or brigandage. Finally he thought of himself, and of how his career in the Church had been permanently blasted by this decision of the Holy Office. He could remain a priest, but he would never gain preferment. It was then that he resigned himself to spending the rest of his life in Mexico, lost in the obscurity of its Toledo with no hope of ever again seeing Leticia; but it was also then that he reaffirmed his belief that the good name of his family might be salvaged by the silver he was determined to find.

Lady Gray Eyes, who had always studied Fray Antonio with interest, saw with some apprehension the significant changes that were taking place in the priest. Where he had once been lively of step and eager for the problems of a new day, he was now dispirited and listless. He seemed particularly afraid of the couriers who brought letters from the capital, and she suspected that he was awaiting bad news to follow on what he had already received. He lost pleasure in conversions, and he took his troops for extended trips into the mountains, always seeking the silver mines that eluded him.

One day upon his return to the fortress-church she went to his quarters and asked him bluntly, "Fray Antonio, what has happened?" and on the spur of the moment he blurted out the story of his father's execution in Salamanca. The look of shock that came over the face of the Altomec woman surprised him.

"Do you mean," she said in a whisper, "that in Spain they burn people alive?"

"Yes," he confessed uncomfortably.

"But the Virgin . . ." she asked, pointing to the statue that graced his bleak wall.

"They do it to protect Her," he tried to explain.

With penetrating eyes the Indian woman looked at him and asked quietly, "So in your country they do exactly what we did in ours?"

"Oh, no!" the young priest protested vehemently. "Even though it was my own father they did it to, I have to admit that it was done to protect . . ."

"The same as we did," the woman replied, looking right at the priest, and at this moment a kind of absolute equality was established between the two, so there was never again any further discussion of baptism.

Because Timoteo Palafox had been safely in the army before his father was executed for heresy, he escaped the generations-long punishment meted out to all members of the heretic's family. But although he could remain in service, he could never be promoted to officer or hold any rank of distinction. In 1529, still unaware that his father had suffered the extreme penalty for his liberal ideas, he reached Mexico City in his bright uniform of ensign, an ambitious and courageous young soldier with an alert mind. Announcing confidently that he was on his way to join his brother in Toledo, he was surprised when Captain Cortés gave different orders: "The Indians in Oaxaca, a big settlement to the south, are proving troublesome. Assemble a company of men and pacify them." Timoteo wanted to turn down this unchallenging task, but

Hernán Cortés was not a governor to whom one could offer objections.

It was therefore to distant Oaxaca that Fray Antonio had to travel to greet his brother, and when he joined him in the mean adobe hut being used as headquarters, he learned that Timoteo had been aboard ship so long in getting to Mexico that he did not know of his father's burning at the stake.

"Terrible news, brother. Father's enemies were remorseless. They hounded him till the Inquisition had to condemn him."

"Burned?" Timoteo screamed.

"Mercy was shown. He was strangled before the fires were lit."

For several minutes Timoteo stormed about the hut, the veins in his neck bulging, and then, choking as the words came out, he swore: "We shall revenge that evil deed. His yellow robe will hang in Salamanca proclaiming our disgrace, yours and mine, but by the strength of God . . ."

"Don't blaspheme."

"By God's strength working in your right arm and mine, we'll cleanse our father's name and ours. Swear to it, Antonio," and in that steaming jungle hut the brothers prepared to take that oath. Standing erect, each man held aloft his badge of office, Antonio his Bible, Timoteo his sword, and swore the vow uttered by the soldier: "We will purify the name of Palafox. Whatever it requires, we will pay the price. That stain will be removed." They lowered their arms and gritted their teeth as if preparing for battle.

Antonio produced a cloth bag he had smuggled from Toledo and emptied its contents upon a rickety table.

"Silver?" Timoteo asked.

"The purest, I'm told. These are the bullets we'll use."

Timoteo, fiery and ready to act, carefully tossed the pellets from hand to hand as if weighing them. "Where was this found?"

"I don't know," the priest replied.

The young officer grabbed his brother by the surplice and shouted, "Then why did you bring me here?"

"To find the mines," Antonio said coldly, unfolding a rough map showing Toledo and the high valley of which it was a part. "The silver seems always to reach us from this area," and with the prescience that marked so much of his work in Mexico he stabbed at the exact spot where the Mineral was later to be discovered.

"Then that's the land we have to have," Timoteo growled, pacing up and down the narrow room.

"That's my intention," the priest agreed.

"This poor land I've already sequestered for the Church." He indicated those barren portions from which the flakes of silver seemed never to come. "These better lands you must secure for our family when you get to Toledo."

"How can I get to Toledo?" Timoteo stormed. "Captain Cortés has sent me here."

"Captain Cortés assigned me to the capital," Antonio replied coldly, "but I reached Toledo. You must do the same."

That night the two brothers drafted six different letters to Cortés, but each seemed lacking in persuasive force. Finally, toward dawn, Fray Antonio decided that Timoteo should send a simple, soldierly appeal, which he proceeded to dictate while Timoteo wrote:

Esteemed Captain,

Since my devout brother, the renowned Fray Antonio, has worked so diligently to bring peace to the Altomecs and glory to your rule, I, Ensign Timoteo Palafox, do petition that I be dispatched with a small troop to protect my brother in his saintly duties among the unconverted. . . ."

The petition succeeded, and in late 1530 Timoteo, now reduced to the ranks because of his father's disgrace, was summoned to Mexico City, where Captain Cortés personally delivered the good news, but the great conquistador did not show enthusiasm as he told the nervous young applicant, "Your petition is granted to go to Toledo to serve as your brother's strong right arm." Before Timoteo could exult, the ruler of Mexico added: "Do not write letters home about this appointment. I've received instructions from Seville following your father's disgrace." He snapped out the words as if he loathed them and their source. "I've been ordered to demote you, Palafox. You can never again occupy an officer's rank in the armies of Spain."

"Permission to sit down?" the young soldier asked weakly.

"Granted. And I'll give you one ray of hope. As an ordinary soldier you can still achieve much, with valor, determination, obedience to command. By being a model for others less intelligent."

"But what will I be called if I'm allowed no rank?"

The two soldiers discussed this for some moments, and it was Cortés who recalled a title once used in the Spanish armies, a word that could be translated into English as something like "sergeant," so that when Timoteo marched west to look for the silver mine of Toledo, he was no longer an ensign destined to become a general; he was plain Sergeant Palafox, burning with anger, hatred and a determination to find the wealth that would buy back his family's reputation.

As soon as the sergeant reached Toledo, he initiated his search for the mine. Accompanied by only a few other soldiers, he tramped river-beds and climbed hills from which he could look down on his brother's fortress-church. He found nothing, and was infuriated by the fact that whenever he came upon Indians in their small outlying villages, a few women in the mean huts were sure to be wearing silver bangles.

"Ask her where she got them," he would shout at his interpreter.

"They were given her."

"By whom?"

"She says her uncle."

"Fetch him!" but when the old man was brought, and even tortured, he would not tell how he had obtained the bracelets and earrings. Enraged, Timoteo would want to lay waste the village to uncover the secret source of the silver, but would be restrained by the other soldiers.

Timoteo had been rampaging through the countryside for less than a month when Fray

Antonio was approached one day by a nine-year-old Indian girl he recognized. It was Stranger, who screamed: "They've taken my grandmother!" and she led the priest to the barracks, where he found Timoteo and four soldiers torturing Lady Gray Eyes, who was strapped prone to a bench.

"What are you doing?" the priest thundered.

"She knows where the silver is," Timoteo snapped.

"Let her go!" his brother shouted, and the woman was unbound. As she struggled to her feet and rubbed her shoulders to relieve the pain, she did not thank the priest but smiled at him with a kind of rueful satisfaction.

"You may go," Fray Antonio said.

"You are acting just as we used to," the queen said as she took her granddaughter by the hand.

In 1532, Timoteo, urged by his brother to find the silver but forbidden by Fray Antonio's piety from using the tortures that might have uncovered it, undertook an expedition to that Valley-of-the-Dead from which the Altomecs had launched their conquest of City-of-the-Pyramid, and here he found more silver bangles than in any other previous area, which convinced him that he was close to the mines he sought. But the Indians in the valley proved wholly intractable. Perhaps on orders from Lady Gray Eyes they refused to speak of silver; they would provide no food, nor would they work for the Spaniards; and finally one young warrior knocked Timoteo down when the latter tried to take his wife.

In retaliation, Sergeant Timoteo Palafox lined up his soldiers and marched down the middle of the valley, killing everyone he encountered and setting fire to every home. Some Altomecs, of course, escaped to the hills, but more than six hundred Indians were killed that day, and from their arms and legs nearly two thousand silver bangles were recovered.

When Timoteo returned to Toledo, he marched his troops into the fortress-church and threw the booty before his brother with the words "Now we're beginning to find silver somewhere." Secret messengers had sped before him to inform Lady Gray Eyes of the massacre, and she was at the side of the priest when his brother delivered the bangles, so that the young soldier's reception was not a pleasant one.

"You wanted silver!" Timoteo shouted defensively.

"But not this way," Fray Antonio replied. "Not by massacring hundreds."

"Getting silver is not easy," Timoteo argued.

"But these were Indians that I had baptized," the priest cried in anguish. "They were part of us."

"They were savages," Timoteo said, "and they attacked us."

"They did not!" Antonio thundered.

"Do you believe her?" the soldier demanded. "Rather than your own brother?"

Fray Antonio, realizing that it was unseemly to fight with his brother before an Altomec witness, said calmly, "There must be no more slaughters, Timoteo."

"They know where the silver is," the sergeant replied ominously. At this, Lady Gray Eyes smiled, causing Timoteo to shout, "Brother, get her out of this city. She's poisoning you."

The extent to which Lady Gray Eyes was influencing the priest was not to become evident for some years, but Timoteo was correct in his estimation of the situation, and he became her avowed enemy as she became his.

For four more years Sergeant Palafox probed the hills for silver and found nothing. Each time he trudged back to the fortress-church his gaunt, stoop-shouldered brother would pace up and down before him as he washed, storming,

"While you fail, our family continues in dis-grace."

"Brother," Timoteo would reply, "I have looked until I'm weary and there is no silver."

"It's right around us," Antonio would cry in frustration.

"They must be bringing it in from the north," Timoteo reasoned.

"No!" Antonio would shout. "Don't ever say that. It's here, under our feet."

Finally, one day in 1536, after such a scene Timoteo replied quietly, "All right. If it's out there, you find it. I'll guard the fortress." And during most of that year the residents of Toledo saw their thin, scholarly priest astride a donkey riding into the hills looking for a treasure that he was destined never to find.

Upon his return from one such fruitless expedition Fray Antonio was ablaze with an idea that in the long run was to prove even more important in establishing the fortunes of the Palafox family than the later discovery of silver. He called his brother to his room and while he washed he explained excitedly, "Timoteo, you must marry a girl from Spain, one with a name so proud that our father's disgrace will be submerged. You must bring her here, and for a wedding gift we'll petition the king for a quarter of a

million acres. The land will be legally ours, and
one day we'll find the mines."

"It's a good idea," the soldier said, "but I
don't know any girls in Spain."

"I do!" the priest cried, "and she's of such
exalted reputation the king will have to grant us
the land." Summoning an Indian artist, he directed the man to paint a likeness of Timoteo,
which he enclosed in a letter addressed to the
marquis of Guadalquivir with a message our
family still owns:

> It seems highly unlikely that a girl as well
> born and as beautiful as Leticia should still
> be unmarried, but on the chance that she
> is, I am writing to request her hand for my
> brother, Captain Timoteo Palafox. Frankly,
> esteemed sir, my father was burned as a
> heretic in Salamanca and there is every
> reason for you to refuse to ally your noble
> family . . .

"Should you mention that?" Timoteo asked.

"With the marquis, it may prove the deciding
point," Antonio replied, without informing his
brother of the marquis's liberal views.

In his impetuous desire to find his brother a
proper wife who could enhance the family for-

tunes, Antonio did not pause to reflect upon the terribly wrong thing he was doing: bringing a woman he had loved to Mexico not for the real reason—that he wanted her to be near him again—but for the ostensible reason that he sought a bride for his brother. He could not fore-see the anguish this must bring him.

But having made one daring move, he found courage to make another: he drafted a second letter to the king himself:

> And so, Sire, in view of the warlike nature of the Altomecs, whose constant incursions threaten Your Majesty's lands, and in view of my constant desire to win these difficult pa-gans to God, I humbly beseech that these rebellious areas be made part of the dowry of the marquis of Guadalquivir's daughter, he being the one who served you so gallantly in your fight against the Moors. If this is done, I assure you that I shall see to it that troops under my control will bring peace, tranquillity and the love of Jesus Christ to this part of your realm.

When this extraordinary letter reached Spain, the king was faced with a dilemma: if he ap-proved of the marriage and the land grant, he ran the risk of infuriating the Dominican leaders of the Inquisition, which had condemned the Palafoxes; but if he denied the petition he would be rejecting one of the men he trusted most and upon whom he had relied in the times of decision, the marquis of Guadalquivir. He could not reach a decision until he restudied Fray Antonio's plea, and then he grasped the nub of the problem: "The priest promises he'll bring new lands under my control and new souls to Jesus Christ. Petition granted. Let the marriage and the dowry go forward." In this duplicitous way the Palafox brothers grabbed their first sizable section of land.

The royal decree authorizing the grant reached Toledo long before Leticia arrived, for her departure from Seville was delayed by protests lodged by the parents of the minor nobleman she had married eight years earlier. He had been a handsome young fellow with an important position in the army, but while on service in the king's dominions in the Netherlands he lost his life in a daring sortie against the Protestant armies. Now his parents wanted his widow, Leticia, and her children to remain with them in Spain.

She had startled them by saying boldly: "The children can stay with you. I shall go to Mexico," and not even her father's caution against this rash judgment dissuaded her. Her arrival in Toledo was further delayed by other considerations imposed by her various relatives, but her dowry was delivered according to the king's schedule.

When the lines of deed were to be officially drawn, Fray Antonio dominated the proceedings to ensure that any lands suspected of containing silver fell into the Palafox personal holdings, while those that had already proved barren went to either the Church or the king. By this stratagem Sergeant Palafox gained possession of enormous stretches of promising land around Toledo plus the virtual ownership of some nine thousand Indians, whom he considered as his slaves and treated as such.

One of the first Spaniards in Mexico to be aware of the power to be gained from land and Indians, Timoteo caused six iron brands to be forged in the form of a large letter P, and he carried these to all parts of his new estate, where they were placed in fires until white-hot, after which they were pressed against the right cheeks of all the Altomecs belonging to him. So for two generations men in Toledo could point to the right cheeks of Indians and say with certainty, "That one belongs to Palafox."

It was Lady Gray Eyes who brought this bar-

barous behavior to Fray Antonio's attention. Dragging a badly scarred peasant woman before the priest, she showed him the distorted face still bloated and discolored from the branding. Antonio, drawing back in horror, asked: "What happened to her?"

"Your brother," Gray Eyes said with obvious revulsion.

"He struck her?"

"Branded her—with a hot iron. Your family initial. That big P."

She spoke calmly and dispassionately, but there was a sadness in her voice and at one point she observed, "When I lay hidden in the cellar with my son's pregnant wife, waiting for Stranger to be born, we used to study the parchment showing your gods and pray for their arrival, because they were the gentlest deities we had ever imagined. When I saw how your men killed, I thought, They must have left their gods in Spain. But then I learned that the people there had burned your father. . . ."

For the first time she told Fray Antonio of how she and the Altomec women had slipped out at night to destroy the Mother Goddess, to whom people had been sacrificed by burning. Looking at him with dark accusing eyes, she cried dolefully, "Six years before you came to this city, we had cleansed ourselves of abominations like the burning of people. Why have you not ended them in Spain?"

Her question was so devastating that Fray Antonio rushed from the room and issued a chain of orders: "Go to the villages. Collect every branding iron with that shameful letter. When you have them all, report to me."

On a day in June he ordered a great fire to be lit and melted all the cruel irons.

In late 1537 the beautiful young widow Leticia de Guadalquivir arrived in Veracruz, whence she made the long upland journey to Toledo, where on a bright sunny morning under a sky that was an impeccable welcoming blue she faced the brothers. At that moment she was more alluring than she had been when Antonio had known her as a self-willed girl in Seville. The years had softened her, made her more of a woman, and the tragedy of her husband's death had given her maturity, but Antonio could see from the imperious manner in which she surveyed her surroundings that she was still determined to be mistress of her own world.

When she moved forward toward the brothers, she went automatically toward Antonio as if to resume their love affair of years ago, but the priest flashed a warning signal with his eyes and an almost imperceptible shake of his head. With a half-smile she turned away from Antonio and moved almost gaily toward Timoteo. "You must be the handsome young man in the painting they sent me," she said, and with the elegant ease she had perfected even as a young girl, she kissed him on the cheek.

That afternoon, with scores of Indians watching and approving, the couple went into the fortress-church, where Fray Antonio was waiting to marry them. I can visualize the three of them as they stood there together on that fateful day, for I often heard about it from my Palafox relatives. My mother-in-law, Doña Isabel, from the Spanish branch, liked to describe the scene: "Four hundred years ago, it seems like only yesterday. Antonio the priest, tall and slim and dark, a solemn man. Palafox, short, rugged, with a grinning countenance, always a soldier. And between them this radiant woman, thirty years old maybe. How tangled their emotions must have been. They say in our family that when the time came for Fray Antonio to recite the marriage ritual he almost fainted, but his brother reached out and steadied him. 'Not here,' the soldier whispered, and the marriage was solemnized." My mother-in-law always ended with that strange word, adding: "What no one noticed at the time was that when Father Antonio ended the marriage

ceremony he cried in a firm voice: 'Captain Palafox, you are now wed to Leticia.' He had no right
to use that word 'Captain,' for Timoteo had surrendered any claim to an officer's rank, but from
that moment on he was Captain to everyone.
Just as Timoteo had stolen the Palafox lands, so
now Antonio stole the name Captain. We're a
bold, clever lot, Norman."

On the night of the wedding Lady Gray Eyes
told her granddaughter, who was then seventeen. "These brothers have done an evil thing,
Stranger."

"What?" the lissome girl with long braids
asked, anxious to learn all she could about the
Spaniards.

"The priest has summoned for his brother a
girl with whom he was once in love," the wise
old woman explained.

"Did he tell you that?"

"Not in words."

"What did you see?"

"The moving forward, the drawing away," the
queen said, and tears came into her eyes.
"These Spaniards make life so hard for themselves. They love a system of gods they can
never sustain. They adhere to principles they
can never understand."

"Why doesn't the priest take the girl, if he's
the one who loves her?" Stranger asked.

"For a Spaniard that would be too simple," the queen replied. And in the succeeding days they watched.

What I am about to relate does not, of course, appear in the chronicles of either the Spaniards or the Altomecs, but it is very much a part of my family tradition, and I heard it first from my own mother, who was certainly not given to idle chatter. For three years, from 1537 to 1540, Fray Antonio Palafox lived in a kind of hell. He was deeply in love with his brother's wife, whom he had known intimately in Seville; yet he himself had officiated at her wedding to his brother and it was with his words that her marriage had been solemnized.

Like King David, he found himself dispatching his general to strange battlefronts, hoping that the enemy would slay him so that Timoteo's wife could revert to him; yet even when the captain was miles from Toledo and Leticia was alone in the fortress-church and obviously eager for the priest to visit her, he could not bring himself to violate his brother's marriage. He would meet Leticia inside the fortress and she would intimate that he would be welcomed in her chambers that night; against his will he would recall the night he had spent with her in the Moorish garden in Seville and he would suffer an agony of desire, but he could never bring himself to

approach her room. As soon as Captain Timoteo's horse could be heard whinnying at the
fortress gate, the priest would mount his donkey
and leave by another exit.

Antonio would go searching for silver, and the
Indians of remote areas saw him often in those
years, a tall, graying, handsome priest of forty-
two. He had once been the most commanding
figure among the Spaniards, but he was now
irresolute, alone and driven by conflicting
desires. On one such trip he camped in Valley-
of-the-Dead, hoping that Altomec survivors of
his brother's massacre might slaughter him in
revenge, but the Indians knew him as their friend
and fed him. Next day he startled them by lining
them up and washing their feet. Through tears
he pleaded for their forgiveness, which they had
already granted. Later, when he wandered off
into the hills, they kept scouts watching over
him, and when news of his unusual behavior
reached Toledo, Captain Palafox thought he
might have to send his crazy brother back to
Spain.

But Lady Gray Eyes had contrary plans, and
when word sped through the fortress that the
mad priest was returning on his donkey, she ran
to the walls and looked down on his forlorn figure. He was gaunt from hunger, and sunken-
eyed with confusion. His long legs dragged in

the dust, and his donkey was in command. Carefully she watched as he dismounted, went to the refectory for food, and repaired to his quarters for a bath. When he reappeared shaven and once more a priest, she kissed her granddaughter on the forehead and whispered, "Now."

A few minutes later the slim young girl, dressed in her simplest gown of linen and with flowers in the tips of her long braids, went to the chapel where the priest was praying in much confusion of soul and said, "Fray Antonio, I have come to be baptized."

The priest looked up and asked, "Has your grandmother at last given her consent?"

"No," replied the girl demurely. "I am doing this of my own will."

The priest clutched her hands. "Why?" he cried joyously.

"Because last night I heard about how you begged the Indians in Valley-of-the-Dead for their forgiveness."

The priest felt hot tears edging their way into his eyes, for it seemed to him that in a world of moral confusion the Indian convert represented a solid point of reference, one that his mind could cling to. He took her triumphantly to the tunnel that pierced the fortress wall and led to the outdoor chapel, where they stood at last before the baptismal font. Normally, Stranger would have had to wait until an assembly of several score had been gathered for conversion because Fray Antonio conducted his baptisms with pomp, but the honest joy at winning the queen's granddaughter inspired him to baptize her at once.

When the rite was concluded, Fray Antonio put his hand once more upon the head of the tall girl and said in a kind of exaltation whose source he did not comprehend, "Henceforth you shall no longer be known as Stranger. Your name shall be María-of-the-Assumption." With that he led her back into the narrow tunnel. When they were beside the huge wall that he had constructed, he felt her close behind him and stopped, and perhaps by accident she bumped into him; they embraced, and there was a tremendous meeting of their mutual hunger, and after more than an hour they emerged into the sunlight of Toledo, the city they would govern together for many decades.

When the Palafox brothers were comfortably settled with their women—Timoteo with the daughter of a Spanish nobleman, Antonio with an Altomec princess—they resumed their search for the hidden silver mine with which they hoped to cleanse their father's shame. One day in 1541, Timoteo was returning empty-handed to Toledo and had reached a point within sight of both the pyramid and the fortress. He started going down a hill he had climbed many times and, in so doing, kicked aside a small rock, which revealed another of a type he had not seen previously. Upon examining it closely, he concluded joyfully that it must be silver ore and ran with it to his brother. The two pulverized the rock and finally reduced it to a small lump of silver.

Attempting to mask his excitement, Fray Antonio asked casually, "Where is the mine?"

"It doesn't seem to be a mine," Timoteo replied.

Fray Antonio bit his lip. "But now we'll surely find the mine."

"I looked, but it was not at hand," Timoteo said, and this was the beginning of the real frustration of the Palafoxes. It is true that between the years 1540 and 1550 Timoteo was to uncover several profitable deposits of silver, and it is a matter of record that for the remaining years of his life he was able to send the king in Madrid an annual gift of about twenty thousand duros, which paved the way for his and his brother's advancement in the army and the Church. But the great mother lode of Toledan silver, which the brothers knew had to exist somewhere in the vicinity, eluded him and often in the evenings his brother, now Bishop Palafox, would unroll his maps and ask once more, "Tell me, Timoteo, have you searched this valley?" Invariably Timoteo had.

In 1544, when it seemed likely that the trivial silver mines so far discovered could be depended upon to produce a steady if limited income, Bishop Palafox began to turn his energies to the third obsession that governed his life. He took his brother to the southern battlements of the fortress-church and pointed to the cactus-ridden wastes that lay beyond what once had been the Altomec City-of-the-Pyramid.

"Down there," the bishop said quietly, "I shall build our new city."

"For a tribe of miserable Indians?" Timoteo asked.

"For the glory of God," the priest replied. "After us, there will be civilized people in this city, and we shall build structures of such splendor they will forever honor the name of Palafox."

"We've already built this fortress," Timoteo protested.

"Can you see that pile of rocks?" the priest asked.

"Beyond the tree?"

"And the others?"

"I can hardly see them," the soldier replied.

"They form the outline for our Hall of Government," Antonio explained.

"It's too far away to defend from the fort," Timoteo warned.

"By the time it's finished, we won't need the fort," the priest replied.

"These Altomecs will never—"

"Facing the Hall of Government," the priest interrupted, "I plan to lay out a large public plaza. Can you see the rocks over there?"

Timoteo tried but failed to visualize the ambitious plan. "You're playing with empty fields."

"They won't be empty long, because I plan to start building right away, a special building along the entire western side of the plaza. It'll be the glory of our city."

"What kind of building?"

"A cathedral," the priest replied.

"You mean from here . . . down to what you call your Hall of Government? You must be insane!"

"When I was in Seville," Antonio replied, "waiting for my ship, I saw their cathedral. Did you bother to see it?"

"I did," Timoteo replied, with some nostalgia.

"When the priests of Seville started that enormous building," Antonio reported, "they announced to their people, 'We are going to build a church so large that all who come after us will cry, 'They must have been insane.' " He paused, then added, "I am touched by that kind of insanity."

"But a building from here to there. Antonio, where will you get the money?"

The priest turned on the battlement to look at his brother. "Why do you suppose I've driven you so desperately to find the silver?" he asked.

"Our family . . ." the soldier stammered. Then he faced his brother and snapped, "You tell me! Why did you draw the map so that the mines would fall in my land . . . and not in the Church's?"

"Because I was determined even then that our family should do the building," the priest replied. "Because I am determined to erase the shame we bear. Do you think I arranged for you to have nine thousand slaves merely for your pleasure? Timoteo, you are going to put those Indians to work not for yourself but for the building of Toledo, so that when you and I are dead, men will say, 'This is the city of the Palafoxes, who served God.' "

In 1544 the real building of Toledo began. The Hall of Government was finished in that year, after which Fray Antonio slipped the viceroy such an enormous bribe in silver that the official

was willing to overlook Professor Palafox's condemnation and appoint his son Timoteo, who
had been demoted by Captain Cortés, to the
rank of governor of the vast Toledo district. At
Timoteo's investiture, his brother whispered:
"The cleansing of our family name has begun."

The spacious central plaza was now laid out
according to Fray Antonio's plan, and in 1549
the first public band concert was held there,
given by Altomec musicians trained by Antonio.
The construction of the vast cathedral was
begun but made no conspicuous headway, for
during the first fifty years its corners seemed so
ridiculously far apart that the casual observer
could scarcely believe that they were all intended for the same edifice. Roads were built;
small churches proliferated; the House of Tile
rose toward the end of the bishop's life; wherever Antonio moved, buildings seemed to spring
up, and they were of such beauty that later historians often speculated as to how this ascetic
priest had acquired his flawless sense of design.
A French professor of architecture said of him,
"From the original fortress-church to the House
of Tile we can follow the orderly progress of a
master builder. Bishop Palafox took an Indian
city and transformed it into a jewel of Spanish
architecture, yet always, in all he did, he showed

respect for Indian building traditions. Toledo is a monument to his solid yet exquisite taste in combining the two cultures."

Antonio was supported in his desire to build by María, who said: "My ancestors were insatiable builders, too. I think all great people must be. They suffer some kind of urge to leave the face of the earth different from what it was when they arrived." And in later years, when the huge government and ecclesiastic buildings were completed, she said, "We have built for the governor and for the priests and for God. Now I want us to build a small, pretty building for my Indians."

And it was she who kept applying moral pressure on the bishop until he agreed to build a convent in which young Indian women could dedicate themselves to the Church and elderly ones find a last home. But, like Antonio, she could not think small, and when the convent was finished it stretched along the entire eastern boundary of the plaza, and flourished there until 1865, when Emperor Maximilian had it converted into his Imperial Theater. During these years of building, María never forgot her grandmother's admonition: "You must seek and find the kind of man who is capable of the love that has marked your family, and if you find him, cling to him forever, more even than you cling to your family, or your god, or your country." She became one of those many flawless wives that the Mexican Indians gave their Spanish conquerors, and from her union with the priest sprang multifold blessings, just as the union of Mexico and Spain produced far more that was beneficial than damaging.

Fray Antonio and María had four children, who launched the Mexican half of the Palafox clan, and one of their three sons became a brilliant churchman who, in time, found his own Indian girl to help him in the task of running the ecclesiastical half of Toledo. It was largely because of the stability that María brought Fray Antonio that he ultimately overcame the shame his family had suffered in Spain and won the title of Bishop Palafox in the New World. His gnawing desire for his brother's wife was easily dissipated when he compared her unsteady, nagging ways with the serenity and helpfulness of his own Indian wife, and before a decade had passed he felt sorry for his brother and almost censured himself for having engineered such an unfortunate marriage.

Antonio never legally married María; there was no convention by which he could have done so, nor was she ever known as his wife. She was simply Doña María, the most gracious of all the women in Toledo. When dignitaries arrived from Mexico City to talk business with the bishop, they could spend three days in argument and never see the stately Indian woman; but once the business was concluded, Bishop Palafox would bring forth his Altomec princess with the introduction "This is Doña María," and from the subtle manner in which she took control it was apparent that in the fortress part of that fortress-church she was mistress.

It was she who organized the final baptism of all Altomecs, except her grandmother, who resisted until her death. The old woman was buried near the grave of her father, General Tezozomoc, and gained immortality in the religious festival that occurred each year on the anniversary of the day when she had marched out of the city with Doña María, bearing a parchment portrait of the Virgin Mary and her Son.

But, most of all, Doña María brought a kind of balance into the life of Bishop Palafox. She showed him how ridiculous it was to avenge a father by trying to find more and more silver, especially when the father had given his life trying to prove that silver must be treated in sensible ways; and if the first Palafox brothers found redemption in Mexico, it was not because they discovered silver deposits but because they fitted themselves solidly into the community and made their part of Mexico a haven of law, religion and good government.

During the sunny years that Doña María spent with the bishop, no Indians were killed in the high valley, and although it is true that those belonging to Captain Timoteo were slaves, they were nevertheless protected by the Church and an ultimate escape from their slavery was provided for.

In 1580, at the age of eighty-two, Bishop Palafox died as happy a man as one could have found in Mexico. One of the reasons why he was able to die in peace was that he had accomplished his various missions: he had wiped the stain of dishonor from his family name; he had pacified the Altomecs and converted them; he had established the city of Toledo and adorned its central plaza with noble buildings. Just before he died, having finished the House of Tile, held to be his architectural masterpiece, Bishop Palafox was planning a new series of buildings and had even talked of constructing a Roman-type aqueduct across some half-dozen miles of hills and valleys so as to bring fresh water into the city. When he died, the walls of the cathedral were twenty feet high. If he had failed to find the mother lode, he and Timoteo had discovered lesser deposits that enabled them to provide their king with riches. But what gave him the greatest consolation was that he knew his work would be carried forward by the surviving members of his well-entrenched family.

A son of Captain Palafox naturally succeeded to the governorship upon the death of his father, thus establishing a precedent that made the Hall of Government practically a Palafox inheritance. In the same manner, a youngster whom the bishop had sired with María was about to be ordained a priest and was obviously destined to become the second Bishop Palafox. To support such men, Captain Timoteo's initial grant of a quarter of a million acres had been enlarged by one means or another to a third of a million and would shortly double itself.

At her husband's death Doña María started her own important work. In her upstairs room at the House of Tile she looked out over the city her bishop had built and she began to reflect upon the strange relationship that had developed between the Spaniards and the Indians. Doña María developed the idea that the greatness of Mexico would be secured by the continued union of Spaniard and Indian, and that if anything conspired against it, the nation would suffer. She was therefore inspired to record the history of her people, and it was this work that became so influential in the development of Mexico, for it gave substance to the claim that at the time of the conquest the Indians were already civilized.

In the many books I have read on the subject, historians have been harsh in evaluating the claim of Spain that it colonized the New World, and particularly Mexico, in order to win souls for God, and the so-called unholy alliance of priest and soldier has often been ridiculed, especially by Protestant writers like my father, who heaped a good deal of scorn upon the Spanish rationalization. But I have studied the records of the Palafox family in an effort to determine exactly how the original brothers operated and what they did with their energies and their silver. Let me admit up front that, yes, Timoteo the hotheaded soldier did brand his Indians, whom he considered his slaves, and, yes, he did direct that massacre of the Altomecs, but in each instance he was condemned by his brother, and in repentance he helped not only to build the new city of Toledo but also to finance its major buildings about the plaza.

How exactly did the brothers spend their income from the small mines? Of every hundred ounces of silver that Timoteo dug out of the Toledo hills, records I have seen proved that about sixty went directly to the king of Spain to support his Catholic opposition to infidel En-

gland; and the great armada that came so close
to subduing England could not have sailed if the
silver of Mexico had not reached Madrid. Of the
remaining portion, thirty of the ounces went to
Bishop Palafox for the building of Toledo and for
the subjugation of the surrounding Altomecs,
and the last ten ounces were kept by the Palafox brothers, sometimes illegally, to purify their
family's reputation.

On himself the bishop had spent little. He
lived frugally, fought the paganism of the Indians
and kept them at the onerous task of piling one
stone upon another for the greater glory of God.
Whenever one of his assistant priests ran into
difficulty in some outlying parish, the bishop was
not hesitant in dispatching his brother's troops
to allay the trouble and chastise the troublemak-
ers.

At the same time, no Indian tribe in Mexico
was more quickly pacified, none was brought
more securely into the bosom of the church, nor
treated with less brutality, than the Altomecs
under the supervision of Bishop Palafox. One of
the first Indians to become an ordained priest in
Mexico was an Altomec from Toledo. The first
home for elderly women was constructed under
the bishop's supervision, and in Toledo it was
safe to walk at night while other areas of Mexico
were still battlegrounds. When I use my Palafox

ancestors as prototypes, I have to conclude that they, at least, and I believe a good many Spaniards like them, gave the Spanish colonies a government that was not noticeably inferior to what England would later provide her settlements in America or France hers in Canada.

In the centuries that followed the death of the original Palafox brothers, there was some confusion about the connections in this vigorous Mexican family, for there were Palafoxes everywhere, but it was generally understood that there were two branches, each with its own inherited characteristics. The descendants of Governor Palafox maintained their tradition of marrying only full-blooded Spaniards, and this branch of the family, to which the present Don Eduardo belonged, watched over the business interests of the clan; the offspring of Bishop Palafox and his Indian princess continued to marry with Indians and produce the Church dignitaries, poets, artists and architects. But it was a significant characteristic of the Palafoxes that the two branches, the pure Spanish and the part Indian, lived in harmony, shared the great wealth of their clan, and looked upon each other as true cousins.

There seemed always to be a Bishop Palafox,

and he seemed always to contract an alliance with some able Indian woman, so that the essential fire of the family remained strong. In 1640 the third bishop finished the cathedral pretty much as his grandfather had planned it nearly a century before. In 1726 one of his descendants built the magnificent aqueduct that ensured the city's growth. And in 1760 it was an Archbishop Palafox who tore down the old façade of the cathedral, replacing it with the marble churrigueresque masterpiece of which I have already spoken.

But before the façade could be erected—it cost four million pieces of silver, what with the renewed carvings and decorations inside—it was necessary for the lay branch of the family to take action, and they did so with spectacular results. In 1737 Ignacio Palafox, of the Spanish branch, was managing the small group of mines. But, like all his ancestors, he still sought the mother lode, which reason told him had to be somewhere in the vicinity.

On returning empty-handed from his ninety-sixth excursion into the surrounding hills, he came upon a rise of ground from which he could look down upon the valley of Toledo and its pyramid. He turned his donkeys loose to graze and sent his servants home with the horses while he stared down at the mines from which a modest amount of silver had been eked out since their discovery in 1538. Infuriated by his family's two hundred years of failure to find the bonanza, Ignacio Palafox reasoned, "Why not approach this problem from an entirely different prospect? If, as we've always thought, there is a hidden lode, where would it have to be if its inconsequential portions cropped out where our present mines are?" He pointed to each of the mines as it stood on church ground and tried to visualize what the structure of the subterranean areas must be, but no pattern evolved.

"It's haphazard," he concluded.

He turned from the valley and looked at his donkeys as they grazed the hillside, and they moved about in haphazard fashion, one following another's tail, the other moving away by himself. "That's good for donkeys," he reasoned, "but suppose that the distribution of silver is not haphazard. Suppose that there has got to be a system?" He reviewed all he knew about veins and deposits but could deduce no logical pattern. That night he did not come down from the hills but stayed behind with his donkeys and for three hard days and nights tried to visualize what the interior structure of the known mines must be in relationship to a mother lode, and toward the evening of the last day a new concept came to him and he said firmly, "We've always been wrong in assuming that the lode would be in the center of these casuals. Perhaps it's off to one side and they erupted upward, drifting off in obedience to some internal gravity." And when he studied the land afresh he saw that at the surface it had a slight but definite slope from west to east. "It's got to be back there," he shouted, "where we've never looked!" And that was the genesis of the deep shaft going straight down more than nineteen hundred feet that my father and grandfather developed and supported in later years, and which now stood abandoned at the Mineral.

Ignacio Palafox dug for nearly six hundred feet without striking silver, and his family concluded he was crazy. His uncle, the current bishop, encouraged him to proceed, but before he gave him anything more than moral support he struck a firm bargain with the miner. "If I supply you with the funds," the bishop proposed, "you must promise that with your first silver you will beautify the cathedral."

"I'll pay for the paint and a little gold leaf," Ignacio promised.

"It isn't a little gold leaf that I have in mind," the bishop replied. "If I advance the money, and if you find silver, I shall want to tear out the whole interior of the cathedral and rebuild it with silver, and I shall want to tear down the old façade and replace it with marble."

The plans were more than Ignacio could digest and he asked weakly, "How much would that cost?"

"Four million pesos," the bishop said, "but in the end you and I would have the most beautiful church in the world."

"To imagine spending millions when you have nothing is easy," the miner said, shrugging his shoulders.

"But I mean to collect," the bishop warned, and the compact was drawn. In the ensuing years the bishop protected Ignacio from the insults of the family, and his prayers kept the miner hopeful. In 1740 the prayers and the pickaxes bore fruit, and Ignacio Palafox uncovered, at a depth of six hundred feet straight down, the lode of silver that was ultimately to produce $800 million. It was distributed according to the agreed proportions: 60 percent to the king; 30 percent to the Mexican Church; and 10 percent to Ignacio Palafox. Of his share the first four million pesos went to fulfill the pledge to the bishop, who, in accordance with the building mania of his ancestors, ripped out the interior of the cathedral, tore down the façade, and replaced them with the silver and marble of which he had dreamed.

These were years of fulfillment for the Palafoxes. Ignacio, thanks to his gifts to the king, was created a conde, and the counts of Palafox played an important role in Mexican history, bolstering a colonial regime that was increasingly threatened by other Mexicans who wished to free themselves from the domination of Spain. The bishop who rebuilt the cathedral was made an archbishop and the joke became current in Toledo that from the days of Fray Antonio to the present, the miter had passed directly from father to son.

Two traditions of the family were maintained: on the count's side male children married only Spaniards; all able boys, whether Spanish or part Indian, were sent across the Atlantic to the University of Salamanca, where there had been Palafoxes in attendance since before the year 1300. By the 1960s, of course, there were no more counts in Mexico, such titles having lapsed after the death of Maximilian, but in Toledo they were still thought of as nobility and they behaved as such. I'm proud to be a member of their family, although up to now I've done little to add to their nobility. But as I finished my review of their gallant record I swore I'd do my best.

THE
BARBERS

AFTER THE DEATH of Paquito de Monterrey in the ring and our nocturnal visit to the catacomb it was two o'clock Saturday morning by the time I returned to my hotel room. As I was preparing to go to bed I chanced to look out the window and was surprised by what I saw. Three men were slipping quietly out of our hotel and heading for the parking lot, and it was the composition of the trio that riveted my attention. Old Veneno Leal was in the lead, with Chucho and Diego trailing, the latter carrying a canvas bag, but Victoriano, the star of their troupe, was missing.

I had an instant response: "If those three are going alone, it certainly has something to do with bulls, some nefarious business that Victoriano must not be involved in. What could that be?" Then it hit me, a once-in-a-lifetime chance to witness something that few aficionados could ever see. Pulling on my pants and jamming my feet into shoes, I ran from my room, leaped down the stairs and ran out to the parking lot to intercept them.

As I had suspected, they did not go directly there but started across the plaza as if heading for the cathedral, looked about to be sure no one was following, then doubled back quickly to the parking lot, where they climbed into their big cream-colored Chrysler, with Chucho at the wheel, Veneno up front beside him and Diego in back. The powerful engine choked, then caught, but before the car could move I jumped out of the shadows and grabbed the open window at the driver's side.

"You going to do a little barbering?" I asked. The three toreros looked at one another and Chucho shrugged his shoulders.

"How did you guess?" Veneno asked.

"Easy. I saw you leave Victoriano behind, so I knew it must have to do with bulls, something illegal maybe that he couldn't afford to be involved in. Then I remembered that the corrals here in Toledo have room for only two sets of bulls. So it was clear that Sunday's animals would have to arrive sometime tonight. And you're off to intercept them. Right?"

"For a norteamericano, you're pretty smart," Veneno growled.

"Can I come along? I've never seen a barbering job." Again Chucho shrugged, whereupon Diego released the latch of the rear handle with his foot and kicked the heavy door open for me.

"Climb in," he said, and we whirled into the night.

When we left the parking lot it was two-fifteen in the morning, but mariachi bands still roamed the streets and stragglers followed them, so we had to edge our car down the street that led up from the cathedral. Once we were free of the mob Chucho floored the accelerator and with a giant roar we ripped past the open-air chapel, where only a few hours before I had been sitting with Mrs. Evans. We threw dust over the last few houses of Toledo, then tore out onto the highway that led west toward Guadalajara, a hundred and forty miles distant. Like all bullfighters, the Leals were aggressive drivers.

In the right front seat, like the grizzled captain of a ship, sat old Veneno, white-haired and rugged in the flickering light that flashed back into the car from trees or poles. Beside him, at the wheel, sat the peón Chucho, an expensive coat slung over his shoulders like a cape. His thin, handsome face resembled a Renaissance portrait from the brush of Ghirlandaio, its features hard and clean, its subdued colors harmonious.

Chucho was a skillful driver, one who obviously loved the feel of a surging car as its power spoke back to him through the vibrations of the steering wheel. His sensitive hands adjusted constantly, taking the big car into one curve after another, always at high speed yet with reasonable safety. But when we had left behind us even the villages that clustered at the edges of Toledo and had crossed the hills that rimmed the high valley, we came upon those long straight reaches that characterize Mexico's rural highways, and Chucho surprised me by stretching himself far back in the driver's seat, working his shoulders as if they had become stiff, and taking his feet off the pedals that controlled the car.

"What are you doing?" I asked in Spanish.

"Cruise control," he explained, indicating a knob on the steering wheel, which he had activated and which would now keep the heavy Chrysler pounding down the road at a constant speed.

"How fast are we going?" I asked.

"Eighty," Chucho replied; I saw that the

speedometer had not been converted to kilometers and that it indicated eighty miles an hour.
Occasional farms leaped out of the darkness as
we whipped past; occasional cattle looked up to
see what was roaring past them. The car sped
on automatically, cutting its gas feed back a bit
when going downhill, increasing it whenever it
felt an uphill pull. Down straightaways we roared
at eighty. Around gentle curves we squealed at
the same speed, and Chucho kicked out the
cruise control to regain command of the car only
when we approached corners that were so tight
that the speed simply had to be cut. Even then,
the banderillero took at sixty-five curves that I
would have been afraid to take at forty.

"Where do you plan to intercept the bulls?" I
asked once when we had negotiated such a
curve and the car had been handed back to the
cruise control.

"The village of Crucifixión," Diego, who was
sitting beside me, explained.

"Are you going to do the job there?" I asked.

"If the foreman isn't along," Diego replied. "If
he is, we'll have to arrange something else."

"Who's Palafox using as his foreman now?"
I pursued.

"As always—Cándido."

When Diego said the name I happened to be
looking at Veneno, sitting stonily in the front

seat, and I saw the old picador's jaw muscles contract.

"If Cándido's along," I said, "your trip's wasted."

"Maybe," Diego replied. "But also maybe we can do business with the old bastard."

"With Cándido?" I laughed.

"With somebody," Veneno growled from his front seat. Without taking his eyes off the road, he said, obviously for my benefit, "After what happened today, we're going to speak to those bulls."

"You mean . . . Paquito?"

The three bullfighters crossed themselves and Veneno growled, "Yes. We are going to talk with the bulls of Palafox, and if Cándido tries to stop us—"

There was an ominous pause, and now I could see Chucho's jaw muscles tightening. None of the Leals seemed willing to comment further on the subject, so I said, "I ask this as a writer—that is, as one who knows nothing really about bullfighting—don't you sometimes reflect that what you're thinking of doing tonight is . . ." I paused with a show of delicacy.

"You mean, do we think it's dishonorable?" Veneno asked.

"I didn't use that word," I countered, "but it's a good one."

"I'll tell you what honor is," Veneno said, still keeping his eyes on the road, and it was fortunate that he did so, for we now approached at great speed the cutoff that would take us south from the Guadalajara highway to the Palafox ranch. It was along this road that we would intercept the bulls at the little village of Crucifixión. To get onto the road we had to negotiate a rather sharp turn to the left and it was apparent that Chucho was reluctant to take the Chrysler away from the cruise control. With the slightest flick of his white head, the old picador indicated to his son that the turn was coming up, and with an equally controlled reaction Chucho indicated that he saw it and that he intended taking the turn at his present speed. This knowledge frightened me and I started to lean forward to protest, but I was restrained by the cool reaction of the bullfighters. They just became a little more attentive, their shoulders slightly tensed, as the car hurtled toward the turnoff. It seemed to me that Veneno and Diego were asking, I wonder if Chucho can manage this? But it never occurred to them to interfere with what he was doing.

Flexing his shoulder muscles and twisting his neck, Chucho adjusted himself in his seat, moved his left foot nearer the brake pedal in case some emergency forced a slowdown, and prepared to swing the surging car into the turn.

At a steady eighty miles an hour we roared up to the cutoff point, edged purposefully to the right, started slipping sideways in a skid, then regained control and thundered ahead on the new road. It was a moment of exquisite uncertainty, followed by a sensation of triumph, and once the turn had been negotiated and we were safe on a road that would not be used much at night, Diego advanced the speed of the cruise control so that we roared south at ninety miles an hour.

"People who follow bullfights," Veneno resumed, as if nothing had happened, "are much concerned about honor and dishonor, and about the worst word you can use for a matador is to say that he is one without honor. Chucho can tell you sometime how it feels to have that word thrown at you."

"A very bad bull in Guadalajara," Chucho observed simply. With his left hand he massaged his right shoulder.

"The bull gore you in the shoulder?" I asked.

"He gored me everywhere." Chucho laughed. "That is, he should have gored me everywhere, but I jumped over the fence."

"In 1912," Veneno began, staring as if mesmerized at the ribbon of road unrolling in a straight line before us, "I went to Spain as picador for the great Mexican matador Luis Freg, may his fighting soul rest in peace." The Leals crossed themselves in memory of one of the bravest and most inept men ever to don the bullfighter's uniform. "Freg was a man of such honor as we see no more. Sixty-seven major horn wounds while I worked for him. In the hospital—out of the hospital—great fight on taped-up legs—back into the hospital.

"Well, in 1914 he was so badly wounded that he simply couldn't fight, so he allowed me to hire out with other matadors and I got a good job with Corchaíto, the Little Cork Boy, and, believe it or not, he was even braver than Luis Freg. It's about his honor that I wish to speak.

"Corchaíto wasn't brave because he was stupid or ignorant. You happen to remember how he exploded onto the bullfighting scene? On a day I'll never forget he was fighting a hand-to-hand with Posada, and on the second bull—they were boxcar Miuras—poor Corchaíto was severely wounded, but he stuffed a rag into the wound and continued to kill his bull. Big ovation and into the infirmary. Then on the third bull Posada, who was a much better fighter, looked at the audience after a fine pass, and the bull took him from behind. With three swift chops the bull killed him, right there in the ring.

"With the senior matador dead and the junior badly wounded, the authorities wanted to suspend the fight, but Corchaíto came out of the infirmary and said, 'These people paid to see six bulls die, and they will see it.' Painfully wounded, he killed Posada's deadly bull, then the fourth, the fifth and the sixth, after which he collapsed and was carried back to the infirmary near death.''

There was a silence as we hurtled southward past sleeping farmhouses, and after a moment I reflected, "I'd say that Corchaíto had honor."

"Yes," Veneno mused. "But that isn't the story I was going to tell."

"You mean there's more?"

"With a man of true honor there's always more," the old picador said. "When I asked Freg for permission to work for a Spanish matador, he leaned up from his hospital bed and asked, 'Which one?' and I replied, 'Corchaíto,' and he said, 'Good. The Little Cork Boy's brave, and I'd hate to see you work for anyone who wasn't.'

"So that day in August, we're fighting in Cartagena with two of the best matadors of the day and Corchaíto says to his troupe, 'Today we're going to kill bulls in the grand style.' On the fifth bull of the afternoon, named Distinguido, he performs magnificently with the cloth—naturals, past the chest, windmills—and he's sure of at least one ear and more likely two. He delivers a good sword thrust, but it was just a little back and to the side. Nevertheless, the bull falls down, mortally wounded, and it's only a matter of the last dagger thrust to finish him off.

"But Corchaíto, as I explained, was a man of honor, and he calls his men together and says in a loud voice so that the people in the sun can hear, 'Get that bull back on his feet. When my bull dies he dies right.' We pulled and hauled and got the bull back on his feet, and this time Corchaíto gave what I thought was a magnificent kill, but when the bull was down the Little Cork Boy made a great show of studying the exact point where the tip of the sword went in, after which he yelled at us, 'Get the bull up again. I'm a matador, and I kill with the sword.'

"So although the bull was legally dead, we prodded him until he staggered to his feet to face the matador for the third time. But you know how fast bulls learn in the last few minutes of the fight. So when Corchaíto came in for the third time with what would have been the perfect kill, this weary, tormented, dying bull neatly hooked him in the groin, twirled him three times on the horn, and threw him against the boards, where he caught him with both horns, tossing him in the air twice more. When we carried Corchaíto to the infirmary, I put my big picador's hat over the gaping hole in his chest so that people in the stands would not faint, but black blood gushed out from the edges of the brim, and before we reached the infirmary he was dead. His heart had been ripped completely in half. That's what honor does for a man."

We thundered down the dark road, carried along by a force that seemed wholly outside ourselves and quite beyond our control. Once we came upon a flock of chickens sleeping on the warm macadam, and for a moment I thought that Chucho would kick out the cruise control and try to lead the Chrysler past the frightened and bewildered fowl, but he apparently decided against this because, gripping the wheel a little tighter, he held the car on its course. There was a wild flutter of chickens, a slamming of feathered bodies against the windshield, but the car sped implacably on. I was reminded of the time Benito Mussolini, in his early days, was being driven at top speed through the Italian countryside with an American newsman—Ralph Ingersoll, I seem to remember. The car struck and killed a village boy, but Il Duce commanded the driver to drive on. To the American he said, "Never look back," and I realized that if Chucho had struck a child and not a chicken he, too, might have driven on without bothering to look back.

"How many men have you seen die in the

ring?" I asked the old picador, who was brushing feathers from his coat.

"First my father. And then Corchaíto. Ignacio Sánchez Mejía. Balderas. Three beginners whose names you wouldn't know, three banderilleros, two picadors and a cushion salesman. Today, Paquito."

We said no more on this subject and for some minutes we tore along the empty road. Whenever we approached a farming village I thought, We ought to slow down for places like this, but Chucho kept the cruise control set at seventy, and as we sped along we sometimes caught sight of astonished peasants who had been sleeping alongside the road until awakened by the thunder of our approach. With sleepy, unbelieving eyes they watched us flash by.

It was about two miles north of such a village that the critical moment of our ride occurred. We were going down a straight stretch of road, completely empty and safe, when from our left just a little distance ahead appeared a lumbering cow about to cross the highway at a point where, if we maintained our speed, we would have to smash into her. In the split second that we four saw the cow, I was the only one who cried out. In English I shouted, "Watch out!"

If we struck this animal at seventy the car

would be destroyed and we would be killed, and if we swerved to avoid her we would be thrown on the pebbled shoulder of the road, where we would die in a smashup.

None of the Leals spoke. They did not even move. With eyes straight ahead, they watched tensely as we careened down on the doomed cow, which now occupied most of the roadway. I could not guess what Chucho would do, but at the last moment he calculated precisely where the cow would be, and with a sudden deft turn of the wheel he elected to take us to the right, past the cow's nose. With exquisite skill he kept our left wheels on the macadam, which prevented the car from skidding, and threw our right wheels far out onto the shoulder, which allowed us to squeeze past safely. Even so, the body of the Chrysler struck the cow in the head, breaking her neck instantly and throwing her wildly back across the highway.

The big Chrysler stopped weaving and settled down. Chucho checked the cruise control and satisfied himself that it was delivering its required power. Diego rolled down his window to study the left side of the car, after which he rolled it back up and reported, "Dented." Old Veneno continued to stare straight ahead.

The Leals had the delicacy of not referring to my outcry at the moment of crisis, and as I studied them I realized that as bullfighters, who faced catastrophe every working day, they had not been much concerned by the near accident. Chucho Leal was driving a high-powered Chrysler at night, and it was his responsibility to negotiate whatever dangers might arise. If he had not long since proved himself equal to the job, Diego would have been at the wheel, and he would have slid past the cow in exactly the same way. Bullfighters were men who lived with danger and had a fine sense of its limits. I did not enjoy such driving nor approve of it, but if one elected to travel with bullfighters, that was the kind of driving one got.

"Are you claiming, Veneno," I finally asked, "that a man like Corchaíto should not have behaved with such honor?"

"That's not the point at all," the old picador said. "Men like Luis Freg and Corchaíto could not have behaved dishonorably if they wanted to. They had no choice. You ever see Freg fight? Sometimes when we got to the ring we had to lift him out of the carriage, his legs were so stiff from bandaging."

It was obvious that we had exhausted this subject for the present, so in silence we approached the little Altomec village of Crucifixión, where the Leals hoped to intercept the bulls of Palafox. From the outskirts it looked like any other grubby little place inhabited by several hundred people, and as our car entered the central area I saw that Crucifixión had the usual plaza with a gloomy saloon lit by a naked bulb. To my surprise we did not stay in this area but rolled quietly down a side street until we reached an inconspicuous spot from which we could survey the deserted plaza.

"We'll wait here," Chucho said.

"Diego," Veneno commanded. "See if the bulls have arrived." From his rear seat the young bullfighter slipped out of the car, carefully closing the door so as to make no noise. As he moved forward he studied the spot where the cow's head had struck. Then he casually sauntered into the plaza.

"What I was trying to say," Veneno abruptly resumed, "is that we should always keep in mind what the end of honor is. My father thrilled Mexico, but the bulls killed him. Freg had honor, and the bulls used him as a pincushion. Corchaíto—he had honor and it broke his heart. That boy today had lots of honor and tonight they're singing songs about it, but he can't hear."

The practical view of honor, so similar to Falstaff's and just as reasonable, made me speculate on what my interpretation of the principle was. I suspected that a defining characteristic of my life was that I had always shied away from the crucial responsibilities—my marriage, the challenge of writing important work or trying to, even the decision as to which country I belonged to. I was no Corchaíto willing to die to prove a principle. I wasn't even a Juan Gómez fighting his relatively little battles with a dignity I had never had. Reflecting on all this, I was not proud of myself, but I pursued the matter no further, for in the square a a commotion arose. I assumed that the bulls of Palafox had arrived, but I was mistaken. From a village even smaller than Crucifixión, as I later learned, a group of Altomecs had carried a workman who had fallen from the roof of a church and nearly killed himself. They had been hiking since sundown and twice the injured man had fainted. Now it was near three in the morning and he was unconscious, probably near death.

"It's somewhere over here!" the bearers shouted, pointing toward the plaza exit that led to our street, and the crowd surged our way. One man broke away from the others and ran up to our car asking, "Is this where the doctor lives?" Before we could answer, the others had caught up with him and we saw the pale face of the wounded man.

"I'm a stranger here," old Veneno said gravely, "but I'll ask." He slowly opened the car door and got down onto the sandy roadway. His austere demeanor impressed the Altomecs and they followed him like dutiful servants.

"Halloooo there!" Veneno cried in a deep voice. "Where does the doctor live?"

There was no reply, and he shouted again. A light came on and a woman screamed, "Stop that noise!"

"Where's the doctor?" Veneno cried again, this time in an imperious tone.

"You're in front of his door," the woman bellowed. "Dr. Castañeda."

The Indians banged on the doctor's door and a light went on upstairs. While we waited for the doctor to appear, I studied his office. It was a low adobe building with windows filthy from the fly-specks of nearly half a century. Above the door, bullet scars showed that General Gurza's men had once rampaged through the nearby plaza firing their revolutionary shots at random, and nearly a fourth of the tiles that had once framed the doorway had been broken or stolen.

A downstairs light flicked on and the door creaked open, displaying a barefoot, suspend-ered old man who was almost as dirty as his windows. He looked exhausted but he made a decent show of welcoming the Altomecs and their miserable burden.

His office consisted of an earthen floor, a few

chairs of unfinished lumber and the inevitable framed photographs of women in black and men with mustaches, all covered with the soot of ages. The inert body of the workman, who looked to be near death, was gently placed upon a rickety uncovered table and Dr. Castañeda began undressing him. Both the thigh bone and the shin of the right leg were broken, so that the leg swung outward like a scimitar, but what was more important, and what the doctor noticed immediately, was that some other bone had punctured the lower part of the man's belly and now stood forth strangely white and free of blood. Dr. Castañeda shook his head, and the Indians, interpreting this sign, whispered among themselves.

What happened next appalled me. The doctor went to a glass case such as shopkeepers use for penny candies, slid back the door, and started rummaging through a pile of filthy medical instruments covered with flyspecks and dust. Forceps, tongue depressors, scissors and hemostats lay jumbled together, and the doctor took whatever he needed from the pile, blew on it, wiped it on his shirt, and went to work. When the tool was no longer needed, it was pitched unwashed back into the glass case to accumulate more dust.

Veneno whispered to me in his grave voice,

"Now you can see why matadors dread being gored outside the big cities. Can you imagine having your guts operated on with those things?" His two sons studied the doctor with fascination, and when I saw Chucho cross himself, I thought: He's probably experienced such medical care in a similar village.

After his initial probing, Dr. Castañeda looked at the Altomecs and said, "There isn't much we can do for this one."

One of the Indians grabbed the doctor's arm and pleaded, "He must live! He has four children."

"Everybody has four children," the old doctor replied. He rummaged in the glass case for another tool and I thought, Years ago this doctor tried to keep his instruments clean—the way he was taught. Now look at him.

Wiping the tool between his arm and his left side, he approached the stricken man to try to force the protruding bone back through the stomach wall, but as he did so the man on the table groaned piteously, jerked his head twice, and died.

"God's blessing," Veneno mumbled. The three Leals crossed themselves, and it seemed to me that in the filthy room at Crucifixión we had been closer to the reality of death than we had been that afternoon in the bullring of Toledo. A bullfighter may not actually court death, but he knows that he is tempting the Grim Reaper, so that death does not come unexpectedly, but a peasant working in his field has a right to expect continued life, at least into his sixties. When death strikes him arbitrarily, it seems more terrible. One of the peasants broke into soft weeping, as if it were part of him that had died. "His brother," one of the Altomecs explained. "And well he might weep, for now he'll have more children to feed."

Down the street from the plaza hurried two men bringing a priest, who was dressed in an ordinary business suit. "The father's here," one of the Indians announced, but the weeping brother said sternly, "No priest will touch my brother."

When the priest was advised of the brother's stand, he hesitated and then turned to leave, but Dr. Castañeda threw his medical implements into the glass case, slammed the door shut and cried, "Father, when a man dies in my house I want a priest." He elbowed his way through the Indians and took the priest by the arm.

"Not for my brother!" the stubborn relative shouted. There was a scuffle, after which the protesting brother was taken away. Dr. Castañeda went up to the man, who was being held by three of the Altomecs, and snarled, "I'm not going to get paid, so he'll die the way I say. He's no longer your brother. He's a corpse on his way to meet God."

"Not my brother!" the imprisoned Indian shouted. "He's on his way to hell!"

"Oh, shut up!" one of the men cried, clapping his hand over his friend's mouth. The priest, ignoring an unpleasantness with which he was familiar, went about his duty of blessing the dead man and commending his soul to heaven, for which Dr. Castañeda thanked him warmly. But when the priest had gone, the brother broke away from his captors, rushed over to the table and spat upon the dead body.

"He's in hell," the brother shouted. "Where he wants to be and where I want to be. He's dead, and he's left four children, and no pig of a priest can help him now."

Veneno startled me by striding across the dirty room and striking the brother across the mouth, knocking him into a corner. "Don't you speak of death and priests like that," the old picador said menacingly, crossing himself.

We returned to the Chrysler and watched in silence as the Altomecs wrapped the dead body in a sheet and started the long hike back to their village. As Dr. Castañeda had predicted, no one had any money to pay him, so he brushed some of the dust off the top of his instrument case, surveyed his miserable office, and turned out the light.

When the funeral procession had returned to the plaza, leaving us alone, I looked beyond the doctor's office and saw how wretched this Indian village was. A garage displayed its broken tools, its dripping water faucet and its unspeakable toilet. A school, farther down the narrow street, was ramshackle, with broken windows.

This was rural Mexico, almost as impoverished and ignored as the worst of what I had seen when reporting on Haiti. It infuriated me to know that the Mexican political party that had run the nation for most of this century had called itself something like the People's Revolutionary Party and had loudly preached social justice for all, winning election after election on that windy promise, but when installed, had proved itself to be a callous oligarchy. A small group of buddies had passed the presidency from one to another, each coming into office with modest means and leaving after six years with hundreds of millions, usually hidden in Swiss banks. The so-called revolutionaries stole the country blind, allowing or even forcing the peasants to sink deeper and deeper into abject poverty. Few nations had been ruled so cynically, which was why so many peasants wanted to escape to the good jobs, houses and food in the United States. I was not proud of what my country had accomplished during my lifetime.

And yet I loved this country, its color, its music, its warm friendships, its handsome cities so much older than those in the United States. I have often thought as I watched my wealthy friends enjoy their privileges that there was no country on earth where a young man of good family whose father had a government job from which he could steal a large amount of money could live better. Of course, he would have to blind himself to the gnawing poverty about him, but apparently that was easy, since so many did it.

I had witnessed this phenomenon in Cuba in the 1950s, when the idle rich were cruelly indifferent to poverty, and it had not surprised me when Fidel Castro had been able to organize his revolution. I had ample reason to despise that same Castro of recent years, for on major matters he had lied to me, encouraging me to make a fool of myself in my reports from Cuba, but I had to admit his drawing power and feared that much of Latin America, always hungry for a savior, would imitate Cuba—even Mexico.

Certainly, looking at this Altomec village of Crucifixión, I had to admit that my gallant Indian ancestors had been pitifully shortchanged by the twentieth century. The material rewards of industrialism had been slow to filter down to the Indians, and whereas Mexico City was lovely and Toledo unique in its charm, beyond them lay a thousand Crucifixións where the Indians were denied almost everything that was required for decent living. Even the names of the villages—Crucifixión, Encarnación, Santiago de Campostela, Trinidad—bespoke the betrayal the Altomecs had suffered, and when I compared the civilization they had built for themselves in the fourteenth and fifteenth centuries with what they had today, I felt they had a right to revolt.

"Why do you suppose villages like this are so poor?" I asked.

"Why?" Veneno snorted in Spanish contempt for anything Indian. "They prefer to live like pigs." He spat out the window.

"I will say this, though," Chucho mused, pointing across the plaza to the towers of a church large enough to serve a population eight times as large as Crucifixión's. "Beyond the church they have a fine country bullring."

"They do!" Veneno cried enthusiastically. "Remember the great afternoon you had here in Crucifixión, Chucho? Bulls of San Mateo."

"La Punta," Chucho corrected quietly. "I'll never forget."

There was a moment of awkward silence, during which I remembered that this notable fight had taken place when it was still uncertain whether Chucho or Victoriano was to become the matador. "You were very strong that day," old Veneno reflected, and I wondered what Chucho was thinking, whether he resented the fact that his father had converted him into the peón, whether he ever experienced the pangs I sometimes suffered because I had wanted to be a novelist but had been sidetracked into journalism.

Our cases were by no means identical. He had been ordered into secondary status; I had carelessly slipped into the security of a field I had not consciously elected. So my fault rested on my own shoulders, and yet . . . and yet, there had been my father's unvoiced assumption that I could not do what he had done. It wasn't a clear case at all. Chucho's father had yelled at him; mine had smiled at me, indulgently.

"Chucho, do you ever regret—" I began, for as a reporter I had steeled myself to ask any question, however intrusive, but before I could finish, Veneno said bluntly, "Here comes Diego."

Running across the plaza with the easy grace that marks bullfighters, Diego looked about to be sure he wasn't being followed, then ducked into our side street and whispered, "The bulls are here."

"Cándido, too?" Veneno asked.

"Cándido," Diego said with finality. "He's at the saloon now."

In the darkness Veneno sucked in his breath, then snapped his fingers and asked, "Clay, you used to know Cándido, didn't you?"

"He worked for my father," I replied.

"Would you proposition him?"

"About barbering?" I asked.

"Yes," Veneno said sharply.

"He won't listen," I warned.

"He's got to listen," Veneno insisted.

"I'll speak to him," I said. "But he loves bulls the way you love your sons."

Veneno and I left the Chrysler and started walking toward the plaza, but we had gone only a few steps when the old picador halted and called for Chucho. "Cándido hates me," Veneno reflected. "I killed one of his bulls once, an ugly beast. As a picador I had no right to do this, and he's never forgiven me. You go, Chucho. To you he might listen."

We went up to the dismal little saloon, where a gang of late-night loafers had gathered to talk with the bull men, and I was approaching the ring of tables when I saw parked along the edge of the plaza a sturdy truck loaded with six rectangular boxes strapped with steel bands. Almost against my will I left the saloon and walked toward the truck, aware that I was being used in an illegal operation of which I did not approve. I knew that shaving horns was a nasty business, and I had come along only to see how it was done, but now I was being conscripted as an active participant, and I was ashamed of myself for being so compliant. When I went up to the boxes I could feel the terrible strength of the imprisoned bulls as they pressed against the sides, or snorted, or kicked the planks. In the darkness I sensed their overwhelming power as they must have sensed my fear. They grew restless and one of the six issued a low bellow that was additionally terrifying.

I was about to move away when I was startled by a firm hand that grasped my shoulder and a familiar, rasping voice, which warned, "Don't bother the bulls!"

I jumped away and looked around to see a tall, thin man dressed in leather pants, shirt tied about his middle, bandanna knotted at his throat and a large sombrero. He now had white hair that he wore in bangs, dark eyes, a seamed face and a large mustache. He must have been past seventy but he had the austere correct manner I had known as a boy. He had once been my closest friend, my most trusted adviser, and he looked now almost exactly as he had in those hectic days at the Mineral.

"Cándido!" I cried. "It's Norman."

He limped toward me just as he had done the first time I had seen him and embraced me. "What brings you here?" he asked soberly.

"Let's go over to the saloon," I suggested, taking him by the arm, but as soon as he saw Chucho he pushed my hand away and asked, "Have you come to this little village at night to talk with me about the bulls?"

"Let's sit down," I pleaded, but he refused.

"Where is he?" Cándido demanded. "Where's the real one? Is he afraid to come out and face me like a man?"

"Wait a minute, Cándido," I begged. "We just wanted to—"

"Ho, Veneno, you evil old man!" Cándido shouted into the darkened plaza. "Where are you hiding?"

"Old friend," I pleaded, as people began to fill the plaza to find out what the noise was about. "Veneno has an idea—"

"I know Veneno's idea," the foreman of the Palafox ranch interrupted. "Pepe!" he bellowed to one of the men drinking at the saloon. "Pepe! Get out your gun and shoot anyone who tries to get near our bulls."

A slim, rangy lad left the saloon, hurried to the truck, and hefted his rifle to stand guard.

"Now damn you, Veneno, have the courage to come out."

There was a long silence, after which a sound was heard of a car door banging. Then white-haired Veneno strode into the plaza, almost as old as Cándido, almost as erect in carriage. He walked across the stones to where Cándido stood and asked bluntly, "Can we work on the bulls?"

Old Cándido looked at him with hatred and cried, "You dare to ask me—?"

Veneno interrupted to say, "There will be money for you."

"You pig!" the foreman cried. "Pepe! Shoot him." The slim boy on the truck made no movement and someone in the crowd laughed. This infuriated Cándido and he said slowly, "Laugh! But do you know why our friend Veneno has hustled through the night to intercept the bulls? Because he is sick with fear."

The crowd drew closer and I watched the picador, who stood erect without a sign of embarrassment. Cándido continued, "Yesterday a man died in the ring in Toledo and Veneno is sick with fear, because on Sunday his son has to face these bulls." He indicated the six beasts of Palafox in the boxes behind him. "And he has come here to bribe me into allowing him to barber these bulls." He allowed the news to sink in, then added contemptuously, "My own bulls."

Veneno still said nothing, whereupon old Cándido did an unexpected thing. He moved close to me but pointed to the picador and said, "And this evil one has been afraid to approach me himself. He sends an American." He pointed at me with disgust, and with a quick twist of his hand pulled out my shirt so that my stomach was exposed, showing a long white scar.

"In the old days," Cándido said, his long mustache bristling with emotion, "this American was a man of honor. Look at that scar! I know he earned it fighting the greatest bull that Palafox ever produced, Soldado."

In the crowd there were some who knew the history of bullfighting, and the unlikely information that an American had once fought Soldado caused real excitement. Stragglers pressed up to see the scar that the legendary bull had left across my stomach more than forty years before.

"You never fought Soldado," a man from the saloon protested.

"I did," I said, tucking in my shirt.

"As a man of honor, Norman Clay," Cándido said to me quietly, "gather your thieves together and go back home."

"It's a simple matter—" I began, but before I could finish my sentence old Cándido, as he had often done when training me, struck me across the face and shouted, "No more!"

The crowd separated, making a path for us, and we retreated to the Chrysler with the sound of Cándido's voice in our ears: "Pepe, keep that gun ready and shoot them if they try to touch the bulls."

We resumed our places as before: Chucho driving, Veneno beside him, Diego in the left rear seat, me in the right. Nobody said anything, then Chucho muttered a prayer, crossed himself and kissed his thumb, as bullfighters always did before starting to drive a car. It occurred to me that earlier, when Chucho had climbed into the Chrysler behind the hotel, he had no doubt said his prayer and crossed himself, so that when he approached the wandering cow at high speed he did not panic as I would have done, but thought: I am in the hands of the Virgin, and if it is fated that I die, I'll die. This might seem incredible to the average American, who has been taught at least the rudiments of highway safety, but not to someone like me who has worked in the Arab countries. Truckers at the start of a long haul will mutter a one-word prayer, "Inshallah," and then roar down the highway with a sign painted across the front of their vehicle that says "Inshallah," the message being "If you get hit by this truck it was Allah's will, not my bad driving."

After preparing his soul for the journey, Chucho edged the big Chrysler into the plaza and past the truck of bulls, where Pepe sat guard with his rifle. Soon we were on the highway back to Toledo, and soon the cruise control was again set at seventy. Before long we roared past the area where the cow had been killed, and her body still lay beside the road. At some villages we dropped down to sixty. At others where the road was straight we kept the control at a steady ninety, and once, when a man seemed about to start across the road ahead of us to encounter instant death, I gasped, after which I too said a little prayer and committed myself to the mercy of the Virgin. The Chrysler roared through the night as if to emphasize the saying "Bullfighting will never be completely safe until matadors stop driving to the plazas."

"Did you really fight Soldado?" Veneno finally asked.

"Yes," I said. I could feel respect building.

"What kind of bull was he?" asked Veneno, who was fascinated by the history of this great animal who had sired so many of the good bulls of Mexican history.

"We hid him in a cave at the Mineral," I explained.

"I know that part," Veneno said. "Was he a quick animal?"

"Very," I said.

"And he gave you the wound?"

"Yes," I laughed. "My mother thought I was going to die."

"Did he turn quickly?" Veneno pursued.

"That's how he caught me," I explained.

"You fought Soldado!" Veneno repeated. "Incredible. I suppose you know that no Mexican can say as much?"

"It's one of the reasons why I love bullfighting," I said. "It's why I wanted to come along tonight. You know, I've never seen the barbering."

"When Cándido struck you—"

"Why didn't I knock him down?"

"Yes."

"Cándido was like a father to me," I said.

"But your father lived for a long time, I believe."

"Yes, but Cándido taught me many of the things that counted."

"He's a man of great honor," Veneno said, "and as you heard, I despise such men."

The Leals spent the rest of the trip devising ways to circumvent old Cándido's honor. When at four in the morning we roared into Toledo they hastened to a side street where they found a veterinary, and after coaching him in what he must do—and paying him well—they hurried to the stockyards at the edge of town, where they borrowed a movable chute and many lengths of rope. Then they went to the bullring, where they slipped into the first corral, which was empty, so as to hide Diego near the shack where the guardian of the bulls was housed while his animals were waiting for their fight. It was from this spot that old Cándido would protect the bulls of Palafox, as he had done for nearly fifty years.

Veneno then led Chucho and me back to the Chrysler, which we hid far down a side street. From beneath the rear seat Chucho took out a sizable canvas bag, and we walked quietly back to a spot across from the bullring, hiding ourselves so that we could oversee the gate to the first corral. I was still reluctant to be an active part of this shady business, but as a writer on assignment to cover a complex story I was not only willing but eager to tag along to see how the dirty work was done. Not an honorable position to be in, but a practical one when Drummond kept demanding "more inside stuff, a more intimate account, proving to the reader that you'd been there."

We were close to the open space in which the

amusements of the festival were clustered, and although it was now almost four in the morning, the visitors to Toledo were enjoying themselves in noisy fashion. Above us spun the Ferris wheel. Around us were the greasy restaurants and beyond lay the shooting galleries, the games, the carousels and the peddlers of spun candy. But the dominant note of the festival continued to be the mariachi bands who strolled back and forth through the festival area, each playing its own tune until dawn.

I had barely become adjusted to the noise when the speedy Palafox truck, with Pepe holding his gun, drove up to the corral gate. Adeptly old Cándido maneuvered the gates of the cages, and one by one the big bulls for the Sunday fight scrambled down the ramp and into the corral where food and water waited. From our hiding place we could hear the muted conversation of the animals as they tried their horns, muscled one another away from the best drinking spot, and settled down.

At this point two things happened. The veterinary appeared out of the darkness to advise Cándido that he must come to the office to certify the health of the animals, and as soon as Cándido left, Diego hit young Pepe over the head with a club. The Leals were now free to proceed with their barbering, and moment by moment I was more deeply involved in their criminal behavior, but I must admit that by now any moral compunctions were dulled. This was exciting business.

Using the trained plaza oxen, who were practiced in maneuvering wild bulls into required positions, the Leals alternately goaded and lured the first bull into the borrowed chute, where they promptly lassoed him about the head and legs, drawing the ropes so tight that the huge head became at last immovable. The Leals then produced their canvas bag, from which they took a set of specialized saws and files. Chucho, taking the saw and working first on the right horn, sawed off three inches of the tip, leaving a blunt cross section the size of a half-dollar.

As soon as the right horn had been trimmed, Chucho moved with his saw to the left horn, and old Veneno took over the principal part of the job. With a big, rough file and a skill that bespoke years of training, he proceded to rasp away all the outside portion of the blunted horn, producing at last a new tip barely distinguishable from the original except that it was three inches shorter with its point about half an inch closer to the inside. It was this latter insignificant alteration that would make the once-powerful bull pliable and ineffective.

If the horn had been merely shortened with

the new tip remaining in the same axis, the bull would quickly condition himself to the change, since a straight charge would merely require three more inches of thrust in the same direction, and with only a few preliminary charges the beast would learn to accommodate himself. But with the horn shortened and the tip moved inward as well, the bewildered animal would be unable to adjust, for he was now required both to lengthen his charge and to point his horn tip slightly outward, and these two things he could not do together. In Spanish this indecent process, which as a fair-minded sportsman I deplored, but in which as a writer I was interested, quite destroyed the natural balance between bull and man, giving all the advantage to the latter, and was known as shaving; those who performed the act were barbers, the greatest of whom was Veneno Leal.

When the picador had finished the rough work on the right horn, he turned it over to Diego, who with an ultrafine emery paper smoothed the new tip until only the most practiced eye could detect that a rasp had been at work. A few drops of oil applied with a cloth restored the sheen, and a handful of earth well rubbed in gave the tip its proper age. By this time Veneno had altered the left horn and Diego switched to it, after which the bull was turned loose to make way for another.

The Leals worked with silent speed, for they had to barber all six bulls if Victoriano was to be protected, since no one could be sure which bulls a matador would draw in a lottery. The pairings being picked blind out of a hat, the system had to be kept honest. Occasionally the agent of a top matador would try to dictate how the bulls would be allocated, and to a degree Veneno had tried to pull that trick against Paquito de Monterrey in the pairings for the first fight, but the young fighter's agent was too smart to permit any such shenanigans. The bull that had killed his young matador had been properly paired and honestly chosen. And when Veneno was faced by a canny manager like Cigarro and a tested matador like Juan Gómez who personally supervised the choosing of his bulls, there was no chance for Veneno to dictate anything. The three bulls his son must face on Sunday would be determined by pure chance, so it was imperative that all six be shaved. None could enter the ring with their horns unbarbered. Silently the men sawed off the horn tips of the second bull, and the third, and the fourth. They had some trouble getting the trained oxen to lure the fifth bull into the chute, but when they finally got him there, they worked with unusual speed and Veneno was not pleased with the result. "Get him out!" he cried nevertheless, and the mutilated bull stormed off to test his new horns. They could hear him chopping away at a board, sometimes missing it by inches, again striking it later than he thought he should. In the thirty-six hours remaining before the fight he would not learn to control his horns, and whichever matador got him in the draw would encounter a relatively easy enemy.

But while the Leals were attempting to corral the sixth bull I heard a commotion in the street and Veneno rasped, "It's Cándido!"

"Police!" the foreman started shouting. "Someone's meddling with the bulls!"

A great cry was raised in the street and people were summoned from the festival. Soon there was a rattling of the gates and it became obvious that if we wanted to escape arrest we had better flee. Abandoning the sixth bull, we gathered our barber tools and ran from the corral, down the alleyway used by the oxen and to the fence over which we jumped to mingle with the noisy crowds still attending the festival. As we ran, we had to leap over the still-unconscious body of Pepe, whose gun lay useless in the dust.

Dodging down streets where the police would

not be, we reached the Chrysler and slumped breathless into our seats, fully aware of the unlawful things we had done but pleased that we had done them so well. Then Veneno brought us back to the real world. "There's one in there we didn't get," and I could foresee that in the thirty-two hours before the drawing for the Sunday fight he would torment himself over the chance that his son might draw the bull with the untrimmed horns.

"Hide the canvas bag," he commanded, and Diego lifted the rear seat and stuffed the barber tools into a prepared hideaway. Then to my surprise the old picador growled, "Chucho, drive us to the bullring."

"Is that wise?" I asked.

"Outsmart the bastards," Veneno said.

We drove up to the crowd that surrounded the first corral and saw, in the glare of the street lamps, old Cándido, his mustache bristling, as he cried, "That damned picador shaved these bulls."

"Hello, Cándido!" Veneno called airily from the Chrysler.

"You! You paid the veterinary to take me away!"

"Away where?" Veneno asked blandly.

"Away from my bulls," Cándido shouted.

"Something happen?" Veneno asked.

The old foreman exploded, but before he could speak the crowd fell back. The police had summoned Don Eduardo Palafox, owner of the bulls, who approached slowly in the glare of the street lamps. "What happened, Cándido?" Palafox asked.

"This one shaved the horns of our bulls," the foreman replied.

"Where were you?" Don Eduardo demanded.

"I was forced by the veterinary to make a report—"

"What veterinary? What report?"

A man was brought forward by the police and Cándido said, "That one—there."

"He's no veterinary!" Don Eduardo scoffed as Veneno smiled. The real veterinary we had approached had been no fool. Rather than get himself mixed up in what might turn out to be a troublesome affair he had enlisted his wife's brother, who had acted the part. It was apparent to all that Cándido had been tricked.

As the crowd laughed, the old foreman, who had failed Don Eduardo, grew bitter with rage, but before he could vent it on Veneno, his young assistant Pepe came up with a flashlight to report, "They shaved only five." He rubbed his head where he had been clubbed and repeated the news: "They shaved only five."

Cándido's rage left him. He stared at Veneno, at Chucho, at Diego and finally at me. "So you missed one. Pepe, which one was it?"

The attendant came over and whispered in Cándido's ear, whereupon the foreman went to Don Eduardo and passed the information along to him. The three men from the ranch began to laugh, and then to point at Veneno and laugh harder and finally to hold their sides to control huge waves of laughter.

"Wait till you see the one you missed!" Don Eduardo said between quakes of mirth. "Oh, Veneno, just you wait."

"I just got here," the old picador said blandly. "You all saw me and my sons drive up."

"There will be no fooling now, Veneno," Cándido said with sudden seriousness. "God has a way of balancing out these things. On Sunday you will stand right here drawing lots and God will give you the bull you failed to shave. And if you knew what I know about that bull you would not sleep for a week."

Cándido's statement struck home, and I could see its corrosive effect on the superstitious old picador. He licked his lips and repeated, "I did nothing. I just got here."

But the three men from the Palafox ranch— Don Eduardo, the owner, Cándido, the foreman,

and Pepe, the apprentice—looked at one another and fell once more to laughing, and their
voices rose higher than the noise of the festival,
and I knew that this derisive laughter would torment Veneno and his sons until the end of the
fight on Sunday.

13

ON THE
TERRACE

ANY FESTIVAL, regardless of what it cele-
brates—music, art, dance, cinema, bullfighting—is blessed if it has one hotel that is so
dominant that it houses the principal contestants, because that hotel then becomes the
focus of activity. Visitors meet there, fans stop
there to gawk at the celebrities, and if the food
happens to be good, experts on gastronomy
come to renew old acquaintances and exchange gossip. For the Festival of Ixmiq such a
gathering place was the House of Tile. What
made the place irresistible was the terrace in

front that was enclosed by the two wings reaching out at attractive angles to make a perfect place for outdoor refreshments and meals.

Saturday began with an agreeable surprise. As I was having my breakfast of a sweet roll and cocoa I heard a pleasant voice at my elbow: "Would you mind if I joined you? Daddy had a few too many last night. He'll sleep late."

It was Penny Grim, bright and fresh in an expensive gray-blue cashmere sweater, a very short tartan skirt and light tan cowboy boots that added just the right touch of understated elegance proper for a sophisticated seventeen-year-old.

"Where'd you get the crocodile boots?" I asked as I invited her to sit with me, and she explained, "There's this character in Tulsa who specializes in cowboy boots, eighteen different kinds of leather."

"How is Tulsa these days?"

"It's a great kicking-off place."

"You leaving?"

"I don't think I'd want to spend my life there." She hesitated, considered the implications of what she'd said and added, "I might come back when I was real old, like maybe fifty, to be near friends."

When she saw me wince, she asked instantly, "Did I offend you?" and I said, "I'm fifty-two and wondering how I can start the real half of my life."

She had the tact to lean back, study me and tap my hand reassuringly. "I'd have thought you were in your thirties."

"You were saying about Tulsa?"

"Nothing much. What are we having for breakfast?"

"Roll and hot chocolate." This made her laugh, and she said, "Maybe you *are* as old as you claim. Hot chocolate!" When the waiter came she asked for some unbuttered toast and a boiled egg.

"Watching your weight?"

"When you're a butterball at thirteen and you discover that boys do not like fat girls, you change your eating habits in a hurry."

Looking at her now, I could not believe she'd ever had problems with her appearance. She was not gorgeous—that implies overblown beauty—but she was very pretty, with a frame that was delicate but Oklahoma tough. She was what I once said of Donna Reed, "American healthy." All in all, she was extremely appealing and I envied the young man who would win her.

When she interrupted my musings with a smile, I said, "I'm still waiting to hear about Tulsa."

"A great place to grow up in. Horses. Exciting oil business. Good schools."

"But—"

"But I wouldn't want to spend the active years of my life surrounded by the people I've always known. I want to go up against the best—in New York—Los Angeles—maybe even London or Paris. Or—I saw this neat TV film on Florence in Italy."

"Doing what in the big city?"

"Participating." Breaking the toast, which had come before her egg, she spoke carefully. "Financially I'd be O.K. There's Daddy's oil money and a trust account Mother left me. I don't want to waste those advantages." She clearly meant what she said, but she still hadn't told me what specifically she intended doing with her life, and I asked about this.

"Plenty of time to figure that out. Four years of college should teach me something."

"Where?"

"Daddy's always wanted me to go to some place he calls respectable. That means in either Oklahoma or Texas. Lately he's settled on S.M.U. in Dallas. He tells me they have a great football team, one you can look up to, and he sees me as maybe their head cheerleader."

"Well, that is a goal," I said.

"I do have the moves, and I guess the figure."

She went through the motions of twirling a baton. "But in high school I had this history teacher—"

"Private school?"

"Yep. Mother insisted. This teacher was an eye-opener, a cobweb-brushing-away wizard. When I learned she had graduated from Smith College in Massachusetts, that made up my mind. I applied for entrance and they accepted me. To get the cobwebs of Tulsa brushed away."

"So it's off to Smith—and New England—and the boys from Harvard and Yale?"

"Not exactly. When Daddy heard what I'd done, he went ape. Had his oil friends back East check Smith out and they reported it was a school that girls went to when they did not want to get married, or couldn't. When he relayed his findings to me he added a clincher: 'And they don't even have a football team.' "

"So the dream of getting a first-class education ended?"

"Don't downgrade S.M.U. A girl can get a fine education there—"

"And an acceptable Texas husband?"

"Well, yes. That does figure in Daddy's speculations—and mine, of course."

"What will you study at S.M.U.?"

"It's not at all sure I'll be going there."

"Entrance problems?"

"No. Mrs. Evans, she's a kind of mother to me—Daddy and her husband were partners in a lot of oil deals—she also looked into Smith, and *her* friends said it was one of the best in American education. She thinks she might persuade Daddy to let me go there."

"And if he refuses?"

She pondered this for some moments, biting her left thumb and looking at me with those odd-colored eyes that matched her auburn hair: "The time does come, you know, Mr. Clay, when a girl becomes a young woman. It comes, I guess, when she's sixteen to eighteen. Then she has to make up her own mind, or she may, as Daddy points out so often in speaking of his deals, 'miss the whole ball game.'" She laughed. "Daddy always speaks in terms of games. He considers me his quarterback, and he does want to do the right thing, but always in his way. My problem right now is that I badgered Daddy to bring me here so that I could meet a matador. But I'm having no luck, and yesterday's tragedy slowed things down. You know Toledo. Can you arrange it?"

"Matadors I do not know intimately, but my uncle is owner of one of the biggest bull ranches in Mexico, and I can certainly fix it for you to go out there for a fiesta tomorrow—"

"Tomorrow's too late. At the fights yesterday, I saw in the stands what the girls call a 'real hunk,' and when I asked who he was, the people next to us said 'Fermín Sotelo, he's fighting tomorrow.' I'd love to meet him. Tried to yesterday, but then the other man got killed and things fell apart." Shivering, she said, "That death was pretty awful. Does it happen often?"

"First one I ever saw. Photographed it every inch of the way. It'll be a sensation in New York."

"Is that all you thought about?" she asked.

"That's my job, to think about such things, with pen and camera."

She was about to say something when she suddenly gasped and whispered, "My God! It's fate. There he is," and when I looked across to one of the two larger tables reserved during the festival for matadors and their troupes, I saw that it was indeed Fermín Sotelo, a lithe, handsome young man who had recently taken his doctorate, so that he was now a full-fledged matador. He'd done well in Mexico and not so well during his first expedition to Spain, and the local impresario had probably picked him up for a reasonable fee to fill the third spot on today's card. His exaggerated swagger, the cocky angle of his dark head, the effusive attention paid to him by his subalterns, all testified to a matador on his way up, and I understood why Penny was so excited about the possibility of meeting him.

"Could you possibly take me over?" she begged. I felt ashamed at having to say "I can't because I don't know him," and I feared she might think I considered her too immature to be involved with matadors. But then I caught sight of León Ledesma in his black cape and I flagged him down: "Don León, pull up a chair. You remember Penny Grim from the catacombs." He joined us, throwing a charming smile at Penny as he reached for the other half of her toast.

"The problem," I explained, "is that this fine young woman is desperately eager to meet a real matador and right over there is Fermín Sotelo having his breakfast. Could you possibly take Miss Grim, who speaks acceptable Spanish, over to his table and tell the matador that she's your niece?"

"I'll do better. I'll tell him she's my adopted daughter and that if he isn't nice to her I'll give him a scathing review."

Enjoying the charade, Ledesma took Penny by the hand and was about to lead her to where Fermín sat with the men of his troupe when they were almost run over by a group of giggling American girls who would later be described as "groupies," a properly ugly name for an ugly life-style. Teenagers mostly, but extending also into the twenties, these footloose young women chased after movie stars, famous athletes, rock groups and, if they could scrape together enough money to get to Mexico, matadors. I had often had the opportunity to watch their noisy assault on celebrities, and the speed with which they would hop into bed with anyone who would let them astounded me. I abhorred the lot. They were an insult to womanhood and an embarrassment to our nation.

This brazen contingent engulfed the matador's table, allowing Ledesma and Penny no chance of breaking through. Returning petulantly to me and bringing Penny with him, León asked, "Why is it, Clay, that every year at Ixmiq we get this flood of beautiful American girls who come down here to find excitement at our festival? Have they no entertainments at home? No attractive young men? No romance?"

Penny, who was proving more adult than I had imagined, answered for me: "You saved the right word till last, Señor Ledesma. Romance. You clever Mexicans have constructed a myth about your country as the home of adventure, starlit nights and guitars." To my surprise she broke into song: " 'South of the border, down Mexico way,' " and he joined in, in Spanish.

The duet broke whatever ice there may have been, for he snapped his fingers and, saying

"Penny, I simply cannot allow those vultures over there to prevent me from taking you to see Matador Sotelo," he rose, flourished his cape and told Penny: "Follow me!" Pushing his huge bulk through the cluster of girls, he elbowed them aside with a curt "I have business with the matador, if you please."

When the girls were scattered, he said to young Sotelo: "Maestro, I bring a friend of mine from Oklahoma, dreadful place, suburb of Texas, which is pretty bad, too. Miss Penny Grim speaks Spanish, saw the fights today and understands the art you practice. May we join you?"

Sotelo, who would have been out of his mind to refuse, jumped up, held a chair for Penny and indicated another for Ledesma, who declined graciously: "No, this is a meeting of young people," and he waddled back to my table.

I could not overhear what the young people were talking about, in Spanish, but they made an enviable pair, he at the beginning of what could prove to be a solid career, she on the verge of achieving the full-blown perfection of a champion rose. Soon their conversation became animated, with Sotelo showing her the various passes he made in the ring and then grabbing a tablecloth to allow her to imitate his hand movements. In doing this he had to place his arms around her, an act that brought no protest from her.

When the demonstration ended, she rose and, bowing with charming dignity, allowed him to kiss her hand. On her way back to our table I noticed that she protected that hand as if the kiss might blow away.

When she was seated, the first thing she did was thank Ledesma: "You were so kind—to move those other girls away."

He bowed, then coughed and said: "What I'm about to look into is heavy material before breakfast, but it's a proper subject for speculation. I've thought," he said in his best pontifical manner, "that the United States is unusually blessed. It has a perfectly dreadful society, dull as a fog over a swamp, but in every direction off its shores it has enticing places to visit. In the east the Caribbean. In the west Hawaii, in the north Alaska and Arctic Canada. And to the south, best of all, Méjico!" He pronounced the name of his new homeland in the Spanish manner, without the x, even though a law had been passed in 1927 making "México," with an x, the official name of the country. "And I can boast because you know, I'm not a Méjican, I'm pure español, which entitles me to a superior attitude." He said this last with a pompous smirk to betray the fact that he realized how preposterous it was.

When he asked Penny what she would be studying, and she replied, "History," he exploded: "What a great thing you've done for me, Don Norman! Allowing me to meet this splendid young woman. She can tell me whether my thesis is correct or not. Is it the historical dullness of American life that makes Hawaii and Méjico so attractive?"

Determined not to allow León to overpower her with his exhibitionism, she said: "If you take pride in pronouncing your Méjico properly you must do the same with our island. It isn't How-wah-yah, it's Huh-vah-ee."

"All right, I stand corrected. Now, tell me why there is this constant exodus of young women from your country to ours."

"There aren't many matadors in Tulsa, Oklahoma."

"And not too many here in Toledo."

"What brings us down, and we drove nearly a thousand miles to get here, is the attraction of a different way of life. To have a taste of it before we marry and settle down."

Her last words were drowned by a noisy commotion caused by the arrival in a gray limousine of a woman remarkable in the history of Mexican bullfighting. "Here she is!" shouted the crowd in the plaza. "¡Conchita! ¡Arriba! ¡Viva!" And up the few steps to the Terrace came a tall, slim woman in her thirties dressed in the costume that a countrywoman whose husband owned vast estates would favor: boots, gray whipcord skirt, embroidered white blouse, covered by a military-style jacket adorned with silver buttons, and on her head one of those broad-brimmed black hats fancied by Spanish horsemen. She presented a commanding figure, and knew it.

Accepting a chair hurriedly offered her at the big central table, she was immediately surrounded by men associated with bullfighting and by others who remained standing nearby. "Who's that?" Penny asked, and I enlightened her about one of the minor glories of the Mexican scene.

"Sometime around 1930 a young Puerto Rican scholar named Cintrón, member of the well-known family that also produced the actor José Ferrer, received an appointment to West Point. While in the United States Army he married an American girl. They had a daughter, named her Conchita. That's her, over there."

"Why are they making such a fuss over her?"

"Like her father, she loved horses and she became skilled in handling them, even as a little girl."

"Does she ride in a circus or something?"

"No, she does something far more remarkable. With the help of experts in Chile and Peru, where her father served, she made herself into a first-class rejoneadora."

"What's that?"

"She fights bulls from horseback." When I heard her gasp in disbelief, I said: "Yes, this afternoon that woman who looks almost frail will sit astride her white horse, use no hands, only her knees, to guide him, and fight a mad bull. Believe me, Penny, she does just that, and when you see her this afternoon you'll be amazed."

"You mean she's fighting today?"

"She's the star."

"I didn't see her name on any of the big posters. Conchita Cintrón?"

"You can see it on the new little ones. Real big. She's on a farewell tour of the Mexican rings, and at the last minute Don Eduardo persuaded her to include Toledo. His big arguing point? 'Conchita, we'll give you a *despedida* so grand you'll never forget it.' "

"What's that?"

"A Mexican-style leave-taking. Going-away party for a matador who will never be back. You'll weep, I guarantee."

"Why would I? I don't know her."

"The band playing 'Las Golondrinas.' The

embraces of old friends. I'm choking up just thinking of it."

"It sounds so unlikely, a Puerto Rican woman fighting a bull here in Mexico."

"Look at me," I told her. "Born and bred in Mexico but making my living in New York and Europe. Or Don León here. Born in Spain, now stuck in Mexico. We never knew where we'd land." Looking at her fixedly, as Ledesma did too, I asked: "Who can guess where a handsome girl like you, with so many privileges, will make her home? Or with whom?"

To deflect attention from herself, she asked: "Is she really that good?"

"Like Babe Ruth in baseball, the best. Número Uno."

"Could I meet her?"

"Sure. We're old friends. I've interviewed her several times for magazines." But I shuddered: "Me try to break through that crowd? I'm not that brave." But she was so insistent on meeting this strange, compelling woman that with some trepidation I took her by the hand and started toward the seemingly hopeless task of breaking through the ring of admirers. When Conchita saw me, she jumped up, crying: "Norman! God bless you, you bring me luck!" and rushed over to embrace me and plant a kiss on my cheek.

"And who's this child? Don't tell me it's your

new bride—you should be ashamed of yourself."

"Daughter of a friend from Oklahoma. She
insisted on paying her respects."

For several minutes my starry-eyed ward
stared at Conchita, but finally she gathered
courage and said: "I love horses. Always had
my own."

"Then you ride?"

"In rodeos, yes."

"Oh, I love rodeos! The clowns, the big
steers, the noise. What do you do in your
rodeo?"

"The barrel race."

"I know it well. Beautiful girls on beautiful
horses, dashing about in mad circles." Suddenly
grasping Penny by her wrists, she said, "For
such riding you must have strong hands," and
Penny said, "I don't. I'm not so hot," at which
point the conversation was ended by the intrusion of groupies who had learned who Conchita
was and were now demanding autographs.

When we returned to our table, Ledesma said
to Penny soberly, as if he were her uncle: "In the
brief time I've known you, Penny—here on the
Terrace, at the corrida yesterday, and especially
watching the way you reacted to the catacombs,
I could see that you were far too intelligent to be
chasing around after Mexican matadors."

"But she's not a matador. She's a—what did you call her, Norman?"

"Rejoneadora," I said and León snapped: "Almost as bad. She's part of the scene, and potentially damaging to a girl like you."

"You don't like women bullfighters?" Penny asked, and he growled: "I deplore them." Then smiling warmly, he nodded across the tables to Conchita, who saluted. "She's not a woman," he said. "She's an angel." Then he resumed his lecture: "Bullfight people lead a rough life. Girls in every town pester them. American girls on vacation can't leave them alone. You can do yourself no good by leaping at them and you might do yourself immeasurable harm." He dropped his avuncular tone and said harshly, "Stay away from the toreros! They're no good for you."

She received this admonition gracefully and with a touch of humor: "A girl can look, can't she?" and he said, "Even looking sometimes gets your eyebrows singed." She seemed so crestfallen that I had to come to her rescue.

"I have napping in my room a matador—well, almost a matador—who might prove acceptable. I'll send him down," and I left her wondering what I might have meant by that.

When I reached my room I rousted Ricardo out of bed: "Get downstairs. Penny Grim wants to talk with you about your experiences as a would-be fighter." He was hesitant at first, and understandably so. "Her father would bash me over the head if I stepped near her," he said, but I reassured him: "Her father tied one on last night and won't become airborne for hours." This brought him no comfort, for he said "I know from experience that drunks can recover instantaneously." But when I added that she'd be easy to find because she was sitting with León Ledesma, he leaped out of bed, dashed into the bathroom, used my shaving brush, my razor and I suspect my toothbrush, and zoomed back to whip on his trousers—as an aspiring torero he could hardly miss an opportunity to talk again with Mexico's foremost critic. Smoothing his hair with my brush, he dashed downstairs while I fell into bed and dropped off almost instantly.

It was about three when I woke up and went down to the Terrace for some light lunch and found that Ledesma had left my table but that Ricardo Martín and Penny were in vigorous conversation. They made an attractive pair, each leaning forward to catch the point the other was making, and I was about to leave them alone, when Penny saw me and invited me to join them. "After all, it is your table. He's been telling me the most fascinating story about how he got into bullfighting." I was about to ask her for details when I saw Mrs. Evans coming in alone, and I asked her to join our table. As the four of us sat there toying with our lunch, because we did not care to eat heavily before the fight, Penny, with an occasional correction from Ricardo, started telling Mrs. Evans and me, with an excitement in her voice that betrayed the fact that she had found Martín a delightful companion, what she had learned from him.

"After Ricardo won his second Purple Heart in Korea, the Marines said: 'With that cluster of ribbons he'd make an ideal recruiter in high schools,' and they brought him back to San Diego."

Ricardo broke in, "I found the work repulsive and started drifting down to Tijuana, and at the age of nineteen I saw my first bullfight, and it provided everything I was looking for. Courage, drama, spectacle, and something as far away from my stupid father and my dipsy-doodle mother as I could get. In 1957 some friends told me: 'The real scene is the April festival in Toledo,' and when they decided to drive down I hooked a ride with them, and when I saw the real thing, three great fights in one weekend, I decided right then, in that plaza out there by the statue of the Indian, that I was going to stay, and come hell or another draft I was going to be a bullfighter."

"How did you live?" Mrs. Evans asked. "What I mean is, how do you live?"

At this point the narrative was broken by the arrival at our table of Penny's father, Ed Grim, whose bloodshot eyes announced that he was in a foul mood and ready for battle. It took him a few minutes to figure out that his daughter was somehow involved with the miserable fellow who had quit the United States Marines to become a bullfighter in Mexico, and when this became clear he heard his sensible Tulsa neighbor, Mrs. Evans, widow of his former partner, explaining, "I've just asked Señor Martín—"

"What's this Señor business? Where'd he get the name Martín? I thought it was honest Martin, from Iowa."

"It's Señor Martín," she insisted, "because he wants to be accepted as a young man who respects Mexican ways. And he's from Idaho, not Iowa." When the oilman grunted, she continued. "I asked him how he earned his living while traipsing around the countryside, trying to be a matador."

"I'd be fascinated to hear," Grim said, and with obvious embarrassment Ricardo explained, "I'm ashamed to say that five months after I made my big resolve to stay here forever, I was back home begging my mother to let me have the small inheritance my grandmother had left for me in her care. When she learned what I wanted to spend the money on, she asked my father if he thought it was a practical idea for me to become a Mexican bullfighter, and when he heard the question he exploded. I listened to him rant and rave, then I said I knew what I wanted to do and he screamed: 'You're no son of mine,' and I snarled back: 'I never was,' and that day I changed my name to Ricardo Martín, partly out of respect and a kind of love for Mother, but also because I couldn't see making my way in Mexico with a name like Caldwell. How are you going to put that on a billboard? But Martin easily becomes Martín, heavy accent on the last syllable, or even Martínez.

"Mom turned out to be a lot smarter than I thought, because she said: 'I'll not allow you to touch that money my mother left for you, but I'll mail you fifty dollars a month.' "

"Glad to hear someone in your family has good sense," Grim said, and I saw Penny kick him.

Ricardo, ignoring the interruption, said, "You'd be surprised how much extra change a guy can pick up down here just by keeping his ears open."

"And his hand outstretched," Grim said.

"Are you making headway?" Mrs. Evans asked, and Ricardo said: "Anyone here know the word *pachanga*? I'm not sure it's in the dictionary, but I'm king of the pachangas.''

"What are they?" Mrs. Evans asked, always curious.

"A brawl. A village brawl in which everyone can participate. It's really a village bullfight without a barricaded ring, without picadors, and without formal costumes. What they do have is some seven- or eight-year-old bull with very big horns but the sharp tips sawed off. Weighs about fifteen hundred pounds, half again the size of a proper bull. If he doesn't get you with his horns he tramples you to death.''

"Sounds rather disorganized," Mrs. Evans said, following the account closely.

"It's a riot, really, not a bullfight," the young man said. "There're two kinds of riots: those organized like the attack on the Bastille: 'Let's get those prisoners outta there'; and those that are totally disorganized, like a real pachanga.''

"Then why do you bother with them?"

Ricardo stopped, looked at her in disbelief and said: "Because the job of a would-be matador is to fight bulls. Any bull, anywhere. In a pachanga, you learn whether you have the courage to get within range of those horns and then stand there with your feet planted and make him drive past you. To take part in the next pachanga I would walk to Oaxaca." The sincerity with which he spoke, this young man who had fought as a Marine in Frozen Chosen and then run away from the security of home again to attempt this dangerous profession, impressed his listeners.

"Is yours a special case, or are there a lot of young men like you?" Penny asked.

"There've always been wandering hopefuls like me. Some of the greatest came up my way, Juan Belmonte in Spain, Juan Gómez here in Mexico. I guess we're universal."

"I mean, Americans?"

"Sidney Franklin made it, a kid from Brooklyn. And Patricia McCormick, a girl."

At this startling information, Grim exploded. "You mean a decent American girl came down here, did the pachanga business you spoke of and became a matador?"

"She did," Ricardo said matter-of-factly. "Fought real corridas and was pretty good."

"The world is going to hell," Ed grumbled. "And you, young lady, stay away from matadors."

She smiled and said, "Señor Ledesma told me the same thing," and Grim said, "That critic gets smarter every minute."

Mrs. Evans wanted to get back to her main

interest. Smiling at Martín, she asked, "You use such good English when you want to. Where did you learn it?"

"Idaho has good schools. Mom made me read."

Mrs. Evans now spoke like a mother: "And you're giving up your education to be a matador?"

"It wasn't much, really. I would never have been a scholar. In the Marines I'd never have become an officer." Looking down at his hands he said: "I wasn't losing much. But I could not risk blowing this one chance to do the big thing."

"If you dreamed of doing something big, why didn't you grab at the G.I. Bill? It helps pay for a veteran's education toward a new job or profession."

"I told you I did."

This was too much for Ed. "You mean you're just *pretending* to go to college so you can be a bullfighter? What kind of kid are you?"

"We settled that yesterday. An ex-Marine who will knock you flat on your ass if you make one false move."

"Penny, let's get out of here. This dump is no place for a decent young girl."

"I'm staying," she said. "I like these people. They're my friends."

"I told you to come with me," Grim repeated,

but Ricardo said quietly, "And she said she was staying. Good-bye, Mr. Grim," and the daughter stayed as the father stormed off.

When he was gone, Mrs. Evans said, "I don't want you people to underestimate Ed Grim. He's a terrific oilman."

"That doesn't give him the right to order everyone around," Ricardo said, and she replied, "Young man. Ed Grim fought the battle to give oil-field workers medical insurance, fair wages, and the right, if they wanted to, to join unions."

"But, of course," Penny said, "having made that grandstand play, he did all he could to bust the union."

"Even so," Mrs. Evans said, "what you see with Ed is basically what you get." Then, turning exclusively to Ricardo, she asked: "So you still dream of doing the big thing?" and he replied, "Yes, because I've watched so many settle for the little thing."

"So what do you do next?" she asked, and he said: "Sneak in the fight tomorrow to see how Victoriano and Gómez handle it. You can always learn if you study the best."

"And in the cold morning-after?"

His face broke into a big smile as he patted Mrs. Evans on the hand. "You really understand bullfighting. Every day is a cold morning-after. Well, on tomorrow morning after the big fight I hurry back to Mexico City to seek out news about the next pachanga. I'll work my way to some village, and one of these days something big will happen."

"And if it doesn't?" Mrs. Evans bored in.

"I'll have to make it happen."

"And how do you do that?"

"I have a plan!"

We sat silent for some minutes—the widow of a Tulsa oilman with ample funds and a fifty-two-year-old journalist with a comfortable income—and we were both struck by the precariousness of Ricardo's financial condition.

Mrs. Evans asked Ricardo: "You said you were going to sneak in to see the fight tomorrow. How?"

"You learn the ways."

I think she was going to lend him some money, but just at that moment Ed Grim came to our table lugging two heavy suitcases and bringing Mr. and Mrs. Haggard behind him with their luggage.

"We're heading north," he announced almost fiercely as if to say "And what are you going to do about it?" He placed one suitcase beside Penny's chair. "We decided that bullfighting is barbaric. We want no more of it. You're coming with us, Penny. And, Elsie, you'd come home, too, if you had any sense."

Without hesitation Penny said quite calmly, "I'm not going." Drawing her suitcase closer to her, she said, "For a long time I've wanted to spend a day at a Mexican ranch, and Mr. Clay told me he could arrange it. I'm staying."

"Now wait a minute!" I protested, "I said that before I knew you were leaving your father and staying behind. Believe me, the Festival of Ixmiq is no place for a seventeen-year-old high school girl on her own."

"I'm almost a college girl and old enough to know my own mind."

Penny was adamant. She would not ride back to Tulsa with her father and the Haggards. She was determined to stay with the matadors, and when her father seemed ready to carry her off to his Cadillac, Mrs. Evans felt she had to intervene. "Chester! I'm staying and Penny can stay with me. She's a big girl now. Come autumn, she'll be away from you anyway."

"But at a decent college. Not in some Mexican pachanga or whatever it's called."

Seeing that he could not budge Penny and that we seemed to be encouraging her to resist him, he became furious, almost tearing his coat pocket to get at his fight tickets for the remaining bullfights. Throwing them on the table, he cried in fury, "Take them, and as for you, Elsie

Evans, your husband must be turning in his grave."

"I think he might be," she said, and then she became the conciliator. "Chester, your little girl is growing up. If Millicent were alive she'd tell you to let her go. And you can do it with the assurance that I'll look after her."

As Ed got in the car, he realized he could not leave his daughter as if he were dismissing her in a fit of temper. Hastily climbing out, he came to where she stood beside me, clasped her in his arms and mumbled: "You're a champion, kid. Don't screw it up." He kissed her, then turned to Mrs. Evans and me and said fiercely: "Keep an eye on her. She's Oklahoma gold."

When Ed and the Haggards were gone Mrs. Evans asked, "Now, how am I going to get my car home? I don't drive anymore." Before waiting for an answer, she pushed the eight valuable tickets into the center of the table, where Penny reached out to grab her pair and tuck them into her small purse. The other six Mrs. Evans turned over to Ricardo, saying, "Since they pertain to bullfighting, they're yours." Leaving them on the table, he arranged them in a neat line. "Six tickets. Two tourists were here about an hour ago begging people on the Terrace to sell them tickets. Fifty bucks for today's fight. A hundred bucks for tomorrow's." When the women gasped, he explained, "After a death in the ring, interest goes way up." Moving the tickets about in patterns, he said, "Four hundred and fifty bucks. Enough to keep me chasing pachangas for a year." Rising abruptly, he went to Mrs. Evans and kissed her. "Mom would approve of you, and so do I," but she said, "Thank Ed Grim, not me."

This amiable discussion was interrupted by the passage through the Terrace of a matador in full costume on his way to fight. He was a man for whom I had great admiration, so I called him over and made introductions: "This is Pepe Luis Vásquez, the Mexican one. He has the misfortune that Spain has its own matador of that name, but this is the good one."

Ricardo was awed at having this fine torero standing beside him. He rose and with his right forefinger indicated various parts of the matador's costume: "Wound here. Wound here. In the trade he bears the honorable title The Pincushion. No matador in recent times has survived the wounds this man has," and he indicated: "Horn here could have been fatal but the medics saved him. Horn through here. Eight or nine horns in the buttocks down here. This leg, that leg."

"Is he telling the truth?" Penny asked, and Pepe Luis bowed and said in good English:

"Under more favorable circumstances, I could prove it." Penny said without changing her tone or her expression, "That would be compelling," and I thought, Señorita Penny knows how to handle herself.

We chatted briefly, and he was a splendid torero of the solid middle group, never a transcendent star but always the man of dignity who faced the bulls as they came. He represented the backbone of the bullfight business, the man who year after year filled the afternoon bill in second or third position, often outshining the stars.

He had barely gone when one of the aging phenomena of the Mexican scene passed through on his way to the arena. It was Calesero, the matador from Aguascalientes who each spring helped the Toledo people put together their program for Ixmiq. He was the gentleman of the profession, a man of exquisite delicacy in the ring, a master of cape work, none better, but never outstanding with the sword. Aficionados came to the plaza in hopes of catching him on a good day when with his cape, his nimble feet and his arching body, slim and artistic in its movement, he would weave miracles with some compliant bull. A man of great dignity, he nodded to me as he passed, and I did not try to intercept him.

So, by the simple device of having shared Ledesma's table at the House of Tile, Mrs. Evans, Penny and Ricardo had seen at close hand the four toreros who were to be in that day's fight: Conchita the adorable; Calesero, the elder statesman; Pepe Luis Vásquez, the valiant; and Fermín Sotelo, the new comet rising above the horizon. It promised to be a rewarding afternoon.

As we rose from our table to start for the bullring, Ledesma and I were detained by the arrival of my uncle, who presented the critic with a moral dilemma: "Don León, I'm aware that neither Calesero nor Pepe Luis has paid you your customary fee."

"They have not," Ledesma said coolly.

"But this festival is important to our city—to me, personally. To help me, trusted friend, to sell tickets for tomorrow's fight, could you bring yourself to speak well of the matadors' performance in today's?"

"Praise them when they haven't paid? Impossible." He turned away, but Don Eduardo could not risk the damage a scornful review might cause.

"León, gentleman of honor, let's admit that they did not give you your fee. Let's admit that they've insulted you. But if I paid their fee, would that make it possible?"

Ledesma ignored my uncle and turned to me: "Señor Clay knows that I respect Calesero and Pepe Luis as men of courage and dignity. Will I be willing to testify to that in this afternoon's fight? Yes, Don Eduardo, I shall do what I can to protect your festival," and without looking back at my uncle he allowed the hand that I could not see to reach backward toward Don Eduardo, who, I am sure, placed some notes in it.

"They are two men of proven honor. I like them. Praise them when they haven't paid? Impossible. Testify to their honorable behavior? I could do no less," and the two old friends shook hands.

It was fortunate for me that we had lingered, for my delay enabled a messenger from Mexican Wireless to hand me instructions from New York:

Clay, Toledo. Photos copy sensational. Mexican study completed. Come on home. Drummond.

As I pondered these words, with the sounds of the festival echoing vaguely in my ears, as if calling me back to the bullring, I sat alone on the Terrace and contemplated the daring of Ricardo Martín in presuming to be a matador and

Penny's willingness to face her father's wrath in her desire to see the completion of the adventure she had planned for so long, and I compared their daring with my timidity, and I was not proud of myself. I wanted to quit writing formula articles, which I could do so easily and so well. I remember a picture story I did when the French were struggling in what was then their Vietnam. With an even hand I cast up the pros and cons, reaching no decision as to who would win or who ought to win. My photographer had taken a great shot of a Vietnamese peasant in his rice paddy looking up at the sun and I titled the story "Pham Van Dong Faces the Future." In other stories I'd had a Korean peasant facing the future, a Pakistani in East Bengal facing the future after one of the great floods that drowned thousands, and everybody else facing the future except me.

What I really wanted to do was write a book as good as my father's about our Indian ancestors, our gallant Spanish bishops, those unforgettable ranks of dead Toledans in the catacomb and especially the revolutions and wars I'd seen in Toledo as a boy. The last idea caused me to cry out: Maybe that's the good one. An American kid at the heart of the Mexican rural revolution, seeing everything and comprehending nothing.

Regardless of what I ultimately decided on, I wanted to get started before it was too late, so while the others marched to the ring, I telephoned Mexico Wireless and sent New York this message.

> Drummond. Glad Paquito fotos words usable. But you're wrong. That doesn't end the Mexico story. It's just beginning. Am staying here.

As I walked to the ring I wished there had been a cameraman to record my progress, with the pots of flowers in the background, the wonderful façade of the cathedral and the statue of my father. I'd title the resulting story "Pham Van Clay Faces the Future."

14

SATURNINE
SATURDAY

A GERMAN TOURIST, proud of his mastery of English and his knowledge of bullfighting acquired in Spain, dubbed the second day Saturnine Saturday, for the six normal fights were dull and sluggish. No one was killed. No one was sent to the hospital for major attention. No ears or tails were granted, nor did aficionados petition for them. And certainly neither the bulls nor the matadors came close to being immortalized. It was a standard dull fight.

I actually enjoyed it, for not having to write about or photograph what I suspected would be

a rather routine corrida, I sat in the second row
with Mrs. Evans on my right, Ledesma on my left
and Penny Grim in the first row in front of us so
that we could share her enthusiasm in watching
two toreros with whom she had actually spoken,
the matador Fermín Sotelo and the rejoneadora
Conchita Cintrón.

If the normal afternoon of six fights was tedious, that adjective did not apply to Conchita's
exhibition, for Don Eduardo kept his promise
that her farewell to Toledo would be unforgettable. From the moment the big gates opened so
that the fighters could parade forth in splendor,
even Ledesma, who did not like rejoneadors,
male or female, had to admit that the woman he
had called an angel was superb in the effect she
created. Riding erectly at the head of the parade
on a large white horse, she was dressed in austere gray—calf-length boots, trousers protected
by heavy leather chaps that reached to her
waist, a general's military jacket over a white
shirt with lace at the cuffs, a delicate cravat tied
neatly at the neck, all topped by a hard-finished
felt hat with a five-inch brim all around, a seven-
inch stovepipe crown and a top severely flat.
She and her prancing steed seemed creatures
from another era.

The stately horse was for the parade only.
The animals on which she would actually face

the bull would be smaller and capable of changing direction instantly, but the parade horse was amazingly effective, for she had trained it for two displays: in crossing the sand in the parade, the animal pranced in what was almost a dance step, first one foreleg stretched forward, then the other; and when Conchita reached our side of the arena, the horse came to where Don Eduardo sat beside Penny Grim and there bowed in elegant style, dropping one knee to the ground, extending the other leg like an elegant courtier genuflecting before his queen.

Penny cried: "He's bowing to me!" and she could be forgiven this error, because I was certain that the horse was bowing to me, and I'm sure Ledesma and Mrs. Evans felt the same. All I can say is that it was some entrance.

The parade over, Conchita wheeled her big white horse and galloped him across the arena and out the big gate, through which she reappeared quickly on a much smaller white horse. Returning to our side of the ring, she waited as the bugle blew, and when the small red door was opened a large black bull roared in, front feet high, horns slashing about to locate an enemy.

Just as matadors on foot run their bull in the opening stages with a big yellow cape, so Conchita, brandishing a long spear with a flag at the far end, placed the lure before the bull, twisting it now and then, allowing the bull to charge it and hook it with his horn. In this maneuver the rider had to have a stout right arm and the horse the ability to anticipate where the deadly horn might strike and avoid it.

"How can she work so close to the bull without getting caught?" Penny asked, and León explained: "It's a matter of intersecting trajectories, the bull going in one direction, the horse at an angle in the other." When the time came for Conchita to place the banderillas and the horse had to make his moves without guidance from the reins because both of Conchita's hands were occupied with the sticks that she must place in the bull's neck muscles while leaning down from her horse, Penny watched the fluid motion of bull and horse as their trajectories converged. The extreme danger and beauty of execution combined to create a breathtaking moment.

"Oh!" Penny cried, clutching my arm. "She's so wonderful—doing a thing like that!" and I could see that she was stunned by the realization that women could perform in areas that had once been the exclusive preserve of men.

On the second pair of sticks the horse won applause by riding up to Penny and bowing its head to her as if she were his princess in an old-time fairy tale, and Conchita gathered her olés by dedicating the banderillas to Penny, who dissolved in ecstatic wonder. Turning back to us, she asked rapturously: "Did you catch that in your camera, Mr. Clay?" and I nodded, which increased her pleasure.

After a superb display of horsemanship in conjunction with that big moving black target, Conchita tried to dispatch the bull using a sharp sword with a very long handle, but as happened nineteen times out of twenty with rejoneadors, she failed, three times. Since this was to be expected, she was allowed to dismount, send her horse back to the corral and finish the fight on foot. Able but not spectacular, she finally succeeded with the help of the man with the short dagger, who cut the spinal cord.

But the despedida was not allowed to end on the downbeat of that banal kill, for as the dead bull was hauled away, Conchita's parade horse was brought back and she stood beside it as a score of dignitaries filed into the ring to pay homage to this radiant woman. The mayor was there, the governor of the state, the general from the barracks, Don Eduardo as owner of the Palafox ranch, León Ledesma as the premier critic, and others from the taurine fraternity. Speeches were made, flowers were presented, and at a signal from the mayor, the band, augmented for this occasion, played Mexico's sad, sweet waltz of farewell, "Las Golondrinas" (The Swallows). As its limpid notes floated across the sands, people began to weep softly, and when a groom stepped forward to lead the white horse out of the arena, a sign that Conchita would never again perform there, Penny's eyes filled with tears.

Then came the climax. From boxes that had been kept hidden two flocks of white doves were released, and as they flew upward in a flutter of wings a woman singer with a throaty voice stepped forward to sing a song that had always affected me deeply—"La Paloma" (The Dove). It was said to have been composed to honor the Empress Carlota as she went into exile after the execution of her husband, Emperor Maximilian. There were lines in this haunting lament that I had always cherished:

> "If to your window there should come a
>   white dove,
> Treat it with tenderness, for it is I,
>   myself."

"Have a tissue," Penny said. "Your nose is dripping."

"Tears," I said. "Look at Ledesma," and his eyes were brimming, too.

Thus did my friend Conchita Cintrón bid fare-well to a town in which she had often performed with elegance and valor. As she left the ring for the last time, Penny sat silent, biting her knuck-les. Then, in a soft voice, she leaned back to tell me: "To meet a woman like her! To have her nod to me from the ring. It was worth the whole trip."

It was unfair to the three matadors on the regular part of the afternoon's fight to have had such an emotional episode precede their ap-pearance, but a despedida had to occur at the end of a torero's exhibition, and since Conchita fought only one bull, her culminating celebration came early. But drab though the following six fights were, they contained such a tremendous surprise for Penny that even her memories of Conchita would be erased when in later years she remembered this day.

Calesero, as I had explained to the Americans when he passed through the Terrace, was an elder statesman of his profession, never the prime minister but always the trusted secretary of state who could be depended on. When he received a fine bull in the draw, he was capable of doing exceptional work, but when, like today, he drew a difficult bull, his accomplishment had to be limited. A few elegant passes, two sets of above-average banderillas but nothing sensa-

tional, and a workmanlike final act—his performance provided nothing for condemnation but
only occasional displays for praise. At the end
he received the polite applause to which he was
entitled, a man of great integrity who had not
had much luck.

Pepe Luis Vásquez could always be depended upon to give a stalwart performance,
and today he started by trying to engage his first
bull as it came out the chute. It was a foolhardy
attempt, for at that early stage the bull had too
much power. It knocked aside Pepe's cape,
then did the same with Pepe. The crowd gasped
when blood showed clearly on his leg, and
Calesero rushed to where the peóns were dragging the wounded man. He was understandably
apprehensive about the extent of the damage,
for the custom of the bullring demanded that if
one of the junior matadors was wounded so
severely that he could not continue, the senior
man—in this case Calesero—would have to
fight his own two bulls plus the two of the injured
matador, a disappointing prospect for both him
and the public, since he was neither a strong
man physically nor one who was likely to provide a spectacular show.

Fortunately the bull's right horn had merely
grazed Vásquez's left leg, but had penetrated
enough to bring a respectable show of blood,

which, fortunately, was stanched immediately in the infirmary. Calesero and Fermín Sotelo, the third matador, conducted the middle passages of the fight, leading the bull to the picadors and then placing the banderillas. By the start of the final segment Pepe Luis was back, bandage showing and ready to take control of the sword work. He was valiant and he was good, bringing the bull perilously close to his chest in a series of passes that brought the first real cheers of the afternoon. But he was not lucky with the sword, and when the colorless fight ended with a protracted attempt to dispatch the bull, the crowd yawned.

Everyone was eager to see what the new man, Fermín Sotelo, would do. He was willing but his bull was not, and it was almost painful to see the young man straining to prove his merit to a new audience but failing even to show that he was competent. It was a dismal performance with not one exciting pass, not one acceptable pair of sticks and a pathetic last act, with the wounded bull walking stolidly about the arena as Fermín tried desperately to end the fiasco. The warning trumpet sounded an *aviso* that the time allowed for this fight was running out, and the period of nervous sweating began.

So when the second *aviso* sounded, Fermín really began desperately to chase his bull and just within the time limit brought him down. It was an ugly termination, which was greeted with an awful silence. No band music. No boos. No cheers. There was just the arrival of the peóns with their mules to tidy up the sand.

"This is certainly a dull set of fights," Mrs. Evans said during the intermission. "My Oklahoma friends were smart to duck out. With a show like this they might have become violent."

"What you've just seen," Ledesma told her, "is an honorable part of the bullfight. It's like one of your baseball games where nothing happens, where the outcome is never in doubt, and no one gives a damn who wins. Or a football game with not one decent run or long pass. One side wins with three field goals that excite nobody. Lovemaking's much the same way, and so are the novels you read. Workmanlike, but who gives a damn?"

"Is that your view of life, Señor Ledesma?"

"Not just my view. It is life. Most of life is damned dull. Remember, in a long season you'll have a lot more boring games than no-hitters, where you're on edge the last four innings."

"But one can hope for more," Mrs. Evans said, "especially if one has driven all the way from Oklahoma. Which reminds me, who's going to drive that damned Cadillac back for me?"

Penny, feeling exalted because Conchita and her horse had bowed to her, expected the excitement to continue at that high level. Turning to me, she asked almost petulantly: "When do the fireworks begin?" and Ledesma answered for me: "Young lady, with your personal interest in the matadors, maybe you had better hope they never begin. On many days, ladies, a matador is perfectly content to see the afternoon drift past. Get it over with and hope for a better day." He smiled at Penny, adjusted his cape and asked: "Isn't it often that way on a date? Get the damned thing over with and hope for someone more exciting next week?"

"How about the ticket price?" Penny asked. "When we're fleeced, aren't we entitled to at least some professionalism?"

"Ah hah! Now you introduce the economic factor. You did, not me, so I'm allowed to look at those unsatisfactory data from the man's point of view. He's taken you out, spent a bundle and the evening is totally blah. Is he entitled to a refund because he chose poorly? Not at all, and neither are you. But in the next three fights something good might happen, like maybe your matador Fermín will oblige us by getting a horn through his esophagus."

"Ugh! Ugh!" Penny cried, bringing her hands over her eyes, but Ledesma was remorseless:

"Those are the answers you're entitled to when you bring up these questions. Let's hope none of you young women marry unsatisfactory husbands and discover in your sixties that's how the ball game is going to end." There was silence.

Then Penny asked tentatively: "Conchita? Was she also as bad as you claim?" and Ledesma replied airily: "In this business rejoneadoras don't count. But if you ask me how her horse did, I'd say passable, verging on acceptable." Then he added: "Of course, if you asked me, 'Are you in love with Conchita?' I'd have to confess, 'Since the first day I saw her perform in Guadalajara.'"

Calesero on his second bull provided one series of his elegant passes in which bull and cape and man seemed to be moving as one about the arena. It was stunning, worth the price of the ticket, but when he sought to duplicate it when his bull came off the picador, he was unable to bring the bull back under control, and the fight ran its allotted twenty minutes having provided nothing else worth remembering.

Pepe Luis Vásquez, his leg bandage now invisible beneath his damaged suit, returned stubbornly to the spot where the first bull had gored him. As the audience leaned forward, he waited till the bull was almost upon him, then dropped to his knees and delivered a farol, swirling the cape up over his head and the bull's. The horn came within inches of his skull but he remained on his knees, pivoted about, brought the bull back in the opposite direction, then flicked the far end of the cape to perplex the bull and keep him fixed till he regained his footing.

This daring act brought well-deserved cheers. He had proved he had courage, and I applauded longer than the others because I could guess what this acknowledgment from the crowd meant to him. Unfortunately he was not able to follow up, for the bull was so intractable that Pepe Luis could give him only the routine passes that led from one part of the fight to the next. But it did not progress rapidly enough and Pepe Luis heard an *aviso.* This spurred him to make a frenzied effort to accelerate, and this led only to further confusion. If someone who hated bullfights had wanted to make a motion picture that would damn the sport, this afternoon would have been ideal. Pepe Luis did not suffer the indignity of seeing his bull go out alive, to be slaughtered in the corrals for beef distributed to the poor, but he did end his fight in the silence with which aficionados demonstrate their boredom.

We'd had five bulls that had looked rather good on the hoof, and three quite acceptable matadors, but there had not been one demand that the matador take a circuit of the ring to garner applause, nor a single handkerchief waved at the judge to demand that the matador receive an ear as a badge of triumph.

As Pepe's gloomy display ended, I watched Fermín Sotelo from my seat with the Oklahomans and could see that he was gritting his teeth in a determination to save the day, especially since Penny would be watching him so intently. Before he left the passageway she called down to him in Spanish: "Buena suerte, matador!" but he stared straight ahead as if he had not heard her. Deflated, Penny turned to ask Mrs. Evans: "Who does he think he is, a performance as rotten as his last one, he has no right—"

"Penny!" I protested. "Think a minute. He's a Mexican in Mexico. His job is to keep his Mexican fans happy, not you. It would look bad for a beginning matador to pay too much attention to a Yankee."

"I saw on television where a famous matador in Spain dedicated a bull to Ava Gardner and people cheered," and I said: "When you come back next year as well known as Ava, you'll get your bull, too."

My attempt at humor did not mollify her, but just before his bull came roaring out, Fermín glanced quickly at Penny, slipping her a wink and a slight nod. When he moved inside the ring to study the bull as it thundered into the center, I heard Penny whisper to Mrs. Evans: "Help me pray for him. Let him be spectacular!" and two Oklahoman hearts accompanied the young man as he went out to redeem himself.

With a bravery equaling that shown by Vásquez when he knelt in the sand, Fermín allowed his péons only two running passes to test the bull, then stepped in boldly to launch a series of veronicas, the exquisite pass named after the saint who had used her veil to wipe the sweat from the face of Jesus as he carried his heavy cross to Calvary. The passes were so beautifully executed that I joined the hundreds who were cheering. "See, Penny!" I cried. "He's going to show us a masterpiece. The kid knows what he's doing."

"He's a man," Penny said. "Look!"

He was in the midst of delivering three perfect chicuelinas, wrapping his cape about himself as the bull approached, so that the animal caught only the last flick of the cape as it disappeared behind the man. These were superlative passes, and I cheered. If I overemphasize work with the big magenta cape at the beginning of a fight and with the little red muleta at the end, it's because I've known bullfighting since I was a boy of eight and have seen all the notable Mexican artists and most of the Spanish masters who came over during our winters. So for me the art of the fight is what the man can do with the cloth, big or little, especially when he unites the bull to him as they move back and forth across the sand. Those are moments of excruciating beauty, which I find in no other sport, and I've seen a lot of them.

But in the cloth work the part I treasure most comes when the bull has charged at the horse and been pushed away by the picador. Confused and for the first time in his life really hurt, the bull breaks free, searching wildly for any enemy he can find, and there stands the matador, waiting and knowing that now he faces an entirely different animal. Up to now the bull has been curious, and passes could be based upon that curiosity, but now he is enraged, his power multiplied, his horns more deadly. It is now that a matador can best display both his artistry and his courage as he lures the maddened bull to six inches from his body. With magic in his wrists and supreme control of his feet, he launches one incredible pass after another until the crowd has to cry "¡Olé!" Sometimes the cape is in front, sometimes at the side, sometimes behind his back, sometimes fluttering like a butterfly, and sometimes dipped with a low chopping motion not lovely in itself but necessary to tire the bull's neck muscles and make him lower his head for the final act.

I love to watch such work and now, as I shared my delight with the Oklahomans, Penny asked almost deliriously in her happiness over Fermín's fine performance: "Could you do that, Clay? You seem to know so much about what other people do," and I replied: "I gave passes like that to Soldado, best bull of them all, and no other bullfighter in the world can claim that," and she was impressed.

I was glad for her that when Fermín began his final work he managed a breathtaking pass that proved him to be a serious matador. Drawing the bull not far from where we sat and keeping the sword behind him in his right hand, with his left he held the cloth very low and led the bull slowly past, flicked the end of the cloth to fix him and pivoted to face him again. Satisfied that he had the animal under control, he raised the cloth almost to his chin, stood erect, and gave one of the great passes of bullfighting, *el pase de pecho* (the pass of the chest, called by some the pass of death). Under any conditions this pass is spectacular, for there is only a hair's breadth between the bull's horns and the matador's head. But in this instance Fermín, convinced that he had a safe bull, attempted the astonishing variation known as "counting the house," that is, ignoring the bull as he thundered past but staring into the stands as if he were indeed checking on the number of paying customers. His luck held. The bull came right at him, head high, and rode past by inches, while Fermín stood his ground, head turned to the side, a detached look on his face that was almost a sneer as he looked directly into the eyes of Penny Grim. I snapped a shot of him as the bull brushed past his studiedly world-weary face. When I look at that face now in the photo, it still astounds me.

With that noble pass I knew that Fermín had clinched the championship of the Saturday fight and perhaps of the entire festival, until I heard Penny cry "Oh, no!" While everyone was lost in admiration of Fermín's impeccable pass of death, the bull, standing alone some distance from us, saw a flutter of cloth in the stands, and drove at it in a fury caused by his earlier frustrations when hitting the cloth rather than the man. Again he found no man, but his right horn did smash into the heavy board barrier and with a sickening snap broke completely off, right at the point where it had been attached to the skull. A sigh rose from the crowd, for it was obvious that he had been ruined for the final act of the fight, the breathtaking moment when the matador must reach directly over the deadly right horn in order to place the sword. With no horn there to create emotional tension, any chance for either danger or art vanished.

In wealthy arenas, where impresarios can afford to keep a spare bull in the corrals for just such emergencies, the bugles would blow, the oxen would come in and the matador's one-horned bull would be led back to his pen and the substitute bull brought in. But the Toledo plaza had no spare, and so this culminating fight of the second day must end in a pathetic display: a skilled matador dispatching an unarmed bull.

"What happens now?" Penny asked, and I said: "Your boy makes the best of a bad business. He kills the bull, but it means nothing—not a contest—no honors here."

"How rotten!" and I saw tears forming in her eyes.

But she had no concept of just how rotten it was going to be, for this apparently impotent bull was about to remind the aficionados of Toledo just how cantankerous a fighting bull of pure Spanish blood can be. This one, his horn gone, knew that he must now defend himself with special vigor, so whenever Sotelo lined up for what ought to have been the easiest kill possible, the bull also lined up, as it were, protecting his vulnerable neck by brushing the sword sideways with his muzzled face or suddenly lifting his bony forehead and knocking the sword up in the air.

In desperation, Fermín tried a few passes to make the bull drop his defenses, but he accomplished nothing. The bull's head remained high and moving in various directions to ward off any attack. "Dispatch him—any way you can," counseled his manager from the passageway, and the crowd began to chant: "Get rid of him! The bugler's getting ready to warn you." But there was also self-controlled Calesero whispering unhysterical encouragement: "Fermín, you can do it. Careful with that other horn, he'll toss it twice as wild." In giving this counsel the older man was obedient to the tradition: "If he doesn't do it, I'll have to." This Calesero was both prepared and willing to do; it was an assignment of honor, but it was also a miserable way to end a fight, so as the younger man approached the bull, Calesero shouted: "Steady, Fermín, you can do it."

I was watching Penny as the promising efforts of her matador turned to ashes, and I could see with what intense participation she followed each disastrous attempt by Fermín to bring some order to this deplorable affair. It was as if she were in the ring with him. But with time pressing down on him and the bull becoming more fractious each moment, the matador's chances of salvaging the afternoon diminished.

Even his peóns started yelling: "Don't try passes. Kill the damn thing," but in maddening frustration Fermín felt honor-bound to give a respectable performance. Aware that he was slipping from hero of the afternoon to goat, he became so desperate that whatever he attempted misfired. I could see Penny with her fists clenched as she kept muttering: "It shouldn't end this way, it shouldn't," and when Mrs Evans reached forward to console her, Penny snapped: "Pray, please. Pray!"

Fortunately for Penny, the bull had taken a stance about as far away, on the sunny side, as he could get, but now, as bulls often did in such disasters, he began a long, slow, plodding march across the arena to where we sat. He seemed to be telling Penny: "You wanted to see me die. Well, here I am," and he stopped right in front of our seats, so everything that followed occurred practically in Penny's lap. The anxious young woman could almost reach out and touch Fermín as he swore and sweated in his frantic effort to terminate this fiasco, but he was able to accomplish so little that we heard the wailing bugle sound, the first *aviso.* "Oh, no! That's so unfair!" She was right. Her matador had been in no way responsible for this calamity. The damned bull itself was responsible, but now the shame of trumpet calls in the fading light of a dying day fell on him, and she sat close enough to him to see each mark of anguish on his face.

The bull was backed against the barrier just below us, with his head and horns pointing out into the arena so that when Fermín tried to attack he was looking straight at Penny, and I was proud of the way she handled herself, not looking away to escape the humiliation of her man but sharing it. Keeping her gaze full upon him, she called repeatedly in Spanish: "*¡Coraje, muchacho!*" (Courage, little fellow) and groaned when each of his efforts failed.

Fermín's task was brutally difficult, for the bull, settled in a spot where he felt confident, still fended off any sword thrust by jerking up his head or swinging his horns to knock the sword away. He was, I thought, much like a skilled baseball player who stands feet apart, bat held short, and successfully fouls off any ball thrown at him, or like a skilled duelist who parries every thrust with what my teacher called "a twist of the wrist."

But now a second disaster occurred, because it was entirely possible for a matador to make a perfect attack on the bull only to have his sword, by sheer bad luck, strike bone. Then the flexible sword would double back, acquire great tension, and spring out of the matador's hand, making a graceful curve over his head and falling into the sand, point down. On certain tragic occasions this flying sword lands not in the sand but in the body of some spectator in the first rows, and death is instantaneous.

When the second *aviso* sounded, Fermín's face grew ashen. Calesero called out: "One sword will do it," and the young fighter, who had never before had such an experience, stopped the trembling in his right arm, planted his feet firmly, twisting his ankles as if digging himself into the sand, rose on his toes, and made three attacks that were flawless, except that each time he hit bone.

Calesero, hoping that Fermín might avoid the indignity of a third *aviso,* told the younger man firmly: "Time left for one more try. Make it good." Fermín decided that his only chance to outwit this knowing bull would be a running pass away from the left horn and a swift sword thrust as he reached a spot between where the horns should have been. Though extremely dangerous and even foolhardy, it might work, he thought, moving off to the bull's right so that his powerful right arm would be free to thrust downward. His movements revealed his strategy and unanimously the other toreros shouted: "Over the horn!" and "From the front!"

As the trumpeter brought his mouthpiece to his lips, Fermín started his run. The third *aviso* ended the fight. In a last gasp of heroism and folly, Fermín attempted the impossible. The bull anticipated his approach and with a wild toss of his head, caught the sword and tossed it in the air. It fell point down in the sand as the trumpeter finished his mournful announcement that the matador had lost his bull and that the oxen would now be brought in to lead it to slaughter in the corrals.

Like many a matador before him who had heard that third *aviso,* which sealed his shame, Fermín wanted to chase after the bull and finish him before he left the arena, but was restrained by Calesero and Pepe Luis. His own banderillero said: "Let him go, Fermín. You did your part. It was that damned wall." So, head down, the young matador returned to the passageway where he had left his brocaded cape and his other swords. As he reached for his gear he heard a voice from the stands and looked up to see Penny. "You were heroic, matador," she said. "Fate stole your bull from you." Her voice wavered as tears choked it, but Fermín's sense of shame was so great he could not look at her.

Turning his back on her as if he wished to be rid of these intrusive Americans, he hurried out of the arena, through the patio de caballos where the horses were kept, and into his waiting limousine. Speeding to the House of Tile, he jumped out, rushed upstairs to his room unwilling to look at anyone, and packed for his escape from this distasteful town and for his long drive north to Torreón, where he would fight tomorrow.

And so the German tourist's aptly named Saturnine Saturday ended, with little having been accomplished and no honors won. The band did not play to signal the end of day, nor did people congregate to discuss the interesting events of the afternoon, for there had been only the few passes of Calesero, the bravery of Pepe Luis and Fermín's *pase de pecho,* thin reward for a long afternoon. In silence the crowd dispersed, not because they were frustrated or disgusted but because the day had never sprung to life.

Ledesma, in bidding us good-bye, said: "Now I have a job harder than any of yours. I've got to report what happened." He smiled at Mrs. Evans and said: "As your talkative American friend, Señor Clay, has no doubt told you, Don Eduardo's paying me to tell the world that today was a four-part triumph."

She groaned: "With this fight no one could justify that," but he replied: "I have to say it. Besides, you will concede that each torero did do some one thing that was meritorious. You see, I never lie. What I do is suppress the ugly truths that might damage Don Eduardo when he's trying to sell tickets to his festival."

The mournful ending fell most heavily on Penny. The others had no justifiable complaints. They had watched a rejoneador do passably well, a rare occurrence, and Mrs. Evans had enjoyed two enlightening conversations, with Ledesma at the hotel and with Ricardo Martín at the corrida. But shortchanged Penny had finally met a matador, had identified with him and been forced to watch him collapse and then walk away. However, I had observed during the last fight that she was a resolute young woman, and now, to my keen delight, she proved it by insisting that we find Fermín. "Let's hurry back to the Terrace before he drives off."

"Where's he going?"

"Torreón, he told me. Has a fight there tomorrow," and she revealed how intensely she had become involved with Sotelo during their brief conversation on the Terrace: "I wanted to borrow Mrs. Evans's Caddy and drive him but he wouldn't allow it. Said matadors did not travel to their fights chauffeured by women. I think he meant, especially not by American women."

When we reached the Terrace, now filled with guests who had attended the fight, Penny asked me to take her to Fermín's room, where we found him in the last stages of packing for his hurried ride north. Ignoring his peóns, who were stowing his matador's gear in specially designed suitcases, she walked to him, quietly embraced him and burst into tears. He consoled her but passed her on to me: "Take care of her. She's a princess," and with no further farewell he hurried to his waiting limousine, with Penny trailing behind. It wasn't a real limo, of course; as a newly fledged matador he couldn't afford that. What he had was a used hearse, big and spacious with room for six and a new paint job hiding the original black. It was a fine conveyance, really, and one in which he could sleep during long trips, if he could keep from thinking: I'm riding in my coffin.

He had expected to jump in the front seat next to the driver and be on his way, but Penny reached him before he could close the door, and I overheard her say in Spanish: "Don Fermín, you were very brave. And that's what I'll always remember about this day and my trip to Mexico."

Like a caring parent, he shoved her firmly back to me and said: "If you're her uncle, look after her. She's lovely." He shut the car door and headed north, the tires of the hearse kicking up pebbles.

As we walked back to the Terrace I put my

arm around her and said: "I'm proud of the way you acted at the fight. This is one you'll never forget. The day you grew up," and she asked almost tearfully: "How could a bull with one horn defend himself with such diabolical skill? And against my matador?" And I said: "That's what he's been bred to do. That's his job."

15

AMERICAN
ANCESTORS:
IN VIRGINIA

When a man has a background consisting of three radically different bloodlines—in my case Mexican Indian, Spanish and Virginian—he has, in each branch, about fifteen hundred generations of ancestors, allotting thirty years to the generation. So, to describe my heritage, I would be free to start almost anywhere in history, and I reached fairly far back to recount the Indian influences, back to the sixth century. But when dealing with my Spanish ancestors I felt it proper to go back only to the early 1500s in Salamanca.

For my American antecedents I can relate everything relevant by starting as late as 1823, when a baby boy was born to the Clay family that operated a cotton plantation near Richmond, the colorful capital of Virginia. Northeast of that city there is a large area of swamps, matted trees, gullies and rotting logs. Called the Wilderness, it is frequented by wild turkeys, feral hogs, beautiful birds and an occasional mountain lion, and its waters provide exceptional fishing. It's a place to stay clear of, but throughout history Clay men were familiar with it and found pleasure in its cool retreats and unexpected beauties.

Our family plantation, Newfields, lay at the extreme northeastern edge of the Wilderness where in the late seventeenth century trees could be felled from relatively flat land, broad fields constructed and cotton grown. To the east lay the rivers that flowed into the Chesapeake and then into the Atlantic, and to the west, through the Wilderness, ran the road that took us to Richmond.

On a spring day in 1823 Joshua Clay ran from his plantation home, leaped on his horse and spurred it down our tree-lined lane, out onto the public road, into the Wilderness and on to Richmond. He galloped through the streets till he came to his club, where he told his fellow members: "It's a boy! I'm registering him for entry into the Virginia Third!" Some of the witnesses had welcomed Joshua himself into the famed regiment forty years before.

As far back as the people of Richmond could remember, the Clays of Newfields Plantation had been known for their ability to handle their land, all two thousand acres of it. They were knowledgeable not only about agriculture and the growing of cotton but also about horseshoeing, carpentry, irrigation and the management of Negro slaves. Joshua Clay had some two hundred slaves, whom he treated decently and from whose labor he built a modest family fortune.

The family's patriotism spoke for itself: Clays had served with Colonel George Washington in his frontier fight against the Indians, with General Washington at Valley Forge, and with Andrew Jackson at New Orleans after the English burned our capital during the War of 1812. Clays had also served in the Virginia government, and one branch of our family had led a settlement party to tame the frontier in Kentucky and had stayed on to help build that state.

In 1823, when my grandfather was born, there was no war in progress in which the Clays could take part. They spent the peaceful years improving their plantation, removing the tall trees that encroached upon their cotton fields, and building strong business relationships with cotton traders in Liverpool. They also did a considerable business with the trees they cut down in the area they called the Wilderness by converting the wood into lumber, which they sold to carpenters in cities like nearby Richmond and Washington. Since the family holdings were only some dozen miles from Richmond, the Clays were often in that lively city. As soon as their newborn son was about two weeks old and able to travel, the family drove him to Richmond to visit with the relatives who preferred city living, and it was there that Uncle Clay, who served as clergyman in the Episcopal Church, baptized the child as Jubal Clay.

The first name had occasioned debate in the family, for the boy's father preferred a more military name like Gideon, whom the Lord had specifically called a mighty warrior; the mother, who was a delicate young woman who loved books and painting and music, begged her husband to allow her to name the boy Jubal, of whom the Bible said: "He was the father of all who play the harp and flute." But when the father looked in Genesis to find that citation he read: "Zillah also had a son, Tubal-Cain, who forged all kinds of tools out of bronze and iron," and so he made a pact with his wife: "You can call him Jubal if you wish, and I'll call him Tubal," and that is how the boy grew up. He could play the musical instruments his mother provided, but he could also work in the smithy to help his father shoe horses and forge the tools a plantation required.

In time the mother's name prevailed, in part because she bore a second son whom her husband was allowed to name Gideon, after the warrior who slew the Midianites. But the christening had little effect because Gideon became a banker.

In 1846, when Jubal was a married man of twenty-three with a son of his own, he was growing dissatisfied with his life helping direct the plantation. With his father's guidance he had made himself into a skilled toolmaker, an inventive engineer and a shrewd manager of slaves, selling off the unproductive workers to unsuspecting neighbors and buying black men and women in their late teens who could bear children while doing fruitful work in the fields. In the evenings he enjoyed playing music with his mother and his wife, the two women playing together on the piano, he on a clarinet imported from Germany. He also enjoyed going to Richmond to discuss affairs with businessmen there, to visit with his brother in the bank, or to attend the various plays and musical entertainments the city provided.

Such pleasant diversions did not, however,

make him neglect his work at the plantation, where his wife, Zephania, was proving as capable as he in managing the female slaves; she taught them sewing, mending, weaving and cooking, so that the Clays lived well, dressed well and dined well. This satisfactory state of affairs might have continued indefinitely had not Jubal, on one of his visits to Richmond, dined with a group of military men who spoke with some heat about events that threatened the recently admitted state of Texas and indeed the entire nation.

"It's intolerable!" a major was saying. "When I was a member of the army's inspecting party, trying to decide how many forts and where we should place our new lands, I heard nothing but complaints about the continual threats Mexico was making against our borders."

"Didn't the Texans thrash the Mexicans pretty badly?" a naval officer asked, and the army man explained: "That fellow named Santa Anna, a brazen sort, who's president of Mexico and their leading general, too, won four or five stupendous victories against the Texans. But under Sam Houston, that fellow in our Senate now, the Texans finally rallied and beat him. Won their independence, too."

"And became a free nation."

"For a while," the army man said. "But don't

make a big thing of it. In the decisive battle less than a thousand men on each side took part. A skirmish, really, but it did the trick. And I must give the Texans credit. They won that battle while losing only six men."

Clay could not believe such figures: "Did you say six?" and the army man said: "I told you it was a skirmish."

Clay persisted: "But you say it's the same Santa Anna who's causing trouble now?"

"When he got back home he refused to acknowledge that Mexico lost the battle, and the war, and Texas. He has hopes of winning it all back from us."

"Any chance?" several of the men asked, and the reply was unequivocal: "He's a damned good military man. If we allow him to get a running start, he could create havoc along our southern border."

"What should we do?"

"I'm told President Polk is just waiting for Santa Anna to move back into Texas. It's American territory now, and"—he banged his right fist into his left palm—"it's war. We move south in overwhelming force and crush that would-be Napoleon." His listeners nodded their approval.

In the discussion that followed, a businessman who collected cotton from many plantations and shipped it to England said quietly: "It behooves everyone in this room to consider the opportunities meticulously. In your mind's eye, draw a picture of our southern border. Alabama, Mississippi and Louisiana don't touch Mexico, but everything west of there does. I believe it's land that can grow cotton, and the part that Mexico holds is the richest of all. Believe me, gentlemen, if we could take this Mexican head-on, whip him properly and force him to accept our terms in the peace treaty, we could take his land and win undreamed-of riches."

When the silence of his listeners indicated that they did not share his vision, he assumed that it must be because he had not spoken clearly, so he elucidated further: "The land we take from Mexico could grow cotton, gentlemen, and where cotton grows you must have slaves, and where will they come from? You can't get them from Africa anymore, or Cuba either. Our laws and British ships prevent that. So where must the new landowners look for their slaves? Not Georgia or the Carolinas. They need every slave they have. Alabama and Mississippi don't have ten extra slaves between them. Where the new owners will have to come is Virginia. We're phasing out of cotton. Every one of you men has slaves to spare. Imagine the prices you'll get if new cotton land opens up!"

Although Jubal Clay was a prudent business-

man who could comprehend the financial advantages a war with Mexico might yield, he was,
like his ancestors, primarily a military man, and
now he asked: "How do you see the situation
developing?" and the army man said: "Talk is
that President Polk will call for volunteers, army
and navy, to go down there and teach those
Mexicans a lesson."

"Where do I go to volunteer?" Clay asked and
the man said: "The public call hasn't gone out
yet, but I can assure you that our Virginia Third
has a few interesting openings, captain or better
if you've had military training."

"Does militia duty count?"

"It sure does. How old are you, Clay?"

"Twenty-three."

"I could sign you up tomorrow, but at your age
you'd have to be a lieutenant."

"My family for generations have been fighting
captains. I couldn't settle for less."

The army man leaned back, studied Clay, lowered his head to stare at the table, then said:
"Well, now. I'd sure like to see our complement
filled out, but a captain? At age twenty-three?"

To the man's surprise, Clay broke into a big
grin. "If you look in your records, you'll see I've
been a member of your regiment since 1823."

"You one of those?"

"Yep." And the recruiter said: "If you mean it,

by this time tomorrow I'll have you a captain in the Virginia Third," and Clay saluted, saying: "Like my father and his father before him."

But as the new captain left the table the businessman who acted as a wholesaler in cotton took Jubal aside and said: "Captain Clay, before you depart for Texas, you should give careful thought about this strategy of selling your slaves to whatever new territory we gather after a victorious war with Mexico. Do the proper thing in the next few years, and you can reap profits for decades."

Had Clay accepted his commission in the Virginia regiment one week earlier he would have seen service where he expected, along the Texan-Mexican border under the command of General Zachary Taylor, who was about to lead the invasion south into the heartland of Mexico. But he missed that assignment in which he would have served with many young men like himself who were destined for glory in the 1860s—Ulysses S. Grant and William Sherman fighting for the North, Jefferson Davis and Robert E. Lee serving the South.

His delay placed him not on a train heading for Texas but on a troopship leaving the navy yard at New Orleans for a speedy trip to Veracruz, where the Americans would fight their way ashore and then march up through jungle roads to Mexico City. When that capital was occupied, the war would be over. Soldiers in the expeditionary force believed they could defeat the Mexicans in about a month and were eager to get the job finished.

Sailing with them would be General Winfield Scott, commander in chief of all American forces in Mexico, sixty years old, white-haired, big in all dimensions and possessed of a furious temper and the conviction that everyone in the government at Washington and the army officers on their way to Mexico were plotting against him. But his military credentials were impeccable: fighting in Canada, heroism in the War of 1812, service against the Indians, and holder of every important position in the peacetime army. He was unquestionably the premier military man in the nation, and he intended his conquest of Mexico to be the glorious capstone to his fighting career and possibly a stepping-stone to the presidency.

Well before the voyage began on the little ship that would take him to his meeting with destiny, Scott started assembling a team he could depend on. Aware that he would require some trustworthy aide to copy the confidential documents with which he would bombard his civilian superiors in Washington, he was on the lookout for such a man. One morning he spotted

Jubal Clay exercising on deck—a fine-looking young fellow, clean-cut, well groomed and most likely with a good education. As Clay ran past Scott growled: "You, young man! Have you a steady hand?" Clay stopped and, turning back, saw the general. "I've shot all my life, sir."

Scott bellowed: "I mean can you write a page that can be read," and Clay said humbly: "Yes."

As Clay worked in the general's crowded quarters he required only a few days to discover that Winfield Scott, secure in the nation's top military job, was pitifully insecure in all personal relations but at the same time ridiculously arrogant. He was, Jubal concluded after a week's work, an impossible fellow, but also a man born to command. He said to himself, It's going to be a stormy war.

He soon learned that Scott hated everyone in a position of power. As a staunch conservative Whig he especially loathed President Polk, a liberal Democrat, but he also despised General Zachary Taylor, another Democrat who acted as if he too hoped to be the next president. His ultimate scorn, however, was reserved for Gideon J. Pillow, a pettifogging lawyer from a small town in Tennessee, who was so ineffectual that Clay could not understand why Scott even bothered with him.

"I'll tell you why," Scott thundered. "Because

he was Polk's law partner, and the president assigned him to my staff to spy on me." After Scott had identified three or four other spies among his generals, Clay asked: "If they're all against you, why did the army put you in command?" and Scott roared: "I'll tell you why. Because they knew I was the best man for the job, the only one who could force Santa Anna to surrender, and that I will do."

Clay, suffering daily proof of Scott's incredible vanity and his determination to fight every official to protect what he deemed his rights, wondered how such a man could lead troops effectively, but when in March 1847 the various American warships congregated in the roads of the heavily fortified harbor of Veracruz, Clay saw what a genius Scott was. "To assault that port with its fortifications," a junior officer said, "would mean enormous losses on our side. I do not want such a battle to start."

Nor did Scott, so with a masterly blockade to keep any Mexican supply ship from sneaking into the wharves, and calling upon all the firepower of his ships, he laid down such a furious bombardment that after a few days the Americans marched ashore, virtually unopposed. It was now a free run up to the altiplano where Mexico City awaited the assault. Clay supposed the march might take two or three weeks, the siege another three weeks, and the surrender sometime in mid-May at the latest.

What a surprise my grandfather had! March went by, then April, May and June, and General Scott was still working his way gingerly through the Mexican jungle, up steep paths, past well-defended forts and formidable cities like Puebla. When the subordinate generals urged more speed, Scott growled: "When I reach the capital I want the battle to be already won. Every advantage should be ours. I want a quick, decisive skirmish."

Clay made good use of this dilatory approach, and in a way he could not have planned. A Mexican scout who had volunteered to lead Scott inland in hopes of gaining American citizenship later, one Pablo Mugica, found that he too had time on his hands, so he offered to teach Clay Spanish, for a fee, and as June eased into July and August neared, Jubal gained a low-level mastery of Spanish that surprised him, and he became valuable in interrogating prisoners.

It was on this long, tedious uphill climb that my grandfather became familiar with Mexico's constant revelation of wonders: the great volcanoes piercing the sky, the matted jungle, the handsome little villages each with its whitewashed walls, the silent valleys, the churches hundreds of years old, and everywhere the peóns in their skimpy white clothes and their donkeys.

The more he saw of Mexico, the more he liked it, and while he never thought of living in such a culturally retarded place, the beauty of the land and the essential charm of the inhabitants' Catholic way of life did attract him, so that when other Americans, sweating up the hills, complained or denigrated the country as a hellhole, he was far from agreeing with them. He was not impressed with the military genius of its leaders, for with their enormous numerical superiority he knew that they should have been able to sweep Scott back into the Atlantic, but the people he met on his marches he liked.

His experiences with Scott as he toiled in the general's headquarters handling paper details were constantly surprising, for Scott seethed with hatred of Polk, Pillow and Zach Taylor as he encountered difficulties. His suspicion that spies lurked within his own staff increased, and for good reason, because he really was surrounded by men, usually political appointees, who hoped that he would fail and sometimes took active steps to try to ensure that he did. But he was also accompanied by trusted regular army generals who were as determined as he to achieve a victory. Always outnumbered and opposed by

first-class artillery under the command of Mexican army officers trained in Europe, Scott's
subordinates acted resolutely and responsibly,
even though their commander in chief seemed
to enjoy abusing them and defaming them in his
written reports. Whenever Clay read Scott's latest diatribe against his generals he wondered
how they could obey his orders.

But Clay also saw the manner in which Scott
sought diligently to identify which of his junior
officers showed promise as potential generals,
and these he praised extravagantly, giving them
choice assignments and then reporting on their
successes to Washington. Years later when
Clay was trying to reach a mature assessment
of Scott as a military man, he wrote: "Reading
his reports on his juniors penned in 1847, it
would seem that he was eager to pinpoint those
young men who would prove the greatest Civil
War generals fifteen years later in 1862. He was
proud of having P.G.T. Beauregard on his staff,
quickly spotted George C. McClellan as promising, and mentioned enthusiastically six or seven
other young men who would become important
generals."

But Scott's shrewdest evaluation concerned
a young engineer named Captain Robert E. Lee.
In the dispatches Clay had to copy he read repeatedly of Scott's high regard for this young

Virginian: "Greatly distinguished himself at the siege of Veracruz . . . indefatigable . . . bravery under heavy fire . . . an officer of great promise." But the dispatch Jubal remembered longest and quoted to his family most often came at the end of a message in which he commended both George McClellan and P.G.T. Beauregard: "Captain Lee, Engineer, also bore important orders from me until he fainted from a wound and the loss of two nights' sleep at the batteries."

Scott required a substantial amount of time to get from Veracruz to the capital, 27 March to 14 September, but once there he achieved a series of stupendous victories, and Jubal saw what a splendid general he was. Nothing gave Jubal more satisfaction than the report he helped draft for headquarters in Washington, for it depicted not only a good general but a great man:

> Since our final victory carried us right to the gates of the Mexican capital, which was poorly defended, we expected General Scott to give us the order: "Rush in, overwhelm the guards and celebrate a well-earned victory." But to our amazement he halted us, conferred with his generals and said in my hearing: "We shall stop here two days to allow the stricken Mexican government time to stabilize, to get their breath and

recover their courage. I order this for two reasons: in the days to come we shall have to consult with these men to work out a sensible peace, and they will behave more sensibly if they have retained their sense of honor. And I have learned from history that when a conquering army bursts into a city after a protracted siege, terrible things are likely to happen. Arson, plunder, murder, rape. These are things that do not happen under my command. We will wait till tempers cool, theirs and ours."

Two days later, as planned, a small contingent of our troops assaulted a minor gate defended by a token force of Mexicans. After a brief skirmish our troops broke through. The Mexicans felt that they had defended the city with honor, and when we marched in to take possession, our troops in order, our flags flying, there was no burning, plunder or rape.

Jubal had one other observation on the Mexican War:

At the final battle of Chapultepec late in the siege, an incident occurred that has always perplexed me. It was a confused affair, which consumed several hours, for the Mexicans had the advantage in numbers and position, but in the end we prevailed. Later we learned that during the battle a group of very young cadets from a military college located on the the hill refused to abandon their advantageous site even though their instructors and the older cadets had fled. With extraordinary heroism these lads temporarily repulsed the American attacks but eventually they were engulfed by our numbers and six died. When word of their patriotism spread through Mexico, they became enshrined in legend as Los Niños Héroes. Years later, when I had become a Mexican, people would ask me: "If you were at Chapultepec during the battle, what did you think of Los Niños Héroes?" and at first I used to say: "We were never aware of them," because it was too painful to consider. But this caused such baleful looks that later I said: "If you'd had one brigade more of those children we'd never have won," and my listeners were gratified by this response.

The reason I emphasize my grandfather's role in the Mexican War and his relationship with General Scott is that this friendship produced an incident which would determine the latter half of his life. Shortly after the end of the hostilities, Scott summoned Jubal and said: "Major Clay, no man on my staff has behaved more admirably than you. You have my complete trust. I'm placing you in command of a dozen cavalrymen and their sergeant for an unusual assignment. I've asked General Santa Anna to issue you a safe conduct to ride northwest of here to Toledo, a mining town with the same name as the town in Spain. I want to know what kind of mines it has, especially whether it's iron or coal. It looks to be about a hundred and eighty miles away. Take money, take food, take ammunition, take your eyes and ears, and Godspeed."

So toward the end of September 1847 my grandfather's party of fourteen rode out from Mexico City toward Toledo, which was almost as far west of the capital as Veracruz had been east, and it had taken them half a year to traverse that distance, but now the fighting was ended and they rode at their pleasure, always attentive to repel snipers or bandits who might try to assault them. It was, as Grandfather loved to tell my father in later years, a trip marked by grand vistas of the volcanoes behind them and the glorious panoramas ahead. They passed historic settlements like Querétaro, saw now and then a small pyramid or other relics of past occupation, and in time they reached the more barren ground covered with cactus, a plant with which the Virginians in the party were not familiar.

In time, when the cooler breezes of November made the weather comfortable, they reached a crest from which they looked ahead to their target, the famous mining city of Toledo, with a large pyramid to the right, a handsome aqueduct running from it into the city limits, inside which stood a central plaza bordered by colonial buildings including a cathedral, and off to one side an imitation of a Roman coliseum built of red boards. When Grandfather tried his Spanish on a man with a mule he said: "That's where they run with the bulls," and when Jubal asked: "And where are the mines?" the man said proudly: "Beyond the city, to the north," and all my grandfather could see was a vague mass of shacks.

"*¿Dónde está la cárcel?*" Jubal asked a man at the edge of the city, and the man surveyed the troop and asked: "*¿Quién es el prisionero?*" for Jubal had confused the word *cárcel,* jail, with *cuartel,* military headquarters or barracks. When the mistake was explained, both sides began to laugh, and the Mexican called over some friends to explain that the American soldiers wanted to

go to jail. Thus my grandfather entered the colonial city of Toledo accompanied by robust
laughter.

The commanding officer of the city's guard
detachment recommended that the Americans
stay at a hostelry that occupied a building famous in the region, the House of Tile, a handsome building facing a fine park to the south and
a spectacular sight on the north, the huge pyramid of Toledo, so that during Jubal's three-week
stay in the city he gazed alternately at the
square, which was only three hundred years old,
or the brooding pyramid, thirteen hundred years
old. Both gave him constant delight.

He had explained to the Mexicans that he had
come to visit their famous mines, and they corrected him: "Only one, señor, but it is big
enough," and when they formed a mounted caravan they took him some seven miles to the
north along a wide but winding road to a nondescript site on a hillside consisting of a group of
low adobe buildings, their roofs made of vines
intertwined with tree branches and plastered
with mud. There was no impressive building that
could have been associated with a major mine,
but there was a large circular area across which
narrow paths ran, and Clay saw that they led to
a vast, dark hole. This was the famed Mineral de
Toledo, as highly regarded in Spain as in Mex-

ico. In Spanish the name was certainly in the plural for the reason that no one could believe that the silver that poured out of Toledo could have come from one mine only.

"Only silver?" Clay asked and the men nodded. "No iron?" and they shook their heads. "Any iron in the hills beyond?" and again they disappointed him. With that quick solution to the problem he had been sent to investigate, he could have marched back to the capital, but instead he made a fortunate decision: "I'd like to see what quality of mine they have," and he tarried in Toledo, finding the citizens willing to help, for they were justly proud of their treasure. They took him to a Spanish engineer from the home country, a wiry, sandy-haired man not over five feet three, who seemed actually delighted to entertain a knowledgeable visitor: "Mine? Engineer?" When Clay said *"Abogado,"* the Spaniard said something that indicated that he liked lawyers, and Clay struck his own forehead: *"Algodón,"* which meant that he raised cotton, and again there was laughter.

The distance from the shack, in which he met the head of the mine, to the open shaft was only some fifteen yards, but the gravity with which the miner led the way and the care he exercised when approaching the open hole made Clay cautious as he moved forward. At this point eight small Indian women came up out of the mine, each with a basket on her head containing what Clay supposed to be some dark ore containing silver.

When the women had passed, their bare feet making no sound, their solemn faces showing no animation, Clay and the engineer moved to the spot from which they had climbed out of the pit, and there the Spaniard indicated a stout board platform where Clay could lie down in a prone position and look down into the Mineral de Toledo. It was an awesome experience: He could see the dark wall of the pit but not the remote bottom where Indian workmen were digging out the ore that their women carried to the top. There was only darkness, a kind of glimpse into hell, for up the shaft from time to time came wisps of gray smoke; someone was burning something far, far down in the bowels of the earth.

Then, slowly emerging from the smoke, perhaps two hundred feet down, came eight more Indian women with baskets on their heads, and as he stared at the weaving pattern their movement created he had the impression that they were walking on air, for he could see no stairway. But when he looked more closely as they climbed higher, he saw what had escaped him before: into the sides of the pit, winding down in an endless spiral so as to achieve a gradual rate of ascent, ran a series of narrow stone steps, which had been cut centuries ago for use by the thousands of Indian men and women who had toiled here.

As Jubal stared at the steps he was appalled to see what a small area they provided for the climbing feet—about eighteen inches square— and how, through the centuries the stone wall of the pit had been worn smooth by the pressure of a million hands as the workers had steadied themselves in their perilous climb. He thought: It must be even more dangerous climbing back down, for then the whole weight of the body pulls you forward and a false step . . . He could imagine himself plunging headlong down that abyss. While he was contemplating the horror of such a death the women climbing the stairs reached the top of the shaft, blinking as sunlight struck them. Stepping out of the pit, they moved along the path to deliver their ore to the smelter without a single pause in their movements, so that Clay judged them to be machines, dependable, manageable and cheap. They reminded him of his Negro slaves chopping cotton, except that the slaves worked in daylight.

By the time the engineer was ready to lead Clay down the shaft and into the mine, my grandfather had prepared himself emotionally to see some great thing, and he was not disappointed, for in later years he often told his family, whether in Virginia or Mexico: "It was one of the most thrilling days of my life, and I seldom use that word."

The mine that year was nearly thirteen hundred feet deep straight down, and the descent was, as he had anticipated, perilous, but the Spaniard showed him how, if he kept his right shoulder pressed against the wall, he could negotiate it with relative ease and safety. But the descent seemed endless, a slow drop into hell; however, when they approached the six-hundred-foot mark, the shaft opened out into a spacious cavern of some magnitude. Indeed a small farm could have been installed here with the rocky roof high enough to permit reasonably tall barns.

"You found a thick lode here?" Clay asked, and when the engineer nodded, Clay said: "But down there it narrows again?"

"Disappears."

Clay halted at the edge of the shaft as it continued downward, as narrow as before, and the magnitude of the decision made at this point more than a century ago stunned him: "You mean, that as the lode began to run out, someone had the courage to argue: 'Down below there must be the other part,' and on that blind hope they dug through solid rock even deeper?"

"The decision wasn't difficult. In Spain the king received a report every month on the progress of the Toledo Mineral. He relied on our silver, and when he saw it running out he gave an order: 'Dig deeper,' and the Indians dug."

When Clay asked: "How much deeper?" the engineer said: "You'll see," and down they went on the same narrow steps, leaning to the right as before to keep their balance. After perhaps a hundred feet of black rock they came to the second cavern, nearly seven hundred feet down, not quite as spacious as before, but still more than a ballroom in size.

"They dug here for years," the engineer said as they descended to the thirteen-hundred-foot level. "This is where they began to come upon the real treasure of Toledo."

As Jubal's eyes became accustomed to the dim light thrown by smoky flares, he saw that he had descended not to a miners' cave but to an underground village placed in a circle well over five hundred yards in diameter. Here some three dozen Indians and their Mexican overseers toiled as if they were on an open field in sunlight. There was a smithy to sharpen the tools that cut away the rock to find the ore; there were vats of water, a flat area that resembled a restaurant with tables; lost in distant shadows were store-

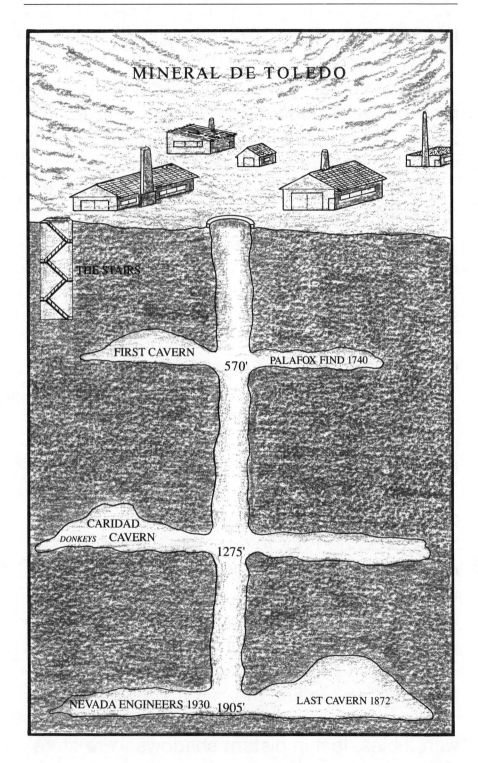

MINERAL DE TOLEDO

THE STAIRS

FIRST CAVERN

570'

PALAFOX FIND 1740

CARIDAD CAVERN

DONKEYS

1275'

NEVADA ENGINEERS 1930

1905'

LAST CAVERN 1872

houses. But what astounded Clay the most was the donkeys bringing large chunks of ore from the cutting face to the area where it would be broken into smaller segments for transportation above.

"How do you get the donkeys in and out? They can't walk down the steps, can they?"

"They don't go out."

"Never?"

"Their bodies are hauled out when they die." And as Clay stared at the donkeys, plodding along in near darkness, his eyes wandered from them to the Indians and he asked: "The Indians? Do they too stay down here perpetually?" and the Spaniard said: "Not by force. They're allowed up if they wish, but that climb is fearful, as you'll see, so some prefer to stay down. Of course, when they grow too old to work, we encourage them to leave, but some prefer to stay and work at little jobs here and there. Some grow fond of their donkeys and stay with them."

"But how do they get the donkeys down here?" Clay asked. The Spaniard asked the workmen if any were due to come down that day and they nodded. After more than two hours during which Clay inspected the cavern, finding one amazing aspect after another, the foreman blew a whistle, whereupon an Indian worker began beating a drum and women stopped their steep climb with their baskets. When activity in the shaft had ceased for about twenty minutes, Clay heard a bumping and a scraping, punctuated by the sound of braying, and in time he saw, in a rope sling that slowly descended, the kicking legs of a protesting donkey. When released, the animal ran about, exploring this rocky pasture on which he would spend the rest of his life. With the ropes thus freed, the miners formed a kind of basket into which were tossed different items no longer required below, and after proper signals were sent by tugging on the rope, the drumbeating began and the huge bundle rose, bumping the narrow walls as it went.

When the women resumed their climb, Clay asked: "Do some of them live down here too?" and the engineer said: "If they've been up and down several times, with loads, they're free to sleep down here. Of course, they go above to have their babies, but even so, a few stubborn ones stay down."

"Do pregnant women climb those steps, with baskets of ore?"

"We watch carefully. When she's in the seventh or eighth month we give her easier tasks aboveground. Like feeding ore into the furnace."

"How long have those steps been there?" Clay asked, and the engineer said: "They tell me the Indians discovered silver here in 1548, so the first steps must have been cut three hundred years ago next year."

"And if one of the women, or the men, slips on a step . . . ?" The Spaniard shrugged and raised his hands upward in a gesture of supreme dismissal, but then he did add: "We've always watched the steps closely, and if we find one where people have fallen from time to time, we bring the stonemasons down and we redo that step, though it takes time and it's costly. Of course, we preach caution going and coming." He explained that more Indians died coming down empty-handed than when climbing up with a load of ore: "They get careless, and they hurry."

"Where do you find the Indians to do this work?" and the engineer said: "Criminals used to be sent here, in the early centuries, but we found they weren't reliable—they were apt to do dreadful things. So the engineers stopped that, too dangerous."

"Then what?"

"Our missionaries persuaded some of their converts to work so they could be near a church, and when we didn't get enough—this was in my time—the soldiers would bring in whole tribes. If you could speak to each of the workers down here, you'd find a dozen different languages."

"Do those brought in by the soldiers ever protest? I mean, in America sometimes our slaves start a rebellion."

"The same here. This mine has seen some incidents, very ugly ones. The entire white staff belowground wiped out, or Indians from one tribe eliminating another tribe. And we have to be watchful. Sometimes a man who's become . . ." He knocked on his head to indicate insanity. "He might lurk in one of the empty caverns we saw coming down, and when he spots a manager he doesn't like or one of the Indians we promoted to a job he wanted, he waits till the man has taken the first step on the stairs, then out he leaps, grabs the man and together they plunge to the bottom."

"Has that happened in your time?"

"Last month. We have to be constantly alert."

What Clay was seeing, especially the delivery of the donkey, made him think: If you can bring the donkey down by those ropes, why don't you haul the ore out the same way? and the Spaniard explained: "Ropes cost money. Use them too often, they fray and break. Besides, it's a long way down here from up there. The women are much cheaper."

When the time came to start the long climb out, Clay was tormented by many visions: some insane Indian grabbing him for the terrible plunge; the donkey that had been sentenced that day to a perpetual service underground; and, most lurid of all, the scene of an entire community living and working and having children deep in the bowels of the earth. As he tried to calculate how many Indians had perished in the Mineral de Toledo, he was suddenly struck by the parallel fate of his slaves at Newfields Plantation. But he was able to salve his conscience: "After all, God has ordained that inferior races must work for the superior. Anyway, the Indians probably have it a lot better here than they did in the mountains." But when he reached the top and climbed out into the sunlight, he felt the cruel pain in his legs, and he thought: How do those little women do it? When he saw the next line of eight crossing the flat ground to the smelter he muttered softly: "You're stronger than I could ever be."

He told his fellow engineer as they parted: "I'll be wanting to see a lot more of your operation. It looks to be in great shape." When he returned to his quarters in the House of Tile a surprise awaited him that would make his expedition a worthy and memorable adventure, for Don Alipio Palafox of the notable Spanish family who had played a major role in converting an ancient Altomec city into a modern Christian one was waiting to welcome him to Toledo, which the

Spaniard considered a Palafox fiefdom. A gracious, vigorous man in his late thirties with a
head of black hair, a smile of white teeth and
skin markedly darker than that of the average
homeland-born Spaniard, he greeted Jubal as if
eager to pay his respects to the conquering
hero: "With that ass Santa Anna leading our
troops, you couldn't escape winning. Did you
ever see a general make more mistakes? Sending his army here and there when he should
have stayed home defending his capital?"

"We were lucky to win," Clay said modestly.
"And it was damned difficult, because your men
fought valiantly."

"Where did you learn to speak such excellent
Spanish?"

"Don Alipio, you've been a diplomat to some
foreign capital. I learned a few words, a few
useful phrases on the march up from Veracruz."

"In that short a time? You must be a genius
with words."

"Don Alipio, how long do you think it took us
to make that march?"

"I have no idea. Out here we didn't follow the
progress of the war. Santa Anna's always in one
or another. How long?"

"March to September. A man can learn a lot
of Spanish in seven months."

As he said this they were resting at a table on

the hotel's open terrace facing the city's central plaza and without braggadocio but with a great deal of family pride, Don Alipio explained why his Palafoxes were important residents: "Two Palafox brothers immigrated here from Salamanca in the 1520s, not long after Cortés. Antonio, the priest, became bishop of Toledo. His brother, Timoteo, the soldier, became a miner. What a pair! The bishop built the first fortress-church; it stood where the cathedral is now, and Timoteo found the silver to pay for it.

"Finding this a profitable way to do the Lord's business and the king's, the brothers then converted the rude church into a fine cathedral. They also built the Hall of Government down at the far end of the plaza, and that fine building over there near the cathedral."

"They sort of boxed in the plaza, didn't they?" and when Don Alipio smiled appreciatively, Jubal said: "Don't tell me they built this hotel, too?"

"A mule train reaching here from Acapulco in 1575, bringing goods from the Manila galleon of that year, misdelivered a package here. No address. Intended for some church somewhere. The Palafox brothers opened it and found that handsome stack of fifty-four blue-and-yellow tiles you now see cemented into that wall."

"The brothers kept them?"

"What else to do? And when the wife of one of them saw the tiles . . ."

"The bishop was married?"

"Captain Clay, five Palafoxes in a row were ordained Bishop of Toledo, each the son of his father. They weren't so finicky in those days. And I'll tell you further. Every one of those five wives was an Altomec Indian. Not a Spaniard among the bunch. That's why I'm rather darker than usual and proud of it. Now, Timoteo's branch of the family always married girls born in Spain, casta pura if you wish, and sometimes there was snubbing back and forth between the wives. Their branch would boast: 'Not a drop of Indian blood in our family,' and the women of my branch would retaliate: 'Our ancestors were queens of this city when Salamanca was populated with cows.' But we men made them quit. We said: 'Your Spanish branch made all the money, but our Altomec branch gave it all to God.' A fair trade."

Clay asked: "Why did your line of priests always choose Altomecs?" and Palafox said: "Simple. They converted the young girls, baptized them, educated them, watched them grow, fell in love with them. These days the two branches are good friends."

After a halt in the conversation Don Alipio said: "I must admit, I take immense pride in the

statue of that Indian out there. One of my ancestors," and he pointed to a stone figure who surveyed his plaza as if he still commanded what
happened here: "It's Ixmiq. Ruled these parts
about A.D. 600. Our tribe was a gentle group,
called affectionately by the others the Drunken
Builders. He and his young men built the original
things that we Palafoxes built upon later." As
soon as he mentioned the name he corrected
himself. "I fell into the habit of thinking of myself
as one of the Palafoxes. Why? Because that
name has persisted. For seven generations, the
first five bishops and two after them, we've
never had anything but an Indian mother in our
line. Maybe I'm more of a descendant of old
Ixmiq than I am of the Palafoxes. Maybe best of
all, an honest mix of both."

Palafox suggested that they take their drinks
to the rear porch of the House of Tile, and as
they passed through the beautiful passageway
decorated from ceiling to floor and across the
ceiling, too, with tiles of many colors, he explained: "Those first tiles that the brothers stole
went only on the walls, but everyone praised
them so much that the women of our family,
Spaniards and Indians alike, fell in love with
tiles, so that every mule train from Veracruz
brought us tiles from Spain—they're the gold
ones. Then one of our women—I don't remem-

ber who—said, 'Bringing tiles from Spain and
Manila is crazy. Our Indians can make better
tiles than those,' and that's how the famous tile
works of Toledo began. All these other colors
you see, made right here."

When they came to the rear veranda, they
made themselves comfortable in chairs brought
from Spain and Palafox said: "Look at that pyramid! How it controls our landscape, and our
thoughts. There was a song my mother used to
sing that goes back to the time of Nopiltzín, the
great king about 900," and he leaned back,
closed his eyes and began chanting in a tongue
Clay did not understand. His voice quavered
and Clay saw that his hands clenched. When he
ended Clay said quietly: "They must be ancient
words," and Palafox said: "They are, and they'd
mean nothing to you. You wouldn't be interested," and Clay said: "Oh, but I would," and his
host chanted softly:

"For thy fame shall perish, Great
        Nolpiltzín, and thou,
    Powerful Tezozomoc, where are thy
        songs of triumph?
No more do I cry aloud in thy praise, but
        rest tranquil
    That ye have marched back to thy
        homes.

Ye whom I bewail, I shall know
nevermore, never again.
I am bereft here on earth that ye now
rest in your homes."

"When was it built?" Clay asked, and Palafox
said gravely: "Year 600 built, 700 defaced, 800
resurfaced, 900 almost wrecked, 1000 a terrible
group of newcomers enlarged and perverted
that noble structure."

"Perverted? I thought that pyramids all over
the world were religious structures."

"We don't like to talk about it. Do you boast
of your religious wars? Or we of our Inquisition?"
They stared at the huge monument for some
minutes, when Clay asked: "What's that little
structure to the left?" and Palafox beamed: "I'll
take you there one day," and Clay asked: "Why
are you being so courteous? Two weeks ago we
were mortal enemies." and Palafox laughed, a
big, embracing chuckle: "Because you and I are
twins. You come here to see what your enemy
is really like. I want to see whether Americans
are really human."

They dined together that very evening, very
late, and on the front veranda, so it was nearly
midnight when Don Alipio broached a subject
about which he had often speculated: "You
must see this plaza, Señor Americano, a con-

stant theater of revolution. I can't believe that your armies overlooked it. In 1151 the new Altomecs subdued the old Drunken Builders. In 1527 the Spaniards routed the Altomecs. In 1811 the Mexicans in this plaza shot the Spaniards, and who will come marching through here next year no man can predict. But the life of the plaza continues, the cathedral, built on the ruins of a fortress, built on the ruins of an Indian holy place, its bells still ring, its glorious façade is world-famous and old Ixmiq still stands there surveying it all."

In succeeding days Don Alipio took Clay to the pyramid, which overwhelmed him with its silver and gold, and to the nearby terrace, which focused attention on how artistic the Altomecs could be when they broke loose from their terrible gods. But what really surprised him was the trip they took on horseback to one of the Palafox ranches seven miles to the southwest. It was not fenced in, since it consisted of open range, but there was a handsome stone gate behind which clustered a group of small mud-and-wattle shacks and ordinary farm buildings. Don Alipio called for a stable boy to fetch fresh horses, which they rode about a mile south where Clay saw on the horizon several jet-black bulls of moderate size—much smaller than his dairy bulls in Virginia or even his milk cows—but with tremendous horns coming straight from the head and parallel to the ground. For the first time in his life Clay was seeing the famous fighting bulls of Spain and he asked the usual questions: "They aren't fenced in?" "If they're not molested, they remain passive." "We can ride among them?" "Yes, they see the horse as another animal, and if the horse doesn't bother them, they won't hurt him. But if you were to dismount, and showed only two legs instead of four, they'd become suspicious and might poke at you with their horns, not in anger, you understand, just in curiosity. But all the same, the horn would go through you, and, pfttt, you're dead."

"Why have fighting bulls here in Mexico?" and Don Alipio had a ready answer: "Whatever happens in Spain becomes popular here, and one of these days we'll have more than just gentlemanly fighters running bulls in the park. We'll have bullrings and men who make their living fighting bulls. Right now, my brother and I are building a ring just beyond the plaza. I'll show you this evening. You're dining with me, remember?"

"Where did you get those bulls?" Clay asked and Don Alipio said proudly: "Way back our family was closely associated with the marquis of

Guadalquivir in Seville. His daughter Leticia came over to Mexico to marry into the Spanish branch of our family. He raised fighting bulls in Spain. To help us get started, the marquis that's living now sent over as a gift a dozen animals seventeen years ago."

"Is that his brand on the animals?" Clay asked, pointing to the big G underlined by an undulating mark representing the Guadalquivir River.

"On the older animals, yes. It's an honorable brand, that one, but look at the younger animals," and when Jubal had a chance to inspect a calf he saw the new brand, a large P with a heavy bar across the foot of the letter. Don Alipio said: "We hope that will become a mark of honor in the plazas of Mexico," and Clay asked: "You expect many to be built?" With great confidence the breeder said: "Many."

"You must have vast acreage here, to allow the bulls to roam wild," Clay said. Palafox replied proudly as they took cool drinks from an Indian who had followed with a bucket: "The original bishop and his thieving brother converted a quarter of a million of what you call acres to our family's use. In twenty-five years it grew to a third of a million, and in 1740 we had more than a million and a quarter acres. Then came the Revolution of 1810, much land was taken from us, and now we have only some five hundred thousand acres." My grandfather was astounded: "That's still enormous. In the States you'd own much of the rich part of Virginia," but Don Alipio cautioned: "Anytime the troops march through the plaza, whssst, there goes another quarter million."

Dinner that night at the city home of the Palafoxes was a rare opportunity for an American intruder to witness the social life of an important Mexican citizen. Within a spacious courtyard surrounded by a high adobe wall topped by jagged fragments of broken glass stood a large house on a rise high enough to permit looking over the top of the wall to the pyramid. Three other Palafox couples would be dining with Don Alipio and his wife, and when Jubal arrived, the others were in the garden enclosed by a high wall and made tranquil by the sound of water as it trickled down over rocks. They were what Clay had supposed a group of Palafoxes would be: the men trim and well preserved from constant life in the saddle, the women well groomed and reserved in manner. He could guess the age of no one but judged that they were all well under sixty. He could see that they were slightly embarrassed, more likely confused, as to why they should have been invited to meet an American army officer with the war less than a month in the past, and they supposed that Clay would speak no Spanish. They were, of course, like most cultivated Mexicans of that day proficient in French, but none spoke English, since it was held to be the vulgar language of business and Americans. But when Don Alipio told them: "The captain is comfortable in Spanish," their reserve softened, and they gradually opened up to a discussion on what terms the peace treaty might contain.

One Palafox man, somewhat older than Don Alipio, warned: "Mexico has adjusted itself to the loss of Texas, but we will never surrender California. We need those ports on the Pacific." Another agreed: "True, we do have Acapulco, but it's not a major port, and it's cut off from most of Mexico by jungles and mountains."

Here Clay made his first observation: "It seemed to me as we tried to march up those endless hills that Veracruz was also cut off from the high plateaus we're on now," and the men wanted to know how the Americans had been able to push through the Mexican defenses. But when Jubal started to explain, he could see that they were not really interested, for as one man said: "In Mexico we have these wars constantly. One can hardly keep up with them," and another said: "Remember how, a few years ago, your father and mine marched out so bravely to crown Iturbide emperor of Mexico? He lasted two years and Santa Anna shot him."

The first speaker corrected him: "No, Santa Anna didn't do the actual shooting. He wasn't even there. But he did turn his men against the emperor and they did the shooting."

At this point, as my grandfather noted in the brief memoir he left his family, they went in to dinner, for it was approaching the time when Mexicans took their evening meal, eleven o'clock at night, and when they seated themselves in the massive sheepskin-covered armchairs at the huge oak table, Señora Palafox said from her place at the foot of the table: "We have a special entertainment for our guest," and signaled to a maid who brought into the dining room a girl of about eight dressed in a national costume of extraordinary charm: flowing skirt reaching to the floor, many lacy petticoats, colorful bodice, lovely shawl, high comb in her hair, and a bright ring on the middle finger of each hand.

"This is our Alicia," Don Alipio said proudly as he placed his arm around her, "our little China Poblana, and now she will explain to our guest from the north the legend of her beautiful dress." In a musical voice the child recited: "Many years ago on the Manila galleon that arrived in Acapulco came this beautiful Chinese lady, dressed as you see me tonight. She came as a slave, but she was so charming that everyone loved her and she married the king, and all the ladies at court had to dress the way she did. And today this is our national costume." Bowing to each of the couples, she curtsied to her mother and left the room.

"A few minor corrections," Don Alipio said. "We never had a king in Mexico since the time of Montezuma, and the ladies were not forced to dress like the Chinese slave. They wanted to, but Alicia was correct, that is our national costume for pretty women," and each of the Palafox wives confessed that even till this day they kept as treasures the China Poblanas they had worn as young girls.

I have spent more time than I probably should have in writing about this evening, and especially the party dress of an eight-year-old girl, but that particular dress became one of the cherished treasures of my family, and Jubal, not an emotional man, wrote shortly before he died: "I was twenty-four that night I dined with the Palafoxes, and I confess I was struck by the peaceful character of their handsome home. They scarcely knew there had been a war."

That night as he tried to sleep in his room at the House of Tile, he lay awake trying to decipher why the Palafoxes were being so atten-

tive. He did not have to wait long for an explanation because the next day the three men who'd
been at dinner came to the hotel and suggested
that he ride with them out to the Mineral, and
when they arrived at the site he had wanted to
revisit, they began to explain how this precious
property, which they owned, could be converted
into one of the world's top mines with the injec-
tion of substantial amounts of American money
and especially engineering skills.

A man whom he judged to be Don Alipio's
brother kept hold of Clay's arm as he explained:
"It's not just money we need, but machines, too.
They make fine ones in Sweden, I'm told. But
above all, we need bright young men like you.
Am I correct that you studied mining?"

"I learned trying it on my land in Virginia, after
reading books sent from England and Germany."

"Is that why your general sent you out here?
Is he a bright man, can he understand a business opportunity when it stares at him?"

Clay replied: "General Scott holds businessmen in contempt," and the Mexicans laughed:
"Like our generals, and what fools they are."

In less than an hour the Palafoxes had shown
Grandfather the entire surface structure of the
Mineral, indicating which buildings and pro-
cesses would be replaced if funds were availa-

ble, and then they asked: "Suppose you were in charge? What would you do?" and Clay said: "Around the entrance to the mine I'd build a stone wall, maybe three feet high, with a gate though which you'd get to the shaft."

"Why would you do that?"

"I like to see things neat. No, what I mean is, there are always certain things that ought to be done, just for their own sake."

The Palafoxes asked: "Would you be willing to go down again?" and Clay said: "I would indeed. That's why I wanted to come. This place is magical," and on the descent he watched carefully to see if he could detect which of the hundreds of stone steps ought to be recut.

In the bottom cavern he saw, as if they were old friends, the donkeys, the Indian men working at the face, the women hefting baskets of ore, the high ceiling and the beginning of the shaft that would take the miners down to where the next cavern would be excavated. As he explored the present one and saw the rude beds used by the men who preferred not to climb back to the top each night, he began to contemplate seriously the improvements a real mining engineer would probably undertake, and he asked one of the Palafoxes: "How difficult would it be to square the sides of the shaft?"

"You mean, all the way down?"

"Yes. It's one of those things that ought to be done."

"You'd better ask him." The man indicated the Spanish engineer, but Don Alipio said firmly: "That one knows nothing," so there was no answer to Clay's question.

"Well," Clay continued, "if the shaft was squared off and we found an engine of some kind, and I'm sure they make them in England, you could have a long rope and a cage at the end, and you could haul the ore up to the smelter."

"What would be the advantage?"

"Well, these women, they wouldn't have to climb up and down those—"

"They've done it all their lives, Captain. That's how they live—I mean, earn their living. If you did it with a machine from England, how would they live?"

On the climb up, Jubal had an opportunity to inspect at eye level each step as he approached it. At the top he told the Palafoxes: "I saw four steps that ought to be recut," and one explained: "We keep careful watch, and if something bad happens, we're there that afternoon."

Grandfather stayed in Toledo three weeks, making excursions out into the country, and on one he came upon Valley-of-the-Dead, from which the Altomecs had launched their conquest of the Drunken Builders, and he appreciated what an enticing sight the buildings of Toledo must have been in 1151, when the strangers swept in to take control. He also visited the Palafox bull ranch again, and twice more he climbed to the top of the pyramid, trying to visualize the fearful things that had occurred there. But most of all he frequented the central plaza, with its fine buildings, and the splendor of this colonial city was impressed in his mind.

When it came time to say good-bye to the Palafoxes, they said they hoped he would report favorably to the general, and he promised he would. He bade farewell to each of the Palafox women, and then saw little Alicia, to whom he bowed deeply: "Farewell, Señorita China Poblana," and he was off.

On the ride back to Mexico City his troops ran into trouble, not from the Mexican army, which had been instructed to honor his safe conduct, but from the bandits who infested all highways and who had learned that an attack on an American unit, while risky, produced rich rewards. About ten miles past Querétaro, where wealthy travelers were often spotted on their way to the capital, the bandits struck, and for nearly half an hour there was heavy firing, but Jubal and the petty officer in charge of the cavalry so ably kept their men under control that the sorties were repulsed with two bandits dead and no Americans killed. It had been a spirited fight, for which Clay would earn another commendation and a medal.

Upon his return to the office he occupied with the other aides he found General Scott in pitiful condition. Still convinced that everyone was plotting against him—and many in fact were—he had ordered the arrest of three of his subordinate generals, including President Polk's personal spy, the infamous General Pillow; but they in turn had brought charges against him. The liberal Democrats in Washington, seeing a chance to spike Scott's conservative Whig ambitions for the presidency, ordered the charges against the three generals dropped, while those against Scott were to be prosecuted with a general court-martial. Clay helped Scott write his protest to headquarters: "Never has a general accomplished so much with so little and in reward has been so savagely abused and humiliated by his superiors."

In later years when Clay told this story he would conclude: "And I wanted to add my postscriptum: 'You ought to be ashamed of yourselves to treat a general this way,' but when I tried to say this to the general himself, he brushed me aside: 'It's what happens when politicians try to direct wars.' "

My grandfather told one more story about his duty with Scott: "At breakfast on the morning I was to leave, Scott was under a kind of military arrest. Charges that he had stolen funds or something like that, and when it came time to say good-bye he said: 'You know, Clay, I never intended being a soldier. Back in 1807 I was admitted to the bar and considered my course in life well set. But I had barely started when the British frigate *Leopard* committed an outrage against our ship *Chesapeake.* I heard about it late in the evening, and that night, with no sleep, I bought a fine charger, rode twenty-five miles in the dark, and borrowed the uniform of a tall trooper. At sunrise I offered myself as a volunteer to a cavalry unit.

" 'I never looked back, Clay, and when this mess is cleared up, which I'm sure it will be, I propose to be the chief officer of the United States military forces.'

" 'How could that be?' I asked in amazement, and he said: 'Because if they have any sense they'll see that I'm the best man available—by far. And they'd have to choose me.' And it happened just as he said. When our Civil War broke out, he was placed in charge of all Union forces, and he did a brilliant job of establishing the great design that defeated us. Three hundred and fifty pounds, subject to fainting fits, suspicious of everyone and hated as few military men have ever been, he was the architect of Union victory, and as a Confederate fighting against his strategy, I cursed every time his name was mentioned."

In the thirteen years between 1848, when he left Mexico, till 1861, when he became intensely concerned about the efforts of the Northern politicians to deprive Southern planters like himself of their right to own and work slaves, Jubal Clay lived a happy life on Newfields, his cotton kingdom northeast of Richmond. Now most of his family's two thousand acres had been cleared of trees that had once formed a part of the Wilderness; carefully cleaned and graded, his cotton was drawing top prices in Liverpool, his slaves were passive again after creating minor disturbances fomented by Northern radicals, and he and Zephania, with their two boys and a girl, lived the stately life of Virginia planters. At home they entertained the gentry of their district and participated in musical evenings in which Jubal's mother, in her seventies, played the piano while Zephania played the cello, an instrument she was still learning to play, and he the flute. Among the neighbors were several fine voices, both male and female, so that varied concerts of high quality could occasionally be offered the neighbors in the county.

But the highlight of any month came when Jubal and Zeph, as everyone called his wife, drove into Richmond for the richer social life there. On these occasions the Clays saw Southern culture at its best. Businessmen trained in the fine universities of the North mingled with religious and political leaders educated at William and Mary or Tom Jefferson's University of Virginia. But any Richmond gathering carried a somber, stabilizing influence exerted by the military men who had been trained at West Point. These were men of honor, who, in those excitable years, were already grappling with some of the gravest dilemmas a man can face: Do I owe my allegiance to the army at whose headquarters I was trained or to my home state, which nurtured me and instilled in me the scale of values to which I subscribe? At one informal meeting in 1860 a colonel named Longstreth who had served in the Mexican War with two junior officers he admired told Clay's social group: "I knew no finer Virginian than young Robert E. Lee, a West Point man devoted to the army, but also a staunch Virginian. If trouble comes, and I'm increasingly sure it will, he'd face a difficult choice. Fight for the North or the South? But I

also watched another type, an aggressive, almost uncivilized lout from some Western state,
name of Grant—he was also West Point—and
I'm sure he'd remain with the North. I liked Lee,
disliked Grant intensely for his lack of any culture whatever, but judged they'd each be honest
military men according to their different lights."

This concept of two men, each a graduate of
West Point, heading in two radically different
directions, and each with ample justification,
fascinated Clay: "Maybe men like me were luck-
ier. We didn't go to West Point to absorb Northern ideas. We stayed home and sharpened our
Virginia, Carolina and Georgia loyalties, then got
our military training on the field, in Mexico. Our
choice is a lot simpler. Let the North make one
false move against us, and it's war."

"Do you expect it?"

"No. I see quite clearly that the commercial
interests of both North and South require a prolonged period of peace." Several in the group
agreed, with one planter named Anderson making an interesting observation: "Of the two nations"—here he pondered the appropriateness
of that term—"yes, I do believe we've become
two nations, whether we wanted it that way or
not, but of the two, the South has far more to
gain by an extended period of peace than the
North."

This differentiation was far from self-evident to most of the listeners, all ardent partisans of the South, and one planter argued: "You'll have to explain that, Anderson. Seems to me that our position, what with our command of cotton, which Europe must have, is secure."

"No," Anderson countered. "The true situation is that each day of peace we have a chance to grow stronger relative to the North."

"Good God, man! Are you trying to argue that the North is stronger than us?"

"Sir, I've said that the present drift of peace is all in our favor. But only a madman would argue that as of the present we're as strong as they are."

This unpatriotic reasoning exasperated the planter: "Anderson! Look at the balance sheet. We've got twice as much money from Europe as the North does. Our financial structure is much sounder, and our system of management and control is superior. We're in a favorable position financially."

Anderson, a studious man in his fifties, had traveled in the North and could not be dislodged from conclusions that he had judiciously developed: "A nation's survival capability is not measured by deposits in a bank. Factories are what count, miles of railway line, shops in cities, and above all, the number of men of fighting age that can be called upon."

"None in the North have men that can fight like ours," another planter argued, to which Anderson replied: "True, but fifteen men who can keep coming at you, one after another as required, must overwhelm the one trained rifleman."

"Now, that's a dangerous theory, brother Anderson," a man in his thirties said. "I signed up yesterday to lead a company in case trouble starts."

"So did I," Anderson said, and the men laughed at the thought of a fifty-year-old volunteering for active duty, but Anderson explained: "I'll be training our young men in military tactics, how one properly trained Southern boy with his good rifle, revolver and saber can hold off fifteen Northerners—for a while."

On the ride back to the plantation that evening Jubal Clay found persistent images forming in his brain: "Trains, factories, unlimited numbers of men. And those figures growing larger every day. Hell, we don't even have a train heading northeast out of Richmond, and won't have one for another ten years." As he plunged into the Wilderness other images appeared: 'New men up there, as he said, piling out of every boat from Europe. No training, no traditions. But there they come. And down here? Half of our men are black and they don't count. More important, they can't be counted upon." As he broke out of the Wilderness and saw the neatly tended boundaries of Newfields, its image superseded all others: "This plantation is what the fight will be about—supposing it comes. An orderly way of life in which a family can grow."

He had always been pleased with the name the old Clays had given their plantation, Newfields, rather than some classical name like Sparta or one like The Oaks or The Pillars. He could picture his ancestors girdling the last tree, pushing it over when it died, lopping off the branches, burning them around the fallen trunk and scattering the fertilizing ashes over the newly formed field. "It must have been exciting," he said to himself as he approached the big house, "to see a new field come into life and to know that it did so through your work. But the delight in seeing that first crop of cotton white as far as you could see on what had once been black forest! That's what a man lives for."

When he reached the portico, gleaming white in the moonlight, he turned his horses over to the Negro groom and hurried immediately to his office, sat in a big chair at his knee-hole desk and rang for the maid: "See if Mrs.

Clay can join me." As he waited for his wife the persistent images returned: "Factories, railroads, men, slaves, fifteen against one." Staring at the walls of his office he thought: From this desk the Clays before me built our little kingdom. They cleared the land, planted the cotton, bought the slaves and handled them properly, found the markets and educated their children. It's inconceivable that I would commit mistakes that would destroy all they accomplished. Nor shall I."

When his wife joined him she immediately asked: "What happened in Richmond?" for she had learned that when Jubal invited her into his study rather than joining her in the pleasant sewing room, she could be sure that matters of gravity were involved.

"Zeph, take the easy chair. This could be a long one."

"Is this about those fields we wanted to buy?"

"I'm talking about all Virginia. The entire South. Maybe the nation itself."

"Jubal, what are you saying?"

"It was one of those questions that cut to fundamentals. A military man, I think he was, talked seriously about North and South. Pointed out that they have the factories to produce weapons and gunpowder. They have the railroads to move them quickly here and there. And they have almost unlimited men to press these advantages."

"But who says we're going to have a war?"

"It seemed to me, Zeph, that all the men at the meeting thought so, and if each had felt free to speak his mind, I do believe that most would have warned: 'The South cannot win, in the long run, if the war drags on, and if the Northern advantages are applied with relentless pressure.' "

"Then why have a war?" He had always appreciated the ground-level common sense with which his wife approached any difficult problem: "If prospects are so bleak for our side, why fight? Can't the differences be reconciled?"

"No! Flatly, no! Those in the North have put themselves in a self-righteous position from which they cannot retreat and save face."

"Is the same true about us?"

"With me it is. I can't agree to a situation in which one day we have two hundred slaves worth a fortune and the next day none and no way to keep this plantation functioning. You simply cannot ask men who have spent their lives building—"

"So you too think war's inevitable?"

"No," he said reflectively, "as traditions in our family affirm, I don't want war. I want to see a rational solution." But then he made a state-

ment I've heard members of the Clay family repeat a score of times in this century: "But if they
threaten your entire way of life you've got to do
something."

They continued all that night, if I understand
correctly from the notes Jubal left, to discuss
the serious problem of how they would function
as a family if Jubal had to volunteer to help fight
a war: "I'm thirty-seven and entitled to major's
rank in the Virginia Third. You're thirty-four and
the ablest woman I know—in all fields. When I
went off to war in Mexico you managed—"

"But this would be a real war, wouldn't it?"

Recalling the fight at Chapultepec, he told
her: "Any war is real. A skirmish of three against
six is real," and this brought him to a major
concern: "If the North is as strong as they say,
and if we're as good fighters as we know we are,
this could be a long war. As years pass—"

"Years?" her voice trembled and said what
he had been afraid to mention: "Our boys would
be old enough . . ." and he nodded. Their older
boy, Noah, was seventeen; his brother, Paul,
fifteen. If the war dragged on, with the North
always throwing in more men, the South would
have to call upon boys as they neared manhood. This realization altered everything.

Zephania spoke first: "Rock-bottom truth.
You think war's inevitable?"

"Yes. Those in the North are determined and we Southerners are resolute. Result? War."

"And you think we would lose?"

"I can't say this to any man—it'd sound like cowardice, but I can tell you the truth. We'd run a great risk."

The Clays sat silent and brooding. When the sun rose, she coughed before starting anew. "Did the men think a war, if it happened, might reach down here?"

"We didn't discuss that. Didn't even mention it."

"Let's think about it. Could the war reach down here?"

"In Mexico I learned one thing. If General Santa Anna starts his war in Texas he must consider the possibility that it will end up in his capital at Mexico City, six hundred and fifty miles farther south."

"Our troops would never let them reach as far as Richmond, surely not."

"Our troops won't want them to reach that far, just as their troops would not expect us to reach New York. But once you cry havoc and let slip the dogs of war you cannot predict at whose house they will bay."

"Oh, Jubal, that's too horrible to contemplate."

"But we *are* contemplating it, and I see this as

our probable future. There will be a war. Those Northerners will insist on it. I shall volunteer, maybe within the week, and then we're in till the end. You've already proved you can run New- fields, so long as the slaves do not take this as an opportunity to rebel. In due course Noah and Paul will be in uniform, which means that you and Grace—she'll be old enough to help—must hold our little kingdom together. And when the war ends, we reassemble in peace and do our best to make up for the time we've lost." After a moment's silence he said: "The fields will need clearing of brush. It does sneak in, you know, if left untended for a while."

The war did come as Jubal Clay had foreseen, but to his surprise it was triggered not by some insolent act of the North but by Southern hot- heads firing on a United States fort in Charles- ton, South Carolina. From that moment there were two flags, the Stars and Bars and the Stars and Stripes; two names, the Confederacy and the Union; and two groups of fighting men, Johnny Reb and Yank.

As expected, Jubal Clay reported for duty as a major in the Virginia Third and quickly became what I called in my wars a light colonel. During the early years of the war he seemed to be fighting incessantly, but since most of the fighting occurred in what was called the Peninsula Campaign, he was often engaged in fights defending Richmond, so that he was on familiar terrain in areas like Mechanicsville and Gaines' Mill. This meant that he sometimes arranged to sneak home to see Zephania and the children. On such trips he repeatedly said: "It's going to be a long war. We're outnumbered badly, but one of our men trained in country shooting is worth six of their raw recruits straight from some overcrowded city, so in the end we have a chance to win."

As he had anticipated, by the end of the second year both his sons had been called to duty. At a trivial skirmish, associated with the great Confederate victory at Chancellorsville, of which the official report said: "We repulsed the Union forces while suffering only minor losses," a loss that was not minor to the Clays was the death of Noah. At another Confederate victory, about which the commanding general said: "Our losses were at the acceptable level," the Clay's younger son, Paul, was among those slain.

Now when Jubal managed a few days at the plantation his task was to console Zephania over the loss of her sons, but she would talk only about the problems of life on the plantation:

"The Northern warships blockade our ports so fiercely that no cotton can be shipped to Europe. Slaves run away to join the Northern armies. Grace's school has closed." Never would she speak of her lost sons, and the loving communication that had always existed between husband and wife perished with the war.

In early May 1864 it was clear that Butcher Grant, as many Confederates called him, intended muscling his way by brute force straight down the peninsula from the Potomac River south of Washington, fording the Pamunkey and Chickahominy rivers and stabbing the heart of the Confederacy by capturing Richmond. If he followed that route his troops would pass close to the Clay plantation but, more important, would then try to penetrate the Wilderness. When Clay heard that and visualized the impenetrable Wilderness he knew, he cried: "That would be insane. Impossible to march an army through there. Scouts couldn't make it," but when he tried to assure the Confederate command that they must have misinterpreted Grant's intentions, they told him: "Maybe we did, but here he comes, straight for the Wilderness." And when they showed him their maps, he understood their next orders: "You know the area, Colonel Clay. Take all your men, get the best engineers you can find, muster the back-woodsmen and make this vital crossroads impossible to attack," and a big forefinger jabbed at a spot Clay knew well, less than eight miles from his home, the insignificant inland settlement with the curious name of Cold Harbor, only ten miles from Richmond and guarding the entrance to that capital.

Clay and a cadre of officers who had hunted the Wilderness as boys and young men borrowed from other units any soldiers who knew the area, and they in turn conscripted woodsmen in their fifties and sixties to help them erect around Cold Harbor a defensive network that could be breached only by piling dead Union soldiers six deep and marching over them. And even when that was accomplished, the surviving invaders would still have to fight hand to hand from below as they looked up into the faces of thousands of Confederate troops armed with the weapons they knew best: rifles, pistols and long knives. If Grant attacked Cold Harbor, he would be sending his men into certain annihilation.

But that was still not enough margin for Clay, so when he judged his ground defenses to be truly impenetrable, he wheeled into position as many cannon as he could muster and placed each one so that it commanded a different approach to the final line of breastwork trenches. No Union soldier would approach Cold Harbor without facing cannon fire from at least three angles, and the cannon would be firing explosive shells filled with a lethal mixture of rusty bolts, bits of iron, lengths of chain, lead pellets and even shards of broken glass.

When I say "impenetrable" I am not referring to these mechanical horrors. I mean that the Wilderness woodsmen, without orders from Clay, had converted the entire area that would have to be traversed into a natural death trap, an abatis, a French word my grandfather did not know, nor did I when I first heard it. An abatis, devised by European peasants to obstruct the lord's cavalry, consisted of bending strong saplings forward into a woven impediment and then with a sharp ax slashing each sapling so that it presented a daggerlike point that could pierce a man through his belly or a horse in one of his four legs.

At twilight on Thursday, June 2, 1864, Colonel Clay, in surveying the defensive works for which he had been responsible, noted with grim satisfaction that all was ready. There were the nine cannon to rake the approaches, each field of fire interlocked with the others. There were the riflemen with their deadly fire. In front were the buried bombs that would explode if a foot touched them, and in front of all that was the abatis, its sharp spikes, hundreds of them, pointing straight at the invaders' bellies. And beyond, to the north along the route the Yankees would have to take if they wanted to march on their way to Richmond, lurked the Wilderness itself— its swamps, its mud, its tangled trees, its miasma, its oppressive June heat, its confusing trails that led back upon themselves. It was to this assignment that General Grant had sent his men with clear, crisp orders that allowed no hesitancy or misinterpretation: "At 0430 on the morning of Friday, 3 June inst. you will assault the defenses at Cold Harbor and secure it for the passage of our troops to Richmond."

In Confederate headquarters at a rough farmhouse behind the crossroads, Colonel Clay said as he lay down for a brief rest at three in the morning of June 3: "Not even Butcher Grant would dare try a frontal assault on what we have here. I pray that our flanks are prepared, because I'm sure he intends driving right at us to make us commit our troops, and then slipping off to the easier terrain on our left." As he said this he looked to the east, where he supposed Grant would veer, and uttered a short prayer: "Dear God, protect our men over there. They may have a very rough day." He had barely concluded this prayer when woodsmen who had been hiding in the Wilderness as scouts rushed into Cold Harbor by a hidden trail they had preserved for this purpose: "My God! They're marching straight at us!" and when Clay shinned partway up a tree to see whether this could possibly be true, he saw to his horror that Grant's troops, in gallant battle formation, were heading directly for the abatis and the interlocking fire of the nine great cannon.

In the first eight minutes of that June morning, three thousand Yankees died. In the next half hour, when the second wave pushed forward over the dead bodies of their comrades, five thousand more died, with not one of Colonel Clay's Confederates dead. Four hours later, at nine in the morning, Butcher Grant issued new orders: "The entire front to resume the attack," but when these insane words reached the line commanders they refused to accept them, even at the risk of suffering grave personal penalties.

Clay, barely a hundred yards from the Yankee lines, heard an enthusiastic Yankee blow his bugle for a massive charge right at the Confederate guns. "Dear Jesus!" Clay cried. "Don't let them!" and when no Yankees left their improvised trenches he wept.

———

It is generally held that one of the best accounts of Cold Harbor is the one my grandfather wrote when he was called back to Richmond to receive a decoration for his tremendous defense of Cold Harbor and I can do no better than to cite it here:

Richmond, 19 June 1864

My Darling Zeph:

I can scarcely believe that the horrifying events of the last few days took place only a few miles from where you and Grace were residing peacefully at Newfields. If my hand trembles in writing it's because I've not slept properly for six days nor washed for five. By the time this reaches you, you'll already know that we've handed the enemy a crushing defeat. Butcher Grant who boasted that he would ride roughshod over us has been knocked back with losses that must make even his savage brain stop and wonder.

When it became apparent that a significant battle might be shaping up about the insignificant crossroads you know so well, Cold Harbor in the Wilderness, General Lee gave me the task of seeing that our batteries were in position to rake a murderous cross fire through every approach, and I used the

Alabamans and Colonel Butler's Virginians to that purpose. . . .

Clay went on to tell his wife about the preparations he had supervised for the protection of the Confederate positions and the carnage they exacted. It's what Grandfather reported in his next paragraphs that has commanded the attention of historians and biographers:

Since the Union charge started at 0430 and lasted only half an hour, it must be clear that the destruction of the enemy troops occurred just before sunrise, which was fortunate timing, since that would allow the Union commanders to appeal for a truce, and this would allow them to leave their lines, come onto the battlefield and take back their dead and wounded, of which there were, lying about the field of fire, not less than a thousand, and my adjutant said, "More like two." If they were to be left out there when the blistering sun rose to bake and scorch them, their pain would quickly grow to agony.

I therefore ordered my men: "Hold your fire when the rescue teams appear," and they were more than ready to obey, because the slaughter they had perpetrated at point-

blank range was permissible under the circumstances, and by that I mean I agreed
with one of my men who said: "If they was
stupid enough to march right into our bullets
with no chance of firing back, they deserved
to die," but none on our side wanted to continue this awful killing. So we waited for the
Union stretcher-bearers to come out and
rescue their wounded. None came.

By ten in the morning the sun was beginning
to beat down with great force and men were
beginning to cry out for water, and medicine,
and stretcher-bearers, but none came. By
noon the heat was quite unbearable, even
for those of us under cover, and you must
understand, Zeph, that the wounded men
between the lines lay so close to our lines
that I could tell whether a fallen man with
no cap was either blond or brunet, and
had I known their names I could have
led to them. It was they who called to me:
"Please! Water! Help!" but there was nothing I could do.

I must explain why I was powerless to help
these poor men. The battle was still under
way. No Union general had applied for a

truce, nor was he likely to, because that would be admitting we had won, and this Grant refused to do. So as the sun went down on Friday the third, a date that will be remembered for our great victory, the wounded out in the field between the lines at last had some relief from the blazing sun. But now, in the cool of the evening when they had time to think, the dreadfulness of their condition became clear. They were to spend the night out on the ground that would gradually become cold, and damp with dew, and miserable, so they began pleading with both their companions to the east and their enemies to the west: "Water! For God's sake, water!" And all that night we heard their cries for the mercy we were powerless to provide.

Zeph, tears fill my eyes and I cannot describe the three days—Saturday, Sunday, Monday—with the sun hotter each long day, the ground more miserable at night and that incessant screaming of the Union men for help. One of my men, a farm boy from near Frederick, was so distraught by the cries— Zeph, they were only ten or fifteen yards away—that he disobeyed my orders and went into the field with a pail of water, but the

Union sharpshooters fired at him. I think they intended to miss, for he scrambled back to our lines. After that, our men shot at them if they tried to work in the field. And still Grant refused to sue for a truce.

On Monday night when the screaming became intolerable, we heard gunfire, and when I inspected with a throw-lantern I saw a Union soldier crawling from one fallen body to another and shooting the men whose badly wounded bodies were beginning to produce blood poisoning and horribly distended bellies. I did a terrible thing in throwing my light upon him, for when one of our men saw what he was doing, shooting his own companions, my man took aim and shot the Samaritan. . . . I can't go on.

Zeph, I'm writing later. Tuesday morning, after four days of this horror, Grant finally conformed to battle rules and asked for a truce, but even then he delayed action and it was past noon on a blistering day before the white flags appeared and the medical teams came out from the Union trenches to rescue the few who remained alive. I calculate that Grant's obstinacy in this affair accounted for an additional nine hundred deaths. And I hope there is a special hell for

such a man, one with great heat and no
water.

> With all my love,
> Jubal

The name Jubal at the end of the letter I've just
quoted prepares the way for an amazing coinci-
dence that would, in years to come, account for
perhaps the most dramatic event in my grandfather's life. The Confederate general in command of Lee's left wing in this gruesome battle
was Jubal Early, a crusty forty-eight-year-old
professional soldier from the Western back-
woods section of Virginia. A skilled cavalryman,
a veteran of many battles, most of them victories, he had watched his namesake Jubal Clay
perform superbly at Cold Harbor, and after the
battle sought out the younger man, who was
flattered to have attracted the attention of such
a grizzled veteran.

"They tell me," General Early said as he dismounted at Clay's temporary headquarters,
"that I'm about to set forth on an undertakin' of
some magnitude, and I would feel more secure
if I could have as one of my adjutants a man like
you." Before Clay could respond, Early added:
"You havin' that sizable plantation out there, I
presume you know how to ride."

"Yes, sir."

"Would you take it kindly if I were to ask General Lee to transfer you to my command?"

"Any Virginian would be proud to ride with you, sir—I especially. I've some scores to settle with Butcher Grant."

"You're the man I want," the general said, and in that informal way Jubal Clay was seconded to Jubal Early. Together they set forth on one of the great adventures of the Civil War, nothing less than an attempt to swing over into the Shenandoah Valley far to the west, gallop up that natural highway, reach almost to the Pennsylvania border, capture Harper's Ferry, and then swing sharply southeast in a mad attempt to capture Washington itself. Seven days after General Grant retreated from Cold Harbor, his tail between his legs, Clay was riding north with General Early to catch a train that would carry them to a pass through the low Virginia mountains. There they would dismount, ride through the hills and reach the Shenandoah, where large units of Confederate cavalry were waiting to start their daring dash north.

Then came the days of glory! Following the tracks of the great Stonewall Jackson, who in 1862 had rampaged up and down this valley, confounding the Union forces sent to destroy him, Early's troops marched into historic Winchester, capital of the Shenandoah, in majestic style one sunny afternoon when the entire population came out to cheer. In front, leading trim ranks of cavalry—"Handsome men in handsome uniforms riding handsome horses," one country editor wrote—came General Early, astride a white horse and resplendent in a uniform famous throughout the South: huge white felt hat adorned with a long snow-white turkey feather, a white coat made of a heavy imported fabric that reached to his ankles, fine boots, highly polished, and a natty gray uniform decorated with medals.

His foot soldiers were presentable, for although their uniforms were nondescript and some were tattered, they were clean from the washing given them by the women who followed such large troop movements, but as they marched, the people of Winchester unhappily noticed that many of the soldiers were boys not much past fifteen, and that an appalling number were barefoot.

The armed might of the parade left such a powerful impression on the watchers that a newspaper reported: "That army could proudly march through the Pearly Gates or storm the portals of Hell," but when the troops bivouacked at dusk, women from Winchester came bringing shoes they had taken from their menfolk.

North of Winchester, Colonel Clay was given the job of leading a work force to dynamite and otherwise destroy the track and bridges of the Baltimore & Ohio Railroad, a line so helpful to Northern troops moving back and forth that it was known as "Grant's cavalry." With cheers and poundings on the back, the Confederates watched as one bridge after another of the hated line twisted upward and fell back in ruins.

As the men tramped over the ground that Stonewall's men had traversed, sucking up vitality from each memorable step they took, they did more. They roared far north of Washington, captured Harper's Ferry and swung east to do battle with the Union general, Lew Wallace, whom they defeated roundly. On July 10, a month after Cold Harbor, the two Jubals, victorious in a score of battles and skirmishes, actually invaded Washington itself. True, it had been done through the backdoor, the extreme northwest corner, but it was a foothold and Clay went to bed believing that when they marched out of the city they would be taking Abraham Lincoln with them as prisoner and that the war would be over. The vision was not extreme, for earlier that afternoon when Clay had directed his sharpshooters to knock off Union troops manning a fort near the Confederate lines, his men had focused their attention and their sights on the

Union soldiers, ignoring the tall civilian who stood with them. It had been President Lincoln, come to see personally whether or not his troops could hold off this bold thrust of General Early. Clay and Lincoln had been no more than thirty yards apart.

But the Union generals reacted too swiftly, and threw into the defense of Washington too many fresh troops for even Jubal Early to think of actually capturing the city. He had to withdraw lest he lose his cavalry, and from the first encampment on the retreat, Clay wrote to his wife:

Darling Zeph,

We've had an unbroken chain of victories. You'd have been proud of me on horseback with General Early. We reached Washington and threw a fearful scare into the Union government, and then I led an excursion into Pennsylvania, where I invested the important town of Chambersburg. I warned them that they must pay indemnity for the savage manner in which they burned the homes of peaceful citizens favorable to our cause. I demanded $25,000 of them, and when they insolently refused to pay, I burned the town.

His wife never received the letter, for when he left his command at Cold Harbor to ride with

General Early, word passed among the Union
solders: "Clay was responsible for those shells
filled with chain and pointed stakes that
wounded so many of our men." They said also:
"And who shot at us when we tried to rescue our
dying men? Clay." As they withdrew from the
field where they had lost so many in so few
minutes, a rage consumed them and when
someone learned that Clay owned the plantation they were passing, infuriated soldiers, ignoring commands from their own officers, dashed
down the line and torched it.

Zephania and her fourteen-year-old daughter
were in the house when the Union men fired
through the windows. The girl ran out out of the
house as soon as the flames started, but her
mother stubbornly refused to do so, remaining
behind to gather precious bits she could not
bear to lose. Disoriented, she even tried to
move the piano to protect it from the spreading
fire, so that when she finally did run for the door,
there was no escape route and she perished.

Her husband, now retreating from his foray
into Washington and his burning of Chambersburg, had to be constantly on the move, so that
no mail reached him with news from home. The
cause of this haste was the arrival in the Shenandoah of a brilliant young cavalryman as commander of the Union forces. Phil Sheridan's rise

from volunteer to general had been spectacular, and his great good luck in battle was proverbial. One of his first acts in the Valley was to pin Early's army down in Winchester, the city that had welcomed the Confederates only a few weeks before. At that time Early had been on his way north to stunning victories: now he was in retreat, seeking to preserve the life of his army and of himself.

Sheridan proved relentless, a determined, dogged killer, and when the fierce battle ended, Early had lost 40 percent of his army; Union losses had been heavy, too, but there was this profound difference: The Northern states could provide an endless supply of new recruits; the South had been drained. And Northern troops marched in bright new shoes designed especially for military use; many of Jubal Early's fifteen- and sixteen-year-old soldiers marched barefoot.

Then in quick succession came a chain of crushing defeats, with Phil Sheridan outsmarting Early repeatedly. The retreat ended one night with the two Jubals eating meager uncooked rations in the deserted schoolhouse of a small village where they could not escape reviewing the bleak situation of their beloved Confederacy. The general said: "We can still win. If we can move our troops down to help Lee defend Richmond, we can exhaust Grant. He's not much of a general, stand and punch." And Clay, his hatred for Grant intensifying with each battle lost, cried: "Isn't there some way we can strike at him direct?" and Early said grimly: "If we can make him come at us, as we did at Cold Harbor, we can wear him down." Clenching his fist, he repeated: "Wear him down! Wear him down!" But each man knew that it was their armies that were being worn down, although neither would admit it.

As they sat in near darkness, an aide delivered a batch of mail to the two officers, and when Clay sorted he found to his surprise that Zephania had not written, but one of the other letters from a neighbor explained why: "It is my sad duty to inform you that Union renegades burned Newfields to the ground. Zephania died in this blaze, but not your daughter, Grace, who is safe with us."

Dumbly he passed the letter along to the general, who read it in silence. Early had never married and believed that men fought best when not encumbered with wives. Repeatedly he refused his officers permission to leave ranks long enough to marry: "Do that when peace comes and your wife can stay with you," but out of respect for Clay's feelings he did not voice this opinion now.

"I've lost it all," Clay said more to himself than

to Early. "My sons, my wife, my plantation."
Such shattering loss was too much: "Oh, God!"
he cried, beating his forehead with both hands.
"This is unfair! Where is there reason in such
accumulation of sorrows?"

It was this conviction that an unreasonable
God had punished him too much and too un-
fairly that drove Jubal Clay into an intimate
friendship with General Jubal Early when the
latter was similarly abused in a crushing letter
from Robert E. Lee informing him that Early's
army was being taken from him and given to a
subordinate. The letter, dated 30 March 1865,
when the world was falling apart, contained
phrases that scalded the grizzled fighter.

> I deem a change of commanders in your
> department necessary. . . . Your reverses in
> the Valley have, I fear, impaired your influ-
> ence, both with the people and the soldiers.
> . . . I have felt that I could not oppose what
> seems to be the current of opinion. . . . I must
> find a commander who would be more likely
> to inspire the soldiers with confidence . . .
> thanking you for the courage and devotion
> you have ever manifested, I am your obedi-
> ent servant,
>
> R. E. Lee, General

The disconsolate pair, united by their hatred for General Grant and their determination to see the Northern forces humbled, staggered toward Richmond for a final defiance. General Early, no longer displaying his white hat with its turkey feather and his long coat, received a minor appointment to which Clay also reported so as to remain close to a man he increasingly admired. Jubal Early was a fighter, a man of honor, and for him to be abused by his own government because the North had the capacity to throw hordes of fresh troops against him was unfair and scandalous.

But Clay also clung to his general for a more personal reason. The linchpins of his life had shattered: He had lost his beloved wife, his stalwart sons, his home and now his national cause. All had vanished, except his daughter, who was adrift, and he had nothing except his honor and his determination to help Jubal Early fight somewhere, somehow. But he was relying upon a weak support, for Early was as bereft as he. But the general still retained an indestructible loyalty to the cause, for when General Lee surrendered the Confederate cause at Appomattox in April of 1865, Early and Clay refused to concede that the war was over. Rejecting the generous offer of parole that the North extended to Southern officers, they said bold and loud: "We're still at

war. We'll never surrender to Butcher Grant,"
and when they refused to take the pledge of
allegiance to what they called the Northern government, they became hunted fugitives. In the
garb of petty farmers they sneaked out of Virginia and, wandering the backroads and living
off the charity of Southern patriots, they crept
down through the Carolinas and Georgia and
westward through Alabama and Mississippi and
into Louisiana, where they hoped to join the
army of Confederate general Kirby Smith, who
was still fighting. But as they entered the state
they heard the sad news: "The general, he held
out as long as possible, last one in the field. But
when the North threw an entire army in to catch
him, he had to surrender. War's over, but we
gave 'em a good fight for it, didn't we?" and
Early grunted: "We did."

When the men asked: "Where you soldiers
goin' now?" Early said: "Texas. They know how
to fight down there," but the Louisiana men said:
"War's over there, too. It's over all through the
South. You'd better go home. Where is it?"

"We got no home," Early said. "Used to be
Virginia, but it's gone," and the two Jubals
drifted into Texas. One evening as they camped
along the Brazos River a local doctor who had
acquired one of the newfangled cameras asked
permission to take their pictures: "You're Con-

federate exiles, aren't you?" When Early said: "I guess you could call us that," the doctor posed them against the trunk of a Southern oak. The photograph found its way into a Texas historical society's collection and in the 1930s when someone was looking through the photos, now brown along the edges, he cried to the librarian: "This has got to be Jubal Early! He came through here," and there the fugitive stood: fifty years old, bearded, flowing cap gone, small one in place atop his balding head, Mexican-type cotton pants held up with a rope, cotton shirt, linen duster as a coat, and in his right hand a long white walking stick to aid him with his rheumatism. Beside him, in similar garb minus the linen duster and the little hat, stood Jubal Clay, lower jaw thrust out as if he dared General Grant to intrude. It's the only photograph of the two Jubals during their self-enforced exile, and it had, as court papers prove, an unintended consequence.

The doctor, proud of the fine work done by his new camera, posted the photograph on the wall of his waiting room, where it was seen by a man with a sharp eye: "Hello! They could be the fugitives that Northern officer is looking for," and when the man from Vermont who had the job of bringing federal law into the State of Texas—a carpetbagger, if you will—saw the photograph of General Early he cried: "That's them!" Eager to grab the reward that had been posted for the fugitives, he called upon the commanding officer of the Northern troops occupying that part of Texas and urged him to capture the Confederates.

The two Jubals would have been taken had not a Negro working as cleaner for the soldiers heard the orders and scurried out the back to the shack in which the two men were hiding. He knew they were Confederates, and he also suspected that they had come from his home state of Virginia, so he did not wish to see them taken by Northerners: "You best be headin' outa here, elsen they cotch you." By the time the Federals reached the area where the photograph had been taken, the two men were on their way to the port of Galveston, where they caught a steamer that smuggled them out of the United States to the Bahamas, the Virgin Islands and finally Cuba, where Early heard exciting news: "Mexico is in turmoil. Emperor Maximilian needs all the help he can get. He'd welcome a trained soldier like you, a general to boot." Early made a snap decision: "Clay, off we go to Mexico. Sooner or later they'll have to fight the United States again, and I want to help them when they do." Using what skimpy funds remained from gifts sympathetic Southerners had given him, he bought a big broad-brimmed hat and had a tailor make him a copy of his famous ankle-length white coat: "I will land in Mexico as a real general." But he was not able to persuade his partner to join him.

"I like Mexico," Clay said. "I see it as a country with a glowing future, but I have a daughter somewhere near Richmond, and I must care for her," so the two Jubals parted at shipside in a Cuban port, the general heading for Mexico, the colonel back to the risk of capture in the States. Theirs had been an adventure in Southern patriotism, and they made their farewells with dignity and mutual respect.

But General Early's invitation to Clay that he join him in Mexico had a mesmerizing effect on the Virginian, for as he worked his way carefully north from Texas to avoid capture, he began to have visions of that silver mine in Toledo, and the lonelier he became, a fugitive hunted on all sides, the more the mine became an obsession: "A man could find refuge there. . . ." And: "If a man found himself without a home, he could work in a mine and build himself a life." But he took no steps to convert that dream into reality, for Virginia called powerfully to him.

Clay's experiences in his defeated Southland were not pleasant. Landing at Savannah, he made his way quietly and in disguise through

Georgia and the Carolinas and into Virginia, at whose threshold he bowed his head in sorrow. As one who had obviously been a soldier who had helped defend the Confederacy, no questions were asked and he was helped by all who met him. In time he was back at Cold Harbor, where he surveyed the battlefield on which he had once played a significant role. Then he trudged the distance to where Newfields plantation had once stood, and there in grief, which swept over him like the fever of an ague, he could see in the ruins his wife, Zephania, as she went about her duties; he could hear the boys at play; he could visualize his daughter in a pinafore, and the house slaves at their chores. All gone, a way of life never to be recovered. From that moment of utter despair, Jubal Clay became a new human being, no longer a Southern planter, no longer a Confederate colonel. Instead, at forty-three, he became a man with ties only to his daughter—and even that cord would soon be brutally cut.

Making his way back to Richmond, he slipped undetected into his club, now fallen on hard times but still populated by his old business and military friends, who gave him a robust welcome when they discovered who he was: "Tell us about Cold Harbor and the defeat you slapped on Grant. How about General Early's gallant campaign up the Shenandoah? What happened to Early when he went into hiding after Appomattox?'' They were surprised and pleased to learn that Clay had remained loyal to Early until the general had escaped to Mexico.

Hearing of Early's latest action, all the members wanted to speak, for each had known some planter friend who had refused to remain in the new United States, where they were forbidden to own slaves and where their gracious way of life had been destroyed. A few had fled to Canada, but most had gone south to Mexico, which they called "a land where freedom is still respected."

"Did you hear that Jake Tomlin has decided to take the jump south?"

"I can believe it. His friend Adams sent back a heartening letter. Land for almost nothing. And thousands of Indians eager to work for almost nothing."

"Did you know that Henry Bailey has moved his cotton handling office to Veracruz? Shipping to his same customers in Liverpool, but now it's Mexican cotton."

"Jubal, I remember that you served with General Scott in Mexico. How did you find it?"

With unexpected vitality, memories of those years in '47 and '48 came tumbling back: "It was a real country, not at all like we used to think. Some of its cities, away from the war, were quite habitable."

"Did you have a chance to see any of them?"

He started to tell of his visit to Toledo but judged it would be tedious to explain why he had been investigating a silver mine.

A man asked: "Would you consider emigrating there? Like the others?"

"I had a chance to go with General Early. I love Virginia. When I get my name cleared, I'd want to work here—rebuild—get things going again."

"You should, Clay," one of the members said. "You're a real hero and we need you." Then he repeated: "A real hero. You must be amazed at what's happened with your daughter."

Clay leaned forward: "What did? I've been looking for her."

"After the fire . . . some of us buried your wife, Jubal . . . the girl came here to a family in Richmond, where I saw her often, a true Southern belle, an honor to our people, and to you, Clay."

"What happened?"

"When the North took over our government they sent down a handsome young man from West Point, a lieutenant, and he worked in the governor's office, that is, their government, not ours. He was a bright fellow, good manners, treated us with respect while some of his seniors from the North were real bastards."

"And then?" Clay asked, afraid to hear the answer.

"Yes, they fell in love. He was invited to all the parties, such as we could afford, and he was widely liked. An excellent young man, except his war background, and they were married."

"Married?" He said the word with such force that for some moments no one dared speak, but then a club member who had also fought at Cold Harbor said: "Young Shallcross served as Grant's aide at Union quarters on the Pamunkey."

For two days my grandfather could not bring himself to visit his daughter, although he was willing to risk capture to see the only remaining member of his family—and capture would be probable if he was identified by an official in the government of occupation. But his curiosity and love for his daughter were so great that on the third day he allowed his fellow officer from Cold Harbor to take him to the small house occupied by Shallcross and his bride. There he waited behind a tree while his guide knocked on the door, was greeted by a man Clay could not see, and entered. Inside, as the man explained later, he arranged a truce of honor: "Captain Shallcross, you know me, Major Abernethy, reprieved by your government."

"Of course, Major. What can I do for you?"

"I know, here in Richmond, where a Confederate officer is hiding who is not reprieved." At these ominous words Shallcross held up both hands: "We no longer hound patriots, misguided though they were. I don't want to hear any more."

"Former Confederates are arrested daily," the major snapped, and Shallcross said: "If they force themselves upon us, if they have criminal records."

"I think you will want to see this one, but I must ask your word of honor once you have seen each other that he can leave freely."

"You didn't need to creep to my house to extract such a promise. Granted." The two soldiers shook hands, whereupon the major went back to the door and signaled. In a moment Jubal Clay edged suspiciously into the small room and stood facing his son-in-law. When neither man spoke, the major said: "Captain Shallcross, I have the honor to present Colonel Clay, late of the Virginia Third."

Shallcross flushed, hesitated, then extended his hand: "You are welcome here, Colonel. I'll call your daughter." In a moment Grace Clay Shallcross entered the room—an elfin girl of sixteen with a waist so small a man could encircle it with his hands. She was, thought Clay, in that first moment of seeing her after three years of painful absence, the kind of woman who would keep the South alive and functioning, for defeat had not touched her, and he saw her as a creature of inestimable worth. But as the four of them sat and talked he felt a hardness supplanting his first sensations of love.

"How was it your mother didn't escape, too?"

"She wanted to save her piano. The men tried to drag her away, but she wouldn't go and finally they had to flee, because of the smoke." She hesitated then added: "We thought that maybe she wanted to die . . . the boys gone . . . the house . . . and maybe you had been killed in the Valley defeats."

"When she died we were still winning. We were in Washington." His voice hardened not against his daughter but against the man she had married. Pointing at Captain Shallcross he asked: "Is it true that he served as General Grant's aide at Cold Harbor?"

Shallcross did not propose to have his young wife answer for him: "I was there, as you were, Colonel Clay. We had great regard for your performance that day. I heard General Grant say so."

"Regard for me? Did he have no regard for his

own troops? That he left them dying out there in the blazing heat?"

Aware that this line of interrogation must end in verbal brawling, Captain Shallcross said: "Colonel, I am honored to have a wonderful woman like your daughter for my wife. And had you been available at the time, I would have come to you as one man of honor to another to ask for her hand. I pray that you will grant it now." Extending his hand, he moved slightly toward Clay.

"For an agonizing moment," reported the ex-Confederate who had arranged this meeting, "the two men looked at each other, Shallcross almost pleading, Clay with growing bitterness, at the end of which he said darkly: 'I must leave this contaminated house, and I shall never in this life see you again, Grace.' With that he stamped from the room."

Before he left Richmond, Clay went to a notary and signed a legal paper giving title to the two thousand acres of the former Newfields Plantation east of Cold Harbor to his daughter, Grace Clay, born on that site in 1850. After filing this with the registrar of such papers and asking that officer to advise her after he had gone, he returned to his lonely room, where he found awaiting him a letter that threw his plans into disarray:

My Dear Col. Clay,

I have heard through the Brackenridges of Richmond that in your despair over the death of your wife and the loss of your home you propose leaving the country. Surely, anyone who realizes the crushing losses you have suffered will understand your decision, and those like me know how you, more than most men, centered the better portion of your life upon the joys you knew with Zephania, your unequaled wife.

But, Jubal, I must remind you that there is a higher duty, and I beg of you to reconsider. Do not leave our homeland. It sorely needs you now. You are an engineer and command the skills we require for the rebuilding of our ravaged lands. There is so much work to be done that if we all labored 'til midnight for the rest of our lives we should barely accomplish a beginning. You above all are needed.

Therefore I implore you, and if I were still your general I would command you, to stay at home and commit yourself to the work at hand. If you plead, "I spent four years fighting the North, must I now help them rebuild what they destroyed?" I can only advise you that the wisdom of the Almighty oftentimes commands a man to do exactly the opposite of what he did ten weeks before, and if he defends his honor there will be no dishonor in obeying the dictates of One mightier than himself. I implore you to stay and work, for I am convinced that it is God's work we do.

But I am mindful of the oppression one suffers when one must live where a particular tragedy has overtaken him, so I want you to leave Cold Harbor and come to Lexington, where our faculty sorely needs your engineering and mathematical skills. You will find a new life instructing our young men whose duty it will be to rebuild the South, and I shall rejoice in having with me once more that dashing, reliable Colonel Clay.

> Yours quietly,
> Robert E. Lee

Reading the letter three times in his hunger to hear once more his commander's grave voice, he satisfied himself that Lee was offering him a teaching job at long-established Washington College, a school of good reputation, and the idea of working with Lee again was so exciting that any thought of sleep was ridiculous. Throwing a jacket over his shoulders, he walked out into the streets of Richmond, the city he had fought so diligently to protect, and the idea of separating himself from the gallant struggle brought tears to his eyes. He visualized Lee as the one man who had gone through four years at West Point without picking up a single demerit—Jubal Early had had nigh two hundred every year—Lee as the bright-eyed captain in Mexico, and, finally, Lee in defeat. It would not be easy to disassociate himself from such a man.

But suddenly the menacing image of Ulysses Grant took possession of his mind, and as it crowded out the gentle memories of Lee he cried aloud: "I cannot live in the same country with that man!" He ran to a friend's house, asked to purchase a horse, which was given him free, and as the sun appeared he rode quietly out of Richmond, still legally a fugitive and aware that never in this life would he again see his beloved city, or his revered commander, or his daughter.

16

AMERICAN ANCESTORS: IN MEXICO

WHEN MY GRANDFATHER landed at Vera-cruz in late 1866 and climbed the famil-iar road he had marched nineteen years earlier with General Scott as they fought their way to Mexico City, he anticipated no difficulty in locat-ing his friend General Early: "Stands to reason. If he's still in that big white hat with the turkey feather and that long white coat, everyone will know where he is." Using his adequate Spanish, he asked a watchman: "Where might I find American soldiers who came down here after our war?'' and the man pointed: "That little church. Many Americans drink there all day.''

When he entered the courtyard of the church, set off by a high adobe wall, he found the Confederates, and one look at the motley crew assured him that he had joined the losers. They were an unkempt lot, unshaven, unwashed, some of their clothes in tatters, but intermixed with that type were a few men of obvious breeding, men who could not tolerate living in a nation governed by men like Butcher Grant. Clay naturally gravitated toward those of his own kind but was prevented from joining them by the others, who showered him with questions: "What battles did you see? What generals did you march with? Did you have to leave America?'' Some rough types not only asked questions, they also demanded answers, and in their eagerness for news of home he detected loneliness and the fear that they might never again see their homeland.

He had to answer them: "I'm a Virginia man, the Yankees burned my plantation, killed my wife and sons. I'm like you. I could never live there with men like Grant in charge.'' The men felt empathy for Clay because all of them were without jobs and some had no money at all. "How do you expect to live, Reb?''

"I'm looking for a friend, When I left him in

Cuba, he told me to meet him here. He'd have something."

"Maybe we've seen him. What's he like?" and when Jubal mentioned General Early, the crowd broke into derisive joking: "Old Jube, got his ass kicked at Winchester, didn't he? When he come here he talked big, cursed Grant, swore he'd never go back, Mexico was his home now."

A wry-faced man from Tennessee with only one arm broke in: "Cut quite a figure with that big white hat and turkey feather, but after three months he told us: 'No sane man could live in this madhouse. They beg this fellow to come over from Europe and be their emperor, and he done a good job, they tell me. But now they want to get rid of him.'"

"General Early, what happened to him?"

"Hightailed it off to Canada. Said it was a decent country a man could respect."

"Did he have any money?" Clay asked, and one of the men said: "His brother, back in the States—he sends him some."

During the few days he was in the capital Clay learned of more than a hundred Confederates who were determined to make Mexico their home, and many of them were unlike the disgruntled drifters in the churchyard. These others had found work. Some had brought considerable sums of money with them or had access to

it through relatives back home, and Clay suspected that such men were going to build a
good life for themselves, especially if they were
able to get hold of property.

One such man from Georgia told him: "Mexicans hate the North just as much as we do. They
welcome us Confederate brothers. If we try to fit
in, they accept us." With a smile he added: "And
they understand our attitude toward our slaves.
Their Indians are about the same but they use
different words."

At the end of numerous similar discussions
my grandfather reached two conclusions, which
he often discussed with my father: "I saw that
Mexico welcomed us only if we had money or a
job, and I saw that neither was available in Mexico City. With that insight I headed for Toledo,
where I hoped the rich Palafoxes might remember me."

They did. When three Palafox men who had
attended that memorable dinner back in 1847
came to talk with Clay at the House of Tile, he
could see they were heavier about the middle
and grayer of hair, for that had been more than
nineteen years ago, and he thought: They, of
course, remember me as little more than a boy,
and now I'm a battle veteran and a fugitive with
lines in my face.

Don Alipio threw his bearlike arms about my

grandfather and cried: "I could see when he was here before that he was a Toledo man, and that one day he'd be back. Well, here you are, and now what?"

They did not waste time with Jubal. The brother who managed the family's money said bluntly: "Yes, nineteen years and we still don't have a decent manager at the Mineral. Señor Clay, destiny has brought you back to us. Can you ride out to the mine with us tomorrow? We seek your counsel." When the four men inspected the shaft—much deeper now but still operated by little Indian women climbing up those incredible stairs—and the smelter and the adobe warehouses, Jubal said: "It's obvious what ought to be done. You haven't even built the stone rim around the mouth of the shaft," and they said: "We talked about it, but our managers never seemed to understand."

Jubal, an honest man, one of the most incorruptible of that tormented period, could not misrepresent himself to the Palafoxes: "I have no plantation any longer, no wife, no children, no country." He paused, laughed and then concluded: "And damned little money. I need a job and I have a powerful feeling about this mine. Often during the war, and later, I thought of those caverns of silver."

A deal favorable to both sides was arranged

that first morning after his arrival in Toledo, but he had barely started the innovations that would preserve this as one of the premier mines of the world when he was diverted by the last thing on earth he needed, another war. One morning Don Alipio came galloping out to the Mineral: "Clay! You must come with us. We may need your skills." On the hurried ride back to town the fifty-eight-year-old man said with the eagerness of a nineteen-year-old: "Querétaro has sent an urgent message. They need all the troops we have. The damned Indians are threatening to shoot the emperor, and we mustn't let that happen."

At the churchyard in Mexico City the Confederate exiles had mentioned an emperor, but Jubal had not been listening: "Has the emperor done a bad job?"

"A splendid one. Exactly what our side wanted when we asked for him."

This sounded so improbable that Jubal asked: "I don't understand," and Don Alipio stared at him in disbelief to think that a learned man from the next country had not even been aware of the tremendous change that had occurred in next-door Mexico: "Didn't you hear? The liberals were making such a mess of this country after you and General Scott left that some of us, men like my brothers and me, from all over Mexico, sent a delegation to the emperor of France—I was a member—and we asked him to find a young prince of good character to come to Mexico as our impartial emperor. He made a handsome choice, Maximilian, royal house of Austria. I was on the committee of three who went to Vienna to offer him the crown. He took it and he and his Empress Carlota, the Belgian princess, have given our country just what it needed, stability."

Clay's mentor wished to explain further but apparently decided that no norteamericano could ever understand Mexican politics, for he shrugged and concluded: "Now they want to shoot him, the best man we ever had."

In Toledo he found more than a hundred militiamen gathered before the cathedral in the plaza, including five other members of the Palafox family, all mounted on sturdy horses. Since Querétaro, known as the western protector of that capital, lay some seventy miles east of Toledo, the informal expeditionary force would require at least two days to reach their target, so a hastily put-together line of mules and their Indian drivers had been converted into a quasi-military train that would bring along tents and food and extra ammunition. Jubal, finding himself by accident part of a military exercise, thought, General Early would never do it this way, on the spur of the moment, but before he could protest to anyone, the Toledo force rode out to rescue their emperor.

The railroad, which had probed into many corners of Mexico, built with English and French money, had not yet reached Toledo, so the dirt road east was maintained in fairly good condition. But even so, by the end of the first long day, Jubal was exhausted, though the Palafox men appeared to be in top condition. As dusk fell, Clay was initiated into a long-established custom of the Mexican military unit. When the troops began to bivouac, a score of peasant women mysteriously emerged with clay pots and a collection of sticks, and before long the preparation of a hot meal of beans, tortillas and shreds of spicy meat was under way. Some of the women had come all the way from Toledo on donkeys, others had joined as the troops rode through their villages; they were the soldaderas, the hangers-on without which no Mexican army could function.

The Palafox expedition, as it was being called, approached the western outskirts of Querétaro on the afternoon of 18 June 1867, but there they were halted by a contingent of heavily armed Indians commanded by an officious white colonel from the southern city of Oaxaca who ordered the invaders to halt. When Don Alipio reined in his horse, the colonel warned him: "No armed troops allowed in the city tomorrow."

"Whose orders?"

"Benito Juárez."

Don Alipio did not spit at the mention of the hated name, but Clay could see that he clearly wanted to. "Are you from Oaxaca?" and when the colonel nodded, Alipio grunted: "I thought so. They're really going to shoot the emperor?"

"The court-martial has condemned him. For the welfare of Mexico."

"Must we remain outside the city?"

"You must."

The Palafox expedition thus came to a halt. But the idea that a decent man like the Austrian archduke, who had labored so diligently to ingratiate himself with the Mexican people, should be executed by a gang of Indians from Oaxaca was so offensive that Don Alipio, who felt responsible for Maximilian, having persuaded the young man to accept the imperial crown, suggested to Clay: "Are you willing to slip through the lines as a private citizen with no weapons?"

"Of course, but for what purpose?"

"To see what's happening."

"What could we do about whatever we do see?"

Don Alipio looked at him as if he were an imbecile: "Do! We give a grave man consolation—that we were there in his moment of agony. Come!" The two men, grabbing a handful of tortillas and leaving their big guns behind, left the guarded highway, slipped along the darkened edge of town, watched for pickets and slipped into the sleeping city. Working their way to the central area, they remained inconspicious until Don Alipio found a way to accost a soldier without arousing suspicion: "Where will it happen?"

"They say they're bringing him to that wall."

"Are you one of the firing squad?"

"They never tell us." Then suspiciously: "Is this one a norteamericano?"

"Came here after the war up there. Citizen of Mexico now."

"Bad war?" the sentry asked, and when Jubal nodded, the man said: "They're all bad."

They slept that night on the steps of a Querétaro church, and well before dawn they became aware of activity within buildings nearby. A troop of soldiers, perhaps fifty, marched out and took positions around a large square, not the central plaza, and with their rifles parallel to the ground they began pushing anyone who had come to see the execution well back of where the shooting would occur.

When the sun was up, officials of various types scurried about the plaza exchanging assurances that all was moving ahead as planned, and three times the group with which Don Alipio and Jubal stood was pushed farther back until the don asked a soldier: "Where can we stand without being moved here and there?" and the young man, assessing Alipio as an important figure, took him to a place cordoned off from the general public. There they waited, and when the June sun was high, so many people started running about at once that Don Alipio whispered: "Now."

From a nearby barracks a troop of a dozen soldiers, neatly uniformed, marched out with long rifles and took a parade-rest posture facing a wall constructed of big stones fitted together by artistic masons in years past. With the arrival of the firing squad, Jubal realized that an execution was really going to occur, and he asked Don Alipio "Why?" The disheartened man deferred to a nearby newspaperman, who was eager to explain: "The ones who brought the young prince here did a good thing. All the European nations supported the plan, which would bring order to Mexico, but in the United States there was always suspicion. You're norteamericano, yes?" When Clay nodded, the man said: "Monroe Doctrine, yes? Doesn't it say no European interference in the New World? Well, when Maximilian arrived, you were too busy with your own war to worry about ours, but once peace came—the North won, didn't it?" This Clay ignored. "When you had time to look south you saw Europe meddling in Mexican affairs and you said: 'This has got to stop!' and once you said that, all the kings in Europe grew afraid. They stopped supporting Maximilian. Result? That firing squad over there."

While the squad waited, some of them white-faced and nervous, people began emerging from what had been the emperor's prison, and they too took positions facing the wall. Finally an officer of some high rank appeared, and he stood close to the file of riflemen. Then came a priest, two soldiers and between them the tall, handsome Austrian whose rule over a nation about which he had known nothing had lasted only three years. Thirty-five years old, he was a striking man who looked imperial—slim, haughty in manner, composed and walking with a steady step and an almost defiant mien. Somewhere in the crowd a voice cried "Long live the emperor," and Jubal, realizing that Don Alipio wanted to echo it, grasped Palafox sternly by the arm and the older man remained silent.

An officer, moving the priest aside, offered Maximilian the customary blindfold but it was rejected. Staring straight ahead as if he wished to see the bullets leaping at him, he stood in sunlight and watched the commanding officer raise his sword, cry out the order, then lower his sword as his men fired their dreadful volley. Many of the bullets must have struck the emperor, for he fell instantly, bravely, and without a cry. The ridiculous adventure of Emperor Napoleon III of France and his fellow European monarchs had ended in tragedy.

As the Palafox group rode back to Toledo, depressed and angry at the way Benito Juárez, Maximilian's Indian opponent, had handled the affair, Jubal thought, We Americans are as responsible for his death as the Mexicans, but he did not voice this opinion. However, when they camped out the first night and the soldaderas moved in with their dishes, Don Alipio said thoughtfully: "The norteamericanos could have saved him, if they had wanted to. But they had other problems," and now Jubal could speak: "With men like Grant in control they'll never be able to do the right thing up there."

During the first half year that Jubal worked at the Mineral, he applied himself so diligently to the task of bringing the operation into modern times that he rarely went into Toledo in the evenings. He ordered machinery from Scotland, new devices for smelting ore from Sweden, and practi-

cal goods from the new industries in the northern United States. He did the last with repugnance, but had to admit that the prices were too
attractive to be ignored. One of his accomplishments that gave him the greatest pleasure, however, was the construction of a neat circular wall
twenty-two feet in diameter and four feet high
enclosing the upper outlet of the shaft, but with
a vast hole in the middle to allow the Indian
women to descend into the mine and then to
climb up with their baskets of ore. No way had
yet been devised for doing this with machinery,
but whenever Jubal caught sight of the women
being used like pack animals he felt frustrated.
"Why can't the men do that work?" he asked
repeatedly and was never satisfied with the answer: "Because in Indian life, time out of mind,
women do the hard work like tilling the maize
and hauling the ore, while men do the work that
requires thinking, like hunting animals, fishing,
fighting the enemy and, in the mines, working at
the face and chopping out the ore in the proper
way."

But one fundamental practice at the Mineral
he did change. In the old days, it was only after
three or four women had fallen to their death
because of some faulty stone in the stairs that
that step had been repaired. Now with Jubal
making the descent and ascent several times

each week, and inspecting each step as he climbed, he saw that the problem had two parts: either the riser was too high, making the downward step dangerous, or the tread was too narrow or lacking a corner, making the foot slip off. By correcting these errors before they could imperil the women, he saved lives.

One day while he was working with the stonecutter, a solitary Indian woman came up the steps and had to pause until the workman finished, and for the first time there in the semidarkness with the great stone-lined hole reaching downward, Jubal spoke with an individual Indian basket carrier. To his surprise she was not reticent, and in response to his interrogations revealed that she was nineteen, born to parents from a village not far from Toledo, baptized by priests in that area and sent by them to the mines as was traditional for young women of that village. She had worked in the shaft climbing up and down with her basket since the age of fourteen and expected to continue till thirty-five or a few years longer and then either to return to the village or to take a job in one of the caverns doing the jobs that centered in those spacious areas.

"Why do you stop at age thirty-five?" Jubal asked, and the young woman had no explanation, but the mason working on the faulty tread

interrupted: "Their legs. They can't climb anymore. Well, they can climb, but not with baskets." He grinned at the woman and said: "I
couldn't climb them either, with that load of
ore," and when Jubal tested the weight he said:
"Me neither."

The woman said she had an Indian name,
which Jubal did not understand, but also a baptismal name given her by the priest: "They said
I was María de la Caridad. We're always María
and another name to make sure the Virgin
Mother looks after us." Her name meant Charity, and by popular custom she was known simply as Caridad. As she repeated the name
Kar-ee-*thath* she gave it such a sweet, melodious sound that Jubal looked for the first time at
her as another human being, a person like his
dead wife, Zephania, who had given her shortened name, Zeph, that same musical lilt, and in
that moment of recognition the basket carrier
became not a slave sentenced to this life of toil
by her Church and her government but an individual person with a character, aspirations and
a soul.

In later conversations with Caridad, Clay
learned that her ancestor many generations
back had been an important Altomec woman
named Lady Gray Eyes, who had destroyed the
terrible ancient gods and paved the way for

Christianity, but Caridad wondered if the new religion was in any significant way better than the old: "It was the priests who discovered the mine and who dug this hole and put us to work for them." But when Jubal made inquiries about that, he learned that it was not Antonio, the first Palafox and the priest, who had done these things, but his brother Timoteo, who had been a kind of businessman and the operator of the mine in its earliest stages. And when he asked about this mystical Lady Gray Eyes, the Palafox men said: "No myth there. She was very real, and she did lead her people away from the hideous old gods and to Christianity. She had a beautiful daughter-in-law, Xóchitl, mother of the amazing Indian woman called Stranger. That one married the first Palafox, so all of us dark ones are her descendants; the light-skinned ones come from the brother who married a Spanish lady, and kept doing it—I mean his descendants married Spaniards, too."

Why, Jubal wondered, did the Palafox line of Lady Gray Eyes' children now live in rural palaces while Caridad's slaved in the mines? Realizing that he lacked enough background to sort out a complicated story, he paid no more attention to it, but something happened in the mine that showed Caridad was an unusual Indian woman and perhaps just as proud as the Palafox men, to whom she was, presumably, distantly related. One day when he was working in one of the deepest caverns where the donkeys were kept, a group of Indian men were trying to fix an intricate network of ropes around a donkey so they could lower it to the newly excavated cavern below. They were having such difficulties with the obstinate beast that the foreman, one Joshua with a big voice, yelled at Caridad, who was nearby: "Don't just stand there like a fool. Help swing that rope." When she tried to pass it under the beast's belly, the donkey kicked, striking not Caridad but Joshua, who responded by knocking Caridad away from the operation and abusing her both physically and verbally. This Jubal could not tolerate, so he moved Caridad aside, told her not to worry, and himself fixed the sling under the animal and helped Joshua lower it to the next level.

Thus occupied, he did not notice the effect of Joshua's attack on Caridad, but when he finished the drop he chanced to look at her, and her face was many shades darker than before and she was biting her lower lip so hard that flecks of blood showed. Judging it prudent not to involve himself in Indian problems, he climbed up the stairs that now showed no danger spots, and by the time he was back at the

smelter he had dismissed the incident altogether.

However, a few days later Indian women
came to his office screaming: "Señor, Joshua
fall down the shaft. Dead." Descending the
stairs rapidly, he reached the cavern that
housed the donkeys to find the dark place in
turmoil. In the first moments of his investigation
he learned that Caridad and others had been
working to affix the sling to another donkey
when Joshua had fallen backward and down the
dark shaft. A woman named María de la Con-
cepción whispered: "Don Jubal, he was no
good," and when he queried the men in the
lower cavern one said: "I saw him fall, and he
cried 'Caridad,'" but this informant also said that
Joshua was no good, and he had not told the
other men of the foreman's last word.

Jubal decided that Caridad had pretty surely
taken revenge on Joshua, and he concluded
further that it was not preposterous to think that
this determined little basket carrier might be descended from some strong-minded woman who
had defied and destroyed the unacceptable ancient gods.

Clay was pleasantly surprised to receive an invitation from the Palafox men to what became almost a recapitulation of that memorable family dinner in 1847, when the owners of the Mineral first broached the possibility of Clay's taking over the management of their mine. The same three couples were guests, and after drinks on the veranda overlooking the pyramid and congratulating Jubal on his accomplishments in improving the appearance and profitability of the Mineral, Don Alipio's wife said as darkness fell: "Alipio, ask the servants to light the flares," and brands soaked in oil were lit along the high wall that enclosed the gardens protecting the house. In this congenial ambience, with birds bidding the world good night, the group passed the hours from seven through eleven discussing the death of Emperor Maximilian and the deplorable consequences for his widow, the Belgian princess.

"I loved her musical name," one of the women said, and in a gentle singsong she recited: "Marie Charlotte Amélie Augustine Victoire Clémentine Léopoldine."

"Did she have no last name?" another woman asked, and the first said: "Seven is enough."

"But you didn't say what happened to her,"

and the doleful answer came: "Tragedy overwhelmed her. She lost her mind, they say."

"Did they shoot her, too?"

"No, Juárez wasn't cruel enough for that.
She's to go into exile, I believe—a sad misad-
venture, but we'll survive, Mexico always does."

At eleven the party moved inside to the spacious dining room with its heavy oak chairs and
silent Indian waiters, but before anyone was
seated, Señora Palafox announced: "We have
late arrivals," and through the wide doorway
came a most handsome couple, both in their
late twenties, the man in a gold-and-blue uniform, the woman in an ingeniously decorated
white dress whose minute stitching in light
brown and gold made it almost shimmer in the
flickering light. "This is our son-in-law Major
Echeverría and his wife, our daughter, Alicia."
Turning to Clay, the mother said: "I think you
met our daughter when you were here before,"
but Clay was speechless, because just then a
maid brought into the room a little girl of seven
or eight dressed in the same exquisite China
Poblana costume her mother had worn in 1847.
As Jubal looked at the child the years passed,
the war vanished, the terrible losses he had sustained were obliterated, and he was again

twenty-four with the stunning victories of General Scott less than three months past.

The protracted dinner, eleven till half past one, was for Clay a mixture of delight and torment, for although he was glad to see Alicia so radiant and happy as a wife and mother, he was distraught to think that a child who had impressed him so indelibly twenty years earlier, and who had lived in his memory ever since as that adorable child in her China Poblana, had graduated into a world from which he was forever barred.

As the amiable chatter swirled about him he wondered: Why am I so fascinated by her? Could it be that she represents all I lost in the fire? Is she Zephania reborn? But he had scarcely phrased the possibility than he dismissed it. No, damn it. It's Alicia herself. My God, how lovely she is! Then he almost broke into laughter at himself for his fanciful daydreaming. It's that damned dress. How that Chinese girl must have agitated the minds of Mexico. How she still agitates me.

His eyes kept focusing on the child, and her mother, noticing this, said rather boldly: "You seem to be fascinated with my daughter's dress. Do you recognize it as one I wore here years ago?"

"I had hoped it was," he replied, and was

about to explain why when Alicia said: "It was my grandmother's. It survived four generations."

Now he found himself gazing furtively at Alicia, and he saw that the promise of unusual beauty she had shown as a child had become reality. Not only did she have exceptional physical beauty but she seemed to have almost a spiritual force. Moreover, she talked sense: "Poor, doomed Carlota, she should have known their irresponsible adventure could come to no good end. No outsider could ever rule Mexico because it's doubtful he could understand us— certainly not an Austrian."

"She was Belgian," Señora Palafox corrected and her daughter said: "I was thinking of Maximilian. He should never have brought a creature like that to this savage land."

Alicia's use of the word "savage" caused her uncles and her father to protest, but she defended her position with spirit: "I see it so. The horror of that pyramid out there. Our great-grandfather Timoteo branding all the Indians on the cheek. What things that infamous Cortés did. And the imbecilities of Santa Anna, eleven different presidents in thirteen years. Let me tell you, we're a doomed land."

Her father said: "Much as I despise Juárez, I think he might bring stability to this country. At least let us pray that he does," and on that hopeful note the dinner ended. And the Palafox men united in telling Clay: "You've exceeded our expectations. Now if we can only get the railroad to come our way, we'll be protected," and Jubal said: "That's up to you, gentlemen. You know the people in control."

When time came to bid the Palafoxes good night and ride back to the Mineral, he said good-bye to Major Echeverría, shaking his hand. When he came to Alicia he bowed, afraid to touch her, but she extended her hand and took his: "We're so glad you came," and he could say nothing. Alicia's daughter in her China Poblana curtsied and said in a piping voice: "We're glad to see you, brave americano," and the group applauded.

In the following days Clay was tormented by the vision of Alicia Echeverría, who reminded him of all he had lost in Virginia: his wife, his home, his way of life and the companionship of his children. At night he slept poorly and in the daytime found little joy in performing the very tasks that the previous week had given him such a feeling of satisfaction. He kept thinking alternately of Señora Echevarría and her eight-year-old daughter, and the child merged into the little Alicia he had seen twenty years before. It was perplexing, but one fact rose constantly before him: Alicia, this vision of perfection, was married to someone else and would forever be unattainable. Yet her presence remained with him, and goaded him into an act so bizarre that he could have explained it to no one.

It had been the custom in Toledo for almost two centuries to have in the month of April a fiesta that filled the plaza with activity. It was the modern version of the ancient celebration that I had come down to photograph in 1961, and although by now it had degenerated—or grown—into primarily a series of three splendid bullfights attended by rich Americans, in my grandfather's day it had retained much of its original religious impulse. In 1868, when he had begun to whip the Mineral into productive order, he happened to ride through town when the fiesta was under way, and normally he would not have been interested in the goods and services on sale, for he needed none of them, but on this day he happened to notice a roving band of musicians whose like he had not heard before. They were wandering minstrels, seven rural men from the outlying villages, and they played music featuring by a steady beat, an elegant use of strings and two of the best trumpeters he had ever heard, and as a military man he had heard many. They also had one violin player gifted with a voice capable of producing a soaring falsetto and he sang like a joyous lark reaching for the heavens.

Clay became so pleased with this music that for some time he followed the musicians as they strolled through the plaza, collecting coins. As he passed an improvised shop peddling dolls, he saw something that caused him to stop abruptly. Forgetting about the musicians, he stared at one fairly large doll, rudely made but dressed in a splendidly sewn China Poblana, each detail of the dress done exactly right. The dress was a work of art, unlike the primitive doll it clothed—it was the best of Mexican workmanship married to the worst.

"How much, señora?" When the keeper of the stall gave a price less than a dollar in American money, Clay said: "I'll take it," and since it was not customary in the plaza for such a purchase to be wrapped, he continued his stroll with the big doll under his arm.

He had gone only a short distance when he heard his name, and turning around he found himself face-to-face with Señora Echeverría and her daughter. In that moment Alicia understood why my grandfather had bought this doll, and she gave Jubal a comforting smile as if to say: I was impressed with you, also. Jubal, realizing that he had betrayed his secret infatuation, felt blood rushing to his face and tried to hide his doll in his arms, but Alicia laid her hand gently on his arm and said: "It's a handsome doll, Señor Clay, and it does look like me when I was her age," and she looked at her daughter, who smiled at the American.

The next months at the Mineral were depressing. Work did not move ahead as planned, production lagged and repairs were not made after Jubal had identified weak spots. Also, he was agitated by the presence of the China Poblana in his quarters and mortified that he had revealed his secret to Alicia. The doll became a self-inflicted wound reminding him that he had lost an important part of any decent life: partnership with a person of the opposite sex.

Clay felt that his spirits might be lifted if he could at least improve the situation at the mine, and it occurred to him that if he could get two trained mechanics he could fix everything required. He remembered the group of Confederate exiles in the churchyard in Mexico City, and consulting with the Palafoxes, he promised them: "If one of you will go to that little church in the capital—it'll be easy to find—and bring me two good American mechanics . . ."

"Why don't you go?" they asked, and he found himself riding to Querétaro and taking the train to Mexico City, but when he located the church where the Confederates had once as-

sembled, he found them gone. Locals he interrogated told him that the Americans now congregated in a series of cantinas, and when he
visited those bars he learned that the good
workers had found jobs right away, while the
others were still waiting for money from the
Southern states and still getting drunk each
night.

"Where could I find two good mechanics?"
Clay asked, and the prospect of steady work
was so inviting to the more responsible of the
Confederates that several who'd held good jobs
in the Old South wanted Clay to consider them.
He picked two men, one from South Carolina
and the other from Alabama, whom he felt he
could trust, and his taking them to Toledo began
the influx of Confederate expatriates that clustered about the Mineral. The two men Jubal
hired proved excellent workmen, who in time
married local women and raised children who
spoke, acted and looked like average Mexicans.
Such families, in turn, attracted other Confederates until the area contained numerous veterans, all of whom considered Jubal Clay their
informal leader and spokesman since he had
been a colonel in America and a foreman in
Mexico.

When the families were settled, the men,
none of whom had American wives, used to

meet occasionally to talk about their activities during the war. Some had been at Gettysburg, others at the devastation of Antietam, but all found grim satisfaction in hearing what Colonel Clay had done in those incredible minutes at Cold Harbor or in the burning of Chambersburg, for as one of the men who had ridden with Jeb Stuart on his impetuous raids said: "Sometimes we won."

These men were disgusted when in 1869 they heard that General Grant had been installed as president because it reminded them that he had always been destined to win. But one Confederate—they never called themselves ex-Confederates, for they would consider themselves to be on active duty till they died—a man with a theological background, consoled his companions: "It proves to me that God really is a Confederate." When a man slow to catch on asked: "What do you mean?" the theologian said: "God is finally punishing the North. Giving them Grant for a president. He'll ruin the country the way he wasted his army."

Gradually this cadre of loyalists surrendered the dream that they might one day return to take up arms against the North, but some vowed that if Canada ever decided to march south, they would flock back to help. Jubal's Southern patriotism flagged somewhat when a newcomer brought shocking news: "General Early has left Canada, accepted a presidential pardon and is now serving as front man for a group of gamblers in New Orleans." Refusing to believe this of his former leader, Clay kept making inquiries till he learned from a reliable source: "Yes, the two generals, Beauregard and Early, are working for a gang of gamblers in Louisiana, but it ain't as bad as it sounds. They been appointed by the state to see the lottery is kept honest. Couldn't find two better guarantees than names like Beauregard and Early."

No matter how hard he worked at the Mineral, Jubal could not lessen his infatuation with Alicia, but history now removed her from his presence. Major Echeverría had associated himself with the rising fortunes of Porfirio Díaz, whom the Palafox men had supported for years, and who showed promise of correcting the excesses perpetrated by the Indian president, Benito Juárez. Now Díaz was about to make his move to stabilize the nation, and Echeverría went with him, taking his wife and family to Mexico City.

But as Alicia left Toledo she did a somewhat surprising thing: when she looked at the China Poblana dress that four generations of girls in her family had treasured, she impulsively wrapped it and attached a hastily penned note: "Señor Clay, you are a dear, loyal man whom we all appreciate. I pray that you will find yourself a good wife and much happiness. This dress is a remembrance. Alicia Palafox Echeverría." Handing the package to one of the family's Indian servants, she said: "Take this to the Mineral and leave it in the room of Señor Clay," and she went off to the capital.

When my grandfather returned to his quarters, he told his family later: "I wondered what this gift could be, because the note was inside. When I opened it and saw the colorful dress I was still confused. But then I read the letter." He never told his family what he had made of Alicia's strange gesture, but I at least know what he did, because I still retain proof. He went to an Indian wood-carver and asked him to make a sturdy doll, the size of an eight-year-old girl. When it was delivered he dressed it in the China Poblana dress, and the doll stayed with him till he died. My father, John Clay, then kept it, and I have it in my apartment in New York.

Alicia's prayer, which Grandfather interpreted as a command that he find himself a wife, arrived at a time when he, too, had begun to think about this, for his Confederate friends who had married Mexican girls were constant proof that even when the Rebel was Protestant and his bride Catholic, a strong union could result. And just at this time, circumstances developed that required him to see more and more of María de la Caridad. No longer a teenager—she was now twenty-four—she had tired of climbing the perilous steps more often than was absolutely necessary and she had taken to sleeping now and then in the lowest cavern, down with the donkeys and the Indian men who elected to remain there permanently. One such man, Elpidio, who had not seen sunlight in years, explained when she asked why he never climbed up: "If the priest sends me here and if Señor Clay makes me work so hard, they have taken the sun from me and I don't give a damn when I die."

This bitter lament so distressed her that the following night she took Elpidio's complaint to Señor Clay, and as he listened to her report of how the Indian men lived in that bottom cavern he began to question the slave-owning mentality he had brought with him from Virginia. For some weeks he did nothing about it, contenting himself with visiting the caverns each day and inspecting the tragic conditions in which the brown-skinned men labored. But one evening as he was about to climb the appallingly inadequate stairway, he felt invisible hands clutching at his throat, and at each step upward the strangulation became more real, until he halted in the topmost cavern, one abandoned more than a century before. Here he formed the self-incriminating judgment: On the day we send them into this mine, we condemn them to death! It was a moment fraught with overwhelming guilt.

The next morning he told the Palafoxes: "There are engines now that can haul a cage up out of the mine loaded with ore and lower it back down with men to work the ore. We must use those, no matter the cost." They agreed, and were pleased when he added: "And they have a new wire rope in place of the bulky manila hemp."

Immediately Clay drew the specifications for a cage capable of negotiating the diameter of the existing shaft, and where the stone sides were close together he appointed workmen to cut away protruding stone. In this way he created one of the first humane mines in Mexico. During this hectic time when the engine was being installed and the diameter widened he saw a good deal of Caridad, who helped by supervising the traffic on the stairs that were soon to be abandoned. He found her extremely quick in comprehending his orders and helpful in explaining Indian traditions and preferences to the other Confederates, so that by the time the new sys-

tem was installed he and Caridad had achieved
such rapport in working together that she became in effect his assistant.

When the conversion was completed and the
new engine from England, appropriately called
a donkey, was bringing ore above ground and
taking workers down, he arranged two celebrations: a fancy one in the House of Tile attended
by local officials, friends of the Palafoxes and a
mariachi orchestra; and a much quieter get-
together of the Confederates, including any living in the area, whether they worked at the
Mineral or not. Jubal, aware that many Mexican
wives would be present, invited Caridad to attend—he wanted to show his gratitude for the
help she had given.

The highlight of the Confederates' party was
a report from a Baptist clergyman from Alabama
who was quietly proselytizing for Prostestantism
among the devout Catholic Indians: "Wonderful
news from the North," he said. "Their President
Grant is proving to be the most corrupt, stupid
and inadequate leader they've ever had. A
thieving ass." After the cheering, a man from an
important family in North Carolina asked with
mock grief: "Why didn't he show those attributes when he was fighting us?"

Jubal saw how easily the Mexican wives fitted
into the gathering, speaking freely, making

jokes, teasing their voluble husbands. One wife who had become proficient in English said: "When I listen to you muchachos I find it difficult to remember that you lost the war." Her husband snapped: "But we took care of you paisanos in 1848," and everyone cheered.

As the party ended, Caridad took Jubal aside and said bitterly in her broken English: "Always the same. You give big party for Palafoxes, mariachi band. You give one for Americans, lots of beer. But nobody do nothing for Indians—we do all the work. You saw it," she stormed. "You not ashamed?"

He was ashamed, but as a Virginia planter he was astounded that a woman who was virtually a slave with a different skin color should have talked to him so bluntly and on a subject so out of line with customary practice. Of course, on his plantation when a job was well done he might have given the slaves a side of beef, and maybe Zephania would have helped her cooks bake some pecan pies, but no slave would ever have demanded any of this—least of all a woman. But the idea was so clearly right that he was humbled. He clasped her hand and said: "You're right in what you say. I need your help." And then he added: "And I need you, too," to which she whispered: "Yes, you do."

At first they did not get married. Quietly she

moved into his quarters and cleaned the place. In the following days each of his two main Confederate workmen, accosting him separately, said: "You'll never regret it," and the two wives told Caridad with considerable firmness: "Learn English."

Their marriage took place in one of the cathedral's ornate chapels, not in the outdoor chapel, where the Indians had attended rites during the rule of the first Palafox bishops, and in due course they had a son, who would become my father. In naming him John, Jubal said: "I've always hated my name, that Old Testament stuff. And I think the names Mexicans give their boy babies are worse: Hilario, Alipio, Cándido. I want the simplest name there is. Sam would be good, but the women would call him Samuel. Maybe John. It's biblical too, but people forget that," and John it was.

When Jubal was older he received a surprising letter from the Cold Harbor post office. It was from Grace Clay Shallcross and said that to her delight, her husband, an important lawyer with government connections thanks to his having been an aide to General Grant, had saved his salary, taken her back to the land she owned at Newfields and built there a replica, no, an improved version, of the old plantation house. The letter ended: "Your spirit dominates the place,

Father, the same fields, the same crops, many of the same Negroes but working for wages now. Please come home and help us enjoy it."

Caridad, who could now read English easily, appreciated the grave threat this letter was to her and did not protest when he burned it without taking down the new address, nor would his son, John, ever visit the place, nor John's son, myself.

The act of Jubal's that had the most lasting effect on Toledo—for in time the silver mine petered out and all he achieved there was lost—was something he did in the 1890s, when he was an old man. While attending the spring fiesta in the plaza it occurred to him that this affair could be made much grander, so he hurried to the Palafox mansion and he and the Palafox men, all very old, made ambitious plans for the next fiesta: "We could have a Tournament of Flowers, for all the poets of the region. There'd be dancers from Oaxaca in their colorful costumes. We could build thirty stalls, all the same size, and store them from year to year." They gave full rein to their imagination, because they knew they would not see many more fiestas. The main innovative idea came from Don Alipio: "My Palafox bulls have become the best in Mexico, no contest. The city wants to make our plaza bigger. We'll help them. And to make the fiesta real, we'll have three grand bullfights, Friday, Saturday, Sunday." Jubal said: "We'll give a hundred-peso prize to the best mariachi band." The men liked the idea, but the Palafoxes who handled funds asked: "Where will we get the hundred pesos?" and Jubal said: "From me. Do you know what my name means in the Bible? The father of all who play the harp and flute." One of the men pointed out: "No harps or flutes in a mariachi band," and Jubal retorted: "Those trumpets make up for them."

When the time came to make colorful posters announcing the celebration, Jubal drew the sketch using the word "Festival," which is pronounced like "Mineral" with a heavy accent on the last syllable. But when the Palafoxes saw his proposal they protested: "There's no such word in Spanish. Fiesta, Festivo, but no Festival." When he asked others, they confirmed that he had used a word that did not exist at that time in formal Spanish, but he was stubborn: "It has a singing sound, and the foreigners who come to Toledo to watch will know what it means," and the name stuck.

My grandfather did not die happy. He was protected by a wonderful wife, his son was now grown and Mexico was at peace under the iron dictatorship of Porfirio Díaz. But then, as if to signal that the good old days were ending, in the northern city of Monterrey an anarchist tried to assassinate Díaz but struck instead the carriage of Colonel Echeverría, killing him and his wife, Alicia. Within three months Díaz had abdicated and the infamous General Gurza was destroying north-central Mexico, with Emiliano Zapata doing the same to the south.

Jubal was distraught. He had thought of Alicia Palafox as a member of his family. At times she was that child of eight in the sacred China Poblana, again the delicately beautiful bride he had seen on his return to Toledo, at other times the gracious woman in the plaza who had caught him buying the doll, or the sensitive person who had sent him the dress and the note, both of which he still kept. I think it is fair to say that in some quiet way these two had loved each other, but maybe I'm searching for a new word. I do know that the memory of Alicia Palafox lives in our family's memory as vividly as on that dreadful day when she was killed and Mexico began to fall apart.

Since I was born in 1909 and left Mexico permanently in 1938, it is obvious that I witnessed the continuing Revolution that scarred the country during those years; however, this passage will be a story not about me but about my father,

John Clay, who saw the tragedies not as a child but as a participating adult. It is also the account of how Toledo reacted to the fighting, for our family lived there throughout the wars. To bring some order to the confusion I shall identify the people who play recurring roles, and some of the stages on which they acted.

Dominant in the rebellion was General Saturnino Gurza, a butterball of a man six feet tall with an enormous belly that protruded from just below his rib cage, but faded away to almost nothing down to where he used a length of rope as a belt. Since he was proud of being a peón, he wore the peón's costume: sandals, unpressed loose white pants, no undershirt beneath his open-necked white shirt, a red bandanna and an enormous white straw sombrero.

He had a face to match his torso—big, round, hair in his eyes and a mustache that drooped below his chin line. On several occasions I heard him give orders, and I remember his coarse voice, which seemed always to end with a sardonic laugh, as if he enjoyed doing the terrible things he did.

Gurza had grown up in poverty in one of the bleak northern Mexican states along the border with the United States, a country for which he developed an abiding hatred. As a boy he had terrorized his companions and at the age of nineteen declared himself to be a colonel, fighting for whoever paid him. By twenty he was a self-appointed general, in which capacity he demonstrated such mastery that he quickly converted himself into a real general. So from boyhood he had been fighting constantly, but against whom or for whom he seemed never to understand. He became famous as the general with two wide bandoleers laden with cartridges crisscrossing his chest, a huge rifle slung in his left hand and a sneer on his lips. When that burly figure stormed into a meeting, it commanded respect.

In his lawless activities Gurza always seemed able to win the support of an army of ragtag dissidents called *los descamisados* (those without shirts), who enjoyed serving under him when he raided the sites between the American border and Mexico City. He also had no trouble taking control of an apparently limitless supply of trains that had now penetrated most parts of Mexico's corners. Regardless of which railroad he stole them from, they all looked alike: a wheezing engine whose water tank could be easily punctured by enemy bullets, maybe one ordinary coach with windows, one baggage car with heavy bars protecting its windows, followed by a string of flatcars—occasionally one would have fencelike sides—and the inevitable caboose in which rode enthusiastic soldiers who found joy in firing at anyone the men on the forward flatbeds had missed. Since three railway lines now crossed in Toledo, one leading to the capital, one to Guadalajara and one to San Luis Potosí, it was inevitable that we would be seeing a lot of General Gurza, whose short name was easy to remember.

In fact, during my childhood the history of Toledo was so entangled with the exploits of this wild man that in my mind Gurza and Toledo have become fused as one entity. His excursions into town were inevitable, for he and his army lived on railroad freight cars, and that brought him to us constantly. I saw his troops in action on four terrifying occasions: in 1914, when the nuns were murdered; in 1916, when he killed five men of my family; in 1918, when he torched the town and murdered our priests; and in 1919, when he destroyed our mine. And there was that fifth excursion when he dandled me on his knee as if were my loving uncle.

There were other visits, of course, for he was always on the move, but he came so often, either chasing or being chased, that specific events and their dates become a blur. What I can state for certain is that in my childhood he was an ogre, in my boyhood a terror, and in my later years a perplexity, the most remarkable Mexican I have known.

In our city the general had clearly identified enemies: the Palafoxes with their big homes and large tracts of land; Mother Anna María, the superior of the convent northwest of town, who had the bad luck to be known as a member of the Palafox family, thus incurring a double enmity; and Father Juan López, an underweight, shifty-eyed village priest with a bad complexion and a burning desire to see his church sponsor and deliver justice to his Indians. In these years Father López served as a minor functionary in the cathedral, which had a cadre of four other priests who discharged the traditional duty of catering to the well-to-do families in the region.

Each of these enemies of the general was associated with some building or buildings, so that whenever he rampaged through Toledo he had no problem finding targets on which to vent his spleen. Mother Anna María's convent was a late-eighteenth-century building erected by the Palafoxes of that day. Situated on a hill north of Toledo, it commanded perhaps the finest view in the district, for one could see not only the pyramid and the smokestacks of the Mineral but also the profile of the city and the rolling countryside. The convent itself was a thing of beauty with secluded cloisters and low towers, but its surroundings alone would have made it special.

Ineffectual Father López worked in the cathedral and lived in meager quarters on its grounds. The Palafox holdings included the Mineral, the big houses behind adobe walls and the bull ranch. But it was the city itself, a kind of self-contained refuge in the vicinity of Mexico City but not contaminated by it, that constituted the major target for an assailant. Any marauding army able to invade Toledo sent a message of fear to the capital: "Might we be next?" so government forces sometimes tried to forestall such attacks by encircling Toledo to defend it, but such futile efforts merely made the conquering armies more vengeful when they marched in as victors.

It would be helpful if I could explain who was fighting whom in those chaotic years, but I was unable to keep such things straight then any more than I can now. In 1911 the dictator Porfirio Díaz was overthrown by the poetic dreamer Francisco Madero, who was soon murdered by more practical people. Then a man named Victoriano Huerta battled for supremacy with a man named Venustiano Carranza, whom my father did not like. When the three famous bandits—Pancho Villa, Emiliano Zapata and Saturnino Gurza—took control, hell broke loose across Mexico. At last Carranza was assassinated and

Obregón resumed power, but he was assassinated, too, and in 1934, a black day in Mexican history so far as the Clay family was concerned, Lázaro Cárdenas, a wild-eyed radical, became president, and our drift to exile began.

I hope you've been able to make sense of all this because, as I said before, I was never able to. What I knew was that General Gurza came and went, and when he came people died, and when he went they lamented their losses. Our first experience with him was in 1914, when I was five years old. One of his open trains approached Toledo from the north, and when a scout galloped into town with the terrifying news "Here comes General Gurza!" my father, who had become manager of the Mineral at my grandfather's death, put my mother and me in an inner room, saying: "No matter what happens, stay here," and he ran off to protect the mine.

Father did not have to worry about this incursion from the north, because the train came on a rickety track well to the west of the pyramid. This put the loaded cars close to the convent, and when our sparse government troops halted the train at the edge of the city, Gurza, in a rage at having been prevented from entering Toledo, led a charge on the undefended convent, broke down the fragile gates, rousted out all the nuns and shot seven. He would have especially liked to execute Mother Superior Anna María, since she was a Palafox, but he could not find her. Loyal nuns at the risk of their own lives had hidden her—they were the ones that Gurza shot.

I was, as I said, five at the time, and although I can remember the horror with which my family heard of this outrage, I did not understand the euphemisms with which Mother and Father discussed the tragedy. They used the Spanish *violado las monjas* (violated the nuns) to describe what had happened before the women were killed, and perhaps it was better that I did not understand, but by the next time Gurza came through I knew that the nuns had been victims of indecent games, rape, torture and shooting. There was much violating of women when Gurza's bullies ransacked a place.

In the aftermath of this obscene attack, Father bought two pistols and coached Mother and me: "They're beasts. Shoot them if they ever come to this side of the pyramid and try to force their way into the house." Taking Mother aside to where they supposed I could not hear, he told her: "If they're about to capture you, use the gun on them. If they're too many, use it on yourself." At the age of six I learned how to load, care for and use a revolver. And at night I had visions of holding off General Gurza, whom I had not yet seen, with my revolver and shooting him dead when he attempted to violate Mother.

I did get to see the general some years later when his dreadful train came down again from the north, this time without opposition. Backing it into town so as to provide a quick getaway if troops from the capital moved in, he rounded up all the citizens, including those of us at the Mineral, and herded us into the plaza. There, on a sunny July day in excessive heat, we sweltered with Father whispering: "Say nothing. Do nothing. Attract no attention," and in abject silence we watched as Gurza's men, working from lists that the officers read, rounded up the landowners of the district, the big ones with more than two hundred thousand acres each, and hauled them into that part of the plaza facing the cathedral. There he put them against the stone wall of one of the towers and shouted accusations against them in a voice so loud it terrified me: "Good people of Toledo! These men, you know them, they stole your lands, threw you off, turned you into slaves. Isn't that right?" and from the listeners came many voices: "Yes, yes!"

Then he cried to one of his officers: "Read the list!" and the man, with no insignia showing that he was an officer, read: "Aureliano Palafox, sixty thousand acres. Belisario Palafox, forty thousand acres. Tómas, twenty thousand acres," and the litany continued to those who owned only a few thousand acres. In later years I remembered those figures and wondered how the Palafoxes had acquired so much land. I was not aware that our acreage extended far into the countryside.

When the list was completed, Gurza cried to one of his men: "How did these thieves get their land?" and the man shouted: "They stole it!"

"From who?"

"From the peóns."

"And what do we do with such thieves of honest people's land?"

"Shoot them!" The heat of the moment was so intense that many voices in the plaza screamed: "Shoot them!"

"My God," Father cried. "They're going to do it!" and he whispered to Mother: "Cover his eyes," and her hand came over my face, but a crack was left and with one eye I watched General Gurza, his bandoleers glistening in the sun, give the order to fire. I saw the muskets jump, the muzzles smoke, and the landowners fall as blood began to stain the foot of the cathedral tower.

Thinking the execution over, Mother dropped her hand, so I clearly saw that one of the owners had not been killed—in later years I would learn that this frequently happened in mass shootings—so now General Gurza whipped out his revolver, went to the wounded man and shot him through the head. Four Palafoxes had been executed—their careful amassing of land, usually with government approval, had signed their death warrants.

The bodies were left in the hot sun until evening, when Gurza gave the crowd permission to return home, but before we left the plaza I had a chance to look closely at the tower wall and saw that it was pockmarked with scars from bullets. In the decade ahead a thousand buildings would suffer similar marks.

How did the public executions affect our family? A kind of numbness spread over us. Father refused to believe that he had seen what happened, for he was revolted by its calculated brutality. He could not eat that night: "I'm still nauseated," he said. The effect on Mother was quite different—it was one of sullen rage. She was, after all, a Palafox, the daughter of Alicia Palafox, that beautiful woman whose China Poblano had so captivated my Grandfather Jubal. Having seen men related to her—one was an uncle—shot simply because they owned land had to be a warning that one day she too might be executed for a similar reason. She thought that perhaps we ought to leave the Mineral, since it was known as a Palafox holding, and she proposed this to Father and me, but we insisted on staying, for as he explained: "This is my job. It's a decent one and I've treated our people fairly." So we clung to our home and our occupation, but now we lived in apprehension, for if seven nuns and nine landowners could be shot without trial—the seven because they were religious, the nine because they owned land— anything could happen.

By the time I was eight, that is, in 1917, I had invented a gruesome game that any child in those turbulent years could have played. From newspapers of the day and the numerous cheap magazines featuring stories about various aspects of the endless war, I began to follow the careers of individual officers whose records attracted my attention, and when the file on some individual officer was completed, I had a representative account not only of his extremely active life but of Mexico in its agony. I had nine such compilations, each a duplicate of the others; the one for a young lieutenant named Fermín Freg stands out in my memory as epitomizing the period:

> 1910   newspaper. Brave Lieutenant Fermín
>   Freg, who led the charge that de-

feated the rebellious enemies of our beloved protector of the nation, Porfirio Díaz.

1911   magazine. Major Freg as loyal defender of Francisco Madero, who had driven the hated dictator Díaz from Mexico.

1913   magazine. Lieutenant Colonel Freg in guard of honor for General Huerta, who ordered the murder of Madero.

1913   small booklet. Colonel Freg, aide-de-camp to General Carranza, who has ousted General Huerta from power.

1914   big book. Generals Prado, Gurza and Rubio signing The Pact of the Three Generals.

1915   large booklet. Colonel Freg in command of the firing squad that executed General Prado.

1916   very big book. General Freg taking salute after great victory at San Luis Potosí.

1917   largest book. Full page in garish color, body of General Freg fusilladed by troops still loyal to General Prado.

The biographies are monotonous in their pre-
dictability. The final photos of men like Madero,
Carranza, Zapata and Obregón, each the recipi-
ent, for a few years, of enormous acclaim, show
the men stained with their own blood, from a
bullet fired by a onetime friend.

I was assisted in this gruesome game by my
grandmother, María de la Caridad, who was now
a widow in her sixties, and as concerned as ever
about the welfare of her family and her Indians,
in that order. She lived with us in warm harmony
and helped Mother raise me. Curiously, she
spoke English better than Mother did and was
determined that I learn it as well as Spanish.
Thanks to her I grew up bilingual without a pronounced accent in either language.

In this memoir I've said that the major characteristic of the Clays of Virginia was their ardent
patriotism, but I myself had never witnessed
this. I was relying upon family legend, but in
1917, while General Gurza was running wild in
our part of Mexico, my father's attention was
diverted to Europe, where the kaiser was trying
to remake the world. When an American expeditionary force was dispatched across the Atlantic
to oppose the Germans, Father growled: "It's
about time," and he met with men in Toledo to

follow the progress of the war. One night he cried out at supper: "If they threaten your way of life, you've got to do something!" and the next day he paid a hasty visit to the American embassy in Mexico City, where he learned that even though he was not an American citizen, he could volunteer for overseas service.

"Could it be with the Virginia regiment?"

"If you pay for the telegram, you'll find out."

When permission was granted he hurried home to Toledo with news that startled us: "The military attaché at the embassy swore me in as an officer candidate. I'm to report immediately to Fort Dix." Then he added, almost as an afterthought: "Graziela, you and Mother can mind the Mineral while I'm gone."

When my mother began to cry, he comforted her and told me: "Watch after her while I'm gone." She sobbed: "You said you never wanted to see the United States again," and he explained: "I'm not doing this for the U.S. I'm doing it for Virginia." And he was off to the hellish ditches of northeastern France.

In his absence our family purchased a map of the battle area and with pins and arrows followed his supposed exploits, and we were fairly accurate in our guesses as to where he was fighting. During the final drive on German positions, what we did not know was that he behaved with valor, winning commendations and medals.

His bravery on the field had an unexpected consequence. As the general pinned the medal on Father's tunic he said: "This makes you eligible for automatic American citizenship," and on the sensible grounds that "in time of trouble, it's better to have two passports than one," he accepted the offer, so that when he returned to the Mineral he could boast: "I'm a Virginian at last."

He had been home only a few weeks in 1918 when Mexico's permanent warfare engulfed him once more, for General Gurza launched his third attempt to capture Mexico City. Local patriots, goaded by a handful of federal troops, tried vainly to halt him north of our city, an act that so enraged him that he drove one of his trains right into the heart of Toledo, used troops from the other train to throw a cordon around the city and began what historians call the Sack of Toledo. He began with the cathedral, that gem of colonial architecture. Bringing up a small cannon, he fired numerous blasts at the eight majestic columns, destroying some completely, shattering portions of others. His men, with great effort, knocked the front doors off their hinges, then rushed inside and with their gun butts smashed decorations in the various chapels. Statuary was crushed, paintings slashed, and the altar

area totally demolished in a frenzy of destruction. In less than an hour, one of the treasures
of central Mexico was a shambles.

When the vandals reached the robing area
where the priests stored their gold-ornamented
festive robes, three young priests who had not
fled Toledo after previous raids tried to protect
these treasures. Enraged, the soldiers knocked
the young men down and then, dragging them
through the gaping front entrance, they shouted
to those on guard in the plaza: "What shall we
do with these?" and General Gurza gave the
answer: "Shoot them!" so within a few minutes
of their capture they were lined up against one
of the walls of the church, and shot by a firing
squad.

Then the rioting began in various parts of the
city. Old buildings were set on fire. Others were
ravaged. Stores were smashed. Women were
raped in the street; at the height of the fury a
man who had once worked for old Don Alipio,
the bull breeder, shouted: "Let's get those
damned bulls!" and he led a large gang of men
waiting in the second train out to the Palafox
ranch, where they methodically slaughtered by
gunfire those proud black bulls that Don Alipio
had imported from Spain. When they were finished, the leader of the gang cried: "Let the
people eat the good meat!" and frightened Indi-

ans who had been watching were told they could butcher the carcasses if they wished, and the herd vanished under the knife.

When the grisly day ended, Toledo had been taught the grim lesson that it must never waver in its support of General Gurza. Its mission accomplished, the train backed away, turned at the edge of town and headed north.

The departure of General Gurza left Toledo in a stupor. Dazed people wandered about trying to assess the damage, and at the Mineral we heard reports of all the terrible things that had happened. My parents were gloomy: "This may be the end of our world. Can Toledo survive such a disaster?" and I could see that Mother felt that there was no future here, but Father reminded her that our family still had its home at the mine and its good health. There were also two surprising survivors of the destruction; against all odds they had kept alive by keeping themselves hidden.

The first was Father López, the scrawny Indian priest at the cathedral. When the fury was at its height, he managed to hide in the small room allotted to Indian priests who served the peóns. They belonged to the cathedral, but were never a true part of it, as their fellow priests refused to acknowledge them. For two days he was afraid to let anyone know he was alive, afraid that Gurza's men might be waiting for him. Unaware that he was the only member of the cathedral priesthood alive, he finally slipped out of his hiding place and tried to mix in unobserved with the people in the plaza. But as soon as he was recognized his appearance was treated as a kind of miracle: "We were sure you were dead. How did you escape?" He deemed it best not to share his secret, and after a while they left him alone, but there was no place for him to go. He knew that the surviving women at the convent had fled, as they were doing over much of Mexico, and he supposed that most of the priests in the Toledo area had been slain in the savage attacks that had been pursued with the hope of driving all Catholic clergy out of Mexico.

Afraid to remain in Toledo lest Gurza and his madmen return, he walked slowly north until he came to the Mineral. I was first to see him and recognized him by his furtive manner: "Dad! It's Father López!" and when my parents joined me they saw it was indeed the priest, but since they had never had anything to do with him they felt no personal responsibility. But Grandmother Caridad said: "He's one of the good ones," and prevailed upon my parents to take him in. Thus the Clay family became the protectors of the last Catholic priest in the region, and, even though they knew the risk they were taking, they gave him a hiding place among the mine buildings and instructed the workmen to tell no one of his presence.

The other survivor of the attack on Toledo involved a more complicated rescue mission. One night Don Eduardo Palafox, accompanied by a foreman from his bull ranch southwest of town, sneaked up past the ruined convent and around the pyramid and, like Father López, came to our door. They had a remarkable story to tell: "They killed all our bulls, wiped out the bloodline. But one male calf has survived. He was with his mother and although Gurza's men killed her, they missed the calf. If we can save him, we can restore the line, if peace ever comes."

"It will," Father said and forthwith took steps to save the valuable animal. That was the year he had introduced automobiles at the Mineral. So it was in a truck that Don Eduardo, his foreman, Father and I rode out to the Guadalajara Road and started for the ranch, but when we reached the cutoff to the left, the one that would have taken us to the main gate, the foreman said: "No, straight ahead six kilometers," and at the designated point he directed Father to turn sharp left over untended ground. After a bumpy ride we reached a spot where two foremen with shaded lanterns were holding the ropes that kept a spirited young calf under control. Deftly they worked the animal into the truck and with this precious cargo the five of us drove back into town.

During the trip to and from the ranch, Father had conversed with Don Eduardo in a low voice that I had trouble hearing. As we reached the western entrance to Toledo they did a daring thing, one so improbable that we laughed about it years later. They drove out to the Mineral, followed Father's directions to a cave hidden behind a pile of slag, and eased the little bull into a neat sanctuary, where fodder was awaiting him. With a snort and a chop of horns that had not yet yet fully sprouted he ran about his new home. "His name," said the foreman, "is Soldado, the little soldier. Protect him. He's precious."

So at age nine I became custodian of one of Spain's best fighting bulls—a young fellow, true, and with only budding horns—and a more exciting pet no boy ever had. He was stubborn and was becoming so powerful that sometimes I was unable to make him go where he didn't want to, no matter how I pushed or pulled. But he obviously liked me and was pleased whenever I rejoined him after an absence. I think he understood that he had to hide in our cave, and although I grew tired of cleaning up after him, I came to think of him as my bull and watched with the satisfaction of a father as he grew more powerful and bull-like.

Occasionally, being careful not to arouse suspicion, the ranch foreman sneaked in to see how Soldado was doing, and when he saw the magnificent promise of the young bull's physique, especially his big chest and slim hindquarters, he told Father: "Time we got him out of here. We think we have a place to hide him in a far corner of the ranch. We'll have a herd reassembled one of these days," and it was that conversation which spurred me to an action that I look back upon with amazement. Aware that I had under my care a fighting bull of pure Spanish caste—for the men reminded me of that repeatedly—I felt a nagging desire to see if he would know how to fight the way the big Palafox bulls had done during the spring festivals in the Toledo bullring.

In time that inquisitiveness became a driving compulsion, so I stole one of Mother's checkered red tablecloths, took it out to the cave, which provided enough light for my experiment, and tried to do the things I'd seen the great matadors do. I held the cloth with two hands, stamped my left foot, and waited for the bull to charge. He did, and with the flat part of his forehead he knocked me flat against the wall so that I fell in a heap. I had seen matadors take knocks like that and get up again, so once more I had my cloth out, held firmly with both hands, and stalked toward the bull. He charged and tossed me right back against the wall. This time the two smacks hurt, both his little horns in my stomach and the stone wall as I smashed into it. But a matador is a man who fights bulls, no matter how they knock him about, so once more I approached my bull, and this time I kept my left hand far out, my right close to my leg, and the bull dove straight for the extended cloth, passing me by a matter of inches.

With no audience to applaud what I knew was a decent pass, I shouted "¡Olé!" to cheer myself, but this attracted the bull's attention before I was ready, and at me he came. Since the tablecloth was now wrapped around me, the bull hit my legs with full force and not only knocked me flat but stomped on me and butted me again with his horns, which if they had been full grown would have killed me for certain. As it was, they were big enough to leave a small scar across my chest.

When my father, Don Eduardo and the foreman came to take the bull back to the ranch and saw that I had been giving passes to Soldado, they were furious. "Don't you know that ruins a fighting bull?" the foreman shouted as he gave me a sharp blow to the head. "You've done a terrible thing," and again he clobbered me.

"¡Basta!" my father cried, pulling me away from further blows, and I have rarely heard that wonderful Spanish word for "Enough!" when I appreciated it more, for the rancher had a heavy hand.

As they herded Soldado back into the truck and allowed me to ride with them out to the ranch the foreman explained that a Spanish fighting bull had unusual intelligence: "Once he fights a man with a cape and makes three or four passes hitting nothing but cloth, he learns that he will not find his enemy that way. And pretty soon he's smart enough to leave the cape alone and drive his horn not at it but for the bundle, the man." The foreman astounded me by what he said next: "So you may have ruined the bull. You've taught him to go for the bundle, and he'll never forget. Three years from now when he goes into the ring, one more dead matador," and I felt sick at having in a sense destroyed my friend.

But Father saved me with a thoughtful observation: "Pedro, think a minute. Soldado will be your seed bull. A jewel of great value. He'll never get into the arena," and when Pedro agreed: "That bull could be sensational as our breeder," I felt better.

As before, we drove past the road leading to the main gate to the ranch until we came to where men waited on horseback, and when we pushed Soldado out of the truck, he rushed about, smelled the horses, recognized them as fellow animals and fell in with them as if he were a docile lamb. As he trotted off to the safety of a far field, his black against the horses' roan, I cried: "Soldado!" but he did not look back at his friend.

Later, as the aficionados of Mexico know, Soldado became the most famous seed bull in their taurine history, sire of bulls that brought glory to the Palafox name. In those years I used to astound men by casually saying: "When I fought Soldado, he knocked me down three times," and they would look at me. I would add: "But I gave him one magnificent veronica," and they would treat me with respect.

While I was at the Mineral protecting my bull from General Gurza, our family's other secret guest, Father López, was endangering both himself and us by resuming his priestly duties even though the countryside was full of people who approved of the government's persecution of priests in what it called "a drive to rid Mexico of the tyranny of Catholicism." On this point, which seemed to tear the nation apart, our family was split three ways. Mother, as a conservative Palafox, was strongly pro-Catholic. Father, as a Virginia Baptist, was pretty firmly against the Catholic Church. And I, who knew little of religion, approved of men like Father López who did good work among his people and disapproved of other priests who ranted at me when I accompanied my mother to Mass. To put it simply, I didn't know what I thought.

What Father López did that endangered us was to move about the rural areas north of the Mineral, quietly assemble small groups of the faithful, and conduct Mass in some barn or kitchen. He wore no clerical garb, of course, and was so scrawny that he sometimes had difficulty convincing the peóns that he really was a priest, and once when I accompanied him I saw tears come into his eyes as he tried to assure the half-dozen people in a small kitchen that he was qualified to bring them the Mass: "Tell them, Norman, tell them who I am," and in my fluent Spanish, which reassured them, I told of his miraculous escape from the murders at the cathedral. Then they clustered about him and he prayed.

Fortunately, he and I were absent on another missionary trip when General Gurza's men made a visit to the Palafox silver mine, and when Father López and I approached the place, he suddenly grabbed my arm and pulled me back. From a vantage point on a hillside we watched what happened.

Eleven soldiers, led by a young officer, stormed into the Mineral and began searching for Father and Mother. Finally locating them, they dragged them out, lined them up against the wall and were about to shoot them as agents of the Palafoxes when Grandmother Caridad came running out screaming "No! No!" One of the firing squad was a local man who had worked with her in the mine and he shouted: "She is one of us!" so the execution was stayed.

Trembling as I hid behind low shrubs on the hill, I watched as Gurza's men tied my parents and my grandmother to a tree to prevent them from interfering with the mission they had been sent to carry out. They took from the backs of three heavily laden mules large bundles of something, and although I couldn't guess what they were, Father López whispered "Dynamite!" and when the bundles were opened I saw the sticks, which were taken to the mouth of the shaft and thrown in. Then a long rope was produced and individual sticks were tied to it, after which it was lowered in the shaft so that the dynamite was evenly distributed down the sides. When all was secure, Gurza's men lit a fuse that ran down beside the rope and at the same time threw four sticks of sputtering dynamite down the shaft. For a moment nothing happened, then came a titanic explosion as the mine blew itself apart.

The blast started fires in the various caverns and now Gurza's men threw into the smoking shaft the pieces of valuable machinery that either Grandfather and his Confederate engineers had constructed or Father had bought from companies in England. The entire apparatus of the Mineral crashed down to the raging fires below. Finally the men cut the wire that operated the cage Father had built, and it went smashing itself to pieces as it careened down the rocky shaft, after which the men hacked the superstructure from which the cage was suspended, and it too went echoing down the hole that would never be mined again.

Their work done, the soldiers released their three prisoners, and from what I saw I could deduce they told my parents they were lucky that old Caridad had been in the house, for as they departed, one of the men kissed her.

When Father López and I crept back to the Mineral, we joined the family members in surveying the ruins, and I think all of us realized that a way of life had ended—at the mine, in the plaza, and in Toledo generally. Father López said: "Whatever priests come back to reopen the cathedral, they'll no longer be able to tell the people what to do and how to think." When Father and I peered down the shaft he told me: "It can never be revived. Look at the steps," and when I said: "But there's still silver down there," he corrected me: "The vein had already begun to peter out. With the cage and the donkey engine gone, we'll never go down there again." And I knew that our famed Veta Madre (the Mother Lode) had expired.

Mother, who had seen so many of her family murdered by Gurza's men, knew that the remaining Palafoxes would be forced to live in vastly different ways, and as a strong woman she was prepared to make the effort. And even I would have to accept changed conditions. Now that the mine no longer functioned, I might have to leave the Mineral. I knew that the school I attended had been destroyed by the rebels, and that the parents of many of my schoolmates had been murdered and their big homes burned, so I could not guess what new arrangements would be made for me. Each of us had a personal reason for despair, but we agreed on one thing: General Gurza was a monster who had ravaged Toledo as if he were some invading barbarian from Central Asia come to reduce the rest of the world to ashes. Father López thought that it was God's responsibility to strike down the murdering infidel. Father growled: "He should be hanged." Mother wept over the murder of her relatives and repeated grimly: "An avenger will come." I spent the hours in bed before falling asleep dreaming of coming upon Gurza in some village, he bloated with pride over his latest outrage, I with two revolvers moving in on him, step by step, remorselessly, and growling in a voice lower than I then possessed: "This is for slaughtering our bulls, you vile animal!" and I had the satisfaction of hearing him beg for mercy as I pulled my forefingers against the triggers.

Gurza must have heard my threat, for he responded by horribly sacking three villages and roaring off toward Sinaloa in his death-dealing train. His continued success, even against the Americans sent against him, was a frustration to the northerners and, dishearteningly, a cause of joy and pride among our own peóns. Father would cry: "Someone must strike him down!" and the family would cheer the idea. But not quite all of us. I noticed that whenever our family and Father López cursed Gurza for his brutality, Grandmother Caridad kept silent, but one day

when reports reached us of three more instances of Gurza's besting General Pershing
and his Americans, she cried jubilantly: "He's
doing the job for all of us!" When we looked at
her with mouths agape, she realized that she
could continue her deception no longer. We
were assembled on a patio with only three enclosing walls, the fourth side left open so that
Father or whoever was in charge of the mine
could watch its operation, and I shall never forget the astonishment we felt when she pointed
to the handsome stone fringes Grandfather had
built around the top of the shaft and said:
"Gurza did a grand thing for Mexico when he
destroyed that place of hell."

Father was so astounded at his mother's
words that he could not speak, but Mother, who
was a Palafox and an important one now that
her uncles and cousins were dead, said: "What
a horrible thing to say!" but Caridad continued
pointing at the shaft, now forever silent, and said
in the kind of resolute voice her ancestor Lady
Gray Eyes must have used when she decreed
the destruction of the Mother Goddess: "It was
an evil place and it had to be destroyed."

Now Father regained control of himself:
"What are you saying, Mother?" and she told
him plainly: "I was conceived in what was then
the lowest cavern—the only place my father and

mother could be together. The workers called it Caridad's Cavern. With the donkeys that would never see the sun I lived down there, and I came up those dreadful steps only to carry silver ore on my head."

"But we built the cage," Father protested. "Those ugly days are gone."

"And why wasn't it built years ago? A hundred lives ago?"

"These things take time," Father López said. With a fury that surprised us, she turned on the priest and said with teeth clenching at times and her hands formed into fists: "You were worse than the managers. Where do you suppose they found their endless supply of Indians? Where did Jubal get the little girls who worked with me? From you priests in the villages, who sent them to the mines, told them that's their work."

"Indians always worked in the mines," Father López said, and for the first time I became aware that he was not backing down when she stormed at him because he was protecting his Church against accusations he had heard before. I was ten years old when these conversations at the Mineral occurred, and although I could not understand fully the complicated arguments of the four adults, I did see that Father defended anything that had happened at the mine, Father López championed his Church, Mother saw the Palafoxes as the people who had always known what was best for Toledo, while Grandmother Caridad said repeatedly that General Gurza was a far better man than they thought he was. At times I had the feeling that they were arguing to convince me, as the only uncommitted person in the group, and I listened with equal attention to whoever was speaking.

Father López, whom no one had ever taken seriously, was especially careful to see that I understood what he was saying, for after participating in some general discussion about Indian rights or landownership, he would take me aside and say: "Can't you see, Norman, that it's the big landowners who give us the money to keep the cathedral working? They have a right to large fields because they know how to use them. An Indian? What does he do with his milpa?" That was the word for a little plot of land owned by one family, and I was hearing it a lot. "On his milpa he grows just enough corn for his wife to make her tortillas. But the big man grows more than his wife can use, and with the money he earns he supports the Church."

When Grandmother caught him talking with me she would drag me away: "Never believe a priest when he talks about anything but Jesus

Christ. Everything else, he looks out only for his Church. And it's the priests that threw us into the shaft."

As the discussions continued I saw that Father was listening attentively to both sides, trying to understand what forced López and Grandmother to see recent events in Mexico so differently. One afternoon as we had lunch outdoors at a spot from which we could see the beautiful aqueduct that one of the bishops Palafox had caused to be built almost two hundred years before, he said slowly, as if each word came separately to his mind: "How lovely they are, the old stone arches of our aqueduct. Carrying life-giving water from the pyramid to the cathedral—from you, Mother, to you, Father López," and for a moment he held the two disputants by their hands. It was in that quiet instant, I can see now, that the idea for his powerful book was born—*The Pyramid and the Cathedral,* the two forces that had accounted for Mexican history up to this point: the ancient religion and the new; the Indian heritage and the importation from Europe.

I think it must have been about three weeks that we remained there among the ruins of the Mineral, for the images of those quiet days live with me still: the tall smokestacks of the smelter breathing no more, the building in which the ore had been crushed silent forever, the great brooding pyramid, the arches of the aqueduct and in the distance the faint outlines of Toledo. It was the landscape of a fairy tale, just before the ogre comes thundering onto the scene to disrupt the dream.

If I am correct in assuming that Father conceived the idea for his book during those three weeks in 1918, he certainly had a lot to work on, for after Father López and Grandmother had argued vigorously, Mother would suddenly remind them that it had been the Palafoxes who had brought civilization and Christianity to Toledo: "They found the Mother Lode and built the Mineral. One of them built the aqueduct. All the buildings you see on the horizon—they built them, too, the schools, the churches. Without them, Toledo would still be a collection of adobe huts." Then she added an afterthought: "And we built the bullring, too, and the ranch where the Palafox bulls are raised," and I could see that she considered the weight of that contribution equal to that of the cathedral.

The desire of the adults to convince me of their arguments never abated, and in the fourth week this tug-of-war led to a dramatic experience, which I remember as if it happened yesterday. It occurred when Father López invited me to accompany him on one of his secret visits to believing Catholics in one of the villages north of the pyramid. We had a long walk in the hot sun, so that when we reached the village we were tired, hungry and thirsty, and I saw how the villagers, so poor they had almost nothing for themselves, scurried about to find food for us. Then Father López suggested that they might like to join him in a reading of the Mass. When they said: "That's why we hoped you'd come," there in the center of the village, with armed men on watch to flash a signal if soldiers who hated the Church approached unexpectedly, this little fellow, wearing no robes to distinguish him and with no cathedral behind him to lend him dignity, took out a little book that could have caused his death had the revolutionaries found it on him. He read the words I knew almost by heart; I had heard them so often with Mother. They meant nothing to me, but to the huddled Indians they meant everything, for when he finished, they clustered about to kiss his hand and place their own hands on the missal. It was an act of faith whose intensity I had never before seen, and when he indicated that the rude service was over, the men and women lingered with us to talk of the bewildering events of recent days.

"Will the Mineral be reopened?"

"His father says no."

"Who is the boy?"

"He's one of us. His grandmother is Caridad, you know her." Indeed they did, and favorably, for they asked: "Will she stay at the Mineral?" and Father López replied: "In these days, who knows anything?"

"I know something," a man in white peasant garb said. "I was in Aguascalientes and the talk was that General Gurza, losing battles against the norteamericanos up on the border, is going to retreat back to Aguas and make his head-quarters there."

"May God spare Aguascalientes if he arrives," a woman cried, and several men crossed themselves, but Father López drew the informant to him: "Who said General Gurza would be bringing his trains south?" and the man replied: "Men from the north who had drifted down to Aguas to escape his soldiers, they rob and kill, you've seen."

Not wishing to walk back to the mine in late afternoon, when military patrols might be operating, we waited till sunset, and as I moved about the village I saw boys who were not much older than me carrying rifles, and any house that I entered at the invitation of the owners gave the impression of a little fortress. "We love Jesus," one of the women told me, "and we'll die rather than allow Gurza's men to destroy our village and our church."

"Why wasn't the Mass held in the church?" I asked and they explained: "It's been nailed shut by the soldiers to keep us out, but we sneak in and say our prayers. But to conduct Mass there with all of us together at one time is too danger-ous." When I started to ask why, a woman drew close, stared into my eyes, and asked: "Didn't you people at the Mineral hear what they did at San Cristóbal?" When I shook my head, she said: "Gurza's troops rushed in, caught people saying Mass, barred the doors and burned the place to ashes."

"The people, too?" I asked, and the woman nodded, as did the others.

In the darkness Father López and I walked back toward the pyramid, then cut to the east to find the Mineral, where my anxious family de-manded to know where I had been. When I said: "Saying Mass with Father López at San Isidro," my mother cried: "Irresponsible, subjecting a boy to such risk," and Grandmother said to Fa-ther López: "Serve you right if they'd caught you. A priest showing off to a small boy," but when the excitement died, my father told me quietly: "You did right. You ought to see every-thing. It's your country, too, but I wouldn't do it often. There are people out there who hate priests."

This melancholy time in our lives was dramatically interrupted by the arrival of a high-powered team of mining experts from Nevada who wanted to explore the lower levels of the Mineral to ascertain whether renewed mining would prove practical. Bringing in their own cage, great spools of lightweight wire cable and a surprisingly effective little donkey engine, they set up what they called a jury rig over the shaft and descended in twos and threes to inspect the caverns. Their activity excited Grandmother so much that she camped by the jury rig to watch the fall and ascent of the cage. On the fourth day she grabbed me by the hand: "They said we could go down," and into the improvised system we climbed, listened to the whistle and started the swift plunge to the depths.

I had been in the lower caverns only once, when it was crowded with Indians and donkeys, and to see it now in its vast emptiness was eerie. "This is where the men slept who never went up the steps," Caridad explained. "This is where I stayed when I was too tired. We kept the donkeys over there." When she was finished with her story, I had a clear understanding of what life had been like in the caverns, but during a quiet spell, while the Nevada men were probing

the spots where work had ceased with the dyna-
miting of the shaft, Grandmother made plans
with the engineers whereby she and I would
climb to the older cavern above us and wait
there for the cage to pick us up at the end of the
workday.

"I want you to know what it was like, Norman.
Especially the stairs," and with her climbing the
rock-hewn steps she had known so intimately,
and holding my hand, we started up. I kept my
left shoulder pressed against the smooth rocky
wall of the shaft and my feet as close to the left
as I could. It was a terrifying experience for a boy
of ten, and as fear began to grip me Caridad
comforted me: "Don't look up. One foot at a
time. Shoulder to the wall," but I could not obey
her, for the speck of light was so far above and
the treads of the steps so small that I panicked,
wedged myself against the wall and whispered:
"I can't." When she turned back to encourage
me, she saw that I really was unable to move, so
great was the terror that gripped me.

She did not attempt to move down to my level;
the tread where I stood was too small for that,
but she did manipulate her own feet so that she
could reach back and assist me. "We'll take it
one at a time," she said, in a voice so comforting
that I felt I had been saved, but when she

wanted to pull me up, I cried: "I want to go down," and her hold on my arm tightened. With an almost fierce determination she said: "Climbing up is easier. Going down I'd not be in front to help."

Paralyzed by fear of the darkness below and the frail wisp of light from above as it bounced off irregularities in the rocky walls of the shaft, I was unable to climb either up or down, but then came the reassuring voice of the old woman who had done it a thousand times, with a heavy load balanced on her head: "Norman, it was always easier for me to climb up than down," and with her steady hand guiding me I resumed my upward movement, one cautious step at a time, while my heart pounded furiously.

In that way we reached the spacious safety of a middle cavern, where we left the stairs and I rejoiced at the freedom of movement I now had. Eager to prove that I had lost my childish fear, I almost leaped here and there, even going to the edge of the shaft to inspect the dreadful stairs I had just climbed. As I stood there, my grandmother said an amazing thing: "When I'm dead they'll tell you about the time an evil man plunged down from the spot where you're standing. They'll say they always thought I had pushed him." She paused, took my hand and said: "I did," and in a rush of words she added: "There are times when you must. When evil men will not listen."

"Must do what?" I asked, and she said: "Whatever has to be done."

Since it would be more than an hour before the Nevada men would be signaling for the cage to haul them back to the surface, we had ample time to explore the cavern that had been the principal center in Caridad's early days, and when we finally rested on a pile of rocks she said: "You hear Father López and your mother talk about how they tried to help the Indians. This is how," she said as she pointed at the cavern bathed in pale light. Grimly she added: "This is how we lived, Norman, and if anybody asks you, you tell them."

She spoke for some minutes without interruption about the plight of the Indians, and then she surprised me by saying with vehemence: "It's all wrong, you know, for us to speak of me as an Indian and of Father López as a Mexican, and you and your father as norteamericanos. We're all mestizos, half and half, and we should recognize that."

When I asked her what she meant, she explained: "When Spaniards came, who came? Men and women and children? No, only men. Are they going to live alone all their lives? No,

no! They marry Indian women, like your Grandfather Jubal marry me. So from the beginning,
all mixed, all half and half. I'm not pure Indian.
I doubt I ever saw a pure Indian in all my life. All
mixed." I said: "Mother tells me her Palafoxes
married only other people from noble families in
Spain. She says she's pure Spanish."

"She like to believe it, but book says: 'All big
Palafoxes in church marry Indian girls.' I think
so."

"Why are you so angry with Father López?"
I asked and she replied: "Not him. He good man
I think. But it was other priests put us Indians
here in the caverns. They tell us it's our duty."
Suddenly she stopped, shivered, and looked at
the shaft with all the fear I'd displayed only fifty
minutes before: "When a woman with a basket
fell from broken steps up there, she start to
scream, we run to where you are, and see her
face as she falls past us. We see her eyes, her
terror, sometimes two a week. If she have no
one who wants her, they bury her back of empty
caves this level."

We sat in silence and then her keen ear detected movement below; the Nevada miners
were sending signals upward to inform us they
wanted to remain below, probably for more exploration, and when Caridad heard this she
seemed to accept it as a fortunate respite, for

she took my hand as we sat near the gaping hole and said in her musical Spanish: "Norman, you mustn't believe what they say about General Gurza. Yes, he does kill people sometimes. Yes, he does burn hateful buildings. But he is a good man. Trust me, Norman, he's a good man."

Since this was too ridiculous to accept, I said: "Father, Mother and Father López, they all say he's a monster. I hate him."

Tugging on my arm, she reprimanded me: "Don't listen to them. Make up your own mind," and she continued: "Mestizos, people like me, we all cheer for him. He does our work for us— punishes the rich, drives out the priests, helps the poor. When the norteamericanos try to catch him, he makes fools of them. He is our hero, Norman, and you will never understand your Mexico if you accept rich men's lies that he's a bad man."

For half an hour she told me of life in the Indian villages, of the misery of peón families who tried to grow a little corn. She explained how the arrival of Gurza's train in an area gave the little people hope and they prayed for his successes.

"You're against the priest, the cathedrals, and now you say you're praying."

"We pray to the Virgin of Guadalupe, not the

priest who asks us for money in the cathedral."

The nice distinctions she was making were too confusing for a ten-year-old boy to untangle but what I do remember was her quiet insistence that General Gurza was a friend of the real Mexico, a point that she hammered home some days later when she privately learned from her Indian friends that Gurza's train was heading for Toledo and might arrive within the next days. To my mystification the women said that he was coming not from the north, as usual, but from the southeast. That night at supper Father said: "I hear that monster Gurza tried an attack on Mexico City but has been driven off. If he retreats this way, he'll be in an ugly mood," and he warned us to beware.

The next day government scouts reported that Gurza was approaching the city, and my parents started boarding up our home and hiding anything of value, but Grandmother was behaving like her usual calm self. While the others were occupied with protecting our property she took me by the hand and started walking along a footpath by the aqueduct into the part of Toledo occupied by the poor people. There for the first time in my life I saw the miserable little houses shared by several families, the grown children with no shoes, the dirty pump from which everyone took drinking water, and the misery of the poor in a nation at war. But as we talked with women that Caridad knew, I got the overpowering feeling that they were hoping that General Gurza would come roaring into their city, for then their lot would be improved. He was their hero, and as I moved among them I could hear them singing the latest ballad composed in his honor:

> "Brave General Gurza!
> He takes his train everywhere.
> Good General Gurza!
> He fights our battle for us.
> Kind General Gurza!
> He gives money to the poor.
> Brave General Gurza!
> He don't fear nobody."

Then, as the rough words with the awkward rhymes increased in volume, I heard a rumbling noise from the southeast corner of the city and men came running to inform us: "General Gurza is coming! His train is at the bend!" and before my grandmother could take me out of danger, the battered train, survivor of a dozen attacks by government troops, Mexican and American, was chugging into the very area where Caridad and I were trapped by the milling peóns, and I was terrified.

But this time it was a much different Saturnino Gurza who visited Toledo. In the battles for Mexico City he had been soundly defeated by troops loyal to newly elected President Carranza, so he was running away to some safe hiding spot, not seeking danger as before. I was standing not twenty feet from where his train wheezed to a halt, and when he jumped off to talk with peóns he hoped would support him, one of the first he met was me. Rumpling my hair with his big hand, he bent over me, his huge sombrero almost smothering my face, the bullets in his crossed bandoleers bumping against me, and asked: "You, young fellow, will you be joining me on the train in a couple of years?" Engulfed by his huge mustache, I was too frightened to speak, for here was the devil himself, goading me, but Caridad poked me, shoved me forward and answered on my behalf: "He'll be with you, General, and he'll be a good one."

"Can you shoot a gun?" he asked, and when Caridad assured him that I was a crack shot, he grabbed a gun from one of his men and handed it to me: "Practice, young fellow. We'll be needing you." In the meantime he would be needing food and medicine and whatever ammunition the city could supply. As his men fanned out to commandeer such supplies, he took a chair from a sidewalk café and cried in a loud voice as he sat in the middle of the street: "Doesn't anyone have a beer for the savior of the city?" and admiring peóns scattered about to find him one.

Having established a glancing acquaintance with me, he continued our conversation as he drank: "What's your name, son?" and Caridad broke in hastily: "González, Victoriano González."

"Victoriano!" he shouted, rumpling my hair again. "An omen! In the north we'll have a hundred more victories." And he took me on his knee, as if he were my father. There I sat with the rifle he had given me across my lap and his bandoleers lending me a military posture.

Aware that he could keep his train in Toledo only briefly, for Carranza's troops in superior numbers were after him, he handed me back to Caridad and said: *"Tenemos cosas que hacer en el norte"* (We have things to do up north). When his foraging troops had stripped the stores of everything, he climbed aboard the old engine that had carried him to so many victories, ordered the engineer to sound the mournful whistle, and chugged slowly out of town, as if reluctant to meet the battles he knew lay ahead.

———

Of course Father heard about our having been
in Toledo when the brawling man he called "the
murdering bandit" rode in, and he reprimanded
his mother for having taken such a risk with me:
"If Gurza had known he was a Palafox, he'd
surely have shot him," so neither Caridad nor I
told him that Gurza had dandled me on his knee
and invited me to join him as soon as I was old
enough to carry a rifle, and there the matter
rested, with me totally confused. Caridad did not
tell him that Gurza had given me a rifle, which
she had hidden.

The one who took the news of Gurza's arrival
and departure with quivering dismay was Father
López, who asked me repeatedly: "You mean,
he brought his train right into the middle of
town?" and when I nodded, he continued: "And
he didn't shoot anyone? His men didn't go on
murdering sprees?"

"They were too busy looking for food."

"No fires set?"

"I told you, they were busy."

In considerable agitation, Father López talked
with Father and Mother about General Gurza
and his effect upon Mexico, especially the Catholic Church: "The more nuns he slays, the more
tenaciously our people cling to their faith."

"You have evidence of that?" Father asked,

and the priest said: "When I visit the little villages, all the citizens, they know me as the man
who helps them keep their faith alive."

"If Gurza's men catch you, they'd put you up
against the wall."

"Nothing new. If they catch you and find
you're a Palafox, the same thing."

"I don't want you to take the boy on any more
of your rounds. It's too dangerous."

"I know, I wanted him to see the real Mexico,
but once is enough." I was listening to this conversation and saw that Father López wanted to
speak further on this subject but decided not to.

That night two men came to the Mineral with
a horrible report, to which all of us listened with
hearts thumping: "Men have come to Toledo
with stories of what happened when Gurza's
men reached San Ildefonso, a small town north
of Aguascalientes. Like what they say he did
here in Toledo. The train came into town. No
gunfire, no rape or murder. But there was stealing of food and emptying of stores. And this was
only the beginning."

"What happened?" Father asked, and I was
looking at Grandmother when the men from
Aguas said: "Horrible. Some of our men in San
Ildefonso, patriots and partisans of President
Carranza, shot at Gurza but missed him and
killed one of his colonels. That was the signal for

the most violent gunfire you ever saw. Just blazing away. And then the rioting and the killing of
all the priests and nuns they could find. Those
of us who escaped decided to ride out to other
towns to warn them. Gurza's men are destroying the heart of the town."

On hearing this, Grandmother clasped her
hands tightly, kept them in her lap, and said
nothing, but Father López insisted on hearing
the details repeated and pestered the Aguas
men with questions: "How many priests did they
find?" When he heard the number he flinched,
and then asked: "And the nuns?"

"Only three. Our people hid the others."

"Dead?"

"Mutilated. Then killed."

In a quiet voice López said: "I think we should
say a prayer for the martyrs," and when we
bowed our heads, Grandmother too, she
clasped my hand and at the close of the impassioned lament whispered Amen with the rest of
us.

The next days were tense, for everyone in
Toledo realized by what a narrow margin we had
escaped the fate of San Ildefonso. This was
emphasized by Father at dinner one night: "You
see, Mother, what might have happened when
you took Norman into town," she retorted: "He
left us in peace, didn't he?"

I could see that Father López was profoundly distressed by this new attack on nuns, for repeatedly he said: "The killing of men, if they fired against his troops, that I can understand, or maybe even to kill a nun if you came upon her suddenly in a mob, but to seek them out like dogs chasing a hare, that's . . ." He never finished his sentence, for his vocabulary had no word adequate to describe that horror.

Later, when he learned that General Gurza had kept his train at San Ildefonso, since the ravaged town was his to command, using it as a base from which he fanned out to punish government troops or drive the Americans out of Mexico, Father López felt that this was a challenge not to the men of San Ildefonso but to God himself: "It's a sacrilege, a work of the Anti-Christ." At supper, which he took with us, always returning from his expeditions at sunset, he repeatedly told my parents: "He really is the Anti-Christ, and God will punish him." I think my parents grew weary of his fulminations because one day Father said: "But, Father Juan, if you are powerless to force God to exact punishment, why not forget the monster?" and López replied: "Maybe it's because God wants us to do his work for him and punish Gurza."

When he saw that the Clays were beginning to regret having taken him under their protec-

tion, he became nervous, staying away over-
night and remaining silent at the table when he
was there. One morning when we had risen
early and he was about to set forth on his missionary work, he took special care to bid me
farewell, as if he were going on a long journey.
I saw that he was unusually disturbed and that
after leaving the Mineral he headed not to the
villages on his normal rounds but to the northwest. I waited till he was gone, then went after
him, remaining well behind him, but because he
always checked the landscape when he went
on his dangerous missions, he chanced to look
behind him and saw me.

Almost joyously he ran back to embrace me:
"Norman, you've come to lend me courage,"
and without explaining what that signified, he
allowed me to walk with him in the morning sunlight as he hiked westward behind the pyramid.
"Where are you going?" I asked as we approached the railroad tracks that led to Aguascalientes, and he replied: "To where God has
called me." And then he surprised me by revealing a wrapped package he'd been keeping
under his cotton shirt: "You must forgive me,
Norman, but I stole your gun," and he showed
me how he had taken it apart, keeping all the
screws and bolts in a paper bag for reassembly.
When he saw my reluctance to lose the gun he

said benignly: "It's an evil gun, Norman, his gun,
the Anti-Christ's, and it would bring you harm.
Give it to me with your blessing," and there beside the tracks where no one could see, I used
a phrase Mother had taught me: "I, Norman,
give thee, Juan, this my gun, and with it my
blessing."

Embracing me and fighting back his tears, this
dear, good priest whom it was not easy to love,
for he was a difficult man of tedious disposition,
embraced me ardently, kissed me on the forehead and whispered: "When you're a man, Norman, never draw back from doing the right thing,
that's the mark of a man." With that he turned
me about, gave me a gentle push on the back
and started me on my way home. I last saw him
walking purposefully along the railroad tracks on
his way north with the gun General Gurza had
given me.

Three days later the news flashed through Mexico, and the United States, too. A shoeless
peasant residing in San Ildefonso, which General Gurza had ravaged the previous week, had
whipped a gun from inside the white camisa that
peóns wore and fired it directly at Gurza from a
distance of only a few feet, killing him instantly.
The dead general's bodyguards were so in-

furiated that they and other soldiers beat the assassin to the point where his corpse was too mutilated to permit identification. But in the days that followed, President Carranza's men, hoping to downgrade their dead enemy's popular support, circulated the rumor that the gun used to commit the murder was one that had been issued to Gurza's troops after the sack of an arms plant near Mexico City, which proved, they said, that the cruel revolutionary had been slain by one of his own men.

Mother and Father deemed this an act of divine intervention, and they intended asking Father López about this. But my shrewd grandmother had another interpretation, which she confided to me privately: "Like an old woman knitting in the sun, General Gurza had used up his skein. He completed his job. He set Mexico free," and then she led me to her tiny room, where, inside a small traveling bag, she had kept hidden a photograph that a man in Toledo had snapped the afternoon I met General Gurza. It showed me perched on his knee, his big face, mustache and huge sombrero close to me as he handed me the gun that I was supposed to use in his defense when I was fourteen. It was an excellent photo.

"Protect it, Norman. Someday you'll be proud you have it, for it could be the last photograph ever taken of our great leader," and together we sang in muted voices the *Ballad of Saturnino* with its insolent marching rhythm:

> "Gallant Saturnino!
> He rode the train.
> Heroic Saturnino!
> He fought Black Jack.
> Stupendous Saturnino!
> He scorned Carranza.
> Immortal Saturnino!
> He brought us freedom."

The last five syllables were sung as a staccato chant, defying the world, and when they ended, as a kind of benediction to General Gurza, Grandmother took back the photo momentarily, studied it, kissed it and told me: "When I labored in the caverns I dreamed of such a man, but I thought he would come on a white horse, like Zapata. This one came on that rusty train."

The rest of my story about the Clays in Mexico can be quickly told. When Father López failed to return, my parents assumed he had been shot in one of the villages he served, and we said no more about him. In time Grandmother learned that the gun General Gurza had given me was

missing, but never asked me about it. The mining engineers from Nevada returned to explore
the mine twice more before giving up, and on
their last visit their leader told Father: "We help
American Petroleum now and then. They have
the big oil fields at Tampico, and they told me
the other day they'd like to find some responsible American . . ."

"I'm only half American. Born a Mexican,
keep that citizenship, too."

"They know. And they asked if I thought you
might be interested in serving as their representative in this middle part of the country."

"What would I be expected to do?"

"If I understand what they said, you'd help
them find skilled labor, or young men who've
had education in the States, maybe send some
up to Texas and Oklahoma."

"No oil wells in Toledo. It seems a curious
job."

"People are in Toledo. A.P. expects to be in
Mexico for the rest of the century, the reserves
are that big. They need someone like you as
part of their team," and when the shrewd men
from American Petroleum came to Toledo to
interview Father, they saw immediately that the
good relations he'd established at the Mineral
were what they needed to safeguard their holdings in Mexico.

Our family did not have to leave Toledo for Father to do the work they wanted, and this allowed him time to write the book that made him famous and caused the statue, *The Pyramid and the Cathedral,* to be erected in his honor at the far corner of the plaza. From our front porch we could see both edifices, and their history was in our bloodstream. It was a noble book, still is, a glimpse into the heart of Mexico, and one of the passages I've cherished is his portrait of Jubal Clay with his Confederate brothers in his final years:

> Each year on the ninth of April those Confederate soldiers who had refused to live under the domination of the North and General Grant, finding refuge here in the salubrious climate of Toledo, would convene in fellowship to mark, not celebrate, the day on which Robert E. Lee surrendered to Butcher Grant at Appomattox Court House.
>
> Someone would propose a toast: "To the day the world ended!" and they would drink in silence, but always someone else proposed: "To the day Canada invades the North and we rush there to help her." This toast they drank with cheers and cries of

"We'll be there!" At the first reunion after the election of Grant as president, Jubal proposed his own toast: "We can take heart from the election of Butcher Grant, because it proves there is a God in heaven. He's giving those bastards what they deserve. Let's watch how he messes up the nation as he did his army at Cold Harbor."

But as the years passed, and the exiles aged, Jubal noted a phenomenon: "Every man who recalled his battle experiences claimed he had fought with either Stonewall Jackson or Jeb Stuart or Massa Robert himself. Since not one of us admitted he had fought under a losing general, I often wondered how we had managed to lose the war."

As time went on, Father proved so invaluable to American Petroleum that the company offered him yearly bonuses in stock, until we became a family with a solid if not spectacular financial footing. As the president of the company once said when delivering the bonus at a staff gathering: "The best thing John Clay ever did for this company was write that book. It proved to the Mexicans that we were not only good people but also a cultured group who appreciated Mexican patterns of life. Clay is our resident Mexican, and we treasure him."

Under Father's guidance mining affairs proved so profitable in central Mexico that American Petroleum decided to probe deeper into our Mineral to see if perhaps some major vein lay hidden far below what was now known as Caridad's Cavern at the thirteen-hundred-foot mark. So the Nevada engineers who had probed in the 1930s returned with new equipment that enabled them to speed down below the nineteen-hundred-foot level, but they found nothing. However, Father's other projects earned the company rich rewards.

You can imagine his dismay when the radical liberal Lázaro Cárdenas became president in 1934 and began threatening to expropriate all foreign petroleum holdings. He told me in the letters he sent me at college—I was a graduate student in those years—that Mexico was plunging headlong into another revolution. That same year he sent me news that Grandmother Caridad had died, "a wonderful fighting woman to the end." He said that she left a cryptic message for me: "Tell Norman to guard that photograph. Each year it becomes more valuable." It was clear that as Mexico became more nationalistic, and more particularly because of its willingness to stand up to the United States on the oil business, Saturnino Gurza was being slowly but surely converted into one of the great national heroes. Those pusillanimous leaders who had opposed him, such as Carranza and Huerta and Obregón, were seen as men to be forgotten, while Gurza grew yearly in stature. Grandmother had been right in her assessment of Mexican history; Father López had been wrong.

But Grandmother's death posed a difficult problem for me, for with her gone I was the only person alive who knew that Father Juan had died a martyr's death, and the knowledge of that truth hung heavily upon me. In those tumultuous days after the assassination of Gurza it was prudent to preserve the secret, for to reveal it might have caused danger not only to our family for having harbored the assassin but to the Catholic Church as a whole for having encouraged, it might seem, this blow against a revered leader. Now the burden of truth lay on me alone, and often as I looked at that remarkable photo, the last ever taken of Gurza, as Caridad had suspected, I watched it become transformed under my very eyes. General Gurza, the man holding me on his knee, had become the father of the new Mexico, and I resolved that sometime, when the occasion was proper, I would reveal both the photograph and the history of the rifle.

In the meantime I had six excellent copies made and kept them in various places.

In 1938 Cárdenas did expropriate the oil wells; American Petroleum was expelled from Mexico, its enormous wealth wiped out by a mere scratching of a presidential pen; and soon thereafter my father, author of the fine book about Mexico, left that country for good. My mother, always a loyal Palafox, refused to join him, but in due course I followed his example, even to the extent of leaving a Palafox wife behind me. Father wanted to bring my mother with us, but she refused to leave the ancestral home of the Palafoxes; an equally weighty consideration was her religion. At her marriage to my father, there had been a mutual understanding that she would remain Catholic but he would be free to elect at some future time whether he wanted to join her church or not. He delayed his decision, and neither he nor Grandmother Caridad applied any pressure on me to join any religion, Mother's Catholicism or Father's Protestantism. Caridad told me when I was eleven: "I've been a good Catholic like all before me, but the only thing it ever did for me was put me down in the mines."

There was no bitterness in our departure, that is, personally. Mother and Father had regard for each other, but Father said he simply could not live in a nation that stole private property with inadequate compensation, and Mother said it was unthinkable that she could ever live in a country like the United States that had stolen not property but the entire northern state of Mexico. When I asked what this meant she said: "I mean the parts you call Texas, New Mexico, Arizona and California. Stole them all and someday we'll march north to gain them back."

Father was not alone in these days of anguished decisions about future lives. I had married a lovely Palafox girl, from the Spanish branch, and she too found it incomprehensible that she would accept exile in America, abandoning all that had made Toledo such a splendid home, with the advantages that accrued to the name Palafox. She refused to join me, so that when Father and I left Toledo for a new home in Alabama, all of us knew that reconciliations were improbable. In those days a man decided where his family should live, so there was not one moment's consideration of the fact that I might want to stay with Mother in Toledo.

Father had chosen Montgomery because it was a fine Southern city populated by reliable people who still believed that the South should have won the War Between the States, as they called it, since they viewed the war as having been fought between two equal national entities—one pro-slavery, one anti. "There was no rebellion, young man," a distant cousin lectured me when I arrived: "It was a war between equals, except that we had all the education and moral training, they had the railroads and the factories."

I was happy in Alabama until I found out that another reason Father had wanted to settle there was that he would be close to Mexico when war started. He was convinced that President Roosevelt would soon march south of the border to take back the oil wells and he wanted to be in on the kill. When it was apparent that the crippled president was indeed planning a war, not against Mexico but against Germany, he told the members of his Confederate Club: "My God! He's fighting the wrong war!" and once more Clay felt betrayed by Northern leadership.

In Montgomery he suffered many regrets, not because of his treatment there, but because he felt it was indecent for him to live on his pension and stock from American Petroleum when he had failed them so signally: "They hired me to help them maintain good relations with the Mexican government, and I had to sit by in impotence when Cárdenas stole our entire operation and hundreds of years of oil reserves. I'm a total failure." And when his New York publishers wanted him to write a foreword for a special edition of *The Pyramid and the Cathedral,* explaining the new Mexico, he told them: "The new Mexico can go to hell." They replied with an urgent letter: "Don't say that in public," and he didn't.

So there you have my family tree. Indian builders back to A.D. 600. Spanish scholars back to 1498. Virginia patriots only to 1823, but you have seen my undefeated grandfather Jubal and my philosopher father, John, in proper detail. As for myself, I was born in Toledo in 1909 to a Palafox mother and a son of a Confederate émigré, lived through the heat of the revolution, and emigrated back to the United States in time to growl: "If Hitler and Tojo think they can destroy our pattern of life, we'd better do something about it." In 1942 I saw duty in the Pacific as an aviator, and in 1950 as a combat correspondent in Korea.

When I felt that I had to abandon my wife in Toledo, a decision that she made, not I, she sensibly had our marriage annulled on grounds that I had refused to live with her, which was technically correct. I regretted my losing her, even mourned it, but there was nothing I could do.

Like the offspring of those other Confederate

soldiers who fled to Mexico in 1866, I have never been able to determine whether I'm a Mexican or a norteamericano. I was born a Mexican citizen and in my formative years led a wildly exciting life there; as an adult I gained American citizenship by virtue of my volunteering for World War II; but I return to Mexico whenever I get a chance, for to visit the plaza of Toledo in moonlight and see that rim of handsome buildings built by members of my Spanish family, or that fabulous Mineral rejuvenated by my grandfather, or the brooding pyramid begun in 650 by restless Ixmiq moves me more deeply than anything I see elsewhere. Even if I went back to Cold Harbor to see where Grandfather Jubal masterminded his half hour of horror, I doubt it would affect me as deeply as a visit to that plaza in which General Gurza committed his crimes and then gave me my gun.

BY
TORCHLIGHT

IT IS the second night of a three-day bull-fight festival that is often the most rewarding. Friendships have been made. Visitors have learned where to find the fashionable places to dine. The spectators now have six different matadors to compare. There is not the pang of regret that sometimes overwhelms the final night. But as day quickly fades after the death of the last bull on Saturday, night arrives with its mystical powers, and nowhere in Mexico or Spain is there a finer plaza in which to celebrate the ending of a festival day than the one in Toledo.

The plaza itself is of such careful proportions, large enough to accommodate big crowds but not so spacious as to prevent intimacy, that it makes being there a pleasure. I know a dozen plazas in the cities of the world, and many, like that of Salamanca, are larger than Toledo's and some, like the one at Cartagena, have more imposing single buildings; others, like the big one in Madrid, played major roles in Spanish and world history, and certainly the majestic Zócalo of Mexico City with its cathedral dedicated to the Virgin of Guadalupe is perhaps the best of all. I do not include the area before St. Peter's in Rome in that comparison, because it has none of the intimacy of a plaza; indeed, it isn't even enclosed on all four sides.

But the plaza in Toledo has one overwhelming mark of superiority: it is scaled with almost magical precision to the human experience, the size and capacities of the human being. You can stand at the statue of Ixmiq at the north end and still keep in touch with what's happening at the statue of my father, John Clay, at the southern end, and if you spot a pretty girl taking her evening stroll at the far end, you have only to wait where you are, for she will soon be passing you.

For many Toledanos the plaza has one serious drawback. The broad avenue that runs down the western length in front of the cathedral has in recent years been rechristened by politicians Avenida Gral. Gurza in honor of the famous bandit who, in other parts of Mexico, is revered as a hero, but who in Toledo is rejected with shudders because of the terror he brought our city.

The word *Gral.* has always fascinated me, for as one travels in Mexico one comes upon one avenue after another named Avenida Gral. Gómez or the like, and this perplexed me until I learned that *Gral.* is an abbreviation of the word *General.* Mexico adores its generals, and any sizable city that does not have an Avenida Gral. This or That is poor indeed. Because my grandmother, a fervent partisan of Gral. Gurza, taught me to respect what the man had been trying to do, I accepted the name of the avenue.

On this lovely night under the stars a wooden theatrical platform, a kind of rustic stage, had been erected on Gral. Gurza where it passed in front of the cathedral, but at the southern end near the statue of my father. On this stage Héctor Sepúlveda, the one-handed poet who had conducted himself so convincingly in the Tournament of Flowers Thursday night, was to direct a pageant he had written entitled *Here in This Plaza,* and from the posters I'd seen I supposed

it would be a Mexican version of a show I had
seen one dark night at the Bastille in Paris. It
was most effective, an artistic mix of previously
recorded fiery orations, music and the sounds of
a mob storming the prison gates, all emphasized by brilliantly synchronized lighting effects.
I thought: The Mexicans are great at such displays, and I had bought my ticket.

Hispanic custom being what it is, the produ-
cers of such an entertainment faced a difficult
decision: "Do we give it at eight in the evening
before the public eats dinner at eleven? Or do
we give it at one in the morning, after the spectators have eaten?" The Altomec poet had wisely
decided on the latter, since he realized that his
audience would be excited after the ending of
the bullfight and would be so engaged in festivities that they would not want to sit still to hear
his performance. It would start at one.

This delay gave me time to watch evening
shadows come creeping over the plaza, and it
was as if each degree of gathering darkness
brought out its own accompaniment of mariachi
bands, for one by one they appeared in various
quarters of the plaza and the surrounding
streets, until they seemed like a gathering of
chattering birds, each singing its own song.

As their music grew, I found deep pleasure in
just sitting there and watching events in the

plaza and on the Terrace. When the Widow Palafox bustled past checking that tables were properly set for the evening meal, I thought: How reassuring it is to see the continuity of ordinary behavior, and as if to demonstrate the truth of this comment, Don Eduardo stopped by to spread lies about his six bulls for the morrow: "Precious, Don Norman, I assure you, if the matadors are equal to the task of making them conform." For the last twenty Ixmiq festivals he had been saying that about his bulls, even when he knew that at best they were only marginal. But as I started to laugh at his fraudulent spiel I remembered how many times in past decades some Palafox bull whom the experts had dismissed as marginal had come storming into an arena and torn the place apart. It did not pay ever to laugh at Don Eduardo—or his bulls.

Sitting momentarily at my table he surprised me by asking: "Norman, do you ever miss Magdalena?"

Since he was referring to one of his nieces, a fine Palafox girl to whom I'd been married for five years, I felt I must speak well of her, but doing so was not difficult because she had been a good wife: "When I'm in the States I almost feel as if I'd never known her. But here in Toledo—looking at that plaza where we courted—my heart could break with longing."

He sighed, for he too remembered Magdalena, one of the best Palafox women of her generation, but now an exile in Madrid: "You should seriously consider, Norman, flying to Madrid and bringing her back to Toledo. And while you're about it, why not bring yourself back?" Since there was nothing I could say, he shrugged, rose and continued his wandering among the tables.

When the two Oklahoma women came onto the Terrace for dinner, I invited them to join me and I quickly saw that young Penny was still grieving over the loss of her matador, for her red eyes showed that she had been weeping. But such regrets ended when León Ledesma came up from the plaza, halted dramatically as he drew his cape around him, and studied the scene as if deciding whether it would be worth his while to mingle with us. His mind was made up by Mrs. Evans, who called: "Señor Critic, what did you write about today's performances"

"Do you really want to hear?" he asked as he joined us, and without waiting for an answer, for it was obvious that he wanted to show off, he said: "Of the divine Conchita I wrote: 'She bade farewell to Toledo and our hearts with the wonderful grace she has always had, and we wept as she departed.' "

"But what did you say of her performance?"

Mrs. Evans asked, and he snapped: "A real critic never bothers with rejoneadors, male or female. I indicated that I loved her, didn't I?"

"And Calesero?"

"A man of honor. A distinguished citizen of Aguascalientes, one of my favorite cities, and a man who can be very good with the cape, but not too good with the kill. Of such men whom I hold in esteem I have two code words, *detalles,* details, and *pinceladas,* delicate brushstrokes. To see Calesero give three of his wonderful passes to a real bull is better than watching some clown have good luck with a compliant one."

"And Pepe Luis Vásquez? I felt respect for that young man."

"And so you should. He's one of those honest workmen who brings basic credit to the art of bullfighting. Always dependable. With him you're sure to see honorable effort, and when he gets a good animal, he wins ears because the heart of the audience is with him. In respecting him, Señora Evans, you become a true aficionada. But what do you suppose I wrote about our newcomer, Don Fermín?"

"Did he pay you?"

"Adequately. My words read better in Spanish. More poetic, more resonant," and he proceeded to read his commentary on Fermín with such dramatic force that she had to stop him: "My Spanish isn't good enough. I don't understand a word you're saying."

"With what I write sometimes it's better that way," he said and folded the paper. "What I said was that this young man has a future as promising as Armillita's or Gaona's at a similar age." When I gasped, for these were two of Mexico's greatest, he snapped peevishly: "I didn't say he *was* as great. Only that he had a chance to be."

"And if he doesn't pay you next time?" Mrs. Evans asked, and he replied: "Then I say: 'Despite the great promise he showed at Toledo, it's now clear that he's a zero, has not fulfilled his potential, no class at all.'"

Mrs. Evans, enjoying the preposterous exhibitionism of this sardonic man, asked: "Will you be coming with us to the pageant tonight?" and he dismissed her with a sneer: "I loathe amateur theatrics." He delivered the Spanish word for *loathe* in four long-drawn-out syllables, *aborrezco,* but then he bowed to the two women and said: "However, to accompany you would be so pleasant that I shall be here to escort you." And he too wandered off.

During the leisurely meal electric lights throughout the plaza were turned off, and in the momentary darkness men ran with flaming brands to light a multitude of torches, devices constructed of some kind of long-burning wick drawing from a reservoir of oil contained in a can. To see these torches emerge like a host of fireflies on a summer night was a return to child-hood innocence. The plaza suddenly became so enchanting that whatever might happen at the pageant would be touched with magic.

It was now toward one in the morning, and I watched the crowd beginning to drift toward the improvised stands facing the cathedral where a built-up wooden stage merged easily with the entry steps to the church. This enabled the eight pillars to be used as part of the scene, and the great doors to be opened and closed as the action required. Thus the entire church would be part of the presentation.

The Widow Palafox came through warning her patrons: "Better start for the cathedral or you'll miss the opening," whereupon Ledesma returned to our table, extended his right arm to Mrs. Evans, his left to Penny, and started the procession through the plaza. Don Eduardo and I trailed behind, arriving at the cathedral just in time to take the seats that had been reserved for us, with Don Eduardo, Ledesma and Penny in the front row, Mrs. Evans and me off to one side in the second. I was not unhappy about this arrangement, for it allowed me an opportunity before the play started to speak about Penny, in whom my interest had grown.

"She seems an admirable girl," I said. "Perhaps a bit raw about the edges, but—"

"Tulsa-raw. When it matures you can get a very powerful person."

"Has she that possibility?"

For some moments she pondered this, then said: "The way she's handled her father recently makes me think so. She's been more mature than I could have been," and she told me how the confrontation had developed. "Ed came home one day while Penny was still in school. Needing a tool he could not find, he suspected it might be in her room. When he got there he didn't find it, but he did see on the wall a big four-color poster of the kind high school kids enjoy. This one showed a fifteen-year-old red-headed nymphet barely clothed, and the caption:

> Sure, blondes have more fun,
> But redheads have it more often.

"He left it there, but when she came home he asked: 'Does that mean what I think it means?' and she said: 'Sure, if you have a dirty mind.' Again he said nothing, but the next day when she returned from school the poster was missing.

"She was outraged: 'I thought we had an agreement you wouldn't trespass on my room,' and he said quietly: 'That's not the kind of sign to be looking at just before you go to sleep.' She had the sense to surrender: 'You may be right, Dad,' and the flash point was avoided.

"But a few days later she told him: 'When the Haggards and Mrs. Evans go down to Mexico next month, I'm going along.'

" 'Not without my permission.'

" 'I'm going, Dad. Don't let's make a big deal of it.'

" 'Why in hell would you want to go to Mexico?'

" 'Because last Sunday's paper said that the Festival of Ixmiq in the little town of Toledo was a highlight of the season.'

" 'Why would you bother with a Mexican festival? It's a backward country to begin with.'

" 'Because they have bullfights, and I'd like to meet a matador.'

"At this poor Ed exploded, called me in as Penny's unofficial guardian and asked, with both of us sitting there: 'Elsie, what's gotten into this child? She wants to drive to Mexico with you to see if she can meet a matador,' and I said: 'When I was her age I was burning to meet John

Barrymore.' And then I added: 'Ed, the obligation of a child is not to make his or her parents happy.'

" 'That's a hell of a rule. What *is* her obligation?'

" 'To develop into a mature woman, with character. To be herself.' It was hard to do, but I told Ed that I thought if my son had had more personal gumption he might be alive today. But when my husband died, poor Peter felt he had to remain home and look after me. I told him: 'Ed. If you want to keep her, let her go. Unless you want her to grow up to be one more oil heiress making a damn fool of herself in New York and Paris.' "

"How did he take that?" I asked, and she said: "He kissed me and said: 'Off we go to Mexico, if I can take it.' Obviously, as you saw, he couldn't. He fled." She chuckled: "So there beside Señor Ledesma we have a young lady who is developing a very strong character. Mexico's been good for her—and for me, too. I needed it as much as she did."

At this point the mariachis ended their overture with a blare of trumpets, after which the one-armed Altomec poet, dressed in the flimsy clothing of a peón, came out from the cathedral, walked down the steps and took center stage, where he declaimed:

"This is the House of God
Built by the Bishops Palafox.
Here is where the laws of God
Were promulgated.
Here we worshiped for four hundred
  years,
Here we were baptized.
Here we were married
Here we paid our tithes
It was a holy place."

Suddenly, from inside the cathedral came three separate groups of three men each dressed in simple black robes and wailing antiphonally, first one group then another:

PRIESTS: We are the three of Toledo.

Now from the front rows of the audience came the heavy voices of two dozen men and women in the peón costume representing the people not only of Toledo but of all Mexico. Their combined voices had great authority:

ALL THE PRIESTS: We are three priests of Toledo.

PEOPLE: May their souls rest in peace.

FIRST PRIEST: We served God and the people of Mexico, as we were instructed.

PEOPLE: May their souls rest in peace.

SECOND PRIEST: We brought mercy to the people, we brought justice.

PEOPLE: These three good men instructed us, they baptized us. And at the hour of death they sped us into the arms of God.

THIRD PRIEST: We are the three who were assassinated against these walls.

At this each group went to a part of the façade at which the executions of 1914 had taken place, as the mariachi musicians played mournful notes:

PEOPLE: May their souls rest in peace, may these good men find eternal peace.

While the priests remained in their positions against the wall, the music became martial, the marching songs I had sung with my grandmother during the Revolution, "Adelita" and "Jesusita en Chihuahua," while from behind the cathedral came a large group of soldiers in tattered uniforms:

SOLDIERS: We are the brave soldiers who saved the city of Toledo.

PEOPLE: May they be awarded medals.

SOLDIERS: For eleven bitter years we fought to save Mexico, and our wives knew us not, our sons were not born.

PEOPLE: Across the barren fields they fought, on the outskirts of the city they skirmished, and they died as they were commanded.

SOLDIERS: But we are also the ones who burned Toledo, who destroyed the cathedral in which we march tonight.

PEOPLE: May their souls rest in peace, the peace they never knew.

SOLDIERS: We are the firing squad that mur-
            dered the priests here against
            the wall, as we were com-
            manded.

PEOPLE: Merciful God, forgive them.

Eight of the soldiers now detached themselves
from the body, raised their rifles, and formed a
firing squad to murder the priests. An officer
took charge, raised his sword as we awaited the
volley, then dropped it . . . in silence. And although there was no explosion of gunfire, the
priests fell. I think we were pleased that we had
been spared the sound of real bullets; it was
only make-believe.

PEOPLE: It was an act that should not
          have happened.

There now came a long reading by the poet in
which he told the other side of the priests' story,
of how they went through the countryside finding Indian villages and converting them in one
gesture to Christianity and slavery in the mines.
A band of Indian women sang and danced their
bitter version of the Conquest:

WOMEN: We danced to the rain god, we
         sang to the gods of nature.

PRIESTS: Then we came to save you.

WOMEN: Before, we never worked in the mines.

PRIESTS: We want you to be good citizens.

WOMEN: We used to stay with our children.

PRIESTS: You are needed in the mines. It is a way of life.

WOMEN: We grow faint. And are long gone in pregnancy.

PRIESTS: You are needed in the cotton fields . . . in the mines.

WOMEN: In the mines we perish. Allow us to be free.

PRIESTS: Silence. Saint Paul has said, in such matters the woman is to be silent. We will advise you. Your life is in the mines.

Now eight soldiers detached themselves from the others and lined up with heavy rifles in a firing position. All the soldiers chanted in extremely slow cadence:

SOLDIERS: Those are the ones in that firing squad, not us, those are the ones who sought seven nuns at the convent.

NUNS: We are the seven of Toledo, the seven who served the people, who cared for abandoned children, who served God in our dozen ways.

SOLDIERS: It was those others who dug out the hiding nuns, not us.

NUNS: When we saw the guns pointed at us, we knew the end was near, but no one cried out or tried to run away. We were in the hands of Jesus.

SOLDIERS: It was those others who did the dreadful thing, it was not us. We did not give the order.

At this point the eight soldiers with guns faced the seven nuns, and the officer in bright uniform appeared with sword raised. As he dropped it the eight riflemen fired, this time with a terrifying explosion, and the seven nuns fell to the ground, with heart-stabbing effect. No longer was it make-believe.

> PEOPLE: God, forgive the soldiers. They did not give the order. God, take to your bosom the seven nuns. They were the brides of Jesus.

Suddenly the mariachis broke into the wildest of the revolutionary songs, creating an impression of troops on a rampage, raping and burning. After this chaotic episode, they played a song about a military train coming into the city. Then a large group of men occupied the stage, with someone looking remarkably like General Gurza in the center:

> GRAL. GURZA: I am the man . . . not the general . . . not the revolutionary. I am the man who had to make decisions.

> PEOPLE: May his soul rest in peace. He was a man of Mexico.

> GRAL. GURZA: I had to burn Toledo. The enemy was close on my heels. I had to deprive them of your city.

> PEOPLE: God will forgive him. It was an act of war.

GRAL. GURZA: It was I who ordered the three priests to be executed. Death to their thieving bishops . . . they were conspiring against us . . . against the revolution.

PEOPLE: May his soul rest in peace. He was a patriot.

GRAL. GURZA: It was not I who ordered the nuns to be shot. He did it, that one in the fancy uniform . . . he did it.

When the officer saluted, some in the audience booed, the seven nuns came alive again, and the firing squad aimed their guns again, but this time Gral. Gurza stepped in front of them and ordered them to lower their rifles as the audience cheered.

GRAL. GURZA: In my anguish I stormed back and forth across the face of Mexico. And in my honor I refused the presidency, for I was only a simple soldier.

PEOPLE: May his soul rest in peace, this patriot.

The poet had expected cynics in the audience to snicker at Gurza's protestations of anguish and simplicity, so he had given the general lines that allowed him to castigate spectators in the front rows:

GRAL. GURZA: Do not laugh at me. Where do you think you are sitting, you with the smiles on your faces? Look at the sign. What does it . . . ? I can't read, but I know that sign. It says Avenida Gral. Gurza. My avenue, my land you're sitting on. The people of Toledo knew what they were doing when they named this avenue after me.

PEOPLE: He is right. He is forgiven. May his soul rest in peace.

GRAL. GURZA: I did not seek peace. I sought the war that would set us free.

PEOPLE: Give this good man peace. He saved us.

What the poet presented next astounded and delighted me, for that afternoon a technician using a ladder must have climbed the statue of my father and hidden a loudspeaker near the mouth, so that when an unseen actor spoke, the words came directly from my father. It was uncanny.

JOHN CLAY: I watched and I wrote.

PEOPLE: He told the truth. He was a norteamericano, but he told the truth.

JOHN CLAY: No man ever came to me in vain. In my house there was refuge.

PEOPLE: He gave refuge to Father López. May both men rest in peace.

JOHN CLAY: I watched and I wrote, I said: "Never will Mexico find peace."

PEOPLE: And he said: "Never can the Indian be educated."

PRIESTS: And he said: "The church begs and steals, deludes and threatens."

PEOPLE: May God have mercy on his soul.

SOLDIERS: And he said: "The army murders and rapes, burns and
steals."

PEOPLE: And he said: "Oh, Mexico! I am
the son of the cactus and the
maguey."

When the light that had been playing on the
statue faded, a tall figure in gorgeous diplomatic
dress, covered with medals, stalked out from
the wings and onto the center of the wooden
stage where, in a voice of gentle reason, he
spoke:

MAXIMILIAN: I too was the stranger who
loved Mexico.

PEOPLE: He tried to govern wisely.

MAXIMILIAN: When the French discarded
me, and counseled me to flee,
I pondered for three days.

PEOPLE: He elected to fight alone, for all
of Mexico. Willingly he marched
toward his grave.

MAXIMILIAN: I did not flinch. I had made my
decision and I did not flinch.

Now the squad of eight, guns at the ready, aimed at Maximilian, and the same officer raised his sword, dropped it and again came the explosion of eight rifles, with Maximilian falling dead.

ALL: May God have mercy upon his soul. May he find peace.

PEOPLE: May his soul find peace, for he was a worthy man.

SOLDIERS: We were called often to form the firing squad. Across Mexico we worked, bringing new patterns of peace.

ONE SOLDIER: But we never chose the victims. We never gave the order. That one did.

THE OFFICER: I did as I was commanded. Our job was to bring peace to Mexico.

PEOPLE: May he too find peace. He did only what he was told.

At the far end of the plaza another microphone activated a loudspeaker near the mouth of the Ixmiq statue, and the distant position coupled with the deep register of tone created a voice from ancient days. But it was not the voice of the Ixmiq I knew, the great builder of the sixth century; it was that of the later Ixmiq, slain by the Spaniards:

IXMIQ: I am Ixmiq, the Indian. I am he who was crucified.

PRIESTS: May God heal his wounds. May the Virgin console him.

IXMIQ: In the hours of my agony no priest consoled me, for it was they who had condemned me.

PRIEST: May this agonized soul find peace.

IXMIQ: When the blood from the gashes on my shinbones ran down to my eyes, no soldier fought for me.

PEOPLE: How could blood from his shins drip down into his eyes?

IXMIQ: The Spaniards crucified me upside down. My head was splitting and my own blood choked me.

SOLDIERS: Rest, Ixmiq, rest.

PEOPLE: Why did they do this to you?

IXMIQ: The priests said that when Jesus was crucified, he rose and went to heaven. When I was crucified, I merely died. I was no god. "See!" they cried. "He is no god."

PEOPLE: How did they prove that?

IXMIQ: They left me hanging on this post for seven months . . . dried . . . feet turning to dust . . . the people could see I had been no god.

SOLDIERS: Rest, Ixmiq, rest.

IXMIQ: Save your consolation—I do not grieve. From my ashes have risen a melodious people.

Here the mariachis played some of the most heavenly music I'd ever heard, with the two trumpeters creating a mood of conciliation.

ALL: He who was crucified has found peace.

IXMIQ: In the plaza of Toledo my soul wanders at night.

ALL: He whose body was finally burned has found consolation.

IXMIQ: And where the cactus and the maguey meet, my dreams and my hopes are entwined.

At this innocuous statement all hell broke loose in the plaza, for at the southern end of the square my father protested in a piercing voice:

CLAY: I wrote those words. You're stealing my words.

At which, from the northern end, Ixmiq replied in that deep voice that seemed to rumble out of the depths of the pyramid.

IXMIQ: And who are you to speak of theft, you half-Spaniard, you half-norteamericano? Did not both parts of you invade my land, and steal everything you saw? Your Spanish half stole my silver, your American half stole my northern lands. Shame on both your halves.

CLAY: And both of us brought you civiliza-
        tion, a gentler religion and cities
        that know good government.

IXMIQ: You brought also the fires that
        consumed me, the warfare that
        has ravaged my lands, the slavery
        of the mines.

CLAY: And we brought you peace.

PEOPLE: May these worthy souls find
        peace. May their arguing over guilt
        stop, for we are all guilty of things
        for which we should be ashamed.

But the two disembodied voices would not stop, and the night was filled with their loud anti-phonal accusations, Ixmiq the Indian challeng-ing all that my Palafox and Clay ancestors had accomplished, with my father in a voice increas-ingly loud rebutting as best he could. It was a metallic debate that filled the plaza, these two long-dead men who had loved this city and its citizens. Finally, with the mariachis sounding tre-mendous chords, the two voices shouted mean-ingless words at each other, and suddenly there was silence, which was broken by the sound of one female voice:

WOMAN: God, bring peace and resolution to these tormented souls, and to all of us, for the truth can never be known.

CLAY: In my ignorance I wrote: "Mexico will never find peace." Forgive me.

IXMIQ: In my vanity I thought we could hold back the Spaniards and the norteamericanos. Forgive me.

PEOPLE: Let the lights that shine about us this night dispel ignorance. Let us find reconciliation and peace.

ONE PRIEST: And may the soul of Ixmiq, who was crucified, sit in the lap of God, beside Jesus, who was also crucified.

The drama of days past was broken by a scene that brought tears to many eyes, including mine, for I could hear Grandmother Caridad speaking. A boxlike structure was pushed out from behind one of the pillars; it contained four little Indian women:

THE WOMEN: This is our cavern. We are the women who toiled in the cavern, year after year, with the sun hidden from us.

FIRST WOMAN: I was taken from my home in the hills. "Work for the glory of God," said the priest, and I was taken.

SECOND WOMAN: I was born in the cavern, I never saw the sun till I was four.

THIRD WOMAN: I lived with the donkeys. They too died in darkness.

FOURTH WOMAN: I fell from that bad step at the top. As I fell I could see my friends working in the caverns as I sped past.

ALL WOMEN: We are the ones who carried silver up the steps to glorify God and the king of Spain.

PEOPLE: May they find rest from their years of toil.

ALL WOMEN: The beautiful silver statues in
the cathedral, the silver ob-
jects, we made them, not the
men at their polishing wheels.

At this a procession of men from the cathedral
came marching with silver ornaments held high,
statues and votary objects:

PEOPLE: See the treasures of our
church!

ALL WOMEN: We carried them on our
heads, our legs buckling from
the burden.

PEOPLE: May the poor women find rest.
May they find sunlight.

The pageant did not end on this mournful note,
for as the mariachi musicians shifted from their
dirge for the women, they broke into the time-
honored folk music of Mexico, one of the richest
and most rhythmic in the world. Then, from the
depths of the cathedral came five tall men costumed as princes of the church:

BISHOPS: We are the Bishops Palafox.
We brought order and dignity
to this plaza.

FIRST BISHOP: I built the church that stood where this grand building now stands.

PEOPLE: God will praise him for such a deed.

SECOND BISHOP: I built the Hall of Government, so we would be wisely ruled.

PEOPLE: The world will praise him for such a sagacious act.

THIRD BISHOP: I built the theater as a convent. It was Maximilian who converted it.

PEOPLE: All who love dance and great oratory will praise you both.

FOURTH BISHOP: I built the House of Tile that we might enjoy good food and fellowship.

PEOPLE: All who love humanity will praise him.

FIFTH BISHOP: I built the beautiful aqueduct, that the city might survive.

PEOPLE: All people of any denomination
must praise that grand act.

As the people praised the bishops the latter responded in an unusual way. In stately measure,
tall and dignified as princes of the church should
be, they slowly moved into a dance in which their
arms did not flail nor their torsos move extravagantly. Instead, with grave dignity they wove and
interwove with one another, gracefully, like slim
trees bending in a soft breeze. It was a strange
dance, but gratifying, for it successfully depicted
the majestic grandeur of the Church and the
contributions of men like the Palafoxes. As the
five bishops, each concentrating on his own
dance, mysteriously brought their tall figures together in a final harmony, something entirely
different filled the stage with an explosive action
that elicited cheers from the audience: out of the
shadows came five small Indian women, each
going to her bishop, with whom she would remain for the duration of the pageant:

BISHOPS: We were not fools. We needed
women to perpetuate our family.

WOMEN: The bishops converted us, baptized us, educated us, watched us
grow, and married us.

PEOPLE: Praise the common sense of man-
kind. May you all find peace and
confirmation.

WOMEN: And with the good bishops whom
we loved, we had many children,
and they helped build this plaza.

PEOPLE: God bless the common sense of
Toledo.

Now the five couples, tall men and little women,
began a dance, simple at first, then more and
more intricate until they had gone through the
full range of Mexican folk dance. Accompanying
the dancers was the loudest mariachi music
possible with constant arpeggios from the two
trumpeters, which filled the plaza with celebration and merriment. No one could fail to see that
the five bishops loved their Indian women, and
that good had come of their marriages. When
the dancing reached a climactic point, the music
suddenly stopped, and in the silence the actors
cried: "May God bless this plaza of Toledo!" I
thought, What an appropriate ending, how fresh
and unsentimental, but my conclusion was pre-
mature, for now the mariachis came forth with a
tremendous three-chord blast, and the stage
was bathed in a golden light while a choir sang
religious music. A solemn voice announced:

"The apotheosis of Paquito de Monterrey, that brave matador," and from the dark interior of the cathedral strode a handsome young man in bull-fight costume, accompanied by his team of three peóns, also in uniform, followed by a huge picador astride a white horse.

The choir sang the newly composed "Lament for Paquito," about the bull that was cruel and unfair and the sainted mother grieving in Monterrey. This brought just a hint of derisive laughter, for it was now widely known that the dead hero's mother had run a call-girl operation in the northern city, but the traditions of the ring had to be observed. They did not attempt to bring a real bull onto the stage, but a man with ferocious black horns attached to his head did appear and with realistic gestures did kill the matador. The choir sang, the two buglers played a rendition of taps that would have opened the gates of heaven, and indeed the big doors of the cathedral swung open, and six men dressed in white carried the corpse inside, followed by the choir.

As the crowd dispersed I sought out Sepúl-veda, the poet, to congratulate him, but before I could do so he forestalled me: "You know, I didn't write the matador part. He forced it on me." At this moment Don Eduardo Palafox came bustling up: "Wasn't that ending magnificent? I wrote it."

"It was quite moving," I said, trying to be polite, and he threw his big arm around me: "Remember! Tomorrow after the sorting of the bulls, everybody out to my ranch. You, too." This last was said to the poet; to me he said: "Be sure the redhead from Oklahoma comes. She'll enjoy it, and we'll enjoy her."

When he was off to invite others to what had become a yearly feature of the festival, I told Sepúlveda: "Your part was exactly right. And I suppose you realize that at the Tournament of Flowers you were also the winner?"

"Yes," he said with a smile. "And do you know why I didn't complain?"

"Why?"

"Because I knew what you judges couldn't know. That tonight this pageant would be given. Which would you choose—the ribbon you were able to award or the passion with which the people of Toledo embraced my play?" He pointed to where some people were kneeling at the cathedral walls to see where General Gurza's bullets had struck the stone. When I looked more closely I saw that among the curious was León Ledesma chaperoning Mrs. Evans and Penny, and I joined them.

"Your father stole the show," Ledesma told me. "A master touch." But Mrs. Evans disagreed: "The dancing of the bishops, either alone or with their wives, how imaginative and how neatly it bound everything together." Penny, cured of her sorrows, said eagerly: "The swaying of those ten bodies, so wonderfully matched, they made me sway with them. I'm so glad you made me come."

Wanting to see the plaza in the moonlight, with the torches gone, I lagged behind and watched Ledesma escort the Oklahoma women back to the House of Tile, where Lucha González was singing in the nearby café and waiters were bringing drinks to the Terrace. It seemed as if at a proper festival everyone met someone with whom companionship was possible or encountered either an image or a concept that had a subjective significance. I had not done so yet, but I could see that all the others had, so I supposed that my turn was still to come. I hoped so.

It was now two-thirty in the morning. The poet had done a masterly job of creating a narrative poem that spoke to the sensibilities of people familiar with what had occurred in their plaza, and I hope that the full text of his pageant might be published locally in book form. As custodian of my father's literary rights, I'd be more than willing to grant permission to quote generously from his *The Pyramid and the Cathedral.* When

I thought about this I realized that copyright extended for only twenty-eight years plus a second twenty-eight, after which anyone could reprint anything without permission. Since the book had first been published in 1920, the fifty-sixth year would be 1976, so I had only fifteen more years of control.

How pleased I was that the poet had made use of my father's statue and his words, for they tied me to this splendid plaza. In front of that little shop I had sat on General Gurza's knee and accepted his gun. On that Terrace my grandfather had met Don Alipio with such fortunate consequences for us, and at the southern corner I had stood proudly in the sun as the statue to my father had been dedicated.

There were uglier moments, too, for here my family had been forced to watch the execution of the priests, here we had found Father López weak from days without food, and in the bullring nearby I had just seen Paquito de Monterrey "killed by Bonito, that unfair and disgraceful bull." On that bench my Palafox wife, young, elegant and beautiful, had told me that just as my Palafox mother would refuse to move to America with Father, so she too would refuse to go with me.

As I strolled the plaza and heard the various

mariachi bands that still played as they wandered through the city, hoping to come upon some nostalgic tourist with his companion who might enjoy a serenade for six or seven dollars, I cried aloud: "I wish that nights like this could continue forever...." One of the mariachis must have heard me, for coming out of the shadows the members of the band gathered about me and the leader, a man wearing a very large sombrero, asked in broken English: "You like maybe one song, good night?" I startled him with my reply: "For ten American dollars, how many songs will you sing for me?" and he replied: "For ten yanqui dollars we will sing till the rooster crows, but you must tell us the songs," and I did.

With each song I named the men clapped: "This one knows!" and we had a master serenade whose numbers were played with such verve and sung with such joy that before we had traversed half the plaza we had an entourage behind us, many joining in the songs as we drifted idly toward the House of Tile: "La Adelita, "Valentín de la Sierra," "La Cucaracha" begging for an extra smoke of marijuana, "The Corrido of General Gurza" with its insults to President Wilson, "Guadalajara," and the two I loved especially, the breathtaking beauty of "Las Golondrinas" and the heartbreak of "La

Paloma." These were the songs I carried with me wherever I went, the golden memories of my years in Mexico.

At the statue of Ixmiq, which an hour ago had come so vividly alive with its declamations, the mariachis, pleased with my appreciation of their songs and with the extra dollars they were in the process of collecting from other tourists who had trailed along, said: "And now, Señor Aficionado, you will dance for us," and on their own they struck into the "Jarabe Tapatío," a wild hat dance. The leader, seeing with approval that I was trying in my clumsy way to do the steps around the rim of an imaginary sombrero tossed on the ground, tucked his violin under his arm, grasped my hand, and joined me in the dance. Round and round we went as the music soared and spectators clapped. I grew dizzy, the lovely buildings of the plaza whirling about as if they too were joining in the dance.

With a wild crescendo the music stopped. The man with the violin steadied me, and I was left looking up at the statue of Ixmiq, who seemed to be smiling in approbation of the uninhibited behavior of his descendant Norman Clay. And in that moment an idea of vast significance came to me: If a man could write the story of this plaza, its tragedies, its soaring triumphs, the fusillade of Gurza's bullets, he would have the history of all Mexico as it had unfolded in my lifetime, and Ixmiq seemed to nod in agreement.

But at that untimely moment the electric lights came on again, the torches died and I thought: Reality can sure knock hell out of dreams.

18

THE
SORTEO

IT WAS about ten Sunday morning when I drove Mrs. Evans back from our exploration of the Mineral, where we left the memory of my Anglo-Saxon ancestors interred in the perpetual hole from which they had wrested so much ore. I was about to deposit her at the House of Tile for a morning nap when she asked pointedly: "And where are you going now?"

I replied: "My father and I always liked to study the bulls on Sunday mornings before a fight. . . ."

"You're going to the bullring?" she asked.

"Yes," I replied, with no enthusiasm, for I could anticipate that she would ask to come along, and I was sure that the curious thing I was about to do would be boring to her, if not incomprehensible.

"Would you be embarrassed if I came along?" she said bluntly.

"I wouldn't be embarrassed," I replied, "because you're a good testimonial for the Tulsa schools. You ask good questions."

"But you don't really want me, do you?"

"You can come if you wish, but I'm sure you'll be bored."

"Why? Isn't it obvious that I've become a bullfight junkie?"

"Don't joke," I laughed.

"What is it you'll be doing?" she asked seriously.

"I'm going to the corrals," I said, "and, like half a hundred other idiots, I'm going to watch six bulls for two hours. That's all."

"Watch them to find out what?" Mrs. Evans asked.

"Before the day is over, the six bulls will be dead. I'll be trying to detect some clue in their behavior that will predict the manner in which they'll die."

"You mean their bravery?" Mrs. Evans asked.

"Among many other things."

"Such as?" she pressed.

"Are you willing to sit and listen?"

"That's how I learn."

I started an explanation that would have bored most people, but not her. "This afternoon there will be six bulls to be fought by two men. How do you divide those six deadly animals into two groups of three each so that neither matador gets all the good ones or all the bad?"

"Are they that different, the bulls?"

"As different as six men chosen at random. So about this time on the big day very knowledgeable men go out to the corrals and study the bulls, compare their good and bad points, try to estimate their probabilities once they rush out into the ring."

"Can they make sensible decisions?"

"Not scientifically, but they can consider questions like: Does the bull have a bad eye? Is he slightly lame in one foot? And especially: Does he favor one horn rather than the other?"

"That takes two hours?"

"It takes a lifetime."

"To what end?"

"The task is to pick one set of three bulls that matches as evenly as possible the other set."

"How do they decide who gets which?"

"That's the beauty of the system. Who do you suppose does the matching? The confidential peóns of the matador. And when the pairings have been agreed upon, each of the branded numbers of the two sets is written on a different piece of cigarette paper, rolled into a tight ball, and placed in a hat. Then the matador's men choose blind from that hat, the lower-ranking matador's man picking first."

"Sounds complicated."

"Don't you see the beauty of it? You're representing your matador, I'm protecting mine. If you pull a fast one and make a trio of bulls infinitely easier to fight than the other, you're free to do so. But when the blind draw comes, think a moment. Chance may decide that your man gets the really lousy set and mine gets the good. You and I have to be honest. You really want to go and watch this game of intellectual sparring?"

"I can hardly wait."

"Will you bring Penny?"

"I think not. The poor child moped about last evening and didn't want to get out of bed today. She was so excited about meeting a handsome matador, and I think she had spun all sorts of notions about a vacation romance." Shaking her head, she said: "A young girl can react badly to such disappointments. She spent the last year trying to figure out who she is and what her chances are with men. At seventeen she's ready for action, and to suffer a setback like this is hard on her. So let's leave her with her teen-age grief. It's part of growing up."

Then, brightly, she said: "Excuse me for a moment, I don't want to feel totally unwelcome at this all-male affair," and she ran into the hotel kitchen, from which she shortly returned with a small basket of sandwiches and wine. At the corrals I was astonished at the way this gracious lady quickly endeared herself to all the habitués, so that we were soon given favorable positions, with her standing with one foot cocked on the baseboard of the corral, staring at the six Pala-fox bulls.

The corrals were large roofless holding pens where the six bulls, blood brothers, were kept for two or three days prior to the fight. When the sorteo, or the sorting, was over, at twelve noon on the day of the fight, each bull would be led to a separate darkened stall, where he would wait five hours till it came his turn to be released from his prison and thrown out into the bright sunlight of the arena. By that time he would be confused, perhaps terrified, and so blazing with anger that he would be willing to fight any object in his way in order to bring some kind of sense and control back into his life.

But now as these siblings, all from one year, 1957, on one ranch, remained with familiar friends whose smells and habits they knew, they were so peaceful they seemed almost tame, but I had to explain one curious aspect of this affair: "See that lone bull over there in a corral by himself? He's from San Mateo, a ranch just as famous as Palafox, and he's a fine animal. He's today's substitute."

"Under what circumstances?" she asked, and I was increasingly impressed with the inquisitiveness of this woman.

"If one of the Palafox bulls should break a horn slamming into the wooden wall or, like yesterday, simply refuses to fight. They send in a team of six or seven oxen, real big beasts, to take him out alive, and in his place they bring in the substitute."

"Sounds sensible."

"But the point I'm making is that if right now you brought that San Mateo bull into this corral, the Palafox bulls would know in an instant that he was not one of them and represented a menace. In two or three minutes that San Mateo bull would be dead. And if you walked in there, in the same two minutes or so you'd be dead because they'd know by smell and look that you posed the same menace."

"Do they ever kill one another, the siblings, I mean?"

"No. Well, maybe once in ten years a ranch may lose a bull that way, but I've never heard of it. Mrs. Evans, remember one fact. These bulls are by nature placid animals. They have no evil desire to kill anyone. They do not go hunting for men. No ranch hands who tend them as they grow up are killed. It's only when they're taken from their milieu and feel themselves endangered that they become powerful enemies."

"I suppose you could say the same for a lot of men."

Standing near us that Sunday morning at ten were some three dozen devotees, men who had been following the great bulls since infancy. Don Eduardo, the breeder of these six, passed idly among the watchers, answering questions and freely giving his guesses as to which bulls would do well. Toward eleven, swarthy Juan Gómez, who would have to kill three of the bulls, sidled up to the corral and gazed with impenetrable Indian solemnity at his potential adversaries. Cronies quickly pressed up to him, asking in hushed whispers: "Which one do you like, for your style, matador?" Always he shrugged his shoulders and continued studying the bulls.

It was Mrs. Evans who first voiced what everyone was thinking, and I suppose that only a woman would have dared to make the comment she did: "One bull has horns so much longer than the others."

The conspiracy of silence was broken, and

we all stared at the conspicuous animal, No. 47, whose horns had not been shaved by the midnight barbers, and he moved in dark grandeur, as if he knew he was different and an adversary of dreadful potential.

"How would you like to get him in the lottery?" an old man joked with Gómez.

"I'll be disappointed if I don't," Gómez replied, not taking his eyes away from the self-contained beast with the sharp horns. "With that one a man could do something." And as I looked at the proud animal I became fascinated by the difference between him and the others, and I started asking questions of Don Eduardo and Cándido, his taciturn foreman, so that during the two hours that we watched I was able to reconstruct for Mrs. Evans the life history of the animal that was attracting so much attention.

In the year 1907, two years before I was born, a favorite cow on the vast ranch lands of the marquis of Guadalquivir, near Seville, gave birth to a male, who was to become favorably known in Mexican bullfighting history as Marinero. For three and a half years this young animal grew strong in the marshes along the river, so that in the summer of 1910, when the future Don Eduardo Palafox, then barely seventeen years old, went with his father to the Guadalquivir ranch to buy a seed bull for the Palafox ranch in

Mexico, the only animal the Mexicans seriously considered was Marinero.

Late that year he arrived in a cage aboard ship at Veracruz and was hauled by railroad to the city of Toledo, from which he was taken, still in his cage, by oxen to the Palafox ranch. Set loose among the Mexican cows, this outstanding bull quickly produced those brilliant animals, bulls and cows alike, that were to add distinguished chapters to the history of Mexican bullfighting. Carnicero, Sanluque, Terremoto, Rayito—they were the Palafox bulls that took innumerable thrusts of the lance and killed many horses, and each was famed as the son of Marinero.

"And this is where I come in," I told Mrs. Evans, "and not as a minor character, I make bold to say. In 1918, when I was nine years old, yet another sacking of Toledo occurred and this time General Gurza's rowdies fusilladed the Palafox herd for beef and during the firing Marinero was killed. Only one of his sons escaped, the calf Soldado who grew up with me in a cave at my father's mine."

"What did you just say?"

"Yes, one of the most famous bulls in Mexican history and I sort of roomed together in a cave. My parents hid him there till Gurza's men retreated north on the train."

"Those must have been dreadful days."

"They were wonderful days. Me and the bull, hiding against the world."

"I meant the Revolution, when Mexico was in such terrible shape. I read about it, and some Oklahoma men marched with General Pershing. But tell me more about you and your buddy."

"It's understandable that I would always feel a sense of identification with this great, dark beast who grew to power at my home, and through him I came to understand the significance of the wild bull who goes forth to fight men on Sunday afternoons. It was Soldado with whom I played while he was still a calf, and later on it was he, growing always bigger, who gave me such a pummeling. I used to take consolation, at bullfights either in Mexico or Spain, in thinking, I'm the only man in the world who can say 'I fought the great daddy of them all.' Of course, I wouldn't have to tell them *when* I fought him or where.

"Yes," I told Mrs. Evans, "that animal who inhabited my cave survived the Revolution to become the celebrated father of the Palafox line. His first son was born in 1920, and after that he sired an impressive line of bulls and cows, whose sons in turn terrorized the bullrings of Mexico. Three of his offspring killed toreros, and many won a place in the chronicles by bravery beyond the average. By 1923 the first grandson of Soldado was born, and ten years later the Palafox ranch was able to provide as many descendants of the original Marinero and his son Soldado as the bullrings of Mexico required."

"When I look at those bulls out there, am I seeing the offspring of your Soldado?"

"Maybe technically, but hereditary strains in animals are like those in human beings. They do run thin. At Palafox, inbreeding was producing big animals with little hearts, and crowds gasped with anticipation when some powerful Palafox bull burst into the ring, but then threw cushions when he proved a coward. The disappointment was greater with Palafox bulls because more was expected of them. So after a year or two of debacles the Palafoxes realized that the Marinero-Soldado strain had run itself out. A new seed bull from Spain was required.

"In the spring of 1933 Don Eduardo's elder brother, Don Fausto, was sent to Seville to purchase another bull from the marquis of Guadalquivir, and since I was his nephew—"

"You're a Palafox?"

"Of course. I was born a Mexican citizen—in this city."

"What are you now?"

"American. Earned it for military duty I did in World War II. As I was explaining, my uncle

Fausto took me to Spain with him, and I helped in the selection of an unusually fine seed bull who rejuvenated the line. And now it gets interesting, because when the imported bull lunged against its restraining cage while being unloaded at the Palafox ranch, it crushed Anselmo Leal so that later he died. So this afternoon, Victoriano will be fighting three bulls of the line that killed his father. You will find that Victoriano will do his best work today. Whenever he fights a Palafox bull, he seems obligated to revenge his father."

"What we have to be careful about," Don Eduardo interrupted, "is that the wild man, Veneno, doesn't kill our bulls before the matador gets to them."

I explained to Mrs. Evans that Veneno had lost both his father and his brother to Palafox bulls and that she would see picador's work this afternoon that she might never see again. She asked Don Eduardo, "Do you mean that the man on horseback can kill a bull?"

"A bull? He'd kill them all if we didn't watch him."

"And now the ladies come into the picture," I said to hold her interest before the sorting began. "Tell her about la Reina, Don Eduardo."

After taking a bite of a sandwich Mrs. Evans had given him from her basket, he said: "In 1942 our bulls were again showing signs of decadence, and normally I'd have gone to Spain for another seed bull, but the war was now on and it was impossible to get a bull across the Atlantic. So we purchased thirty cows from the Piedras Negras ranch, a Mexican ranch, and these scrawny, ferocious Mexican cows brought new life to the Palafox breed."

"The cows were important," I explained, "because it's from them the bulls get their courage."

"But you've been talking about all these bulls—Marinero, Soldado, the one you selected at the Guadalquivir ranch. I thought it was the bulls that were important."

"They are," Don Eduardo interrupted. "For build and horn structure and stamina—yes, we look to the bulls for that. But Norman just told you about the period around 1933 when we produced enormous bulls. Some of the best-looking ever seen in Mexico. And they weren't worth a damn. Because what a fighting bull needs more than anything else is courage. And that he gets only from his mother."

Mrs. Evans pointed at the bull with the unshaved horns and asked incredulously: "You mean to say that his sons—"

"He'll never have any sons," Don Eduardo interposed. "He's a fighting bull."

"Hasn't he ever . . ." Mrs. Evans began hesitantly.

"Of course not. That bull's never seen a cow or been near a man on foot or done anything but spar with other bulls on the range." Don Eduardo said these words in a rather loud voice, and as he did so his foreman Cándido quietly looked about to see if anyone had overheard. Satisfying himself that his employer's words had done no harm, the solemn foreman looked reproachfully at Don Eduardo, who caught the message and looked quickly about to see if there had been any Mexican eavesdroppers. In a much lower voice he said: "Nothing has been allowed to detract the attention of that bull from his job."

"But his courage comes from his mother?" Mrs. Evans persisted.

"Always," Don Eduardo assured her, and it seemed to me that with this information Mrs. Evans straightened her shoulders slightly, as if she had long suspected that with humans, too, it was the mothers who determined the nature of their sons' courage.

"In January of 1947," Don Eduardo said enthusiastically, "one of the great cows of Palafox history was born, a mean, scrawny, knock-kneed, sharp-horned female named la Reina, the Queen. Her ancestry included Marinero, the great original bull of Guadalquivir; and Soldado, who grew up in Clay's cave; but from her Mexican mother she reached back to those fierce, ugly animals from the days of Hernán Cortés. Reina was a notable cow, one of the bravest ever to breed in Mexico."

It was now approaching twelve, when the actual sorting would begin, so I told hastily of how the Palafoxes discovered they had a great cow on their ranch. When this scrawny little lady was two years old, Don Eduardo gave a sumptuous party at the ranch. It was the year 1949 and peace had returned to the world and money was easy. The actor John Wayne was present, as were the American and British ambassadors, and the festivities covered three days, on the last of which the guests assembled at the ranch's bullring for a testing of the year's cows. In charge was white-haired Veneno, who appeared on horseback with an oaken lance that contained a short steel barb. He was attended by his son Victoriano and by the senior matador Armillita, while in a silent box under the improvised stand sat Don Eduardo and his foreman Cándido taking brief but vital notes.

At a sign from Don Eduardo the rough gate leading to the corral was opened and a spindly-legged little heifer of two called Flora was let into the ring, across which she could spy a man on horseback. There was an anxious moment of silence, when everyone asked, "Will she be brave?" for this first moment was the most decisive. If the cow hesitated too long before charging, or if when she did charge she moved haltingly, it was obligatory to mark her down as cowardly and to prevent her from being bred to the ranch's best sires. Her sons, inevitably, would be cowardly and of no use in the ring.

As this first cow came into the sunlight, she saw the mysterious figure in the distance and charged like a thunderbolt. No one cheered but all sighed. The fiery little animal struck at the horse and felt Veneno's barb rip at her shoulder. Stunned, she drew back.

There had been no cheering for her initial bravery because her second test was now at hand, and this must be conducted in silence, without the frenzied encouragement that voices might provide. The little cow had been hurt and blood trickled from her shoulder. She pawed the earth with her left foot and Don Eduardo thought: "Looks bad. Looks like she's a dust-thrower." He looked apprehensively at Cándido, who stared straight ahead, praying that the cow would prove brave.

Tentatively the young cow moved toward the horse, then stopped as she felt the twinge of pain in her shoulder. Then, before the audience was ready, she exploded at the horse and drove with breathless fury at the animal and at the lance, which again jabbed into her shoulders. Some of the Hollywood people cheered and were promptly admonished by the Mexicans, who saw what the Americans had not: as soon as the second prod of steel struck home the little cow leaped about and then moved away. She wanted no more of the contest and nothing that Veneno could do would lure her back. She was not a brave cow and her sons would never bring glory to themselves and the ranch. In fact, she would have no Palafox sons.

"Nothing," Cándido scratched in his book, and the cow's destiny was settled.

This irrevocable decision did not, of course, terminate the testing of the cow. Veneno, in disgust, spurred his horse from the ring and dismounted outside while Armillita and Victoriano, the two matadors, practiced their cape work on the little animal. It was a sunny morning, and the flourishing of the capes as they flashed in the brilliant light was poetic and explained why the matadors were so accomplished when facing real bulls. Fifteen, twenty times they practiced the same pass, with the little cow charging back and forth with pleasing animation, for as she had shown in her first wild charge across the ring, she was essentially a brave little animal and she fought the capes with distinction, so that some of the Americans cried: "What a wonderful animal!" But Cándido and Don Eduardo knew that she had shied away from the punishing lance, which proved that her courage extended only to a point, beyond which she was a coward.

At this moment Don Eduardo interrupted my history lesson to explain: "The reason meticulous testing of the cow is essential, Señora Evans, is that there is no way to test a bull."

"Aren't they taken into the ring at two years old, too?" she asked.

"Oh, no!" Don Eduardo replied. "If a two-year-old bull was fought with a cape for even two minutes, he'd remember that trying to gore the cape got him nowhere. Deep in his little brain he'd hoard that discovery, and two years later, when he faced a man in a formal fight, he'd know instinctively that if he struck the cape he'd still find nothing. So after one or two futile passes, he'd leave the cape and head right for the man. He'd kill the matador every time."

"You mean that none of those bulls"—she indicated the six who were to be fought that afternoon—"has been tested?"

"Good God, no!"

"If it were discovered that Don Eduardo had tested his bulls with a cape," I explained, "the matadors would refuse to fight them."

"Tested bulls would kill matadors every after-noon," Don Eduardo agreed.

"Then all you know about those bulls—" Mrs. Evans began.

"Is what their mothers told us," Don Eduardo replied.

"Well," I said, "when the bull's two years old we sometimes tease him from horseback and try to upset him with poles."

"Why?" Mrs. Evans asked.

"To see if he'll fight back. But this is out on the open range, and he probably never realizes that there's a man on the horse. He's not hurt, and the only memory he retains is of a four-legged enemy. That's why, in the real fight, he's usually so ready to charge at the horse."

"But all that we really know," Don Eduardo repeated, "is what we find at the testing of his mother."

"The cow Reina that you were telling me about," Mrs. Evans suggested. "How did she test?"

Don Eduardo became expansive. "John Wayne came down to sit with me before this cow came out and I had to say, 'We haven't shown you a brave one yet, but in this business we always have hope,' and when the door to the corral opened and this skinny little cow came bursting in I thought, Maybe this one! and when the testing was over I had tears in my eyes. It was like . . ." He stopped and blew his nose. "Cándido, tell the American lady about Reina."

The dour foreman looked at Mrs. Evans as if to say: You couldn't possibly understand, and said nothing, so Don Eduardo blew his nose again and said: "Mrs. Evans, if you ever had a son who proved himself to be brave—"

I saw that this was becoming too emotional and said dryly: "Mrs. Evans had a son—very brave. He died in the war."

Instead of halting Don Eduardo, this information had quite the opposite effect. Clutching Mrs. Evans's hands he cried, "You did! Then you know what I'm talking about. It's a terrible thing, Mrs. Evans, a terrible and moving thing to see courage and to know that it can be transmitted from mother to son. This cow Reina, she was maybe the skinniest of the lot, but when she saw that horse on the other side of the ring . . . dust didn't bother her, nor sunlight nor the long lance. She broke into a gallop and struck the horse seven times. Her shoulders were a mass of blood but she kept coming back again and again. Veneno knocked her over, smacked her in the tail with the lance, charged the horse at her, did everything indecent, but she kept driving at him. I finally had to yell, 'Get that goddamned horse out of there,' but we couldn't get the horse out because she followed him wherever he went and we couldn't open the gate.

"So we called Armillita into the ring to take her away with his cape, thinking to sneak the horse out when she was engaged elsewhere, but on the first pass she knocked Armillita aside and went right back to the horse. So we put another matador into the ring and when the two of them kept the little cow off to one side we finally got the horse out.

"She was bleeding a lot, but now she settled down to fight the capes, and she was like a dream. Cándido, tell them!"

The lanky foreman waved his right hand back and forth several times and repeated, "Like a dream."

"What impressed us most, however, was the way this cow began to learn. She had hit Armillita on her first charge, and now she started to gain ground with each charge. Soon she was coming very close and Armillita laughed and said: "I've had enough," and he tried to walk away, but she kept after him. So I called in some of the aspirants who haunt these testings, and one after another they fought the cow, and she knocked them over like cups tumbling down from a stall in the market. Her horns weren't long enough to do much damage, but her heart—"

"Is she still living?" Mrs. Evans asked in the pause.

"She's famous in Mexico," I said. "I don't remember the details. Her first bull was immortalized by Armillita—just about the fanciest show in the last twenty years. What happened with the others?"

Don Eduardo was eager to talk: "Her first two throws were cows, just as brave as she was. Her first bull was Relampaguito, Little Lightning Bolt. As Norman said, immortalized. Her second bull, her third bull—immortalized. Her fourth bull was born in 1957, the best of the lot. Sangre Azul, Blue Blood."

"Was he immortalized, too?" Mrs. Evans asked.

I was looking at Don Eduardo when she asked this, and he winced in a way that showed his reluctance to discuss the matter, and I could not guess what had happened with Sangre Azul, for although I was a Palafox through my mother and a member of the family because of my marriage to one of Don Eduardo's nieces, I was not privy to the secrets of the bull ranch. I was eager to hear about the great bull, but Don Eduardo was reprieved from having to explain by the noisy arrival of León Ledesma, who appeared flourishing his black cape.

Coming immediately to Mrs. Evans he said:

"You've been here for hours, I can see it. Those in the know appear only at twelve, when the action begins."

"Those of us really in the know," I said jokingly, "want to study the bulls to see how we would sort them out—to check our guesswork against the later facts."

"And what have you wizards with the key to the animal kingdom seen that excites you?"

From my pocket I brought out a small card on which I'd written down the various scraps of information I'd either deduced for myself or been told by others more knowledgeable. "These seem to be the facts," I said and reminded Mrs. Evans that she could see the number of each bull branded clearly on its flank.

No. 29. 448 kilos/986 pounds. Shaved. Overage. 4 years, 3 months. Sluggish.

No. 32. 450 kilos/990 pounds. Shaved. Skittish. Favors left eye. Quick reaction.

No. 33. 433 kilos/953 pounds. Shaved. Placid, allows others to shove. Explosive???

No. 38. 463 kilos/1019 pounds. Shaved. Heavy, slow. More ox than bull. Powerful.

No. 42. 444 kilos/977 pounds. Shaved. Small horns. Very quick. Weak left foreleg.

No. 47. 473 kilos/1041 pounds. Unshaved. Monster. Eager to attack. Dangerous.

Quick to absorb details, Ledesma said: "Interesting set, well chosen, Don Eduardo, to fit the styles of the two matadors," and as he gave a rapid review of the figures I was struck by his perspicacity.

"Obviously there are two that must be separated, both heavy—38 big and slow would be ideal for Victoriano, 47 even bigger and powerful horns, ideal for Gómez." He then analyzed which bulls Veneno would want for his son, and which Cigarro, as spokesman for Gómez, would want for him.

"Gómez is here," Mrs. Evans said. "Won't he pick for himself?"

"Never. The picking of the bulls is always done by the agent. Gómez is one of the few matadors who attend the sorting."

In the few minutes before noon I asked Don Eduardo to hold our places while I showed Mrs. Evans one of the gracious elements of the taurine world, a bronze plaque that addicts had paid for years ago to commemorate a historic fight and had set into the wall of the sorting area:

Homage of the aficionados of Toledo
to the great Mexican matador
Juan Silveti
remembering his complete fight given in
this plaza on 25 December 1931

with the bull Explosión of
Palafox

"I saw that fight," I told Mrs. Evans. "Silveti was unforgettable. A Mexican redneck. Always dressed in public in a charro uniform, Mexican cowboy, with a huge sombrero and a cigar. But he could fight, as he proved that day. One writer said: 'Our beloved Juan tied a golden ribbon about the bull's horns and led him where he wished.' And that was about it." There were other plaques, too, making this almost a hall of fame, for through the years the best matadors had come to the Festival of Ixmiq, which had been built into an important event, I told her, by my grandfather.

Now the bartering began, with Veneno and Cigarro exercising every skill to ensure that the two groups of three would be evenly matched, for as I had explained when we first reached the corrals, neither side could be sure which set it would get in the draw, so it had to be honest. At the end of a lot of haggling, with several additional experts throwing in their judgments, it was agreed that the pairings would be 29, 38, 42 in one group, 32, 33, 47 in the other, and when this was announced, Ledesma told us knowingly: "Now Veneno starts to sweat, because he must be desperately afraid that his boy Victoriano will draw that second group, the one containing Forty-seven, that unshaved bull."

Again Ledesma was right, for after each set of numbers had been written on a thin sheet of cigarette paper, rolled into a tight wad and placed in a hat provided by the keeper of the corrals, Veneno, as representative of the younger matador in terms of promotion to senior status, made the sign of the cross, and raised his eyes to heaven. Not daring to look at the fateful hat, he allowed the corral keeper to guide his hand to it. Fumbling inside for a moment, trying to detect in some mysterious way the favorable wad of paper, he took one, meticulously unfolded it, and stiffened. For Victoriano he had picked the second set of three, the one with the deadly bull No. 47.

At that moment I suffered the most extraordinary sensation. My right forefinger started twitching, as if eager to start photographing Victoriano's fight with the deadly bull in anticipation that a tragedy would occur that I could use as the high spot of any second article I might write if something significant occurred today. Never in the history of bullfighting, so far as I could remember from Cossío, the world authority on the subject, had two toreros ever been killed in one fight or even in one protracted festival, so I could not reasonably anticipate the murder about which I'd planned my article, but I did have a right to speculate on what dramatic events might unfold when two matadors of such contrasting styles met those fine exemplars of the Palafox breed. The name of the ranch played a significant role in my guessing because the Palafox bulls had proved they could kill matadors, but Victoriano's lot would be the more dangerous, for he would have to fight the bull with the unshaved horns.

Veneno, aware that he had served his son poorly, now took frantic steps to see if he could rectify the draw. Edging close to Cigarro, he whispered: "Gómez does great work with big bulls. I could let you have Forty-seven," but the Indian's agent whispered back: "You really want to get rid of those horns, don't you?" and he walked away, leaving Veneno with an even greater determination to get rid of that deadly bull.

Ledesma, Mrs. Evans and I had heard parts of the above exchange, and we could fill in the other arguments, but as Ledesma explained: "The sorteo is the one absolutely honest part of the bullfight. The bull's horns can be fixed, as you've seen. The ranch can slip in a bull that's overage, like Number Twenty-nine, clearly more than four years. The judge can award ears that haven't been earned. And even the critic"—he bowed politely—"can on occasion be sub-verted. And as for the matadors and picadors, they can be guilty of abominable trickery, but the sorteo is inviolate. It's conducted honestly and Veneno should be ashamed of himself for trying to upset this one in order to protect his son."

The six bulls were led back into the individual stalls where they would await the bugle that called each one in turn to the entrance gate. Now the substitute from the other ranch was led to his stall, and the bulls in effect left the pre-fight area, but in their absences Ledesma said ominously: "In daylight, Veneno lost his fight. His man is still saddled with that tremendous bull. But in darkness he's sure to have some card to play."

When I asked: "Now what does that mean?" he replied: "We'll keep a watch on the evil one, and maybe you'll learn something more about our national pastime." He smiled at me, aware that he had ended with a phrase usually re-served for American baseball. He was a learned rascal, but I had no idea what his words meant.

At twelve-twenty that Sunday morning the sort-ing was over, but as men stood around arguing probabilities, Don Eduardo circulated among them, inviting certain friends out to his ranch for the afternoon festivities that would occupy the four hours till the start of the fight. When he reached Mrs. Evans, Ledesma and me, he said: "It would not be a fiesta without you. Please bring the little Oklahoma redhead," but Mrs. Evans asked: "Would a girl like Penny fit in at such an affair?" and Don Eduardo clasped her hands: "Dear Mrs. Evans, a famous Mexican movie starlet will be there, not much older than Penny. They'll form an international pair, Mexican and norteamericana." He pressed his invitation with such obvious sincerity that I told Mrs. Evans: "Let's see if we can persuade her to quit her mourning for love lost." To my surprise Mrs. Evans said: "We really should, you know. She spent a fortune putting together a wardrobe for such an outing in the country. It'd be ridiculous to waste it," and when we returned to the Terrace she tossed me the keys to her Cadillac and said: "You'll find two huge cases in the trunk. Please bring them up to our room."

When I opened the trunk I found exactly what she had described, an enormous suitcase and a big round leather hatbox. When I lugged them upstairs to the hotel room, I found Penny still abed, pillow rumpled, eyes downcast. "I didn't ask for them," she mumbled, and in reply Mrs. Evans spoke not to her but to me: "Mr. Clay, please open the boxes," and when I did I saw tags showing that everything had recently been purchased from the Dallas Neiman-Marcus, the West's leading department store, and I thought: I'll bet the two cases cost more than what's in them, maybe four hundred dollars each.

"Please empty them," Mrs. Evans said. "Let her see what she's throwing away." As I removed the contents of the cases I learned what it meant to be the daughter of an Oklahoma oil millionaire, for the items were not only exquisite, each in its own way, but also grotesquely expensive. When the Hispanic adviser in Dallas assembled the outfit, she had told Penny: "You'll be the star of any fiesta you wish to attend," and indeed there was every reason to think she was right. The stunning ensemble was based, Texas style, on her silvery gray boots, a wildly expensive South American skin tanned to perfect flexibility.

"But you already have those alligator boots. Why these?" asked Mrs. Evans.

For the first time since we entered the room, the listless girl in the bed, covers drawn under her chin, showed interest: "Flexible," she said. "Twist them." When I did, the boots responded as if they were made of some exotic cloth, not leather. "Girls who work in rodeos need boots like that," she added.

"Have you ever worked in a rodeo?" I asked. "Wrestling calves and all that?"

"Barrel races. I'm fairly good when I have my own horse."

Continuing with the first big bag, I produced a pair of heavy socks of a lighter gray. These would come to her knees. And then came an extraordinary short skirt in a muted blue, made of some fabric I could not identify but still carrying the price tag: $485. It seemed little bigger than my hand and contained no decoration whatever; it had a dull, slightly roughened finish, which indicated that the weaver had paid careful attention to his cloth. Its quiet elegance made Penny, wearing only a skimpy undergarment, jump out from beneath her covers and grab the skirt from my hands.

"I'll wait outside," I said, but she laughed: "No need. I wear less than this in gym class."

Even so, I turned my back on her as she slipped into the various items I handed her, each of which was perfection, exactly right for a day in the country. The blouse I handed her was beyond my experience. Of some exotic South American weave, it was decorated with a host of hand-embroidered pale blue-and-gold flowers, so subtle they were barely visible. Over this she wore a form-fitting jacket of the thinnest pliable leather adorned with small bronze studs, which

was not garish but soberly dignified. The last
item in the big case was an alpaca scarf so
fragile it weighed nothing in my hand; she tied it
loosely about her neck, then said: "Now for the
best part," and she pointed to the round case.
From it I lifted a woman's sombrero, an elegantly molded felt that had been created by a
cowboy's hatter in Tulsa, whom Penny had visited six times before he was satisfied that his
finished product cast proper shadows on her
lovely face. When she tilted the sombrero properly and smiled at me, I said: "It would have
been criminal to leave you here," and she
looked so appealing with wisps of red hair
sneaking out from under the hat that I was
prompted to make an observation that I hoped
the two women would not consider macabre: "I
want to photograph you, Penny, as you put on
the jacket, the scarf and the sombrero. In a
room like this, two days ago, I photographed
Paquito as he dressed for his death. You're
dressing for your life."

"And what do you mean?"

"In that costume, something good's bound to
happen."

She took off the garments to put them on
again while I snapped her picture. She was satisfied, I'm certain, that indeed some exciting surprise awaited.

On our way down to the car I whispered to Mrs. Evans: "What did that outfit cost, would you guess?"

"I don't need to guess. I had one like it when I was younger. Maybe eighteen hundred dollars, counting the two cases."

"I should think that would assuage a lot of grief."

"When you're seventeen, nothing assuages a love wound, but a Jason Cree sombrero helps. My husband had three. I still have two."

For the entertainment of guests who attended the periodic testing of cows the Palafox ranch had a small wooden arena that was a duplicate of the big ones in which real fights were held, as well as a tastefully landscaped garden under whose big trees a lavish barbecue could be served. There was also a spacious recreation room with two pool tables and chairs made of highly polished bull's horns with leather seats and raw-wool cushions. Around the walls, each on a hardwood plaque, ranged the heads of nine bulls that had brought glory to the name of Pala-fox. Beneath each of the dark heads with their glistening horns appeared in neat lettering the name of the bull, what he had achieved to gain immortality, the arena in which it had occurred, the matador who had fought him and the date. To visit each of these bulls in turn was to relive the glories of the ranch and its line of bulls.

"Torpedo, 11 febrero 1881," read Mrs. Evans, "todos los trofeos, Mazzantini, Plaza de México." When she asked what the Spanish meant, Don Eduardo said proudly: "All the trophies. Awarded by the judge to the matador that performed miracles. Two ears, tail, a hoof."

In 1903 Ciclón had killed a young matador in Guadalajara, and in 1919 Triunfador had proved he was entitled to that name by dominating the plaza at Monterrey, knocking down five horses, sending to the infirmary all three matadors who tried, one after another, to subdue him, and defending himself to the last.

Then Mrs. Evans, one of the sharpest-eyed women I'd ever met, said: "But these two have no mention of the plazas," and Don Eduardo explained: "They're two I told you about, two of the greatest. Our seed bulls, Marinero from the marquis of Guadalquivir in 1910, and Domador in the 1950s. They were too valuable to be sent to plazas. We wanted to keep them alive."

Don Eduardo then showed us a display that he said would amuse us: "I doubt there's ever been a fight like this one. This great bull Tormento was given in the sorting to one of the mercurial characters in Mexican bullfight history, Lorenzo Garza, the formidable izquierdo, left-hander. Temperamental as a bumblebee. On a good day he would justify his name, Lorenzo El Magnífico, on a bad he could be dreadful. With Tormento he ascended to the highest cloud in the heavens, more than magnificent. Ears, tail, hoof, six rounds of the plaza, flowers strewed where he stepped. Then, with the second bull, who might have been just as good as the first, he was so deplorable, so inadequate, that a great riot started with cushions and chairs filling the plaza. Sixteen brawny men jumped into the arena to beat him up, but seventeen policemen rushed in to rescue him. Look at the two photographs taken by a friend of mine."

The first showed El Magnífico garnering a level of praise that few athletes ever know; the second revealed the arena filled with debris, rioting bullies and police in phalanx formation. Same matador, same bulls, same Sunday afternoon, same spectators. "That's bullfighting," Don Eduardo said. "An inexact science."

Now Mrs. Evans cried out: "Here's your bull, Mr. Clay," and when I joined her there was Soldado looking down at me, and I was afraid to speak lest my voice break.

Then I heard her voice from another part of the room, for she walked fast: "I don't see

Reina, and you said she was one of the greatest of all."

"We don't hang cows on our walls. It wouldn't look right to the men drinking here."

Then I said: "For the last three days I've heard about your really great bull, Sangre Azul." To Mrs. Evans I explained: "Blue Blood," and she said, rather abruptly, I thought: "Thank you."

After a reflective pause, as if it pained him to speak, Don Eduardo said: "He was born in 1957, branded in '58 and faced the men on horseback with lances in March of '59."

"How did he test?"

"Phenomenal. That's when we knew we had a tremendous bull. A year ago we had already nominated him to be our lead bull for this year's Ixmiq, and as he put on weight and his horns steeled into their length and position, he became what we all agreed was the perfect Palafox bull. Not too heavy, he was going to come in at Festival time at about four hundred fifty kilos—what's that in pounds?"

"As always, 2.2 pounds to the kilo, so let's say just under a thousand pounds."

"Very strong up front, nicely tapered at the rear, but very strong hind legs for pushing."

"He wasn't in the corrals today. What happened?"

Don Eduardo leaned back, thought and after a while called to the men tending bar: "Have we a photo of Sangre Azul?" and when one was provided it showed a majestic bull at top fighting power, exactly as Don Eduardo had described him. Then, to answer the question, he began hesitantly: "It's a delicate subject to discuss with a lady present, but in the bull world, you know, we have an occasional bull called a maricón." Unable to continue, he pointed to me: "Explain it, Clay," and I said as delicately as I could, for in 1961 the subject was not openly discussed: "Bulls inherit a strong genetic tendency to mount other animals. If there are no cows available, sometimes you'll see a bull try tentatively to mount one of his brothers. It's not uncommon, and the bull receiving the attention handles it easily by moving away."

"So far it's understandable."

"But occasionally," Don Eduardo broke in, "every ranch will produce a bull to which this normal activity becomes not a youthful exploration but a fixation. The bull becomes a maricón—what's the word, Clay?"

"Spanish slang for male homosexual."

"Goodness! You're telling me that this handsome creature was a maricón?"

"No, damn it. What I'm trying to say," Don Eduardo blurted out, "is that the splendid bull you saw this morning, Number Forty-seven, is an incurable one. But we didn't detect it soon enough. He pestered many of the bulls in his generation, but they fended him off easily. However, two unfortunate things happened. Number Forty-seven developed a positive fixation on Sangre Azul, who fought him off every time he tried to mount. This infuriated the bigger bull, and one afternoon last January when both bulls were at their greatest, a magnificent pair for this year's Ixmiq, Number Forty-seven pursued Sangre Azul all about the grazing field, until Azul had enough. Turning on Forty-seven before anyone could separate them, Azul drove right at him, hurt him badly, whereupon Forty-seven lashed out with those huge horns and killed Azul.''

No one spoke, then after we had studied the photograph of the exceptional bull, Mrs. Evans said: ''So Número Cuarenta-y-siete has already killed an enemy. Will he remember that when he comes out this afternoon?''

''We cannot say,'' Don Eduardo replied. ''But we did not broadcast the news that the fight between the two bulls had occurred, and we've certainly kept it secret that our prize bull lost.''

I learned later that just about the time Mrs. Evans and I reached this point in our conversation at the ranch, Veneno, in his room at the House of Tile, was on the telephone to a friend of his, the great banderillero Rolleri, now manager of the ring at San Luis Potosí: "Rolleri, what do you know about that bull the Palafox people were so proud of, Sangre Azul I think they called him?"

"Not much, Veneno. I saw him in the campo last year, a handsome animal. Predicted at the time: 'That one will yield ears.' "

"Can't you think of anything else? This is important."

"Now, wait a minute! In February, maybe March, I met a boy who works at Palafox, and I asked him: 'How's your great bull Azul Something doing?' and all he said was 'He went.' I don't know what he meant."

"I know damned well what he meant," Veneno snarled, "but not what it signifies. Today we have a full plaza."

"Buena suerte," Rolleri said. Veneno replied: 'In this dirty business a man makes his own good fortune, or his matador gets killed.'

As far as we could reconstruct his movements on that busy afternoon, as soon as Veneno left the phone he hurried out to the bullring, where he slipped into the area where the bulls were guarded and casually asked a young fellow from the Palafox ranch: "When Sangre

Azul died, did Don Eduardo mount the head?"

"No. He was sick about the loss of such a bull."

"Which one killed him?"

"That damned maricón," the boy said bitterly, and he pointed to the stall holding No. 47.

"Oh, Jesus!" Veneno muttered to himself. "The one we missed in the barbering. The one that has already killed another bull." He ran to his car and drove at breakneck speed to the cement factory at the far edge of town where he made a great noise till he roused an assistant manager: "I need one oversize bag of cement, right now. A building under way."

When it was produced, it was so heavy it took both him and the workman to load it into the back of his car, and on the way back to town it became even heavier, for he stopped by a small stream and, using a pail in which he often carried sandwiches during a long trip from one fight to another, he soaked the bag until it was dripping wet and far too heavy for one man to handle. He then drove back to the ring, parked his car near the patio in which the picadors kept their horses, greeted them and told a young fellow who tended the Leal horses, "When you get a chance, bring it in from the car," and he hurried off to dress in his heavy picador's gear for the fight that would begin shortly.

———

At the ranch, when we were led to the little ring in which the testing would take place—it could seat no more than sixty—Penny could not be aware that shortly she would be goaded into proving that her expensive charro's costume was not merely for display. After we were settled, Don Eduardo asked the mariachis he had imported to sound a flourish and, borrowing their microphone, he announced: "We are not offering a formal tienta—that means a testing, our norteamericano friends. That takes too much time and too many cows. But we are going to throw three or four of our best cows into our little ring, and I've asked our dear friend Calesero of Aguascalientes—you saw him yesterday, and if you wish you may applaud him again. He's agreed to supervise our little exhibition, but as you see, he's not dressed in his bullfight costume. That's saved for real fights. We call it *traje corto*—short dress, clothes he'd wear at his ranch."

The crowd applauded as Calesero moved to the center of the ring. He was a handsome man who would soon "cut his coleta," the ritual act signifying his formal retirement from bullfighting; it consisted of cutting the wisp of hair matadors wear at the nape of the neck. He wore ordinary ranch shoes of some expensive make, work pants neatly folded up from the bottom so as to show two inches of white inside fabric above the shoe top, a white shirt buttoned at the neck, a shoestring black tie fastened to the shirt at the belt so that it hung straight, a short jacket of the kind that generals wear, and a sombrero cordobés; a rather small black hat not so large as a regular sombrero. He was a figure from the early years of the last century, adding dignity to the afternoon.

After he bowed to the audience in the stands and to the many more from the countryside who crowded in against the fence, he indicated that his colleague for the show should come forward, and I was surprised to see a young man, not yet a full matador, who would be in the ring that afternoon. I told Mrs. Evans and Penny, "That one should not be here. He should be in his hotel room, resting." When they asked why, I explained: "When only two matadors share the bull, mano a mano like today, there must be, for safety's sake a third matador on hand, in case the first two get knocked out before the afternoon ends. Sobresaliente they call him from the Spanish *sobre* (over) and *saliente* from the verb *salir* (to go out), so the word really means substitute."

"If he shouldn't be here, why is he?" Mrs.

Evans asked, and, making inquiries, I learned that this young Pepe Huerta, eager to please anyone important in the bullfight world, had allowed Don Eduardo to bully him into appearing briefly at the noontime fiesta: "After a few passes he'll motor back to town to dress for the fight. Don Eduardo has a car waiting." So we would be seeing not only Calesero but also this apparently promising young aspirant. A bugler from the mariachi band sounded the traditional call: "Send in the bull!" and the gate swung open to release a two-year-old cow who looked as if she had just been shot from the mouth of a heavily charged cannon, for after a quick look around she galloped with great fury right at Calesero, who stood his ground, unfurled his cape, and led her past.

Turning with speed, she came back at him, and with practiced skill he led her past again, then delivered her with expert passes into the jurisdiction of Huerta, who also gave her a pair of passes. Having struck nothing but cloth, she was so frustrated and bewildered that she stopped to reconnoiter, and this provided time for Don Eduardo to signal that the first two of the amateurs who wanted to test their skills against the cow could replace the two matadors, and into the ring rushed two boys about fifteen armed with borrowed capes and hoping to dominate the cow as the matadors had done. But now the little cow had adversaries more her size and, also, she had learned something from those first futile charges. Driving at the first boy, she again hit only cloth, but in a swift turn she was upon him again before he could reset his feet, and down he fell like a bowling pin. Thus encouraged, she headed for the second lad, who could do nothing with her, and for the next moments at least one of the boys was always on the ground and sometimes both of them.

The boys were called from the ring to applause for their bravery, and the signal was given that all who wished could jump into the ring with or without capes and try to dodge the galloping cow. It was a gay and lovely frolic, with the cow making one hit after another, and enjoying it as much as the young men.

But now the bugle sounded, the ring was cleared of everyone except the two matadors, who deftly led the excited and triumphant cow to the exit, where she kicked her heels, tried to charge Calesero again, and disappeared to loud applause as Don Eduardo said on the loudspeaker: "You've seen a real Palafox cow. Her sons will be brave."

A second was brought in, and after a few passes from the professionals two more young fellows were invited to show their skills, and they were much like the first pair. When their feet were firmly set they knew how to use their capes, but when the spirited cow turned quickly, the young matadors were not prepared. I explained to Mrs. Evans and Penny that the cow really had no horns—that is, none that had reached a point of development where they pointed forward: "So getting hit by the cow is much like getting struck by a flat object. It pushes you about but it doesn't puncture."

As I said this the third cow was allowed in, and when Calesero saw in the first pass that she charged straight and hard and true, he motioned to young Huerta to take her to a far part of the ring. He then astounded Penny and Mrs. Evans by coming to the stands and addressing the movie starlet in Spanish: "Divine señorita, will you help me to conquer this brave bull?" To the delight of the crowd she agreed, left the stands, kicked off her high-heeled shoes and grabbed one end of a long red cloth while Calesero held the opposite end, about five feet away. In this formation the two marched slowly, breathlessly across the sand while young Huerta used his cape to point the cow in the direction of the oncoming enemy. Then the sobresaliente retired while remaining close enough to rescue the actress if anything went wrong.

Nothing did. The cow saw the fluttering cloth,

lunged at it, struck it exactly in the middle, and
passed both the actress and the matador. It was
a lovely action, with the aspect of a fairy tale. I
thought: He's like a medieval knight, she's like
a princess wearing a hennin, that conical headdress topped with a veil. And the little cow is
really a fierce dragon.

Penny must have had similar thoughts, for as
the exhibition ended, she cried to no one in particular: "I could do that!"

"What did you say?" Don Eduardo asked, and
Penny said almost as a challenge to the actress:
"I could do that. Any cowgirl could."

"Are you a cowgirl? Like a cowboy?"

"Sure."

Don Eduardo called for Calesero and they
spoke at the barrier, then the matador, with a
grand gesture, extended his right hand to
Penny, and without any urging from me or Mrs.
Evans, she rose, nodded to the guests and
started down to the sand, but as she passed me
she whispered: "You were right. These clothes
are too good to waste."

Trying to protect her, I grabbed a wrist and
whispered: "You don't have to do this," and she
whispered back: "If she can do it, so can I."

"But she's a movie star. She's supposed
to—"

Brushing my hand aside, she said: "I wasn't

thinking of her. It's Conchita," and with the agility of a schoolgirl in gym class, she vaulted over the railing and into the ring.

As the crowd cheered, Calesero graciously asked in broken English if she cared to take off her boots as the actress had done, and she replied in Spanish: *"No es necesario. Se hicieron para esto"* (Not necessary. They were made for this.).

As Penny and her matador started their slow march toward the cow I thought: What an exquisite scene. An elderly matador about to retire with honors, a beautiful young woman with spirit, and each costumed exactly right. The red cloth! The eager animal! With my automatic I took six rapid-fire pictures, and with the last one caught Pepe Huerta whispering to Penny just before the cow came up: "Feet firm. Don't move. Hold the cape tight."

She obeyed, tensing both her wrists and her jaw as the cow roared between the two, but now came the critical part, for Huerta yelled at Penny: "Turn with her! Plant your feet! Hold tight!" and again the cow smashed right into the middle of the cape, but this time she turned with such incredible swiftness that Penny had no time to prepare. The cow was upon her, butting her sharply in the right leg and tossing her into the air, but she did not fall back onto the sand, for Huerta caught her, held her in the air, and delighted the crowd by kissing her on the cheek as he stood her back up.

"Toro!" warned the crowd, for the cow, seeing this new center of action, was bearing down on the pair, but Calesero deftly interposed himself in front of Penny and led the cow away.

I supposed that this was the end of Miss Grim's performance, but I was mistaken. Ashamed of having allowed herself to be knocked down, she recovered her end of the cape, handed the other end to Huerta and indicated that she at least was ready for another charge. Now it was Calesero who stood at her side, coaching: "Feet firm. Hold tight," and it was either her skill or Huerta's, but the cape had been placed perfectly, for the cow roared safely past, but again, even before Calesero could reposition Penny, the little beast was upon her from the rear. This time Penny went up in the air, and this gave Huerta a chance to catch her before she crashed. As he planted her gingerly back on the ground, he again kissed her, then held her hand aloft as he coached her in taking a turn of the arena to wild applause from the watchers. And that is the way Penny Grim of Tulsa, an incoming freshman at S.M.U., met her third torero in three days, and had twice been kissed by him.

As she stood close to him at the railing, waiting for the fourth cow to be let in, I thought: What
a handsome pair they make! Two young people,
bright-eyed, full of vitality, each leaning toward
the other. The quaint essence of youth!

My attention was diverted by Ricardo Martín,
who had obviously learned of the tienta through
the bullfighters' grapevine and now wormed his
way in with hopes of making at least a few
passes with a real animal. Undetected by Don
Eduardo's guards, he now edged toward the
arena, saw that Huerta was paying more attention to Penny Grim than to the bull, snatched a
red cloth that had been draped over the railing,
and with an athletic leap landed in the ring to
face a still-vigorous and determined animal.
Lacking the stick that would normally have held
his muleta open, he had to rely on the most
difficult passes in the repertory: limp cloth low in
the left hand, right hand behind the back, moving slowly toward the cow and stamping his right
foot softly to provoke the charge. It was risky,
even with a cow, but he performed the ritual so
perfectly and with such style that watchers
began to clap. The cow charged and Martín remained immobile except for the slow motion of
his left hand as the cow swept past. Then, like
a real matador, he turned quickly but with an

economy of movement and presented the cloth again, low, slowly, gracefully.

In those magical moments he announced to the taurine world that he knew what he was doing and on his third pass, even better and closer than before, I heard some around me saying: "He knows, that one."

Calesero came to him and embraced him, leading him personally back to a seat beside Mrs. Evans. When the exhibition ended, Ricardo tried to steal the red cloth he had borrowed but was detected by one of Don Eduardo's men, who said boldly: "If you don't mind, I'll take that." In great humiliation Ricardo had to surrender it. But at that moment Mrs. Evans stepped in and asked the functionary: "What is the muleta worth?" for she had already learned that word, and the man said: "They're not cheap, the proper ones, the way they're cut and stretched. Ten dollars." And he showed her how what seemed to be a simple square of cloth had a pocket in it for holding the stick or sword that the matador used and also how small washers were sewn into the fringe to keep it from blowing about in a wind. "If it blew up, covering the matador," the man said, "he would become the unprotected target and might be killed. This is an important piece of cloth."

"You've explained it beautifully. Here's ten dollars and the cloth belongs to him." When the exchange was made and Martín tucked the muleta into his shirt, León Ledesma looked at me quizzically and I nodded, which meant: "That's right, León, he hopes to be an espontáneo this afternoon," and the big man groaned: "Not two in two days. The gods are punishing me."

As we passed out of the ring toward our cars, which would take us back to the bullfight, the workman who had tried to take the red cloth from Ricardo overtook us and grabbed Martín by the arm, and for a moment I feared there might be a brawl. But the man had brought a matador's stick, the kind whose point fitted in the pocket of the cloth. It was about three feet long, too much by far to hide under a shirt when one was going to try an espontaneo. But this one had been sawn in half and brought back together by a clever system of hinges and screws. Folded, it could be hidden and when reconstituted in full length as one climbed over the red fence into the ring where the bull waited, it would be a helpful tool.

"*¿Hoy día, quizás?*" the workman asked. (Today, maybe?)

"*Sí.*"

"Buena suerte." And he left us to ride back to the bullring with workmen from the ranch.

On our ride back Mrs. Evans asked Ledesma to share the rear seat with her while I drove her Cadillac with Penny perched beside me, and I heard Mrs. Evans say: "It's pretty obvious that Ricardo's going to try to get into the ring this afternoon, isn't it?"

"He and about six others," replied Ledesma.

"But if he does leap in, and if he does as well with the bull as he did with the cow, will you say so in your report?"

"I don't deal in such matters. Nothing ever comes of such an act."

"I'm told that's how Gómez got started."

"He's one in a thousand—ten thousand."

"But let's suppose he does something spectacular, would you then say so?"

"I told you I don't deal—"

I cannot say for sure what happened, because I could see their heads in my mirror but not their hands, but I'm fairly certain that money was exchanged, paper money, and after a long silence, Mrs. Evans asked: "In your sober opinion, Señor Ledesma, what would it cost an American boy to become an apprentice and then a matador, always providing he had the talent?"

"Well now!" and he began to reel off numbers that staggered me. "First the basics. Two suits, five thousand dollars. Swords, capes, muletas, thirty-five hundred. The special cape for the entry parade, twenty-five hundred. Then the recurring fees, your peóns and picadors, three thousand dollars a fight. Tips to everyone, six thousand dollars. And then the important things, publicity, including the critics, five thousand dollars. Manager maybe as much as eighteen thousand dollars. So when you are looking at one of our top matadors, Mrs. Evans, you are looking at big money."

"But with a beginner, if one wanted to do it on the cheap?"

"That's the way I'd do it. If you had a winner, someone who could get contracts, not many but a few. Secondhand suits, swords as available, maybe as little as nine thousand dollars."

"Could an American make a real dent, at nine or ten thousand dollars?"

"Six or seven try each year, probably on less. I know of two who tried real hard on twice that much. They all failed."

"Have any succeeded?"

"Within severe limits, two or three."

"If young Martín does get into the ring this afternoon, will you be able to tell by whatever he accomplishes whether or not he has a chance?"

"Mrs. Evans, be realistic. If he tries, you'll see total chaos. He'll be lucky if he even gets near the bull. The peóns won't allow it."

"But if he should?"

"You've been a tonic in this festival. And I've grown quite fond of you. So I will give you my opinion free, such as it is. So ask away."

"What I want to know, if he does well, will you say so in print?"

"I've already promised you I'll say something favorable about the testing at the ranch. I've drafted the opening lines. 'Yesterday at the Palafox Ranch I saw Calesero in his *traje corto* perform his arabesques with the sturdy cows of Don Eduardo, but the highlight of the ab-breviated tienta was the well-regarded nor-teamericano aspirant Ricardo Martín, who proved once again that he knows how to handle the muleta. He is definitely a young man to watch.' "

"Have you seen him before?"

"No, but it sounds better that way, a more considered judgment."

At this point I again lost sight, literally, of what-ever transaction occurred, but when it was concluded, Ledesma said: "But only if he actually gets near the bull." And on those terms I drove the Cadillac into the parking lot and headed for the bullring, unable even to guess what might be about to happen.

19

SOL Y SOMBRA

RELIEVED TO LEARN that my account of the tragedy at Izmiq-61 was in New York and that my photos had been delivered by air, I was free to attend the final fight as a spectator. I took along my notebook and cameras, on the odd chance that something memorable might happen, but my major concern was to see that my Oklahomans had a meaningful conclusion to their stay in Toledo. I had grown attached to Mrs. Evans, who seemed to have all the best attributes of a mother, and I was aware that had I been a couple of decades younger I'd been paying more than casual attention to Penny. So it was a privilege for me to stand outside the bullring with them as crowds gathered for the culminating mano a mano between Victoriano and Gómez.

"The two gates, this Sol and that Sombra, symbolize the fight," I told them as we marked the sharp difference between the two groups of aficionados using those gates. "You'll notice that those with tickets reading Sol, a motley crowd, use the one leading to the cheaper seats. They'll sit facing the sun, which can be damned bright in Toledo this time of year. Look at how they bring hats with brims or eyeshades to keep out the glare. Even so, they'll be uncomfortable during the first three bulls, but they watch with pleasure as the sun starts to disappear behind the upper tiers of the ring."

"Do they pay a lot less over there?" Penny asked, and I said: "You bet, but now look at these coming in with Sombra tickets. Well dressed and scrubbed. Entering by a gate adorned with that statue of a Palafox bull. They'll enjoy protection from the sun through the entire fight, for their ticket means shade. You don't have to be a snob when you're sitting in comfort here in Sombra to think: Look at those poor slobs over there in that blazing sunlight. Such thoughts even occur in Christian minds! 'I'm in heaven, they're in hell.' The extra pesos you pay to get seats in the shade are well spent. You ladies will be in shade."

There was a third entrance reserved for a few privileged people like Ledesma the critic and Clay the journalist. We could enter by the gate used by the matadors, but whereas they remained in a holding area until time for their processional entrance, Ledesma and I could slip through an even smaller red door that gave entrance to the narrow space between the tiers of seats and the sandy arena in which the bulls would be fought. This narrow passageway was called in Spanish the callejón, and many incidents during the fight would occur here. The manager would whisper suggestions to his matador. Functionaries would carry out orders from the president high in his box overlooking everything. Occasionally a bull would leap over the barrier separating the passageway from the arena and create havoc in the narrow space, which was supposed to be a refuge. In what looked to be a safe passageway men could be killed.

On this day I would not be using the privileged entrance, for I had no reason to be down in the passageway. I could sit in a seat behind the two Oklahomans, and it was fortunate that I was there because Penny gave me a commission.

Leaning back from her front-row seat she whispered: "Mr. Clay, that substitute matador at the ranch told me the big matadors might let him place one pair of sticks, maybe. If he does, he promised me: 'Mexico will not see a better pair this season,' so if it happens, do catch a photograph," and she added softly: "I would like that."

Mrs. Evans also gave me her commission in a voice even more subdued: "If Ricardo tries it, photograph everything," and I replied: "If I have enough film." She warned: "You'd better have."

As the minute hand on the arena clock crept toward five, the band of ten instruments high in the rafters began a traditional bullfight march, then suddenly stopped to allow their two trumpeters to sound the call that officially started the afternoon. A big gateway on the far sunny side of the arena opened partially and out rode a man in an ancient costume astride his white horse, which high-stepped in a slow dance to our side. There the man picked up a ceremonial key with which he galloped back full speed to open the red door through which the bulls would enter the arena. Then the big doors opened fully and into the sunlight stepped the three matadors followed by their troupes, including two mounted picadors for each matador. Trailing behind came a dozen men wearing white shirts who were called *monos sabios* (trained apes) whose job it was to clean up the arena after each of the six separate fights.

This entry scene was like nothing else in sport or spectacle. Even the most jaded aficionado had to be thrilled by the sight of the three matadors so handsome in their special capes, resplendent in color and decoration and used only for this entry march, followed by the peóns, each also wearing the best cape he could afford. When they reached our side, Victoriano, at the height of his public acceptance, came to where the actress we had seen at the ranch sat and with a bow offered her his cape, and at the same time Pepe Huerta, the substitute, came to Penny Grim and offered her his somewhat tattered cape, which she also spread out. The difference between the two capes was immediately and almost cruelly obvious: $2,800 to $69. But the audience applauded the two gestures, and both the matador and substitute posed momentarily before the two women as we snapped our shutters. The afternoon was off to a memorable start.

But then Juan Gómez, almost fighting to establish and maintain his role as a major matador, eclipsed the other pair, for he waited till they had made their presentations, then marched slowly to where Lucha González sat and with the gestures of a grandee at the court of Versailles presented her with his rather shopworn cape as spectators whispered: "She's the flamenco singer, Lucha. She danced in that movie, remember? Some years back," and the arena applauded.

Now at a signal from the president the bugler sounded his plaintive call, an echo from centuries that spoke of battle and death. The sound created an ominous mood, and as it wailed away into silence, the little red door across from us opened, and out roared the first Palafox bull of the afternoon, head high, legs pumping, horns jabbing this way and that in search of targets. The fight had begun.

Gómez ran to his first beast, the one we had described as having "small horns but quick movements," and tried to set the pattern for the afternoon by attempting a series of stately passes, but the bull did not comply. The animal was not cowardly, for when the well-padded horses came out it attacked them furiously, but again, when Gómez tried to lead the bull away for a set of really fine passes with the cape wrapping around his body as the bull roared past, there was no bull roaring anywhere, and the matador's attempts to make something happen proved not only fruitless but also just a bit ridiculous. The bad afternoon started for Gómez at that moment, but worse was about to happen, for now the intricate strategy of a hand-to-hand fight intruded.

When Gómez, having demonstrated that he could do nothing with his first bull, stepped away, Victoriano was on hand to sweep in, unfurl his cape and give the bull a series of brilliant passes that evoked cheers throughout the plaza. "Damn that bull," I would hear Gómez muttering to his peóns. "Why charge at him and not me?"

With the picadors it was the same. After the first pic, not a good one, Gómez tried to lead his bull away for some fancy passes, but the animal would not respond. Now the bandy-legged little Indian faced the cruel decision: ask the president to move the fight on to the next stage, knowing the bull had not been adequately tested, or deliver him to the second picador in hopes that this one would do the necessary job. But, if the bull did attack the second picador, then Victoriano was entitled to try his luck with passes. Gómez evaluated the situation only briefly, then allowed Victoriano his chance, and the graceful younger man again received a bull ready to cooperate. Victoriano gave him two sets of exquisite passes in which the cape became part of a flowing sculpture, the bull a friend to the matador, not an enemy.

With the sticks Gómez was adequate, but not exceptional, nor could he afford to hire men who were, so on this first bull he placed a desultory pair, but then felt obligated to offer Victoriano a chance to display what he could do, and the fans applauded this gesture. But it turned out poorly for the Indian, because poetic Victoriano drifted across the sand like an angel, rose on his toes and placed a pair so elegantly that the crowd cheered.

There was always a brief interval between the placing of the last sticks and the final stage of the fight, and in this pause Ledesma came to where we were sitting, pushed his big head between Mrs. Evans and Penny and whispered to me: "Norman, you'd better come down here with me," but I demurred: "I'm happy with these two." Severely he said: "There may be something you should see," and with those cryptic words he lured me away from the Oklahomans and down into the passageway, from where we watched Gómez try to do something with his bull.

The animal, somewhat confused by previous happenings, did not arrive at the end of his day suitable for the kind of passes and close-in work at which Gómez excelled. Juan accomplished little with the red cloth and failed three times to drive the sword home. As the bull was dragged out he heard what the reporters called divisos, or a division of opinion: a few cheers for his bravery and effort to do well, many jeers for having failed.

It was as if the drab first fight had been a forgivable prologue to the real afternoon, for the second bull, belonging to Victoriano, seemed to have been sent by Don Eduardo to prove that any Palafox bull carried with him the possibility of a superb performance. At the sorting that day I had noted No. 33 as "Placid, allows others to shove. Explosive???"

I was privileged to see this fight through the eyes of Ledesma, who allowed me to look over his shoulder as he jotted down a running series of notes to aid him when he wrote his critique: "Vic. two beautiful verónicas. Gómez finally does something. Leads toro off 2 fine walking passes. Vic. magnificent banderillas. Band plays. Gómez only regular. Vic. opens faena farolazo de rodillas. [Starts final stage on knees with swirling pass over his head]. Gets better, better. Muleta held behind back, bull under his arm, inches. A decent kill, but bull stands. One jab with the dagger sword. Bull falls. Dianas [traditional music of applause.] Wild cheering. An ear. Another ear. More dianas. Cheers. Tail.

Tour of the arena. Another. Another. He invites Don Eduardo to join him. Triumphant. Note his clever placement of toro."

When I asked what that last note meant, I was treated to another example of why it was rewarding to be near Ledesma at a taurine affair. He not only loved the gallantry of the bullfight world but also served as the recorder of its more sardonic elements: "Always watch how Victoriano places his bull during a fight. Whenever he feels capable of giving a fine series of passes, he directs his peóns to bring the bull over here to Sombra, so that the high-paying customers can marvel at his artistry. When he has a bull with which he can do nothing, his men lead it over to Sol and leave it there. Victoriano goes over, gives a few bad passes and dispatches the bull as quickly and ineptly as possible. Sol gives meaningless cheers, Sombra pays the rent. He likes rich people, but, of course, so do I."

"Do other matadors behave any differently?"

"Gómez. Watch the way he orchestrates his fight. When he has a great series of passes in prospect, he takes his bull to the Sol, because those are the people who support him, the people who know what real bullfighting is. With them, no sham or fancy-dancy."

"Where did you hear such a word?"

He laughed: "I once escorted a Hollywood startlet who was mad about Mexico. She taught me."

When I watched how the two matadors used the broad expanse of sand to do their work I saw that my earlier instinct had been accurate: Ledesma was right. Victoriano was indeed the artist of Sombra, Gómez the man of Sol.

The little Indian, having been forced to listen to the triumphant cheers for his opponent, was challenged to outperform him, and he certainly tried, but his valiant work on his second bull, the one we had spotted as being overage, was still unrewarding. For him the afternoon was degenerating into a debacle. One splendid moment, unfortunately, did not involve Gómez. True to his promise to Pepe Huerta, the substitute whom management had picked up on the cheap from Guadalajara, he allowed the young aspirant to place the second pair of sticks, having himself messed up the first pair. The eager substitute must have been rehearsing what he would do this day, if he got a chance to show the skills he knew he had but which others did not recognize. He took the sticks, decorated with garish purple tissue paper wrapped about their length, strode manfully to where Penny sat above him in the front row, and with the sticks in his left hand he pointed the barbed ends at her and announced he was dedicating his performance to her. The crowd cheered, and Penny, sitting with his frayed entrance cape still gracing the railing, started shouting in a most unladylike voice: "Mr. Clay! Mr. Clay! Get the photo!"

Heart pounding, nerves alert, wearing the one decent suit of lights he owned, Pepe went out toward the middle of the arena and started that long, dreamlike stalk toward the bull, feet together, jumping up and down now and then to hold the bull's attention. Fortunately, considering what Pepe had planned, the bull initially remained cautiously immobile, watching the thin figure approach with his arms extended over his head, until finally, with a mad rush, he came out of his defensive position driving right at the man. At that moment Huerta ran toward the bull, made a complete 360-degree turn to the right, and wound up facing the now bewildered bull only a few feet away. Up in the air leaped the man, sticks still high above his head, and with a deft turn and twist of his body he escaped the horns but left himself high enough in the air to enable him to place the barbed sticks exactly in the neck muscle behind the horns.

My automatic camera had caught some dozen shots of those last electric moments.

One that showed the full drama and grace of that last turn and downward dip of the sticks would be widely circulated in Mexico as The Pair of Toledo. In a poster-size reproduction paid for by Penny Grim it would come to rest on the wall of her dormitory room at S.M.U. in Dallas; beside it would be a small shot of Huerta dedicating the famous pair to her. It had happened. She had come to Mexico hoping to meet a bullfighter and she had found a champion.

Huerta's performance did nothing to help Gómez, because when Juan tried the third pair he looked almost pathetic in comparison with what the substitute had just done. And with the sword at the end he was brave but luckless. This time at the unsatisfactory kill there were not even divisos; they were all boos.

The pause after the third bull was like the midpoint of a baseball game in the United States when the groundkeepers run out to smooth the diamond, for now the big gate on the sunny side opened to admit two teams of mules dragging behind them heavy bags that leveled out the sand. Since the horses wore cockades in their manes and their drivers wore blue shirts, they made a colorful show and concluded their work at the far side of Sombra, from where they galloped in a mad chariot race to see which team would reach the exit gate first. After cheering the winner and booing the loser, the crowd was ready for the festival to resume.

Victoriano's second bull was almost a replica of his first, except that this time he was awarded only the two ears. The crowd made a noisy demand for the tail also, and when it was not granted, they made the triumphant matador circle the arena twice to wild cheering. I watched him as he passed and suspected that fear was hiding just below the joy he was entitled to show: "There's still that big one to face. The killer." I knew from past experiences with matadors that he was already beginning to sweat, and I put new film into my camera to be ready for what was likely to be the climax of the afternoon.

I missed Gómez's lackluster performance with his third bull, because before it started, León Ledesma tugged at my sleeve: "We may be able to see something not many witness," and he led me quietly to the sunny side of the arena, where we ducked furtively through a little red door into the darkened area in which the bulls were housed after the sorting. In their individual stalls only two of the six bulls remained, No. 38, the big sluggish oxlike fellow that Gómez was about to fight, and No. 47, the unshaven one who had killed Sangre Azul. As we stood in the shadows where we would not be observed, the gate enclosing No. 38 was jerked open with a loud bang while a man at the front end made a huge noise by rattling on the bars. The big bull, more than a thousand pounds of muscle and power, came rushing out of his cage and down the narrow passageway that would take him into the arena. Just as he left the darkness a workman with a steady hand reached down from a safe position and jabbed into the bull's neck muscles a short, sharp dart bearing a small ribbon showing the colors of the breeder's ranch, and this sudden sting caused the animal to leap forward. This one apparently made a great entrance, snorting and charging, for the crowd roared its approval, but I lost interest in him, for Ledesma was guiding me to another spot from which we could look into the cage holding the last bull, the killer.

Standing almost face-to-face with the bull, I desperately wanted to photograph that great head—black, powerful, quick little eyes, and those deadly horns, straight, unmarred and unshaven—but when I moved my camera into position Ledesma knocked it away and indicated with a nod of his head that others were in this darkened area too, high above, looking down from a perch that placed the bull's rear quarters directly under them.

Because of my long acquaintance with

Veneno, I knew he was capable of doing anything to give his son even a slight advantage
against a deadly enemy, but I could not have
guessed at the outrageous move he was about
to make. Perhaps he was going to shoot a mild
tranquilizer into the bull. No, his tactic was far
more primitive, one sometimes used when a
matador knew he had to face a fearful adversary, a strategy I had heard of but never expected to see.

Immediately after the close of Victoriano's triumphant fight with the fourth bull, Veneno had
hurried to the area where the picadors kept their
horses and the reserves in case one got killed
or incapacitated during the fight. There he had
waiting for him Diego and Chucho dressed in
their uniforms, and together they had dragged
from its hiding place the extremely heavy sack
of cement that had been soaked in water. Heav-
ing and huffing, they had hoisted it aloft to the
runway overlooking the bulls' cages, and there
they had positioned it directly over the rear hip
joints of No. 47. Now, with Gómez about to start
the third portion of his last bullfight, they were
ready.

Within ten minutes, this powerful bull would
explode into the arena and start looking for Victoriano with his needle-like horns, but Veneno
intended him to reach the ring with his power to

kill sharply reduced. As Ledesma and I watched in silence, we heard the picador whisper "Now," and the three Leals shoved the bag of cement forward, inch by inch, then "Ugggh!" and it fell with a thud on the most vulnerable part of the bull's rear end where the hind legs were joined to the hip. Ledesma and I, only a few feet away, heard the heavy weight hit the bull and watched as the wet bag slumped for a moment on the bull's back, then slipped to the ground. We heard the bull grunt and watched as he tried to exercise his suddenly painful rear quarters, and after a few irritated shakes of his legs, he adjusted to the new pain and was again ready to defend himself. But Veneno and his sons could now be sure that when he reached the ring he would have lost that extra degree of explosive energy that made a big bull so dangerous. This one would be slowed down, not enough to lame him but more than enough to retard him when trying to use his rear legs for that sudden burst of energy which could destroy horses and men.

As Veneno and his sons climbed down from their perch and hastened to their positions for the final fight, I wondered if Victoriano, who stood to profit from their furtive efforts, was aware that his bull had been so damaged that the fight would be unfair. I hoped that he was not, for I saw him as a man striving to be honorable, but in the treacherous world of bullfighting, who could be sure?

As León and I crept back from our spying mission, we heard the dismal trumpet wail the first aviso to Gómez warning him: "Speed it up, matador! Time's awasting!" and before Ledesma and I could regain our places in the passageway, the second aviso sounded. We arrived in time to see the poor Indian sweating as he tried vainly to work this devilish No. 38 into position where it could be finished with the sword, but the bull refused to cooperate, even though badly wounded by the matador's previous thrusts. Slowly, planting its feet carefully and solidly, it staggered on, a foe of tremendous vitality who refused to lie down and die.

In desperation, Gómez called for the sword that ends in not a point but a dagger and with it he tried to cut the spinal cord with one thrust into the spot behind the horns where the cord joined the head. This was a most difficult operation requiring skill and luck. He had neither, and as he tried repeatedly, with sweat rolling down his face, the crowd began a monotonous chant with each thrust: *"Tres, cuatro, cinco, seis . . ."* It was humiliating and disheartening, but Gómez did not allow the jeers to hurry or distract him. On the ninth try he placed his feet properly, as always, gripped the cloth in his left hand so the bull could see, and steadied the nerves in his right arm. Just as the trumpeter started his final aviso, the dagger hit home and the bull dropped dead spectacularly. Juan Gómez turned to salute the president high in his box and that official nodded back. Both knew what a hellish job it was to kill a powerful bull who refused to die.

Ledesma and I were back in the passageway when the clarion sounded for the final bull. After what we had just seen we were eager to watch how he reacted. He came thundering in looking for enemies but, noticeably to us at least, he avoided pushing off with his right rear leg; it was clear that a new and sudden pain was affecting his charge. I was surprised to see how quickly he mastered that pain, or ignored it, for by the time he reached where we waited, he was galloping at what looked like full strength. The three young Leal men—Veneno of course was in the corrals astride his horse awaiting his call to action—must have observed with relief that their bull seemed just a bit slower than expected; in a crisis this fraction of a second might make the difference between life and death.

Keeping my eyes riveted on the bull, with whom I now identified, my right forefinger waiting on my camera to photograph his fight against pain and devious adversaries, I watched as he stabbed at the giddy capes twisting on the ground before him. Until the matador stepped into the ring to take charge, it was a rule of the bullring that the peóns could run the bull only with the cape held in one hand so that it dragged. This provided the matador an opportunity to study how the bull reacted, and now Victoriano ran into the arena to launch whatever good passes he could while the bull was still in a voluntary chasing mood. He acted wisely, for when the animal saw the cape that had been on the ground now fluttering in the air, he interpreted it as a new kind of enemy and lunged at it exactly as the matador had planned. The thousand pounds of fire and muscle passed properly into the folds of the cape and out the other side, then quickly turned to catch the foe it had somehow missed. As it spun around I spotted the defect in the beast. Its right leg hesitated for the flick of a second, and the return charge was delayed just long enough for Victoriano to reset his feet and execute another fine pass.

Satisfied by these explorations that the bull was compliant, he now made one of those instant decisions that are the wonder of bullfighting: he would attempt one of the most dangerous and beautiful of all the passes, the *mariposa* (butterfly). Boldly he threw the cape over his head so that it came down behind his body, leaving nothing protecting his face, heart and stomach area. One thrust of the horns there and he was dead. Only two rather small triangular areas of cape were exposed to the bull, one guided by the left hand, one by the right, and these he began to show the bull in a tantalizing pattern. Now the left was visible and the bull looked in that direction. Then the left disappeared and the right came into view, tempting the bull to turn first here then there. The matador backed across the arena with the bull following as if the two were performing a ballet, a pas de deux of death. Then, without warning, the bull made a wild dive at the left square of cape and passed under the arm of the matador, who spun as the bull went past, so as to present the right corner of the cape still held behind his back. Twice more the bull charged the bit of cape, not the man, who at the end of the last pass twirled the cape with one hand and turned the bull into a knot, leaving him motionless and perplexed. It had been a masterly performance and the crowd cheered both partners of the dance.

At this point the clarion sounded and into the ring came old Veneno astride his enormous white horse, accompanied by a second picador who had apparently been given instructions to stay clear so that the bull always struck at

Veneno's horse and not his. The bull, who in the campo would have ignored the horse and had often done so when in the companionship of other bulls, now saw the mounted man as the only adversary in the ring and began a powerful drive that would have carried him straight into Veneno with overwhelming velocity. Victoriano, seeing the peril his father would face if the bull struck him with that accumulated force, deftly stepped forward with his cape, and slowed the bull's forward motion before delivering him close to his father. Now Veneno demonstrated why he was, even at his age, one of the finest picadors in Mexico. Leaning far forward to keep the bull away from his horse, he jabbed his oaken staff with its triangular steel point deep into the neck muscle. When it was well seated, he leaned even farther forward till he was right over the horns, still pushing downward, still trying to revolve the pic so that its barb could do the most damage, destroying most of the bull's power before the final act when Victoriano would have to face him alone.

The president, seeing what Veneno was attempting, ordered the trumpeter to sound a warning that this first pic should now end, whereupon Veneno treated the crowd to the comedy act of dancing the carioca. Maneuvering his horse by knee pressure, he kept it always positioned so that the bull could not break loose and run away, while with his stout right arm he kept punishing the bull, indeed almost destroying him, and at the same time indicating to the president that he was doing his best to obey orders. It was, I thought, much like the raucous masquerade performed by professional wrestlers in which the villain drags the hero into a corner where the referee cannot see what's happening and then gouges the man in the eye, bites his ear, strangles him, and knees him in the groin. When the referee admonishes him, he throws both hands in the air and cries: "Who? Me?" Wrestling and bullfight crowds enjoy such nonsense.

When Veneno finally allowed the bull to run free, his son ran in with his cape and performed a new series of handsome passes in such a way that the bull was left a free choice as to which picador to attack this time. The second picador, still under orders, maneuvered his horse so that the bull had to go back to Veneno, who repeated his crushing performance. I thought that by this time the bull was markedly favoring his right hind leg, but I was mistaken; he was merely gathering strength for one mighty thrust. When it came, without warning, the bull bowled over both Veneno and his horse as if they had been made of straw. Sensing that it was the fallen man, not the horse, who was his abuser, he lunged at the defenseless old man. Veneno was in the most perilous position possible: if a horn caught him while lying flat on the solid earth, there would be no bouncing off or sliding away—that horn would pierce him and pin him to the ground. It was a fearful moment as Pepe Huerta and the peóns of both Victoriano and Gómez sped out to confuse the bull with their flashing capes.

He was not deceived. Almost as if he were brushing aside the capes, he continued to lunge at the fallen picador, but now a new defender rushed in. It was Gómez, cape flapping in front of him like an old woman drying a sheet on a sunny day, whose bold gesture saved the fallen man. Slowly the bull followed Gómez, able at any moment to pierce the cape and kill the little Indian, but somehow Gómez continued to lure him away. Spectators who knew anything about bullfighting knew what a heroic act the Indian had performed; even those who had counted his disgrace a few minutes before—"*Cinco, seis*"— now sat mute in wonder at his bravery.

Victoriano, still confident of his eventual triumph over the difficult little fellow, sought to hammer home his victory by first placing an admirable pair of banderillas and then arrogantly marching over to where Gómez waited. Holding the second pair of colorful sticks in his right hand, he raised his left forearm parallel to the ground, rested the sticks upon it like a votive offering, and invited the Indian to try his luck on this fine Leal bull. Gómez, taken by surprise and aware that he was no match for Victoriano in this part of the fight but always gallant, accepted the challenge. Taking the sticks from Victoriano's arm, he came to where I waited with my camera and said, "Pañuelo?" When I handed him my handkerchief he asked Ledesma the same question and received his handkerchief with an honest blessing from the big man in the black cape: *"Buena suerte, matador."* Gómez nodded gravely, for he was about to risk his life.

Striding out in his bowlegged way to where everyone could see, he stuck the two handkerchiefs in his mouth, took the two banderillas in his hands, and broke them off a few inches from the barbs, reducing them from twenty-six inches to six. Then, wrapping the jagged ends in cloth, and holding both banderillas in the right hand, he began the slow, fatal march toward the bull. *"Eh, toro"* I heard him call. "*Toro*!" and when at last the bull reacted, Gómez ran in a wide circle, carefully calculating where he would intercept the bull's charge. When that spot was reached he leaped high in the air, leaned in over the horns and with one hand jabbed the two barbs directly on target. It was a superb performance, one that could have been done only by a very brave man, but he paid a fearful price, for as he completed his miracle his left foot struck the bull's lagging right rear foot and he stumbled slightly, enough to give the bull a chance to turn back and rip deeply into his right groin.

In a flash, peóns from both sides rushed out, protecting him with their swirling capes, then stood guard while medical attendants swarmed in to carry him to the infirmary beside the chapel. There practiced medics cut the leg of his trousers, cleaned the ugly gash without administering an anesthetic, and dusted the gaping hole with "the bullfighter's friend," Dr. Fleming's penicillin. In the old days a matador with a wound like this died four days later of septicemia. Now a wounded man lived, so when the doctors hastily sewed up the hole, they could predict with confidence: "You'll live, but you're finished for today." A junior doctor attending Gómez whispered to a nurse: "And for this year." So Juan Gómez's Ixmiq-61 had truly ended in disaster. There would be no triumphant season in Madrid this summer and in the stands Lucha González, anticipating the gravity of the wound, groaned: "Oh hell," for she saw her chance of becoming a flamenco singer in Spain once again delayed, if not destroyed.

———

In the ring other changes had occurred. Now the inexperienced Pepe Huerta became more important; if anything should happen to Victoriano Leal, Huerta would be obligated to fight the last bull to a conclusion. Victoriano, realizing he and Huerta were now partners, invited the young aspirant to place the third pair of banderillas, which he did with less flair than the first time but well enough to gain applause.

That was the last light moment of the afternoon, for now a frightened Victoriano, with no Veneno to protect him, had to march out and tackle this powerful bull whose right rear leg might be weakened but whose heart seemed more resolute than before. This bull knew how to defend himself. Despite his apprehension, Victoriano remained the gallant. Striding matador fashion to where the actress sat behind his handsome parade cape, he raised his bullfighter's black cap with its two end points, held it straight toward her, and dedicated the bull to her. Then, in the time-honored tradition of the bullring, he turned his back on her, threw his cap insolently over his left shoulder and stalked out to do battle. The actress, although unprepared for this abrupt conclusion to the dedication, caught the cap and pressed it to her lips, where she would keep it as the last moments of the festival unwound.

Victoriano's task was to kill this bull expeditiously with the least possible exposure to those lethal horns. The bull's task was to defend himself to the last breath of his pounding lungs, the last swipe of his practiced horns. And each had a store of tricks to neutralize the other's devices.

When Victoriano tried, in deference to his exalted position and his performance so far, to give his bull at least a couple of decent passes, the animal, now tired and aching from strange afflictions, refused to comply and would not budge from the defensive position he had taken. Veneno, now coaching from the passageway, cried: "Finish it, however you can," but this prudent counsel of surrender only encouraged the matador to attempt one last pass to show his dominance over even this difficult beast. When the bull saw him approaching he waited till the critical moment, then swung his forequarters about and lashed out with his saberlike right horn, catching Victoriano in the right leg. From my vantage point I could see that it was a serious wound, one that would require stitches, but I judged it would not be disabling like the one taken by Gómez.

As Veneno gathered his bleeding son in his

arms for the trip to the infirmary I could hear him whispering, "You'll live. You'll not lose your leg." He had learned that it was vital in these first moments to prevent the wounded torero from thinking that he might die. "You'll live, Victoriano. You'll be back next year, bigger than ever."

While the matador was being carried out the far gates, Mrs. Evans was whispering: "I think I see Ricardo getting ready to make his move." The young American had edged himself into a position from which he might leap over the barricade and dash into the ring while others were preoccupied with the confusion, and at Mrs. Evans's prompting I readied my camera, but nothing happened.

The ring was now clear except for one side where the bull, who remained motionless, protected himself by keeping his back to the wooden barrier that hemmed the arena. Toward him, marching slowly across the sands, came the substitute, Huerta, whose task it was to kill this immensely dangerous bull. The young man did not know what Ledesma and I knew, that No. 47 had killed the great bull Sangre Azul, but he was aware that 47 had already sent two of Mexico's major matadors to the hospital. He moved cautiously, trying to determine what he could do that Victoriano, a much more experienced man, had failed to do. He was in no hurry for this test of his skill.

This hesitancy gave young Ricardo Martín, the same age as Huerta, the opportunity he needed. After secretly reconstituting his folded stick and jamming its spiked end into the far corner of his red muleta, he nodded slightly to both Mrs. Evans and Penny, who flashed him the thumbs-up sign. He then vaulted the barrier, and before any peóns or officials could intercept him, was upon the bull and dropping to his knees. From this position he accepted the charge of the bull, passed him handsomely, as the crowd roared approval. Then he whirled about, still on his knees to take a return charge, which again he handled with a flourish. Martín, realizing that he faced two fights, one against the bull, the other against the horde of men who were trying to drag him off to jail, fought a skillful and courageous two-front battle, first running so fast that no one could catch him, then doubling back at enormous risk to himself and throwing a few hasty passes at the bull, who was so confused by the racket about him and the flashing bodies that he continued to attack the one thing he did understand, that red cloth.

In this chaotic warfare, now further confused by six frantic policemen running about, Ricardo had one important factor in his favor: The others were terrified by those long, unshaved horns. Courageous though they might normally be, they would chase this deadly bull just so far; when they saw those horns turning in their direction they backed off. In this harum-scarum situation Ricardo managed three sets of two passes each, enough to throw the stands into a frenzy.

After the third pair, which left the bull standing rigid amid the confusion, Ricardo reached forward, patted the bull between the horns and strode away in the affected posturing of a matador. In this moment of carelessness two policemen grabbed him, and off he was dragged to a holding pen from which he would be taken to jail after the festival ended. He left to cheers. Both valiant and knowing, he had not been a reckless, feckless espontáneo but an aspiring torero, and the crowd knew the difference.

When quiet was restored, once again Pepe Huerta started toward the agitated bull. But once more he was interrupted, for through the red gate on the far side used by matadors hobbled Victoriano, his leg tightly bandaged so blood did not flow, his torn trouser leg awkwardly pinned together, his walk steady though limping, his hands empty and his bullfighter's cap long gone, moving purposefully to intercept Chucho and Diego, who rushed to meet him. Reaching for his sword and with the red muleta

draped over his left arm, he started for the waiting bull. On the way I heard him tell Pepe Huerta:
"It's my responsibility." When the younger man
could not hide his disappointment, Leal assured
him: "I'll help you get a fight, but this one is
mine." and the young man had to retreat, surrender his sword, and resume his cape.

When Veneno saw what his son was about to
attempt, to kill this dangerous bull, he became
frantic: "No! Your leg won't be steady. No, Victoriano!" for he knew that any bull that had
knocked down two horses and two men would
remember those victories and try to kill any man
who approached. Victoriano must be protected
from self-destruction.

But his son had found new courage, and I
heard him dismiss his father: "It's my bull, and
I'll finish him." Turning his back on Veneno, he
limped out to certify his independence.

Alone in the middle of the ring he was no
longer a pirouetting marionette manipulated by
others but a lone man facing a deadly task. The
fight was between a gallant beast who had been
mistreated by forces he could not comprehend
and a new man who had found himself. Four
times the bull had gained victories over horses
and men, and twice the matador had garnered
laurels for his stylish fights against his first two

bulls, only to be wounded by his third. It would be an even fight.

Then came the moment in Ixmiq-61 that I will always remember, even though my camera was unable to catch it, for its significance was not aesthetic but moral. When Victoriano came to face his enemy, he found him exactly where he wanted, before the Sombra seats, a spot from which he had launched most of his memorable faenas. But when he approached No. 47, the great bull slowly turned and started hunting for that fortunate spot which he dimly remembered as the one from which he had sent both Gomez and Victoriano to the infirmary. It seemed incredible that a dumb animal could identify in this strange arena those spots where he'd had minor triumphs and those others where he'd suffered, but in fight after fight, Spanish bulls exhibited that uncanny sense. If No. 47 could take refuge in his chosen spot, he had a chance for victory.

Slowly, as the sun disappeared, he started a plodding march across the full diameter of the arena, attacked by a dreadful pain he could not understand and trailed by a determined matador who suffered from his own wounds. As the shadows lengthened in the arena the two adversaries, beast and man, limped to their destiny.

This time the bull's chosen refuge was in the Sol, where he took a position with his aching rear jammed against the wooden barrier. From here he would not be easily dislodged, and all of us who had been allowed to watch from the passageway in Sombra now scurried to be near the bull as he prepared to defend himself in Sol. Of this tense crowd, only Ledesma and I knew how the bull had been damaged, and I, at least, was praying: "Protect yourself, old fellow. You've won your fight." Ledesma, seeing moisture glistening in my eyes, said: "It can get rather emotional, no?" and he directed me to watch closely the way in which Victoriano proposed to solve his deadly riddle: how to lure that bull out of his defensive stance.

When I saw Victoriano, a man who had befriended me, approach the bull, I thought: Let him do well, but I realized that I was cheering both the bull and the man, and understood that what I meant was: Let this fight end honorably.

Slowly, as in the old days, Victoriano walked toward the bull, not running from the side as in his recent cowardly days, and he moved with such authority that the bull tried to decipher what kind of threat this adversary posed, and in doing so moved his hindquarters slightly away from the defensive barrier. His inquisitiveness doomed him, because once he deserted his haven he was vulnerable, and now had to twist and turn to keep facing his enemy. This allowed Victoriano to tease him into an acceptable stance, and in that moment the matador went in boldly, bravely for a masterly kill, but the wily animal was waiting, and with a toss of his powerful head he used the smooth side of his left horn to hammer Victoriano in the chest, knocking him flat.

From old Veneno's vantage it looked as if the bull had gored his son, so with a frenzied leap, and followed immediately by his other sons, he ran to save his fallen matador with flashing capes. When the Leals had Victoriano upright but unsteady, they insisted that he quit the fight and allow them to carry him back to the infirmary, but he brushed them aside, asked for his fallen sword, and said simply: "Now I know his tricks. This fight is over," and he went back to face the bull.

Anticipating the animal's weakening attempts at self-defense, the elegant matador exuded an aura of invincibility, for he did everything right to lure the bull out of his refuge, then to profile in the face of the deadly right horn and go over it to lodge the sword deep and true. The bull staggered, looked around frantically and searched on trembling feet for his attacker.

Technically the bull was dead, for the steel

went through one lung and close to the heart, but his terrifying determination to fight on was so great that he refused to obey the message of death coursing through his sorely damaged body: "Lie down, brave bull. You defended yourself. Don't breathe so deep. Lie down."

He refused. Staggering about in a grotesque dance of death, he tried with his damaged rump to relocate that comforting fence but failed. So, as if his three good legs were oak trees in some meadow, he dug in where he was and refused to surrender.

It was a sight that those of us who saw it from the passageway will never forget. We could reach out across the fence and touch him. Victoriano, in an act of compassion and respect for his great bull, went up to him, placed his hand on the bull's forehead between the horns, and gently pushed him down. The legs crumpled, the knees buckled and, with a final attempt at lunging forward, the bull died.

Slowly, painfully, his face ashen from loss of blood, all energy drained, Victoriano hobbled back across the arena to present himself to the president high in his box. Sword in his left hand, muleta draped across his left forearm, he raised his right like some ancient gladiator reporting to his emperor: "I have complied," whereupon Veneno and his sons gathered him in their arms and started for the infirmary. As they carried him past the mob in Sol cheers began.

Soon the entire plaza was demanding that he be awarded a turn of the ring, so with dianas playing, he freed himself from the men who were carrying him and started the triumphal parade, but he turned not to his cheering supporters in Sombra but back to where No. 47 was about to be hauled away. Halting the mules, he indicated that this tremendous bull who had defended himself so nobly must share the honors, and these two wounded warriors toured the ring in glory.

As they passed the breeder's box, Victoriano saw Don Eduardo Palafox, afraid that he might not be called out to join the triumph, jumping up and down like a nervous schoolboy who had to go to the bathroom. When the matador looked in his direction with a nod so slight that no one could see it, if indeed it was a nod, Don Eduardo catapulted from the box and joined the glorious procession as flowers and gifts poured down.

As they approached the exit gate on their turn, Victoriano remembered when he was a lad starting his career. Hobbling to where the police watched approvingly, he called: "Bring out the boy!" When his demand was augmented by shouts from the crowd, Ricardo Martín was produced in handcuffs and, with Victoriano sponsoring him, he made a turn of the ring in which he had performed so intelligently and so well. Manacled hands raised above his head, he acknowledged the cheers, but when he came to Mrs. Evans he stopped and blew her a kiss, for in his mind he had dedicated the bull to her.

Long after others had left the ring, I remained inside the passageway, leaning with my arms on the barrier that had protected me from the horns, and as I stared at the gate through which Victoriano and No. 47 had made their exit, I wondered what force in their lives had driven them to perform so heroically. Man and beast were incomparable, a pair of adversaries whom destiny had ordained for this festival, and I mumbled: "They performed for you, Clay, to remind you of the principles by which a life should be led."

20

THE
HOUSE OF
TILE

I F SATURDAY NIGHT was, as I said earlier,
the happiest night of a festival because
looming obligations could be ignored, Sunday
night after the close of the last fight was clearly
the most depressing, for now a return to normal
life and its tensions became inescapable. This
was particularly true of Ixmiq-61, because the
last fight had been such an emotional affair that
a letdown was inevitable, and as participants in
the festival gathered in desultory manner at the
various tables on the Terrace, one could detect
a certain vacancy in their eyes, as if the fires of

the last three nights had left only smoldering embers.

It was a night of bittersweet experiences, none more intense and complex than the one I became involved with when I took my seat at a table at which Penny Grim was talking agitatedly with León Ledesma, who was apparently telling her things she did not want to hear. "Tell her, Norman, what these American girls who cluster about the matadors like bees seeking honey are called."

"You said it in the car this afternoon, they're camp followers."

"There's a harsher, more accurate word. In Spanish we say *putas.* Translate it for her."

"Whores." When I saw her blush I added: "But I'd not use that word myself."

"What would you use?" Ledesma asked with a touch of his familiar acid.

"I think 'giddy young girls away from the restraints of home' would cover it."

"I'll accept that, if you insist on being old-womanish. But this young girl is not giddy, and with Mrs. Evans and you and me on hand, she's certainly not free from the restraints of home."

"You talk as if you were my guardians," Penny broke in. "I sent my father home, and I do not care to take directions from you—none of you. I have a date with him tonight, and I intend keeping it."

Now I understood. In some clever way during the testing at Don Eduardo's, Pepe Huerta, while holding the cape with Penny or standing beside her at the barrier, had arranged to take her out after the fight, and she was waiting for him to come down from the room the Widow Palafox had allowed him to move into for a few pesos. Ledesma was determined that she not join, symbolically, the tawdry collection of young women waiting to grab hold of any torero they could land. Matadors were preferred, peóns acceptable if they were young, picadors too old and fat. A young would-be matador like Pepe Huerta might be the top prize, for he would carry with him a sense of drama and romance, the young man aspiring to greatness.

"I sympathize with you, Penny," I said, to Ledesma's disgust. "He's a handsome young fellow, and that pair he placed, that whirling dervish bit—you might spend a lifetime at the plazas and never see the likes of that."

"Did you get it on film?" she asked, and the intensity in her voice betrayed how keenly interested in Huerta she was.

"I must have caught more than a dozen shots,

rapid fire, in color. I promise to make you an enlargement of the two best."

"I would like that," and she touched my arm with such vibrancy that for an instant I wished she were interested in me and not in the young bullfighter. "Send them to me. Don't just promise."

"I will." As I said this I saw Pepe Huerta come onto the terrace freshly showered and with the neat dress and narrow black tie that toreros favor as one of the marks of their profession. When he bent to kiss Penny's hand, I saw that at the nape of his neck he had a long tuft of hair carefully dressed in the little knot known as the coleta. One of the saddest days in a matador's life comes when, to the accompaniment of "Las Golondrinas," that incredibly lovely song of farewell, he marches to the middle of the arena during his last fight to allow the next senior matador to take a long pair of shears and cut his coleta, signifying that his life as a matador has ended. I've seen the ceremony twice and wept each time with no embarrassment, for everyone else was weeping, too. So when I saw that young Pepe was already wearing the coleta, I knew he took his profession seriously and that Penny was in the presence of a real torero.

It was fascinating to watch how perfectly these two young people meshed, the excited girl, the hesitant but proud young man in the first stages of his profession. As they sat beside me they seemed once more to lean toward each other, as they had at the testing. It was as if some supernatural force was acting upon them, and I found myself wishing that Mrs. Evans were here to dampen the ardor, for it was clear to me that this mutual attraction was getting way out of hand, with me powerless to control it.

Ledesma was equal to the task. "I'm so glad you decided to stop by, Pepe. That was a tremendous pair you placed today."

"I hope the photographers caught it."

"They couldn't miss. It'll be in all the papers." The two men were speaking in Spanish, but since Penny had studied that language in school, and Ledesma had excellent English and Huerta a respectable smattering, the conversation flowed easily. Penny said: "Mr. Clay told me he had more than a dozen shots, in color." Shyly she added: "He promised to send me a pair—for my room."

"It's too bad the espontáneo spoiled that last bull," Ledesma said. "You might have done something with that one—before he became unruly because of the crowd in the ring."

Huerta instantly transferred his interest to a dissection of the fight: "I'm sure I could have handled that bull. Did you notice how he had

slowed down in pushing off with his hind feet
when he started his charge? Veneno had really
punished him with the lancing. Slowed down like
that, I could have managed him."

Ledesma looked at me and nodded. Then,
turning to Pepe, he asked: "And what brings you
to our table?"

"At the tienta, Señorita Penny—" He pronounced her name with a delightful, musical accent.

"Don't you know her last name?" Ledesma
asked coldly.

"She told me, Penny," the young man said
hesitantly.

"You don't know her last name, but you come
here—"

"Señor Ledesma, she invited me."

"If her father were here, you'd ask his permission, wouldn't you?"

"Yes . . . yes. I would look for him, but she said
he'd gone home."

"And left her in my care. I am—what you
might call—her sobresaliente father."

With his adroit use of this bullfight term, which
specifically identified the young would-be matador, the critic warned the aspirant that he must
not pursue this matter of escorting Penny Grim,
but the Oklahoma girl did not feel herself bound
by this threat from the critic.

"I asked him to take me to see the celebrations," she told us, pointing to the plaza and the carousel.

Suddenly everyone's attention was deflected by the appearance of the two Leal brothers, who were quickly surrounded by squealing young women who had hoped to date their young brother Victoriano.

"Is he still in the hospital?" a blonde asked.

"Is he badly wounded?" cried another girl.

"Will he be able to fight again?" Their questions tumbled out in a mix of Spanish and English, and after some minutes of confusion, the two Leals allowed the girls to drag them off into the heart of the plaza. From the hotel doorway, their father, white-haired Veneno, watched his sons coping with a situation that occurred frequently: surrounded by adoring young women, mostly from the States.

"That is what you must not be," Ledesma said coldly as the obstreperous girls disappeared beyond the statue of Ixmiq. And to the young torero he said with even more coldness: "You have no engagement tonight, Pepe. I am this girl's father, and she is too young to accompany you unattended." As I listened to this astonishing performance I realized that he was speaking like the dutiful son of a Spanish family of good breeding. He was protecting his younger sister, who could not be allowed to wander off without a dueña, and if Mrs. Evans had been thoughtless enough to leave the girl without proper chaperoning, he, Ledesma would have to correct that social error.

Penny, of course, did not see it that way. She had taken a strong liking to this highly acceptable young man. She had been thrilled by his magical performance with the sticks, and since she had for some time in Tulsa been accustomed to going out at night with her various youthful suitors, she expected to do so here. So despite what Señor Ledesma said, she proposed to keep her date with the sobresaliente, but when she rose to do so, she came up against twin stone walls: Spanish custom and bullfight tradition.

Ledesma knew that he might be powerless to halt Penny, accustomed to her Oklahoma freedoms, but in disciplining young Pepe Huerta he was all-powerful. If the latter ignored the critic's direct orders, Ledesma had the capacity to forestall Huerta's rise in bullfight circles. He could pass the word to the impresarios not to bother with Pepe: "No talent. One pair doesn't make the man. You can skip him," and he would be skipped. Worse, he would be blackballed. Years would pass and he would receive no invitations

to fight in the important arenas. Huerta knew I
knew, and most of all, León Ledesma knew, that
what this boy did in the next few moments could
determine his career.

"I apologize, Señor Ledesma. I should have
asked your permission." Rising and turning to
Penny, he said: "You were very brave this afternoon. I shall always remember."

With a cry that brought an ache to my heart,
for I had forgotten how powerful emotions can
be when one is seventeen, Penny rose, threw
her arms about Huerta, and kissed him on the
cheek, holding on to his left hand when she
finished. "I'll have the pictures Mr. Clay took. I'll
follow your career, Pepe, and I'll cheer you when
you become famous. This was so wonderful. It
could have been so wonderful," and she fell into
her chair and put her face in her hands.

I indicated to Pepe that he should leave and,
bowing to Ledesma, he did. As soon as he was
gone, Penny rose to go to her room, but Ledesma grabbed her arm and pulled her back down:
"We'll have no climbing out of windows,
Señorita Grim. You'll wait here with me till Mrs.
Evans returns from wherever she is."

I left them sitting there in silence as I hurried
from the Terrace to see if I could overtake
Huerta. I caught up to him under a lamplight

where we spoke for some minutes: "You were very good today, Pepe. That's enough. It might lead to something."

"We did have an understanding. She did ask me."

Because of my own spotty track record I felt qualified to tell him: "Sometimes a man has to take it in silence when he loses his girl."

"Maybe I shouldn't have been there at all. The Terrace is for matadors."

"After a pair like yours today, you can sit any-where. But now what?"

"Who knows? I don't get many fights."

"How many a season?"

"Maybe six. I think that pair today, if any of the newspapers prints it, that might help."

"Pepe, I could see you were going to try something special, so I took a series of rapid-fire shots, and if they turn out and my magazine prints a series, you'll get a lot more than six."

"Don't lose the film."

"And now what?"

"I have to get my gear. My parade cape, a fine old one, borrowed from a man in Guadalajara. A bull caught him, he don't fight anymore."

"And when you get your stuff?"

"I go to the station where the trucks leave for Guadalajara. The drivers know me. The Sunday-night runs. I'll be home by dawn."

"Pepe, I'm going to earn a lot of money on those shots of you. Let me give you your share now."

Proudly he refused: "I get by. My mother lets me live with her. I do all right."

"Pepe, damn it. You earned the money. It's your legal share."

"You mean, like a salary?" For this question he used the Spanish word *sueldo,* and I said eagerly: "That's it, your *sueldo,*" and with a dignity that made me ashamed to look in his eyes, he accepted two ten-dollar bills.

When I returned to the Terrace I saw that Mrs. Evans had arrived in a fury and was behaving like the enraged widow of an Oklahoma oil millionaire: "Clay! How are we going to get that poor boy out of jail?"

"They have some eighteen thousand witnesses that he broke the law, nearly ruined the finale to the festival."

"Trivial. Fine him and set him loose."

"Fine him? Where would he get the money to pay it?"

"I'll help him. He's a fine lad, conducts himself well, and I will not see him rot in a Mexican jail."

"Mrs. Evans! He's in Mexico because he wanted to be here. And he's in jail because he was willing to take the risk of being arrested. Knew the penalty when he leaped into the ring. He won't rot."

Receiving no comfort from me, she importuned the Widow Palafox who reassured her: "It's not like the old days. They don't mistreat young men in jail no more. Two nights to scare him, he's free."

"Would your cousin, Don Eduardo, be able to help?" and the widow said: "He helps everyone. He runs Toledo," and upon urgings from Mrs. Evans she telephoned the ranch owner, who soon appeared: "What can I do?"

When Mrs. Evans started to explain, he cut her off: "I was there, remember? I saw what he did to my best bull. Almost ruined our festival. Let him rot in jail, two, three months. Teach him a lesson."

She could not accept this and spoke of appealing to the American ambassador in Mexico City, to whom she had brought a letter of introduction from influential friends in the oil business. This threat finally made an impression on Don Eduardo, for he summoned the widow and asked: "You say he's in our jail?" and when she nodded he rose, signaled to me and said: "We must see what we can do to get his release. But there will be the matter of the fine. Have you any money, Norman?"

"Not at this hour. Tomorrow, when the banks open—"

"I have traveler's checks," Mrs. Evans said, and she accompanied Don Eduardo and me to the jail at the far end of town. There, amid the obstreperous drunks who had been picked up at the festival and a group of prostitutes who had come into town from Mexico City, we found Ricardo Martín sitting quite contentedly with three young Mexicans about his own age. He was relating in fairly good Spanish his experiences with Victoriano's bull, making passes with his right hand as the imaginary bull swept past. He was, as they say, feeling no pain. He'd made it into the ring. He'd attacked his bull under great difficulties and had satisfied himself and others that he knew what bullfighting was. Not many young men his age enjoyed comparable success, and he could afford two or three days in confinement.

Mrs. Evans, who had visualized him in some medieval torture chamber, was disarmed when she found him reasonably at ease, but nevertheless she pursued her mission of freeing him: "What are the charges?"

The jailer shrugged, looked at Don Eduardo, and made no reply, but when she pestered him he growled: "I don't make charges. They bring him here, he's my problem. You want him out, that's your problem."

Don Eduardo agreed and said he'd call a lawyer, who appeared with a court official who explained that the charge was disturbing the peace at a public assembly, which involved five days in jail if found guilty, and everyone had seen that he was guilty. But if Ricardo paid his fine, the jailer could release him tonight.

"How much is his fine?" Mrs. Evans asked, and the official hesitated, then said tentatively, as if testing the water: "Two thousand five hundred dollars American."

I gasped and so did the others, including Ricardo, but Don Eduardo exploded: "Ridiculous! Make it two hundred," and, deferring to Palafox, the official said: "All right, two hundred, but in dollars."

When Mrs. Evans unzipped her wallet and produced two traveler's checks, which she signed with an impatient flourish, the official asked Don Eduardo: "Will I be able to cash these at the bank—in the morning?" and my uncle said: "Better than pesos." To us he added: "In the old days I'd have stormed in here, head of the Palafoxes, and told them what to do, not asked, and there would have been no traveler's checks exchanging hands, believe me." He sighed. "Maybe the new days of responsible democracy are better, but I doubt it. No government account will ever see any part of the two hundred dollars. He'll give the jailer twenty-five, keep the rest for himself, and nobody's hurt."

When Ricardo was turned over to us, he asked permission to go back and say good-bye to his cellmates, and when this was granted he asked Mrs. Evans if she could lend him five dollars to buy his fellow prisoners some bottles of Coke, and she gave him the money. We then drove back to the Terrace, where Mrs. Evans rapped out a series of orders: "I'd like that table in that private corner. Clay, see if you can find the Widow Palafox, she's needed. Ricardo, wait over there for a few minutes, if you will." When all was done to her satisfaction, with the Widow Palafox seated at her elbow, she revealed her purpose in assembling us at the table: "I'm stuck down here with my Cadillac and no one to help me drive it back to Tulsa. Do I dare hire Ricardo to drive me home? I'd like to know what you think."

Don Eduardo's and my response was negative, the widow's mildly positive, and when the votes were on the table, as it were, Mrs. Evans became specific: "The plays you see, the movies about young drifters doing terrible things to older women. Do I dare risk it? Obviously I want to, but how can we tell if he's a stable young man and not some psycho, as the young people say?"

Don Eduardo made a cautionary observation: "The land between here and the Texas border can be pretty rough. There are old-time bandits really, it's no Easter holiday."

"That's exactly why I need a man to help me."

"Norman here, I'd trust him to be your companion."

"I'm sorry, no way I could take the time," I protested. "They're yelling for me in New York right now."

"Or I could let you have one of my men from the ranch who's been a long time with me—completely trustworthy." He was speaking in English to be more persuasive, but Mrs. Evans was still wavering: "I wonder if I dare trust him."

The widow said: "I've been watching him. He don't drink. He seems like a nice young man. If it was my car involved, I'd risk it. But with you, Mrs. Evans, they tell me you have money, you would face added risks."

"Why are you proposing this crazy thing?" Don Eduardo asked, and to my surprise she said: "Call Señor Ledesma over. He's working too hard on his notes. And he may have some thoughts on this." When I went to invite León to join us, he brought Penny along, and Mrs. Evans shocked us all by what she proposed.

"Señor Ledesma knows that for the last few days I've been asking questions to determine what it might cost to finance a young American who wants seriously to become a Mexican matador."

"Good God!" Don Eduardo cried. "Have you lost your senses?" to which she replied: "My son was about Ricardo's age when he died, and he always wanted to do some big thing, but lacked the time to even know what it was. Ricardo does know. He wants to be a bullfighter. It may be a stupid ambition, but it's real. He proved that twice today at your fiesta, Don Eduardo, with a little animal, and in the ring with an enormous one. I decided then I'd help."

"Can none of you norteamericanos talk sense with this woman?" Don Eduardo asked.

To my astonishment, it was Penny who butted in with an opinion: "At her age and with her money, if she wants to do something that she's always wanted to do, she'd better do it now. How much would it cost?" and I could see that she was captivated by the idea of anyone's becoming a matador. Mrs. Evans deferred the question to Ledesma, who recapitulated the figures he'd given earlier: "So you see, it could be done in first-class style, maybe twenty thousand dollars—"

"Ridiculous!" I cried. "Don't even consider it, Mrs. Evans."

"I'm not," she said. "But I certainly am considering quite seriously backing him to the extent of five thousand the first year. Properly administered, this would give him a fighting chance. Señor Ledesma told me, after Ricardo's performance in the ring, that he'd act as my banker-accountant. He says it would be worth the effort—not insane at all."

"I think it's insane," Don Eduardo harrumphed. "Hard enough for a Mexican boy to become a torero. I've watched them try and fail. But a norteamericano? That's really crazy."

"If I was proposing to give some talented girl a scholarship to become a medical doctor, you wouldn't think me crazy. Well, let's consider this a graduate fellowship to a talented boy."

"Not a fellowship, Mrs. Evans. He hasn't graduated from anywhere. This would be a shot in the dark."

"I rather think that warfare in Korea and the pachangas of rural Mexico, if I have the right word, constitute a reasonable equivalent to a college education."

"Have you told him?" Don Eduardo asked, and she said: "Not yet. First I want your approval of having him drive me home," and she demanded a yes-no vote from each of us, and when it came out four yeses—León's, the widow's, Penny's and her own—against two noes, Don Eduardo's and mine, she cried almost triumphantly: "That settles it! Mr. Clay, please fetch Ricardo and let's tell him the good news."

But as I started for the other table, Don Eduardo pulled me back down and said in Spanish: "We must prevent this good woman from committing a terrible error." Before we could give her a word of warning Mrs. Evans proved that she knew more Spanish that we had supposed, for almost condescendingly she smiled at my uncle and me. "I'm grateful to you men. You've been so kind." Then she turned to Penny and León: "And you've become something like my own children. I'll always cherish the time we've had together. But . . ." She said this with heavy emphasis, "I came to Mexico because I wanted to experience something beyond wearing widow's weeds and watching television in Tulsa." Placing her hand on mine she said: "That tableau at the cathedral last night, it was worth at least a week of television."

When she paused, no one jumped in to rebut, so she admitted: "When my Tulsa friends abandoned me with scornful words the other day, I cried a bit, then stamped my foot and said: 'They did me a favor, damn it!' Made me judge my problems alone . . . made me realize I was facing the rest of my life, and that Tulsa bridge parties were not going to be sufficient. I didn't know it when I drove out of Tulsa, but I was searching for someone like that boy over there."

"He's a grown man," Don Eduardo grumbled, "and sadly mixed up."

"So was my son, but I loved him. And now, Mr. Clay, bring him here."

When I led him to our table Mrs. Evans did not risk having one of us speak first. Vigorously she said: "Ricardo, as you must have guessed, we've been discussing you and we've reached two decisions. Starting within half an hour I want you to drive me and Penny back to Tulsa. I'll pay expenses and give you something for your time. And starting from when you get me home, I'll set aside five thousand dollars for your first year— to help you become a matador. I know you have the talent, we've seen that, and now you'll have the opportunity." Before he could express his amazement she said: "No, consider this a normal educational grant, bestowed in memory of my son, Roger. And now let's pack."

As she rose to go, she saw León Ledesma looking at her admiringly, for he approved of the steps she was taking, and impulsively she picked up his hands and kissed them: "León, you're the one honest human being in bullfighting, you and the bull. All the rest is horribly corrupt. Don Eduardo here sends overage bulls to the arena. I heard how Victoriano's family shaved the horns of the bulls, and Mr. Clay told us about the ton of wet cement dropped on the back of the one bull that wasn't diminished. The arena manager cheats everyone, and the ticket scalpers cheat the public. Only you stand forth clean and honest. Openly you accept pay, and openly you deliver. Tell me, I know you favored Gómez in the fight today. Will you say so in your column?"

"When Gómez pays, I write."

"But out of decency, you must say something."

"About his artistry, nothing, About his bravery in trying to finish Victoriano's job for him, a great deal."

"And about Ricardo, will you throw in a word or two about how well he made his passes during the fracas?"

"You paid me, didn't you? Do you want to read it?" He tossed the copy he'd already completed on the table, but she refused to take it: "I'll trust you, León. Everyone else does," and she pushed aside his big hat and leaned down to kiss him.

Then she smiled at all of us: "It really was a festival, wasn't it?" and she hurried upstairs to pack.

When the three travelers returned to the Terrace before climbing into the Cadillac, Ledesma nudged me and whispered: "I can't believe it. You saw me struggling to protect Penny's virtue from an attack by a Mexican would-be matador, but now her own protectress literally throws her into a high-speed luxury car with an American would-be matador. The world is crazier than I realized." His outburst caused me to study young Penny as she came down the stairs with the two cases containing her bullfight costume, and she seemed more alive and vibrant than ever despite her sadness and the red about her eyes. Mrs. Evans, noting my interest, said: "Thank you, Mr. Clay. You've been like a father to her," and I said archly: "You misread the signals."

As Penny moved to pack her gear, I thought: How much extra baggage she's taking home— death in the arena, ghosts in the catacombs, a handsome centaur riding his horse with no hands while he fought a wild bull, a magical Indian trumpeter, the five little wives of Palafox bishops dancing like little angels, and that incredible pair by Pepe Huerta, dedicated to her. And now to ride more than a thousand miles through spectacular cactus lands in the companionship of a good-looking war veteran who knows his own mind!

"What are you thinking?" Mrs. Evans asked, and I said: "She returns home so vastly different from what she was when she came. Two years older in four days of festival."

"That's not the significant change. This morning after Penny and I had a long talk I telephoned my friends at Smith College and told them: 'My ward, Penny Grim—I'm speaking for her father, too—she's changed her mind, I'm glad to say. She now wants to enter Smith next September. Deposit will be in the mail Tuesday."

"Does her father know about this?" I asked, and she said: "No."

"He's going to be furious," I warned. "He was all set for her to be a cheerleader at S.M.U."

"You're wrong, Mr. Clay. Ed won't be furious. He'll be blustery. He knows in his heart I'm doing the right thing."

"But taking her north with Ricardo. That's asking for trouble."

"Indeed it is. Mr. Clay, that girl you've seen has problems you've never dreamed of. One day she's going to be immensely wealthy. She must learn now to make the right choices, analyze the men she'll meet, seed her head with ideas that will mature. When she reaches Smith with hundreds of attractive men from Amherst next door and Yale and Harvard not far off, each one of them knowing she's worth millions, she'll have to be wise beyond her years."

As we walked to the car and saw Ricardo at the wheel and Penny scrunched down in the backseat, I said to Ledesma: "That little girl knows exactly what's happening—and she's enjoying every minute."

"You're wrong, Norman. She stopped being a little girl in the bullring this afternoon when Pepe Huerta dedicated his marvelous pair to her. Right now she's terrified. The grandness of life suddenly exploding in her face, and she wondering what it will mean."

Guessing that we were talking about her, she lowered her window, blew us a pair of kisses, and headed home.

As the Cadillac sped north on the road that would take them to the Texas border at Laredo, the Widow Palafox, standing with Ledesma and me, said: "When I watched Penny stuff that hatbox in the trunk, I almost screamed."

"Why, for heaven's sake?" Ledesma asked, and she explained: "Years ago I saw this movie, Roberto Montgomery it was, a soft-speaking young man, attaches himself to two lonely women, only luggage he has is a hatbox, just like hers. Gradually we learn it holds a woman's head. I won't be able to sleep tonight."

When the Widow Palafox and Ledesma left us, I was not unhappy to be left alone with Don Eduardo, for even at this late point in the festival I had an important matter I wanted to discuss with him: "Do you happen to carry with you a key to your museum?" He said: "Naturally. I run it," and I asked if he'd accompany me there, since I wanted to give him something he might treasure. When he said: "I never tire of seeing that place, the soul of our city," I hurried up to my room to fetch the gift, and as I did I noticed that Ricardo, whom I had allowed to share my room at no cost to himself, had taken with him my shaving cream and toothpaste, but had thoughtfully left my good shaving brush.

It was only a short walk up Avenida Gral. Gurza to the abandoned church that Don Eduardo, with help from the poet Aguilar, had transformed into the Museo Palafox. When we reached its locked portal the Don did not bother to use his key but banged on the oaken door crying: "Aguilar! Open up!" and when the sleepy man obeyed, an act he was accustomed to performing, my uncle led me into his taurine museum with its tasteful displays. Here were the heads of Palafox bulls that had brought distinction to the brand. Their horns highly polished with a mixture of wax and shellac, they seemed as ready to defend themselves in death as they had been in life, and I noted those who had killed their matadors.

Leading me to an inner room Don Eduardo said: "Look at us! Are we not a handsome lot?" and there, staring down at me exactly as the bulls had done, were portraits of my ancestors reaching far back into Palafox history—the bishops, the generals, the builders of the family fortune. I was startled by the fact that there were no women, and when I questioned the Don about this, he said frankly: "In our history it was the men who counted. They carried the name forward." Then he said with pride: "But we weren't parochial, not at all," and he pointed to two oversize photographs of Jubal Clay and my father, John. They too had played major roles in the Palafox heritage, and as I studied their familiar countenances I wondered if there would ever be reason to add my photograph to the display. I had married a Palafox but had left her for Alabama, or, to tell the truth, she had left me to remain in Toledo.

Turning to the business at hand, I took from a carefully prepared folder a large copy, made by a professional, of a photograph that I de-

scribed in this way: "A historical picture. Important to the Palafoxes. Your museum should
have it."

"What is it?" he asked, eyeing the folder suspiciously.

"An exciting photograph."

"Does it show the stages of the Mineral? We
could use shots of that, especially the caverns."

"It's something quite different," I said, and
revealed a reproduction of the lifelike photograph my grandmother had given me of General
Gurza with me perched on his knee and the gun
between us.

Uncle Eduardo, whose family had been made
to suffer so much by Gurza, growled: "Is that
who I think it is?" and I asked: "And who do you
think that boy is on his knee?"

"Could that be you?" he mumbled as he
pushed the picture away, touching only the
edge, as if it were contaminated.

"Let me explain. Gurza gave me that gun to
use to defend him when I reached fourteen."

"I'm amazed you even touched it."

"And that little woman is Grandmother Caridad."

"She was an Indian. Didn't know any better."

"And what do you think happened to that
gun?"

"Something bad, I hope."

"Grandmother brought it home, and Father López, that skinny priest we kept in hiding at the Mineral, stole it, smuggled it north to San Ildefonso and used it to assassinate General Gurza."

"Somebody ought to build a monument to that gun, but Gurza? His picture in this museum, in this town? Not in my day!" and with a quick move he grabbed the photograph from my hands, tore it into bits and threw them on the floor. "We allow no obscenity here."

Dismayed by this rejection, I went to the door and called back: "Glad I didn't bring you the original. Years from now you'll wish you had it."

At first I thought he hadn't heard me, for when I looked back I saw him standing over the shreds of photograph trying to grind them into the tile flooring with his heavy boots. But he had heard my bitter farewell, because as I left he shouted: "Don't you dare send me the original. I'll rip it up, too. And if you bother to come next year, don't bring your Oklahoma oil people. No sense of history. Just money. They disgust me."

But when I tried to slam my way out I opened the wrong door and saw something so horrible that I uttered an involuntary scream. There, towering above me in the darkness, its hideous features illuminated only by a weak shaft of light from the room I had just left, was a terrifying head covered with snakes and resting atop a distorted body that seemed to contain all the monstrous symbols dreamed up to frighten children.

"Rather frightening, eh?" Don Eduardo asked, grinning at my reaction.

"What is it? Seems to be alive."

"The Mother Goddess, the Altomecs called her in the days just before Cortés. That's the goddess the women in your branch of the family, Lady Gray Eyes and her team, destroyed a few years before the first Bishop Palafox arrived."

Taking another peek at the horrible thing, I asked weakly: "How did you get such a big statue in here? Tear down a wall?"

"She was delivered in fragments. A German archaeologist found her broken pieces buried deep beside the pyramid, where she fell. We assembled her in that room."

"Do you allow schoolchildren in there? They'd be terrified."

"No. We keep her hidden from them until they're older. But we do not keep her hidden from our minds because she was part of our history, too. Especially a part of your heritage, Norman, seeing that you're from the Indian part of our family."

Risking another glimpse of the horror, I said: "It was time Cortés arrived with a breath of sanity," but he corrected me: "Remember, it was the women in your family who destroyed that evil bitch."

When I returned to the Terrace, feeling injured by the brutal rejection of my gift, and my nerves frayed by the sight of the hideous Mother Goddess, I felt the need for human companionship. Searching the tables, I could find no one with whom to discuss the events of the past five days. Mrs. Evans was gone. The Widow Palafox, exhausted by the unremitting work she'd had to do at her hotel, was asleep, and the two heroes of the last day, Victoriano and Gómez, were in the hospital. Ledesma, I supposed, was busy writing his reports of the festival, and I was abandoned in a town filled with confusing memories and ghosts.

Then, from the cheap café at the far end of the Terrace, came the brassy voice of Lucha González chanting her would-be flamenco, and I was drawn to her as though to a magnet. The attraction could never be said to involve art, for I deplored her singing and her dancing was worse, but I felt compassion for her: Poor, mesmerized woman, when her matador took that horn in the groin, there went his chance for a season in Spain and hers for a shot at Madrid's flamenco scene. She must must known that two more years of Mexico would finish her chances—Gómez fighting in the minor plazas, she condemned to the cheap cafés.

When she saw me standing by the door, she motioned for me to take a chair at a table already crowded, and when her number ended, she came to join me, drawing up a chair: "I spent half an hour with Juan in the hospital. It's a deep wound. No more fights this year. There won't be that trip to Spain which he was sure to get—the mano a manos with Victoriano have been very popular." She did not weep, but her eyes were heavy with weariness. "Well," she said with a show of brightness, "in time he'll mend, and thank God I still have my voice, and I can dance. I'll continue to get work."

"Yes, you will, Lucha," I assured her. "Cafés need singers and dancers. You're one of the best."

"I couldn't leave him," she said, "not even if I received a call from Spain. We need each other, and Cigarro will always find some way for us to earn a living."

When the café manager saw her sitting with me he did not reprimand her for not singing, but he did look at her and nod slightly. Wearily she rose, patted me on the head and resumed her sad performance.

I would probably have left the café had not
León Ledesma arrived at this moment. As I motioned for him to join me, Lucha broke into a
noisy song about a girl from Acapulco and León
cried with enthusiasm: "That's what I need after
this long day's work. The sorting at noon, the
testing at the ranch, the bag of wet cement in
the afternoon, Ricardo in jail where he belonged, Mrs. Evans gone and my stories written.
And now to hear the Jenny Lind of Toledo! What
a nightcap! Let's find a spot near her."

Throwing her a kiss, he watched as a waiter
located a table near the stage at which two men
were sitting. I heard the waiter ask: "Would you
mind if Señor Ledesma, he's the famous bullfight critic—"

The men jumped up, said effusively that he
was their favorite writer on bulls, and asked
what he thought of Victoriano's amazing afternoon: "Would you permit us to buy you and your
friend a copa?" León said that would be most
kind and then asked if he could not buy *them*
one, and soon the four of us were blood relatives. When Ledesma explained: "This one was
born in Toledo, but was smart enough to get out,
and is a Palafox by birth," they insisted on toast-
ing me with a bottle of the best Rioja.

And then something occurred that was unexpected. It was nearly five in the morning, but

many who had enjoyed the festival still lingered. They applauded noisily when Lucha finished her turn and came to sit with us but actually cheered when a frail, elderly man took her place, accompanied by a young male guitarist. As soon as he saw them, Ledesma leaped up, ran onto the stage, embraced the old man and dragged him to our table: "This is Pichón. When I was a young man in Barcelona he was the best chanter of flamenco the city had. How did he get his name, Pichón? A torch singer, like Lucha here, was singing 'La Paloma.' And he cried: 'Palomas—doves—are soft white birds for teary-eyed women. I'm what the Americans call a soot-covered pigeon!' and the name stuck, Pichón."

They spoke of Barcelona for a few minutes, after which León asked: "And what do you sing for us in this cold, gray dawn?" and the man said, as he returned to his stool by the guitarist: 'Peteneras.' " Both Ledesma and I fell silent, for this is one of the great flamenco songs of human heartbreak. How can I explain it to someone who isn't Spanish? An older man sitting on a chair in the plaza of a Spanish village sees a beautiful young woman, distraught, coming his way, and he sings such heartfelt words that they speak for all villages, all unhappy women. But you must hear the words as Pichón and the

other great singers of Spain would sing them—
in a beery voice, as if hesitant about intruding
. . . an immense difference between the singer
and the girl, but close in the way their hearts
beat:

> "Where are you going, pretty Jewess,
>   Dressed in such fine robes?"

> "I'm going for Rebeco,
>   Who is in the synagogue."

> "You won't find him there, pretty Jewess,
>   For he is off to Salamanca."

> "Ah me! Have they called him
>   To the Inquisition? Woe's me!
> He will not see this pretty dress."

Just an old man, a chair, a guitarist standing
nearby, and five of us at a wooden table drinking
Rioja: Lucha, Ledesma, me and the two Mexican men who had bought the wine. As the chant
rolled on in its simple words and rhythms, we
were in another time, another place, and when
Pichón passed on to other songs, always in that
husky voice of a laborer coming in from the
fields at the close of day, Ledesma started
speaking in a voice as rudely poetic in its way as
Pichón's had been.

"I heard him first in Barcelona, 1931, when things were good in Spain. I had made a start with the local papers, poetry, music, bullfights. The whole world was before me. And, with my regular salary, the tapas bars at night, and the singers, it was a world that would continue forever.

"One night I asked the singer: 'What song is that?' and he asked: 'Do you like it?' and when I said: 'Yes,' he said: 'You have a good ear. It's "Peteneras," ' and I asked: 'What does that mean?' and he said: 'The name of a pretty Jewess,' and I asked: 'Then why in the plural?' and he said: 'Her name is Petenera, but what I sing is a mix of many songs named for her, so it's got to be plural.'

"Then General Franco came along, and those of us who wanted to remain free were sent to fight in the little mountain town of Teruel, where the fate of the world was being decided. Hellish battle. I was on the losing side. Father, mother, brothers all killed by the Falangists, I fled to Mexico."

The memory of those tragic days had a curious effect, for he stopped, stared at me as if he had never seen me before and said bitterly: "Yes, you visitors from the North who are so carefully educated and have good doctors, you enjoy coming here and acting in a condescending way to all things Mexican. But let me tell you, on dark nights I do two things. I weep for Teruel and all I lost there. God, how I would like to go back and reclaim it. Then, in my sorrow I have to admit it will never happen, but with new joy in my heart I give thanks for Mexico. In all the world, Mexico was the only place that would accept men like me who had opposed Franco. This land is sanctified. Ten thousand government officials in Mexico are verified saints. They took us in against the judgment of the entire world. So, Mr. Norman Clay, do not come down here to our festival and ridicule us. Mexico had courage when you did not."

The two Mexicans said: "Yes, in the 1930s Mexico debated a long time about admitting Spanish liberals like you, Señor Ledesma, but we did." León pointed to Pichón and said: "Him, too," and as he finished a set of songs the men motioned for him to join us.

"Tell them how we met," Ledesma said, and the old man explained: "When the bad times came I crept out of Barcelona and slipped into Mexico on a freight ship, God knows how. No papers, no money. I was singing for drinks and tortillas in the capital when this one came, with his black cape—"

Ledesma interrupted: "First money I earned in Mexico I went to a tailor and told him: 'I want a black cape that will make me look like a Span-iard.' This is the third edition, same tailor."

"Why?" I asked and he said: "Because in Spain I was a liberal and proud of it—never tried to hide it, even at the risk of my life. Here I would be a Spaniard and never try to hide it. Well, anyway, as soon as I heard Pichón's voice I knew he was my old friend. He's never made a rich living, but wherever we Spanish exiles meet, someone pays for Pichón to sing, and when he does tears come and we long for home."

This mention of homesickness caused him to lean back, his black cloak wrapped around him, his hat pulled forward, his voice slow and dreamlike: "The end of any fiesta is heartbreak time. Have any of you ever attended the great fair of Pamplona in northern Spain?" None of us had. "Eight days of the best bullfights in the world, in my judgment. That's where they run in the streets with bulls chasing them."

"I've seen pictures," one of the men said. "Lunacy."

"On the last night, after eight days of friend-ship and drinks and bulls, it's over, so what do the people do? They light candles, each person has his own candle, and they parade like ghosts in a suddenly dead city, and as they wind their way through the narrow streets they chant: 'Pobre de mí. Poor me,' with such sadness you'd

think the end of the world had come and not just
the end of the festival." He paused. "During my
first Pamplona I'd run with the bulls and fallen in
love with an English girl who had left, so that
when I chanted 'Pobre de mí' I really meant me,
and I imagined that all the others were grieving
specifically for me."

The café manager, seeing both his singers
seated at our table listening to León, bustled
over: "One of you sing! This is a café. Here we
sing."

When Pichón volunteered, Lucha told us:
"Gómez not hurt too bad. Maybe miss two,
three fights. I gotta sing, keep money coming."
But as in all her conversations with people with
any kind of power, she came quickly to her main
subject: "Gómez getting hurt, it hurts me too.
With his success we were gonna visit Spain for
sure. He fight, I do flamenco." Both Ledesma
and I knew that the possibility of her finding a job
in Spain, where there would be hundreds of
women younger than her, prettier, better dancers, and infinitely better singers, were nil, but
despite what people like us told her, she persisted in believing that once she landed in Madrid, doors would spring open.

"Pichón!" she cried from her chair beside me.
"The song I dance to," and she moved to the
tiny stage with the guitar player in the corner,

Pichón in his chair, and she in the crude spotlight. Then, waiting to catch the beat of words and music, she began her version of a flamenco dancer in a Seville café. It was pitiful, so lacking in elemental force or feeling that none of us wanted to watch, but as she proceeded a kind of forgiveness anesthetized my critical judgment. We were in Spain, listening to true flamenco in some authentic Sevillian café. The guitar and Pichón were so real that they masked the grotesqueries of Lucha González, and I thought: She's like those bulls. Life crops her horns and drops a ton of wet cement on her, but she keeps singing—to help a man who will never take her to Spain.

"Poor kid," I said to Ledesma. "She'll never get to Madrid. When will you be going back?" and he gave the answer he had to repeat a dozen times a year when people asked that question: "Not till Franco dies, and it looks as if he'll live forever."

As he said this Lucha stopped her clumsy dancing and resumed her singing, which was so painful after Pichón's masterly performance that Ledesma grimaced and turned his back to the stage. The harsh dismissal made me protest: "It hurts to see anyone's dream go up in smoke."

"Norman! She never had a legitimate dream. Never a chance of coming true."

"I've heard worse singers. She might have made it."

"Norman, dear friend. In Spain no flamenco artist tries to both sing and dance. He sings, she dances. Lucha's been tormenting herself with a pathetic fantasy, and I can stand no more of this self-deception." Rising abruptly, he stalked out into the clean predawn air.

Unwilling to be alone on this mournful night, I went after him, with the two Rioja men trailing. When I caught up he growled: "Where are we heading?"

"I want to say good night to that statue down there—of my father. Did you know that my grandfather found refuge here in 1866 the same way you did in 1939?"

"Seems to me I heard that your father and you left Mexico—took back American citizenship."

"Not 'took it back.' Fought like hell to win it back. Him in World War One, me in Two."

"Why did you feel it necessary to turn your back on Mexico?"

"Couldn't abide the way you people stole the oil wells we legally owned."

"Do you ever still think of yourself as Mexican?"

"When I'm busy in the States, Mexico is ten thousand miles away. But when I return to this plaza . . ."

As we walked, León and I made believe our forefingers were candles and sang "Pobre de mí," and soon the men with the Rioja joined us, and in that formation we reached Father's statue.

In the darkness I said: "León, you and my grandfather are twins. Fugitives from tyranny. Refugees always longing for home, gathering with others to share songs, weeping in the night over past glories . . ."

I had summarized his life so accurately and, in a sense, my own that neither of us found it necessary to speak further on the subject, but I felt the need for serious talk, so I proposed: "Let's go a few steps farther. To the bullring. And you tell me honestly what we saw there today."

As we walked the short distance to the low circular building where, only a few days ago, I had seen those first posters proclaiming Ixmiq-61, the man with the bottle of Rioja said: "I can tell you what we saw. The rebirth of a great Mexican matador. Victoriano was stupendous." In Spanish that four-syllable word, *estupendo,* carries wonderful resonance, far more than our rather drab three-syllable one.

The other stranger agreed: "He came alive. Fought as in the old days. Thrilling."

But as was his habit, which made him such a respected commentator, it was Ledesma who nailed down the significance: "Always start with the bull. We saw one who could not be defeated, no matter what we did to him. We saw that damned Indian Gómez do what he had to do and lose his chance for Spain. And yes, we did see Victoriano become a matador de toros and not a dancing master. So much to see in that squat, ugly building where honest dreams are pursued and satisfied."

At this moment it seemed that a gigantic incandescent light burst through the fading night sky, illuminating the images I had been collecting since coming to Toledo five days ago: the pyramid with its grotesque gods, the cathedral with its martyred priests, the graceful aqueduct, our Mineral with its endless chain of climbing women, and above all, this plaza with its rampaging soldiers. Illuminated by this astounding light, the mosaic acquired special meaning, for me: If No. 47 could be true to himself to the last, if Gómez could risk his career doing what he had to do, if Lucha can keep singing even as the dream fades, and if Victoriano can remake himself, I can certainly tackle the task that has confronted me for so long. Then, as I broke out of the trance that had possessed me, I saw that my mystical light was nothing more than the rising sun, and I was jolted back to reality.

"Rioja man! Where's the telegraph office?" I

demanded. When we got there we banged on the door to wake the operator, and I handed him an extra five dollars to dispatch an urgent message to New York: "It'll reach them just as they open shop," I told Ledesma, and he said: "Norman, it's a solid message."

> Drummond. I believe you owe me nine months' sabbatical at half-pay. I'm taking it. There's more to Mexico than bullfights and I propose finding what. Am airmailing you Cassette Twenty-nine, ten, twelve great color shots incredible pair banderillas. 360 degree turn in air over horns of tremendous bull. Pick six for spread across two pages. *Así torean los grandes.* (Thus fight the great ones.) Kid is Pepe Huerta, aspirant, Guadalajara, nary a peso, rented suit, but a comer. Please use. Norman.

For me Ixmiq-61 did not end that Sunday night in April, because later in August while I was in Mexico City researching in archives for the book I was attempting to write, I could not forget the insolent manner in which Uncle Eduardo had torn up his copy of that rare photograph of General Gurza and me, so I interrupted my work and wrote a fiery ten-thousand-word article about General Gurza's last raid on Toledo, how Father

López survived the first raid and the massacres of his fellow priests, the manner in which my family had hid him and the running debate between López the scrawny priest and Grandmother Caridad the lay revolutionary. I then related the incidents of my meeting with the general and how the photograph came to be, with the fateful gun so clearly displayed.

And in a story never before told by a Clay, neither in Mexico nor the United States, I gave full details of the assassination of Gurza by Father López and proved by the photograph of the gun that the general had been killed by one of his own guns, or, at least, by one he had stolen from the munitions plant near Mexico City.

When published with a score of grisly photographs of the rape of Toledo, the execution of the nuns and especially my documentation of how Gurza, an infuriating enemy of the United States, had died, numerous historians rushed into print with confirming evidence. The result was that the photograph my grandmother had given me reached an audience that would have pleased her, but also confused her, because in my account she was clearly the person who engineered the death of her hero. She had accepted the gun from Gurza, had brought it home, had kept it in a place from which Father López could steal it, and had forestalled any investigation by the police. I was glad I had been goaded into telling the story, for it illuminated the history of both the Palafoxes and the Clays.

I published the piece in early September. By Christmas it had reached all Spanish-speaking countries, and in late January 1962 this letter from Toledo was delivered to me in Mexico City:

Mi Querido Sobrino Norman [Dear Nephew]

I must have been out of my mind when I tore up that stupendous photograph of General Gurza, you and the rifle. I see it wherever I go, thanks to your fine article and the reproductions that have been made throughout the world. Everyone who comes to our museum asks to see the original and all we have is a bad copy from a Spanish magazine with added color for effect, a horrible show.

Please, please send us at least a good copy, and if you are generous enough to let us have the original, we'll have the mayor confirm it as a city treasure, and we'll print copies for schoolchildren who visit us.

We have tremendous plans for Ixmiq-62. Both Victoriano and Gómez have signed contracts to appear. Calesero will come down from Aguas, and Fermín Sotelo will

return to repeat his triumph. I have personally commissioned Héctor Sepúlveda, the
one-armed poet whose work you liked, to
write a pageant based on your photograph,
The Life and Death of General Gurza. We
Palafoxes despise him, but since you've
made him our local hero, we have to accept
him. Sepúlveda and I have agreed on two
features, although I did most of the talking.
A highlight of the show will be a powerful set
of lights focused on the little shop where you
and Gurza sat that day, and we've picked a
fine soldier who marched with Gurza and
took part in the first two sacks of Toledo,
very realistic, he looks like Gurza. My granddaughter has a boy about nine years old who
will play you. We have a gun from that period, such guns abound in Toledo, and it will
be a historic moment. I asked Sepúlveda to
write speeches for Gurza and you but he
said he felt I could do it better, and I'm working on them.

By popular demand we will again close the
pageant with the *Apotheosis of Paquito de
Monterrey,* and I have personally visited that
city and located his sainted mother. She has
agreed to come to Toledo for the night of the
pageant and will appear in mourning as she

sends the soul of her son to heaven. I will also write her speeches.

The entire committee felt it would add a great deal if you could attend Ixmiq-62 as a highly regarded son of Toledo, and it would be even better if you would persuade those wonderful people from Oklahoma to return. They made a most favorable impression, especially the girl who fought our cow with such style.

Your admiring Uncle Eduardo

Universally revered novelist JAMES A. MICHENER was forty before he decided on writing as a career. Prior to that, he had been an outstanding academic, an editor, and a U.S. Navy lieutenant commander in the Pacific Theater during World War II. His first book, *Tales of the South Pacific,* won a Pulitzer Prize and became the basis of the award-winning Rodgers and Hammerstein musical *South Pacific.* In the course of the next forty years Mr. Michener wrote such monumental bestsellers as *Sayonara, The Bridges at Toko-Ri, Hawaii, The Source, Iberia, Texas, Alaska, Journey,* and *Caribbean.*

Decorated with America's highest civilian award, the Presidential Medal of Freedom, Mr. Michener has served on the Advisory Council to NASA, holds honorary doctorates in five fields from thirty leading universities, and has received an award from the President's Committee on the Arts and Humanities for his continuing commitment to art in America.